The Canterbury Tales

Geoffrey Chaucer

The Canterbury Tales

❦

Edited with Introductions, Bibliographies,
Footnotes and on-page Glossaries by

DR LESLEY A. COOTE
Lecturer in Medieval & Renaissance Studies
University of Hull

Wordsworth Poetry Library

Publisher's Dedication

For my husband Anthony John Ranson
with love from your wife, the publisher.
Eternally grateful for your unconditional love.

Introducer's Dedication

To David for his help and encouragement,
to Jonathan for his sense of humour, and
to my Chaucer students for their enthusiasm,
all of which have contributed greatly
to the making of this book.

Readers who are interested in other titles from
Wordsworth Editions are invited to visit our website at
www.wordsworth-editions.com

For our latest list and a full mail-order service, contact
Bibliophile Books, 5 Datapoint, South Crescent, London E16 4TL
TEL: +44 (0)20 7474 2474 fax: +44 (0)20 7474 8589
ORDERS: orders@bibliophilebooks.com
WEBSITE: www.bibliophilebooks.com

First published in 2002 by Wordsworth Editions Limited
8B East Street, Ware, Hertfordshire SG12 9HJ
Text revised 2012

ISBN   978 1 84022 692 8

Typeset in Great Britain by Antony Gray
Printed and bound by Clays Ltd, St Ives plc

CONTENTS

INTRODUCTION

Geoffrey Chaucer

It is not known precisely when Geoffrey Chaucer was born, but the evidence of later documents suggests a date of around 1340. His father, John, was a vintner, a wine merchant. John and his wife Agnes lived in the ward (district) known as Vintry (from the French *vin*, or Latin *vinum*, meaning 'wine'), in the City of London. There are no records of Chaucer's schooling, but he appears in 1357 as a page in the household of Elizabeth, Countess of Ulster, wife of Lionel, Duke of Clarence, second surviving son of Edward III, then King of England. How Geoffrey came to be a page in the household of the third most important lady in England (after the queen and Princess Joan, wife of the Black Prince) is unknown, but the Chaucers lived in a high-status area, with important and wealthy neighbours, and it may be that, as a survivor of the Black Death, John Chaucer had inherited unexpected wealth from his dead relatives.

Chaucer next appears in France, in the invading English army of 1359, when he was taken prisoner and ransomed. The king paid the large sum of sixteen pounds towards his ransom. In 1366 Chaucer was in what is now Spain, possibly in connection with the Black Prince's expedition to help Pedro the Cruel (who appears as a tragic 'example' in The Monk's Tale). By the end of that year Chaucer had returned to England, and he married Philippa Roet, the daughter of Sir Payne Roet, a Flemish knight. Philippa was the sister of Katherine Swynford, who was governess to the children of the king's fourth son, John of Gaunt. Katharine became Gaunt's mistress, and eventually his wife. At the time of her marriage, Philippa Chaucer was lady in waiting to Queen Philippa of Hainault, Edward III's wife. Chaucer thus gained more important connections in the royal family, which would prove useful on the death of Princess Elizabeth, when Chaucer appears to have enjoyed the patronage not only of her husband, but also of Gaunt. By 1367 Chaucer was a member of the royal household, with Gaunt as his patron. One of Chaucer's earlier works, *The Book of the Duchess*, is a memorial to John of Gaunt's first wife, Blanche of Lancaster.

In 1372 Chaucer made his first journey to Italy, visiting Genoa and Florence. This would have been his first contact with the early

Renaissance, and with the works of Dante, Petrarch and Boccaccio. He was probably chosen for diplomatic work because of his knowledge of languages, French and Italian in particular. It is now accepted that he probably learned his Italian in London, rather than on these embassies to Italy.

From 1374 Chaucer lived in a house over Aldgate, one of the northern gates of the City of London, awarded to him rent-free for life by the Mayor and Aldermen. This coincided with his appointment as Controller of Customs in the Port of London. Living close to the royal household at the Tower of London, Chaucer was also employed as an envoy during this period, visiting France and Italy, where he went again in 1378 to negotiate with Bernarbo Visconti of Milan and his son-in-law, the English mercenary captain Sir John Hawkwood (Bernarbo is another of the monk's *exempla*).

By the late 1380s Chaucer had farmed out his customs duties to deputies, and was appointed a Knight of the Shire and a Justice of the Peace for the County of Kent. The beginning of this period coincided with the Peasants' Revolt of 1381, when the 'peasants' under Wat Tyler, Jack Straw, and the priest John Ball entered London, caused chaos, ransacked carefully chosen buildings such as Gaunt's palace at the Savoy, and massacred many members of the Flemish community. Chaucer would have been grateful to survive, particularly in view of his association with Gaunt. Around this time Philippa Chaucer died, and her husband probably 'rode out' the political crisis of 1388/9, when Richard II and the Lords Appellant fought for control of the kingdom, maybe on his estates in Kent. It was also during this period that Chaucer conceived the idea of *The Canterbury Tales*, and began work on the collection.

In July 1389 Chaucer came out of semi-retirement to be Clerk of the King's Works, supervising the building works of Richard II in and around London. He supervised the building of new fortifications at the Tower of London, including the Byward Tower and the reinforced quayside, which can still be seen. In 1391 he gave up this post, and took up the sinecure of deputy forester of North Petherton in Somerset. During the last years of Richard II, Geoffrey Chaucer was a recipient of grants from both Richard and Henry, Earl of Derby, eldest son of Gaunt. In 1399 Derby became King Henry IV, when he deposed Richard and had him murdered. In that year, Chaucer moved to a house in the precincts of Westminster Abbey, where he was a pensioner. It is for this reason that Chaucer was buried in the Abbey after his death in 1400. The spot where he was buried was only later designated as 'Poet's Corner'.

In his lifetime Geoffrey Chaucer played many different parts: merchant's son, courtier, knight, diplomat, civil servant, customs official, citizen of London, representative of the 'county' community of Kent, and – in a strictly 'non professional' capacity – poet and writer. This varied background is evident in the diversity of life which he depicts in *The Canterbury Tales*. Was he also a pilgrim? At some point in his life, very likely . . .

The Canterbury Tales

When Geoffrey Chaucer conceived the idea for *The Canterbury Tales* there had been collections of stories before, but Chaucer's was different, not simply because the writer was a literary genius but because it was written in English. Chaucer would have learned how to write poetry, to 'endite', as part of his noble upbringing at the court of the Countess of Ulster, and possibly also his languages – at the very least he would have learned French. He may have attended the Inns of Court at some point, at least for a year, as 'gentil' young men often did, in order to learn something about the law. What is remarkable about Chaucer is that – as far as we know – he did not write poetry in all of the languages he *could* use. His contemporary, John Gower, wrote in English, French and Latin. Instead, he chose to write in English, and he used his knowledge of French and Italian to enrich his own vernacular. The closest analogue to Chaucer's story collection was written in Italian, *The Decameron*, *c.*1350 by Giovanni Boccaccio (1313–75). In *The Decameron*, a group of young Italians escape into the countryside to avoid the plague (the Black Death of 1348), and pass the time by telling stories. Although there is no evidence that he had read *The Decameron*, Chaucer certainly knew *The Decameron,* and the similarities between the two collections suggest that he had been influenced by the Italian work. In Italy Chaucer had seen the beginnings of the Renaissance, and witnessed poets such as Boccaccio writing literature to ensure their own immortality, and to glorify their cities or states. It may be that Chaucer wanted both to immortalise himself as an author (to gain a place in the House of Fame) and also to glorify his own city, London, and his own country. Thus at the beginning of the Prologue the pilgrims come from all over England to London, to go to Canterbury to visit the tomb and shrine of the 'holy blissful martyr', Thomas Becket. St Thomas was the 'unofficial' patron saint of England, preferred to the more military 'foreigner' St George, who had been introduced by Edward III during the war with France. Although based upon stock types and not representative of all degrees of late fourteenth century society, it is possible that the Canterbury pilgrims represent the main types whom Chaucer himself might have seen in the city.

Boccaccio's story-tellers are static (they sit down and tell stories), whereas Chaucer's are in motion. The pilgrimage may have been chosen as a very English form of leisure activity, or simply because it was within Chaucer's immediate experience. It is an inspired choice of format, because the collection itself is also a pilgrimage. For the writer and the reader/hearer, it is a pilgrimage towards salvation, during the course of which they are invited to observe different lives and different values, and to measure these against their own. The whole culminates in the parson's magnificent statement on how to obtain absolution, and therefore salvation. In his choice of a pilgrimage motif, Chaucer may have been influenced by reading the bestseller of his day, William Langland's *Piers Plowman*, which features the pilgrimage of an individual towards his own, and his people's, and Cristendom's, salvation. However, he may simply have been reflecting the importance of pilgrimage as an ideal, and its popularity as a recreational activity, in his own society. Pilgrimage was an important part of popular devotion, and those who could not go might depute this to someone else, or undertake a 'virtual' pilgrimage, reciting the liturgies associated with each stage on a pilgrimage journey. *The Canterbury Tales* could be seen in this light, as a 'virtual' pilgrimage for the reader.

The Canterbury Tales were not a complete work at Chaucer's death. Some pilgrims do not tell stories, and the surviving stories are difficult to arrange. The collection was not finished: the host's original statement is that the pilgrims will tell two tales each, one on the way to Canterbury and another on the way back. The pilgrims only tell one tale, and some pilgrims, for example the ploughman and the yeoman, do not tell stories at all. Subsequently, the stories were made up into a collection, but it was not at all obvious to the compilers how this should be done, and different manuscripts have different arrangements. There is no indication that Chaucer left any instructions about how the stories were to be collected together. Some tales – for example, those of the knight, miller and reeve – obviously follow one another, but others are less easy to locate. This edition presents one possible arrangement; there are others.

Most of the *Tales* are written in five-stress rhyming couplets. A few: The Monk's Tale, The Prioress's Tale, The Second Nun's Tale, The Clerk's Tale and The Lawyer's Tale, are written in stanzaic form. The Monk's Tale is written in eight-line stanzas, and the others in seven-line stanzas, a form which became known as 'rhyme royal', generally indicative of the education and status of the tellers. Chaucer has matched these subjects well to reflect the character of the person who tells them. He was able to do this because of his remarkable ability to understand the construction of poetry, and the nature and function of genre. The fabliau stories, for example, match the humble origins of their speakers, and the nature of their, frequently coarse, contents. Chaucer always uses genre in order to subvert it, as in the brilliant Nun's Priest's Tale, where the simplest genre of all becomes the medium for arguably the most complex of all the *Tales*.

Unlike most medieval authors, we can 'know' quite a lot about Geoffrey Chaucer's life, which was relatively well documented because of the public nature of his employment. His contemporary Langland was the most popular author of his generation, but nothing is now known about him; even his name is probably a pseudonym. Because Chaucer was a royal client and a civil servant, his life has left many records, none of which have anything to do with his poetry, but because he appears to us as a 'real' person, it is easier to relate his life to his work. The fact that his work is more accessible than Langland's, for example, is due to his far more flexible use of form and language, the liveliness of his stories, the continued relevance of the issues he raises; and his endless, apparently non-judgemental, fascination with human life and human society.

Reading Chaucer: Rhyme, Metre and Language

Most of *The Canterbury Tales*, and the linking sections between them, are written in couplets; that is, they are based upon a format in which every two lines are linked by end-rhymes. Thus, in the first four lines of the General Prologue:

> Whan that Aprille with his schowres **swoote**
> The drought of Marche hath perced to the **roote**
> And bathud every veyne in suich **licour**
> Of which vertue engendred is the **flour**

The last words of the first two lines rhyme, then the next two; and so it continues.

The exceptions to this are the stanzaic tales, in which the rhyme is arranged slightly differently, on a pattern of ababbcc, where the first and third lines rhyme at the end, as do the second, fourth and fifth. The sixth and seventh lines rhyme with one another, like a couplet. For example, from The Second Nun's Tale:

> Thou Mayde and Moder, Daughter of thi **Sone**,(a)
> Thow welle of mercy, synful soules' **cure**;(b)
> In whom that God for bounte chees to **wone**(a)
> Thou humble and heyh over every **creature**;(b)
> Thow nobelest so ferforth our **nature**(b)
> That no disdeyn the Maker had of **kynde**(c)
> His Sone in blood and fleissh to clothe and **wynde**.(c)

This is varied in The Monk's Tale, the stanzas of which have eight lines, a sign that the monk considers himself different from, more erudite than, the other pilgrims:

> And hanged was Cresus, this proude **king**(a)
> His real tour might him not **availe**;(b)
> Tegredis, ne noon other maner **thing**(a)
> Ne can I synge, crie, ny **biwayle**;(b)
> But for that Fortune wil alway **assayle**(b)
> With unwar strook the regnes that ben **proude** –(c)
> For whan men trusteth hir, than wil sche **faile**,(b)
> And cover hir brighte fac with a **clowde**.(c)

The form is achieved by the addition of an extra (b) rhyme between the final two lines.

The poetry also relies for effect on the distribution of stress, that is, of strong syllables, within the line. Chaucer uses five stresses within the line, which makes the line very flexible, as it allows the writer to rearrange the distribution of weak syllables as it suits his purpose. This makes the English appear more 'natural':

> **Whan** that **Apr-il-**le with his **schow**res **swoote**
> The **drought** of **Marche** hath **per-ced** to the **roote** . . .

The only tale in which Chaucer departs from this stress-pattern is The Tale of Sir Thopas, in which he uses a three- and four-stress line, which helps to render the tale awkward and formulaic, and adds to its downright silliness:

> Yet **lest**neth, **lord**ynges, **to** my **tale**
> **Mer**ier **than** the **night**yngale

There are two tales written in prose: The Tale of Melibee and The Parson's

Tale. Prose was the language for serious writing, such as histories, chronicles and works of scholarly authority. These two tales are, in fact, didactic treatises, and as such, prose is the correct form in which they should, according to late medieval literary convention, be written.

Spelling

There were no English dictionaries in the Middle Ages, as English had ceased to be a high-status language after the Norman Conquest in 1066. In addition, English has many dialects, some of them impenetrable to people speaking another (Chaucer plays on this in the reeve's tale). Medieval spelling may appear very strange at first, but its peculiarities do become familiar after reading for a fairly short time. Many words and expressions are glossed in the text, but here are a few general rules which will help with the most common spelling problems encountered by the modern reader.

'y' frequently occurs where we would expect 'i':

lynage (lineage); lyve (live)

these may be interchangeable: ryden/riden

or there may be an 'i' instead of 'y': worthi (worthy)

'i' sometimes occurs where we would expect 'e': yit (yet)

or 'e' where we would expect 'i': geve (give)

'u' is frequently added before 'n' after 'a':

daunce (dance); chaunce (chance)

'c' is frequently added before 'h' after 's': sche (she); schort (short)

an extra 's' is sometimes added before 's':

Englissche (English); fresshe (fresh)

an extra 'o' is sometimes added before 'o': schoo (shoe); noo (no)

The past participle is frequently prefixed by 'y', as in y-ronne (run); y-wedded (wedded/married); y-seen (seen); y-goon (gone).

In words such as moo (more) oo or o (one), the consonants at the end of the word are missing.

Some Frequently Encountered Words

hem = them; here = their;

quod, or quoth (the 'd' and 'th' are interchangeable) = says, or said

poeple = people

'Invisible' Changes

In order to render the text easier to read, I have made changes to the transcription which are not apparent to the reader. The scribe of the manuscript almost always writes 'j' in the same way as 'i', but I have substituted 'j' where this accords with modern usage. Similarly, 'v' is almost always written 'u' by the medieval scribe, but I have substituted 'v' where this accords with modern usage. Capital 'F' is written 'ff' in the manuscript, but I have replaced this with the upper-case version. I have, of course, added modern punctuation, and have replaced the medieval genitive 'es' with the possessive apostrophe (e.g. knightes = knight's), in accordance with modern usage.

I have given proper names capital letters, whereas in the medieval original the use of upper case letters for proper names is erratic.

'Thorn' and 'Yogh'

Throughout the manuscript, 'th' is usually represented by the Old English letter 'thorn', represented by the symbol 'Þ'. I have replaced thorn with the modern 'th', in order to make the text easier for the modern reader.

Less frequently, the medieval scribe has represented 'g', 'y' or 'gh' by the Old English letter 'yogh', represented by the symbol 'ð'. I have replaced these with the appropriate modern equivalent, but have indicated where I have done this by placing the modern letters in italics.

Punctuation

Medieval punctuation, where there is any, consists of a series of dots and slashes (virgules), indicating the length of a pause. For example, / equates roughly with a modern comma, and // with a full stop. This manuscript uses one or two dots in the same manner, but only in the prose tales, i.e. those of Melibee and the parson. In order to make the text more intelligible, I have added modern punctuation throughout.

Roman Numerals

I have retained the roman numerals used by the medieval scribe, but these are 'translated' in the marginal glossary.

Reading Aloud

Medieval people customarily read aloud, even when by themselves. When a scribe copied a manuscript, he would read it aloud, then write down what he *heard*, not necessarily what he *saw* on the page. It is much easier to understand Middle English if it is read aloud. If you read it out loud, even quietly to yourself, you will find that the words often *sound* like what they mean, even if they appear strange when you *look* at them.

Pronunciation

We cannot, of course, know exactly how Medieval English was pronounced, although it is possible to extract clues from the material by studying the way in which words rhyme, for example. Medieval English developed from Old English, which was a Germanic language, in which vowel sounds were far more 'pure' than they are in modern English, which uses dipthongs extensively in the pronunciation of vowel sounds. It is extremely difficult to represent pronunciation in writing, but these basic observations should help.

'Short' vowels, such as 'i' (give), 'a' (tap), 'o' (dog), 'e' (bet), were pronounced much more closely as they are in modern French or German, towards the front of the mouth. Long vowels, such as 'a' (father), 'e' (meer), 'o' (bone), 'i' (spine), also used pronunciation more akin to modern French than modern English, in which these vowels have become dipthongs; ('ar', 'ea', 'ow', 'ie'). In Medieval English, such dipthong-sounds are largely represented by two letters, indicating the resulting sound.

'Ch' is pronounced as in Scottish 'loch', and 'cht' as in Scottish 'nicht'. The resulting whole sounds rather more like a modern Continental language than modern Standard (Southern) English. The recordings made by the Chaucer Studio offer a very good idea of what the stories may have sounded like originally, and can be listened to while reading the printed text. The Studio's website is:

http://www.creativeworks.byu.edu/chaucer/about.aspx

How this Book is Arranged

This book is based upon a course for beginners in Chaucer Studies, run by the editor at the University of Hull, and is arranged in order to be as user-friendly as possible. The text, notes and glossarial information are all on the same page. With a few exceptions, each tale has a short introduction, a specialised bibliography and a plot summary. Although limited in size, the introduction sets out some of the main themes and questions concerning the tale, which may be followed up by using the bibliography. Books included in the General Bibliography, at the beginning of the book, are not repeated, although these include work on most of the tales in the collection. The plot summary is intended to stimulate interest in the tale, to aid selection, and to be a framework for the tale to be read in Medieval English.

This edition is based upon the text of British Library MS Harley 7334, a manuscript produced, probably in a London workshop, within ten years of Chaucer's death in 1400. It therefore represents a version of *The Canterbury Tales* which was being read shortly after the final composition date. There is evidence that in the fifteenth century it was owned by relatives of the Haute family of Ightham Mote in Kent, then in the sixteenth century by members of the Hampden family, first cousins of the Sidneys of Penshurst (a family with strong literary connections, notably Sir Philip Sidney and Ben Jonson), also in Kent. The manuscript is decorated with red and blue ink, and has initials in red, blue, pink and green, with initials and borders embellished with gold leaf.

Some text is missing from the Harley Manuscript, in particular the transition between The Squire's Tale and The Franklin's Tale. This has been supplied from the 'Ellesmere' Manuscript (San Marino CA, Huntington Library MS EL 26 C9).

The stories have been ordered according to what can be surmised from the texts themselves. There are three major groupings. The first group, comprising the knight, the miller, the reeve and the cook, are obviously the first of the stories, and should be placed at the beginning. Another group, comprising the second nun, the canon's yeoman, the manciple and the parson, come at the end, as the pilgrims near Canterbury. The third group, comprising the shipman, the prioress, 'Geoffrey' and the monk, must be situated at the centre of the pilgrimage; the monk tells his tale near Rochester, which is roughly halfway along the pilgrimage route. The lawyer's tale and the clerk's tale are freestanding and unattached, while the wife of Bath, friar and summoner belong together. As these are linked by subject matter, the clerk and the lawyer are usually placed on either side of this group, after the cook. I have placed the lawyer first, but others may have the clerk. As the second section of the *Tales* has a more serious aspect, I have kept the romances of the squire and the franklin, which are paired stories, in the first half, following the clerk and merchant (also a pair). I have, though, moved the physician and the pardoner into the second half, before the second nun, due to the linked theme of 'transformation'. This gives a more balanced set of stories, with the central group remaining in a 'central' position. This may not, of course, have been the case if Chaucer had provided the other stories.

The notes in this book have been kept to a minimum, and relate only information necessary to the understanding and enjoyment of the stories, mainly literary and socio-historical background. Those who wish to pursue the subject further will find more detailed notes, and the rest of Chaucer's works, in Larry D. Benson (ed.), *The Riverside Chaucer*, Oxford, Oxford University Press, 1987.

At the end of each introduction, there are question-based topic suggestions, and topic 'keywords' to give some ideas on how the subject matter might be expanded, while enabling links to be made between the tales.

General Bibliography

David Aers, *Chaucer*, Brighton, Harvester, 1986

V. Allen and A. Axiotis (eds), *Chaucer: Contemporary Critical Essays*, Basingstoke, MacMillan, 1997

Malcolm Andrew (ed.), *Critical Essays on Chaucer's Canterbury Tales*, Oxford, Oxford University Press, 1991

Peter Beidler (ed.), *Masculinities in Chaucer: Approaches to Maleness in The Canterbury Tales and Troilus and Criseyde*, Cambridge, D. S. Brewer, 1998

Alcuin Blamires, *Chaucer, Ethics, and Gender*, Oxford, Oxford University Press, 2006

—— *Women Defamed and Women Defended*, Oxford, Clarendon Press, 1992

Piero Boitani and Jill Mann (eds), *The Cambridge Chaucer Companion*, Cambridge, Cambridge University Press, 1986

Derek Stanley Brewer, *A New Introduction to Chaucer* (second edition), New York, Longman, 1998

Peter Brown, *A Companion to Chaucer*, Oxford, Blackwell, 2000

T. L. Burton and John F. Plummer (eds), *'Seyd in forme and reverence', Essays on Chaucer and Chaucerians in Memory of Emerson Brown* Jr, Provo, UT, Chaucer Studio Press, 2005

Ardis Butterfield (ed.), *Chaucer and the City*, Woodbridge, Suffolk and Rochester, NY, D. S. Brewer, 2006

Andrew Cole, *Literature and Heresy in the Age of Chaucer*, Cambridge, Cambridge University Press, 2008

Carolyn P. Collette, *Species, Phantasms, and Images: Vision and Medieval Psychology in The Canterbury Tales*, Ann Arbor, Michigan University Press, 2001

Edward I. Condren, *Chaucer and the Energy of Creation: The Design and the Organization of The Canterbury Tales*, Gainesville, University Press of Florida, 1999

Helen Cooper, *The Structure of The Canterbury Tales*, Athens, University of Georgia Press, 1984

Robert M. Correale and Mary Hamel, *Sources and Analogues of the Canterbury Tales: Volumes 1 and 2*, Woodbridge, Suffolk and Rochester, NY, D. S. Brewer, 2002 and 2005

Susan Crane, *Gender and Romance in Chaucer's Canterbury Tales*, Princeton, Princeton University Press, 1994

Dolores L. Cullen, *Chaucer's Pilgrims: The Allegory*, Santa Barbara, CA, Fithian Press, 2000

W. A. Davenport, *Chaucer and his English Contemporaries: Prologue and Tale in The Canterbury Tales*, Basingstoke, Macmillan, 1998

Carolyn Dinshaw, *Chaucer's Sexual Poetics*, Madison, University of Wisconsin Press, 1989

Steve Ellis, *Chaucer: An Oxford Guide*, Oxford, Oxford University Press, 2005

Ruth Evans and Lesley Johnson (eds), *Feminist Readings in Middle English Literature: The Wife of Bath and All her Sect*, London, Routledge, 1994

Susanna Fein and David Raybin (eds.), *Chaucer: Contemporary Approaches*, University Park, Pennsylvania State University Press, 2010

William K. Finley and Joseph Rosenblum, *Chaucer Illustrated: Five Hundred Years of The Canterbury Tales in Pictures*, New Castle, DE, Oak Knoll Press, 2003

Douglas Gray (ed.), *The Oxford Companion to Chaucer*, Oxford and New York, Oxford University Press, 2003

R. Hanna and T. Lawlor (eds), *Jankyn's Book of Wikked Wyves*, Athens, University of Georgia Press, 1997

Elaine Tuttle Hansen, *Chaucer and the Fictions of Gender*, Berkeley, University of California Press, 1992

Wendy Harding, *Drama, Narrative and Poetry in The Canterbury Tales*, Toulouse, Presses Universitaires de Mirail, 2003

Carol Falvo Heffernan, *The Orient in Chaucer and Medieval Romance*, Woodbridge, Suffolk and Rochester, NY, D. S. Brewer, 2003

—— *Comedy in Chaucer and Boccaccio*, Woodbridge, Suffolk and Rochester, NY, D. S. Brewer, 2009

John Hines, *The Fabliau in English*, London, Longman, 1993

Laura F. Hodges, *Chaucer and Costume: The Secular Pilgrims in The General Prologue*, Cambridge, D. S. Brewer, 2000

Amanda Holton, *The Sources of Chaucer's Poetics*, Aldershot and Burlington, VT, Ashgate, 2008

Simon Horobin, *The Language of the Chaucer Tradition*, Cambridge and Rochester, NY, D. S. Brewer, 2003

Peggy A. Knapp, *Chaucerian Aesthetics*, Basingstoke and New York, Palgrave Macmillan, 2008

Leonard Michael Koff and Brenda Deen Schildgen, *The Decameron and The Canterbury Tales*, Madison, NJ, Fairleigh Dickinson University Press; London and Toronto, Associated University Presses, 2000

Laura C. Lambdin and Robert T. Lambdin, *Chaucer's Pilgrims: An Historical Guide to the Pilgrims in The Canterbury Tales*, Westport, CT, and London, Greenwood Press, 1996

Seth Lerer, *Chaucer and his Readers: Imagining the Author in Late-Medieval England*, Princeton, Princeton University Press, 1993

Geoffrey Lester, *Chaucer in Perspective: Middle English Essays in Honour of Norman Blake*, Sheffield, Sheffield Academic, 1999

B. W. Lindeboom, *Venus' Owne Clerk: Chaucer's Debt to the Confessio Amantis*, Amsterdam and New York, Rodopi, 2007

Frances McCormack, *Chaucer and the Culture of Dissent: The Lollard Context and Subtext of The Parson's Tale*, Dublin, Four Courts Press, 2007

Jill Mann, *Chaucer and Medieval Estates Satire*, Cambridge, Cambridge University Press, 1973

—— *Feminizing Chaucer*, Cambridge, D. S. Brewer, 2002

Priscilla Martin, *Chaucer's Women: Wives, Nuns and Amazons*, Basingstoke, Macmillan, 1990

Mark Miller, *Philosophical Chaucer: Love, Sex, and Agency in The Canterbury Tales*, Cambridge and New York, Cambridge University Press, 2004

Colin Morris and Peter Roberts (eds), *Pilgrimage: The English Experience from Becket to Bunyan*, Cambridge and New York, Cambridge University Press, 2002

Susan Signe Morrison, *Excrement in the Late Middle Ages: Sacred Filth and Chaucer's Fecopoetics*, Basingstoke and New York, Palgrave Macmillan, 2008

Marijane Osborn, *Time and the Astrolabe in The Canterbury Tales*, Norman, Oklahoma University Press, 2002

Lee W. Patterson, *Temporal Circumstances: Form and History in the Canterbury Tales*, Basingstoke and New York, Palgrave Macmillan, 2006

Helen Phillips, *An Introduction to The Canterbury Tales: Fiction, Writing, Context*, Basingstoke, Macmillan and New York, St Martin's Press, 2000

—— (ed.), *Chaucer and Religion*, Woodbridge, Suffolk and Rochester, NY, D. S. Brewer, 2010

S. H. Rigby, *Chaucer in Context: Society, Allegory and Gender*, Manchester, Manchester University Press, 1996

Ian Robinson, *Chaucer and the English Tradition* (second edition), Harleston, Edgeways, 2004

Anne Rooney, *Geoffrey Chaucer: A Guide through the Critical Maze*, Bristol, Bristol University Press, 1989

J. Stephen Russell, *Chaucer and the Trivium: The Mindsong of The Canterbury Tales*, Gainesville, University Press of Florida, 1998

Larry Scanlon, *Narrative, Authority and Power: Medieval Exemplum and the Chaucerian Tradition*, Cambridge, Cambridge University Press, 1994

Brenda Deen Schildgen, *Pagans, Tartars, Moslems and Jews in Chaucer's Canterbury Tales*, Gainesville, Florida University Press, 2001

R. Allen Shoaf, *Chaucer's Body: The Anxiety of Circulation in The Canterbury Tales*, Gainesville, Florida University Press, 2001

Paul Strohm, *Social Chaucer*, Cambridge, MA, Harvard University Press, 1989

Michelle Sweeney, *Magic in Medieval Romance from Chrétien de Troyes to Geoffrey Chaucer*, Dublin, Four Courts Press, 2000

N. S. Thompson, *Chaucer, Boccaccio and the Debate of Love: A Comparative Study of The Decameron and The Canterbury Tales*, Oxford, Oxford University Press, 1999

Diana Webb, *Medieval European Pilgrimage, c.700–c.1500*, Basingstoke and New York, Palgrave, 2002

Siegfried Wenzel (ed. and trans.), *Preaching in the Age of Chaucer: Selected Sermons in Translation*, Washington, DC, Catholic University of America Press, 2008

Edward Wheatley, *Mastering Aesop: Medieval Education, Chaucer and his Followers*, Gainesville, University Press of Florida, 2000

Nigel Wilkins, *Music in the Age of Chaucer, with Chaucer Songs* (second edition), Woodbridge, D. S. Brewer, 1999

Digital and Neo-Chaucer

Both *The Canterbury Tales* and *The Decameron* were adapted for film by Italian director Pier Paolo Pasolini, as part of a trilogy which also included *The Arabian Nights*. Pasolini's version highlights the dark, apocalyptic background and the fairy fantasy elements, while foregrounding the colourful, exuberant – and coarse – life of the comic tales.

P. Pasolini, *The Canterbury Tales*, BFI Video, 2011

Agnès Blandeau, *Pasolini, Chaucer and Boccaccio: Two Medieval Texts and their Translation into Film*, Jefferson, NC, London, McFarland, 2006

Pamela Clements, 'Neomedieval Trauma: The Cinematic Hyperreality of Geoffrey Chaucer's Canterbury Tales', in *Neomedievalism in the Media*, edited by Pamela Clements and Carol Robinson, Lampeter, Edwin Mellen, 2012, pp. 35–54

The BBC has produced two versions of *The Canterbury Tales*. The first, and best, is the animated version, produced by Eastern European animators, and voiced by well-known actors. This version is also available in Middle English.

Various authors, *The Canterbury Tales*, BBC, 2005

The second, more recent version is an adaptation of selected stories in a modern setting. Some of these 'work' better than others, in particular The Shipman's Tale and The Clerk's Tale.

Various authors, *The Canterbury Tales*, BBC, 2004

http://www.bbc.co.uk/drama/canterburytales

Kevin J. Harty, 'Chaucer for a New Millennium: The BBC Canterbury Tales', in *Mass Market Medieval: Essays on the Middle Ages in Popular Culture*, edited by David W. Marshall, Jefferson, NC, and London, McFarland, pp. 13–27

Electronic, parallel text editions

http://www.librarius.com/cantales.htm

http://www.canterburytales.org

William Caxton's early print version:

http://www.bl.uk/treasures/caxton/homepage.html/

A modern multimedia Canterbury pilgrimage:

http://guardian.co.uk/books/2012/may/04/chaucer-canterbury-tales-2012-multimedia

And a 'fun' site: Geoffrey Chaucer Hath a Blog . . .

http://www.houseoffame.blogspot.com

Brantley L. Bryant, *Geoffrey Chaucer Hath a Blog, Medieval Studies and New Media*, Basingstoke, Palgrave Macmillan, 2010

Canterbury Cathedral (official site):
http://www.canterbury-cathedral.org

THE GENERAL PROLOGUE

It is April, a time of fertility and invigoration, when people feel the urge to fall in love, to travel, and to go on pilgrimage. 'Geoffrey', on a pilgrimage to Canterbury, arrives at the Tabard Inn, in Southwark, on the south bank of the Thames. During the evening, twenty-nine others arrive, also on a pilgrimage to Canterbury, and are described by 'Geoffrey'. All of the pilgrims decide to travel as a group. The host of the inn, one Harry Bailly, suggests that they should avoid boredom on the trip by telling stories, two each, one on the way, and one on the way back. The teller of the best story will win a supper at the other pilgrims' expense on their return. Harry will accompany them to Canterbury, and he will be the judge. The pilgrims agree to this, and the pilgrimage begins . . .

'Geoffrey' does not begin his account of the pilgrimage by giving a description of the pilgrims themselves, or his own circumstances, but with a pastoral description of spring: its warmth, its sweetness, its noises, its general seductiveness. In so doing he immediately initiates an ambiguity which will be the feature of *The Canterbury Tales*. People go on pilgrimage for a variety of reasons, not all of them spiritual, not all of them holy. It is a feature of the *Tales* that this ambiguity is not only always present, but is not presented in a negative light, any more than is the sensuality of spring, or the urge to travel and to socialise. It is not wrong, but simply human, to be seduced, whether by the spring, the characters or the narrative, and to be human is to carry the divine potential for salvation. There is not one of Chaucer's characters, not even the pardoner, who is beyond salvation, although all are ambiguous and imperfect.

It is generally accepted that Chaucer's descriptions of the Canterbury pilgrims are based on the tradition of 'estates satire'. This medieval genre features characters representative of different occupations and social classes. These are not individualised, and usually represent the short-comings of the occupation or class they represent, thereby inviting moral examination and criticism by the reader. Although his pilgrims do conform to this pattern, Chaucer departs from the tradition in the detail of his descriptions and in the sympathetic treatment his characters receive from the narrator. The ordering of the descriptions also introduces problems if this is to be seen as pure 'estates satire'. Chaucer's pilgrims appear to be individualised, although careful examination reveals that many of their characteristics are based upon contemporary stereotypes. For example, the character of the friar is based upon 'anti-fraternal' satire, often produced by members of the regular clergy, who felt threatened by the friars' popularity as preachers and confessors. In this form of satire, friars are frequently portrayed as mercenary beggars who wheedle their way into houses by means of their relationship with the women, who are frequently seduced by them, and to whom they give trinkets. They then spend the proceeds on good living. The wife of Bath is based upon stereotypical wives in misogynist literature on the miseries of marriage. The knight and the squire both illustrate the principles of chivalric knighthood and gentility, just as the poor parson illustrates the principles of being a true Christian and a good shepherd of the faithful. Chaucer, however, manages to convey the impression that these are real people, real individuals whom one might meet on a pilgrimage. He does this partly by his use of detail to give colour and 'roundness' to the descriptions, and also by his use of detail to convey the character of the individual. Thus the prioress carries a rich, ornamental rosary with an ambiguous message, *amor vincit omnia* ('love conquers all'), to suggest she may be more of a well-brought-up lady who likes to be seen as a heroine of romance than a bride of Christ. Another device used to individualise the characters has become known as Free Indirect Discourse, which consists of the actual words of the character being reported by the narrator as part of his own narrative. Thus 'Geoffrey' gives an opinion on the monk which is not really his own, but a report of what the character has himself said:

> What schulde he studie and make himselve wood
> Uppon a book in cloystre alway to powre,
> Or swynke with his handes, and laboure
> As Austyn byt: how schal the world be served?

'Geoffrey' also notes that he thought the monk's opinion was good. This is contrary to the tradition of estates satire, which is moral and judgemental; it reveals the faults of each of the groups in society in order to pass judgement upon them. Neither Chaucer, nor 'Geoffrey', ever passes judgement in this way. The readers/hearers are left to make up their own minds about the morality of the characters and their viewpoints.

Other works in which the world is presented in terms of an overview of members of society are William Langland's *Piers Plowman*, where the world is described as a field, and the anonymous *Winnere and Wastoure*, where the world is a battleground between the moral forces of getting and spending. Another variant on the 'estates', which is very close to Chaucer's list of characters, is the Dance of Death, represented in literature by John Lydgate's early fifteenth-century *Dance of Maccabree*. The list of characters in this poem is even closer to Chaucer's list than those in Langland's prologue.

The characters are not presented in any particular order, although the reader/hearer might be led to expect a traditional ordering when the knight is presented first. The knight is presented as a paragon of his estate, as are the parson and the ploughman. This has been taken to indicate that Chaucer retains the structure of the three orders of society; those who fight, those who pray, those who work. If this is so, it provides a stable frame of reference around which the others move, indicating the standard of which all of them fall short. The assumption has been questioned, however, in the generally ambiguous context of the *Tales* as a whole. The knight may be a mercenary, or someone who pursues a fruitlessly violent lifestyle at the expense of his lands and people at home, and the parson may be heretical, or at least heterodox.

The chief impression given by the General Prologue is one of movement and vitality. 'Geoffrey's' world, like that of his audience, is a world in motion. The characters are all lively, none are passive, and all are 'winners' in the sense of potential and actual profit-makers, in their world. Even nefarious churls such as the miller, the pardoner, the summoner, the reeve and the manciple know how to make a profit, licit or illicit. It is hard to believe that either 'Geoffrey', or Chaucer himself, actually *dislikes* any of them; all, even the summoner, have at least one potentially attractive quality. There is also a sense of the commentator's sheer enjoyment of the pilgrims' diversity, in which the variety of life itself is celebrated. The pilgrimage itself conveys the impression of continual motion, into which the reader/hearer is drawn, as is 'Geoffrey' himself. All of these devices make it easier for the audience to identify with the pilgrims, as the audience would like to see themselves also as successful members of society. Their profit will be gained from reading the *Tales*, a process which will lead to self-knowlege, and ultimately towards their own salvation.

Topic Keywords

Medieval society/ estates satire as genre/ costume/ pilgrimage/ medieval inns/ medieval cities, London and Canterbury

Further Reading

Malcolm Andrew, 'Context and Judgement in the General Prologue', *Chaucer Review*, 23, 1989, pp. 316–37

Jon Cook, 'Carnival and *The Canterbury Tales*: Only Equals May Laugh', in *Medieval Literature: Criticism, Ideology and History*, edited by David Aers, New York, St Martin's Press, 1986, pp. 181–3

Helen Cooney, 'The Limits of Human Knowledge and the Structure of Chaucer's General Prologue', *Studia Neophilologica*, 63, 1991, pp. 147–59

Helen Cooper, 'Langland's and Chaucer's Prologues', *Yearbook of Langland Studies*, 1, 1987, pp. 71–81

Laura Lambdin, Robert Lambdin and Elton Smith, *Chaucer's Pilgrims: An Historical Guide to the Pilgrims in The Canterbury Tales*, Westport, CT, Greenwood Press, 1996

Colin Wilcockson, 'The Opening of Chaucer's General Prologue to *The Canterbury Tales*: A Diptych', *Review of English Studies*, 50, 1999, pp. 345–50

❦ Whan that Aprille with his **schowres swoote**   *showers sweet*
The drought of Marche hath **perced** to the roote,   *pierced*
And **bathud** every **veyne** in suich **licour**   *bathed; vein; liquid*
Of which **vertue engendred** is the **flour**:   *vigour; conceived; flower*
Whan **Zephirus eek** with his swete breeth   *the west wind; also*
Enspirud hath in every **holte** and **heeth**   *inspired; wood; heath*
The tendre croppes, and the yonge soune[1]
Hath in **the ram** his halfe cours y-ronne –   *Aries*
And smale **fowles** maken melodie,   *birds*
That slepen al night with open **yhe**,   *eye*   **10**
So **priketh** hem nature in **here corages**.   *quickens; their natural desires*
Thanne longen folk to gon on pilgrimages,
And palmers for to seeken straunge **strondes**   *shores*
To **fern halwes kouth** in sondry londes.   *foreign holy places; well-known*
And specially, from every **schires** ende   *shire's*
Of Engelond, to Canturbury they wende,
The holy blissful martir[2] for to seeke,
That hem hath holpen whan that they were **seeke**.   *sick*
Byfel that in that sesoun on a day,
In Southwerk, at the **Tabbard** as I lay   *Tabard (inn)*   **20**
Redy to wenden on my pilgrimage
To Canturbury, with ful **devout corage**,   *steadfast intent*
At night was come into that hostelrie
Wel nyne and twenty in a companye
Of **sondry** folk, by **aventure y-falle**   *various; chance; fallen*
In **felaschipe**, and pilgryms were thei alle,   *fellowship*
That toward Canturbury wolden ryde.
The chambres and the stable weren **wyde**,   *roomy*
And wel we weren **esud** atte beste.   *accommodated*
And schortly, whan the sonne was to reste,   **30**
So hadde I spoken with hem **everychon**   *each one*
That I was **of here felawschipe anon**.   *one of their fellowship; very soon*

---

1 The sun was considered to be 'new' at the vernal (spring) equinox.
2 St Thomas Becket, murdered in 1170 in Canterbury cathedral by knights of Henry II. Becket was the unofficial 'patron saint' of England, and his shrine was the most famous of England's holy places.

And **made forward** erly to aryse,   agreed
To take oure weye ther, as I yow **devyse** –   recount
But **natheles** whiles I have tyme and space,   nevertheless
Or that I **ferthere** in this tale **pace**,   before; farther; travel
Me thinketh it **acordant** to resoun   in agreement with
To telle yow alle the **condicioun**   state
Of eche of hem, so as it semed me,
40   And **which** they weren and of what **degre**,   what they were like; status
And **eek** in what **array** that they were inne –   also; clothing
And at a knight than wol I first bygynne
A knight ther was, and that a worthy man,
That from the tyme that he ferst bigan
To ryden out, he lovede chyvalrye,[3]
Trouthe and honour, fredom and curtesie,
Ful worthi was he in his lordes **werre**,   war
And therto hadde he riden, **noman ferre**,   no-one further
As wel in Cristendom as **hethenesse**,   heathen lands
50   And evere honoured for his worthinesse.
At **Alisandre** he was whan it was wonne;[4]   Alexandria
Ful ofte tyme he hadde **the bord bygonne**   sat at the head of the table
Aboven alle nacions in **Pruce**;[5]   Prussia
In **Lettowe** had **reyted** and in **Ruce**.   Lithuania; campaigned; Russia
No **cristen** man so ofte of his degre: Christian
In **Gernade** atte siege hadde he be,   Granada
At **Algesir**, and riden in **Belmarie**;   Algeciras; Morocco
At **Lietys** was he, and at **Catalie** –   Turkey (places in)
At many a noble **arme** hadde he be   feat of arms
60   Whan thei were wonne, and in the **greete see**   Mediterranean
At **mortal** batailles hadde he ben fiftene,   deadly
And foughten for oure feith at Tramassene[6]
In lystes thries, and **ay** slayn his **foo**.[7]   always; foe (enemy)

3 Chivalry; the code of honour and way of life associated with the noble and 'gentle' life.
4 The knight's campaigns are all connected with the crusading ideal.
5 The Teutonic knights feasted those who crusaded with them. The 'head' of the table was the place of most honour.
6 In north Africa.
7 'he had jousted three times' (the list is the board which separates two jousting knights).

This ilke worthi knight hadde ben also
Somtyme with the lord of Palatye,[8]
Ageyne another **hethene** in Turkye; against; heathen (non-Christian)
And evermore he hadde a **sovereyn prys**, great reputation
And though he was worthy he was **wys**, wise
And of his **port** as meke as a **mayde**. bearing; maiden
He never yit no **vilonye** ne sayde evil thing 70
In al his lyf unto no maner **wight**. person
He was a **verray parfit**, gentil knight. truly perfect
But for to telle you of his **aray** – clothing
His hors was good, but he was nou*gh*t **gay**. richly caparisoned
Of **fustyan** he wered a **gepoun**, coarse cloth; tunic
Al **bysmoterud** with his **habergeoun**, besmattered; mail shirt
For he was late comen from his **viage**, journey
And wente for to doon his pilgrimage.
With him ther was his sone, a yong **squyer**,
A **lovyer** and a lusty bacheler, lover 80
With lokkes **crulle as** they were layde in presse. curly; as if
Of twenty yeer he was of age, I gesse.
Of his stature he was of **evene lengthe**, average height
And **wondurly delyver** and gret of strengthe, wonderfully lithe
And he hadde ben some tyme in chivachie[9]
In **Flaundres**, in **Artoys** and in **Picardie**; Flanders; Artois; Picardy
And **born him wel** as in so litel **space**, bore himself well; time
In hope to stonden in his lady grace.[10]
Embrodid was he **as it were a mede**, embroidered; like a meadow
Al ful of fresshe **floures**, white and reede. Flowers 90
Syngynge he was, or **flowtynge**, al the day. playing the flute
He was as fressh as is the **moneth** of May. month
Schort was his **goune** with sleeves long and wyde: gown
Wel koude he sitte on hors and faire ryde.
He **cowde** songes wel make, and **endite**, knew how to; write poetry
Lustne and **eek** daunce and wel **purtray** and write. listen; also; draw
So hote he **lovede** that by **nightertale** loved; night-time
He sleep **namoore** than doth a nyghtyngale.[11] no more

8 A north African potentate, presumably Muslim.
9 An armed raid, many of which were carried out by English knights in France.
10 In the hope of impressing his lady.
11 The nightingale sings at night.

Curteys he was, lowly and **servysable**,	courteous; willing to serve

100 And **carf byforn his fadur** at the table[12]   carved in front of his father

A **yeman** had he and servantes **nomoo**   yeoman; no more

At that tyme, for him **lust** ryde soo: wanted to

And he was clad in **coote** and hood of grene.   coat

A **shef of pocok arwes**, bright and **kene**,[13]   sheaf of peacock arrows; sharp

Under his belte he **bar** ful **thriftily**.   carried; fittingly

Wel **cowde he dresse his takel** yomanly.   knew how to look after his gear

His **arwes drowpud** nought with fetheres lowe,   arrows; fell short

And in his **hond** he bar a mighty bowe.   hand

A **not heed** hadde he, with a broun **visage**.   close-clipped (hair); face

110 Of woode craft cowde he wel **al the usage**.   how to do it

Upon his arme he bar a gay **bracer**,   arm guard

And by his syde a swerd and a **bokeler**,

And on that other side a gay **daggere**,

Harneysed wel and scharp as poynt of spere.   decorated

A Cristofre on his brest of silver **schene**;[14]   bright

❦ An horn he bar, the **bawdrik** was of grene –   sheath

A **forster** was he, sothely, as I gesse.   forester

Ther was also a **nonne**, a prioresse,   nun

That of **hire smylyng** was **ful** symple and coy: her smiling; very

120 Hire grettest **ooth** nas but, 'by Seynt Loy'[15],   oath

And sche was **clept** Madame **Englentyne**.   called; eglantyne (a sweet herb)

Ful wel sche sang the servise **devyne**,   divine

Entuned in hire nose ful **semyly**,   intoned; seemly/becomingly

And Frensch sche spak ful faire and **fetysly**,   fashionably

Aftur the scole of Stratford atte Bowe,[16]

For Frensch of **Parys** was to hire **unknowe**.   Paris; unknown

At mete wel y-taught was sche withalle –[17]

Sche **leet** no morsel from hire lippes falle,   let

Ne wette hire **fyngres** in hire sauce deepe.   fingers

12 Part of a young knight's training was to serve at his lord's table.
13 The arrows were dressed, that is fledged, with peacock feathers.
14 The image of St Christopher, patron saint of travellers.
15 St Eligius, goldsmith and patron of metal-workers, a 'fashionable' saint.
16 The convent of Stratford-at-Bowe was favoured by rich merchants for their
   daughters: royal and noble girls were mostly entered into the convent at Barking.
17 'she had been well taught to eat with good manners'

Wel cowde sche **carie** a morsel and wel **keepe**   pick up and eat; take care   130
That no drope **fil** uppon hire brest: fell
In curtesie was sett al hire lest.[18]
Hire **overlippe wypud** sche so clene,   top lip; wiped
That in hire cuppe was no **ferthing** sene   small speck
Of **grees**, whan sche dronken hadde hire draught.   grease
Ful semely **afture** hir mete sche **raught**,   after; reached for
And **sikurly** sche was of **gret disport**,   definitely; very social
And ful plesant and amyable of **port**,   manner
And peyned hire to counterfete cheer[19]
Of court, and ben **estatlich** of manere,   dignified   140
And to ben holden **digne** of **reverence**.   worthy; being looked up to
But for to speken of hire conscience –
Sche was so charitable and so **pitous**   full of pity
Sche wold weepe, if that sche sawe a mous
Caught in a trappe, if it were **deed** or bledde.   dead
Of smale houndes hadde sche, that sche fedde
With **rostud fleissh** and mylk and **wastel breed**;   roast meat; white bread
But sore wepte sche if oon of hem were deed,
Or if men smot it with a yerde smert,   stick; smartly

❦ And al was conscience and tendre herte.   150
Ful semely hire **wymple y-pynched** was.   headdress; pinched/pleated
Hire nose streight, hire **eyen** grey as glas,   eyes
Hire mouth ful smal, and therto softe and reed.
But sikurly, sche hadde a fair forheed: truly

❦ It was almost a **spanne brood**, I trowe,   handspan; broad/wide
For hardily sche was **not undurgrowe**.   not skinny
Ful fetys was hire **cloke** as I was **waar**:   very fashionable; cloak; aware
Of **final** coral about hire arme sche **baar**   fine; wore
A **peire of bedes**, **gaudid** al with grene,   rosary; large green stones
And theron heng a **broch** of gold ful **schene**,   brooch; bright   160
On which was first y-writen a crowned 'A',
And after that **Amor vincit omnia**.   'love conquers all'
Anothur nonne with hire hadde sche,
That was hire **chapelleyn**, and prestes thre.   deputy

18 'All her concern was to maintain courtesy'
19 The counterfeiting of cheerfulness, especially at meals, was an essential sign of
    good manners.

A monk ther was, a fair for the maistrie,[20]
An outrydere that loved **venerye**,[21]   hunting
A manly man, to ben an abbot able.
Ful many a **deynte** hors hadde he in stable,   fine
And whan he rood, men might his bridel heer
170   **Gyngle** in a whistlyng wynd, so cleere,   jingle
And eek as lowde, as doth the chapel belle
Ther as the lord was keper of the **selle**.   cell (subordinate monastery)
The reule of Seynt Maure or of Seint Beneyt[22]
Bycause that it was old and **somdel streyt**,   somewhat strict
This **ilke** monk **leet forby hem pace**,   same; let them pass by
And helde aftur the newe world the space.[23]
He gaf nat of that text a pulled hen[24]
That seith that hunters been noon holy men,
Ne that a monk whan he is **cloysterles**   away from his cloister
180   Is likned to a fissche that is watirles:
This is to seyn, a monk out of his cloystre –
But **thilke** text hild he not worth an **oystre**.[25]   this same text; oyster
And I seide his opinion was good –
What schulde he studie and make himselve **wood**   mad
Uppon a book in **cloystre** alway to **powre**,   cloister; pour/ read intently
Or **swynke** with his handes and laboure   work hard
As **Austyn byt**: how schal the world be served?   Saint Augustine; bad/ordered
Lat Austyn have his swynk to him reserved!
Therfore he was a **pricasour** aright: horseman
190   Greyhoundes he hadde, as swifte as **fowel** in flight.   birds
Of **prikyng** and of huntyng for the hare[26]   riding

❦ Was al his **lust** – for no cost wolde he spare.   desire
I **saugh** his sleves **purfiled** atte hond   saw; fur-lined
With **grys**, and that the fynest of a **lond**;   fur; land
And for to **festne** his hood **undur** his **chyn**   fasten; under; chin

20 'a fine figure of a man'
21 A monk who rode out to granges and other properties to check on them, take
   rents etc.
22 Two forms of monastic rule; most English monks were Benedictines.
23 'adhered to the new world'
24 'He didn't give a pulled hen for that text'
25 Oysters were common in medieval times.
26 This could be sexual innuendo – the 'hare' was the female pudendum.

He hadde of gold y-wrought a curious **pyn**:   pin/brooch
A **love knotte** in the **gretter ende** ther was.   lover's knot; thicker end
His heed was **ballid** and schon as eny glas,   bald
And eek his face, as he had be **anoynt**.   anointed
He was a lord ful fat and in good **poynt**.   condition   200
His **eyen steep** and rollyng in his **heed**,   eyes; well-defined; head
That **stemed** as a **forneys of a leed**.   steamed; lead-lined furnace
His bootes **souple**, his hors in **gret estat**;   supple; really good condition
Now certeinly he was a fair **prelat**.   prelate; churchman
He was not pale, as a **forpyned goost** –   tortured spirit
A fat swan loved he best of eny **roost**.   roast (meat)
His palfray was as broun as eny **berye**   berry
A **frere** ther was, a wantoun and a **merye**;   friar
A lymytour, a **ful solmpne** man.[27]   very solemn/dignified
In all the ordres foure[28] is noon that **can**   knows   210
So moche of **daliance** and fair **langage**.[29]
He hadde y-made many a fair mariage
Of yonge **wymen** at his owne cost:[30]   women
Unto his ordre he was a noble **post**.   pillar
Ful wel biloved and familier was he
With frankeleyns **over al in his cuntre**,   throughout his region
And eek with worthi women of the toun,
For he hadde power of confessioun,
As seyde himself, more than a **curat**,   curate
For of his ordre he was **licenciat**.   licensed   220
Ful sweetly herde he confession,
And plesaunt was his absolucion.
He was an **esy man to give penance**   he gave light penances
Ther as he wiste han a good pitance,[31]
For unto a **poure** ordre for to **geve**   poor; give
Is signe that a man is wel **y-schreve**,   forgiven (after confession)
For if he **gaf**, he **dorste** make **avant**,   gave; dared; claim
He **wiste** that a man was repentant –   knew
For many a man so hard is of his **herte**,   heart

27 A friar licensed to beg.
28 The four main orders of friars in England: Franciscan, Dominican, Carmelite, Augustinians.
29 social intercourse; language/speech.
30 The implication is that he had to, as he had made them pregnant.
31 'where he thought he'd get a good financial reward'

230 🍃 He may not wepe though him **sore smerte**.   hurts deeply
Therefore in stede of wepyng and prayeres,
Men **mooten** given silver to the pore freres.   may
His **typet** was ay **farsud** ful of knyfes   sleeve; stuffed
And pynnes, for to give faire **wyfes**,   wives/women
And certayn he hadde a mery **noote**;   voice
Wel couthe he synge and pleye on a rote.[32]   he knew well how to sing
Of yeddynges he bar utturly the prys.[33]
His nekke whit was as the flour delys;[34]
There to he strong was as a champioun[35].

240 He knew wel the tavernes in every toun,
And every **ostiller** or gay **tapstere**,   landlord; barmaid
Bet than a **lazer** or a beggere –   better; leper
For unto such a worthi man as he
Acorded not, as by his **faculte**,   it was not suitable; status
To have with **sike** lazars aqueyntance.   sick
It is not honest, it may not **avaunce**   be advantageous
For to **delen** with such **poraile**,   'hang around' with; poor people
But al with riche and sellers of **vitaille**!   foodstuffs
And overal **ther** eny profit schulde arise   where

250 **Curteys** he was and **lowe** of servyse.   curteous; humble
Ther was no man nowher so vertuous;
He was the best begger in al his hous,
For **thorgh** a **widewe** hadde but **oo schoo**,   although; widow; one shoe
So plesaunt was his '*In principio*'[36],
Yet wolde he have a **ferthing or** he wente –   farthing (a small coin); before
His purchase was bettur than his rente.[37]
And **rage he couthe**, and pleye as a **whelpe**   he knew how to sport; puppy
In lovedayes[38], ther couthe he mochil helpe,[39]
Forther was he not like a **cloysterer**,   poor monk

32 A medieval stringed instrument.
33 'he was the greatest of performers'
34 The fleur-de-lys or lily-flower, heraldic symbol of the king of France. The friar is associated elsewhere with 'Frenchness'.
35 'He was as strong as a champion (fighter of judicial duels) in this respect'
36 One of the prayers from the liturgy which he sang.
37 'his 'perks' were worth more than his pay'
38 Times when disputes were settled, and people were accorded – in a holiday atmosphere.
39 'when he knew a lot about helping'

With a thredbare cope[40] as a **pore scoler**, poor scholar 260
But he was like a **maister** or a pope: academic
Of double worstedewas his **semy cope**,[41] short coat
That rounded was **as a belle out of presse**. like a bell out of a press
Somwhat he **lispede** for wantonnesse, lisped
To make his Englissch swete upon his **tunge**, tongue
And in his harpyng whan that he hadde sunge.
His **eyen** twynkeled in his heed aright, eyes

❦ As don the sterres in the frosty night.
This worthi lymytour was called 'Huberd'.
A marchaunt was ther with a forked berd; 270
In **motteleye** high on horse he sat, multi-coloured clothing
Uppon his heed a **Flaundrisch bever** hat, Flemish; beaver
His **botus clapsud** faire and **fetously**. boots; clasped; well
His **resons** he spak ful solempnely, statements
Swownynge alway the encres of his wynnyng.[42]
He wolde the see were **kepud** for eny thing defended
Bitwixe **Middulburgh** and **Orewelle**.[43] Middelburg; Orwell
Wel couthe he in eschange scheeldes selle.[44]
This worthi man ful wel **his witte bisette**, used his wits
There wiste no man that he was in **dette**, debt 280
So **estately** was he of **governaunce**, respectable; bearing
With his bargayns and with his **chevysance**: dealings
Forsothe he was a worthi man withalle – truly
But, **soth to say**, I **not** what men him calle.
truth to tell; didn't know (ne wot)
A clerk ther was of **Oxenford** also, Oxford
That unto logik hadde long y-go.[45]
Also lene was his hors as is a rake[46]
And he was not right fat, I undertake,
But lokede **holwe** and therto **soburly**. very thin; gravely/seriously

40 A priest's cloak, worn when saying Mass.
41 Worsted was the finest woollen cloth.
42 'always talking about the extent of his profits'
43 Middelburg in the Netherlands and the Orwell estuary, in Suffolk – in other words, the North Sea.
44 'He knew well how to sell shields (measures of exchange) in the exchange'
45 'taken up the study of logic long ago'
46 'his horse was as skinny as a rake'

290 Ful thredbare was his **overest courtepy**,	outermost covering
For he hadde nought geten him yit a benefice,	
Ne was not worthy to haven an office;	
For him was lever have at his beddes heed	he would rather
Twenty bookes, clothed in blak and **reed**,	red
Of **Aristotil** and of his philosophie,	Aristotle
Then robes riche, or **fithul**, or **sawtrie**.	fiddle; psaltery
But although he were a **philosophre**,	learned man
Yet hadde he but litul gold **in cofre**,	in his chest
But al that he might gete and his frendes sende,	
300 On bokes and his lernyng he it spende,	
And **busily** gan for the soules pray	earnestly
Of hem that gaf him wherwith to **scolay**.	study
Of studie tooke he most cure and heed,	
Not **oo** word spak he more than was neede:	one
Al that he spak, it was of heye **prudence**,	wisdom/'gravitas'
And schort, and quyk, and ful of gret **sentence**.	learning/importance
Sownyng in moral manere was his speche,[47]	
And gladly wolde he lerne, and gladly teche.	
A sergeant of lawe, **war** and **wys**,	careful; wise
310 That often hadde ben atte **parvys**	St Paul's porch (parvise)
Ther was also, ful riche of excellence.	
Discret he was and of gret reverence;	
He semed such, his wordes were so wise.	
Justice he was ful often **in assise**,	at the assises
By patent and by **pleyn** comission,	full
For his science and for his heih renon –[48]	
Of fees and robes had he many oon.	
So gret a **purchasour** was ther no wher noon;	purchaser/buyer
Al was **fee symple** to him, in effecte –	complete ownership
320 His purchasyng might nought ben to him suspecte.[49]	
Nowher so besy a man as he ther **nas**,	was not (ne was)
And yit, he semed **besier** than he was.	busier
In termes hadde **caas** and **domes** alle,	cases; judgements
That from the tyme that kyng were falle,[50]	

47 'his speech was very moral in its tone'
48 'because of his learning and his high reputation'
49 'there were never any flaws in his purchase agreements'
50 The death of a king (some manuscripts say 'King William', ie William I) but could mean any king before Edward III (1327–1377).

Therto he couthe **endite** and **make a thing**.   draft; make a legal document
There couthe no man pynche at his writyng,[51]
And every statute **couthe he pleyn by roote**.   he knew fully by heart
He rood but **hoomly** in a **medled coote**,   ordinarily; multi-coloured coat
Gird with a **seynt** of silk with **barres** smale –   belt; stripes
Of his array telle I no lenger tale.   330
A **frankeleyn** ther was in his companye;   franklin (free landholder)
Whit was his berde as the **dayesye**;   daisy
Of his complexion he was **sangwyn**;   ruddy
Wel loved he in the morn a sop of wyn.[52]
To lyve in **delite** was al his **wone**,   pleasure; custom
For he was Epicurius' owne sone,[53]
That heeld opynyon that **pleyn delyt**   sheer enjoyment
Was **veraily felicite** perfyt.   truly; happiness
An **houshaldere** and that a gret was he –   householder
Seynt Julian he was in his contre.[54]
His breed, his ale, was alway **after oon**;   the best   340
A better **envyned** man was no wher noon.   stocker of wine
Withoute bake **mete** was never his hous,   food

❦ Of **fleissch** and **fissch** and that so plentyuous,   meat; fish
Hit **snewed** in his house of mete and drynk,   snowed
Of alle deyntees that men cowde **thynke**,   imagine
Aftur the **sondry** sesons of the yeer;   various
He chaunged hem at mete and at soper.
Ful many a fat **partrich** had he **in mewe**,   partridge; in his birdhouses
And many a **brem** and many a **luce** in **stewe**.   bream; pike; fishpond   350
Woo was his cook but if his sauce were
Poynant and scharp, and redy al his **gere**.   tasty; utensils
His table **dormant** in his halle alway   standing
Stood redy, covered, al the longe day.
At **sessions** ther was he lord and sire;   sessions (court)
Ful ofte tyme he was knight of schire.[55]

---

51 'Nobody was able to fight fault with his drafts'
52 'a piece of bread dipped in wine'
53 Epicurus, the Roman who believed that the pursuit of pleasure was everything.
   The franklin is dedicated to the pursuit of pleasure.
54 Saint associated with hospitality.
55 Knight of the Shire – one of the county's elected representatives in Parliament.

	An **dulas** and a **gipser** al of silk	dagger; purse
	Heng at his **gerdul**, whit as morne milk.	girdle/belt
	A **schirreve** hadde he ben, and a **counter** –	sheriff; auditor
360	Was nowher such a worthi **vavaser**.	propertied gentleman
	A **haburdassher** and a carpenter,	haberdasher
	A **webbe**, a **deyer**, and a **tapicer**,	weaver; dyer; tapestry-maker
	Weren with us **eek**, clothed in **oo lyvere**	also; one; livery (uniform)
	Of a solempne and gret **fraternite**.	guild fellowship
	Ful freissh and newe his gere **piked** was,	decorated/finished
	Here knyfes were **y-chapud** nat with **bras**	mounted; brass
	But al with silver wrought ful clene and wel,	
	Here **gurdles** and here **pouches** every del.	girdles/belts; pockets
	Wel semed eche of hem a fair **burgeys**	burgess (well-to-do townsman)
370	To sitten in a geldehalle on the **deys**.[56]	raised end of the hall
	Every man for the wisdom that he can[57]	
	Was **schaply** for to ben an aldurman,[58]	worthy
	For **catel** hadde they inough and rente,	possessions
	And eek here wyfes **wolde it wel assente**.	would agree
	And elles certeyn hadde they ben to blame;	
	It is right fair for to be **clept**, 'Ma Dame',	called; 'my lady'
	And for to go to vigilies al byfore,[59]	
	And han a **mantel rially** y-bore.	cloak; royally
	A cook thei hadde with hem **for the nones**,	for the duration (of pilgrimage)
380	To boyle **chiknes** and the **mary** bones,	chickens; marrow
	And poudre marchant tart and galyngale.[60]	
	Wel cowde he knowe a draught of **Londen** ale.	London
	He **cowde** roste, **sethe**, **brille**, and frie,	knew how to; simmer; boil
	Make **mortreux**, and wel bake a pye.	stews
	But gret harm was it, as it **semede** me,	seemed to
	That on his **schyne** a **mormal** hadde he,	chin; ulcer
	For blankmanger he made with the beste.[61]	
	A schipman was ther, **wonyng** fer by weste;	living

56 Guildhall – a special building where the members of the trade fraternity would
   meet both socially and for fraternity business, and hold special festivities.
57 'in his own opinion'
58 Alderman – the highest town or city officials, from whom the mayor was elected.
59 'in front of everyone else'. The vigil is a special church service, usually for festivals.
60 Two forms of spice used in cookery.
61 White meat: pounded white meat, such as veal.

For ought I **woot** he was of **Dertemouth**. — knew; Dartmouth
He rood upon a **rouncey as he couthe**, — nag; as well as he knew how — 390
In a gowne of **faldyng** to the kne; — woollen cloth
A dagger hangyng on a **laas** hadde he — lace
Aboute his nekke, under his arm a-doun.
The **hoote somer** had maad his **hew** al broun, — hot summer; colour
And certeinly he was a good **felawe** – — companion
Ful many a draught of wyn had he drawe
From Burdeuxward, whil that the **chapman** sleep:[62] — merchant
Of nyce conscience took he no keep.
If that he foughte and hadde the **heigher** hand — upper
By water he sente hem hoom to every land.[63] — 400
But of his craft to **rikne** wel the tydes, — reckon/judge
His **stremes** and his dangers him bisides, — currents
His **herbergh** and his mone, his **lodemenage**, — harbours; navigational skill
Ther was non such from Hulle to Cartage.[64]
Hardy he was, and wys to undertake,
With many a tempest hath his **berd** ben **schake**. — beard; shaken
He knew wel alle the **havenes** as thei were — harbours
From Scotland to the **Cape of Fynestere**, — Cap Finisterre
And every **cryk** in **Bretayne** and in Spayne: — creek; Brittany
His barge **y clepud** was the 'Magdelayne'.[65] — called — 410
Ther was also a doctour of **phisik** – — physic/medicine
In al this world ne was ther non him lyk,[66]
To speke of Phisik and of Surgerye,
For he was groundud in astronomye:
He **kepte** his pacient **wondurly** wel — cared for; wonderfully
In houres by his magik naturel.
Wel cowde he fortune the ascendent[67]
Of his ymages for his pacient.
He knew the cause of every **maladye**, — sickness

---

62 Bordeaux was a centre of the Anglo-French wine trade.
63 That is, he threw them overboard.
64 This could be Cartagena in Spain or Carthage in Africa – the former is perhaps more likely.
65 Magdalene, after St Mary Magdalene.
66 'There was no doctor like him in the whole world'
67 The doctor used his knowledge of astronomy/astrology to care for his patients – using the stars and the zodiac to calculate times and methods of treatment.

420   ❦ Were it of cold, or hete, or moyst, or drye,
      And where thei **engendrid** and of what humour.[68]   caused
      He was a **verrey** parfit **practisour**.   truly; practitioner
      The cause y-knowe and of his harm the roote,[69]
      Anon he gaf the syke man his **boote**:   remedy
      Ful redy hadde he his **apotecaries**,   apothecaries (chemists)
      To sende him **dragges** and his **letuaries**,   drugs; medicines
      For eche of hem made othur to **wynne**;   make money
      Here frendschipe nas not newe to begune.[70]
      Wel knewe he the olde Esculapius,[71]
430   And Deistorides, and eek Rufus,
      Old Ypocras, Haly and Galien,
      Serapyon, Razis, and Avycen,
      Averrois, Damascen and Constantyn,
      Bernard, and Gatisden, and Gilbertyn.
      Of his diete **mesurable** was he,   moderate
      For it was of no **superfluite**,   excess
      But of gret norisching and digestible.
      His studie was but litel on the Bible.
      In **sangwyn** and in **pers** he clad was al,   red; blue
440   Lyned with taffata and with **sendal**;   silk
      And yit he was but **esy** in **dispence** –   careful in spending
      He kepte that he wan **in pestilence**,   during the Plague
      For gold in phisik is a **cordial**;   medicine
      Therfore he lovede gold in special.
      A Good Wif was ther of byside **Bathe**,   Bath
      But sche was **somdel deef**, and that was **skathe**.   somewhat deaf; a shame
      Of cloth makyng sche hadde such an **haunt**,   skill
      Sche passed hem of Ypris and of Gaunt.[72]
      In al the parisshe wyf ne was ther noon
450   That to the offryng **byforn** hire schulde goon,   before

---

68 It was believed that the four humours, with their qualities of cold, hot, moist and
   dry, ruled the human body and its moods.
69 'when he knew the cause and root of his (the patient's) illness'
70 'their friendship was not newly begun (ie they had known one another for some
   time).
71 Aesculapius, Rufus, Hippocrates, Haly, Galen, Serapion, Rhazes, Avicenna,
   Averroes, Damascenus, Constantine, Bernard, John of Gaddesden, Gilbertus
   Anglicus – all writers on medicine known (or attributed) in the medieval West.
72 Ypres and Ghent – great cloth-making, and cloth-trading, centres in Flanders.

And if ther dide, certeyn, so **wroth** was sche   angry
That sche was thanne **out of alle charite**.   in a really bad mood
Hire **keverchefs** weren **ful fyne of grounde** –   headcloths; finely textured
I durste swere they **weyed** ten pounde   weighed
That on a Sonday were upon hire heed.
Hire **hosen** were of fyn scarlett reed,   hose/stockings
Ful **streyte y-teyed**, and schoos ful **moyste** and newe.   tightly tied; supple
Bold was hir face, and fair, and reed of **heewe**.   colour
Sche was a worthy woman al hire lyfe;
Housbondes atte chirche dore hadde sche **fyfe**,   five   460
Withouten othur **companye** in youthe –   not to mention; lovers
But therof needeth nought to speke as **nouthe** –   now
And **thries** hadde sche ben at Jerusalem.   thrice/three times
Sche hadde **passud** many a straunge streem: passed
At Rome sche hadde ben, and at Boloyne,[73]
In Salice at Seynt Jame, and at Coloyne.
Sche **cowde moche** of wandrying by the weye.   knew a lot about
Gattothud was sche, **sothly** for to seye.   gap-toothed; truthfully
Uppon an **amblere** esely sche sat,   ambling horse
Wymplid ful wel, and on hire heed an hat   with a headcloth   470
As brood as is a **bocler** or a **targe**,   small shield; round shield
A foot **mantel** aboute hire **hupes** large,   over-skirt; hips
And on hire feet a paire of **spores** scharpe.   spurs
In **felawschipe** wel cowde **lawghe** and **carpe**.   company; laugh; chatter
Of remedyes of love sche knew **perchaunce**,[74]   perhaps
For of that art sche knew the olde daunce.
A good man was ther of religion,
And was a pore **person** of a toun,   parson
But riche he was of holy thought and **werk**.   works/deeds
He was also a lerned man, a clerk,   480
That Crist's gospel gladly wolde **preche**.   preach
His **parischens** devoutly wold he teche.   Parishioners
Benigne he was and wondur diligent,   gentle/kindly

---

73 Rome, Bologna, Celicia and Cologne – all major centres of pilgrimage in Western
   Europe in the Middle Ages.
74 Ovid's *Remedia Amoris* would have been known to Chaucer's courtly audience –
   this appears to be an instance of tacit understanding between the poet and his
   original readers/hearers. Taken literally, of course, it means methods of gratifying
   sexual urges.

And in aversite ful pacient,

And such he was y-proved ofte **sithes**.   times

Ful loth were him to curse for his tythes[75]   he was very unwilling

But **rether** wolde he geven, out of dowte,   rather

Unto his pore parisschens aboute,

Of his **offrynge** and eek of his **substance**.   offering/collection; living

He cowde in litel thing han **suffisance**.[76]   sufficient

Wyd was his parisch and houses fer **asondur**,   apart

But he left nat, for reyn ne thonder,

490 In siknesse and in meschief to visite

The **ferrest** in his parissche, moche and lite[77],   farthest

Uppon his feet, and in his hand a **staf**,   staff

❦ This noble ensample unto his scheep he gaf,

That ferst he **wroughte** and after that he taughte;   did

Out of the gospel he **tho** wordes caughte,   those

And this **figure** he added yit therto,   example

That if golde ruste what schulde **uren** doo,   iron

For if a **prest** be foul on whom we truste,   priest

500 No wondur is a **lewid** man to ruste.   lay (not clergy)

And schame it is, if a preste **take kepe**,   take notice

A **schiten** schepperd and a clene schepe.   filthy

Wel mighte a prest ensample for to give

By his clennesse how that his scheep schulde lyve.

He sette not his benefice to **huyre**,   hired it out

And lefte his scheep **encombred** in the **myre**,   stuck; mud

And ran to London unto Seynte Poules[78]

To seeken him a chaunterie for soules,[79]

Or with a **brethurhede** be with holde,   guild/fraternity

510 But dwelte at hoom and kepte wel his **folde**,   sheepfold

So that the wolf ne made it not **myscarye**.   go wrong

He was a schepperde and no **mercenarie**,   hired soldier

And though he holy were and vertuous,

75 Tithes – the tenth of a person's income which should be paid to the parish priest.

76 'He knew how to make do with a little'

77 'the greatest and the least'

78 St Paul's Cathedral, in the City of London.

79 A chantry – a chapel or altar founded for a paid priest to pray for the souls of the departed (usually relatives of the founder/s).

He was to **senful** man nought **dispitous**,	sinful; spiteful
Ne of his speche **daungerous** ne **digne**,	bullying; haughty
But in his teching discret and benigne,	
To drawe folk to heven by clennesse,	
By good ensample, was his busynesse.	
But it were eny persone obstinat,[80]	
What so he were of high or lowe **estat**,	status
Him wolde he **snybbe** scharply **for the nones**.	rebuke; right away
A bettre preest I trowe ther no wher non is.[81]	
He **waytud after** no pompe ne reverence,	took account of
Ne maked him a **spiced** conscience,	sophisticated
But Crist's **lore**, and his apostles twelve,	teaching
He taught, and ferst he folwed it himselve.	
With him ther was a ploughman, his brothur,	
That hadde y-lad of dong ful many a fothur.[82]	
A trewe **swynker** and a good was hee,	hard worker
Lyvyng in **pees** and parfiyt charitee.	peace
God loved he best with al his trewe herte;	
At alle tymes, though him **gamed** or **smerte**,	pleased; hurt
And thanne his neighebour right as himselve.	
He wolde **threiss**, and therto **dyke** and **delve**	thresh; ditch; dig
For Crist's sake, with every **pore wight**	poor person
Withouten **huyre**, if it laye in his might.	payment
His tythes payede he ful faire and wel,	
Bathe of his owne **swynk** and his catel.	both; labour
In a **tabbard** rood upon a **mere**.	sleeveless tunic; mare
Ther was also a **reeve** and a **mellere**,	reeve; miller
A **sompnour** and a pardoner also,	summoner
A maunciple, and my self: ther was no **mo**.	more
The **mellere** was a stout **carl** for the nones,	miller; churl
Ful big he was of braun and eek of boones,	
That **prevede** wel, for **over al ther** he cam,	proved; wherever
At **wrastlyng** he wolde have alwey the ram.	wrestling
He was schort **schuldred**, broode, a **thikke knarre**;	
	shouldered; well-built fellow
Ther nas no dore that he nolde heve of harre,[83]	

520

530

540

80 'But if anyone was disobedient'
81 I believe there is no better priest anywhere'
82 'spread many a load of dung'
83 'there was no door he couldn't heave off its hinges'

Or breke it with a **rennyng** with his heed.   running into it
His berd as ony sowe or fox was reed,
And therto **brood** as though it were a spade.   broad
550 Upon the **cop right** of his nose he hade   very top
A **werte**, and theron stood a tuft of **heres**,   wart; hairs
Reed as the **berstles** of a **souw's** eeres.   bristles; sow's
His **nosethurles** blake were and wyde;   nostrils
A swerd and a **bocler baar** he by his side.   small shield; carried
His mouth as wyde was as a gret **forneys**,   furnace
He was a **jangler** and a **golyardys**,   talker; teller of bawdy tales
And that was most of **synne** and **harlotres**.   sin: debauchery
Wel cowde he stele corn and **tollen thries**,   charge three times
And yet he hadde a thombe of gold, parde.[84]
560 A **whight cote** and **blewe** hood **wered** he: white coat; blue; wore
A **bagge pipe** cowde he blowe and **sowne**,   bagpipe; play
And therwith al he brought us out of towne.
A gentil **maunciple** was ther of a temple,[85]   manciple
Of which **achatoirs** mighten take exemple   buyers
For to be wys in **beyyng** of **vitaille**,   buying; food/supplies
For whethur that he payde or took by **taille**,   credit
Algate he **wayted** so in his **achate**   was watchful; purchasing
That he was ay **biforn**, and in good state.   ahead
Now, is not gat of God a ful fair grace
570 That such a **lewed** man's wit schal **pace**   unlearned; outsmart
The wisdom of an heep of lerned men:
Of **maystres** hadde **moo** than thries ten,   masters/academics: more
That were of lawe expert and **curious**,   skilled
Of which ther were a **doseyn** in an hous,   dozen
Worthi to be **stiwards** of rente and lond   stewards
Of any lord that is in Engelond,
To make him lyve by his **propere good**,   own resources
In honour, **detteles**, **but if** he were **wood**,   without debt; unless; mad
580 Of lyve as **scarsely** as he can desire,   cheaply
And able for to helpen al a schire
In any **caas** that mighte **falle** or **happe**,   situation; befall; happen

84 The miller's 'golden thumb' was proverbial – implying dishonesty, and a certain
    amount of (cunningly assisted) luck.
85 An Inn of Court, possibly the Temple in London. The manciple was an officer in
    charge of purveying supplies.

And yit this maunciple **sette here aller cappe**.	hoodwinked them all
The reeve was a **sklendre**, **colerik** man,[86]	thin; full of choler
His berd was schave as **neigh** as ever he can,	closely
His heer was by his eres **neigh** y-schorn,	near to
His top was **dockud** lyk a prest **biforn**;[87]	
Ful longe wern his **leggus** and ful lene,	legs
Al like a staff, ther was no calf y-sene.	
Wel cowde he kepe a **gerner** and a **bynne**;	barn; bin (for storing grain etc)
Ther was non auditour cowde **on him wynne**.	get the better of him 590
Wel **wiste** he by the drought and by the reyn,	knew
The yeeldyng of his seed and of his greyn.	
His lordes scheep, his **neet**, his **deyerie**,	cattle; dairy
His **swyn**, his hors, his **stoor** and his **putrie**	pigs; horses; poultry
Was **holly** in this reeve's governynge,	wholly
And by his covenant gaf the **rekenynge**	account
Syn that his lord was **xxti yeer** of age.	twenty years
Ther couthe noman bringe him **in arrerage**;	in arrears
Ther nas baillif, ne **herde**, ne othur **hyne**,	herdsman; servant
That they ne knewe his **sleight** and his **conynge**:	slyness; cunning 600
They were **adrad** of him as of the deth.	afraid
His **wonyng** was ful fair upon an **heth**,	home; heath
With grene trees y-schadewed was his place:	
He cowde bettre than his lord purchase.	
Ful riche he was y-stored prively;[88]	
His lord wel couthe he plese subtilly,	
To geve him and **lene** him of his owne good,	lend
And have a thank, a cote, and eek an hood.	
In youthe he lerned hadde a good **mester**,	mystery/craft
He was a wel good **wright**, a carpenter.	craftsman 610
This reeve sat upon a wel good **stot**,	horse
That was a **pomely** gray, and highte Scot.	dappled
A long **surcote** of blew uppon he hadde,	over-tunic
And by his side he bar a rusty **bladde**.	blade
Of Northfolk was this reeve of which I telle,	
Byside a toun men callen Baldeswelle.[89]	

86 Choler was the dominant humour in his body, thus producing the character he describes in the prologue to his *Tale*.
87 docked (cut very short); at the front.
88 'he had privately stored away a fortune for himself'
89 Bawdeswell, between Norwich and Lynn.

Tukkud he was as is a frere aboute,[90]
And ever he rood the **hynderest** of the **route**.   hindmost; company
A **sompnour** was ther with us in that place,[91]   summoner
That hadde a fyr reed cherubyn's face,[92]
620   For **sawceflem** he was, with **eyyen narwe**,   pimpled; small eyes
As **hoot** he was, and lecherous as a **sparwe**,   hot; sparrow
With **skalled browes** blak and **piled** berd;   scabby eyebrows; patchy
Of his **visage** children weren **aferd**,   face; afraid
Ther nas quyksilver, litarge, ne bremston,[93]
Boras, ceruce, ne oille of Tartre noon,
Ne **oynement** that wolde clense and **byte**,   ointment; burn
That him might helpen of his **whelkes** white,   pustules
Ne of the **knobbes** sittyng on his cheekes.   boils
Wel loved he garleek, oynons, and ek leekes,
And for to drinke strong wyn, reed as blood,
630   Than wolde he speke and crye as he were **wood**.   mad
And whan that he wel donken hadde the wyn,
Than wolde he speke no word but **latyn**.   Latin
A fewe termes hadde he, tuo or thre,
That he hadde lerned out of som **decree** –   decree (official document)
No wondur is, he herde it al the day,
And eek ye knowe wel how that a jay
Can clepe 'watte', as wel as can the Pope –[94]
But who so wolde in othur thing him **grope**,   quiz
Thanne hadde he **spent** al his **philosophie**:   exhausted; learning
640   Ay '*Questio quid juris*' wolde he crye.[95]
He was a **gentil harlot** and a kynde,
A bettre felaw schulde men nowher fynde.
He wolde suffre for a quart of wyn
A good felawe han his **concubyn**   mistress
A twelve moneth, and excuse him **atte fulle**,   entirely

90 'His outer garment was tucked into his belt'
91 An official in a Church court, often dealing with moral offences.
92 Cherubim – angels with fiery faces.
93 Mercury (quicksilver), a lead compound, sulphur (brimstone), borax, white lead
   and cream of Tartar (sometimes still used in cooking), made into a paste and
   used as ointments.
94 Probably an imitation of the jay's raucous call; implying that the summoner is
   merely repeating phrases he has learned in the manner of a talking bird.
95 A phrase used in court when determining cases.

And prively a fynch eek cowde he pulle,[96]
And if he fond **owher** a good felawe,   anywhere
He wolde teche him for to have non awe,
In such a caas, of the archedekne's curs,[97]
But if a mannes soule were in his **purs**,   purse   650
For in his purs he scholde punyssched be:
'Purs is the ercedekne's helle,' avowed he,
But wel I **woot** he lyeth right in dede;   understand
Of cursyng oweth ech gulty man to drede,
For curs wol **slee**, right as **assoillyng** saveth;   kill; absolution
And also **ware** hym of a *significavit*:[98]   beware
In **daunger** he hadde at his owne assise   awe
The yonge girles of the Diocise,[99]
And knew here **conseil** and was al here **red**.   secrets; counsel
A garland had he set upon his heed,   660
As gret as it were for an **ale stake**;   sign of an alehouse
A **bokeler** had he maad of a cake.   small shield
With him ther rood a gentil pardoner
Of Rouncival, his frend and his **comper**,[100]   companion
That streyt was comen from the court of Rome.
Ful lowde he sang, 'Com hider, love, to me'.
The sompnour bar to him a **stif burdoun**;   strong accompaniment

❧ Was nevere **trompe** of half so gret a soun.   trumpet
This pardoner hadde heer **as yelwe as wex**,   as yellow as wax
But smoth it heng, as doth a **strike of flex**;   hank of flax   670
By **unces** hynge his lokkes that he hadde,   strands (one ounce)
And therwith he his schuldres overspradde;
Ful **thenne** it lay by **culpons**, on and oon.   thin; bigger strands
An hood for jolitee wered he noon,
For it was **trussud** up in his **walet**:   bundled; bag

---

96 A colloquial phrase of uncertain meaning. It could mean that he could divest
   someone of their possessions, or it may have a sexual connotation (as in 'he
   was a pheasant-plucker').
97 The archdeacon was the bishop's representative in matters of moral law such as
   those dealt with by the Summoner.
98 An order for sending someone to gaol.
99 Diocese; the geographical limits of a bishop's jurisdiction.
100 The Augustinian hospital of St Mary of Roncesvalles, in the City of London.
    Indulgences (pardons) were being sold from there in the 1380's.

Him thought he rood al of the newe get.[101]
Dischevele **sauf** his cappe, he rood al **bare** –   without; bareheaded
Suche glaryng **eyyen** hadde he as an hare.   eyes
A **vernicle** hadde he sowed on his cappe,   image of St Veronica
680 His walet lay byforn him in his lappe,
Bret ful of pardon come from Rome al hoot.   brimful
A **voys** he hadde as smal as eny **goot**;   voice; goat
No berd ne hadde, he never scholde have;
As smothe it was as it ware **late y-schave**.   just been shaved
I **trowe** he were a geldyng or a mare,[102]   believe
But of his craft fro Berwyk unto Ware[103]
Ne was ther such another pardoner,
For in his **male** he hadde a **pilwe beer**,   bag; pillowcase
Which that he saide was oure lady's **veyl**;   veil
690 He seide he hadde a **gobet** of the **seyl**   chunk; sail
That Seynt **Poetur** hadde whan he wente   Peter
Uppon the see til Jhesu Crist him hente.[104]
He hadde a cross of **latoun**, ful of stones,   latten (a form of brass)
And in a glas he hadde pig's bones,
But with thise **reliques** whanne that he fand   relics (saints' remains)
A pore parson dwellyng uppon land,
Upon a day he gat him more moneye
Than that the parson gat in monthes tweye,
And thus with **feyned** flaterie and **japes**   pretended; tricks
700 He made the parson and the poeple his apes.
But trewely to tellen atte laste,
He was in church a noble **ecclesiaste**;   churchman
Weel cowde he rede a lessoun or a storye,
But **altherbest** he sang an **offertorie**,   best of all; offering
For wel he wiste whan that song was songe,
He most preche and wel **affyle** his tunge,   smooth
To **coynne** silver as he right wel cowde,   coin
Therfore he sang ful meriely and lowde.
Now have I told you schortly in a clause,

---

101 'he thought he was the height of fashion'
102 Gelding; a castrated male horse.
103 Berwick (on the Anglo-Scottish border) and Ware (in Hertfordshire, just north
     of London).
104 'until Jesus Christ called him (to be an apostle)'

Thestat, tharray, the nombre, and eek the cause   the status, clothing   710
Why that assembled was this companye
In Southwerk at this gentil ostelrie   hostelry/inn
That highte the Tabbard, faste by the Belle,   was called; near
But now is tyme to yow for to telle
How that we bare us in that ilke night[105]
Whan we were in that ostelrie alight,
And aftur wol I telle of oure viage,   journey
And al the remenant of oure pilgrimage.
But ferst, I pray you of your curtesie,
That ye ne rette it nat my vilanye,   attribute; wickedness   720
Though that I speke al pleyn in this matere,   plainly
And telle you here wordes and here cheere,   their
Ne though I speke here wordes propurly,   their own
For preye knowen, also wel as I,   as well as I do
Who so schal telle a tale aftur a man,   as someone tells it
He most reherce as neigh as ever he can   relate
Every work, if it be in his charge,
Al speke he never so rudely ne large,   though; crudely; plain
Or elles he moot telle his tale untrewe,
Or feyne thing, or fynde his wordes newe.   pretend; make up   730
He may not spare, though he were his brothur –   hold back
He most as wel sey oo word as anothur.   one
Crist spak himself ful broode in holy writ,   plainly
And wel ye woot no vilanye is it.
Eke Plato seith, who so that can him rede   knows how to himself;; advise
The wordes mot be cosyn to the dede.
Also, I pray you to foryeve it me,   forgive
Al have I folk nat set in here degre[106]
Here in this tale as that thei schulde stonde,   as they should be
My witt is thynne, ye may wel undurstonde.   740
Greet cheere made oure ost us everichon,   host; every one
And to the souper sette he us anon: supper
He served us with vitaille atte beste;   food and drink
Strong was the wyn and wel to drynke us leste.   liked
A semely man oure ooste was with alle   manly; host
For to han been a marchal in an halle.   marshal (household officer)

105 carried on/went about things; same.
106 'If I have not presented people as they are'

A large man was he, with **eyyen stepe** –   *eyes bright*
A fairere **burgeys** in ther noon in **chepe**.[107]   *burgess; Cheapside*
Bold of his speche and **wys**, and wel y-taught,   *wise*
750   And of **manhede lakkede** he right naught.   *manhood; lacked*
Eke therto he was right a mery man,   *also*
And after soper playen he bygan,
And spak of myrthe among othur thinges,
Whan that we hadde **maad oure rekenynges**,   *paid our bills*
And sayde thus, 'Lo, lordynges, trewely,
Ye ben to me right welcome hertily,
For by my trouth, if that I schal not lye,
I ne saugh this yeer so mery a companye
At oones in this **herbergh** as is now.   *lodging*
760   **Fayn** wold I **do yow merthe**, wiste I how – *gladly; amuse you*
And of a **merth** I am right now bythought   *amusement*
To **doon you eese**, and it schal coste nought.   *keep you amused*
Ye gon to Caunturbury, God you speede,
The blisful martir **quyte you youre meede**;   *reward you*
And wel I woot, as ye gon by the weye,
Ye schapen yow to talken and to pleye,
For, trewely, comfort ne merthe is noon
To ryde by the weye domb as a **stoon**,   *stone*
And therfore wold I make you disport
770   As I seyde **erst**, and do you som confort;   *before*
And if yow liketh alle, by **oon** assent,   *one*
Now for to standen at my juggement,
And for to **werken as I schal you seye**,   *do as I tell you*
Tomorwe whan ye riden by the weye,
Now, by my **fadres** soul, that is deed,   *father's*
But ye be merye, **smyteth of** myn heed. *if you're not; cut off*
Hold up youre hond, withoute more speche.'
Oure counsel was not longe for to **seche**;   *seek/ask*
Us thoughte it nas nat worth **to make it wys**, *to think about it*
780   And graunted him withoute more **avys**,   *discussion*
And bad him **seie** his **verdite** as him **leste**. *tell; verdict; liked*
'Lordynges,' **quoth** he, 'now **herkeneth** for the beste, *said; listen*
But taketh not, I pray you, in disdayn.

107 A market, one of the best-known streets in London: 'chepe' means simply 'market'.

This is the poynt; to speken schort and playn
That ech of yow, **to schorte with youre waye**,

> to make your way seem shorter

In this **viage** schal telle tales **tweye**

> journey; two

To Caunturburiward, I mene it so,
And homward he schal tellen othur tuo,
Of **aventures** that ther han bifall;

> events/happenings

And which of yow that **bereth him best of all**,

> does it best   790

That is to seye, that telleth in this caas
Tales of best **sentence** and of **solas**,

> serious content; pleasure

Schal have a soper at your alther cost,[108]
Here in this place, sittynge by this post,
Whan that we comen ageyn from Canturbery;
And for to make you the more mery
I wol my **selven** gladly with you ryde,

> self

Right at myn owen cost, and be youre **gyde**,

> guide

And whoso **wole** my juggement **withseie**

> will; question

Schal paye for al we spenden by the weye;

> 800

And if ye **vouchsauf** that it be so,

> grant

Telle me anoon, withouten wordes moo,
And I **wole erely schappe me** therfore.'

> will get ready early

This thing was graunted, and oure **othus** swore

> oaths

With ful glad herte, and prayden him also
That he wolde **vouchesauf** for to doon so,

> grant

And that he wolde be oure governour,
And of oure tales **judge** and reportour,

> judge

And sette a souper at a certeyn **prys**,

> price

And we wolde rewled be **at his devys**

> how he wished   810

In heygh and lowe; and thus by oon assent
We **ben acorded** to his juggement.

> agreed

And therupon the wyn was **set** anoon –

> served

We dronken and to rest wente **echon**,

> each one

Withouten eny **lengere tarying**.

> waiting longer

Amorwe, whan that the day bigan to sprynge,

> in the morning

Up **roos** oure ost, and was oure **althur cok**,

> rose; other cock

And **gaderud us togidur** all in a **flok**,

> gathered us together; flock

And forth we riden, a litel more than **paas**,

> walking pace

---

108 'at the expense of the rest of you'

820   Unto the waterynge of seint Thomas,[109]
      And there oure ost bigan his hors **areste**,   pull up
      And seyde, 'Lordus, herkeneth if yow lest;
      Ye **woot** youre **forward** and I it you **recorde**,   know; agreement; take note
      If **evesong** and **morwesong** acorde,   evening service; morning service
      Lat se now who schal telle ferst a tale,   let us see
      As ever I moote drinke wyn or ale,
      Who so be rebel to my juggement,
      Schal paye for al that by the weye is spent.
      Now **draweth cut**, er that we forther **twynne**,   draw lots; depart/move along
830   Which that hath the schortest schal bygynne.'
      'Sire knight,' **quoth** he, 'maister and my lord,   said
      Nowe draweth cut, for that is myn acord.
      Cometh ner,' quod he, 'my lady prioresse,
      And ye, sire clerk, lat be your **schamfastnesse**.   modesty
      Ne studieth nat ley hand to every man;[110]
      Anon to drawen every **wight** bigan,   person
      And schortly, for to tellen as it was,
      Were it by **aventure**, or **sort**, or **cas**,   chance; luck; design
      The soth is this – the cut **fil** to the knight,   fell
840   Of which ful glad and **blithe** was every wight,   happy
      And telle he moste his tale, as was **resoun**,   reasonable
      By **forward** and by **composicion**,   agreement; understanding
      And ye han herd – what needeth wordes moo?
      And whan this goode man **seigh** that it was so,   saw
      As he that wys was and obedient
      To kepe his forward by his fre assent,
      He seyde, 'Syn I schal bygynne the game,
      What, welcome be thou, cut, **A Goddus name**!   in God's name
      Noe lat us ryde, and herkneth what I seye.'   now
      And with that word we riden forth oure weye,
      And he bigan, with right a merie chere
      His tale, and seide right in this manere.

---

109 A landmark on the Canterbury road.
110 'put your hand in'/ 'draw a lot'

THE KNIGHT'S TALE

Theseus, Duke of Athens, is returning home from a successful campaign against the Amazons. He has defeated them and forced their queen, Hippolyta, to marry him. She accompanies him back to Athens with her young sister Emelye. On the way, Theseus is accosted by a group of Theban women, whose husbands have been killed by the tyrant Creon, who will not permit them to be buried. Theseus defeats and kills Creon, but Creon's two nephews, Palamon and Arcite, are pulled still alive from a pile of corpses. They are taken back to Athens by Theseus, sentenced to perpetual imprisonment, and warned that they will be executed if they try to escape. One day, Palamon looks out of their prison window and sees Emelye, immediately falling in love with her. He tells Arcite, who then does the same. Although sworn brothers, they become enemies for love of Emelye. Eventually, Arcite is released through the intercession of Theseus's friend Perotheus, but he returns to Athens to be close to Emelye, where, altered in appearance and under an assumed name, he rises to a high position in Theseus's court. Palamon escapes from prison, and chances to meet Arcite in a clearing in the forest, where they agree to fight. Theseus also chances to enter the clearing as they fight, and Palamon discloses Arcite's identity. Their lives are saved by the intercession of Hippolyta and Emelye, and Theseus allows them to fight a tournament instead. They have a year to raise troops. Before the tournament Palamon, Arcite and Emelye go the temple of their favoured deities to pray for a suitable result. Emelye is told that she will marry, and both lovers believe they will win. Learning that Arcite will be victorious, Venus (Palamon's deity) pleads for her knight with Saturn, ruler of sudden death. Softened by Venus's tears, Saturn causes Arcite's horse to stumble as he celebrates winning the contest. Arcite is fatally injured, and dies a protracted and painful death. The philosophical underpinnings of the story are explained by the wise old counsellor, Egeus. After a while, Palamon and Emelye are married, and Palamon returns as ruler to Thebes.

'Were it by aventure, or sort, or cas . . . the cut fil to the knyght' (GP 838–9). Behind the ambiguity of 'Geoffrey's' statement lies the fact that the idea of, and the theology of, a divinely-ordered world was deeply ingrained in English society, even at the end of the fourteenth century. The knight politely accepts the invitation to go first in the storytelling contest, and thus his social position, without question and without pride. He is, after all, both 'parfit' and 'gentil' (GP 72), the perfect representative of his class. His story is, like the knight himself, his position in society and the ideologies he represents, grounded in history, tradition and a succession of learned writers and thinkers from the classical past to his own day (what the wife of Bath will later refer to as 'auctoritee') – 'Whilom, as olde stories tellen us' (KT 1). This opening line leads the audience to expect a romance epic, as these frequently employ similar strategies (for example, in *Sir Orfeo* and *Sir Gawain and the Green Knight*). These entertainments were particularly associated with the 'gentil' class, although they were also, in Chaucer's time, enjoyed by the socially aspirational middle classes, and even the very notion of 'gentil' will be eventually be brought into question by Chaucer's other pilgrims.

The knight's story has the characteristics, therefore, of both epic and romance. It has (among other tropes and qualities) the broad scale, the coalescence of the natural and the supernatural, the interaction between public and private lives, and the spectacular 'set pieces' of epic. On the other hand, it has lovers and their rivalries, unforeseen catastrophes and coincidences, and the chivalric encounters and the developmental, *bildungsroman* qualities of romances. The story of Thebes was very popular during the Middle Ages (John Lydgate's *Sege of Thebes* is an early fifteenth-century version of the original story), and the background for this version is classical epic (the *Thebiad* of Roman writer Statius), filtered through the courtly lens of the contem¶ porary Italian writer, Giovanni Boccaccio. The Knight's Tale, which originally stood on its own, freely adapted from Boccaccio's *Il Teseida*, may have been written as early as the 1380s. It was not written specifically for inclusion in *The Canterbury Tales*.

Chaucer creates a tale in which the hot-blooded and hot-headed young lovers of chivalric romance are continually challenging and threatening the world of the epic king, with its battles between nations and its focus on the concerns of national and international politics. Epic is a genre of older men, romance of the young, and the knight's tale plays with the tensions and interactions between the two genres, using philosophy to reach an uneasy resolution between them. The fissures implicit in the genre are implied, ready to be exposed by the miller. The knight's own son, the squire, resembles the young protagonists Palamon and Arcite, with his active chivalry in France and his love-longing, and will attempt to tell a 'romance' story. The tale has, therefore a potential social reading, which medieval people, used to reading allegorically, would quickly have understood. In Chaucer's day, London was often claimed by writers to be 'new Troy' and the collapsed timespace identifying the classical Greek city/state of Athens with the contemporary kingdom/city of England and London was a feature of English culture. A classical Greek funeral pyre is composed of wood hewn from English trees (KT 2041–7), and Chaucer introduces the spectacle of a tournament, which might be an event from Greek history, or something performed and staged for a contemporary audience: Chaucer had overseen such a tournament, complete with mock amphitheatre, to celebrate the marriage of King Richard II of England and Anne of Bohemia in 1382. It may be that the knight's image of King Theseus appearing god-like, on the throne of state (KT 1655–6), is based on a memory of that occasion. Richard II, we are told, also liked to sit in state in Westminster Hall, the building of which Geoffrey Chaucer also oversaw, as the master of the king's 'works'.

Theseus is an ideal ruler, an example of the rulership qualities defined in medieval advice literature, exemplified by 'mirrors' of kingship and the *Secreta secretorum*, advice on how to be a good ruler supposedly given to the young Alexander by his mentor, Aristotle. He is contrasted with the tyrant Creon and the ruler of the gods, Saturn, both cruel 'kings' who are driven by whims, and who fail to consider the general good of the people over whom they hold power. Theseus is chivalric – he can lead fighting men, and shows chivalric pity and mercy to women and the powerless, such as Palamon and Arcite. Above all, he is just and prudent, carefully weighing even decisions taken on the spur of the moment in response to weeping women. He enforces the divine quality of order in his realms, imposing the authority of bloodless rules on a fierce and bloody quarrel. He has progressed from his early devotion to 'the reede statue of Mars' (KT 116), which he can still utilise when required, to the maturity required of the perfect ruler. In this, he resembles young Arcite, whose potential will not be realised due to his tragic early death.

The horrific details of Arcite's injuries and the process of his death introduce an element of shock and horror into the story. Besides being a comment on the consequences of the fact that the young are prone to fall victim to (in the eyes of the older generation) 'silly', often violent and overblown, quarrels and passions, it also indicates a critique of the violence which lay behind the ideals of knighthood and chivalry. These ideals were being re-evaluated at a time when the French war was unpopular and unproductive, the crusade had been devalued due to the Bishop of Norwich's 'crusade' in Flanders in 1383, and 'pacifists' such as the poet John Gower and the followers of radical theologian John

Wyclif were questioning the validity of all violence, even capital punishment. In such an atmosphere, Chaucer's knight can be seen as anachronistic. Chivalry is a code of violence and conflict, and Palamon and Arcite only seem to come to life when they have something to fight over. They fight over Emelye like 'dogs over a bone', and threaten the ordered society which Theseus has built. Women also constitute a threat of destabilisation, not only passively by causing conflicts between men, but actively by publicly weeping and begging for changes in policy. A king could not break his word, so weeping women also enabled him to change his mind without loss of face. Both Philippa of Hainault (who pleaded for the lives of the burghers of Calais before Edward III in 1347) and Anne of Bohemia (who pleaded on behalf of the City of London before Richard II in 1391) helped their husbands to 'concede' mercy to declared enemies. However, the gods of Palamon and Arcite are active, whilst Diana, the goddess of Emelye, is depicted in a passive role, communicating decisions rather than soliciting them. Although Emelye is an Amazon, and thus brown-skinned and without one breast, she is described as a white-skinned, red-cheeked courtly love object when Palamon and Arcite see her from their prison window.

The Knight's Tale is deeply philosophical. It is the secular equivalent of The Parson's Tale, with which it 'bookends' the whole collection. Chaucer drew heavily on the *De consolatione philosophiae* of the fifth-century philospher Boethius, which he translated into Middle English as *Boece*. The main theme of this is the transitoriness of human life, and the fickle whims of the goddess Fortuna, who turns the Wheel of Fortune according to her whims, so that anyone who commits himself to her will rise to good fortune and happiness, then fall to ill fortune and misery. Boethius's was a Platonic philosophy, grounded in the belief that humans are 'the playthings of the gods', and yet he was a Christian, believing that the man who remained faithful, and did not espouse Fortuna, would eventually achieve God's mercy and a place in heaven. Chaucer has both ideas in play in The Knight's Tale. Overall, this is a tale based on pagan philosophy and pagan understandings of warring, pretentious and 'cruel' gods, but the speech of the 'wise old man' (a feature of classical epic) Egeus at the end is a masterly fusion of this with Christian ideas, with the divine order of the Chain of Being (by which God holds all Creation together in harmony) fused with the transitory nature of human life (Arcite will see how stupid love is when he looks down on it all after death). This fusion was first achieved by twelfth-century theologians on the rediscovery of Greek philosophy by the West, and continued to play an important part in later medieval 'thought'. The knight is a crusader. Like the parson, he uses the gifts and qualities he has in order to 'do' the best he can, a reflection of the tendency towards affective religion – the belief that what is inside is more important than outward observance – in the later fourteenth century.

The knight reveals the results of the education deemed suitable for his class and position in society. The Knight's Tale is the product of an élite international culture, which remains in artistic masterpieces such as the crown of Anne of Bohemia and the Wilton Diptych. Its representation of ideals of knighthood and rulership reflect the concerns of a group of individuals and families at the top end of European society. Below them, society was dynamic, shifting and turbulent, and Chaucer's knight is, accordingly, subject to an immediate challenge from 'below'.

Key Questions

What are the features of epic and of romance? How do they interact in this story? Which is the more dominant, and why?

Why would people in fourteenth-century England want to think of their present in terms of the classical past?

What kind of ruler is Theseus? How does he resemble (or not) the pagan gods, or the Christian god? What qualities should a young man retain, develop and lose on the way to maturity? In what ways would rulership be important to the knight, or to members of Chaucer's audience?

What are the essential qualities of knighthood? Are they valorised or criticised (or both) in this story? Is the tale inherently misogynist?

How well (or not) do pagan and Christian ideologies co-exist in this story? How do the pagan deities compare with Christian saints, and with the Christian god? How does the knight's philosophy/theology compare with the parson's?

Topic Keywords

Epic and romance genres/ knighthood, chivalry and tournaments/ courtly love and the socio-cultural position of women/ medieval philosophy/ medieval medicine/ medieval kingship/ the classical past in the Middle Ages

Further Reading

Laurel Amtower, 'Mimetic Desire and the Misappropriation of the Ideal in The Knight's Tale', *Exemplaria*, 8, 1996, pp. 125–44.

David Anderson, *Before the Knight's Tale: Imitation of Classical Epic in Boccaccio's 'Teseida'*, Philadelphia, PA, Philadelphia University Press, 1988

David Benson, 'The Knight's Tale as History', *Chaucer Review*, 3, 1969, pp. 107–23

Brooke Bergan, 'Surface and Secret in The Knight's Tale', *Chaucer Review*, 26, 1991, pp. 1–16

Piero Boitani, 'The Genius to Improve an Invention: Transformations of The Knight's Tale', 1992

Derek Brewer, 'Chaucer's Knight as Hero, and Machaut's Prise d'Alexandrie', in *Heroes and Heroines in Medieval English Literature*, edited by Leo Carruthers, Cambridge, Boydell and Brewer, 1994, pp. 81–96, pp. 81–96

John Burrow, 'Chaucer's Knight's Tale and the Three Ages of Man', in *Medieval and Pseudomedieval Literature: The J. A. W. Bennett Memorial Lectures*, Perugia, 1982–3, edited by Piero Boitani and Anna Torti, Cambridge, D. S. Brewer, 1984, pp. 91–108

Paul Clogan, 'The Knight's Tale and the Ideology of the Roman Antique', *Medievalia et Humanistica*, 18, 1992, pp. 129–55

Bruce Kent Cowgill, 'The Knight's Tale and the Hundred Years' War', *Philological Quarterly*, 54, 1975, pp. 670–9

Susan Crane, 'Medieval Romance and Feminine Difference in The Knight's Tale', *Studies in the Age of Chaucer*, 12, 1990, pp. 47–63

Robert Epstein, ' "With many a floryn he the hewes boghte": Ekphrasis and Symbolic Violence in The Knight's Tale', *Philological Quarterly*, 85, 2006, pp. 49–68

John Finlayson, 'The Knight's Tale: The Dialogue of Romance, Epic, and Philosophy', *Chaucer Review*, 27, 1992, 126–49

Robert Emmett Finnegan, 'A Curious Condition of Being: The City and the Grove in Chaucer's Knight's Tale', *Studies in Philology*, 106, 2009, pp. 285–98

Louise O. Fradenburg, 'Sacrificial Desire in Chaucer's Knight's Tale', *Journal of Medieval and Renaissance Studies*, 27, 1998, pp. 47–75

Alan T. Gaylord, 'The Role of Saturn in The Knight's Tale', *Chaucer Review*, 8, 1974, pp. 171–90

Marc S. Guidry, 'The Parliaments of Gods and Men in The Knight's Tale', *Chaucer Review*, 43, 2008, pp. 140–70

Robert S. Haller, 'The Knight's Tale and the Epic Tradition', *Chaucer Review*, 1, 1966, pp. 67–84

Margaret Hallissy, 'Writing a Building: Chaucer's Knowledge of the Construction Industry and the Language of The Knight's Tale', *Chaucer Review*, 32, 1998, pp. 239–59

Keiko Hamaguchi, 'Domesticating Amazons in The Knight's Tale', *Studies in the Age of Chaucer*, 26, 2004, pp. 331–54

Mark H. Infusino and Ynez Violé O'Neill, 'Arcite's Death and the New Surgery in The Knight's Tale', *Studies in the Age of Chaucer*, 1, 1984, pp. 221–30

Stewart Justman, ' "Auctoritee" and The Knight's Tale", *Modern Language Quarterly*, 39, 1978, pp. 3–14

R. E. Kaske, 'Causality and Miracle: Philosophical Perspectives in The Knight's Tale and The Man of Law's Tale', in *Traditions and Innovations: Essays in British Literature of the Middle Ages and the Renaissance*, edited by David G. Allan and Robert A. White. Newark, Del., University of Delaware Press, London and Toronto, Associated University Presses, 1990, pp. 11–34

Ebbe Klitgård, *Chaucer's Narrative Voice in The Knight's Tale*, Copenhagen, Museum Tusculanum Press, 1995

Barbara Kowalik, 'Genre and Gender in Chaucer's Knight's Tale', in *Studies in Literature and Culture in Honour of Professor Irena Janicka-Swiderska*, edited by Maria Edelson, Lódz, Lódz University Press, 2002, pp. 100–10

Catherine La Farge, 'Women and Chaucer's Providence: The Clerk's Tale and The Knight's Tale', in *From Medieval to Medievalism*, edited by John Simons, Basingstoke, Macmillan, and New York, St Martin's Press, 1992, pp. 69–81

Edgar Laird, 'Cosmic Law and Literary Character in Chaucer's Knight's Tale', in *Literary Nominalism and the Theory of Rereading Late Medieval Texts: A New Research Paradigm*, edited by Richard Utz, Lewiston NY, Mellen, 1995, pp. 101–15

Thomas H. Luxon, ' "Sentence" and "solaas": Proverbs and Consolation in The Knight's Tale', *Chaucer Review*, 22, 1987, pp. 94–111

T. McAlindon, 'Cosmology, Contrariety and The Knight's Tale',
    Medium Ævum, 55, 1986, pp. 41–57

James H. McGregor, 'The Knight's Tale and Trecento Italian
    Historiography', in *The Decameron and The Canterbury Tales*, edited
    by Leonard Michael Koff and Brenda Deen Schildgen, Madison, NJ,
    Fairleigh Dickinson University Press, London and Toronto,
    Associated University Presses, 2000, pp. 212–25

William A. Madden, 'Some Philosophical Aspects of The Knight's Tale',
    College English, 20, 1960, pp. 193–4

Ilan Mitchell-Smith, ' "As olde stories tellen us": Chivalry, Violence,
    and Geoffrey Chaucer's Critical Perspective in The Knight's Tale',
    Fifteenth-Century Studies, 32, 2007, pp. 83–99

Bruce Moore, ' "Allone, withouten any compaignye": The Mayings in
    Chaucer's Knight's Tale', *Chaucer Review*, 25, 1991, pp. 285–301

Daniel M. Murtaugh, 'The Education of Theseus in The Knight's Tale',
    SELIM, *Revista de la Sociedad Española de Lengua y Literatura Inglesa
    Medieval*, 10, 2000, pp. 141–65

Charles Muscatine, 'Form, Texture, and Meaning in Chaucer's Knight's
    Tale', *Publications of the Modern Language Association*, 65, 1950, pp.
    911–29

R. H. Nicholson, 'Theseus's "ordinaunce": Justice and Ceremony in
    The Knight's Tale', *Chaucer Review*, 22, 1988, pp. 192–213

Judith C. Perryman, 'The "false Arcite" of Chaucer's Knight's Tale',
    Neophilologus, 68, 1984, pp. 121–33

Stephen H. Rigby, *Wisdom and Chivalry: Chaucer's Knight's Tale and
    Medieval Political Theory*, Leiden, Boston, MA, Brill, 2009

Lois Roney , *Chaucer's Knight's Tale and Theories of Scholastic
    Psychology*, Tampa, South Florida University Press, 1990

Edward C. Schweitzer, 'Fate and Freedom in The Knight's Tale',
    Studies in the Age of Chaucer, 3, 1981, pp. 13–45

Mark Sherman, 'The Politics of Discourse in Chaucer's Knight's Tale',
    Exemplaria, 6, 1994, pp. 87–114

Robert Stein, 'The Conquest of Femenye: Desire, Power and Narrative
    in Chaucer's Knight's Tale', in *Desiring Discourse: The Literature of
    Love, Ovid through Chaucer*, edited and introduced by James Paxson
    and edited by Cynthia Gravlee, Selinsgrove, PA, Susquehanna
    University Press, 1998, pp. 188–205

Melvin Storm, 'From Knossos to Knight's Tale: The Changing Face of Chaucer's Theseus', in *The Mythographic Art: Classical Fable and the Rise of the Vernacular in Early France and England*, edited by Jane Chance, Gainesville, University of Florida Press, 1990, pp. 215–31

Linda Tatelbaum, 'Venus' "citole" and the Restoration of Harmony in Chaucer's Knight's Tale', *Neuphilologische Mitteilungen*, 74, 1973, pp. 649–64

Sylvia Tomasch, 'Mappae Mundi and The Knight's Tale: The Geography of Power, the Technology of Control', in *Literature and Technology*, edited and introduced by Mark Greenberg, and edited by Lance Schachterle, Stephen Cutcliffe and Steven Goldman, London, LeHigh University Press, 1992, pp. 66–98

Tory Vandeventer Pearman, 'Laying Siege to Female Power: Theseus the "Conqueror" and Hippolita the "Asseged" in Chaucer's The Knight's Tale', *Essays in Medieval Studies*, 23, 2006, pp. 31–40

Scott Vaszily, 'Fabliau Plotting against Romance in Chaucer's Knight's Tale', *Style*, 31, 1997, pp. 523–42

Winthrop Wetherbee, 'Romance and Epic in Chaucer's Knight's Tale', *Exemplaria*, 2, 1990, pp. 303–28

William F. Woods, 'Chivalry and Nature in The Knight's Tale', *Philological Quarterly*, 66, 1987, pp. 287–301

—— ' "My sweete foo": Emelye's Role in The Knight's Tale', *Studies in Philology*, 88, 1991, pp. 276–306

Dorothy Yamamoto, 'Heraldry and The Knight's Tale', *Neuphilologische Mitteilungen*, 93, 1992, pp. 207–15

❦ **Whilom**, as olde stories tellen us,   *once upon a time*
Ther was a Duk that **highte** Theseus –   *was called*
Of **Athenes** he was lord and governour,   *Athens*
And in his tyme **swich** a conquerour   *such*
That gretter was ther non under the sonne.
Ful many a riche **contre** hadde he wonne,   *country*
That with his wisdam and his **chivalrie**   *feats of arms*
He conquered al the **regne** of **Femynye**,   *kingdom; Amazonia*
That **whilom** was **y cleped** Cithea,   *formerly; called*
And weddede the queen **Ypolita**,   *Hippolita*   10
And brought hire hoom with him in his contre,
With moche **glorie**, and gret solempnite,   *pomp*
And **eek** hire yong suster Emelye;   *also*
And thus with victorie and with melodye
Lete I this nobel duk to Athenes ryde,   *permit*
And al his **ost** in armes him biside;   *army*
At certes if it nere to long to heere,[1]
I wolde **han** told you fully the manere   *have*
How wonnen was the regne of Femenye
By Theseus and by his **chivalrye**,   *knights*   20
And of the grete bataille for the nones,
Bytwix Athenes and Amazones,
And how **asegid** was Ypolita,   *besieged*
The faire hardy **Quyen** of Cithea,   *queen*
And of the **feste** that was at hire weddynge,   *feast, or festivity*
And of the tempest at hire hoom comynge –[2]
But al that thing I most as now forber;[3]
I have, **god wot**, a large feeld to **ere**,   *God knows; plough*
And **wayke** ben the oxen in my plough;   *ready*
The **remenant** of the tale is long ynough –   *rest*   30
I wol not **letten** eek non of al this **rowte**.   *hinder; company*
Lat every felawe telle his tale aboute,

---

1 'and certainly, if it did not take too long to hear'
2 A similar storm accompanied the arrival of Richard II's wife, Anne of Bohemia, to England in 1382.
3 'I must restrain myself from telling all that now'

And lat see now who schal the soper wynne;
And ther y-laste I wolde agayn begynne.

  ❦ This Duk of whom I make mencion,
Whan he was **wenen** almost unto the toun,   come
In al his wele, and in his most pride,
He was **war**, as he cast his **eyghe** aside,   aware; eyes
Wher that ther kneled in the hye weye
40   A companye of ladies, **tweye and tweye**,   two by two
Ech **after other** clad in clothes blake: like the other
But such a cry and such a **woo** they make   mourning
That in this world **nys** creature lyvynge,   there is not
Ther herde such another **wementynge**,   wailing
And of that cry ne wolde they never **stenten**,   cease
Til they the **reynes** of his bridel **henten**.   reins; seized
'What folk be ye that at myn hom comynge
Pertourben so my feste with cryenge?'   disturb
Quod Theseus, 'Have ye so gret envye
50   Of myn honour, that thus compleyne and crie?
Or who hath yow **mysboden** or offendid?   done wrong
And telleth me if it may ben **amended**;   put right
And why that ye ben clad thus al in blak?'
The oldest lady of hem alle spak,
When sche had **swowned** with a **dedly chere**, swooned: deathly pallor
That it was **routhe** for to seen or heere: pity
And seyde, 'Lord, to whom fortune hath geven
Victorie, and as a conquerour to lyven;
Nought greveth us youre glorie and honour,[4]
60   But we **beseken** mercy and **sucour** –   beg for; help
Have mercy on oure woo and oure distresse:
Som drope of pitee, thurgh youre gentilnesse
Uppon us wrecchede women lat thou falle,
For **certus**, lord, ther nys noon of us alle   truly
That sche **nath** ben a duchesse or a queene –   has not
Now be we **caytifs**, as it is wel seene;   wretches
Thanked be Fortune and hire false wheel,[5]

---

4 'your glory and honour deos not upset us'
5 In medieval iconography, Fortune is often depicted as a woman holding a wheel,
  on which humans rise and fall. Those who rise have good fortune, those who fall
  suffer ill fortune.

That noon estat assureth to ben weel;[6]
And certus, lord, to **abiden** youre presence,   wait for
Ther in the temple of the goddesse **Clemence**,   Clementia (mercy)   70
We han ben waytynge al this fortenight.
Now helpe us, lord, syn it is in thy might!
I, wrecche, which that wepe and wayle thus,
Was **whilom** wyf to Kyng Capaneus,   sometime
That **starf** at Thebes – cursed be that day! –   died
And alle we that ben in this array
And maken all this lamentacioun,
We leften alle oure housbondes at the toun
Whil that the sege ther aboute lay;
And yet the olde Creon, **welaway**,   alas   80
That lord is now of Thebes the citee,
Fulfilde of **ire** and of iniquite,   anger
He for **despyt** and for his tyrannye,   spitefulness
To do the **deed** bodyes **vilanye**   dead; harm/insult
Of alle oure lordes, which that ben y-slawe,
Hath alle the bodies on an heep y-drawe,
And wol not **suffren** hem by noon **assent**,   allow; agreement
Nother to be y-buried nor y-brent,   neither
But maketh houndes ete hem in despite.'
And with that word, withoute more respite,   90
They **fillen gruf**, and criden pitously,   fell prostrate
'Have on us wrecched women som mercy,
And lat oure sorwe synken in thyn herte!'
This gentil duke doun from his **courser** stepte,   horse
With herte pitous, whan he herde hem speke,
Whan he **seyh** hem so pitous and so **maat**,   saw; downcast
That whilom weren of so gret estat;
And in his armes he hem alle up **hente**,   lifted
And hem comforteth in ful good entente,
And swor his oth, as he was trewe knight,   100
He wolde do so **ferforthly** his might   wholly
Upon the tyraunt Creon hem to **wreke**,   avenge
That al the poeple of Grece scholde speke
How Creon was of Theseus y-served,

6 'status is no assurance of good fortune'

As he that hath his deth right wel deserved.
And right anoon, withoute any **abood**,   delayed
His baner he desplayeth, and forth rood
To Thebes-ward, and al his **oost** bysyde: army
No ner athenes wolde he go ne ryde,   no closer to
110 Ne take his **eese** fully half a day,   rest
But onward on his way that nyght he lay,
And sente anoon Ypolita the queene,
And Emelye hir yonge suster **schene**,   bright
Unto the toun of Athenes to dwelle –
And forth he **ryt**, ther is no more to telle.   rode

🍂 The **reede** statue of Mars[7], with spere and **targe**,   red; small round shield
So schyneth in his white baner large
That alle the feeldes gliteren up and doun[8]
And by his baner was born his **pynoun**   pennant
120 Of gold ful riche, in which ther was **y-bete**   beaten
The Minatour which that he **slough** in Crete:[9]   slew
Thus ryt this Duk, thus ryt this conquerour,
And in his oost of chevalrie the flour,
Til that he cam to Thebes, and alight
Faire in a feeld wher as he thoughte to fighte –
But schortly for to speken of this thing –
With Creon, which that was of Thebes kyng,
He faught, and slough him manly as a knight
In pleyn bataille, and putte his folk to flight;
130 And by assent he **wan** the cite aftur,   conquered
And rente doun bothe wal and sparre and raftur,
And to the ladies he restored agayn
The bones of here housbondes that were slayn,
To do **exequies** as was **tho** the **gyse**:   funeral rites; then; custom
But it were al to long for to **devyse**   relate
The grete clamour and the waymentyng
Which that the ladies made at the brennyng

---

7 Mars, the Roman god of war.
8 The banner glistens as it is carried through the fields; or, the whole surface of the
   banner glistens ('field' also refers to the surfaces on a coat of arms).
9 Theseus killed the Minotaur, half man, half bull, in the Cretan labyrinth, to save
   the lives of Greek hostages who were being fed to it.

Of the bodyes, and the grete honour
That Theseus, the noble conquerour,
Doth to the ladyes, whan they from him wente –   140
But **schortly** for to telle is myn entente –   quickly/sparingly
Whan that this worthy Duk, this Theseus,
Hath Creon slayn and Thebes wonne thus,
Stille in the feelde he took al night his reste,
And dide with al the contre as him **leste**   wished

❦ To ransake in the **cas** of bodyes dede,   heap
Hem for to streepe of **herneys** and of **wede**,   armour; clothing
The **pilours** diden businesse and **cure**   scavengers; care
After the bataile and **disconfiture**.   defeat
And so **byfil** that in the cas thei founde,   it happened   150
Thurgh girt with many a grevous blody wounde,
Two yonge knightes **liggyng** by and by,   lying
Bothe in **oon armes** clad ful richely;   the same coat of arms
Of whiche two Arcite hight that **oon**,   one
And that othur knight **hight** Palamon.   was called
Nat fully **quyk**, ne fully deed they were,   alive
But by her **coote armure** and by here **gere**   surcoat (with arms); arms
Heraudes knewe hem wel **in special**,   especially
As they that weren of the blood **real** –   royal
Of Thebes, and of **sistren** two y-born –   sisters   160
Out of the **chaas** the pilours han hem torn,   heap
And han hem caried softe unto the tente
Of Theseus, and ful sone he hem sente
T'Athenes, for to dwellen in prisoun
Perpetuelly – he wolde no **ranceoun**.   ransom
And this Duk, whan he hadde thus **y-doon**,   done

❦ He took his host, and hom he ryt anoon,
With **laurer** crowned as a conquerour;   laurel
And there he lyveth in joye and in honour
Terme of his lyf – what wolle ye wordes **moo**?   the rest of his life; more   170
And in a **tour**, in angwische and in woo,   tower
This Palamon and his felawe Arcite,
For evermo – ther may no gold hem **quyte**.   save/ransom
This passeth yeer by yeer and day by day,
Til it fel **oones** in a **morwe** of May,   once; morning

That Emelie, that fairer was to seen
Than is the lilie in hire stalkes grene,
And fresscher than the may, with floures newe,
For with the rose colour **strof** hire **hewe** –   fought; colour
180 I **not** which was the fyner of hem two.   do not know
Er it was day, as sche was wont to do,
Sche was arisen and al redy **dight**,   dressed
For May wole have no **sloggardye** anyght.   laziness
The sesoun **priketh** every gentil herte,   arouses
And maketh him out of his sleepe **sterte**,   start/awake
And seith 'Arys, and do thin observaunce!'
This maked Emelye han remembraunce
To do honour to May, and for to ryse:
Y-clothed was sche fressh for to **devyse**,   tell
190 Hire **yolwe** heer was **browdid** in a **tresse**,   yellow; braided; pigtail
Byhynde hire bak – a yerde long, I gesse –
And in the gardyn at the sonne **upriste**,   rising
Sche walketh up and doun wher as hire liste;
Sche gadereth floures **party** whyte and reede,   multicoloured
To make a certeyn gerland for hire heede,
And as an aungel hevenly sche song.
The grete tour that was so thikke and strong
Which of the castel was the cheef dongeoun,
Ther as this knightes weren in prisoun –
200 Of which I tolde yow and telle schal –
Was evere joynyng to the gardeyn wal,
Ther as this Emely hadde hire **pleyynge**.   disport
Bright was the sonne, and cleer that **morwenynge**,   morning
And Palamon, this woful prisoner,
As was his **wone** by leve of his **gayler**,   custom; gaoler
Was risen, and **romed** in a chambre on heigh,   walked
In which he al the noble cite **seigh**,   saw
And eek the gardeyn ful of braunches grene,
Ther as the fresshe Emelye the **scheene**   bright
210 Was in hire walk, and romed up and doun.
This sorweful prisoner, this Palamon,
Gooth in the chambre romyng to and fro,
And to himself compleynyng of his woo,
That he was born ful oft he seyd, 'Alas!'
And so byfel, by **aventure** or **cas**,   chance; fortune

That thurgh an wyndow thikke and many a barre
Of **yren**, greet and squar as eny sparre,   iron
He cast his eyen upon Emelya,
And theer with al he **bleynte** and cryed, 'A!'   blinked
As that he **stongen** were unto the herte,   stung   220
And with that crye Arcite anon up sterte,
And seyde, 'Cosyn myn, what **eyleth** the,   ails
That art so pale and deedly for to see?
Why **crydestow**? who hath the doon offence?   did you cry out
For goddes love, tak al in paccience
Our prisoun, for it may non othir be;
Fortune hath geven us this adversite.
Som wikke aspect or disposicioun
Of Saturne, by sum constellacioun,[10]
Hath geven us this, although we hadde it sworn,   230
So stood the heven whan that we were born.
We moste endure it – this is the schort and pleyn.'
This Palamon answered, and seyd ageyn,
'Cosyn, for sothe, of this opynyoun
Thou hast a veyn ymaginacioun;[11]
This prisoun caused me not for to crye,
But I was hurt right now **ynigh** my **yhe**,   through; eye
In to myn herte, that wol my **bane** be,   killer
The fairnesse of the lady that I see
Yonde in the gardyn, rome to and fro,   240
Is cause of my cryyng and my wo.
I **not** whethur sche be womman or goddesse,   do not know
But Venus is it sothly, as I gesse.'
And ther withal on knes adoun he **fil**   fell
And seyde, 'Venus, if it be youre wil
Yow in this gardyn thus to transfigure
Birform me, sorwful wrecched creature,
Out of this prisoun help that we may **scape**,   escape
And if so be oure destyne be **schape**   predetermined
By eterne word, to deyen in prisoun;   250
Of oure **lynage** haveth sum compassioun,   family
That is so lowe y-brought by Tyrannie.'

10 'some evil configuration in the stars, according to our horoscope'
11 'you are wrong in thinking that this is what is wrong'

And with that word Arcite gan espye
Wher as this lady romed to and fro,
And with that sight hire beaute hurt him so,
That if that Palamon was wounded sore,
Arcite is hurt as moche as he, or more,
And with a sigh he seyde pitously,
'The freissche beaute **sleeth** me sodeynly   kills
260   Of hir that rometh yonder in the place;
And but I have hir mercy and hir grace,
That I may see hir, **atte leeste weye**,   at the very least
I nam but deed – ther nys no more to seye.'
This Palamon, whan he tho wordes herde,
Dispitously he loked and answerde,
'Whether **seistow** in ernest or in play?'   do you say this
'Nay,' quoth Arcite 'in ernest in **good fey**.   good faith
God helpe me so me lust ful evele pleye!'[12]
This Palamon gan **knytte his browes tweye**.   frowned
270   'Hit nere,' quod he, 'to the no gret honour,[13]
To me that am thy cosyn and thy brother:
I swore ful **deepe**, and eek of us to other,   solemnly
That never for to deyen in the payne,[14]
Thil that deeth departe schal us twayne,
Neyther of us in love to hynder other,
Ne in non other cas, my leeve brother,
But thou schuldest trewly **forther** me   help
In every caas, and I schal forther the;
This was thyn othe, and myn **eek** certayn –   also
280   I wot right wel thou darst it nat withsayn –
Thus art thou of my conseil out of doute,
And now thou woldest falsely ben aboute,
To love my lady whom I love and serve,
And evere schal **unto** myn herte **sterve**.'   until; die
'Now certes, fals Arcite, thou schal not so!
I loved hir first, and tolde the my woo,
As to my **counseil** and to brother, sworn   confidant
To **forthere** me, as I have told biforn;   help

---

12 'I don't want to play'
13 'it is no great honour to you'
14 'may we die in pain'

For which thou and I bounden as a knight,
To helpe me, if it lay in thi might;   290
Or elles art thou fals, I dar wel sayn.'
This Arcite ful proudly spak agayn,
'Thou schalt,' quoth he, 'be rather fals than I;
But thou art fals, I telle the, uttirly:
For paramour I loved her first, then thowe,
What wolt thou sayn – thou **wost** it not yit now,   know
Whether sche be a woman or goddesse:
Thyn is affecioun of holynesse;
And myn is love as of a creature,
For which I tolde the myn adventure,   300
As to my cosyn and my brother sworn:
I **pose** that thou lovedest hire biforn.   posit
Wost thou nat wel the olde clerkes **sawe**,   saying
That 'who schal geve a lover eny lawe'[15] –
Love is a grettere lawe, by my **pan**,   skull
Then may be geve to eny **erthly** man.   mortal
Therfore posityf lawe- and such decre –[16]
Is broke alway for love in ech degree.
A man **moot** needes love **maugre his heed**;   must; despite his wariness
He may nought **fle it**, though he schulde be deed.   run away from it   310
Al be sche mayde or be sche widewe or wyf,   whether
And that is nat likly al thy lyf,
To stondon in hire grace no more schal I,[17]
For wel thou **wost** thy selven **verrily**,   know; truly
That thou and I been dampned to prisoun
Perpetuelly: us **gayneth** no raunsoun.   benefit
We stryve as doth the houndes for the boon –
They foughte alday and yit here part was noon.
Ther com a kyte, whil that they were wrothe
That bar awey the boon bitwixe hem bothe.[18]   320
And therfore at the kynges court, my brother,
Eche man for himself – ther is non other.
Love if the **list**, for I love, and **ay** schal;   like/wish; ever

15 'no-one can make a lover abide by any law'
16 Not natural law, but man-made statute
17 'you are no more likely to stand in her grace all your life than I am'
18 A fable of Aesop.

And sothly, **leve** brother, this is al.   dear
Eke in this prisoun moote we endure,
And **every** of us take his **aventure**.'   each; chance
Gret was the stryf and long bytwixe hem tweye,
Yif that I hadde **leysir** for to seye,   time
But to the effect; it happed on a day –
330 To telle it yow as **shortly** as I may –   briefly
A worthy Duk, that *highte* Potheus,   was called
That felawe was to the duk Theseus
Syn thilke day that they were children **lyte**,   little
Was come to Athenes, his **felawe** to visite,   friend
And for to pleye as he was wont to do,
For in this world he loved noman so,
And he loved him as tendurly agayn;
So wel they loved, as olde bookes sayn,
That whan oon was deed, sothly to telle,
340 His felawe wente and soughte him doun in helle;
But of that story **lyst me nought** to write.   I don't want
Duk Potheus loved wel Arcite,
And hadde him knowe at Thebes yeer by yeer,
And **fynelly** at requeste and prayer   eventually
Of Potheus, withoute any raunsoun,
Duk Theseus him leet out of prisoun,
Frely to go wher him lust over al,
In such a **gyse** as I you telle schal.   way
This was the **forward**, playnly to **endite**,   agreement; tell
350 Bitwixe Theseus and him Arcite,
That if so were that Arcite were founde
Evere in his lyf, by daye, night, **oo stounde**,   any moment
In eny contre of this Theseus,
And he were caught, it was acorded thus;
That with a swerd he scholde **lese** his **heed** –   lose; head
Ther nas noon other remedy ne **reed**:   counsel
But took his leeve, and homward he him spedde –
Lete him be war, his nekke **lith to wedde**!   is his surety

360 ❧ How gret a sorwe suffreth now Arcite!
The deth he feleth thorough his herte **smyte**!   strike
He wepeth, wayleth, and cryeth pitously;

To **slen** himself he **wayteth** pryvyly.[19]
He seyde, 'Allas, the day that I was born!
Now is my prisoun werse than was biforn!
Now is me schape eternally to dwelle
Nought in purgatories but in helle![20]
Allas that ever knewe I Potheus!
For elles had I dweld with Theseus,
Y-fetered in his prisoun for evere moo;
Then had I ben in **blis** and nat in woo!   *happiness* **370**
Only the sight of hir whom that I serve,
Thogh nat I hir grace may nat deserve[21]
Wold han sufficed right ynough for me.
'O dere cosyn Palamon,' quod he,
'thyn is the victorie of this **aventure**,   *happening*
Ful bisfully in prisoun to endure.
In prisoun – nay, certes, but in paradys –
Wel hath fortune **y-torned** the **dys**   *turned; dice*
That hath the sight of hir, and I the absence:
For possible is, **syn** thou hast hir presence,   *since* **380**
And art a knight a **worthe** and an able,   *worthy*
But by som cas, syn fortune is chaungeable,
Thou maist to thy desir som tyme atteyne,[22]
But I that am exiled and **bareyne**   *barren/devoid*
Of alle grace, and in so gret dispeir
That ther nys water, erthe, fyr, ne eyr,
Ne creature that of hem maked is,[23]
That may me helpe ne comfort in this,
Wel ought I **sterve** in **wanhope** and distresse,   *die; despair*
For wel my lyf and al my jolynesse!   **390**

❦ Allas, why **playnen** folk so in comune,   *complain*
Of **purveance**, of god, or of fortune,   *provision*

---

19 kill; awaits (an opportunity)
20 Purgatory, where the souls of the dead are held in limbo, being cleansed before admission to the company of the blessed.
21 'Though I know I do not deserve her grace'
22 'You may at some time get what you desire'
23 Medieval medicine stated that all creatures were made of the same four elements as the natural world

That geveth hem ful ofte in many a **gyse**   way
Wel better than thei can hemself **devyse**.   imagine

❦ Som man desireth for to have richesse,
That cause is of his **morthre** or gret **secknesse**,   murder; sickness
And som man wolde out of his prisoun **fayn**,   gladly
That in his houris of his **mayne** slayn. [24]   household men
Infinite harmes be in this mateere –
400 We wote nevere what thing we prayen heere. [25]
We faren as he that dronke is as a mous:
A dronke man wot wel he hath an hous,
But he **not nat** which the righte wey is thider,   doesn't know
And to a dronke man the wey is **slider**.   slippery
And certes, in this world so faren we.
We seeken faste after **felicite**,   happiness
But we goon wrong ful ofte, trewely
This may we **seyen** alle, and namely I,   say
That **wende** have had a gret **opinioun**   thought to; idea
410 That yif I mighte skape fro prisoun,
Than had I be in joye and perfyt **hele**,   health
Ther now I am exiled fro my **wele**,   good fortune
Syn that I may not se yow, Emelye,
I nam but **deed** – ther nys no remedye.'   dead

❦ Upon that other syde Palomon,
When he wiste that Arcite was agoon,
Suche sorwe maketh that the grete tour
Resowneth of his grete **yollyng** and clamour.   echoes; yelling
The pure **feters of his schynes** grete   fetters on his legs
420 Weren of his bitter salte teres wete.
'Allas!' quod he, 'Arcita, cosyn myn,
Of al oure strif, god wot, the **fruyt** is thin!   benefit
Thow walkest now in Thebes **at thi large**,   in freedom
And of my woo thou gevest litel **charge**!   care/thought
Thou maiste seen, thou hast wysdom and manhede,
Assemble al the folk of oure kynrede,
And make a werre so **scharpe** in this cite,   bitter

24 'at his appointed time'
25 'we never know what we are asking for'

That by som aventure, or by som **trete**,   treaty
Thou mayste hire wynne to lady and to wyf,
For whom that I most needes leese my lyf!   **430**
For as by wey of possibilite,
Syn thou art at thi large, of prisoun free,
And art a lord, gret is thin avantage –
More than is myn that **sterve** here in a kage –   die
For I moot weepe and weyle whil I lyve,
With al the woo that prisoun may me gyve,
And eek with peyne that love me geveth also,
And doubleth al my peyne and al my wo.'
Therwith the **fuyr** of jelousye **up sterte**   fire; rose up
Withinne his brest, and **hent** him by the herte,   seized **440**
So **wodly** that **lik was he to byholde**   madly; he looked like
The box tree, or the **asschen** deed and colde.   ashes
Tho seyde he, 'O goddes cruel, that governe   then
This world with byndyng & with worde eterne,
And writen in the table of Athamaunte[26]
Youre **parlement** and youre eterne **graunte**:   decision; decree
What is mankynde more to yow holde
Than is a scheep that **rouketh** in the folde?   cowers/hides
For sleyn is man right as another beste,
And dwelleth eek in prisoun and arreste,   **450**
And hath seknesse and greet adversite,
And ofte tymes **gilteles, parde**!   guiltless; by God
What governaunce is in youre **prescience**,   foreknowledge
That gilteles tormenteth Innocence?
And yit **encrecith** this al my penaunce,   increases
That man is bounden to his **observaunce**,   duty
For goddes sake to letten of his wille,[27]
Ther as a beste may al his lust fulfille;   whereas
And whan a beste is deed he ne hath no peyne,
But man after his deth moot wepe and pleyne,   **460**
Though in this world he have care and woo;
Withouten doute it may stonde so.
The answer of this I **lete** to **divinis**,   leave; divines/theologians

26 'adamantine tablet' (table of adamantine, hardest of minerals).
27 'to fail of his desire'

But wel I **woot** that in this world gret **pyne** is.   know; wo
Allas! I se a serpent or a theif,
That many a trewe man hath doon mescheef
Gon at his large and wher him **lust** may turne,   go about freely; likes
But I moste be in prisoun, thurgh Saturne,[28]
And eek thorough Juno, jalous and eke **wood**,   angry/mad
470   That hath destroyed wel **neyh** al the blood   nigh
Of Thebes, with his **waste** walles wyde,   laid waste
And Venus sleith me, on ther syde,
For jelousye and **fere** of him Arcyte!'   fear

❦ Now wol I stynte of Palamon **alite**,   a little (while)
And lete him stille in his prisoun dwelle;
And of Arcita forth than wol I telle.
The somer passeth, and the nightes longe
Encrescen double wise the peynes stronge   increase doubly
Bothe of the lover and the prisoner –
480   I **noot** which hath the **wofullere cheer**,[29]
For, schortly for to sey, this Palomon
Perpetuelly is dampned in prisoun,
In **cheynes** and in **feteres** to be **deed**,   chains; fetters; dead
And Arcite is exiled upon his **heed**[30]
For everemo, as out of that contre,
Ne nevere **mo** schal se his lady fre.   more
Now loveres, **axe** I this question,   ask
Who hath the worse, Arcite or Palamon?
That on may se his lady day by day,
490   But in prisoun he **moot** dwelle alway: must
That other may wher him lust ryde or go,
But seen his lady schal he never mo.
Now **deemeth** as you **luste**, ye that can,   decide; will
For I wol telle forth as I bigan.

❦ Whan that Arcite to Thebes come was,
Ful ofte a day he **swelte** and seyde, 'Alas!'   became faint
For seen his lady schal he nevere mo,
And, schortly to concluden al his wo,

28 'through Saturn . . . and also Juno'; he blames the gods for his plight.
29 don't know; more miserable time
30 'on pain of losing his head'

So moche **sorwe** had never creature   sorrow   500
That is or schal, **until that** the world wol **dure**.   as long as; endure
His sleep, his mete, his drynk, is him **byraft**,   denied
That lene he **wexe**, and drye as eny **schaft**.   grew; stick
His eyen **holwe**, **grisly** to biholde;   hollow; unpleasant
His hewe **falwe** and pale as asschen colde;   yellow
And solitary he was, and ever alone,
And dwellyng al the night making his moone:
If he herde song or instrument,
Then wolde he wepe, he mighte nought be **stent**;   stopped
So feble were his spirites and so lowe,   510
And chaunged so, that no man **couthe** know   could
His speche, nother his **vois**, though men it herde,   voice
And in his **gir** for al the world he **ferde**,   manner; went
Nought oonly lyk the lovers maladye
Of hertos, but rather lik **manye**,[31]   madness
Engendrud of humour malencolyk,[32]   born/caused
Byforne in his selle fantastyk;[33]
And schortly was al **up so doun**,   upside down
Botte **abyt** and eek **disposicioun**   clothing; manner
Of him, this woful lovere, Daun Arcite.   520
What schulde I alway of his wo **endite**?   recount
Whan he endured hadde a yeer or **tuoo**   two
In this cruel torment, peyne, and woo,
At Thebes in his contre, as I seyde,
Upon a night, in sleep as he him leyde,
Him thought that how the **wenged** god Mercurie[34]   winged
Byforn him stood, and bad him to be **murye**.   merry
His slepy **yerd** in hand he **bar** upright,[35]
And hat he **wered** upon his **heres** bright: hat; hair
Arrayed was this god, as he tooke keepe,   530
As he was whan that Argous took his sleep,[36]

31 A form of love-sickness.
32 The humours affected the human mood. Melancholy, or black bile, makes Arcite
   melancholy and weak.
33 'The brain-cell (part of the brain) which imagines'
34 Mercury, messenger of the gods, had wings on his ankles, on his shoulders and
   on his helmet.
35 staff (which caused sleep); carried.
36 Argus had a hundred eyes, but Mercury sent him to sleep.

And seyde, 'To Athenes schalt thou **wende** –   go
Ther is the **schapen** of thy wo an ende.'   ordained
And with that word Arcite **wook** and **stert**,   awoke; sat up
'Now, trewely, how sore that me **smerte**,'   pains
Quod he, 'To Athenes right now wol I fare,
Ne for the drede of deth schal I not spare
To see my lady that I love and serve –
In hire presence I **recche** nat to **sterve**!'   care; die
540 And with that word he caught a gret **myrour**,   mirror
And saugh that chaunged was al his colour,
And saugh his visage was in another kynde:[37]
And right anoon it ran him into mynde
That, **seththen** his face was so disfigured   since
Of **maladie**, the which he hath endured,   sickness
He mighte wel, if that he bar him lowe,[38]
Lyve in Athenes everemore **unknowe**,   unrecognised
And see his lady wel neih day by day;
And right anon he chaunged his **aray**,   clothing
550 And clothed him as a pore laborer,
And al alone save oonly a squyer,
That knew his **pryvyte** and al his **cas**,   secrets; situation
Which was disgysed pourely as he was,
To Athenes is he go the **nexte** way,   quickest/closest
And to the court he went upon a day,
And at the gate he **profred** his **servyse**,   offered; service
To **drugge and drawe** what so men wolde devyse.[39]   water
And schortly on this **metier**, for to seyn,   matter
He fel in office with a chambirleyn,
560 The which that dwellyng was with Emelye,
For he was wys and couthe some aspye
Of every s[er]va[n]t which that he hight:[40]
Wel koude he hewen wood and water bere,
For he was yong, and mighty for the nones,
And therto he was long and big of bones,
To doon that any wight him can devyse.

37 'he looked completely different'
38 'acted in a lowly manner'
39 do lowly work and draw
40 'he saw the talents of every servant that he had'

A yeer or two he was in this servyse,
Page of the chambre of Emelye the bryghte,
And Philostrate, he seyde that he hight:
But half so wel byloved a man as he   570
Ne was ther never in court of his degree –
He was so gentil of his **condicioun**,   bearing
That thoruhout al the court was his renoun.
They seyde that it were a **charite**   mercy/gracious gift
That Theseus wolde **enhaunsen his degree**,   raise his status
And putten him in **worschipful** servyse,   honourable
Ther as he might his **vertu** excersise;   noble qualities
And thus withinne a while **his name spronge**,[41]
Bothe of his dedes and of goode **tonge**,   speech
That Theseus hath taken him so neer,   580
That of his chambre he made him squyer,
And gaf him gold to mayntene his degree,
And eek men brought him out of his contre
From yeer to yer ful pryvyly his **rente** –   money to live on
But honestly and **sleighly** he it spente,   cunningly
That no man wondred how that he it hadde.
And thre yeer in this wise his lyf he ladde,
And bar him so in pees and eek in werre,
Ther nas no man that Theseus **hath** so **derre**.   held; dear
And in this blisse lete I now Arcite,   590
And speke I wole of Palamoun alyte.

❦ In derknes, and orrible and strong prisoun,
This seven yer hath seten Palomon,
Forpyned what for woo and for destresse.   borne down
Who feeleth double sorwe and hevynesse,
But Palomon, that love **destreneth** so,   hurts
That **wood** out of his **witt** he goth for wo,   mad; wits
And eek therto he is a prisoner
Perpetuelly, nat oonly for a yeer?
Who couthe ryme in Englissch propurly   600
His martirdam? Forsothe, it am nat I.
Therfore I passe as lightly as I may –
Hit fel that in the seventhe yeer, in May,

41 'he made a name for himself'

The midde night, as olde bookes seyn,
That al this storie tellen more pleyn:
Were it by **aventure** or **destene**,   *chance; destiny*
As whan a thing is schapen it schal be,
That some afture the mydnyght Palomon,
By helpyng of a **freend**, **brak** his prisoun,   *friend; escaped from*
610 And fleeth ther rite fast as he may goo,[42]
For he had give drinke his gayler soo,
Of a **clarre** maad of certeyn wyn,   *claret*
With nercotykes and opye of Thebes fyn,[43]
That al that night, though that men wolde him schake,
The gayler sleep; he mighte nou*g*ht awake.
And thus he fleeth as fast as ever he may;
The night was schort, and fast by the day
That **needes cost** he moste himselven hyde;   *of necessity*
And **til** a grove ther **fast** besyde,   *to; close*
620 With **dredful** foot than stalketh Palomon,   *fearful*
For schortly this was his opynyoun:
That in that grove he wolde him hyde al day,
And in the night then wolde he take his way
To Thebes-ward, his frendes for to preye
On Theseus to helpe him to **werreye**,   *wage war*
And **schortelich**, **or** he wolde lese his lyf,   *briefly; either*
Or wynnen Emelye unto his wyf:
This is theffect of his **entente** playn.   *intention*
Now wol I torne unto Arcite agayn,
630 That litel **wiste** how nyh that was his **care**,   *knew; sorrow/trouble*
Til that fortune hath brought him in the snare.

The busy larke, **messager** of May,   *messenger*
Salueth in hire song the **morwe** gray,   *greets; morning*
And fyry Phebus ryseth up so bright[44]
That the orient laugheth of the light,
And with his stremes dryeth in the **greves**   *branches*
The silver dropes hongyng in the leeves;
And Arcite, that is in the court **ryal**   *royal*

42 'as fast as he could go'
43 'drugs and opium'
44 Phebus, the sun.

With Theseus, his squyer principal,
Is risen and loketh on the mery day,   640
And for to doon his observance to May,
Remembryng of the **poynt** of his desire,   object
He on his **courser**, **stertyng** as the fire,   war horse; agitated
Is riden in to feeldes him to **pleye**,   disport
Out of the court were it a myle or **tweye**,   two
And to the grove of which that I yow tolde
By aventure his wey he gan to holde,
To make him a garland of the **greves**,   leaves/greenery
Were it of **woodbynde** or hawthorn leves,   woodbine
And lowde he song agens the sonne **scheene**,   bright   650
'May, with al thyn floures and thy greene,
Welcome be thou, O faire freissche May,
In hope that I som grene gete may!'
And fro his courser, with a lusty herte,
Into the grove ful lustily he sterte,
And in a pathe he romed up and doun,
Ther by **aventure** this Palamoun   chance
Was in a busche that no man might him see:
Ful sore **afered** of his deth was he.   afraid
No thing knew he that it was Arcite –   660
God wot, he wolde have **trowed** it ful lite –   God knows; believed
But **soth** is seyde, **goon ful many yeres**   truth; for many years
That feld hath eyen and the woode hath eeres.[45]
It is **ful fair** a man to **bere him evene**,   a good idea; stay calm
For al day men **meteth atte unset stevene**.   meet by chance
That was so **neih**, to **herken** of his **sawe**,   near; listen (to); saying
For in the busche he **stynteth** now ful stille.   stops
Whan that Arcyte had romed **al his fille**,   as much as he wanted
And songen al the Roundel lustily,
Into a **studie** he fel sodeynly,   contemplation 670
As **deth** the loveres in **here queynte geeres**,   do; their own way
Now in the **croppe**, now doun in the **breres**,   leaves; briars
Now up now doun as boket in a welle;
Right as the Fryday, sothly for to telle –
Now it schyneth, now it reyneth faste;
Right so **gan** grey Venus overcaste   began

45 'The field has eyes and the wood has ears' (a proverb)

The hertes of hire folk, right as hir day[46]
Is **grisful**, right so chaungeth hire **aray**:   gray; clothing
Selde is the Fryday al the wyke **ilike**.   seldom; similar to
680   Whan that Arcite hadde song, he gan to **sike**,   sigh
And sette him doun withouten eny more.
'Alas,' quod he, 'that day that I was bore!
How longe, Juno, thurgh thy cruelte,
Wiltow **werreyn** Thebes the citee!   be at war with
Allas! Y-brou*gh*t is to confusioun
The blood royal of Cadme and Amphioun[47] –
Of Cadmus which that was the first man –
Of his lynage am I, and his ofspring
By **verray lyne**, and of his stok ryal;   true lineage
690   And now I am so **caytyf** and so **thral**   wretched; servant
That he that is my mortal enemy,
I serve him, and am his squyer **pourely**.   of low status
And yet doth Juno me wel more schame,
For I dar nought **byknow** my owne name;   admit
But ther as I was wont to **hote** Arcite,   be called
Now hoote I Philostrate, nou*gh*t worth a myte!
Allas, thou **felle** Mars! Allas, Juno!   dread
Thus hath youre ire oure lynage **fordo**,   destroyed
Save oonly me and **wreccid** Palomon,   wretched
700   That Theseus martyreth in prisoun!
And over al this, to **slee** me utterly,   slay
Love hath his fyry dart so brennyngly
Y-stykid thorugh my trewe, **careful**, herte   full of care/troubled
That schapen was my deth **erst than** my **scherte**!   before; shirt
Ye slen me with youre **eyhen**, Emelye!   eyes
Ye ben the cause wherfore that I dye!
Of al the **remenant** of al myn other care,   rest
Ne sette I nou*gh*t the **mountaunce** of a tare   weight/value
So that I couthe do ought to youre plesaunce!'[49]
710   And with that word he fel doun in a traunce

46 Another proverbial statement – just as the weather is variable on Friday, so
   Venus (who is particularly associated with Fridays) creates variable moods in her
   subjects, ie. those who love.
47 Cadmus and Amphion were co-founders of the city of Thebes. Arcite identifies
   himself with them, and with the city. Ironically, he and Palamon are also a 'pair'.
49 'I hold everything else of very little value except that I might make you happy'

A longe tyme, and afturward up sterte
This Palamon, that thou*g*hte thurgh his herte
He felt a cold swerd sodeynliche glyde.
For ire he **quook**, he **nolde** no lenger abyde:　　　quaked/shook; would not
And whan that he hath herd Arcite's tale,
As he were wood, with face deed and pale,
He sterte him up out of the bussches thikke
And seyde, 'Arcyte, false traitour **wikke**!　　　　　wicked
Now art thou **hent**, that lovest my lady so!　　　　caught
For whan that I have al this peyne and wo,　　　　　　　720
And art my blood, and to my counseil sworn,
And I ful ofte have told the heere **byforn**,　　　before
And hast **byjaped** here the duke Theseus,　　　　tricked
And falsely chaunged hast thy name thus –
I wol be deed, **or elles** thou schalt dye!　　　　　or else
Thou schalt not love my lady Emelye!
But I wil love hire oonly, and nomo;
For I am Palomon, thy mortal **fo**;　　　　　　　foe/enemy
And though that I no **wepen** have in this place,　　weapon
But out of prisoun am I stert by grace,　　　　　　　730
I drede not that **other** thou schalt dye　　　　　either
Or thou ne schalt not love Emelye!⁵⁰
Chese which thou wilt, for thou schalt not **asterte**'　leave
This Arcite, with ful despitous herte,
Whan he him knew, and had his tale herde,
As **fers** as a lyoun, pulleth out a swerde,　　　　fierce
And seide thus, 'By god that sitteth above,
Nere it that thou art silk and **wood** for love,　　mad
And eek that thou no **wepne** has in this place,
But out of prisoun art y-stert by grace,　　　　　　　740
That thou ne schuldest deyen of myn hond,⁵¹
For I defye the **seurte** and the bond　　　　　　pledge
Which that thou seyst I have maad to the –
For, **verray** fool, thenk that love is fre.
Al I wol love hire, **mawgre** al thy might –　　in spite of
But for thou art a gentil, perfiyt knight,
And **wenest** to **dereyne** hire by batayle,　purposes; gain right to her

50 'you will either die, or you will not love Emelye'
51 'If you hadn't had no weapon you would have died by my hand'

Have heere my trouthe – tomorwe I nyl not fayle,
Withouten **wityng** of eny other **wight**,   knowledge;person
750 That heer I wol be founden as a knight,
And bryngen **harneys** right ynugh for the,   arms and armour
And ches the best and **lef** the worst for me;   leave
And **mete** and drynke this night wol I bryng,   food
Ynough for the, and cloth for thy beddyng;
And if so be that thou my lady wynne,
And sle me in this wood that I am inne;
Thou maist wel have thy lady as for me.'
This Palomon answereth, 'Graunt it the!'
And thus they ben departed til **amorwe**,   the next morning
760 Whan ech of hem had leyd his feith **to borwe**.[52]   in pledge

❦ O Cupide, out of al charite!
O **regne**, that wolt no **felaw** have with the!   rule; companion
Ful **soth** is seyde, that love ne lordschipe   truth
Wol not, **his thonkes**, have no **felaschipe**.   thankfully; companionship
Wel **fynden** that Arcite and Palamon!   discover
Arcite is riden anon to the toun,
And on the morwe **or** it were daylight,   before
Ful privyly two **harneys** hath he **dight**,   arms and armour;got ready

❦ Bothe **sufficaunt** and **mete** to **darreyne**   suitable; fight
770 The **batayl** in the feeld betwix hem tweyne.
And on his hors, as he was **born**,   carried
He caryed al this harneys him byforn,
And in the grove at tyme and place **y-sette**,   fixed
This Arcite and this Palamon ben mette.
Tho changen gan here colour in here face,   then
Right as the hunters in the **regne** of Thrace,   kingdom
That stondeth in the **gappe** with a spere,   ambush (for game)
Whan honted is the lyoun or the bere,
And **hereth** him comyng in the **greves**,   hears; greenery
780 And breketh both the **bowes** and the leves,   boughs
And thenketh, 'Here cometh my mortel enemy –
Withoute faile he mot be deed or I;
For eyther I mot slen him at the **gappe**,   clearing

52 ie they had each given their word to one another.

Or he moot slee me, if it me myshappe.'
So **ferden** they in chaungyng of here **hew**.   fared; colouring

❧ As fer as eyther of hem other knew,
Ther nas no, 'Good day,' ne no **saluyng**:   greeting
But streyt, withouten wordes rehersyng,
Every of hem helpeth to armen other,   each
As frendly as he were his own brother,   790
And thanne with here scharpe speres stronge,
They **foyneden** ech at other longe.   set their spears in rest
Tho it semed that this Palomon   then
In his fightyng were a wood lyoun;
And as a cruel tygre was Arcite,
And as wilde boores **gonne** they **smyte**,   began to strike out
That **frothen** white as **fome** fro the wood: froth; foam
Up to the **ancle** they faught in here blood,   ankle
And in this wise I lete hem fightyng well;
And forther I wol of Theseus tell.   800

❧ The **destyne**, **mynistre general**,   destiny; chief minister
That **excused** in the world over al   oversaw
The **purveans** that God hath seye byforn,'   providence
So strong it is that, though the world had sworn
The contrary of a thing by 'ye' or 'nay',
Yet som tyme it schal **falle** upon a day   happen
That falleth nought **eft** in a thousend yeere;   often
For certeynly oure appetites **heere**,   here (in this world)
Be it of pees, **other** hate, or love,   or
Al is it **reuled** by the sight above.   ruled   810
This **mene** I **by** mighty Theseus,   say . . . about
That for to **honte** is so desirous;   hunt
And namely the grete **hert** in May,   hart (mature male deer)
That in his bed ther **daweth** him no day   dawns
That he nys clad, and redy for to ryde,
With **hont**, and horn, and houndes him byside,   huntsman
For in his hontyng hath he such **delyt**,   delight/pleasure
That is his joye and his appetyt,
To been him self the grete hertes **bane** –   downfall
For after May he serveth now Dyane.[53]   820

53 Diana, goddess of the hunt.

❦ Cleer was the day, as I have told **or** this,   before
And Theseus, with alle joye and blys,
With his Ypolita, the fayre queene,
And Emelye, clothed al in greene,
On hontyng be thay riden **ryally**,   royally
And to the grove that stood **faste** by,   close
In whiche ther was an **hert**, as men him tolde,   hart
Duk Theseus the **streyte** wey hath holde;   quickest
And to the **launde** he rydeth him ful right,   clearing
830 Ther was the hert y-wont to have his flight;
And over a brook, and so forth in his weye,
This duk wol have of him a **cours** or tweye[54]   run
With houndes, which as him lust to comaunde.
And whan this Duk was come into the launde,
Under the same he loketh right anon;
He was **war** of Arcite and Palomon,   aware
That foughten **breeme** as it were boores tuo: savagely
The brighte swerdes wente to and fro
So hidously, that with the leste strook
840 I semeth as it wolde felle an **ook**:   oak
But what they were, nothing yit he **woot**.   knew
This duk with **spores** his courser he **smoot**,   spurs; struck
And at a stert he was bitwix hem tuoo,
And pulled out a swerd and cride, 'Hoo!
Nomore up peyne of leesyng of your heed![55]
By mighty Mars, anon he schal be deed
That smyteth eny strook that I may seen!
But tellith me, what **mestir** men ye been   kind of
That ben so **hardy** for to fighten heere,   bold
850 Withoute **jugge** or other officere,   judge/marshal
As it were in a lyste **really**.'[56]   royally
This Palamon answerd hastily,
And seyde, 'Sire, what nedeth wordes mo?
We han the deth deserved bothe tuo!
Tuo woful wrecches ben we, and caytyves,

54 'the Duke wanted to have a run or two at him'
55 'on pain of losing your head'
56 'at a joust'

That ben **encombred** of oure owne lyves;   burdened
And as thou art a rightful lord and juge,
Ne geve us neyther mercy ne refuge,
But sle me first, for Seynte Charite,
But sle my felaw eek as wel as me –   860
Or sle him first, for though thou knowe him **lyte**,   little
This is thy mortal fo – this is Arcite,
That fro thy lond is banyscht on his heed[57]
For which he hath **y-served** to be deed;   deserved
For this is he that come to thi gate,
And seyde that he **highte** Philostrate.   was called
Thus hath he **japed** the many a yer,   fooled
And thou hast maad of him thy cheef squyer:
And this is he that loveth Emelye,
For sith the day is come that I schal dye,   870
I make pleynly my confessioun
That I am the woful Palamoun,
That hath thi prisoun broke wikkedly –
I am thy mortal foo, and it am I
That loveth so **hoote** Emely the bright,   strongly
That I wol dye present in hire sight.
Therfore, I aske deeth and my **juwyse** –   sentence
But slee my felaw in the same wyse,
For bothe we have served to be slayn.'

❧ This worthy duk answerde anon agayn,   880
And seide, 'This is a schort conclusioun!
Your owne mouth, by your owne confessioun,
Hath **dempned** you bothe, and I wil it recorde.   condemned
It needeth nought to pyne yow with the corde –[58]
Ye schul be deed, by mighty Mars the **reede**!'   red
The queen anon, for verray womanhede,
Gan for to wepe, and so dede Emelye,   began
And alle the ladies in companye.
Gret pite was it, as it thought hem alle,
That ever such a chaunce schulde falle,   890

57 'banished on pain of losing his head'
58 'to elicit a confession by torture with the rope (cord)'

For gentil men thei were and of gret **estate**,   social status
And nothing but for love was this debate;[59]
And saw here bloody woundes wyde and sore,
And all they cryde, the less and the more,
'Have mercy, lord, upon us women alle!'
And on here bare knees **anoon** they falle,   immediately
And wolde have kissed his bare feet right as he stood,
Til atte laste **aslaked** was his mood,   steadied
For pite renneth sone in gentil herte;[60]

900 And though he for **ire quok** and **sterte**,   anger; shook; trembled
He hath it al considered **in a clause**:   very quickly
The trespas of hem bothe and hire cause;
And although his ire here gylt **accused**,   pressed
Yet he in his **resoun** hem bothe excused,   reasoning/rational thought
And thus he thought, that every **maner** man   sort of
Wol help himself in love, if that he can;
And **eek** delyver himself out of prisoun,   also
And eek in his hert he had compassioun
Of women, for they wepen ever in oon,   for

910 And in his gentil hert he thought anoon,
And sothly he to himself seyde, 'Fy
Upon a lord that wol have no mercy,
But be a **lyoun** bothe in word in dede,   lion
To hem that ben in **repentaunce** and **drede**,   repentance; fear
As wel as to a proud **dispitous** man   spiteful
That wol **maynteyne** that he first bigan.   stand by (his story)
That lord hath litel of **discrecioun**   judgement
That in such caas **can** no **divisioun**,   knows; difference
But **wayteth** pride and humblenesse **after oon**.'   values; alike

920 And schortly, whan his ire is over gon,
He gan to loke on hem with eyen blake and light,
And spak these wordes al in hight,
'The god of love – a, benedicite!
How mighty and how gret a lord is he!
Agayns his might ther **gayneth** non obstacle.   avails
He may be **cleped** a god of his miracle,   called

59 'this quarrel was about nothing but love'
60 'pity rises quickly in the gentle/sensitive heart' (probably another proverbial
   saying).

For he can maken **at his owen gyse**   *in his own way*
Of every herte, **as him lust devyse**!   *just as he wishes*
Lo! Her is Arcite and Palomon,
That **quytely** were out of my prisoun,   *free*   930
And might have lyved in Thebes ryally,
And witen I am **here** mortal enemy,   *their*
And that here deth **lith** in my **might** also,   *lies; power*
And yet hath love, **maugre** here **eyyen** tuo,   *despite; eyes*
Y-brought hem hider bothe for to dye!
Now loketh, is nat that an heih **folye**!   *foolishness*
Who may be a fole, **if** that he love!   *unless*
Byholde, for goddes that sitteth above –
Se how they **blede** be they nought wel arrayed;[61]   *bleed*
Thus hath here lord, the god of love, hem payed   940
Here wages and here fees for her servise,
And yet **wenen** they to ben wise   *believe*
That serven love, for ought that may bifall.
But this is yette the beste game of alle –
That sche for whom they have this jelousye
Can hem therfore as moche thanke as me![62]
Sche **woot** no more of al this **hoote fare**[63]
By god, than wot a cuckow or an hare!
But al moot be **assayed**, hoot or colde –   *tried out*
A man moot ben a fool, other yong or olde:[64]   950
I **woot** it by myself **ful yore a gon**,   *a long time ago*
For in my tyme a servant was I on:
And **sythen** that I knewe of loves peyne,   *since*
And wot how sore it can a man **destreyne**,   *afflict*
As he that hath often ben caught in his lace,
I you forgeve **holly** this **trespace**,   *wholly; trespass*
At the request of the queen that kneleth heer,
And eek of Emely my suster deere;
And ye **schullen** bothe anon unto me swere   *shall*
That never ye schullen my **corowne dere**,   *crown; attempt*   960
Ne make werre on me night ne day,

61 'see how they'd bleed if they weren't so well armoured'
62 'ought to thank them as much as she does me'
63 understands; passionate business
64 'a man has no choice but to be a fool (for love)'

But be my freendes all that ye may;
I yow forgeve this trespas **every dele**.'   entirely
And they hym sworen **his axing** faire and weel,   what he asked
And him of lordschip and of mercy prayde,
And he hem graunted mercy, and thus he sayde,

❦ 'To speke of **real lynage** and riches,   royal lineage
Though that sche were a queen or a **prynces**;   princess
Ilk of yow bothe is worthy, **douteles**,   each; without doubt
970 To wedde when tyme is; but natheles
I speke as for my suster Emelye,
For whan ye have this stryf and jelousye,
Ye woot youre self sche may not wedde two
At oones, though ye foughten ever mo:
That oon of yow, or be him loth or leef,[65]
He may go pypen in an ivy leef.[66]
This is to say, sche may nought have bothe,
Al be ye never so jelous ne so **lothe**:   hateful (of one another)
For thy I put you bothe in this **degre**,   for this reason; judgement
980 That ilk of you schal have his destyne
As him is **schape**, and herken in what wyse –   predestined
Lo, here your end – of that I schal **devyse**.   outline

❦ My wil is this: for playn conclusioun,
Withouten any **replicacioun**,   repetition
If that you liketh, tak it for the best
That **every** of you schal go wher him lest,   each
Frely, withouten raunsoun or **daungeer**,   threat
And this day fyfty **wykes**, far ne neer,   weeks' time
Everich of you schal bryng an hundred knyghtes,
990 Armed for lystes **up at alle rightes**,   in every way
Al redy to **derayne** hir by batayle;   decide possession
And thus **byhote** I you withouten fayle,   promise
Upon my trouthe, and as I am a knight,
That **whethir** of you bothe that hath might –   whichever
This is to seyn, that whethir he or thou

65 'whether he likes it nor not'
66 'may go and pipe in an ivy leaf' (another proverb)

May with his hundred, as I spak of now,
Sle his **contrary**, or out of lystes dryve –   opponent
Him schal I geve Emelye **to wyve**,   as a wife
To whom that fortune geveth so faire a grace.
The lyste schal I make in this place, [67]   1000
And god so wisly on my sowle **rewe**,   have mercy
As I schal **even** juge ben and **trewe**.   impartial; reliable
Ye schul non othir ende with me make,[68]
That oon of yow schal be deed or take:
And if you thinketh this is wel y-sayde,
Say yaire avis and holdeth yow apayde.[69]
This is youre ende and yaire conclusioun.
Who loketh **lightly** now but Palamon?   cheerfully
Who spryngeth up for joye but Arcite?
Who **couthe** telle, or who couthe endite   knows how to   1010
The joye that is made in this place,
Whan Theseus hath don so faire a grace,
But down on knees wente every **wight**,   person
And thanked him with al here hertes might;
And namely the Thebanes **ofte sithe**.   many times
And thus with good hope and with herte blithe
They taken herre leve and homward they ryde,
To Thebes, with olde walles wyde.

❦ I trow men wolde it **deme** necligence,   consider
If I forgete to telle the **dispence**   expense   1020
Of Theseus, that goth so busily
To maken up the lystes **rially**.   royally
A, such a noble theatre as it was:
I dar wel say that in this world ther **nas**.   was not
The **circuite** ther was a myle aboute;   circumference
Round was the **schap** in maner of compaas,   shape
Ful of degre the height of sixty **paas**,   paces
That whan a man was set in **o degre**   one position
He **letted** nought his felaw for to se.   prevented

67 The list is the barrier between two jousting knights, but here means 'tournament
   ground'.
68 'neither of you can make any other form of bargain me'
69 'give your opinion and be satisfied'

1030 ❧ Estward, ther stood a gate of marble **whit**;   *white*
Westward such another in opposit:
And schortly to conclude, such a place
Was non in erthe so litel space.
In al the lond ther nas no craftys man
That geometry or **arsmetrike** can,   *arithmetic*
Ne **purtreyour**, ne **kerver** of ymages,   *painter; carver*
That Theseus ne **gef** hem **mete** and wages,   *gave; food*
The theatre for to maken and devyse;
And for to don his right and sacrifise
1040 He estward hath, upon the gate above,
In worship of Venus, **goddes** of love,   *goddess*
Don make an **auter** and an **oratory**:   *altar; oratory/chapel*
And westward, **in the mynde** and in memory   *thinking of*
Of Mars, he hath y-maked such another,
That coste largely of gold a **fother**:   *cartload*
And northward, in a **toret** on the walle,   *turret*
Of alabaster whit and reed **coralle**,   *coral*
An oratory riche for to see
In worship of Dyane, goddes of chastite,
1050 Hath Theseus **y-wroght** in nobel **wise**.   *made; fashion*
But yit had I forgeten to devyse
The nobil **kervyng** and the **purtretures**,   *carving; painting*
The **schap**, the **contynaunce**, of the figures   *shape/form; appearance*
That weren in the oratories thre.

    ❧ Furst, in the temple of Venus thou may se,
Wrought in the wal, ful pitous to byholde,
The broken slepes and the **sykes** colde,   *sighs*
The sacred teeres and the **waymentyng**,   *mourning*
The fuyry strokes, and the desiryng
1060 That love's servants in this lyf enduren,
The **othes** that by her **covenants** assuren.[70]
Plesaunce and hope, desyr, foolhardynesse,
Beaute and youth, **baudery** and richesse,   *reckless mirth*
Charmes and sorcery, **lesynges** and flatery,   *lying*
Dispense, busynes and jelousy;   *expenditure*

70 with oaths; promises/agreements

That werud of yolow guldes a gerland,[71]
And a cukkow sittyng on hire hand: [72]
Festes, instruments, cards and daunces,
Lust and **array**, and al the circumstaunces   clothing
Of love, which I **rekned** and **reken** schal;   counted; recount   1070
Ech by other were peynted on the wal,
And **mo** than I can make of mencioun.   more
For **sothly**, al the mount of Setheroun,[73]   truly
Ther Venus hath hir principal dwellyng,
Was schowed on the wal here portrayng,
With alle the Gardyn and the lustynes.
Nought was forgete the porter, Ydelnes,[74]
Ne Narcisus the fayr, of yore agon,[75]
Ne yet the foly of Kyng Salomon,
Ne **eek** the strengthe of him Hercules,   also   1080
Th'enchauntements of Medea and Cerces,
Ne of Turnus, of which the hard fuyry corage;
The riche Cresus, caytif in servage;
Thens may we see that wisdom and riches,
Beaute ne **sleight**, strength ne hardynes,   cunning
Ne may with Venus holde **champetye**,   power-sharing
For as sche **lust** the world than may sche **gye**.   likes; guide
Lo, al this folk y-caught were in hire **trace**,   snare
Til thay for wo ful often sayde, 'Allas!'
Sufficeth this ensample, oon or tuo,   1090
And though I **couthe rekon** a thousend mo.   could count
The statu of Venus, glorious for to see,
Was naked, **fletyng** in the **large** see;   floating; wide
And fro the navel doun al covered was
With **wawes** grene, as bright as eny **glas**.   waves; mirror
A **citole** in hire right hond hadde sche,   musical instrument
And on hir heed ful semely for to see,
A rose garland fresh and wel smellyng,

71 'wore a garland of yellow marigolds'
72 A cuckoo, the symbol of adultery.
73 Citheron, meaning the island of Cythera, where Venus rose from the sea.
74 Idleness, keeper of the garden gate in the Romance of the Rose
75 Examples of love and wealth: Narcissus fell in love with his own reflection,
   Solomon had lots of wives, Medea and Cerces cast spells to gain their loves, and
   Croesus was fabulously rich but a prisoner.

Above hir heed hir **dawes fleyng**.   doves flying
1100 Biforn hir stood hir sone, Cupido:
Upon his **schuldres** were wynges two,   shoulders
And blynd he was, as it is often seene.
A bowe he bar, and **arwes** fair and greene.   arrows

❦ Why schul I nought as wel telle you alle
The portraiture that was upon the walle
Within the temple of mighty Mars the **reede**?   red
Al peynted was the wal in length and **breede**,   breadth
Like to the **estres** of the grisly place   hidden corners
That hight the gret tempul of Mars in **Trace**.   Thrace
1110 In that colde and in that frosty regioun,
Ther as Mars hath his **sovereyn mancioun**,   chief residence
First on the wal was peynted a foreste,
In which ther dwelled neyther man ne beste,
With knotty, **knarry**, **bareyn** trees olde,   gnarled; barren
Of **stubbes** scharpe and hidous to byholde,   stumps
In which ther ran a **wymbul** in a **swough**,[76]
As it were a storme schuld berst every bough;
And downward on an hil, under a **bent**,   slope
Ther stood the tempul of Mars **armypotent**,   powerful in arms
1120 Wrought al of **burned** steel, of which **ventre**   burnished; the entrance
Was long and **streyt**, and gastly for to see;   narrow
And therout cam a **rage** of such a **prise**   draught (of wind); blast
That it maad al the gates for to rise.
The northen light in at the door schon,
For wyndow on the walle was ther **noon**   none
Thorugh the which men might no light discerne.
The doores wer all ademaunts eterne,[77]
Y-clenched over, toward and endelong,[78]
With iren tough; and for to make it strong
1130 Every piler the tempul to **susteene**,   sustain/support
Was tonne greet of iren bright and schene.[79]
Ther saugh I furst the derk ymaginyng
Of felony, and al the **compassyng**.   carrying out

76 (sound of) running water; wind
77 'eternal adamant': the world's strongest stone
78 'bound horisontally and vertically'
79 'as big as a ton (a large barrel)'

The cruel **ire**, as reed as eny **gleede**,   anger; burning coal
The **pike purs**, and eek the pale **drede**;   pickpocket; fear
The smyler with the knyf under his cloke,
The **schipne** brennyng with the blake smoke,   ship
The tresoun of the murtheryng in the bed,
The open **weres** with woundes al **bibled**,   wars; bloody
Kuttud with boody knyf and scharp manace;   1140
Al ful of **chirkyng** was that sory place.   groaning
The **sleer** of himself yet saugh I there,   killer
Here herte blood hath bathed al his **here**;   hair
The nayl y-dryve in the **scholde** a-nyght,   head
The cold deth, with mouth gapyng upright.
A-myddes of the tempul set **Meschaunce**,   in the middle; ill luck
With sory comfort and evel contynaunce.
I saugh woundes laughyng in here rage,
The hunt strangled with wilde **bore**'s corage,   boar
The sowe **freten** the child right in the cradel,   eaten 1150
The cook y-skalded, for al his long ladel,
Nought beth forgeten by the **infortune of Mart**;   Mars's baleful influence
The carter **over-ryden** with his cart –   ridden over
Under the **whel** ful lowe he lay adoun.   wheel
Ther were also of **Mart's divisioun**   protected by Mars
The barbour and the **bowcher** and the smyth,   butcher
That forgeth scharpe swerdes on his **stith**.   anvil
And above, **depeynted** in a tour,   depicted
Saw I Conquest, sittyng in gret honour,
With the scharpe swerd over his heed   1160
Hangynge by a sotil twyne threed.
Depeynted was ther the **slaught** of Julius[80]   slaughter
Of grete Nero and of Anthonius;
Al be that **ilke** tyme they were unborn;   same
Yet was here deth depeynted **ther byforn**,   before (their births)
By manasyng of Marcs right by figure;[81]
So was it schewed right in the purtreture
As is depeynted in sterres above,

80 Julius Caesar, Nero and Antonius, emperors of Rome (not yet founded at the time depicted in the Arcite and Palamon story).
81 'by the threat of Mars in the heavens'

Who schal be slayn, or elles deed for love.
1170 Sufficeth oon ensample in stories olde –
I may nat **rekene** hem all, though I wolde.   recount

❦ The statue of Mars upon a carte stood
Armed, and loked grym as he were **wood**;   mad/madly angry
And over his heed ther schyneth two figures
Of sterres, that been **cleped** in **scriptures**   called; writings
That oon Puella, that other Rubius.[82]
This god of armes was arayed thus:
A wolf ther stood byforn him at his feet,
With eyen **reed**, and of a man he **eet**.   red; ate
1180 With **sotyl pencel** depeynted was this storie   skilful pencil
In **redoutyng** of Mars, and of his glorie.   glorifying

❦ Now to the temple of Dyane the chaste
As schortly as I can, I wol ne haste
To telle you al the descripcioun.
Depeynted ben the walles, up and doun,
Of huntyng and of **schamefast** chastite: modest
Ther saugh I how woful Calystope[83]
Whan that Dyane was **agreved** with here,   annoyed
Was turned from a woman to a **bere**;   bear
1190 And after was sche **maad** the **loode sterre**.   made; pole star
Thus was it peynted, I can say ne **ferre**:   further
Hire son is eek after, as men may see.
Ther saw I Dyane turned in til a tree –[84]
I mene nou*gh*t the goddes Dyane,
But Peneus' dou*gh*ter, the whiche **hight** Dane.   was called
Ther saugh I Atheon an hert y-maked,[85]
For vengeance, that he saugh Dyane al naked:
I saugh how that his houndes han him caught

82 Lines and dots in geomancy (a form of fortune-telling performed by scribbling lines and dots), joined to give Puella and Rubeus, indicators of the aspects of Mars.
83 The nymph Callisto.
84 Daphne, turned into a tree to protect her chastity from Apollo.
85 Acteon saw Diana bathing, and was turned into a stag, then killed by his own hounds.

And **freten** him, for that they knew him naught. *eaten*
Yit y-peynted was a litel forther more 1200
How Athalaunce huntyd the wilde bore,[86]
And Melyagre, and many another story,
The which me list not drawe into memory.
This goddess on an **hert** ful hy **he seet**, *hart/stag; she sat*
With smale houndes at hire feet,
And undernethe her feet sche had the moone;
Wexyng it was, and schulde wane soone.
In **gaude** green hire **stature** clothed was, *yellowy; statue*
With bowe in honde and arwes in a **cas**. *sheath*
Hir eyyen caste sche ful lowe adoun, 1210
Ther Pluto hath his derke regioun.[87] *where*
A woman travailyng was hire biforn,
But for hire child so longe was unborn
Ful pitously, 'Lucyna!'[88] gan sche calle,
And seyde, 'Help, for thou mayst best of alle!'
Wel couthe he peynte **lyfly** that it was wrou*gh*t; *lifelike*
With many a **floren** he the **hewes** bought. *florin (gold coin); colours*
Now ben thise listes **maad**, and Theseus, *made*
That at his grete cost **arayed** thus *furnished*
The temples and the theatres every del, 1220
Whan it was don it liked him right wel.
But stynt I wil of Theseus alite,
And speke of Palomon, and of Arcite.

❧ The day approcheth of her **attournyng**, *fighting in tournament*
That every schuld an hundred kni*gh*tes bryng,
The batail to **derreyne** as I you tolde, *decide*
And **til** Athenes, her covenant to holde, *to*
Hath every of hem brought an **C** knightes, *hundred*
Wel armed for the werr **at all rightes**, *completely*
And **sikerly** ther **trowed** many a man, *surely; swore* 1230
That never **siththen** that this world bigan, *since*
For to speke of knighthod, of her **hond**, *deeds*
As fer as god hath maked see or lond,

86 The huntress Atalanta and the hunter Meleager.
87 Pluto, Roman god of the underworld, land of the dead.
88 The name of the moon, Diana.

Nas of so fewe so good a company –
For every **wight** that loveth **chyvalry**,   person; knighthood
And wold, his thankes, have a **passant name**,   great reputation

❦ He preyed that he might be of that game.[89]
A! **Wel** was him that therto chosen was;   fortunate
For if ther telle tomorwe such a **caas**,   event
1240   I knowe wel that every lusty knight
That loveth **paramours**, and hath his **might**,   passionately; strength
Wer it in Engelond or elleswhere,
They wold **thare thankes wilne** to be there;   really want
To fighte for a lady, bendicite!
It were a lusty fighte for to see;
And right so ferden they with Palamon.
With him ther wente knyghtes many oon,
Som wol ben armed in an **haburgoun**,   hawberk (mail coat)
In a bright brestplat and a **gypoun**,   jupon (padded tunic)
1250   And som wold have **a peyre plates** large,   plate armour
And som wold have a **prys** scheld or a **targe**;   Prussian (Pruce)
Som wol ben armed on here legges **weel**,   well
And have an ax, and eek a mace of steel.
Ther nys no newe gyse that it was old:[90]
Armed were they as I have told,
Everich after his owen opinioun.

❦ Ther **maistow se** comyng with Palomon   you may see
Sigurge himself, the grete kyng of Trace –
Blak was his berd, and manly was his face.
1260   The cercles of his eyen in his heed,
They gloweden bytwixe **yolw** and reed,   yellow
And lik a griffoun loked he aboute,[91]
With **kempe** heres on his browes stowte;   combed
His lymes **greet**, his **brawnes** hard and stronge,   great; muscles
His schuldres brood, his armes rounde and longe,
And as the **gyse** was in his contre,   manner
Ful heye upon a **chare** of gold stood he,   chariot

---

89 'involved in the tournament'
90 'there is no new fashion but that it was old'
91 Heraldic beast with a lion's body with an eagle's head.

With foure white **boles** in a **trays**. | bulls; yoke
In stede of **cote armour** in his **harnays** | heraldic device; armour
With **nayles yolwe** and bright as eny gold, | nails; yellow 1270
He had a **bere** skyn, **cole** blak for **old**; | bear; coal; age
His lange heer **y-kempt** byhynd his bak – | combed
As eny raven fether it schon for blak.[92]
A **wrethe** of gold, **arm gret** and huge of **wight**

wreath; arm-thick; weight

Upon his heed, set ful of stones bright,
Of fyne **rubeus** and of fyn **dyamaunts**. | rubies; diamonds
Aboute his **chare** wente with white **alaunts**, | wolfhounds
Twenty and mo, as grete as eny **stere**, | steer
To hunt at the lyoun or at the **bare**, | bear (or boar)
And folwed him, with **mosel** fast ybounde, | muzzle 1280
Colerd of gold, and towets fyled rounde.[93]
An hundred lordes had he in his **route**, | company
Armed ful wel, with hertes stern and stoute.

❧ With Arcita, in stories as men fynde,
The gret Emetreus, the kyng of **Inde**, | India
Uppon a steed bay trapped in steel,[94]
Covered with cloth of gold, **dyapred** wel, | patterned
Cam rydyng lyk the god of armes, Mars.
His coote armour was of a **cloth of Tars**, | silk
Cowched of perlys, whyte, round and grete: | decorated with pearls 1290
His sadil was of **brend** gold newe bete. | burnished
A **mantelet** upon his schuldre hangyng, | short cloak
Bret ful of rubies reed and **fir sparkelyng**.[95]
His crispe **her lik rynges was y-ronne**, | hair in ringlets
And that was yalwe, and gliteryng as the sonne.
His nose was heigh, his eyen were **cytryne**, | lemon
His lippes rounde, his colour was **sangwyn**. | ruddy
A fewe **frelines** in his face **y-spreynd**, | freckles; sprinkled
Betwixe yolwe and somdel blak **y-meynd**; | mixed
And as a lyoun he his lokyng caste: | 1300

92 'it shone as black as any raven's feather'
93 'wearing gold collars with round lead-rings'
94 'in steel horse-armour'
95 crammed; sparkling like fire

Of fyve and twenty yeer his age I **caste**.   guess
His berd was wel bygonne for to sprynge,
His voys was as a **trumpe** thunderynge.   trumpet
Upon his heed he wered a **laurer** grene,   laurel wreath
A garlond freisch and lusty for to sene.
Upon his hond he bar, for his **delyt**,   pleasure
An Egle tame, as eny **lylie** whyt.   lily
An hondred lordes had he with him ther,
Al armed, **sauf** here hedes, in her **ger**   except; armour
1310 Ful richely in all maner thinges;
For trusteth wel, that dukes, erles, kynges,
Were **gadred** in this noble companye   gathered
For love, and for **encres** of chivalrye.   enhancing
Aboute the kyng ther ran on every part
Ful many a tame lyoun and **lepart**;   leopard
And in this wise this lordes, **all and some**,   one and all
Been on the Sonday to the cite come
Aboute prime, and in the toun alight. [96]
This Theseus, this duk, this worthy knight,
1320 Whan he had brought hem in to this cite
And **ynned** hem everich **at his degre**,[97]
He festeth hem, and doth so gret labour
To **esen** hem and do hem al honour,   make them comfortable
That yit men **wene** that no mannes wyt   believe
Of non estat that cowde **amenden it**.   do it better
The mynstralcye, the servyce at the feste,
The grete giftes to the most and leste,
The riche aray of Thebes, his **paleys**,   palace
Ne who sat first ne last upon the deys,[98]
1330 What ladies fayrest ben or best daunsyng,
Ne who most **felyngly** speketh of love;   sensitively
What **haukes** sitten on the perche above,   hawks
What houndes lyen in the floor adoun –
Of al this make I now no mencioun,
But of theffect that thinketh me the beste:
Now comth the poynt, and herkneth if you leste.

96 Early morning, between six and nine o'clock.
97 accommodated; according to his status
98 Dais, the raised platform at the end of hall, where the host and most honoured
   guests sat.

❦ The Sonday night, **or** day bigan to springe,   before
When Palomon the larke herde synge,
Although it were nought day by houres tuo,
Yit sang the larke, and Palomon also.   1340
With holy herte and with an heih corage,
He **roos** to **wenden** on his pilgrymage,   rose; go
Unto the blisful Cithera **benigne** –   kindly
I mene Venus, honorable and **digne**.   worthy
And in here hour he walketh forth a **paas**   steadily
Unto the lystes, ther hir temple was,
And doun he kneleth, and with humble cheer,
And **herte sor**, and seide as ye schal heer,   painful heart

❦ 'Fairest, O fairest, O lady myn, Venus!
Doughter of Jove and spouse to Vulcanus,[99]   1350
The **glader** of the mount of Citheroun!   gladdener
For thilke love thou haddest to Adeoun,[100]
Have pite on my bitter teeres smerte,
And tak myn humble prayer to thin herte!
Allas! I ne have no langage for to telle
Theffectes, ne the torments of myn helle!
Myn herte may myn harmes nat **bewreye**:   disclose
I am so **confus** that I may not **seye**.   confused; tell
But mercy, lady bright, that knowest wel
My thought, and felest what harm that I **fel**.   feel 1360
Consider al this, and **rew** upon my **sore**   have mercy; hurt
As wisly as I schal for evermore
Enforce my might, thi trewe servant to be,
And **hadde werre** alday with chastite.   fought against
That make I myn avow, so ye me helpe.
I **kepe** nat of armes for to **yelpe**,   care; boast
Ne nat I aske tomorn to have victorie,
Ne renoun in this caas, ne veyne glorie
Of pris or armes, **blowyng up and doun**,   praised far and wide
But I wolde have ful possessioun   1370
Of Emelye, and dye in thi servise.
Fynd thou the maner how, and in what wyse

99 Vulcan, the deformed smith-god, husband of Venus.
100 Adonis, one of the lovers of Venus.

I **recche** nat, but it may better be   care
To have victorie of him, or he of me,
So that I have my lady in myn armes;
For though so be that Mars be god of armes
And ye be Venus, the goddes of love,
Youre **vertu** is so gret in heven above.   power
Thy temple wol I worschipe evermo,
1380   And on thin auter, wher I ryde or go,
I wol so sacrifice and fyres **beete**.   light
And if ye wol nat so, my lady sweete,
Than pray I the tomorwe, with a spere,
That Arcita me thurgh the herte **bere**,   pierce
Thanne rekke I nat, whan I have **lest** my lyf,   lost
Though that Arcite have hir to his wyf.
This is theffect and ende of my prayeere –
Gif me my love, my blissful lady deere.'
Whan **thorisioun** was doon of Palomon,   prayer
1390   His sacrifice he dede render that anoon
Ful pitously, with all circumstances.
Al telle I nat as now his observances,
But at the last the statu of Venus schook,
And made a signe, wherby that he took
That his prayer accepted was that day –
For though the signe schewed a delay,
Yet wist he wel that graunted was his **boone**,   request
And with glad herte he wente hym hom ful soone.

❦ The thrid hour in equal that Palomon
1400   Bigan to Venus' temple for to goon,
Up roos the sonne, and up roos Emelye;
And to the temple of Dian gan sche **hye**.   make her way
Hir maydens that sche with hir thider **ladde**   took
Ful redily with hem the fyr they hadde,
Thencens, the clothes, and the **remenant** al[101]
That to the sacrifice **longen** schal;   belong
The hornes ful of **meth**, as is the gyse –   mead
Ther lakketh nought to do here sacrifise.
Smokyng the temple, ful of clothes faire,   censing

101 the incense; everything else

This Emelye, with herte **debonaire**,   light/genteel 1410
Hir body **wessch** with watir of a welle –   washed
But howe sche did I **der** nat telle,   dare
But it be eny thing in general – [102]
And yet it were a game to here it al.
To him that meneth wel it were no **charge**,   trouble
But it is good a man be **at his large**.   unrestrained
Hir brighte her was **kempt untressed** al,   combed loose
A corone of a grene **ok cerial**   serial oak (species)
Upon hir heed was set, ful fair and meete.
Tuo fyres on the **auter** gan sche **beete**,   altar; kindle 1420
And did hir thinges, as men may biholde,
In state of Thebes and the bokes olde.
When **kynled** was the fyre, with **pitous** cheere   kindled; piteous
Unto Dyan sche spak, as ye may heere.

❦ 'O chaste goddes of the woodes greene,
To whom bothe heven and erthe and see is seene;
Queen of the regne of Pluto derk and lowe,
Goddes of **maydenes**, that myn hert has knowe   virgins
Ful many a yeer → ye **woot** what I desire: know
As keep me from the **vengans** of **thilke yre**   vengeance; same; anger 1430
That Atheon **aboughte** trewely.   bought
Chaste goddesse, wel wost thou that I
Desire to ben a mayden al my lyf,
Ne never wol I be no love ne wyf.
I am **yit**, thou **wost**, of thi company;   still; know
A mayden, and love huntyng and **venery**,   the skill of hunting
And for to walken in the woodes wylde,
And nought to ben a wyf and be with chylde;
Nou*gh*t wol I knowe the company of man.
Now helpe me lady, **sythnes** ye may and kan,   since 1440
For the **formes** that thou hast in the,   different aspects
And Palamon that hath such love to me,
And **eek** Arcite that **loveth** me so sore: also; loves
This grace I praye the, withoute more –
And sende love and **pees** betwix hem two,   peace
And fro me torne awey here hertes, so

102 'only in a very generalised way'

That al here hoote love and here desire,
Al here besy torment and al here fyre
Be **queynt**, or turned in another place;   quenched
1450 And if so be thou wol do me no grace,
Or if my destyne be schaped so
That I schal needes have on of hem two,
So send me him that most desireth me.
Biholde, goddes of **clene** chastite,   pure
The bitter teeres that on my cheekes falle.
Syn thou art mayde and keper of us alle,
My **maydenhode** thou kepe and wel conserve,   virginity
And whil I lyve, a mayde, I wil the serve.'

🌿 The fyres **bren** upon the **auter cleer**   burn; altar; bright
1460 Whil Emelye was in hire pryer,
But sodenly she saugh a sighte **queynt**;   unusual
For right anon **on** of the fyres **queynt**,   one; went out

🌿 And **quyked** agayn, and after that anon   flared
That other fyr was **queynt**, and al a-gon: quenched
And as it queynt it made a whistelyng,
As doth a **wete brond** in his brennyng,   wet; (fire)brand
And at the brondes end out ran anoon
As it were bloody **dropes**, many oon: drops
For which so sore **agast** was Emelye   afraid
1470 That sche wel neih mad was, and gan to crie;
For sche **ne wiste** what it signifyed –   did not know
But oonly for feere thus sche cryed,
And wepte that it was pite to heere.
And ther withal Dyane **gan appeere**,   appeared
With bow in hond, right as a hunteresse,
And seyd, 'A, daughter! **Stynt thn hevynesse!**   put away your sadness
Among the goddes hye it is affermed,
Thou schalt be wedded unto oon of **tho**   those
That have for the so moche care and wo:
1480 But unto which of hem, may I nat telle.
Far wel! For I may her no lenger dwelle.
The fyres which that on myn auter bren
Schuln the declare, **or** that thou go **hen**,   before; away
Thyn **adventure** of love, as in this **caas**.'   Fortune; situation

[And with that word, the arwes in the **caas**]   quiver
Of the goddesse clatren **faste** and rynge,   loudly
And forth sche went, and made a vanysschynge:
For which thus Emelye **astoneyed** was,   astonished
And seide, 'What amounteth this? Allas![103]
I put me under thy proteccioun,   1490
Dyane, and in thi **disposicioun**.'   keeping
And hoom sche goth anon the **nexte** way –   closest
This is theffect, ther nys no more to say.

❦ The next hour of Mars folwynge this,
Arcite to the temple walkyd is,
To fyry Mars to doon his sacrifise,
With al the rightes of his **payen** wise,   pagan
With pious herte and heih devocioun.
Right thus to Mars he sayd his **orisoun**:   prayer
'O stronge god, that in the **regnes** cold   kingdoms/region 1500
Of **Trace** honoured and lord art thou holde,   Thrace
And hast in every **regne** and every land   kingdom
Of armes al the bridel in thy hand;
And hem **fortunest** as the lust devyse –   give good luck to
Accept of me my **pitous** sacrifise.   pitiful
If so be that my youthe may deserve,
And that my might be worthi to deserve
Thy godhed, that I may be on of thine,
Then pray I the to **rewe** on my **pyne**,   have pity; hurt
For **thilke payne** and that hoote **fuyre**,   same; pain; fire 1510
The which **whilom** thou **brendest** for desyre,   formerly; burned
Whan that thou **usedest** the gret **bewte**   possessed; beauty
Of faire freissche Venus that is so free,
And haddest hir in armes at thy wille;
And though the ones on a tyme **myfille**,   had ill luck
When Vulcanus had caught the in his caas,
And **fand** the **liggyng** by his wyf – allaas!   found; lying
For thilke sorwe that was in thin herte,
Have **reuthe** as wel upon my peynes **smerte**.   pity; sharp
I am yong and **unkonnyng**, as thou **wost**   unknowing; know 1520
And, as I **trowe**, with love offended most   swear

103 'what's all this about?'

That ever was eny lyves creature;
For sche that **doth** me al this wo endure. — causes
Me rekketh never whether I synke or flete,[104]
And wel I woot **or** sche me mercy **heete** — before; promise
I moot with **strangth** wyn hir in the place; — strength
And wel I wot, withouten help or grace
Of the, ne may my strangthe nought **avayle**. — do any good
Then help me, lord, to **man** in my batayle, — 'be a man'
1530 For thilke fyr that **whilom brende** the, — once burned
A wel as this fire now brenneth me:
And **do** tomorn that I have the victorie – — make it
Myn be the **travail**, al thin be the glorie. — labour
Thy soverein temple wol I most honouren
Of any place, and alway most labouren
In thy **pleasance** and thy craftes strong, — to please you
And in thy tempul I wol my baner **hong**, — hang
And all the armes of my companye;
And evermore unto that day I dye
1540 **Etern** fyr I wol bifore the fynde: — eternal
And **eek** to this avowe I wol me bynde – — also
My berd, myn hoer, that hangeth long adoun,
That never yit ne felt offensioun
Of rasour ne of schere, I wol the give,[105]
And be thy trewe servaunt whiles I lyve.
Lord have rowthe uppon my sorwes sore –
Gif me thy victorie – I aske no more.'

❦ The preyer **stynt** of Arcita the **strange** – — ended; strong
The hynges on the tempul dore that hange,
1550 And eek the dores, **clatareden** ful fast; — clattered
Of which Arcita saw, what was **agast**: — astonished
The fyres brenden on the auter bright,
That it gan al the tempul for to light.
A **swote** smel anon the ground up **gaf**, — sweet; gave
And arcita anon his hand up **haf**; — lifted
And more **encens** into the fyr yet cast, — incense
With othir rightes, and than atte last

104 'I don't care whether I sink or float'
105 'that was never offended by razor or scissors'

The statu of Mars bigan his hauberk ryng,   *mail surcoat*
And with that soun he herd a murmuryng,
Ful lowe and dym, and sayde this, 'Victorie!'   1560
For which he gaf to Mars honour and glorie;
And thus with joye and hope wel to fare,
Arcite anoon unto his **furie** is fare,   *fight*
As **fayn** as **foul** is of the bright sonne: *glad; bird*
And right anon such stryf is bygonne
For that grauntyng in the heven above,   *because of*
Bitwix Venus, the goddes of love,
And Marcs, the sterne god armypotent,
That Jupiter **was busy** it to **stent**;   *tried hard; stop*
Til that the pale Saturnes the colde,   1570
That knew so many of aventures olde,
Fond in his experiens an **art**,   *ability*
That he ful sone hath plesyd **every part**;   *each party*
And **soth** is sayd, **eelde** hath gret avantage: *truth; old age*
In eelde is bothe wisdom and **usage**,   *experience*
Men may the eelde at ren but nat at rede.[106]
Saturne anon, to stynte stryf and drede,
Albeit that it be agayns his **kynde**,   *nature*
Of al this stryf he can remedy fynde.
'My deere dou*g*hter Venus,' quod Satourne,   1580
'My cours, that hath so wyde for to tourne,
Hath more power than woot eny man.
Myn is the **drenchyng** in the see so **wan**;   *drowning; dark*
Myn is the prisoun in the derke **cote**;   *cell*
Myn is the stranglyng & hangyng by the throte,
The murmur and the cherles rebellyng,[107]
The **groynyng** and the **pryve** empoysonyng.   *groaning; secret*
I do vengance and pleyn **correctioun**   *punishment*
Whiles I dwelle in the signe of the lyoun.[108]
Myn is the **ruen** of the **hihe** halles,   *ruin; high* 1590
The fallyng of the toures and the walles

106 'men may out-run but not out-counsel old age'
107 A possible reference to the 1381 Peasants' Revolt.
108 A reference to the course of the planet Saturn, this time in the sign of Leo, the lion.

Upon the mynour or the carpenter.[109]
I slowh Sampson in schekyng the piler,[110]
And myne be the **maladies** colde,   illnesses
The derke tresoun and the **castes** olde: plots
Myn lokyng is the fadir of pestilens.
Now wepe nomore, I schal do my diligence
That Palomon, that is myn owen knight,
Schal have his lady, as thou him bihight.

1600 Thow, Marcs, schal helpe his kni*gh*t – yet nevertheles,
Bitwixe you ther moot somtyme be pees,
Al be ye nou*gh*t of oon **complexioun**,   temperament
That ilke day causeth such divisioun.
I am thi **ayel**, redy at thy wille –   grandfather
Wepe thou no more, I wol thi **lust** fulfille.'   desire
Now wol I stynt of the goddes above,
Of Mars and of Venus, goddes of love,
And tell you as pleinly as I can,
The grete effecte for that I bigan.

1610 ❦ Gret was the **fest** in Athenes that day,   festivity
And eek that lusty sesoun of that May,
Made every wi*gh*t to ben in such **plesaunce**,   happy mood
That al the Monday jousten they and daunce,
And spende hit in Venus' heigh servise[111]
But **by the cause** that they **schulen** arise   because; had to
Erly **a-morwe** for to see that fight,   in the morning
Unto their rest wente thay at nyght,
An on the morwe, whan the day gan spryng,
Of hors and herneys, noyse and clateryng,

1620 Ther was in the **oostes** al aboute,   armies
And to the paleys rood ther many a **route**   group
Of lordes, upon steede and on **palfreys**.   expensive 'riding' horses
Ther mayst thou see **devysyng** of herneys   preparation
So **uncouth** and so riche, **wrought** – & wel –   unknown/exotic; made
Of goldsmithry, of **browdyng** and of steel.   embroidery

109 Miners were used during seiges, to dig tunnels which undermined the walls of
    a besieged castle or town.
110 Sampson pulled down the roof on the Philistines and on himself.
111 In the pursuit of courtly love (ie. a variety of activities from illicit lovemaking to
    polite flirtation).

The scheldes bright, testers and trappures,[112]

Gold beten **helmes**, hauberks and cote armures, · helmets

Lordes in **paraments** on her **coursers**, · rich robes; warhorses

Knightes **of retenu** and eek squyers, · retained (paid by a lord)

Naylyng the speres and helmes **bokelyng**, · fastening (with buckles) 1630

Girdyng of scheeldes with **layneres** lasyng. · lanyers/laces

Ther, **as need is**, they were nothing **ydel**: · as was necessary; idle

Ther **fomen** steedes on the golden bridel · foam

Gnawyng, and faste **armurers** also, · armourers

With fyle and hamer prikyng to and fro.

Yemen on foote and **knaves** many oon, · yeomen; servants

With schorte staves, as thikke as they may goon;

Pypes, trompes, **nakers** and **clarionnes**, · drums; trumpets

That in the batail blewe **bloody sownes**; · bloodcurdling; sounds

The paleys ful of pepul, up and doun, · 1640

Heer thre, ther ten, **haldyng her questioun**, · discussing

Dyvynyng of this Thebans knightes two. · forecasting

Som seyden thus, som seyd, 'It schal be so',

Som heelde with him with the blake berd,

Som with the **ballyd**, som with thikke hered. · bald

Som sayd he loked grym, as he wold fight –

'He hath a **sparth** of **xxti** pound of **wight**': · axe; twenty; weight

Thus was the halle ful of devynyng.

Lang after that the sonne gan to spryng,

The gret Theseus, that of his sleep is awaked · 1650

With menstralcy and noyse that was maked,

Held yet the chambre of his paleys riche, · stayed in

Til that Thebanes knyg*h*tes both **y-liche** · alike

Honoured weren, and in paleys fet.

Duk Theseus was at a wyndow set,

Arayed **right as** he were god in **trone**: · as if; throne

The pepul **presed** thider was ful sone, · crowded

Him for to seen and doun him reverence,

And eek **herken** his **hest** and his sentence. · listen to; command

An heroud on a scaffold made a '**Hoo!**' · 'Ho!' 1660

Til al the noyse of the pepul was **y-do**. · finished

And whan he saugh the pepul of noyse al stille,

Thus **schewed** he the mighty duke's wille. · revealed

112 Horse armour.

❧ 'The lord hath of his heih **descrecioun**,   judgement
Considered that it were destruccioun
To gentil blood to fighten in this wise,
Of **mortal** batail now in this **emprise**.   deadly; endeavour
Werefor to schapen that they schuld not dye,
He wol his firste purpos modifye.
1670 No man therfore, up peyne of los of lyf,
No maner **schot**, ne **pollax**, ne schort knyf,   arrow; poleaxe
Into the lystes sende or thider bryng,
Ne schort swerd for to **stoke** with the poynt bytyng,   poke/jab; nor
No man ne drawe, ne bere by his side,
Ne noman schal to his felawe ryde
But oon **course** with a scharpe spere – [113]   attack
Feyne if him lust on foote himself to **were**;   thrust; protect
And he that is **at meschief** schal be take,   in trouble
And nat slayn, but be brought to the stake
1680 That schal be **ordeyned** on eyther syde;   set up
But thider he schal by force and ther **abyde**.   remain
And if so falle a cheveuten be take[114]
On eyther side, or elles **sle** his **make**,   kill; opponent
No lenger schal the turneynge laste.
God sped you – goth forth and **ley on faste**,   'get to it'
With long swerd and with mace: fight your fille.
Goth now your way – this is the lord's wille.'

❧ The voice of the poepul touchith heven;
So lowde cried thei with mylde **steven**,   voice
1690 'God save such a lord, that is so good!
He **wilneth** no destruccioun of blood!'   wishes
Up goth the trompes and the melodye,
And to the lystes ryde the companye
By **ordynaunce** thurgh the cite large,   order
Hangyng with cloth of gold, and not with **sarge**.   rough cloth (serge)
Ful lik a lord this nobul Duk cam ryde,
These tuo Thebans on eyther side,
And after rood the queen and Emelye,

---

113 'no man shall ride (ie tilt in the joust) against another with a spear (or lance)
more than once'
114 'one of the two main combatants'

And after hem of comunes after here degre.[115]
And thus they passeden thurgh that cite,   1700
And to the lystes came thei **bytyme** –   eventually
It nas not of the day yet fully pryme[116]
Whan sette was Theseus, riche and hye,
Ypolita the queen and Emelye,
And other ladyes in here degrees aboute.
Unto the **settes** passeth al the **route**;   seats; company
And westward thorough the gates of **Mart**,   Mars
Arcite, and eek the hundred of his part,
With baners is y-entred right anoon;
And that **selve** moment Palomon   same 1710
Is under Venus, Estward in that place,
With baner whyt and **hardy cheer** of face.   stern aspect

❦ In al the world, to seeke up and doun,
So **even**, withoute variatioun,   equal
Ther **nere** suche companyes **tweye**;   were not; two
For ther nas non so wys that cowthe seye[117]
That any had of other avauntage
Of worthines, ne staat, ne of age,
So evene were they chosen, **for to gesse**,   as it appeared
And in two **renges** faire they **hem dresse**:   ranks; draw up 1720
And whan he names **y-rad** were everychon,   read
That in here nombre **gile** were ther noon,   guile/trickery
Tho were the gates **schitt** and cried lowde,   shut
'Dooth nowe your **devoir**, yong knightes proude!'   work
The heralds leften here **prikyng** up and doun: riding
Now ryngede the tromp and clarioun.
There is no more to say, but Est and West
In goth the speres in to the rest.[118]
Then seen men who can **juste** and who can ryde –   joust
In goth the scharpe **spere** into the side: spur 1730

115 'common' people; according to their status – meaning probably 'the chief
    citizens', rather than the more lowly members of the population. Chaucer is
    describing a civic procession as it would have occurred in later fourteenth-
    century London.
116 'it was early, about seven or eight in the morning'
117 'there was none so wise that could not say'
118 They raised them ready for battle.

Ther **schyveren** schaftes upon **schuldres thyk**;　　break; broad shoulders
He feeleth thurgh the herte-span the prik.
Up sprengen speres on twenty foot on hight,
Out goon the swerdes as the silver bright,
The helmes ther **to-hewen** and to schrede,　　　　hacked about
Out **brast** the blood with **stoute stremes** reede,　　burst; strong flow
With mighty maces the bones thay **to-breste**.　　　　burst
He thurgh the thikkest of the throng gan **threste**:　　thrust
Ther stomblen steedes strong, and doun can falle –

1740 He rolled underfoot, as doth a balle:
He **feyneth** on his foot with his **tronchoun**　　stabs; shaft (of spear)
And him hurteleth with his hors a doun –
He thurgh the body hurt is and **siththen** take,　　afterwards
Maugre his heed, and brough*t* unto the stake.　　despite his care
As **forward** was, right ther he most abyde:　　　　agreed
Another **lad** is on that other syde,　　　　　　　　led
And som tyme doth Thebanes twoo
Togider y-met, and wrought his **felaw** woo.　　companion/opposite
Unhorsed hath ech other of hem tweye:

1750 Ther nas no Tygyr in the vale of Galgopleye,[119]
Whan that hir whelp is stole whan it is **lite**,　　little
So cruel on the hunt as is Arcite,
For jelous hert, upon this Palomon
Ne in Belmary ther is no **fel** lyoun,[120]　　　　fierce
That hunted is, or for hunger wood,
Ne of his prey desireth so the blood,
As Palomon to sle his foo Arcite.
This **jelous** strokes on here helmes byte;　　eager
Out renneth blood on bothe sides **reedes**.　　red

1760 Somtyme an ende ther is on every dede,[121]
For er the sonne unto the reste went
The strong Kyng Emetrius gan **hent**　　seized
This Palomon, as he faught with Arcite,
And his swerd in his **fleissch** he did byte,　　flesh
And by the force of **xxti** he is take,　　twenty
Unyolden, and **y-drawe** unto the stake:　　dragged

119 An unidentified place.
120 A place in North Africa (in what is now Morocco).
121 'At some time there's an end to everything'

And in the **rescous** of this Palamon,   rescue
The stronge Kyng Ligurgius is born adoun,
And kyng Emetreus, for al his strengthe,
Is **born** out of his sadel his swerd's lengthe;   lifted 1770
So hit him Palomon, or he were take –
But al for nought – he was brought to the stake.
His hardy herte might him helpe nou*ght*;
He most abyde whan that he was caught
By force, and eek by **composicioun**.   agreement
Who sorweth now but Palomon,
That **moot** no more gon agayn to fight;   may
And whan that Theseus had seen that sight
He cryed, 'Hoo! Nomore – for it is doon!
Ne noon schal lenger unto his felaw goon!'[122]   1780
I wol be trewe juge and nou*ght*e **partye**:   partial
Arcyte of Thebes schal have Emelye,
That hath by his fortune hire y-wonne!'
Anoon ther is noyse bygonne,
For ioye of this so lowde and heye withalle,
It semed that the listes wolde falle.
What can now fayre Venus doon above?
What seith sche now, what doth this queen of love?
But wepeth so, for wantyng of hir wille,[123]
Til that her teeres in the lystes **fille**.   fell 1790
Sche sayde, 'I am aschamed, douteles.'
Satournus seyde, 'Dou*ght*er, hold thy pees.
Mars hath his wille, his knight hath his boone,
And by myn heed, thou schalt be **esed** soone.'   comforted
The trompes, with the lowde mynstralcy,
The **herawdes**, that ful lowde **yolle** and cry,   heralds; yell
Been in here **iuye** for Daun Arcyte –   joy
But herkneth me, and **stynteth** but a lite.   wait; little
Which a miracle bifel anoon –
This Arcyte fersly hath don his halm adoun,[124]   1800
And on his **course**, for to schewe his face,   courser/warhorse
He **priked endlange** in the large place,   rode from end to end

---

122 'No-one shall fight his opposite number any more'
123 'for not getting her way'
124 'had torn off his helmet'

Lokyng upward upon his Emelye,

And sche agayn him cast a frendly yye –   eye

For women, as for to speke in comune,   general

Thay folwe alle the favour of fortune –

And was all his cheer and in his hert.

Out of the ground a fyr infernal stert,   from hell

From Pluto send at the request of Saturne,

1810 For which his hors for feere gan to tourne,

And leep asyde and foundred as he leep,   leaped; stumbled

And or that Arcyte may take keep,   look out

He pight him on the pomel of the heed,[125]

That in that place he lay as he were deed,   dead

His brest tobroken with his sadil bowe: front part of the saddle

As blak he lay as eny col or crowe,   coal

So was the blood y-roune in his face.   running

Anon he was y-born out of the place,   carried

With herte sore, to Theseus' paleys.

1820 Tho was he corven out of his harneys,   then; cut; armour

And in a bed y-brought ful fair and blyve,   with haste

For yit he was in memory and on lyve,   conscious; alive

And alway cryeng after Emelye.

Duk Theseus and al his companye

Is comen hom to Athenes, his cite,

With all blys and gret solempnite,   cheerfulness

Al be it that this aventure was falle,   thing had happened

He nolde nought discomfort hem alle.   didn't want to

Men seyde eek that Arcita schuld nought dye,

1830 'He schal be helyd of his maladye.'   healed; sickness

And of another thing they were as fayn –   glad

That of hem all, ther was noon y-slayn.

Al were they sore hurt, and namely oon

That with a spere was thirled his brest boon.   pierced; bone

To other woundes and to broken armes,

Some hadde salve and some hadde charmes,   oinment

Fermacyes of herbes and eek save   medicines

They dronken, for they holde here lyves have.

For which this noble duk, as he wel can,

1840 Comforteth and honoreth every man,

125 hit himself; front of saddel; head

And made revel al the lange night
Unto the straunge lordes, as it was right.
Ne thar was holden no **discomfytyng**, injury
But as a justes or as a **turneing**. tournament
For sothly ther was no discomfiture,
For fallyng is but an adventure;
Ne to be lad with **fors** unto the stake, force
Unyolden and with twenty knightes take – without yielding
A person allone, withouten moo,
And **rent forth** by arme, foot and **too**, dragged there; toe 1850
And eek his steede **dryven forth** with staves driven off
With foote men, bothe yemen and knaves –
It was **aretted** him no **vylonye**, accounted; crime
Ne no maner man held it no cowardye.

❦ For which Theseus lowd anon **leet crie** ordered to be announced
To **stynten** al rancour and al envye, cease
The **gree** as wel on o syde as on other, victory
And every side lik as other's brother.
And gaf hem giftes **after here degre**, according to their status
And fully heeld a feste dayes thre, 1860
And conveyed the knightes worthily
Out of his toun **a iournee** largely, a day's ride
And hom went every man the righte way:
Ther was no more, but, 'Far wel, have good day!'
Of this batayl I wol no more **endite**, recount
But speke of Palomon and of Arcyte.

❦ Swelleth the brest of Arcyte, and the **sore** hurt
Encresceth at his herte more and more. increases
The **clothred** blood, for eny **lechecraft**, clotted; medical skill
Corrumpith, and in his **bouk** y-laft, corrupts; torso 1870
That nother veyne blood ne venutusyng,[126]
Ne drynk of herbes may ben his helpyng,
The vertu expulsik or animal,[127]
For thilke vertu cleped natural
Ne may the venym voyde ne expelle.[128]

126 'blood letting . . . cupping'
127 'impulse to vomit'
128 'no natural power may void or expel the poison'

The **pypes** of his **lounges** gan to swelle,   tubes; lungs
And every **lacerte** in his brest adoun   muscle
Is **schent** with venym and corrupcioun: destroyed
Him **gayneth** nother for to get his lyf,   benefits
1880 Vomyt upward ne dounward laxatif;
Al is to-broken thilke regioun,
Nature hath now no dominacioun:
And certeynly, where nature wil not **wirche**,   work
Far wel, phisik – go ber the man to chirche![129]
This al and som, that Arcyte moste dye,
For which he sendeth after Emelye,
And Palomon, that was his cosyn deere.
Thanne seyd he thus, as ye schul after heere:

❦ 'Naught may the woful spirit in myn herte
1890 Declare, A, **poynt** of my sorwes smerte   cause
To you, my lady, that I love most,
But I byquethe the service of my **gost** –   spirit
To you, aboven every creature,
Syn that my lyf may no lenger **dure**.   last
Allas, the woo! Allas, the peynes strong
That I for you have suffred, and so longe!
Allas, the deth! Allas, myn Emelye!
Allas, departyng of our companye!
Allas, myn hert's queen! Allas, my wyf!
1900 Myn hert's lady, ender of my lyf!
What is this world? What asken men to have?
Now with his love, now in his colde grave
Allone, withouten eny companye!
Far wel, my swete! Far wel, myn Emelye!
And softe take me in your armes tweye
For love of God, and herkneth what I seye.
I have heer with my cosyn Palomon
Had stryf and rancour many a day y-gon,
For love of you, and eek for jelousie;
1910 And Jupiter so wis my sawle **gye**   guide
To speken of a servaunt proprely,
With all circumstaunces trewely,

129 'farewell, doctor – go carry the man to church (ie to bury him)'

That is to seyn; trouthe, honor and knighthede,
Wysdom, humblesse, astaat and by **kynrede**,   family
Fredam and al that **longeth** to that art,   belongs
So Jupiter have of my soule part,
As in this world right now he know I non
So worthy to be loved, as Palomon,
That servith you, and wol do al his lyf –
And if that ye schul ever be a wyf,   1920
Forget not Palomon, that gentil man.'
And with that word his speche faile gan,
For fro his herte up to his brest was come
The cold of deth, that him had overcome,
And yet moreover in his armes twoo
The vital strength is lost, and al **a-goo**;   gone
Only the intellect, withouten more,
That dwelled in his herte, sik and sore,
Gan fayle whan the herte feste **deth**,   dies
Duskyng his eyyen two and fayled breth: darkening 1930
But on his lady yit he cast his **ye**.   eye
His laste word was, 'Mercy, Emelye!'
His spiryt **chaunged** was, and wente ther   translated
As I cam never, I can nat tellen wher.
Therfore I stynte – I nam no **dyvynistre**:   theologian
Of soules fynde I not in this registre,
Ne me list nat thopynyouns to telle
Of **hem**, though that they **wyten** wher **they** dwelle.   them; know; i.e. souls
Arcyte is cold, ther Mars his soule gye –
Now wol I speke forth of Emelye.   1940

🍂 **Shright** Emelye and howled Palomon,   shreiked
And Theseus his sustir took anon,
Swownyng, and bar hir fro the **corps** away –   swooning; body
What helpeth it to **tarye** forth the day,   wait
To telle how that sche weep bothe eve & morwe?
For in swich **caas** wommen can have such sorwe,   occasion
Whan that here housbonds ben from hem ago,
That for the more part they **sorwen** so,   sorrow
Or elles fallen in such maladye
That atte laste certeynly they dye –   1950
Infynyt be the sorwes and the teeres

Of olde folk and folk of **tendre yeeres**.   tender years (ie young)
So gret a wepyng was ther noon certayn
Whan Ector was y-brought al freissch y-slayn,[130]
As that ther was for deth of this Theban:
For sorwe of him ther weepeth both child and man.
At Troye, allas, the pite that was there!
Craccyng of cheekes, **rendyng** eek of here –   scratching; tearing
'Why woldist thou be deed?' this wommen crye,
1960 'And haddest gold ynow*gh*, and Emelye?'
No man mighte glade Theseus,
Savyng his olde fader Egeus,
That knew this worldes **transmutacioun**,   changeability
As he hadde seen it **torne** up and doun;   turn
Joye after woo and woo aftir gladnesse,
And schewed hem **ensample** and likenesse.   example(s)

❦ 'Right as ther deyde never man,' quod he,
'That he ne lyved in erthe in som degree,
Yit ther ne lyved man,' he seyde,
1970 'In al this world, that som tyme he ne deyde.
This world nys but a thurghfare, ful of woo,
And we ben pilgryms, passyng to and froo.
Deth is an ende of every worldly **sore**.'   pain
And over al this, yit seide he **mochil** more;   much
So this effect ful wysely to **enhorte**,   encourage
The peple that schulde hem **recomforte**.   feel better

❦ Duk Theseus, with al his **busy cure**,   diligent effort
Cast busyly wher that the **sepulture**   tomb
Of good Arcyte may best y-maked be,
1980 And eek most honurable **in his degre**.   according to his status
And atte last he took conclusioun
That ther as first Arcite and Palomon
Hadden for love the batail hem bytwene,
That in the **selve** grove, **soote** and greene,   same; sweet
Ther as he hadde his amorous desires,

---

130 Hector, prince and hero of Troy, was killed by Achilles. Sold back to the
     Trojans for his weight in gold, his body was returned to Troy, accompanied by
     great mourning.

His compleynt, and for love his hoote fyres,
He wolde make a fyr in which th'office   funeral rites
Funeral he might al **accomplice**;   carry out
And **leet comaunde** anon to hakke and hewe   ordered
The okes old,and ley hem on a **rewe**,   row   1990
In **culpons** wel arrayed for to **brenne**.   piles; burn
His officers with swifte foot they **renne**,   ran
And ryde anon at his comaundement;
And after this Theseus hath y-sent
After a **beer**, and it al **over spradde**   bier; covered
With cloth of golde, the richest that he hadde;
And of the same sute he clad Arcyte –
Upon his hondes were his gloves white,
Eke on his heed a crowne of **laurer** grene,   laurel
And in his hond a swerd, ful bright and kene.   2000
He leyde him, **bare the visage**, on the beere;   bare-faced
Therwith he weep, that pite was to heere:
And for the poeple schulde see him alle,
Whan it was day he brought hem to the halle,
That **roreth** of the cry and of the soun.   resounds
Tho cam this woful Theban Palomoun,   then
With **flotery** berd and **ruggy asshy heeres**   waving; rough ashen hair
In clothis blak, y-dropped al with teeres;
And passyng other of wepyng, Emelye,
The **rewfullest** of all the companye.   most pitiful 2010
In as moche as the service schulde be
The more nobul and riche in his degre,
Duk Theseus **leet** forth thre **steedes** bryng,   ordered; horses
That trapped were in steel al glityryng,
And covered with armes of Dan Arcyte.
Upon the steedes, that weren grete & white,
Ther seeten folk, of which oon **bar his scheeld**;   carried his shield
Another his spere up in his hondes heeld;
The **thridde** bar with him his bowe **turkeys** –   third; Turkish
Of **brend** gold was the **caas** and eek the herneys,   burnished; quiver/case 2020
And riden forth **a paas** with sorwful **chere**   slowly; countenance
Toward the grove, as ye schul after heere.
The noblest of the grekes that ther were,
Upon here schuldres carieden the beere,
With **slak paas** and **eyhen reed** and **wete**,   slow pace; eyes; red; wet

Thurghout the cite, by the **maister** streete,   main
That sprad was al with blak and wonder hye –
Right of the same is al the stret **y-wrye**.   draped
Upon the right hond went olde Egeus,
2030 And on that other syde Duk Theseus,
With vessels in here hond with gold wel fyn,
As ful of hony, mylk, and blood, and wyn.
Eke Palomon, with a gret companye,
And after that com woful Emelye,
With fyr in hond, as was that tyme the **gyse**,   custom
To do thoffice of funeral servise.

  ❦ He*y*h labour and ful gret apparailyng[131]
Was at the service and at the fyr makyng,
That with his grene top the hevene **raughte**,   reached (ie the fire)
2040 And twenty fadom of brede tharme straughte.[132]
This is to seyn, the **boowes** were so **brode**.   boughs; broad
Of **stree** first was ther leyd ful many a **loode**,   straw; load
But how the fyr was makyd upon highte
Ne eek the names how the trees **highte**   were called
As ook, fyr, birch, asp, aldir, holm, popler,[133]
Wilw, elm, plane, **assch**, box, **chesteyn**, **lynde**, laurer,[134]
Mapul, **thorn**, beech, hasil, **ew**, **wyppyltre** –   hawthorn; yew; dogwood
How they weren **felde** schal nou*g*ht be told for me,   felled
Ne how the goddes **ronnen** up & doun,   ran
2050 **Disheryt** of here **habitacioun**   disinherited; dwelling
In which they **whilom woned** in rest and pees –   formerly lived
Nymphes, faunes and **amadryes**;[135]
Ne how the beestes and the **briddes** all   birds
Fledden for feere whan the woode was falle,
Ne how the ground **agast** was of the light   astonished
That was nought **wont** to see no sonne bright,   used
Ne how the fyr was **couchid** first with **stree**,   laid; straw
And thanne with drye stykkes, **cloven** in three,   split

131 'strenuous labour and really full preparation'
132 ' the arms were twenty fathoms broad on either side'
133 'oak, fir, birch, aspen, alder, holm-oak, poplar'
134 'willow, elm, plane, ash, box. chestnut, linden, laurel'
135 Hamadryads (wood nymphs).

And thanne with greene woode and **spicerie**,   herbs and spices
And thanne with cloth of gold and with **perrye**,   precious stones 2060
And gerlandes hangyng with ful many a flour,
The **myrre**, **thensens** with also gret odour,   myrrh; incense
Ne how Arcyte lay among al this,
Ne what richesse aboute his body is,
Ne how that Emely, as was the gyse,
Putt in the fyr of funeral servise,
Ne how sche **swowned** whan sche made the fyre,   swooned
Ne what sche spak, ne what was hire desire,
Ne what jewels men in the fyr tho cast,
Whan that the fyr was gret and **brente** fast,   burnt 2070
And how som caste hir scheeld and summe her spere,
And of here **vestiments** which that they were,   clothes
And cuppes ful of wyn and mylk and blood
Unto the fyr, that brent as it were **wood**,   mad/crazy
Ne how the **Grekoys**, with an huge route,   Greeks
Thre tymes **ryden** al the fyr **aboute**   rode; around
Upon the lefte hond, with an heih schoutyng,
And thries with hir speres claterynge,
And thries how the ladyes gan to crye,
Ne how that **lad** was homward Emelye,   led 2080
Ne how Arcyte is brent to **asschen** colde;   ashes
Ne how that **lych wake** was yhold;   funeral celebration
Al **thilke** night ne how the Grekes pleye   that same
The **wake pleyes**, kepe I nat to seye   funeral games
Who **wrastelth** best naked, with oyle **enoynt**,   wrestles; anointed
Ne who that bar him best in no **disoynt**:   problem
I wol not telle eek how that they ben goon
Hom **til** Athenes, whan the pley is **doon** –   to; over
But schortly to the poynt now wol I wende,
And maken of my longe tale an ende.   2090

❦ By **proces** and by lengthe of certeyn yeres,   procession (of events)
Al styntyd is the **mornyng** and the teeres   mourning
Of all Grekys by oon general assent.
Than semed me ther was a **parlement**[136]   parliament

136 Obviously not a parliament in Athens, but here Chaucer is transposing the
    institutions of his own time on to the ancient Greek past.

At Athenes, on a certeyn poynt and cas,
Among the which poyntes spoken was
To han with certeyn contrees alliaunce,
And have fully of Thebans **obeissance**;   obedience/submission
For which this noble Theseus anon
2100 Let senden after gentil Palomon,
Unwist of him what was the cause and why,   he did not know
But in his blake clothes, sorwfully,
He cam at his commaundement **in hye**:   on high (ie Theseus)
Tho sente Theseus for Emelye.
Whan they were sette and **hussht** was al the place,   quiet
And Theseus **abyden** hadde a space   waited
Or eny word cam fro his wyse brest,
His eyen set he ther, **as was his lest**,   as he liked
And with a sad **visage** he **syked stille**,   face; sighed softly
2110 And after that right thus he seide his wille:

❦ 'The Firste Moevere of the cause above,[137]
Whan he first made the fayre cheyne of love,[138]
Gret was theffect, and **heigh** was his **entente**,   noble; intention
Wel **wist** he why and what therof he **mente**,   knew; meant
For which that faire cheyne of love he **bond**   bound
The fyr, the watir, **eyr**, and eek the lond,   air
In certeyn boundes that they may not flee.
That same prynce and moevere eek,' quod he,
'Hath **stabled** in this wrecched world adoun   established
2120 Certeyn dayes and duracioun
To alle that **er engendrid** in this place,   are; conceived
Over the day they may nat **pace**;   step/live
Al **mowe** they yit wel here dayes **abregge**,   may; cut short
Ther needeth non auctorite **tallegge**,   to set forth
For it is preved by experience:
But that **me lust** declare my **sentence**,   I want to; judgement
Than may men wel by this ordre discerne
That thilke moevere **stabul** is and **eterne**;   stable; eternal
Wel many men knewe, **but it be** a fool,   unless he be
2130 That every **parthe dyryveth** from his **hool**,   part; derives; whole

137 The initial creator.
138 The Chain of Love, said to bind the universe together.

For nature hath nat take his bygynnyng
Of no partye ne **cantel** of a thing,   portion
But of a thing that parfyt is and stable,
Descendyng so til it be **corumpable**;   corruptible
And therfore of his wyse **purveaunce**,   foresight
He hath so wel **biset** his **ordenaunce**   established; order
That **spices** of thinges and **progressiouns**   species; processes
Schullen endure by **successiouns**,   one after the other
And nat eterne be, withoute lye –
This **maistow** undertand and se **at ye**.   may you; with your eyes   2140

❦ Lo, the ook, that hath so long **norisschyng**   growing
From tyme that it **gynneth** first to spring,   begins
And has so long a lyf, as we may see,
Yet atte laste wasted is the tree.
Considereth eek, how that the harde **stoon**   stone
Under oure foot, on which we trede and goon,
Yit wasteth it as it **lith** by the weye;   lies
The brode ryver somtyme **wexeth** dreye: becomes
The grete tounes see we **wane** and **wende** –   fade; pass away
Than may I see that al thing hath an ende.   2150

❦ Off man and woman se we wel also,
That **wendeth** in oon of this termes two;   passes on
That is to seyn, in youthe or elles in age –
He **moot be deed** – the kyng, as schal a page: must die
Sum in his bed, som in the deepe see,
Som in the large feeld, as men may se,
Ther helpeth naught; al goth **thilke** weye –   same
Thanne may I see wel that al thing schal deye.
What maketh this, but Jubiter the kyng,
The which is prynce and cause of all thing,   2160
Convertyng al unto his **propre wille**,   turning; own will
From which he is **dereyved**, **soth** to telle,   derived; truth
And her is agayn no creature of lyve,[139]
Of no degre avayleth for to stryve.[140]

139 'no creature lives twice'
140 'it doesn't help at all to struggle (against this)'

❦ Than is it wisdom, as thenketh me,
To maken vertu of necessite,
And take it wel that we may nat eschewe,[141]
And namely, that that to us all is **dewe**;   due (ie death)
And who so **gruccheth** aught he doth **folye**,   complains; foolishness
2170 And rebel is to him that al may gye.[142]
And certeynly, a man hath most honour
To deyen in his excellence and flour,
Whan he is **siker** of his goode name,   sure
Than hath he doon his **freend** ne him no schame;   friend
And gladder might ought his freend ben of his deth,
Whan with honour is **yolden** up the breth,   yielded
Thanne whan his name **appeled** is for age;   faded away
For al forgeten is his **vasselage**.   prowess
Thanne is it best **as far** a worthi fame,   by far
2180 To dye whan a man is best of name –
To **contrary of** al this is wilfulnesse.   argue against
Why **grucchen** we? Why have we **hevynesse**   complain; misery
That good Arcyte, of chyvalry the **flour**,   flower
Departed is with worschip and honour
Out of this foule prisoun of this lyf?
Why gruccheth heer his cosyn and his wyf
Of his wel fare, that loven him so wel?
Can he hem thank? Nay, God woot, **never a del**,   not at all
That bothe his soule and eek himself offende,
2190 And yet they may here lustes nat amende.

❦ That may I conclude of this longe **serye**,   argument
But after wo, I **rede** us to be merye,   advise
And thanke Jubiter al of his grace,
And **or** that we departe fro this place,   before
I **rede** that we make of sorwes two   counsel
O parfyt joye, lastyng ever mo;   one
And loketh now, wher most sorwe is herinne,
Ther wol we first **amenden** and bygynne.   put right
Sustyr,' quod he, 'this is my ful assent,
2200 With al **thavys** heer of my parlement,   the opinion

141 'accept cheerfully what we can't change'
142 'and is a rebel to him who can control all'

That gentil Palomon, your owne knight,
That serveth yow with herte, wil and might,
And ever hath doon syn fyrst tyme ye him knewe,
That ye schul of your grace upon him **rewe**,   take pity
And take him for your housbond and for lord –
Leve me your hand, for this is oure **acord**.   Agreement2
Let see now of your wommanly pite;
He is a kyng's brothir's sone, **pardee**,   by God
And though he were a pore **bachiller**,   young knight
Syn he hath served you so many a yeer,   2210
And had for you so gret adversite,
Hit most be considered, trusteth me,
For gentil mercy aughte passe right.'[143]
Than seyde he thus too Palomon ful right,
'I trowe ther needeth litel sermonyng
To make you assente to this thing.
Com neer and tak your lady by the hand.'
Bitwix hem was y-maad anon the bond
That **highte** matrimoyn or mariage,   is called
By alle the **counseil** and the baronage.   council 2220
And thus with **blys** and eek with melodye,   happiness
Hath Palomon y-wedded Emelye,
And God, that al this wyde world hath **wrought**,   made
Send him his love, that hath it deere y-bought;
For now is Palomon in al his **wele**,   good fortune
Lyvynge in blisse, richesse and in **hele**,   health
And Emely him loveth so tendirly,
And he hir serveth also gentilly,
That never wordes hem bitweene
Of **gelousy**, ne of non othir **teene**.   jealousy; strife 2230
Thus endeth Palomon and Emelye,
And God save al this fayre companye. Amen.

Here endeth the knight's tale.

---

143 'mercy ought to come first'

THE MILLER'S PROLOGUE AND TALE

The host asks the monk to tell a tale next, but the miller, who is drunk, intervenes. In order to avoid trouble, the host allows him to continue.

An Oxford carpenter named John has a pretty, sexy young wife called Alison, and a lodger, an attractive young man named Nicholas, who is a student with an interest in music, astrology and women. Both Nicholas and the parish clerk, Absolon, wish to seduce Alison. Alison agrees to spend the night with Nicholas, if he can think of a plan whereby they can get away from her husband. Nicholas pretends that he has been given secret knowledge, in a dream, that a second Noah's flood is imminent, and that John can use this foreknowledge to save himself, Nicholas and Alison. John sends away the servants, and arranges for the trio to spend the night in large tubs suspended from an outhouse roof. They will then float when the floodwaters overwhelm the town. While John is asleep and snoring in his tub, Nicholas and Alison creep off to bed. However, Absolon comes to the window, begging Alison to respond to his love. Unable to make him go away, she offers to kiss him. She puts her naked backside out of the window, and Absolon kisses it. Horrified, he crosses the road to a smithy run by his friend Gervase, who allows him to borrow a red-hot ploughshare. Absolon climbs to the window, and Nicholas puts out his backside, then farts in Absolon's face. Absolon buries the plough-share in Nicholas's backside, Nicholas cries for water, and John cuts the ropes, thinking that the flood has come. He falls to the floor, breaking his arm. John is chased through the streets by his mocking neighbours, who have been persuaded by Nicholas and Alison that he is mad.

'Geoffrey' notes that the knight's tale is appreciated by most of his fellow pilgrims, in particular by the 'gentils' among them. It is noble, worthy, educated; all factors associated with the teller, and with the class he represents. The host then turns to the monk, who is next in rank among the 'religious' pilgrims, as the knight is the highest-ranking lay person present (the prioress is passed over, as she is a woman). Thus, the host proves that the lottery was a fiction; when the miller speaks out, he is told to be patient, and to give way to a 'bettre man' (MT 23). We are not told any more about the lot-drawing – maybe the miller is indignant about the 'cut' being ignored. Class deference seems to be the catalyst for his intervention, a likely remembrance of the turbulence and violence of the Peasants' Revolt of 1381, which Chaucer would have experienced at first hand if he had been at home in Aldgate when Wat Tyler and Jack Straw's men entered the City of London through the gate below. The miller is a rowdy, tough and outspoken 'stout carl', which must have been the 'gentil' perception of the many who were seeking, and winning, their freedom from serfdom during the twenty years which followed the Revolt. The miller's drunkenness is a behaviour which both challenges and subverts accepted social and religious morality. It would 'offend' the secular 'gentils' (it makes the miller rude and disobedient to his social superiors) and the religious (it robs a man of his divinely-instituted reason and leads to lewdness and demonic acts). The miller, as a working man on holiday, does not care about anyone's susceptibilities, and gets drunk anyway. The host, like King Theseus, remains in control, but allows the miller to go on in order to avoid trouble.

The miller's story is a fabliau, a form of narrative found all over Western Europe, notable for the coarseness of its tropes and imagery, and of its language. Most of the fabliaux which survive in English-language versions (as opposed to Anglo-French) are in *The Canterbury Tales*. Although fabliaux characters are usually urban bourgeoisie, farmers, lower clergy, students, squires and women, they were originally aristocratic entertainment, which enabled members of the upper echelons of society to laugh at the lewdness of those below them, particularly those with aspirations to rise higher in society. Chaucer's very interesting ploy is to place these stories into the mouths of those who are usually the butt of the joke – his middle- and lower-class pilgrims. In the mouth of the miller the fabliau becomes a form of lower-class fightback.

In fabliaux, the streetwise, the sly and the crafty usually triumph over the conventionally wise and the virtuous. The pilgrims are expecting, therefore, that the student will contrive to 'swyve' the young woman behind her husband's back, especially when 'heende Nicholas' is introduced (MT 94). The miller, however, uses the fabliau form to produce a parody of The Knight's Tale, with some unexpected twists. Although drunk, he must have been listening very closely. He introduces a second lover in order to reproduce the Palamon/Arcite contest: two lovers fighting for the right to fuck (not marry) a beautiful young woman (who is by no means unwilling), and an older man (her husband, rather than her guardian), who must not allow the situation to get out of hand. Unfortunately, this 'ruler' is ineffective, uneducated and a fool, who attempts to control his wife by keeping her in close confinement. To make matters worse, he is an old fool, married to a very pretty eighteen-year-old.

Alison, the miller's 'love heroine', like Emelye, is described in terms of natural beauty, but hers is the beauty of the fields, the farmyard, the orchard. She is a 'primerole', a 'kyde or calfe' and a 'perionette tree' (MT 163, 155, 143), which makes her, obviously, ripe and ready for plucking. As well as her visible beauty, she is described in terms of how she smells, tastes and feels, making her beauty available to the senses. Although her outward appearance is described in detail, we are told nothing of 'who' she is, of her 'privetee', except as far as this is revealed by a 'licorous eyye' (MT 139). Alison, like Emelye, is depicted in a way which renders her passive, and yet Alison is the most active of all the characters in the tale. Emelye's inner thoughts and desires, her 'privetee', are unacknowledged and unfulfilled, although they are stated in the knight's story, unlike Alison, whose 'privetee' is not revealed, but who gets what she wants without cost at the end of the miller's riposte. In his tale, it is the men who pay.

Of the two young men in the story, Absolon, the clerk, is the more courtly. His is, however, the clumsy and affected courtliness of the aspirant, rather than the result of noble *nourriiture* (upbringing). His devotion to the Virgin Mary is diverted to sexual desire for a married woman, his religious worship turned to love worship. He succeeds only in making a fool of himself. Nicholas, like Arcite, is the more forceful of the two. He is educated, a student, and therefore perhaps 'gentil' in origin, but he diverts his learning (which is supported financially by his family and friends) into the dubious channels of experimental science. It is by this means that he is able to take advantage of illiterate men like John. His scheme to cuckold his landlord is based on the blasphemous exploitation of John's genuine love for his wife, his naivety, and his simple, but genuine, religious beliefs. Unfortunately, Nicholas's pride induces him to push the joke too far, and he ends up with a severely wounded backside. The tale's moral, as far as there is one, is that men are made fools by calculating women, thus proving the miller's dictum that men should never invade their women's 'privetee'.

The world of the miller's tale is an urban one, the student lodger and John's trips to Oseney suggesting the university town of Oxford. It is also a world of music and sound. The miller himself plays the bagpipes, and both Nicholas and Absolon play instruments and sing. Nicholas and Alison have sex to the accompaniment of the chapel choir singing. Although this world is without the chivalric trappings of the knight's, it is not without melody, or art. It is not less cultured, merely 'differently' cultured. Its people work hard, play hard, and have practical concerns. In this environment it is Absolon's courtly love songs which seem out of place; there is no time for philosophy.

Key Questions

Is it possible to relate the miller and his story to the social history of the time?

What can this story tell us about the medieval urban environment?

How does Chaucer manipulate the fabliau form, and why? How can this be compared with The Knight's Tale?

What is the miller implying about chivalry and courtly love? How does Alison compare to Emelye, and to the 'courtly love' lady? Are the characters stereotyped? How does the humour work . . . who is really the butt of the joke, and what is the joke, anyway?

Topic Keywords

Fabliau genre/ medieval women/ medieval town life/ experimental science and the world of dreams/ popular religion/ medieval universities/ medieval music

Further Reading

Gila Aloni, 'Extimacy in The Miller's Tale', *Chaucer Review*, 41, 2006, pp. 163–84

Timothy D. Arner, 'No Joke: Transcendent Laughter in the *Teseida* and The Miller's Tale,' *Studies in Philology*, 102, 2005, pp. 143–58

Helen Barr, 'Laughing at the Body in The Miller's Tale,' *English Review*, 6, 1996, pp. 38–41

Peter G. Beidler, 'Dramatic Intertextuality in The Miller's Tale: Chaucer's use of characters from medieval drama as foils for John, Alisoun, Nicholas and Absolon', *Chaucer Yearbook*, 3, 1996, pp. 1–19

Frederick M. Biggs, 'The Miller's Tale and *Decameron*, iii, 4', *Journal of English and Germanic Philology*, 108, 2009, pp. 59–80

—— 'A bared bottom and a basket: A New Analogue and a New Source for The Miller's Tale', *Notes and Queries*, 56, 2009, pp. 340–1

Louise M. Bishop, ' "Of Goddes pryvetee nor of his wyf": Confusion of Orifices in Chaucer's Miller's Tale,' *Texas Studies in Literature and Language*, 44, 2002, pp. 231–46

Alcuin Blamires, 'Philosophical Sleaze? The 'strok of thought' in The Miller's Tale and Chaucerian Fabliau', *Modern Language Review*, 102, 2007, pp. 621–40

David Boyd, 'Seeking Goddes pryvetee: Sodomy, Quitting and Desire in The Miller's Tale', In *Words and Works: Studies in Medieval English Language and Literature in Honour of Fred C. Robinson*, edited by Peter Baker and Nicholas Howe, Toronto, University of Toronto Press, 1998, pp. 243–60

María Bullón-Fernández, 'Private Practices in Chaucer's Miller's Tale', *Studies in the Age of Chaucer*, 28, 2006, pp. 141–74

Glenn Burger, 'Erotic Discipline . . . or Tee Hee, I Like my Boys to be Girls: Inventing with the Body in Chaucer's Miller's Tale', in *Becoming Male in the Middle Ages*, edited and introduced by Jeffrey Cohen and edited by Bonnie Wheeler, New York, Garland, 2000, pp. 245–60

Howell Chickering, 'Comic Meter and Rhyme in The Miller's Tale', *Chaucer Yearbook*, 2, 1995, pp. 17–47

Joseph A. Dane, 'The Mechanics of Comedy in Chaucer's Miller's Tale', *Chaucer Review*, 14, 1980, pp. 215–24

Kara Donaldson, 'Alisoun's Language: Body, Text and Glossing in Chaucer's Miller's Tale', *Philological Quarterly*, 71, 1992, pp. 139–53

Thomas J. Farrell, 'Privacy and the Boundaries of Fabliau in The Miller's Tale', *Journal of English Literary History*, 56, 1989, pp. 773–95

Alan J. Fletcher, 'The Faith of a Simple Man: Carpenter John's Creed in The Miller's Tale', *Medium Ævum*, 6, 1992, pp. 96–105

Shannon Forbes, 'To Alisoun now wol I tellen al my love-longing': Chaucer's Treatment of the Courtly Love Discourse in The Miller's Tale', *Women's Studies*, 36, 2007, pp. 1–14

Jesse M. Gellrich, 'The Parody of Medieval Music in The Miller's Tale', *Journal of English and Germanic Philology*, 73, 1974, pp. 176–88

Carol Falvo Heffernan, 'Chaucer's Miller's Tale and Reeve's Tale, Boccaccio's *Decameron*, and the French Fabliaux', *Italica*, 81, 2004, pp. 311–24

David Johnson, 'The Flemish Analogue to Chaucer's Miller's Tale: Three Notes', *Notes and Queries*, 40, 1993, pp. 445–9

Robert E. Lewis, 'The English Fabliau Tradition and Chaucer's Miller's Tale', *Modern Philology*, 79, 1982, pp. 241–55

Karma Lochrie, 'Women's Pryvetees and Fabliau Politics in The Miller's Tale', *Exemplaria*, 6, 1994, 287–304

Linda Lomperis, 'Bodies that Matter in the Court of Late Medieval England and in Chaucer's Miller's Tale', *Romanic Review*, 86, 1995, pp. 243–64

Mark Miller, 'Naturalism and its Discontents in The Miller's Tale', *Journal of English Literary History*, 67, 2000, pp. 1–44

Barbara Nolan, 'Playing Parts: Fragments, Figures, and the Mystery of Love in The Miller's Tale', in *Speaking Images: Essays in Honor of V. A. Kolve*, edited by Robert F. Yeager and Charlotte C. Morse, Asheville, NC, Pegasus Press, 2001, pp. 255–99

Joseph D. Parry, 'Interpreting Female Agency and Responsibility in The Miller's Tale and The Merchant's Tale', *Philological Quarterly*, 80, 2001, pp. 133–67

Lee Patterson, ' "No man his reson herde": Peasant Consciousness, Chaucer's Miller and the Structure of *The Canterbury Tales*', in *Literary Practice and Social Change in Britain 1380–1530*, edited by Lee Patterson, pp. 113–55, Berkeley, University of California Press, 1990

Daniel F. Pigg, 'The Carpenter's "ernest of game": A Re-evaluation of Noah's Flood in The Miller's Tale', in *Geardagum*, 15, 1994, pp. 41–53

Edward Schweitzer, 'The Misdirected Kiss and the Lover's Malady in Chaucer's Miller's Tale', in *Chaucer in the Eighties*, edited by Julian Wasserman and Robert Blanch, Syracuse, Syracuse University Press, 1986, pp. 223–33

William Woods, 'Private and Public Space in The Miller's Tale', *Chaucer Review*, 29, 1994, pp. 166–78

And thus bygynneth the prologe of the millere

❧ Whan that the knyht had thus his tale y-told,
In al the **route** was ther yong ne old   *company*
That he ne seyde it was a noble story,
And worthi to be **drawen in memory**;   *kept in the memory*
And namely the **gentils**, **everichoon**.   *every one of the gentlefolk*
Oure host **tho lowh** and swoor, 'So moot I goon;   *then; laughed*
This goth right wel! **Unbokeled is the male**.   *the bag is undone*
Lo! Se now, who schal telle another tale?
For trewely, this game is wel bygonne.   **10**
Now telleth, now, Sir Monk, if that ye **konne**,   *know*
Somwhat to **quyte with** the knight's tale.'   *equal*
The myller, that for **drunken** was al pale,   *drunkenness*
So that **unnethe** upon his hors he sat,   *hardly*
He wold **avale nowther** hood ne hat,   *remove; neither*
Ne abyde no man **for his curtesye**,   *out of good manners*
But in Pilate's voys he gan to crye,[1]
And swor by armes and by blood and bones,
"**I can** a noble tale for the nones,   *know*
With which I wol now quyte the knight's tale!'   **20**
Oure host saugh wel how dronke he was of ale,
And seyde, 'Robyn, **abyde**, my **leve** brother –   *wait; dear*
Som bettre man schal telle us first another.
Byd and let us **werken thriftyly**.'   *wait; do things fittingly*
"By God's soule," quod he, "that wol nat I!
For I **wol** speke or elles go my way.'   *want to*
Oure host answered, 'Tel on, **a devel way**!'   *in the devil's name*
Thou art a fool, thy wit is overcome!'
'Now **herkneth**,' quod this myller, '**al and some** –   *listen; one and all*
But first I make a protestacioun,   **30**
That I am dronke, I knowe wel by my **soun**;   *sound*
And therfore, if that I **mys speke** or seye,[2]

---

1 The actor playing Pilate in mystery plays had a loud voice
2 'don't speak or say something properly'

Wite it the ale of Southwerk, I you preye –   blame it on (Southwark ale)
For I wol telle a legende and a lyf,[3]
Bothe of a carpenter and of his wyf,
How that the clerk hath set the wrightes cappe.'   hoodwinked the carpenter

🔥 The reve answered, and seyde, "Stynt thi clappe!

reeve; stop your talking

Let be thy lewed drunken harlottrye!   lewd or ribald behaviour
It is a synne, and eek a greet folye
40   To apeyren eny man, or him defame,   injure
And eek to brynge wyves in ylle name: wives; bad
Thou mayst ynowgh of other thinges seyn.'[4]
This dronken miller spak ful sone ageyn,
And seyde, "Leeve brother Osewold,   Oswald
Who hath no wyf, he is no cokewold,   cuckold
But I seye not therfore that thou art oon;
Ther been ful goode wyves many oon,
And ever a thousand goode agayns oon badde –
That knowest thou wel thyself but if thou madde.   go mad
50   Why art thou angry with my tale now?
I have a wyf, parde, as wel as thow: by God
Yit nolde I, for the oxen in my plough,   wouldn't (ne wolde)
Take upon me more than ynough:
Though that thou deme thiself that thou be non,   consider
I wol bileeve wel that I am oon.   believe
An housbond schal not be inquisityf
Of goddes pryvete, ne of his wyf.
So that he fynde God's foysoun there,   plenty
Of the remensunt needeth nought enquere.'[5]
60   What schuld I seye, but that this proud millere,
He nolde his wordes for no man forbere,   keep back
But tolde his cherlisch tale in his manere.   vulgar/coarse
Me athinketh that I schal reherce it heere;   regret; repeat
And therfor, every gentil wight, I preye,   person
For God's love as deme nat that I seye   consider
Of yvel entent, but for I moot reherse   repeat

---

3 A saint's legend and life was the story of their life and deeds
4 'there are plenty of other things to talk about'
5 'if he gets enough of God's bounty, he shouldn't inquire about the rest'

Here wordes, all be they better or werse,

Or elles **falsen** som of my **mateere**.   falsify; material

And therfor, who so **list** it nat to heere,   wants

Tourne over the **leef** and **cheese** another tale,[6]   leaf; choose   70

For he schal fnde **ynow**, bothe gret and smale,   enough

Of **storial** thing that **toucheth** gentilesse,   historical; refers to

And eek more **ryalte** and holynesse.   royalty

Blameth nat me if that ye cheese **amys** –   wrongly

The miller is a cherl, ye know wel this.

So was the reeve, and othir many mo,

And harlotry they tolden bothe two.

Avyseth you, and put me out of blame,   be careful

And men schulde nat make **ernest** of game.   something serious

Here endeth the prologe of the miller   80

And bygynneth his tale

❦ **Whilom** ther was dwellyng at **Oxenford**   formerly; Oxford

A riche **gnof**, that gestes heeld to boorde;[7]   churl

And of his craft he was a carpenter.

With him ther was dwellyng a **pore scoler**,   poor scholar

Had lerned art, but al his **fantasye**[8]   inclination

Was torned for to lerne **astologye**;   astrology

An cowde a certeyn of conclusions

To deme by interrogaciouns,[9]

If that men **axed** him in certeyn houres   asked   90

Whan that men schuld han **drought** or ellys **schoures**,   drought; showers

If that men axed him what schulde bifalle   happen

Of every thing – I may nou*g*ht reken hem alle.   list

This clerk was **cleped** heende Nicholas –[10]   called

6 Here Chaucer reveals that he is expecting these stories to be read as an
  anthology, in the form of a book.

7 He took in paying guests/ lodgers.

8 He had studied for the Bachelor of Arts degree.

9 Refers to the method of learning by question and answer – he could put
  questions in order to get the required answers.

10 'heende' has many meanings – noble, gracious, useful, pleasing, and simply
  'nice'. Chaucer plays upon all of these possible meanings in his portrayal of
  Nicholas.

Of **derne** love he **cowde** and of **solas**;	knew; secret/illicit; amusement
And therwith he was sleigh and ful **prive**,	secretive
And lik a mayden **meke** for to se.	coy/quiet
A chambir had he in his hostillerye	
Alone, withouten eny compaignye,	
100 Ful **fetisly y-dight** with herbes **soote**,	carefully set out; sweet
And he himself as swete as is the roote	
Of **lokorys**, or eny **cetewale**,	liquorice; spice
His almagest and bookes gret and smale,[11]	
His **astrylabe**, **longyng** for his art;	astrolabe; belonging
His **augrym stoones** leyen faire apart[12]	
On schelves **couched** at his beddes heed;	arranged
His **presse** y-covered with a **faldyng reed**.	cupboard; red cloth
And al above ther lay a gay **sawtrye**	psaltery (stringed instrument)
On which he made **a-nightes** melodye,	at night-time
110 So swetely that al the chambur rang.	
And **Angelus ad virginam** he sang,	the angel to the Virgin
And after that he sang the kyng's note[13] –	
Ful often **blissed** was his mery throte.	blessed
And thus this sweete clerk his tyme spente,	
After his frend's fyndyng and his rente[14].	

❦ This carpenter had weddid newe a wyf,	
Which that he loved more than his lyf.	
Of eyghteteene yeer sche was of age;	
Gelous he was, and heeld hir **narwe in cage**,	jealous; strictly (as in a cage)
120 For sche was wilde and yong, and he was old,	
And demed himself be lik a cokewold.[15]	
He knew nat Catoun, for his **wit was rude**,[16]	knowledge; simple
That **bad** man schulde wedde his **similitude**;	advised; like
Men schulde wedde aftir here **astaat**,	condition
For **eelde** and youthe ben often **at debaat**.	old age; in dispute

11 Almagest, by Greek author Ptolemy, was one of the foundations of medieval astronomy
12 augury stones (for predicting the future)
13 Unidentified; possibly a piece of music, maybe a sexual euphemism
14 'according to what his friends gave him, and his own income'
15 'he thought he might be cuckolded'
16 Cato's *Distichs*, or sayings – very well known in the Middle Ages (part of a basic education in Latin grammar).

But syn that he was brou*g*ht into the snare,
He moste endure, as othere doon, his care.
Faire was the yonge wyf, and ther withal,
As eny **wesil** hir body **gent** and smal;   weasel; delicate
A **seynt** sche wered, **barred** al of silk,   girdle; striped   130
A **barmcloth eek**, as whit as morne mylk   apron; also
Upon hir **lendes**, ful of many a **gore**,   loins; gather
Whit was hir smok, and **browdid** albyfore,   embroidered
And eek byhynde on hir **coler** aboute   collar
Of coleblak silk, withinne and eek withoute,
The tapes of hir white **voluper**   cap
Weren of the **same sute** of hire **coler**;   same type as her colour
Hir **filet** brood, of silk y-set ful heye,   head-band
And certeynly sche hadd a **licorous** eyye;   lecherous
Ful **smal y-pulled** weren hir **browes** two,   finely plucked; eyebrows 140
And tho were bent and blak as a **slo**.   sloe (a berry fruit)
Sche was wel more blisful on to see
Than is the newe **perionette** tree,   pear
And softer than the wolle is of a **wether**,   young sheep
And by hir **gurdil** hyng a purs of **lethir**,   belt; leather
Tassid with silk, and **perled** with **latoun**. tassled; decorated; latten
In al this world, to seken up and doun,
Ther nys no man so wys that couthe **thenche**   think/imagine
So gay a **popillot**, or such a wenche;   little doll
For brighter was the **smylyng of hir hewe**   the brightness of her presence 150
Than in the tour the noble y-forged newe.[17]
But of hir song, it was as lowde and **yerne**   eager
As eny **swalwe chiteryng** on a **berne**.   swallow; chattering; barn
Therto sche cowde skippe and make game,
As eny **kyde** or calfe folwyng his **dame**.   kid; mother
Hir mouth was sweete as **bragat** is or **meth**,   sweet wine; mead
Or hoord of apples layd in hay or heth.
Wynsyng sche was as is a joly colt,   frisky
Long as a mast and upright as a bolt.
A **broch** sche bar upon hir **loue coleer**,   brooch; low collar   160
As **brod** as is the **bos** of a **bocleer**;   central 'knob' of small shield
Hir schos were laced on hir legges hey*g*he –

17 The noble was a gold coin, and the Tower of London housed the royal mint,
   where coins where produced.

Sche was a **primerole**, a piggesney*ghe*,[18]   primrose
For eny lord have **liggyng** in his bedde,   lying
Or yet for eny good yeman to wedde.

❦ Now, sire, and eft sir, so **bifel** the **cas**   happened; situation
That on a day this heende Nicholas
Fil with this yonge wyf to rage and pleye,
Whil that hir housbond was at Oseneye,[19]
170   As clerkes ben ful **sotil** and ful **queynte**,   sly; cunning
And pryvely he caught hir by the **queynte**   genitals
And seyde, 'I wis, but if I have my wille,
For derne love of the, **lemman**, I **spille**.'   lover/beloved; am lost
And heeld hir harde by the **haunche** boones,   thigh
And seyde, 'Lemman, love me **al at ones**,   now
Or I wol dye, as **wisly** God me save.'   surely
And sche sprang out as doth a colt in **trave**,   frame
And with hir heed she **wried** fast away,   turned
Y-seyde, 'I wol nat kisse the, by my **fey**!   faith
180   Why, let be!' quod sche, 'Lat be, thou Nicholas!
Or I wol crye out, "Harrow" and "Allas"!
Do wey your handes, for your curtesye!'   take away
This Nicholas gan, 'Mercy!' for to crye,
And spak so faire, and **profred** him so faste,   made her an offer
That sche hir love him graunted atte laste,
And swor hir oth, by Seynt Thomas of Kent,[20]
That sche wol be at his comaundement
Whan that sche may hir **leysir** wel aspye.   opportunity
'Myn housbond is so ful of jelousie,
190   That but ye wayten wel and be **pryve**   secretive
I woot right wel I am but **deed**,' quod sche.   dead
'Ye mosten be ful derne as in this caas.'[21]
'**Ther of ne care the nought**,' quod Nicholas,   don't worry about that
'A clerk hath **litherly byset his while**,[22]

18 Probably a flower, popularly known as a 'pig's eye', but the species has not been
     identified.
19 Village outside Oxford, with a large Augustinian abbey
20 St Thomas of Canterbury
21 'you must keep really quiet about this'
22 'a clerk has wasted his time if he can't'

But if he cowde a carpenter bygyle.'   trick a carpenter
And thus they ben acorded and y-sworn,
To wayte a tyme, as I have told biforn.

❦ Whan Nicholas had doon thus every del,
And **thakked** hire aboute the **lendys** wel,   smacked; loins
He kist hir sweet, and taketh his sawtrye,
And pleyeth fast and maketh melodye.   200
Than **fyl it thus** that to the parisch chirche   it so befell
Crist's **owen** werkes for to **wirche**,   own; do
This goode wyf went on an **haly** day;   holy (holy day = holiday)
Hir forheed schon as bright as eny day,
So was it **waisschen** whan sche **leet** hir werk.   washed; finished

❦ Now ther was of that chirche a parisch clerk,
The which that was **y-cleped** Absolon: called
Crulle was his heer, and as the gold it schon,   curly
And **strowted** as a fan, right large and brood,   spread out   210
Ful streyt and evene lay his joly **schood**.   hair
His **rode** was **reed**, his eyyen gray as **goos**;   complexion; red; goose
With Powles wyndowes corven in his schoos.[23]
In his hoses reed he went **fetusly**,   properly/ neatly
Y-clad he was ful **smal** and propurly,   cleanly
Al in a **kirtel** of a fyn **wacht**,   tunic; pale blue
Schapen with **goores** in the **newe get**,   tucks; latest fashion
And therupon he had a gay **surplys**,   surplice
As whyt as is the **blosme** upon the **rys** –   blossom; bough
A mery child he was, so God me save;   220
Wel **couthe** he lete blood and **clippe** and schave,   knew how to; cut (hair)
And make a chartre of lond and acquitaunce.[24]
In twenty **maners** he coude skip and daunce,   ways
After the scole of oxenforde, tho –
And with his legges **casten** to and fro,   shooting out
And pleyen songes on a smal **rubible**,   rebec
Ther to he sang somtyme a lowde **quynyble**;   counter-tenor
And as wel coude he pleye on a **giterne**.   cithern

23 Leather shoes with holes carved in the shape of window tracery
24 Legal documents – besides cutting hair and letting blood, Absolon also acted as a
   scribe.

In al the toun nas brewhous ne taverne
230 That he ne visited with his solas,
Ther as any **gaylard tapster** was –   jolly barmaid
But soth to say he was somdel **squaymous**   squeamish (about)
Of fartyng, and of speche **daungerous**.   fastidious
This Absolon, that joly was and gay,
Goth with a **senser** on the haly day,   censer
Sensing the wyves of the parisch fast,
And many a **lovely** look on hem he cast;   full of love
And **namely** on this carpenter's wyf;   especially
To loke on hire him thought a mery lyf,
240 Sche was so propre, sweete and licorous –
I dar wel sayn, if sche had ben a mous
And he a cat, he wold her **hent** anoon.   seize

    ❦ This parisch clerk, this joly Absolon,
Hath in his herte such a love longyng
That of no wyf ne took he noon offryng;
For **curtesy**, he seyde, he wolde noon.   good manners
The moone at night ful cleer and brighte schoon,
And Absolon his giterne hath y-take,
For **paramours** he seyde he wold awake,   being madly in love
250 And forth he goth, jolyf and amerous,
Til he cam to the carpenter's hous
A litel after the cok had y-crowe,
And **dressed** him up by a **schot** wyndowe   positioned himself; hinged
That was under the carpenter's wal;
He syngeth in his voys gentil and smal,
'Now, deere lady, if thi wille be,
I praye yow that ye wol **rewe** on me.'   have pity
Ful wel acordyng to his gyternyng
This carpenter awook, and herde him syng,
260 And spak unto his wyf, and sayde anoon,
'What, Alisoun? **Herestow** not Absolon,   Do you hear
That chaunteth thus under oure **boure** smal?'   bedroom
And sche answerd hir housbond ther withal,
'Yis, **God woot**, John, I heere it **every del**.'   God knows; every bit/all

❦ This passeth forthe, **what wil ye bet than wel?**

<blockquote>what will you have better than good</blockquote>

Fro day to day this joly Absolon
So **woweth** hire that him is wo bigon.   woos
He waketh al the night and al the day,
To **kembe** his lokkes brode, and made him gay.   comb
He woweth hire by **mene** and by **brocage**,   go-between; agent   270
And swor he wolde ben hir owne page.
He syngeth crowyng as a nightyngale,
And sent hire **pyment**, **meth** and spiced ale,   sweet wine; mead
And wafres pypyng hoot out of the **gleede**;   fire
For that sche was of toune he **profred meede** –   offered money
For som folk wol be wonne for richesse,
And som for **strokes**, som for gentillesse.   fighting
Som tyme to schewe his **lightnes** and **maistrye**   agility; skill
He pleyeth Herode on a scaffold hye-[25]
But what **avayleth him** as in this caas?   good is to him   280
Sche loveth so this heende Nicholas,
That Absolon may **blowe the bukkes horn** –   go blow his horn
He ne had for al his labour but a skorn.
And thus sche maketh Absolon hir ape,
And al his ernest torneth to a **jape**.   joke

❦ Ful **soth** is this proverbe, it is no lye,   true
Men sayn right thus: 'Alway the **ney slye**   nearby, sly one
Maketh the **ferre leef** to be loth.'   far loved one; lose out
For though that Absolon be **wood** or **wroth**,   mad; angry
Bycause that he fer was from here sight,   290
This Nicholas hath **stonden in his light**.   stood in his light
Now, bere the wel, thou heende Nicholas!
For Absolon may wayle and synge, 'Allas!'
And so bifelle it on a Satyrday,
This carpenter was gon to Osenay,
And heende Nicholas and Alisoun
Acordid ben to this conclusioun,
That Nicholas schal **schapen** hem a **wyle**,   devise; trick
This sely jelous housbond to **begyle**;   trick
And if so were this game went aright,   300

25 He took part in mystery plays

Sche schulde slepe in his arm al night:
For this was hire desir and his also.
And right anoon, withouten wordes mo,
This Nicholas no lenger wold he tarye,
But doth ful softe into his chambur carye
Bothe **mete** and drynke for a day or **tweye**,   food; two
And to hir housbond bad hir for to seye,
If that he **axed** after Nicholas   asked
Sche schulde seye sche **wiste** nat wher he was;   knew
310 Of al that day sche saw him nat with eye –
Sche **trowed** he were falle in som **maladye**.   believed; sickness
For no cry that hir **mayden** cowde him calle,   female servant
He **nolde** answere, for nought that may bifalle.   would not

❦ This **passeth forth** that **ilke** Satyrday   happened; same
That Nicholas stille in his chambre lay,
And eet and drank and dede what him **leste**,   wanted
Til Soneday the sonne was gon to reste.
This sely carpenter **hath gret mervaile**   wondered greatly
Of Nicholas, or what thing may him **ayle**,   make ill
320 And sayde, 'I am **adrad**, by Seynt Thomas;   afraid
It **stondeth nat aright** with Nicholas.   all isn't well
God **schilde** that he deyde sodeinly –   forbid
This world is now ful **tykel sikerly**;   changeable; surely
I saugh to day a **corps y-born** to chirche,   body; carried
That now on Monday last I saugh him **wirche**!   working
'Go up,' quod he unto his **knave** anoon,   manservant
'**Clepe** at his dore and knokke with a **stoon**.   call; stone
Loke how it is, and telle me boldely.'
This knave goth him up ful sturdily,
330 And at the chambir dore whil he stood
He cryed, and knokked as that he were wood.
'What how, what do ye, Mayster Nicholay?
How may ye slepen al this longe day?'
But al for nought – he herde nat **o** word.   one
An hole he **fond** right lowe upon a **boord**,   found; floorboard
Ther as the cat was wont in for to creepe,
And at that hole he loked in ful deepe,
And atte laste he hadde of him a sight.
This Nicholas sat ever gapyng upright,

As he had loked on the newe moone.[26]   as if   340
Adoun he goth, and tolde his mayster soone
In what **aray** he sawh this ilke man.   state
This carpenter to **blessen him** bygan,   cross himself
And seyde, 'Now help us, Seynt Frideswyde,
A man **woot** litel what him schal **betyde**:   knows; happen
This man is falle with his astronomye
In som **woodnesse**, or in som agonye: madness
I thought ay wel how that it schulde be –
Men schulde nought know of God's **pryvyte**.   private business
Y-blessed be alwey a **lewed** man,   unlearned   350
That **nat but oonly his bileeve can**.   knows only his faith
So **ferde** another clerk with astronomye;   fared
He walked in the feeldes for to **prye**   look
Upon the sterres, what ther schulde bifalle,
Til he was in a **marle** pit y-falle –   clay
He saugh nat that – but yet, by Seint Thomas,
Me reweth sore for heende Nicholas.   I'm very sorry
He schal be **ratyd** of his studyyng   berated
If that I may, by Jhesu, heven kyng.
Gete me a staf, that I may **underspore**   lever up   360
Whil that thou, Robyn, hevest up the dore.
He schal out of his studyyng, as I gesse.'
And to the chambir dore he **gan him dresse**:   made his way
His knave was a strong **karl**, for the noones,   fellow
And by the hasp he **haf** it up at oones,[27]   heaved
And in the floor the dore fil doun anoon.
This Nicholas sat stille as eny stoon,
And ever he **capyd** upward to the **eyr**.   gaped; sky
This carpenter **wende** he were in despeir,   thought
And **hent** him by the schuldres **mightily**, seized; powerfully 370
And schook him harde, and cryed **spitously** –   desperately
'What, Nicholas! What, how, man – loke adoun!
Awake and thynk on Crist's passioun!
I **crowche** the from elves and from wightes.'   bless
Ther with the **nightspel** seyde he anon rightes   nightspell
On the foure halves of the hous aboute,

26 Gazing on the new moon was said to cause stupefaction.
27 'he pulled it off the hinges'

And of the **threisshfold** of the dore withoute –	threshold
'Lord Jhesu Crist and Seynte **Bendight**,	Benedict
Blesse this hous from every wikkede **wight**.	person
380	For nyghtes verray the white paternoster;	
Wher **wonestow** now, Seynte Peter's **soster**?'[28]	do you live; St Peter's sister
And atte laste heende Nicholas	
Gan for to **syke sore**, and seyde, 'Allas!	sigh deeply
Schal al the world be lost **eft sones** now?'	immediately
This carpenter answerde, 'What **seystow**?	are you saying
What! Thenk on God as we doon, men that **swinke**.'	work
This Nicholas answerde, '**Fette** me drynke,	fetch
And after wol I speke in **pryvyte**	secrecy
Of certeyn thing that toucheth the and me.	
390	I wol telle it non other man, certeyn.'	
This carpenter goth forth and comth agayn,	
And brought of mighty ale a large quart.	
Whan ech of hem **y-dronken** had his part,	drunk
This Nicholas his dore gan to **schitte**,	shut
And dede this carpenter doun by him sitte,	
And seide, 'John, myn host ful leve and deere,	
Thou schalt upon thy **trouthe** swere me heere	troth
That to no wight thou schalt this **counsel wreye**,	advice; betray
For it is Crist's counsel that seye;	
400	And if thou telle it man, thou art **forlore**,	lost
For this vengaunce thou schalt han therfore,	
That if thou wreye me thou schalt be **wood**.'	mad
'Nay, Crist forbede it, for his holy blood,'	
Quod **tho** this sley man, 'I am no **labbe** –	then; gossip/'looselips'
Though I it say, I **am nought leef** to gabbe.	don't like to talk loosely
Say what thou wolt, I schal it never telle	
To child ne wyf, by him that harwed helle.'[29]	

28 These are examples of semi-religious charms/prayers, commonly used for protection from harm and illness. Although officially frowned upon by the Church, they were – and remained – intrinsic to common culture.

29 Christ – traditionally he harrowed hell by going down to hell between his death and resurrection to free those who had died in faith before his birth, such as the Old Testament patriarchs

❦ 'Now John,' quod Nicholas, 'I wol not lye;
I have y-found in myn astrologye,
As I have loked in the moone bright,   410
That now on Monday next, at quarter night,
Schal falle a **reyn**, and that so wilde and wood,   rain
That half so gret was never Noe's flood.[30]
This world,' he seyde, 'more than an hour
Schal ben **y-dreynt**, so hidous is the **schour**.   drowned; shower
Thus schal mankynde **drenche** and leese his lyf.'   drown
This carpenter answered, 'Allas, my wyf!
And schal sche drenche? Allas, myn Alisoun!'
For **sorwe** of this he fel almost adoun,   sorrow/sadness
And seyde, 'Is ther no remedy in this caas?'   420
'**Whe**, yis, for gode,' quod heende Nicholas,   why
'If thou worken wolt by good **counsail**,   advice
I undertake, withouten maast and sail,
Yet schal I saven hir and the and me.
Hastow nat herd how saved was Noe,
Whan that our lord had warned him biforn
That al the world with watir schulde be **lorn**?'   lost
'Yis,' quod this carpenter, '**ful yore ago**'   a long time ago
'Hastow nought herd?' quod Nicholas also,
'The **sorwe** of Noe with his **felaschipe**   trouble; friends/companions 430
That he hadde **or** he gat his wyf to schipe?   before
Him hadde **wel lever**, I dar wel undertake,   much rather
At thilke tyme than all his **wetheres** blake,   sheep
That sche hadde a schip hirself allone.
And therfore **wostow** what is best to doone –   you know
This **axeth** hast, and of an hasty thing   requires
Men may nought **preche** or make taryyng.   talk about
Anon, go gete us fast into this **in**   now; house

A knedyng **trowh**, or elles a **kemelyn**   trough; beer tub
For ech of us, but loke that they be large,   440
In which that we may row as in a barge,
And have therin **vitaille suffisant**   food; sufficient
But for **o** day, **fy on** the remenant.   one; never mind

30 God destroyed the world because of people's sins, but saved Noah and his family
   because he was faithful

The water schal **aslake** and gon away   abate
Aboute **prime** upon the nexte day: nine o'clock
But Robyn may not **wite** of this, thy knave,   know
Ne ek thy mayde, Gille, I may not save.
Aske nought why, for though thou aske me,
450   I wol nat tellen God's pryvete.
Sufficeth the, but if that thy witt madde,
To have as gret a grace as Noe hadde:
Thy wyf schal I wel saven out of doute.
Go now thy wey and speed the heer aboute,
And whan thou hast for hir and the and me
Y-goten us this knedyng tubbes thre,
Than schalt thou hange hem in the roof ful **hie**,   high
That no man of oure **purveaunce aspye**;   preparation; see
And whan thou thus hast doon as I have seyd,
And hast oure vitaille faire in hem y-leyd,
460   And eek an ax to **smyte** the corde a-two   cut
Whan that the water cometh, that we may goo;
And breke an hole an hye upon the **gable**,   gable (of the roof)
Into the gardynward, over the stable,   towards the garden
That we may frely passen forth oure way
Whan that the grete **schour** is gon away.   shower
Than schaltow swymme as mery, I undertake,
As doth the white **doke** aftir hir drake.   duck
Than wol I clepe how Alisoun, how Jon,
Beoth merye, for the flood passeth anon;   will be
470   And thou wolt seye, 'Heyl, Maister Nicholay!
Good morn! I see the wel, for it is day.'
And than schul we be lordes al oure lyf
Of al the world, as Noe and his wyf.
But of oo thing I warne the ful right –
Be wel avysed of that ilke nyght
That we ben entred in to schippes boord[31]
That not of us ne speke not a word,
Ne **clepe**, ne crye, but be **in his preyere**,   call; at prayer
For it is God's owne **heste** deere   order
480   Thy wyf and thou most hangen **fer a-twynne**,   far away from each other
For that **bitwixe** you schal be no synne,   between

31 'when we have gone on board our ships'

No more in lokyng than ther schal in **dede**:	deed
This **ordynaunce** is seyd, so God me speede.	order4
Tomorwe at night, whan men ben aslepe,	
In to our knedyng tubbes wol we **crepe**,	creep
And sitte ther **abydyng** God's grace.	waiting for
Go now thy way, I have no lenger **space**	time
To make of this no lenger sermonyng.	
Men seyn thus: 'Send the wyse, and sey no thing.'³²	
Thou art so wys, it needeth nat the teche –³³	490
Go, save oure lyf, and that I the **byseche**.'	beg

🐝 This seely carpenter goth forth his way;³⁴	
Ful **ofte** he seyd, 'Allas!' and, 'Weylaway!'	often
And to his wyf he told his **pryvete**;	secret
And sche was **war**, and knew it **bet** than he	aware; better
What al this **wente cast** was, for to seye,	ingenious plot
But **natheles** sche **ferd as** sche schuld **deye**,	nevertheless; acted as if; die
And seyde 'Allas! Go forth thy way anoon!	
Help us to **skape**, or we be ded **echon**!	escape; each one
I am thy verray, trewe, wedded wyf –	500
Go, deere spouse, and help to save oure lyf!'	
Lo! **Which** a gret thing is affeccioun:	what
A man may dye for **ymaginacoun**,	imagining
So deepe may impressioun be take.	
This seely carpenter bygynneth **quake** –	shake
Him thenketh **verrayly** that he may se	truly
Noe's flood come **walking** as the see,	surging
To **drenchen** Alisoun, his hony deere.	drown
He weepeth, wayleth, maketh **sory cheere**;	looks miserable
He **siketh** with ful many a **sory swough**,	sighs; deep groan 510

And goth and geteth him a knedyng trough,	
And after that a tubbe and a kymelyn,	
And pryvely he sent hem to his **in**,	house
And **heng** hem in the roof in **pryvete**.	hung; secretly

---

32 'be wise, and say nothing'
33 'you don't need to be taught (that)'
34 Not necessarily 'silly', but a term of familiarity, meaning 'foolish', but 'endearing'
   at the same time.

His owne **hond** than made **laddres** thre,   hand; ladders
To clymben by the **ronges** and the **stalkes**,   rungs; uprights
Unto the tubbes hangyng in the **balkes**;   beams
And hem **vitayled** both trough and tubbe   provisioned
With breed and cheese, with good ale in a **jubbe**,   jug
520 Suffisyng right ynough as for a day.
But or that he had maad al this **array**,   preparation
He sent his knave and eek his wenche also
Upon his neede to **Londoun** for to go;   London
And on the Monday, whan it drew to nyght
He **schette** his dore, withouten candel light,   shut
And dressed al this thing as it schuld be;[35]
And schortly up they **clumben** alle thre.   climbed
They seten stille wel a forlong way
Now, 'Pater Noster, clum,' quod Nicholay,
530 And, 'Clum,' quod Jon, and, 'Clum,' quod Alisoun.[36]
This carpenter seyd his **devocioun**,   prayers
And stille he sitt and **byddeth** his prayere,   said
Ay waytyng on the reyn, if he it heere.   always waiting for the rain
The **deede** sleep, **for verray busynesse**,   deep; because of his exertions
Fil on this carpenter, right as I gesse,   fell
Abowten courfew tyme or litel more,
For **travail** of his **goost** he groneth sore,   labouring; spirit
And eft he **routeth**, for his heed **myslay**.   snores; is uncomfortable
Doun of the laddir stalketh Nicholay,
540 And Alisoun, ful softe adoun hir spedde;
Withouten wordes mo they goon to bedde,
Ther as the carptenter was wont to lye,
Ther was the revel and the melodye.
And thus **lith** Alisoun and Nicholas,   lay
In busynesse of myrthe and of solas,
Til that the belles of laudes gan to rynge[37]
And **freres** in the chauncel gan to synge.[38]   friars

35 'and arranged everything as it should be'
36 Pseudo-Christian religious 'charms'
37 The second service of the morning, around daybreak.
38 Chancel, at the east end of the church.

❧ This absolon ful joly was and light,
And thoughte, 'Now is tyme wake al night,
For sikerly I sawh him nought styryng   550
About his dore syn day bigan to spryng.[39]
So mote I thryve, I schal at cok's crowe[40]
Ful pryvely go knokke at his wyndowe,
That **stant ful lowe** upon his **bowres** wal.   stands very low; bedroom
To Alisoun than wol I tellen al
My love longyng, for yet I schal not mysse
That **atte leste wey** I schal hir kisse;   at the very least
Som maner comfort schal I have, parfay –   by my faith
My mouth hath **icched** al this longe day –   itched
That is a signe of kissyng atte leste;   560
Al nyght I **mette** eek I was at a feste.   dreamed
Therfore I wol go slepe an hour or tweye,
And al the night than wol I wake and pleye.'
Whan that the firste cok hath crowe anoon,
Up ryst this jolyf lover Absolon,
And him **arrayeth** gay **at poynt devys**;   dresses; with great care
But first he cheweth greyn and lycoris[41]
To smellen swete: **or** he hadde **kempt** his heere,   before; combed
Under his tunge a 'trewe love' he beere[42],
For therby **wende he** to be gracious.   he thought   570
He rometh to the carpenter's hous,
And stille he stant **und** the schot wyndowe –[43]   under
Unto his **brest** it **raught**, it was so lowe,   chest; reached
And softe he **cowhith** with a **semy-soun**:   coos; gentle little noise
'What do ye, hony comb, swete Alisoun?
My fayre **bryd**, my swete **cynamome**?   bird; cinnamon
Awake, **lemman** myn, and speketh to me.   beloved
Wel litel thynke ye upon my wo,
That for youre love I **swelte** ther I go.   grow weak
No wonder is if that I swelte and swete;
I morne as doth a lamb after the **tete**.   teat/nipple   580

---

39 Absolon has been watching for signs of John's absence – 'he' is the carpenter, in
   this case.
40 'as I hope to thrive'
41 To keep his mouth sweet (like chewing peppermints)
42 A herb, to sweeten his mouth.
43 Window with a hinge, so it was glazed or had a shutter.

Y-wis, lemman, I have such **love-longyng**,   truly; lovesickness
That like a **turtil** trewe is my moornyng;   turtledove
I may not ete more than a **mayde**.'   girl
'Go fro the wyndow, jakke fool!' sche sayde,
'As help me God, it wol not be **com paine**!   come and kiss me
I love another, and elles were I to blame,
Wel bet than the. By Jhesu, Absolon!
Go forth thy wey, or I wol cast a **stoon**,   stone
590   And lete me slepe, **a twenty develway**!'   in the name of twenty devils
'Allas,' quod Absolon, 'and weylaway,
That trewe love was ever so **bysett**!   ill-favoured
Thanne kisseth me, **syn** it may be no **bett**,   since; better
For Jesus love, and for the love of me.'
'Wilt thou than go thy way therwith?' quod sche.
'Ye, **certes**, lemman,' quod this Absolon.   indeed
'Than mak the redy,' quod sche, 'I come **anon**.'   now
This Absolon doun sette him on his knees,
And seide, I am a lord **at alle degrees**,   in every degree
600   For after this, I hop,e ther cometh more;
Lemman, thy grace and, swete **bryd**, thyn **ore**.'   bird; mercy
The wyndow sche undyd, and that in hast.
'Have doon,' quod sche '**com of** and speed the fast,   hurry up
Lest that our neygheboures the aspye.'
This Absolon gan wipe his mouth ful drye.
Derk was the night as **picche** or as a **cole**:   pitch; coal
Out atte wyndow putte sche hir **hole**,   arsehole
And Absolon, him fel no bet ne wers,[44]
But with his mouth he kist hir naked **ers**   arse
610   Ful **savorly**: whan he was **war** of this,   with great relish; aware
Abak he sterte, and thought it was **amys**;   not right
For wel he **wist** a womman hath no **berd** –   knew; beard
He felt a thing al rough and long **y-herd**,   haired
And seyde, 'Fy! Allas! What have I do?'
'Te hee!' quod sche, and clapt the wyndow to,
And Absolon goth forth **a sory paas**:   dragged slowly away
'A berd! A berd!' quod heende Nicholas,
'**By God's corps**, this game goth fair and wel!'   by God's body

44 'nothing better or worse happened to him'

This seely Absolon herd every **del**,   bit
And on his lippe he gan for angir byte,   620
And to himself he seyde, 'I schal the quyte!'[45]

❦ Who rubbith now, who **froteth** now his lippes,   rubs
With dust, with sand, with straw, with cloth, with **chippes**,   chippings
But Absolon, that seith ful ofte, 'Allas!
'My soule **bytake** I unto **Sathanas**,   give; Satan/ the devil
But me were lever than all this toun,' quod he,
'Of this **dispit awroken** for to be.[46]   insult; avenged
Allas,' quod he, 'Allas, I nadde **bleynt**!'   turned away
His hoote love was cold and al **y-queint**,   quenched
For fro that tyme that he had kist her ers,   630
Of **paramours** ne **sette** he nat a **kers**;   lovemaking; valued; piece of cress
For he was **helyd** of his **maledye**.   healed; illness
Ful ofte paramours he gan deffye,
And wept as doth a child that is **y-bete**.   beaten
A **softe paas** went he over the strete,   with soft tread
Unto a smyth men **clepith** Daun **Gerveys**,   call; Gervase
That in his forge smythed **plowh** harneys;   plough
He **scharpeth schar** and **cultre** bysily.[47]
This Absolon knokketh al **esily**,   quietly
And seyde unto Gervays, and that anoon –   640
'What! Who art thou?' – 'It am I, Absolon!'
'What? Absolon! What! For Crist's swete **tree**!   cross
Why ryse ye so **rathe**, benedicite!   early; God bless us
What **eyleth** you, some gay **gurl**, god it **woot**,   ails; girl; knows
Hath brought you thus **upon the verytrot**!   hot-foot
By Seinte **Noet**, ye wot wel what I mene!'   Neot
This Absolon **ne roughte nat a bene**   didn't hold worth a bean
Of al this pleye; no word **agayn** he **gaf**,   counter/against; gave
For he hadde **more tow on his distaf**   more to worry about
Than Gerveys knew, and seyde, 'Freend so deere,   650
That hote **cultre** in the chymney heer,
As **lene** it me, I have therwith to doone: lend
I wol it bring agayn to the ful soone.'

45 'I'll get my own back on you!'
46 'I'd rather have my revenge for this insult than all this town'
47 sharpens ploughshares; culters (blades)

Gerveys answerde, 'Certes, were it gold,
Or in a **poke** nobles al untold,   pocket
Ye schul him have, as I am trewe smyth.
By Cristes **fote**, what wil ye do therwith?'   foot
'Therof' quod Absolon, 'be as be may –
I schal wel telle it the tomorwe day.'

660 And caughte the cultre by the colde stele;
Ful soft out at the dore he gan it stele,
And wente unto the carpenter's wal.
He **cowheth** first, and knokketh therwithal   coos
Upon the wyndow, right as he dede **er**.   before
This Alisoun answerde, 'Who is ther,
That knokkest so? I warant it a theef!'
'Why nay,' quod he, 'God woot, my sweete **leef**!   love
I am thyn Absolon, O my derlyng.
Of gold,' quod he, 'I have the brought a ryng:

670 My mooder gaf it me, so God me save –
Ful fyn it is, and therto wel **y-grave** –   engraved
This wol I give the, if thou me kisse.'
This Nicholas was rise for to **pysse**,   piss
And thought he wold **amenden** al the **jape**;   increase; joke
He schulde kisse his ers **or** that he **skape**.   before; escape
And up the wyndow **dyde** he hastily,   pulled
And out his ers putteth he **pryvely**   secretly
Over the buttok to the **haunche** bon,   thigh
And therwith spak this clerk, this Absolon:

680 'Spek, sweete bryd, I **wot nat** wher thou art!'   don't know
This Nicholas anon let **flee** a fart,   fly
As gret as it had ben a **thundir dent**,   thunderclap
And with that strook he was almost **y-blent**;   cut in half
And he was redy with his **yren hoot**,   hot iron
And Nicholas amyd the ers he smoot.
Of goth the skyn **an hande brede** aboute,   a hand's breadth
The hoote cultre **brente** so his **toute**,   burnt; rump
And for the **smert** he **wende** for to **dye**:   smarting pain; believed; die
As he were **wood** anon he gan to crye,   mad

690 'Help! Watir! Watir! Help, for God's **herte**!'   heart
This carpenter out of his slumber sterte,
And herd **on** crye, 'Watir!' as he wer wood,   one/someone
And thought, 'Allas! For now cometh Noe's flood!'

He sit him up withoute wordes **mo**,　　　　　　　　　　more
And with his ax he smot the corde **a-two**,　　　　　　in two
And doun he goth, he **fond nowthir to selle**;　　stopped for nothing
No bred, ne ale, til he com to the **selle**　　　　　　　ground
Upon the floor, and ther **aswoun** he lay.　　　　　unconscious
Up styrt hir, Alisoun and Nicholay,
And cryden, 'Out and harrow!' in the strete.　　　　　　　　700
The neyghebours, bothe smal and grete
In **ronnen**, for to **gauren on** this man　　　　　ran; stare at
That **yet** aswowne lay, both pale and wan,　　　　　　still
For with the fal he **brosten** had his arm;　　　　　broken
But stond he muste, to his owne harm,
For whan he spak, he was **anon born doun**　immediately shouted down
With heende Nicholas and Alisoun.　　　　　　　　by
They tolden every man that he was wood –
He was agast and **feerd** of Noe's flood　　　　　afraid
Thurgh fantasie, that of his vanite　　　　　　　　　　710
He hadde y-bought him knedyng tubbes thre,
And hadde hem hanged in the roof above,
And that he preyed hem, for God's love,
To sitten in the roof **par compaignye**.　　　　to keep him company
The folk **gan lawhen** at his fantasye:　　　　began to laugh
Into the roof they **kyken** and they gape,　　　　stare
And torne al his harm into a **jape**;　　　　　　joke
For whatsoever the carpenter answerde,
Hit was for nought: no man his resoun herde.
With **othis** greet he was so sworn adoun,　　　　oaths　720
That he was **holden** wood in al the toun;　　believed to be
For every clerk anon right **heeld** with othir.　　　agreed
They seyde, 'The man was wood, my **leeve** brother.'　　dear
And every man gan **lawhen** at his **stryf**.　　laugh; trouble
Thus **swyved** was the carpenter's wyf,　　　　fucked
For al his **kepyng** and his **gelousye**,　　watchfulness; jealousy
And absolon hath kist **hir nethir ye**,　　the eye of her behind
And Nicholas is **skaldid** in his **towte** –　　scalded; rump
This tale is doon, and God save al the **route**.'　　company

Here endeth the Miller's tale,

THE REEVE'S PROLOGUE AND TALE

The reeve is angry with the miller, because his tale was about the cuckolding of a carpenter, and he is himself a carpenter by trade. In response, he insists upon telling a tale about the tricking of a miller. He is an old man now, although he still has an active sexual urge, but old men's desires are channelled into four different streams: boasting, lying, anger and covetousness.

At Trumpington near Cambridge there lives a miller (Symkyn), who delights in swindling his customers. In particular he enjoys swindling the manciple of a local college, as this enables him to be contemptuous of those who are far more educated than himself. Symkyn and his wife, who is the daughter of a parson and thus well-connected locally, are both proud, especially the haughty wife. They have an infant son, and a daughter (Malyne) who is still unmarried, although she is twenty years old. This is because Symkyn wants to marry her 'well', due to her higher-class heritage and the dowry she will receive from her grandfather. When the manciple of the college falls very ill, Symkyn is able to cheat the college of even greater amounts, and to boast about it publicly. Two students from the North of England, John and Aleyn, ask the manciple for permission to go to the mill with the college's wheat, to make sure that they are not cheated. The manciple agrees, they go to Symkyn's mill, and the miller swears to himself that he will cheat them, no matter what they can do. While the students are watching their wheat being ground, Symkyn unties their horse, which runs to the fen with the wild mares. Catching their horse takes the students until the evening. In the meantime, Symkyn has his wife bake a cake with some of the students' meal, and his daughter Malyne hides it. The students offer to pay for a night's lodging, so the miller lets them sleep in the same room with himself, his wife and Malyne. Before going to bed, the family all have too much to drink. Kept awake by the snoring of Symkyn and his wife, Aleyn decides he will get some reparation for their material losses by 'swyving' the daughter, and he makes his way into her bed. Hearing them, John feels unmanned and ashamed, so he decides that he will try to do the same with the miller's wife. When the wife leaves the room to piss, John moves the cradle with the baby in it to the foot of his own bed. When the wife comes back, she gets into bed with John, who has vigorous sex with her (which she enjoys very much). As morning comes, Aleyn goes back to what he thinks is John's bed, boasting about what he has done with Malyne. However, it is the miller's bed (it had no cradle because John had moved it). When Symkyn springs up to attack him, Aleyn falls over onto the miller's wife, and she wakes. She picks up a large stick, and accidentally hits the miller over the head, mistaking Symkyn's bald head for the clerk's close-fitting white hood. Malyne and Aleyn stage a tearful 'mock-romance' farewell, and the students make their escape with the cake, as Malyne has revealed the hiding place to Aleyn.

With the intervention of Oswald the reeve, Chaucer's stories and their tellers begin to take on a life of their own, threatening to break free of the host's control (and maybe the author's). The phrase 'A litel ire in his herte is laft' (RT 9) refers the audience to beginning of the miller's tale, when Oswald ostentatiously supported the opinion of his social 'betters' over the dubious moral content of any narrative which might be forthcoming from the drunken miller. This is what might be expected from a socially aspirational member of the lower classes, but the audience also knows that Oswald got rich by stealing from his lord, while maintaining a pleasant, fawning face towards him. The reeve, therefore, will answer the miller with a fabliau story of his own, one which has been manipulated in order to deliver a moral message. (Chaucer's use of the fabliau genre is interesting, here. He has introduced characterisations and possible moral questions to his version of a story known elsewhere as 'Le menier et les deux clers', in which the main emphasis is given to stratagems and how they are planned and carried out. He also introduces elements of split-second timing and the use of space we would now associate with farce.) The host is angry at Oswald for not taking to heart the admonition not to make 'ernest' out of 'game', which is in danger of undermining the storytelling project altogether. He tells the reeve not to preach, as they have reached Deptford already, and he is wasting time.

Oswald attributes his own share of the seven deadly sins to the 'avanting, lyyng, angur, covetyse' (RT 31), which are natural to old men like himself. He makes a feature of the difference between his sexual urges, which are still those of a young man, and his physical impotence. The story sets Symkyn at odds with the young students. The reeve appears to identify with the students in this tale, using their sexual activities vicariously to satisfy his own frustrated libido. The virility of the students is stressed by the vigour of their horse, chasing the mares in the fen, but there is also a theme of impotence (the horse is gelded). The sharp, pointed objects hanging at Symkyn's belt may cover an inability to use the instrument they hide to any useful effect.

Oswald's students may be outsiders in Symkyn's home but, being northerners with a distinctive dialect, they are doubly outsiders. The reeve, too, is an outsider – he lives on a heath (which has been seen as the home of devils). He is an outsider to the 'southern' pilgrims, being a North Norfolk man, with a distinctive dialect with some affiinity to northern English forms. It was unusual to use dialect in this way in English medieval literature, as everyone assumed that 'correct' English was their own. Chaucer deals with this by widening the geographical gap between students and miller. Their accent is of the far north, Northumberland, and is therefore distinctive enough to be recognisably 'different' from his more southerly readership. In French, where the idea of 'correct' language was far more developed, dialect was frequently used to comic effect in fabliaux.

The students are also educated, and the miller, like John the Carpenter, is contemptuous of educated men. He is proud of his ability to trick them, a point he presses home with his suggestion that they can make the room bigger by 'talking up' some extra space. As educated men are higher in social status there is, as with the miller, an element of class envy in play here. Symkyn's wife is the illegitimate daughter of a parson, a man of education and gentle birth. He has used his church's wealth to buy her marriage to Symkyn, who is proud of her gentry-class origins. This duality is apparent in Malyne, who has some noble features, such as grey eyes, along with her father's 'camus' nose and wide hips. The parson wishes to arrange a suitably high-status wedding for Malyne, and the first concern for her father, after learning that she has lost her virginity, is that he will not now be able to marry her so well. The name of the miller is a diminutive of Simon, referring to Simon Magus, who offered the apostle Peter money in return for the ability to work miracles, giving rise to the term 'simony', making payment in return for ecclesiastical preferment. In the background of the story is both ecclesiastical abuse, and the misuse of education. In the miller's tale, educated young men are tricked along with illiterate older ones, but here the educated are triumphant. The reeve, like all socially aspirational peasants, would be aware of the value of education . . . he owes his position to his practical literacy.

The women in the tale are both sexually used, although they may not have been seen as 'abused' by a medieval audience, especially in the light of the reeve's use of the fabliau form. His description of Malyne includes signs that she is sexually receptive, such as the camus nose and the narrator's calling her a 'wench'. However, he also says that when Aleyn jumps on top of her, it was too late to cry out. This may be his observation, or the excuse she gives to her father afterwards. Besides, her parents were both in a drunken sleep. Whether this is in fact a rape is a matter open to debate and individual opinion, but Malyne appears to have enjoyed her adventure as much as her mother. It is her father and grandfather who will lose out. Malyne may now not receive the parson's inheritance, and her father will have to provide for her, as well as his baby son. The miller's wife had not had such enjoyable sex for ages. However, Malyne is the only member of this family (despite their clerical associations) to have some evidence of a moral compass. Her parting from Aleyn takes the form (however debased by the fabliau genre) of an *aube*, a parting song famiiar to Chaucer's audience from courtly love poetry. It is she who reveals to Aleyn the whereabouts of his wheat.

At the end, Oswald supplies a moral, 'a trickster will himself be tricked', but as he is himself dishonest and a trickster, in passing judgement on the miller he is also passing judgement on himself. He takes delight in the students' tricking of the miller and their avenging themselves on his wife and daughter. He sees himself as avenged and recompensed – on the miller, and maybe on the rest of the world – in their acts.

Key Questions

How does Chaucer manipulate/use the *fabliau* genre, maybe as seen by a comparison with the story's analogues?

Is the story anti-clerical?

Does the reeve take a misogynist view of the women in the tale, or are they sympathetic (wronged?) characters in their own right?

How 'moral' is the story? Is this appropriate for the reeve himself?

Topic Keywords

Medieval universities/ simony and the Church/ medieval women/ fabliau genre/ medieval English dialect and language/ medieval East Anglia/ social life (town and country)/ medieval law/ medieval technology

Further Reading

Joseph L. Baird, 'Law and The Reeve's Tale', *Neuphilologische Mitteilungen*, 70, 1969, pp. 679–83

Gay L. Balliet, 'The Wife in Chaucer's Reeve's Tale: Siren of Sweet Vengeance', *English Language Notes*, 28, 1990, pp. 1–6

Jeffrey Baylor, 'The Failure of the Intellect in Chaucer's Reeve's Tale', *English Language Notes*, 28, 1990, pp. 17–19

Peter Beidler, 'The Reeve's Tale and its Flemish Analogue', *Chaucer Review*, 26, 1992, pp. 283–92

—— 'Chaucer's Reeve's Tale, Boccaccio's *Decameron*, ix, 6, and two "soft" German analogues', *Chaucer Review*, 28, 1994, pp. 237–51

N. F. Blake, 'The Northernisms in The Reeve's Tale', *Lore and Language*, 3, 1979, pp. 1–8

D. S. Brewer, 'The Reeve's Tale and the King's Hall, Cambridge', *Chaucer Review*, 5, 1971, pp. 311–17

Peter Brown, 'The Containment of Symkyn: The Function of Space in The Reeve's Tale', *Chaucer Review*, 14, 1980, pp. 225–36

Roger T. Burbridge, 'Chaucer's Reeve's Tale' and the fabliau "Le Meunier et les deux clers" ', *Annuale mediaevale*, 12, 1971, pp. 30–6

M. Copland, 'The Reeve's Tale: Harlotrie or Sermonying?', *Medium Ævum*, 31, 1962, pp. 14–32

Bruce Kent Cowgill, 'Clerkly Rivalry in The Reeve's Tale', *Studies in Medieval Culture*, 29, 1991, pp. 59–71

Holly A. Crocker, 'Affective Politics in Chaucer's Reeve's Tale: "Cherl" Masculinity after 1381', *Studies in the Age of Chaucer*, 29, 2007, pp. 225–58

Sheila Delany, 'Clerks and Quitting in The Reeve's Tale', *Medieval Studies*, 29, 1967, pp. 351–6

Rodney Delasanta, 'The Mill in Chaucer's Reeve's Tale', *Chaucer Review*, 36, 2002, pp. 270–6

Deborah Ellis, 'Chaucer's Devilish Reeve', *Chaucer Review*, 27, 1992, pp. 150–61

Peter Goodall, 'The Reeve's Tale, "Le Meunier et les deux Clers" and the Miller's Tale', *Parergon*, 27, 1980, pp. 13–16

Susanna Greer Fein, 'Lat the children pleye': The Game Betwixt the Ages in The Reeve's Tale,' *Studies in Medieval Culture*, 29, 1991, pp. 73–104

Joseph Grennen, 'The Calculating Reeve and His Camera Obscura', *Journal of Medieval and Renaissance Studies*, 14, 1984, pp. 245–59

Carol Falvo Heffernan, 'Chaucer's Miller's Tale and Reeve's Tale, Boccaccio's *Decameron* and the French fabliaux,' *Italica*, 81, 2004, pp. 311–24

Stewart Justman, 'The Reeve's Tale and the Honor of Men', *Studies in Short Fiction*, 32, 1995, pp. 21–7

R. E. Kaske, 'An Aube in The Reeve's Tale', *Journal of English Literary History*, 26, 1959, pp. 295–310

Ian Lancashire, 'Sexual Innuendo in The Reeve's Tale', *Chaucer Review*, 6, 1972, pp. 159–70

Bruce Moore, 'The Reeve's Rusty Blade', *Medium Ævum*, 58, 1989, pp. 304–12

Glending Robert Olson, 'The Reeve's Tale and "Gombert" ', *Modern Language Review*, 64, 1969, pp. 721–5

Alessandra Petrina, 'Seeing, Believing and Groping in the Dark: A Reading of The Reeve's Tale', in *Thou Sittest at Another Boke . . .*, *English Studies in Honour of Domenico Pezzini*, edited by Giovanni Iamartino, Maria Luisa Maggioni and Roberta Facchinetti, Milan, Polimetrica, 2008, pp. 223–36

John Plummer, 'Hooly Chirches Blood: Simony and Patrimony in Chaucer's Reeve's Tale', *Chaucer Review*, 18, 1983, pp. 49–60

Nicole Nolan Sidhu, ' "To late for to crie": Female Desire, Fabliau Politics and Classical Legend in Chaucer's Reeve's Tale', *Exemplaria*, 21, 2009, pp. 3–23

Joseph Taylor, 'Chaucer's Uncanny Regionalism: Rereading the North in The Reeve's Tale', *Journal of English and Germanic Philology*, 109, 2010, pp. 468–89

William F. Woods, 'The Logic of Deprivation in The Reeve's Tale', *Chaucer Review*, 30, 1995, pp. 150–63

—— 'Symkyn's place in The Reeve's Tale', *Chaucer Review*, 39, 2004, pp. 17–40

Susan Yager, ' "A whit thyng in hir ye": Perception and Error in The Reeve's Tale', *Chaucer Review*, 28, 1994, pp. 393–404

And bygynneth the prologe of the Reeve

❦ Whan folk hadde **lawhen of this nyce caas**   laughed at this silly story
Of Absolon and heende Nicholas,
Dyverse folk dyversely they seyde,[1]
But for the most part they **lowh** and pleyde.   laughed
Ne at this tale I **sawh** no man him **greve**,   saw; take offence
But it were **oonly Osewald the Reeve**.   except
Bycause he was of carpentrye craft
A litel **ire** in his herte is **laft**.   anger; still there
He gan to **grucche** and **blamed it a lite**,   complain; was a bit angry at it   10
"**So theek**," quod he, "ful wel coude I the **quyte**,   as I thrive; pay back
With bleryng of a prowd myller's **ye**,[2]   eye
If that me **luste** speke of **ribaudye**,   wanted to; coarseness

❦ But **yk** am old, me list not pley for age;   I (Norfolk dialect)
Gras tyme is doon, my foddir is now forage;[3]
My **whyte top** writeth myn olde yeeres,   white hair
Myn hert is **al so moulyd** as myn heeres,   as mouldy
And yit I fare as doth an **open ers** –   medlar (a fruit)
That **ilke** fruyt is **over lenger the wers**,   same; worse as it gets older
Til it be **rote** in **mullok** or in **stree**.[4]   rotten; rubbish; straw   20
We olde men, I drede so fare we –
Till we be **roten** can we nat be **rype**,   rotten; ripe
We hoppen alway whil the world wol **pype**;
For in oure wil ther **striketh ever a nayl**,   a tune still plays
To have an **hoor heed**, and a greene tayl[5]   a white head
As hath a leek, for though oure might be doon
Oure wil **desireth** folye **ever in oon**;   continues to desire
For whan we may nat do, than wol we speke –
Yet in oure aisshen old is fyr y reke.[6]

1 Different people reacted differently.
2 'Hoodwinking of a proud miller'
3 'My fodder is now forage' – 'I'm getting too old to do my own grazing'.
4 Straw is the covering for the floor – so, 'is thrown away'.
5 A green tail; a sexual metaphor – my head is old but my genitals are still frisky.
6 There's still fire under our spent ashes.

30   Foure **gledys** have we, which I schal devyse: burning coals
     Avanting, **lyyng**, **angur**, **covetyse**.[7]
     This foure **sparkys longen** unto **eelde**:   sparks; belong; old age
     Oure olde **lymes mowen** be **unweelde**,   limbs; may; unwieldy
     But wil, ne schal nat fayle us, that is **soth** –   truth
     And yet I have alwey **a colt's toth**.   a young man's desires
     As many a yeer as it is passed henne
     Syn that my tappe of lyf bygan to renne,[8]
     For **sykirlik** whan I was born anon   surely
     Deth **drough** the tappe of lyf and **leet** it goon,   drew/pulled out; let
40   And now so longe hath the tappe y-ronne,
     Til that almost al empty is the **tonne**.   barrel
     The streem of lyf now droppeth on the **chymbe**.   rim
     The sely tonge may wel rynge and **chimbe**   chime
     Of wrecchednes that passed is ful **yoore** –   a long time ago
     With olde folk, **sauf dotage**, is no more.'   except senility

     ❦ Whan that oure host had herd this sermonyng,
     He gan to speke as lordly as a kyng,
     And seyde, 'What amounteth al this wit?
     What, schul we speke alday of holy wryt?
50   The devyl made a reve for to preche,
     Or of a **sowter** a schipman, or a **leche**!   cobbler; physician
     Sey forth thi tale, and tarye nat the tyme![9]
     Lo, heer is **Depford** and it is passed **prime**.   Deptford; after nine o'clock
     Lo, Grenewich, ther many a **schrewe** is inne –   villain
     It were **al tyme** thi tale to bygynne!'   about time

     ❦ 'Now, sires,' quod this Osewold the Reeve,
     'I pray yow alle that noon of you him **greeve**,   get upset
     Though I answere and somwhat **sette his howve**,   make a fool of him
     For **leeful** is with force to **schowve**.   lawful; shove
60   This dronken myllere hath y-tolde us heer
     How that **bygiled** was a carpenter –   tricked
     Peraventure in scorn, for I am **oon** –   perhaps; one

     7 'boasting, lying, anger, covetousness'
     8 'When I was born the bung was taken out of my barrel of life, and now its almost
        empty. It used to spurt but now it drops on the rim' (an obvious sexual
        metaphor).
     9 'don't waste time'

And by your leve I schal him **quyte** anoon,   get my own back
Right in his **cherl's** termes wol I speke.   vulgar
I pray to Godde his nekke **mot tobreke**!   may; break
He can wel in myn eye see a **stalke**   stalk (of wheat, corn etc)
But in his owne he can nought seen a **balke**.'   plank/beam

Here endeth the prologe of the Reve

And here bygynneth his tale

℣ At Trompyngtoun, nat **fer** fro Cantebrigge,[10]   far   70
Ther goth a brook, and over that a **brigge**,   bridge
Upon the whiche brook ther **stant** a **melle** –   stands; mill
And this is verray **soth** that I you telle.   truth
A **meller** was ther dwellyng many a day;   miller
As eny **pecock** he was prowd and gay.   peacock
Pipen he coude, and fisshe, and nettys **beete**,   play the bagpipes; mend
And turne cuppes, **wrastel** wel, and **scheete**. [11]   wrestle; shoot
Ay by his belt he **bar** a long **panade**,   always; carried; curved sword
And of a swerd, ful **trenchaunt** was the blade;   sharp
A joly **popper** bar he in his **pouche**.   dagger; pocket   80
Ther was no man for perel durst **him touche**;   danger; dare
A Scheffeld **thwitel** bar he in his hose.   knife (of fine Sheffield steel)
Round was his face and **camois** was his nose,   pug or squashed
As **pyled** as an ape was his skulle.   bald
He was a market beter at the fulle;[12]
Ther durste no **wight** hand upon him **legge**,   person; lay
That he ne swor anon he schuld **abegge**.   pay
A theef he was, forsooth, of corn and **mele**,   meal/coarse flour
And that a **sleigh** and **usyng for** to **stele**.   sly/cunning; used to; steal
His name was **hoote deyvous** Symekyn.[13]   called; proud   90
A wyf he hadde, come of noble kyn;
The **persoun** of the toun hir fader was.   parson
With hire he gaf many a panne of bras
For that Symkyn schuld in his blood **allye**.   join (by marriage)

10 Trumpington, a village which is now a suburb of Cambridge.
11 Possibly 'drink others under the table'.
12 Someone who caused trouble on market day, probably in the public bar.
13 The diminutive of Simon.

Sche was **y-fostryd** in a nonnerye, — raised
For Symkyn wold no wyf, as he sayde,
But sche were wel **y-norissched** and a **mayde**, — brought up; virgin
To **saven** his **estaat** and **yomanrye**. — preserve his yeoman status
And sche was proud and **pert** as is a **pye**; — impudent; magpie
100 A ful fair sighte was ther on hem two –
On **haly** dayes bifore hir wolde he go, — holy (holidays)
With his **typet** y-bounde aboute his heed, — trailing tip of his hood or hat
And sche cam aftir in a **gyte** of **reed**, — gown; red
And Symkyn hadde hosen of the same.
Ther durste no wight **clepe** hir but, '**Madame**'; — call; my lady
Was noon so **hardy** walkyng by the weye, — bold
That with hir dorste rage **or elles pleye**, — flirt/have fun
But if he wold be slayn of Symekyn,
With panade, or with knyf or boydekyn;
110 For **gelous** folk be perilous everemo, — jealous
Algate they wolde here wyves **wende** so. — at any rate; believed
And **eek** for sche was **somdel smoterlich**, — also; somewhat; soiled
Sche was as **deyne** as water in a **dich**, — dignified; ditch
As ful of **hokir** and of **bissemare**. — haughtiness; scorn
Hir thoughte ladyes oughten hir to **spare**, — respect
What for hir **kynreed** and hir **nortelrye** — family; upbringing
That sche had lerned in the nonnerye.
A dou*gh*ter hadden they betwix hem two
Of **xxti** yeer, withouten eny **mo**, — just twenty years old; more
120 Savyng a child that was of **half yer age**; — six months old
In cradil lay and was a **proper page**. — handsome little boy
This wenche **thikke** and wel y-grown was, — well-built
With camoys nose and **eyyen** gray as glas, — eyes
And buttokkes brode and brestes round and hye –
But right fair was hir **heer**, I wol nat lye. — hair
The persoun of the toun, **for** sche was feir, — because
In purpos was to maken hir his heir, — decided
Both of his **catel** and his **mesuage**, — animals; property/real estate
And straunge made it of hir mariage. — was very fussy about
130 His **purpos** was to bystow hir **hye**,[14]
Into som worthy blood of **ancetry**; — ancestry (an 'old' family)
For holy chirche good moot be despendid

14 intention; to a high-status husband

On holy chirche blood that is descendid.[15]
Therfore he wolde his joly blood honoure,
Though that he schulde holy chirche devoure.

❦ Gret **soken** had this meller **out of doute**,   monopoly; without doubt
With whete and malt of al the lond aboute,
And namely ther was a gret **collegge** –
Men clepe it the Soler halle of Cantebregge;[16]   college
Ther was here whete and eek here malt y-grounde,   140
And on a day, **it happen on a stounde**,   it happened once upon a time
Syk lay the mauncyple on a **maledye**;   illness
Men wenden **wisly** that he schulde dye,   surely
For which this meller **stal** both mele & corn   stole
A thousend part more than **byforn**,   before
For ther biforn he stal but **curteysly**,   as was 'socially acceptable'
But now he is a theef outrageously;
For which the wardeyn **chidde** and made **fare**,   grumbled; a fuss
But therof sette the meller not a tare –[17]
He crakked **boost**, and swor it was nat so.   boast   150
Thanne weren there poore **scoleres** tuo,   scholars
That dwelten in the halle of which I seye;
Testyf they were, and lusty for to pleye,   headstrong
And oonly for here mirthe and revelrye
Uppon the wardeyn **bysily they crye**   they pestered
To geve hem leve, but a litel **stound**,   while
To go to **melle** and see here corn y-grounde;   mill
And hardily they dursten ley here nekke[18]
The meller schuld nat **stel hem** half a pekke[19]   steal from them
Of corn, by sleighte ne by force hem **reve**,   take   160
And atte last the wardeyn gaf hem leve.
John **hight** that oon and Alayn hight that other,   was called
Of o toun were they born that highte Strothir,[20]   one

15 'for Holy Church's possessions must be spent on the blood that is descended
   from Holy Church'
16 The Soler Hall, or King's Hall, became part of Trinity College, Cambridge.
17 'the miller didn't care a weed about that'
18 They 'lay their heads on the block'.
19 A small amount.
20 A village in Northumberland.

Fer in the north, I can nat telle where.
This Aleyn maketh redy al his gere,
And on an hors the sak he cast anoon –
Forth goth Aleyn the clerk, and also Jon,
With good swerd and with **bocler** by her side.   buckler (small shield)
Johan knew the way, **that** hem needith no gyde,   so that
170 And at the mylle the sak a-doun he layth.
Alayn spak first, 'Al heil, Symond! In faith,
How fares thy faire doughter and thy wyf?'
'Alayn welcome,' quod Symond, 'by my lyf!
And Johan also! How now, what do ye heere?'
'By God,' quod John, 'Symond, neede has na **peere**.   equal
Him falles serve himself that has na **swayn**,   he must; servant
Or elles he is a **fon**, as clerkes sayn.   fool
Oure mancyple, as I **hope**, wil be deed,   think
Swa werkes ay the **wanges** in his heed,   so; teeth
180 And therfore I is come, and eek Alayn,
To grynde oure corn and carie it ham ageyn.
I prey you speed us in al that ye may.'
'It schal be doon,' quod Symkyn, 'By my fay.
What wol ye do whil that it is **in hande**?'   being done
'By God, right by the **hoper** wol I stande,'   hopper
Quod John, 'and se how that the corn **gas** inne;   goes
Yet sawh I never, by my fader kynne,
How that the hoper **waggis** to and **fra**.'   wags; fro
Aleyn answerde, 'John, and wiltow swa?
190 Than wol I be bynethe, by my **croun**,   crown (of the head)
And se how that the mele fallys doun
Into the trough – that schal be my **desport**,   amusement
For Jon, in faith, I may be of your sort –
I is as ille a meller as ere ye!'[21]
This mellere smyleth for here **nycete**,   silliness/ignorance
And thought, 'Al this is doon but for a wyle;
They **wenen** that no man may hem **bigile**,   believe; trick
But by my thrift, yet schal I **blere here ye**,   hoodwink them
For al here sleight and al here **philosophie**.   learning
200 The more queynte **knakkes** that they make,   tricks
The more wol I stele whan I take.

21 I'm as bad a miller as you are.

Insteed of mele yet wol I geve hem **bren** –   bran
The grettest clerks beth not wisest men,
As whilom to the wolf thus spak the mare –
Of al her art ne counte I nat a **tare**.'   weed
Out at the dore he goth ful **pryvyly**:   secretly
Whan that he saugh his tyme, sotyly
He loketh up and doun til he hath founde
The clerkes hors, ther as it stood y-bounde,
Behynde the mylle under a **levesel**,   outbuilding   210
And to the hors he goth him faire and wel;
He **strepeth** of the bridel right anoon,   strips
And whan the hors was loos he gan to goon
Toward the fen, there wilde mares renne;[22]
Forthwith wil he thurgh thikke and eek thurgh thenne.
This meller goth agayn, and no word seyde,
But doth his **note** and with the clerkes pleyde   business
Til that her corn was fair and wel y-grounde,
And whan the mele was **sakked and y-bounde**,

                                            put in sacks and tied up
This John goth out and fynt his hors **away**,   gone   220
And gan to crye, 'Harrow, and weylaway!
Oure hors is lost, Aleyn, for goddes **banes** –   bones
Step on thy feet! Cum on, man, **al at anes**!   immediately
Aleyn, your wardeyn hath his **palfray lorn**!'   lost his expensive horse
This Aleyn al forgeteth mele and corn –
Al was out of his mynd his housbondrye.
'What wikked way is he gan?' han he crye.
The wyf cam lepyng inward with a **ren**;   run
Sche seyde, 'Allas, your hors goth to the fen
With wylde mares, as fast as he may go!   230
Un thank come on his heed that band him so,   ill luck
And he that bettir schuld han **knyt** the **reyne**!'   tied; rein
'Allas!' quod John, 'Aleyn, for Crist's **peyne**,   agony
Leg doun thi swerd and I sal myn **alswa** –   lay; also
I is ful wight, God wat, as is a ra![23]

---

22 The fens are the flat country around Cambridge and Ely – now farmland, in the
   Middle Ages they were more like bog- and swamp-land, the haunt of eel
   fishermen, reedcutters and wildfowlers. This was not a good place to have to
   chase one's horse and catch it.
23 I'm a lithe as a roe, God knows.

By God's hart, he sal nat **scape** us **bathe**!   escape; both
Why nad thou put the **capil** in the **lathe**?   horse; outbuilding/barn
Il hail, Aleyn – by God, thou is a **fon**!'   ill luck; fool
This sely clerkes speeden hem anoon
240   Toward the fen, bothe Aleyn and eek Jon,
And, whan the myller sawh that they were gon,
He half a busshel of the flour hath take
And bad his wyf go knede it in a cake.
He seyde, 'I trowe the clerkes ben aferd;
Yet can a miller **make a clerk's berd**   trick a clerk
For al his art! Ye, lat hem go here way –
Lo! Wher they goon! Ye, lat the children play!
They get hym nat so lightly, by my croun!'
This sely clerkes ronnen up and doun,
250   With 'Keep, keep! Stand, stand! Jossa, **ware derere**!   look out behind
Ga wightly, thou and I sal keep him heere!'   go vigorously
But schortly, til that it was verray night
They cowde nat, though they did al here might,
Here **capil cacche**, it ran away so fast;   horse; catch
Til in a **diche** they caught him atte last.   ditch
Wery and wete as bestys in the reyn,
Comth sely John, and with him comth Aleyn.
'Allas,' quod John, 'that day that I was born!
Now are we **dryve til hethyng** and to scorn!   driven to contempt
260   Oure corn is stole, men **woln** us **foles** calle,   will; fools
Bathe the wardeyn and eek our felaws alle,   both
And namely the myller, weyloway!'
Thus pleyneth John, as he goth by the way,
Toward the mylle and **bayard** in his hand.   the horse
The myller sittyng by the fyr he **fand**,   found
For it was night and **forther might they nought**;

    they couldn't do any more

But for the love of God they him **bisought**   asked for
Of **herberwh** and of ese, **as for her peny**.   lodging; as they could pay
The myller sayd agayn, 'If ther be eny,
270   Swich as it is, yit schul ye have your part.
Myn hous is **streyt**, but ye han lerned art;   narrow
Ye **conne** by argumentes make a place   know how
A myl brood of twenty foote of space.
Let se now, if this place may suffyse,

Or make it **rom** with speche, as is your gyse.'   big enough; way
'Now Symond,' seyde this John, 'by Seynt Cuthberd[24]
Ay is thou mery, and that is fair answerd.
I have herd say men suld take of twa thinges:
Slik as he fynt or tak slik as he bringes;[25]
But specially I pray the, host ful deere,   280
Get us som mete and drynk and mak us cheere,
And we wol paye trewly **at the fulle**;   in full
With empty hand men may **na hawkes tulle**.   no hawks lure
Lo! Heer our silver, redy for to spende.'
This meller into toun his doughter sende,
For ale and breed, and rosted hem a goos,
And band her hors – he schold no more go loos;
And in his owne chambir hem made a bed,
With **schetys** and with **chalouns** fair y-spred,   sheets; blankets
Nat from his owen bed ten foot or twelve.   290
His doughter had a bed al by hirselve,
Right in the same chambre by and by:
Hit mighte be no bet, and cause why?[26]
Ther was no **rommer** herberw in the place.   larger
They sowpen and they hem to **solace**,   relax
And dronken ever strong ale atte beste.
Aboute mydnyght wente they to reste –
Wel hath the myller vernysshed his heed;[27]
Ful pale he was for dronken, and nat **reed**.   red/ruddy
He **yoxeth**, and he speketh thurgh the nose,   belches   300
As he were **on the quakke or on the pose**.   had a head cold or was hoarse
To bed he goth, and with him goth his wyf;
As eny jay sche light was and jolyf.
So was his joly **whistel wel y-wet**;   he'd wet his whistle (drunk)
The cradil at hire bed's feet is set,
To rokken and to give the child to **souke**.   suck
And whan that dronken was al in the **crouke**,   jug
To bedde went the doughter right anon,

24 Saint Cuthbert – particularly apt for a Northerner, as he was especially venerated
   in the North-East – his shrine was in Durham Cathedral.
25 Such as he finds and such as he brings.
26 'It might be no better, and do you know why?'
27 Pickled his head – got very drunk.

To bedde goth Aleyn and also Jon.

310 Ther nas no more, him needed no **dwale** –   sleeping draught

This meller hath so **wysly** bibbed ale,   dutifully

That as an hors he snortith in his sleep,

Ne of his tayl bihynd took he no keep.[28]

His wyf a **burdoun** a ful strong,   accompaniment

Men might her rowtyng heeren a forlong;[29]

The wenche routeth eek, **par companye**.   in company

Aleyn the clerk, that herd this melodye,

He pokyd John and seyde, '**Slepistow**?   are you asleep

Herdistow ever **slik** a sang er now?   did you hear; such3

320 Lo! slik a **conplyng** is betwix hem alle –   compline (evening service)

A wilde fyr upon thair bodyes falle!

Wha herkned ever swilk a **ferly** thing!   who heard; marvellous

Yet thei **sul** have the flour of ille endyng.   shall

This lange night **ther tydes me na rest**,   I can't rest

But yet **nafors**, al sal be for the beste,   never mind

For, John,' sayd he, 'as ever mot I thryve,

If that I may, yone wenche sal I **swyve**:   fuck

Som esement hath lawe schapen us,[30]

For, John, ther is a lawe that says thus;

330 That if a man in a point be agreved,

That in another he sal be releeved.

Oure corn is stoln, sothly, **it is na nay**,   it can't be denied

And we have had an **ylle fitt** today,

And syn I sal have nan **amendment**,   **restoration**

Agayn my los I sal have **esement**.

By God's **sale**, it sal nan other be.'[31]   soul

This John answerd, 'Aleyn, **avyse the**!   be careful

The miller is a **parlous** man,' he sayde,   dangerous

'and if that he out of his sleep **abrayde**,   awake

340 He mighte do us both a **vilonye**.'   harm

Aleyn answerd, 'I count it nat a flye!'[32]

And up he roos and by the wenche crepte;

28 He also farted (but also a sexual metaphor).
29 'you could hear her snoring a furlong away'
30 Easement: the plaintiff may not have satisfaction in the complaint he has made, but may obtain satisfaction in some other way.
31 'it won't be otherwise'
32 I don't consider it worth a fly.

This wenche lay **upright** and **faste** slepte   flat on her back; soundly
Til he so neih was, or sche might aspye,
That it had ben to late for to crye;
And schortly, for to seye, they weren at oon –[33]
Now pley, Aleyn, for I wol speke of Jon.
This John lith stille a forlong whyle or two,
And to himself compleyned of his woo.
'Allas!' quod he, 'This is a wikked **jape**!   joke   **350**
Now may I say that I am but an ape;
Yet hath my felaw somwhat for his harm –
He hath the myller's doughter in his arm;
He **auntred him** and has his needes **sped**,   dared; met
And I lye as a **draf sak** in my bed.   sack of rubbish
And when this jape is tald **another day**,   **told**
I sal be halda a **daf**, a **cokenay**.   fool; weakling
Unhardy is unsely, as men saith:[34]
I wol arise and **auntre it**, in good faith.'   take a chance
And up he ros, and softely he wente   **360**
Unto the cradil, and in his hand it **hente**,   grasped
And bar it softe unto his bed's feet.
Soone after this the wyf hir **routyng leet**,   stopped snoring
And gan awake, and went hir for to pisse,
And cam agayn, and gan hir cradel mysse;
And groped heer and ther, but sche fond noon.
'Allas!' quod sche, 'I had almost **mysgoon**!   gone wrong
I had almost goon to the clerk's bed.
Ey, **benedicite**! Than had I **foule** y-sped!'   God bless us; evilly
And forth sche goth til sche the cradil fand,   **370**
And fand the bed, and thoughte nat but good
Bycause that the cradil by hit stood.
Nat knowyng wher sche was, for it was derk,
But fair and wel sche creep in to the clerk,
And lith ful stille, and wolde han caught a sleep.
Withinne a while John the clerk up leep,
And on this goode wyf **leyth on ful sore**;   began to have vigorous sex
So mery a fytt ne hadd sche nat ful yore[35]

---

33 'the two were one'
34 He who doesn't dare doesn't win...
35 'she hadn't had such a good time in ages'

He **priketh** harde and deepe, as he were mad.   pricked (rode)
380 This joly lyf han this twey clerkes had
Til that the thridde cok[36] bygan to synge.
Aleyn **wax** wery in the dawenynge,   grew
For he had **swonken** al the longe night,   worked hard
And seyd, 'Farwel, Malyn, my sweete wight –
The day is come, I may no lenger **byde**;   stay
But evermo, wher so I go or ryde,
I am thyn owne clerk, so have I **seel**.'   good fortune
'Now, deere **lemman**,' quod sche, 'Go, farwel!   love
But or thou go, o thing I wol the telle:
390 Whan that thou wendist homward by the melle,
Right at the entre of the dore byhynde
Thou schalt a cake of half a busshel fynde,
That was y-maked of thyn owen mele,
Which that I **hilp** myn owen self to stele –   helped
And, goode lemman, God the save and kepe!'
And with that word almost sche gan to weepe.
Aleyn uprist and thought, 'Er that it **dawe**   dawn
I wol go crepen in by my felawe.'
And fand the cradil with his hand anon.
400 'By God!' thought he, 'Al wrong I have y-goon!
My heed is **toty** of my swynk tonyght,   befuddled
That makes me that I ga nou*gh*t aright.
I wot wel by the cradel I have mysgo –
Heer lith the myller, and his wyf also.'
Forth he goth in **twenty develway**   in the name of twenty devils
Unto the bed, ther as the miller lay.
He **wende** have **crope** by his felaw Jon;   thought; crept
And by the myller in he crepe anon,
And caught him by the nekke, and soft he spak,
410 And seyde, 'John, thou **swynes**hed, awak!   pigshead
For Crist's sowle, and here a noble game!
For by that lord that **cleped** is Synt Jame,   called
As I have thries in this schorte night
Swyved the myller's doughter **bolt upright**   'flat out'
Whiles thou has as a coward ben **agast**!'   afraid

36 The cock crowed for the third time.

'Ye, false harlot!' quod this mellere, 'Hast?
'A, false traitour! False clerk!' quod he,
'Thou schalt be **deed**, by God's dignite!   dead
Who durste be so bold to **disparage**   devalue
My doughter, that is come of hih lynage?'   420
And by the **throte bolle** he caught Aleyn,   epiglottis/Adam's apple
And he **hent him dispitously** ageyn,   grabbed him angrily
And on the nose he smot him with his **fest**;   fist
Doun ran the blody streem upon his brest.
And in the floor, with nose and mouth to-broke,
They **walweden** as pigges in a **poke**,   wallowed; sack
And upon they goon, and doun they goon anon,
Til that the miller stumbled at a ston,
And doun he felle bakward on his wyf,
That **wyst** nothing of this nyce stryf,   knew   430
For sche was falle asleep a litel wight
With Jon the clerk, that waked al the night.
And with the falle right out of slepe sche **brayde**.   woke
'Help! Holy Croys of Bromholme!'[37] sche sayde,
'In manus tuas, Lord, to the I calle!'[38]
Awake, Symond! The feend is in thine halle!
My hert is broken! Help! I am but deed!
Ther lythe upon my wombe and on myn heed!
Help, Symkyn! For this false clerkes fight!'
This John stert up as fast as ever he might,   440
And grasped by the walles to and fro
To fynde a staf, & sche sturt up also,
And knewe the **estres** bet than dede Jon,   nooks and crannies
And by the wal sche took a staf anon,
And sawh a litel glymeryng of a light,
For at an hool in schon the moone light;
And by that light sche saugh hem bothe two,
But sikirly sche **wiste** nat who was who,   knew
But sche saugh a whit thing in hir **ye**,   eye
And whan sche gan this white thing aspye,   450
Sche wend the clerk had wered a **volupeer**,   white cap

37 A famous object of pilgrimage in Norfolk.
38 'Into your hands. Lord', a final prayer of the dying.

And with a staf sche drough hir **neer and neer**,   nearer and nearer
And wend have hit this Aleyn atte fulle –[39]
And smot this meller on the **piled** sculle: bald
And doun he goth, and cryeth, 'Harrow! I dye!'
This clerkes beeten him wel, and leet hym lye,
And **greyth hem** wel, and take her hors anon,   got dressed
And eek here mele; and hoom anon they goon.
And at the millen dore they tok here cake,
460   Of half a **buisshel** flour ful wel y-bake.   bushel
Thus is the prowde miller wel y-bete
And hath y-lost the gyndyng of the whete,
And payed for the soper everydel
Of Alyen and of John, that beten him wel.
His wyf is swyved and his doughter **als**.   also
Lo, such it is a miller to be fals!
And therto this proverbe is seyd ful soth –
He thar nat weene wel that evel doth.[40]
A gylour schal him self bygiled be;[41]
470   And God, that sittest in thy mageste,
Save al this comaignie gret & smale –
Thus have I quyt the miller in his tale.

her endeth the Reeve's tale

39 'thought she hit Aleyn "full on" '
40 'He who does evil had better not expect good (to happen to him)'
41 A trickster will himself be tricked.

THE COOK'S TALE

The cook has perceived the hidden malice in the reeve's tale: he says he will now tell a tale about his own city – London. The host says he had better make it a good story, because the pilgrims might remember the substandard food he has sold to them over the years. Besides, he had better not make it come too close to the truth, because a joke which comes too close to the truth just isn't funny.

An apprentice called Perkin Revellour loves riot, women and taverns, and spends some of his time in Newgate prison as a result. He has a group of young friends who behave in the same way, in particular a friend whose partner is a prostitute. Eventually his master decides to withhold the written certificates which will allow him to practise his craft at the end of his apprenticeship, on the grounds that this would simply be putting a rotten apple into the barrel of his craft . . . (here the story breaks off).

The story was probably intended to develop into a comic tale or fabliau, like those of the miller and reeve. The story does not, however, develop past the descriptive phase, so the entire plot is lost. The interest in the fragment which remains is largely historical, centering on the relationship between 'revel' and 'riot' in the life of the city of London in Chaucer's day. None of Chaucer's fabliaux are set in London, although London was where he grew up and spent much of his life. The world of the apprentice is violent and rowdy, and anti-authoritarian in a political as well as a social sense, resulting in frequent nights in the Newgate cells for Perkin and his friends. The tale reveals the dual nature of the city's life, with respectable merchants, gentry, clerks and tradespeople, and the nocturnal existence of its 'underclass', which those in authority struggle to control. This is a chaotic world far more sinister and dangerous than that of the miller's Nicholas and Alison, one which ultimately reflects the nature of the cook and his profession: he works in the kitchen among the 'knaves' yet he produces fine food for the ceremonial table of wealthy guild officials. On a class level, therefore, this story reveals the lives of the poor who support the lifestyles of those richer and higher born than themselves. Despite the rich, decadent appearance of his work, the cook is a drunk with a 'mormal' on his chin, who cannot even stay on his horse.

There is some implication in surviving manuscripts that Chaucer originally intended the cook to tell the story of an outlaw hero, Gamelyn. However, with his choice of this particular prologue and tale, Chaucer has brought his audience from the educated, chivalric, noble lifestyle of the knight, via the independent suburban miller and the reeve of a country house, to the tenements and back alleys of one of Europe's great metropolitan cities.

Key Questions

Is this story suitable for the cook? Why/why not?

What does this story, and its prologue, tell us about city life in Chaucer's day? Does it have implications about age and/or class?

How might have it developed? What was Chaucer trying to do?

Topic Keywords

Medieval city life/ crafts and guilds/ food and drink

Further Reading

David Boyd, 'Social Texts: Bodley 686 and the Politics of The Cook's Tale', *Huntington Library Quarterly*, 58, 1996, pp. 81–97

Olga Burakov, 'Chaucer's The Cook's Tale', *Explicator*, 61, 2002, pp. 2–5

Daniel Pinti, 'Governing The Cook's Tale in Bodley 686', *Chaucer Review*, 30, 1996, pp. 379–88

V. J. Scattergood, 'Perkyn Revelour and The Cook's Tale', *Chaucer Review*, 19, 1984, pp. 14–23

William Woods, 'Society and Nature in The Cook's Tale', *Papers on Language and Literature*, 32, 1996, pp. 189–205

❦ The Cook of Londoun, whil the Reeve **spak**,   spoke
For joye he thought he **clawed** him on the bak.   scratched
'Ha, ha!' quod he, "For Crist's passioun!
This meller hath a scharp conclusioun
Upon his argument of **herburgage**!   lodging
Wel seyde **Salomon** in his langage,   Solomon
'Ne bryng nat every man into thyn hous;
For herburgage by night is perilous.
Wel aught a man **avised** for to be   careful
Whom that he brought into his **pryvyte**.   secrets/private space   10
I pray to God so gyf my body **care**,   sorrow/pain
Yif ever, **siththe** I **highte Hogge of Ware**,   since; was called; Roger of Ware
Herd I better myller **set a werke**!   duped
He hadde a **jape** of malice in the derke.   trick/joke
And therfore, if ye **vouche sauf** to heere –   grant
But god forbede that we **stynten** heere –   stop
A tale of me that am a **pouer** man,   poor
I wol yow telle, as wel as I kan,
A litel **jape** that **fel** in oure cite.'   joke; happened
Oure host seyde, 'I graunt it the;   20
Now telle on, Roger, & loke it be good –
For many a pastey hastow lete blood
And many a 'Jakk of Dover' hastow sold
That hath be twyes hoot and twyes cold![1]
Of many a pilgrym hastow Crist's **curs** –   curse
For thy **persley** they faren yet the wors   parsley
That they have eten with the **stubbil goos**,[2]   stubble-fed goose
For in thy schoppe is many a flye loos.
Now, goode gentil Roger by thy name,
But yit I pray the, be nought **wroth** for game.'[3]   angry   30
'Thow saist ful **soth**,' quod Roger, 'by my faith;   truthfully

---

1 Different ways of selling pies and pasties in an unsaleable condition, by drawing
  off the juices and reheating ('Jack of Dover' is a type of pie).
2 The manuscript here says 'teen' instead of 'eten', which does not make sense.
3 'Don't be angry – it's all said in fun'

But 'soth play, quad play,' as the Flemyng saith.'[4]   *true play is bad play*
Be thou nat wroth, or we departe her,   *before we leave*
Though that my tale be of an hostyler.   *innkeeper*
But natheles, I wol not telle it yit,
But or we departe it schal by quyt.'[5]
And ther withal he lowh, and made chere,   *laughed; was happy*
And seyde his tale, as ye schal after heere.

❧ A prentys dwelled whilom in oure citee[6]   *apprentice; once upon a time*
40   And of a craft of vitaillers was he.   *provisions merchants*
Gaylard he was, as goldfynch in the schawe,   *gay (merry); greenwood*
Broun as a bery, and a propre felawe,   *handsome fellow*
Qith lokkes blak and kempt ful fetously.   *hair; combed well*
Dauncen he cowde, wel and prately,   *prettily*
That he was cleped 'Perkyn Revellour'.
He was as full of love and paramour
As is the honycombe of hony swete,
Wel were the wenche that mighte him meete;
For whan ther eny rydyng was in Cheepe,[7]   *procession*
50   Out of the schoppe thider wolde he lepe.
Til he hadde al that sight y-seyn   *seen*
And daunced wel, he nold nat come ageyn.   *would not*
And gadred him a meyne of his sort,   *group; similar people*
To hoppe and synge, and make such disport;
And ther they setten stevene for to meete,   *appointed*
To pleyen atte dys in such a strete;   *dice*
For in the toun ne was ther no prentys
That fairer cowde caste a peyre dys   *pair of*
Than Perkyn couthe, and therto he was free
60   Of his dispence, in place of pryvyte.   *secret place*
That fand his mayster wel in his chaffare –   *found; business*
For often tyme he fond his box ful bare.   *empty*
For such a joly prentys revelour,   *reveller*
That haunteth dys, revel, or paramour,   *lover*

---

4 or 'if it's too close to the truth it isn't funny'
5 'it shall be finished before we leave'
6 An apprentice – a young man learning a craft or trade, whilst lodging with a
   master. 'Our citee' is London.
7 Chepe was the centre of the city's mercantile area.

His maister schal it in his schoppe **abye**,   feel the effects
Al have he no part of the mynstralcye.
For thefte and **ryot** be **convertyble**;   riotous living; interchangeable
Al can they pley on giterne and rubible,[8]
Revel and trouthe as in **a lowe degre**,   someone of low status
They be ful **wroth** al day, as ye may see.   contrary (with one another)   70
This joly prentys with his mayster **bood**,   abode (lived)
Til he was oute **neygh** of his **prentyshood**,   nearly; apprenticeship
Al were he **snybbyd** both erly and late,   told off
And somtyme lad with revel into Newgate.[9]
But atte laste his mayster him bythought,
Upon a day whan he his **papyr** sought,   certificate to practice
Of a proverbe that saith this same word,
'Wel bette is roten **appul** out of **hord**   apple; hoard
Than it **rote** al the **remenaunt**;   rots; rest
So fareth it by a ryotous servant –   80
Hit is ful lasse harm to **late him pace**,   let him go (sack him)
Than he **schend** al the servauntes in the place.'   ruin
Therfore his mayster gaf him **acqueyntaunce**,   aquittance (paid him off)
And bad him go, with sorwe and **meschaunce**.   ill luck
And thus the joly prentys had his leve –
Now let hym ryot al the night or leve,

(here the text breaks off)

8 Stringed instruments.
9 A prison in the city of London.

THE LAWYER'S TALE

The host asks the 'man of law' to tell a tale. The lawyer, with either genuine or assumed humility, says he cannot possibly tell a story as well as Geoffrey Chaucer, and lists some of Chaucer's better-known works. He speaks of the evils of poverty, contrasting it with the easy life of the wealthy; he would rather die than be poor. He says he doesn't know any stories, but by chance he has heard this one from a merchant not long ago.

A group of merchants from Syria visit Rome in the course of their business. There they hear about, and meet, the emperor's beautiful daughter, Constance. On their return they tell the Sultan about her, and he determines to marry her: he even converts to Christianity in order to be considered eligible by her father. Despite Constance's entreaties, the emperor agrees to the marriage, and Constance, always obedient to her father, is forced to marry the Sultan. The Sultan's evil mother, who really wants to rule in his place, gathers together all those who do not wish to renounce their Muslim faith. They kill the Sultan and everyone at the wedding feast, except Constance, who, although alone, is under God's protection. Constance is cast adrift in a rudderless boat with some provisions, and she is eventually washed ashore in Northumberland. She is given a home by the local constable and his wife Hermengild, who becomes a Christian. When Hermengild performs a miracle at Constance's behest the constable also converts. A local knight falls in love with Constance, but she refuses him, so he slits Hermengild's throat one night, 'plants' the knife on Constance and accuses her of the murder. In court before King Aella of Northumbria she is saved by a miracle, and Aella becomes a Christian. Later, he marries Constance and they have a son, Maurice. Aella's evil mother conspires to kill Constance and her son by accusing her of giving birth to a monstrous child. The trick is effected by the destruction and replacement of a letter telling Aella the good news of the child's birth. Constance and her son are set adrift . . . this time she lands, by God's help, back in Italy. Lodging with her aunt and uncle, who do not recognise her, Constance allows her son to attend a feast with the emperor and King Aella, who happens to be visiting Rome. Aella recognises his son, and then is reunited with Constance, who is also reunited with her father. The emperor takes Maurice as his heir. When Aella dies, Constance returns to Rome to live with her father.

With the lawyer's prologue, the host manages to regain some control over the storytelling 'game'. He demonstrates his astrological knowledge, with a bit of proverbial philosophy added, while basically telling the pilgrims that they should not waste 'storytelling' time. We are not told whether the lawyer is the next in line according to the lottery which took place at the beginning, or if the host is just attempting to put the whole thing on to a more ordered course. The pilgrim he selects is representative of the educated, wealthy, (rapidly, upwardly) socially mobile class of the legal professional, some of whom (like the lawyer Henry Scogan, to whom he wrote a wryly humourous *Envoy*) were among Chaucer's close friends. The lawyer's tale may be full of 'in jokes', and the same gentle irony, which is apparent in the *Envoy to Scogan*, but many will not be recuperable. The story's stress on the legal position of women (as the possessions of men, unless they happened to be 'dangerous' dowagers) and the need for documentary evidence reflects the profession of the teller. A lawyer would realise the precarious nature of evidence such as the 'birth announcement' letter, victim of a messenger's drunkenness. He would also be aware of the ease with which evidence could be falsified, and false testimony given. The lawyer's plentiful supply of references is understandable in the light of the essential requirement for precedent in the legal process. The storytelling lawyer's tendency to 'overdo' his referencing may be a joke at the expense of the legal profession, which Chaucer would have expected to amuse his legally-minded friends.

The story of Constance is similar to the medieval 'legends' of female saints, in which the heroine patiently and faithfully suffers intolerable torments, to be rewarded at the end with a place in heaven. God frequently uses the heroines of saints' legends and lives to perform miracles and/or proclaim their faith, like Cecilia in the second nun's tale, or he performs miracles on their behalf. Constance's story can hardly be said to involve her own *deeds*, as she does very little except in obedience to male commands. She complains of her powerlessness when she learns that she is to be married to the Sultan, she encourages Hermengild to restore the blind man's sight, and she engineers Aella's meeting with Maurice. For the rest of the story, however, she remains both passive and dumb. Constance is shown being obedient, moderate, temperate, modest, loving and caring towards her family and towards the disadvantaged, and especially being a good, caring mother. When she acts, she defends herself and her faith against accusers, and acts as a peacemaker between men. Her attempts to influence her situation are also passive; she refuses to reveal her identity to those with whom she lodges (although the point of this is never made clear). The only point at which she really rouses herself to violent action is when she is threatened with physical rape, but in this case she is once again the victim, and does not succeed through her own strength, but that of God, as the narrator makes clear.

The action of the plot is carried forward by the men who become associated with Constance, and by their mothers. Because the women are pagan matriarchs, they are able to be aggressive in ways not allowed to the young Christian female, who must conform to Christian ideals. It is her father's decision to send Constance to Syria, which launches her into an alien landscape, and sets off the series of tragedies which befall her. It is men – the constable and the senator – who decide to take her into their homes, where she keeps company with other women. The manipulation or destruction of their sons by older women is a feature of romance (as is the aggressive pagan woman). In fact, the men in this story are not as powerful as they initially seem to be. Unlike the knight's tale, where all the characters are moved arbitrarily by fortune and the whim of the gods, Constance's God has a purpose for her life. Through Constance's presence God is able to perform miracles and ensure the conversion of kingdoms. None of the characters is anything other than a stereotype or a cipher; even Constance is simply a representation of female virtue. The landscape over which they move is similarly featureless. This heightens awareness of the operations of the divine, and it is God who is the hero of this romance 'life'. He guides Constance's boat, he saves her from her assailants, he creates the circumstances in which she will survive and be a vehicle for the spread of the Christian faith, and in the end he engineers the meeting which will enable her reward. Through her passivity, and her silence (speaking only when she really needs to do so, such as in defending her faith and pleading her innocence), Constance is as much a 'vessel' as the ship in which she is carried.

This story is also an example of the romance trope in which a princess is set adrift in a rudderless boat, such as *La Bone Florence of Rome*. The boat with no steersman, such as the boat which guides Galahad and Perceval towards the Holy Grail, frequently appears in the Arthurian legends. The falsely accused woman who is saved by a dramatic miracle, usually resulting in the death or maiming of the accuser, is a feature of the medieval saint's life, both male and female. All of these romance and hagiographical tropes are combined in this story. However, unlike the saints, Constance's reward is a secular one, and in the end she does not ascend to paradise to receive her heavenly crown, but dwells in happy retirement in her father's house, with her son safely installed as the next emperor. This final, earthly rest is remeniscent of many actual noble dowagers (such as Edward IV's mother Cecily Neville) in the fourteenth and fifteenth centuries. In this, Constance is also demonstrating the acceptable face of widowhood, unlike those who (like Henry V's widow Catherine of Valois) married inappropriately or who, like the Sultaness, attempted to wield political power through their sons. True to the intersection of the secular and the holy in medieval life and literature, this is an exemplum for female conduct which is grounded both in this world and the next.

Key Questions

Is Constance believable as a 'real' woman, or does she represent a quality (constancy) only? Is she a woman, or a saint? Is she a stereotype?

How does the story represent the 'other', i.e. the muslim, the heathen, the exotic and foreign?

How 'active' is Constance's passivity?

What part does God/Christianity play in the story?

How does this tale compare with the clerk's (similar) tale of Griselda?

Topic Keywords

Medieval women/ hagiography and saints' lives/ the foreign and the exotic/ medieval geography/ medieval law

Further Reading

Ann Astell, 'Apostrophe, Prayer and the Structure of Satire in The Man of Law's Tale', *Studies in the Age of Chaucer*, 13, 1991, pp. 81–97

Anna Baldwin, 'The Man of Law's Tale as a Philosophical Narrative', *Yearbook of English Studies*, 22, 1992, pp. 181–9

Morton W. Bloomfield, 'The Man of Law's Tale: A Tragedy of Victimization and a Christian Comedy', *Publications of the Modern Language Association of America*, 87, 1972, pp. 384–90

Paul M. Clogan, 'The Narrative Style of The Man of Law's Tale', *Medievalia et Humanistica*, 8, 1977, pp. 217–33

Helen Cooney, 'Wonder and Immanent Justice in The Man of Law's Tale', *Chaucer Review*, 33, 1999, pp. 264–87

Christine F. Cooper, ' "But algates therby was she understonde": Translating Custance in Chaucer's Man of Law's Tale', *Yearbook of English Studies*, 36, 2006, pp. 27–38

Robert B. Dawson, 'Custance in Context: Rethinking the Protagonist of The Man of Law's Tale', *Chaucer Review*, 26, 1992, pp. 293–308

Sheila Delany, 'Womanliness in The Man of Law's Tale', *Chaucer Review*, 9, 1974, pp. 63–72

Carolyn Dinshaw, 'The Law of Man and its Abhomynacions', *Exemplaria*, 1, 1989, pp. 117–48

John Dugas, 'The Legitimisation of Royal Power in Chaucer's Man of Law's Tale', *Modern Philology*, 95, 1997, pp. 27–43

Patricia Eberle, 'The Question of Authority and The Man of Law's Tale', in *The Centre and its Compass: Studies in Medieval Literature in Honour of Professor John Leyerle*, edited by Robert Taylor, James Burke and Patricia Eberle, Kalamazoo, Kalamazoo Medieval Institute Publications, 1993, pp. 111–49

Robert T. Farrell, 'Chaucer's Use of the Theme of the Help of God in The Man of Law's Tale', *Neuphilologische Mitteilungen*, 71, 1970, pp. 239–43

Angela Florschuetz, ' "A mooder he hath, but fader hath he noon": Constructions of Genealogy in The Clerk's Tale and The Man of Law's Tale', *Chaucer Review*, 44, 2009, pp. 25–60

Melissa Furrow, 'The Man of Law's St Custance: Sex and the Saeculum', *Chaucer Review*, 24, 1990, pp. 223–35

Laurel L. Hendrix, ' "Pennannce profytable": The Currency of Custance in Chaucer's Man of Law's Tale', *Exemplaria*, 6, 1994, pp. 141–66

William C. Johnson Jr, 'The Man of Law's Tale: Aesthetics and Christianity in Chaucer', *Chaucer Review*, 16, 1982, pp. 201–22

Yvette Kisor, 'Moments of Silence, Acts of Speech: Uncovering the Incest Motif in The Man of Law's Tale', *Chaucer Review*, 40, 2005, pp. 141–62

Albert C. Labriola, 'The Doctrine of Charity and the Use of Homiletic "Figures" in The Man of Law's Tale', *Texas Studies in Literature and Language*, 12, 1970, pp. 5–14

Robert Enzer Lewis, 'Glosses to The Man of Law's Tale from Pope Innocent III's *De Miseria Humane Conditionis*', *Studies in Philology*, 64, 1967, pp. 1–16

Kathryn Lynch, 'Storytelling, Exchange and Constancy: East and West in Chaucer's Man of Law's Tale', *Chaucer Review*, 33, 1999, pp. 409–22

Robert Lynch, 'Heteroglossia and Chaucer's Man of Law's Tale', in *Bakhtin and Medieval Voices*, edited by Thomas Farrell, Gainesville, University of Florida Press, 1995, pp. 81–93

Roger E. Moore, 'Nominalistic Perspectives in Chaucer's The Man of Law's Tale', *Comitatus*, 23, 1993, pp. 80–100

Marijane Osborn, *Romancing the Goddess: Three Middle English Romances about Women*, Urbana, IL, University of Illinois Press, 1998

Michael R. Paull, 'The Influence of the Saint's Legend Genre in The Man of Law's Tale', *Chaucer Review*, 5, 1971, pp. 179–94

David Raybin, 'Custance and History: Woman as Outsider in Chaucer's Man of Law's Tale', *Studies in the Age of Chaucer*, 12, 1990, pp. 65–84

Kevin Roddy, 'Mythic Sequence in the Man of Law's Tale', *Journal of Medieval and Renaissance Studies*, 10, 1980, pp. 1–22

Susan Schibanoff, 'Worlds Apart: Orientalism, Antifeminism and Heresy in Chaucer's Man of Law's Tale', *Exemplaria*, 8, 1996, pp. 59–96

R. A. Shoaf, ' "Unwemmed Custance": Circulation, Property and Incest in The Man of Law's Tale', *Exemplaria*, 2, 1990, pp. 287–302

Hope Phyllis Weissman, 'Late Gothic Pathos in The Man of Law's Tale', *Journal of Medieval and Renaissance Studies*, 9, 1979, pp. 133–53

Marjorie Elizabeth Wood, 'The Sultaness, Donegild, and Fourteenth-Century Female Merchants: Intersecting Discourses of Gender, Economy and Orientalism in Chaucer's Man of Law's Tale', *Comitatus*, 37, 2006, pp. 65–85

Douglas Wurtele, ' "Proprietas" in Chaucer's Man of Law's Tale', *Neophilologus*, 60, 1976, pp. 577–93

❦ Owre hoste **sawh** that the brighte sonne   saw
The arke of his artifical day hath y-ronne[1]
The fourthe part of half an hour, and more.
He **wist** it was the threttenthe day   knew
Of April, that is messanger to May,
And sawe wel that the schade of every tree
Was in the lengthe the same quantite
That was the body erecte that caused it[2]
And therfore by the same schadwe he took his **wit**,   understanding
That Phebus, which that schoon so fair and bright,[3]   10
Degrees was xlv clombe on hight,[4]
And for that day as in that latitude
Hit was ten of the clokke, he gan conclude;
And sodeynly he **plight** his hors aboute.   turned

❦ 'Lordynges,' quod he, 'I warne you, **al the route**,   the whole company
The fourthe **party** of this day is goon;   part
Now, for the love of God and of Seint John,
Leseth no tyme as forthe as ye may.[5]
Lordynges, the tyme passeth, night and day,
And **stelith** fro us **what** pryvely slepyng,   steals; that which   20
And what thurgh necligence in oure wakyng,
As doth the streem that torneth never agayn,
Descendyng fro the mounteyn into playn.
Wel can **Senek** and many philosopher   Seneca
Bywaylen tyme more than gold in **cofre**;[6]   chest
For losse of **catel** may recovered be,   animals
But losse of tyme **schendeth** us,' quod he.   ruins
'It wil nat come agayn, withoute drede,

1 Here 'Geoffrey' describes in detail how to tell the time, using the elevation of the sun (Phebus), the length of shadows and the time of year.
2 ie the shadows were the same length as the objects which cast them.
3 Phoebus Apollo, god of the Sun, whose chariot carried the sun across the sky each day in Greek and Roman belief.
4 'had ascended (in the sky) by forty-five degrees'
5 'lose as little time as you possibly can'
6 'mourn the passing of time'

Nomore than wol Malkyn's **maydenhede**,   virginity`
30   Whan sche had lost it in hir **wantownesse**.   Wantonness
Let us nat **mowlen** thus in ydelnesse.'   go mouldy

❦ 'Sir man of lawe," quod he, 'so have ye blisse,[7]
Telle us a tale anon, as **forward** ys.   agreed
Ye be submitted, thurgh your fre assent,
To stonden in this **cas** at my juggement.   situation
Aequyteth yow, and holdeth youre byheste,[8]   discharge your debt
Than have ye doon your **devour**, atte leste.'   duty

❦ 'Host,' quod he, "**depardeux**, I assent;   by God
To **breke forward** is nat myn entent.   break the agreement
40   Byheste is dette and I wol holde fayn[9]
Al my byhest, I can no better sayn;
For such lawe as a man geveth another wight
He schuld him selve usen hit by right – [10]
Thus wol oure text, but natheles certeyn
I can right now non other tale sayn
That Chaucer, **they** he **can** but **lewedly**   though; knows; poorly
On metres and on rymyng, certeynly
Hath seyd hem in such Englisch as he can
Of olde tyme, as knoweth many man;
50   And yif he have nought sayd hem, **leeve** brother,   dear
In **o bok**, he hath seyd hem in another;   one book
For he hath told of lovers up and doun,
Moo than Ovide made of mencioun
In his Epistelles that be so olde – [11]
What schuld I tellen hem, syn they be tolde?
In youthe he **made of** Coys and Alcioun,   made poems about
And **siththen** hath he spoke of everychon   since
These noble wyfes and these lovers eeke:
Whoso wole his large volume seeke

7 'as you hope to be happy'
8 'and keep your promise'
9 'a promise is a debt and I will gladly keep all my promise'
10 'the way in which a man judges another should be the way in which he judges
   himself'
11 Ovid's letters by famous women (the Heroides).

Cleped the 'seintes legendes of Cupide'[12]   60
Ther may he see the large woundes wyde
Of Lucresse, and of Bablioun Tysbee,
The sorwe of Dido for the fals Enee,
The tree of Philles for hir Demephon,
The **pleynt** of Dyane and of Ermyon,   lament
Of Adrian and of Ysyphilee;
The barreyn yle stondyng in the see
The dreynt Leandere for his Erro;
The teeres of Eleyn, and eek the woo
Of Bryxseyde and of Ledomia,   70
The cruelte of the queen Medea;
The litel children hangyng by the **hals**   neck
For thilke Jason that was of love so fals.
O Ypermystre, Penollope and Alceste,
Youre wyfhood he comendeth with the beste;
But certeynly no worde writeth he
Of thilke wikked ensample of Canace,
That loved hir own brother synfully –
On which corsed stories I seye, 'Fy!' –
Or elles of Tyro Appoloneus,   80
How that the cursed Kyng Anteochus
Byreft his doughter of hir maydenhede –
That is so horrible a tale as man may reed –
Whan he hir threw upon the pavement:[13]
And therfore he, **of ful avysement**,   after careful consideration
Wolde never wryte in noon of his **sermouns**   writings
Of such **unkynde** abhominaciouns,   unnatural
Ne I wol non reherse, if that I may –
But of my tale, how schal I do this day?

12 The Legend of Good Women: the examples which follow appear in Chaucer's
   earlier work.
13 The tragic stories referred to here are those of Lucrece (raped by Tarquin), Thisbe
   (lover of Pyramus), Dido (deserted by Aeneas), Phyllis, Deianira (wife of Hercules,
   who inadvertently killed her husband), Hermione (lover of Orestes), Ariadne
   (rejected lover of Theseus), Hipsipyle, Hero (lover of Leander, who drowned in
   the Hellespont trying to reach her), Helen of Troy, Briseis (lover of Achilles),
   Laodamia (lover of Protesilaus). The wicked stories are those of Medea (lover of
   Jason, later rejected by him), and Canace. The faithful wives are Hypermenestra,
   Penelope (wife of Ulysses) and Alcestis (wife of Admetus).

90   Me were loth to be **lykned**, douteles,   likened
      To Muses, that men **clepen** Pyerides –   call
      Methamorphoseos wot what I mene[14]   Metamorphoses
      But natheles I **recche** nat a **bene**   value; bean
      They I come after him with **hawe bake**;   though; baked haws (berries)
      I speke in prose, and let him rymes make.'
      And with that word he with a **sobre cheere**   solemn mood
      Bygan his tale, as ye schal after heere.

                  Explicit prologus incipit fabula
                                    the prologue ends, the tale begins

      ❦ O hateful harm, condicioun of **povert**,   poverty
100   With thurst, with cold, with honger so **confoundyd**,   confused/upset
      To asken help it schameth in thin hert.
      If thou non aske, with neede so art thou woundyd,
      That verray neede unwrappeth al thy woundes hyd –
      Maugre thyn **heed** thou most for **indigence**   despite; care; utter lack
      Or stele, **or** begge, **or** borwe thy **dispence**.   either..or..or; living
      Thow **belamest** Crist and seyst full bitterly   blamest
      He **mysdeparteth riches temporal**;   shares unfairly; worldly riches
      And thyn neyhebour thou wytes syngully,[15]
      And seyst thou hast to litel and he hath al;
110   'Parfay,' seystow, 'som tyme he **rekne** schal,   by my faith; pay
      Whan that his tayl schal **breenen** in the **gleede**,   burn; glowing coals
      For he nought helpeth the needful in his neede.'

      Herkneth what is the **sentens** of the wyse –   judgement
      'Bet is to dye than have indigence;
      Thy **selve** neyghebour wol the despyse.   very
      If thou be pore, farwel thy **reverence**.'   esteem
      Yet of the wys man tak this sentence –
      'All the dayes of pore men be **wikke**;   evil
      Bewar, therfore, **or** thou come to the **prikke**.   before; end

      14 Pyerides – another name for the nine Muses. The reference is to Ovid's
         Metamorphoses, where many of the stories mentioned by the Man of Law,
         including references to the Muses.
      15 'single out for accusation'

Yif thou be pore, thy brother hateth the,   120
And alle thy frendes fleeth fro the'.
O riche **marchaunds**, ful of **wele** be ye!   merchants; prosperity
O noble prudent folk, as in this cas,
Youre bagges beth nat **fuld** with **ambes aas**,   filled; twin aces
But with **sys, synk**, that **renneth on your chaunce** – [16]
                                                six, five; riding your luck
At Crystemasse wel mery may ye daunce!

Ye **seek** land and **se** for youre **wynnynges**;   search; sea; profits
As wyse folk as ye knowe alle **thastates**   situations
Of **regnes**; ye be fadres of tydynges,   kingdoms
Of tales both of pees and of **debates**.   Conflicts   130
I were right now of tales **desolat**   entirely lacking
Nere that a marchaunt gon siththen many a yere[17]
Me taught a tale, which ye schal after heere.

In **Surrie** dewelled **whilom** a companye   Syria; once upon a time
Of **chapmen** riche, and therto **sad and trewe**,
                                merchants; assiduous and truthful
That **wyde where** sent her **spycerye**, [18]   far and wide; spices
Clothes of gold and satyn riche of hewe.
Her **chaffar** was so **thrifty** and so newe,   merchandise; useful
That every wight had **deynte to chaffare**   sought to trade with them
With **hem**, and eek to selle hem of here ware.   140

Now fel it that the maystres of that sort[19]
Han **schapen hem** to Rome for to **wende**:   planned; go
Were it for **chapmanhode** or for **disport**,   business; pleasure
Non other message **nolde** they thider sende,   would not
But came hemself to Rome; this is the ende.
And in such place as thought hem **avantage**   advantageous
For here **entent**, they tooke her **herburgage**.   purpose; lodging

16 Good 'throws' on a pair of dice.
17 'many years ago'
18 They appear to have been mercers, trading in luxury goods.
19 'those with authority in the group'

Sojourned have these marchaunts in the toun
A certeyn tyme, as fel to **here plesaunce**; *as they were pleased to*
150 But so bifell that thexcellent renoun
Of the emperour's dou*ght*er, Dame Constaunce,
Reported was, with every circumstaunce,
Unto these Surriens marchaunts; in such **wyse** *form*
Fro day to day, as I schal you **devyse**. *tell*

This was the comyn voys of every man,
'Oure emperour of Rome, **God him see**, *God save him*
A doughter hath, that **sith** the world bygan, *since*
To rekne as wel hir goodnes as hir **bewte**, *beauty*
Nas never such another as was sche.
160 I prey to God hir save and **susteene**, *keep*
And wolde sche were of al Europe the queene.

In hire is **hye** bewte withoute pryde, *great*
Yowthe withoute **grenhed** or folye, *immaturity*
To alle hire werkes vertu is hire gyde;
Humblesse hath slayne in hir **tyrannye**, *evil nature*
Sche is myrour of all curtesye,
Hir herte is verrey chambre of holynesse,
Hir hond mynistre of fredom and **almesse**.' *generosity*

And al this voys is **soth**, as God is trewe – *true*
170 But now to purpos let us turne agein –
These marchants have doon fraught hir shippes newe
And whan they have this blisful mayde **seyn**. *seen*
Home to Surrey be they went agein,
And doon here **needes** as they have don **yore**, *business; formerly*
And lyven in **wele**; I can you say no more. *prosperity*

Now fel it that these marchaunts stooden in grace
Of him that was the **sowdan** of **Surrye**; *sultan of Syria*
For whan they come fro eny straunge place
He wolde, of his benigne curtesye,
180 Make hem good chere, and busily **aspye** *seek*
Tydynges of sondry **regnes**, for to **lere** *kingdoms; learn*
The wordes that they mighte seen and heere.

Among other thinges specially
These marchaunts him told of Dame Constaunce,
So gret noblesse, in ernest, so ryally,
That this Sowdan hath caught so gret plesaunce
To have hir figure in his remembraunce,[20]
And al his **lust** and al his **besy cure**   desire; diligent effort
Was for to love hir, whiles his lyf may **dure**.   last

Par aventure in thilke large booke   perhaps   190
Which that is cleped the **heven** y-write was   heavens
With sterres, whan that he his burthe took,
That he for love schulde have his deth, allas![21]
For in the sterres clerere then is glas
Is wryten, **god woot**, whoso **cowthe** it rede,   God knows; knows how to
The deth of every man, withouten drede.

In sterres many a wynter therbyfore
Was write the deth of Ector and Achilles,
Of Pompe, Julius, er they were y-bore;[22]
The stryf of Thebes and of Ercules,   200
Of Sampson, Turnus, and of Socrates
The deth, but mennes wittes ben so dulle
That no wight can wel rede it at the fulle.

This sowdan for his pryve couseil sent,
And schortly, of this mater for to **pace**,   progress
He hath to hem declared his entent,
And seyd hem certeyn but he might have grace
To have Constance withinne a litel space,
He nas but **deed**, and charged hem in **hyhe**   dead; haste
To schapen for his lyf som remedye.   210

Dyverse men divers thinges seyde,   various
The argumentes casten up and doun;

20 'he couldn't get her out of his mind'
21 'perhaps his death was written in the stars'
22 Pompey, Julius Caesar (victor over Pompey), Hector and Achilles (heroes on
   opposing sides in the Trojan War), Sampson (the biblical Jewish hero), Turnus
   (enemy of Aeneas) and Socrates, the Greek philosopher executed with hemlock
   on a charge of 'corrupting youth'.

Many a **subtyl resoun** forth they **leyden**.   *careful argument; presented*
They spekyn of magike and of **abusioun**,   *deception*
But fynally, as in conclusioun,
They can nought seen in that non avantage,
Ne in non other wey, save in mariage.

Than sawgh they ther in such difficulte,
By wey of resoun, to speke it al playn,
220 Bycause that ther was such **dyversite**   *difference*
Bitwen here bothe **lawes**, as they sayn,   *laws of religion*
They **trowe** that, 'No cristen prince wold **fayn**   *believed; gladly*
Wedden his child under our lawe swete,
That us was taught by **Mahoun** oure prophete'   *Mahomet*

And he answerde, 'Rather than I **lese**   *lose*
Constance, I wold be Cristen douteles;
I **moot** be heres, I may non other **cheese**.   *must; choose*
I pray you, haldeth your arguments in pees;
Saveth my lyf, and beth nat **recheles**.   *careless*
230 **Both** geteth hire that hath my lyf **in cure**,   *but; in her care*
For in this wo I may no lenger **dure**.   *endure*

What needeth gretter **dilatacioun**?   *expansion*
I say, by **tretys** and **ambassatrye**   *petitions; embassies*
And by the Pope's mediacioun,
And al the chirche and al the chyvalrye,
That in destrucioun of **mawmetrye**,   *idol-worship*
And in **encresse** of Crist's lawe deere,   *expansion*
They ben **acordid**, as ye schal after heere,   *agreed*

How that the Soudan and his baronage,
240 And all his lieges schuld y-cristned be;
And he schal have Constance in mariage,
And certeyn gold – I **not** what quantite –   *don't know*
And therfore founden they **suffisant seurte**.   *enough security*
This same acord was sworn on every syde:
Now, fair Constance, Almighty God the **guyde**!   *guide*

Now wolde som men **wayten**, as I gesse,   *expect*
That I schulde tellen al the **purvyaunce**   *supplying of necessaries*

That the emperour of his gret noblesse
Hath schapen for his doughter, Dame Constaunce;
Wel may men knowe that so gret **ordynaunce**   ceremonial   250
May no man telle in so litel a clause,
As was **arrayed** for so high a cause.   set forth

Bisschops ben schapen with hir for to wende,
Lordes, ladyes, and knightes of renoun,
And other folk **ynowe** – this is the ende;   enough
And **notefied** is thurghout the toun   notified/proclaimed
That every wight, with gret devocioun,
Schulde preye Crist that he this mariage
Receyve in **gree**, and spede this **viage**.   favour; journey

The day is come of hire departyng –   260
I say, the woful day that than is come,
That ther may be no **lenger taryyng**,   longer; waiting
But fortheward they **dresse** hem **alle & some**:   get ready; one and all
Constance, that with sorwe is overcome,
Ful pale **arist** and **dresseth hir** to wende,   arose; got ready
For wel sche saugh ther nas non other **ende**.   conclusion

Allas! What wonder is it though sche wepte,
That schal be sent to straunge nacioun,
Fro freendes that so tenderly hir kepte,
And to be bounde undur subjeccioun   270
Of oon, sche knew nat his condicioun;[23]
Housbondes ben al goode, and han be yore[24] –
That knowen wyfes; I dar say no more.

'Fader,' sche seid, 'thy wrecched child Constaunce,
Thy yonge doughter, fostred up so softe;
And ye, my mooder, my soverayn plesaunce,
Over al thing **outaken** Crist on **loft**;   except; on high
Constance your child hir **recomaundeth** ofte   commends
Unto your grace, for I schal into Surrye;
Ne schal I never see you more with **ye**.   eye   280

23 'she didn't know what he was like'
24 'husbands are all good, and have always been so' (sarcasm intended).

Allas, unto the **barbre** nacioun   *barbarian*
I most anoon, **sethens** it is your wille;   *since*
But Crist, that **starf** for our redempcioun,   *died*
So geve me grace his hestes to fulfille.
I, wrecched womman, no fors they I spille;[25]
Wommen ben born to **thraldam** and **penaunce**,   *servitude; punishment*
And to ben under man's governaunce.'

I trowe at Troye whan Pirrus brak the wal[26]
Or Ileon that **brend** Thebes the citee,[27]   *burned*
290 Ne at Rome for the harme thurgh Hanibal[28]
That Romayns han **uenquysshed** tymes thre,   *conquered*
Nas herd such tender wepyng for pite,
As in the chambur was for hir partyng;
But forth sche moot, whether sche weep or syng.

O first mevyng, cruel firmament![29]
With thy **diurnal sweigh** that **crowdest** ay   *daily motion; presses*
And hurlest al fro est to **occident**   *west*
That naturelly wold hold another way
Thyn crowdyng sette the heven in such array
300 At the bygynnyng of this fiers viage,
That cruel **Marcs** hath slayn this marriage!   *Mars*

Infortunat ascendent tortuous,
Of which the lord's helples falle, allas,
Out of his angle into the derkest hous!
O Mars, Atteryere, as in this caas![30]

25 'as I'm a woman it doesn't matter if they sacrifice me'
26 Pyrrhus, sometimes mentioned as the son of Achilles.
27 Ilion, Greek name for Troy.
28 Hannibal, the Carthaginian general.
29 The Prime Mover, or the first, and outermost, of the nine spheres which medieval
   astronomers believed surrounded the earth. These were supposed to move in
   harmony with one another; Chaucer is here suggesting that the contrary,
   discordant, motions of the heavenly spheres are about to cause Constance's life
   to go wrong.
30 The scribe of the manuscript has not understood the astrological/astronomical
   references, and has written 'Atteryere', thinking it to be a proper name, instead
   of 'atazir', an astronomical term for a planet in association with nativity, or birth
   horoscope.

O feble moone, unhappy been thi **paas**!   course
Thou **knettest** the ther thou art nat **receyved**;   you join up; welcomed
Ther thou were wel, fro thennes artow weyved.³¹

Inprudent emperour of Rome, allas!
Was ther no philosopher in al thy toun?   310
Is no tyme bet than other in such caas?
Of viage is ther noon **eleccioun**,   choice
Namly to folk of heigh **condicioun**,   rank
Nought whan a roote is of a birthe y-knowe?³²
Allas, we ben to **lewed** or to slowe.   ignorant, unlearned

To schippe is brought this woful faire mayde,
Solempnely, with every circumstaunce.
Now, 'Jhesu Crist so be with you,' sche sayde.
Ther nys nomor but, 'Farwel, fair Custaunce.'
Sche peyneth hire to make **good contienaunce**;   look cheerful 320
And forth I lete hire sayle in this manere,
And torne I wol agein to my **matiere**.   story

The moder of the Sawdan, ful of vices,
Aspyed hath hir sones **playn entent**,   clear intention
How he wol **lete** his olde sacrifices;   give up
And right **anoon** sche for hir counseil sent,   immediately
And they hen come to knowe what sche ment.
And whan asembled was this folk **in fere**,   together
Sche sette hir doun, and sayd as ye schal heere.

'Lordes,' quod sche, 'ye knowen **everichon**,   each one of you 330
How that my sone **in poynt is** for to **lete**   is at the point of; leave
The holy lawes of oure Alkaroun.³³
Ye ben God's messangere, **Makamete**,   Mahomet

---

31 'you are taken away from where you 'belonged''
32 Such tragedy might be avoided if a horoscope could be calculated and used. The
   horoscope was based on knowledge of the precise date of birth, but this should
   be possible for a person of suitably high status, whose birth would be recorded.
33 The Koran, holy book of Islam. Medieval romances assume that Muslims worship
   false gods – Termagaunt, Apollon, and sometimes Mahound (a corruption of
   Mohamet).

But oon avow to grete God I **hete**;   vow
The lyf schuld rather out of my body stert
Or Makemete's law go out of myn hert.   before

What schal us tyden of this newe lawe   what will happen to us
But thraldam to oure body, and penaunce,
And afterward in helle to be drawe,
340 For we **reneyed** Mahound oure **creaunce**.   renounced; creator
But lordes, wol ye **maken** assuraunce   give
As I schal say, assentyng to my **lore**,   teaching/instructions
And I schal make us **sauf** for evermore.'   safe

They sworen and assenten every man,
To lyf with hir and dye, and by hir stonde,
And everich in the beste **wise** he can,   way
To strengthen hir schal al his frendes **fonde**.   call upon
And sche hath **emprise** take on honde,   enterprise
Which ye schul heere that I schal **devyse**,   explain
350 And to hem alle sche spak in this wyse:

'We schul first feyne ous Cristendom to take;
Cold watir schal nat greve us but **alite**, [34]   a little
And I schal such a fest and revel make
That as I trow, I schal the Sowdan **quyte**.   pay back
For though his wyf be cristned never so white,
Sche schal have need to waissche away the **rede**,   red
They sche a font of watir with hir **lede**.'   bring

O **sowdones**, root of iniquite!   sultaness
Virago, thou Semyran the secounde! [35]
360 O serpent under **feminite**!   the likeness of a woman
Lyk to the serpent deep in helle y-bounde! [36]
O feyned womman, alle that may confounde
Vertu and innocence, thurgh thy malice
Is bred in the, as nest of every vice!

34 The water of baptism.
35 Semiramus, an evil queen.
36 Satan, serpent of the garden of Eden, now in hell.

O Satan, envyous **syn thilke** day   since; the same
That thou were chased fro oure heritage![37]
Wel knewest thou to wommen the olde way!
Thou madest Eve to bryng us in **servage**;   servitude
Thou wolt **fordoon** the Cristen mariage.   destroy
Thyn instrument, so weylaway the while,   370
Makestow of wommen, whan thou wolt **bygyle**.   you make; trick

This Sawdones, whom I thus blame and **wary**,   curse
Let prively hir counseil gon his way.
What schuld I in this tale lenger tary?
Sche rideth to the Soudan on a day,
And seyd him that sche wold **reney hir lay**,   abandon her faith
And Cristendam of prest's handes **fonge**,   receive
Repentyng hir sche hethen was so longe,

Bysechyng him to doon hir that honour
That sche most have the Cristen men to feste.   380
'To plesen hem I wil do my labour.'
The Sowdan seith, 'I wol do at your **heste**.'   request
And knelyng, thanketh hir of that requeste.
So glad he was, he nyst nat what to **seye**;   say
Sche kyst hir sone, and hom sche goth hir weye.

Arryved ben the Cristen folk to londe
In Surry, with a gret solempne **route**,   company
And hastily this Sudan sent his **sonde**,   message/order
First to his moder and al the regne aboute,
And seyd his wyf was comen, out of doute,   390
And preyeth hir for to ride **agein the queene**,   to meet the queen
The honour of his regne to susteene.

Gret was the **prees** and riche was **tharray**   press (crowd); dress
Of Surriens and Romayns, mette **in feere**.   together
The moddur of the Sowdan, riche and gay,
Receyved hir with al so glad a cheere

37 A reference to the ending of the Creation story in Genesis, where the serpent is
cursed by God.

As eny moodir might hir doughter deere,
And to the nexte citee ther bysyde
A **softe paas** solempnely thay ryde.   gentle pace

400 Nought trow I the triumphe of Julius,[38]
Of which that Lukan maketh moche bost,
Was **ryaller** ne more **curious**   more regal; carefully contrived
Than was thassemble of this blisful **oost**;   host/crowd
But this Scorpioun, this wikked **goost**,   spirit
This Sowdones, for al hir flateryng,
Cast under this ful mortally to styng.   intended

The Sawdan comth himself sone after this,
So **really** that wonder is to telle,   royally
And welcometh hir with joy and blys,
410 And thus with mirth and joy I let hem dwelle –
The fruyt of this mateir is that I telle.
Whan tyme com men thought it for the best
That **revel stynt**, and men goon to her rest.   merrymaking ceased

The tyme com, the olde Sowdonesse
Ordeyned hath this fest of which I told;
And to the feste Cristen folk hem **dresse**,   go/attend
In general the both yong and old
Ther men may fest and **realte** byholde,   royalty
And **deyntes** mo than I can of **devyse** –   luxuries; tell
420 But al to deere they bought it, **ar** they ryse.   before

O **sodeyn** wo, that ever art successour   sudden/unexpected
To worldly blis! **Spreynd** is with bitternesse   sprinkled
The ende of our joye, of oure worldly labour!
Wo occupieth the **fyn** of oure gladnesse!   end
Herken this counseil, for thyn **sikernesse**:   safety
Upon thyn glade dayes, have in thi mynde
The **unwar woo** that cometh ay bihynde.   unexpected sadness

38 Lucan recorded Julius Caesar's victory over Pompey in Lucan's epic poem,
Pharsalia.

For schortly, for to tellen at o word,
The Sawdan, and the Cristen everichone,
Ben al to-hewe and stiked atte bord,[39]   430
But it were Dame Constaunce allone.   except
This olde Sowdones, this cursed crone,
Hath with hir frendes doon this cursed dede,
For sche hirself wold al the contre **lede**.   rule

No ther was Surrien noon that was converted,
That of the counseil of the Sawdon **woot**,   knew
That he was al to-hewe, or he **asterted**,   fled
And Constaunce have they take anon **foot hoot**,   in the utmost haste
And in a schippe **stereles**, God it woot,   rudderless
They have hir set, and **bad** hir lerne to **sayle**   told; sail   440
Out of Surry, ageinward to **Ytaile**.   Italy

A certein tresour that sche thider **ladde**,   brought
And, **soth** to sayn, **vitaile** gret plente,   truth; provisions
They have hir geven, and clothes **eek** sche hadde;   also
And forth sche sayleth to the salte see.
O my Constaunce, ful of **benignite**!   kindness/gentleness
O emperour's yonge doughter deere!
He that is Lord of fortun be thi **steere**!   steersman/pilot

Sche **blesseth hir**, and with ful pitous voys   crossed herself
Unto the **croys** of Crist than seyde sche,   cross   450
'O **cler**, O **welful auter**! Holy croys!   bright; lifegiving altar
Rood of the Lamb's blood, ful of pite,[40]   cross
That **wissh** the world fro old iniquite!   washes
Me fro the **feend** and fro his **clowes** keepe,   devil; claws
That day that I schal **drenchen** in the deepe!   drown

Victorious **tre**, proteccioun of **trewe**,   cross; true believers
That oonly were worthy for to bere
That kyng of heven, with his woundes newe,
The white lamb that hurt was with a spere,
Flemer of feendes out of him and here,   banisher   460

39 'hacked to pieces and killed at the table'
40 The rood is an image of the cross with the crucified Christ (the Lamb of God)
   hanging on it.

On which thy **lymes** feithfully extenden,   limbs
Me kepe, and gif me might my lyf to **menden**!'   amend/make better

Yeres and dayes **flette** this creature   float
Thurghout the see of Grece, into the strayte
Of **Marrok**, as it was hir **adventure**.   Morocco; chance
O, many a sory mele may sche **bayte**!   eat
After hir deth ful ofte may sche **wayte**,   expect
Or that the wilde **wawe** wol hir dryve   wave
Unto the place ther as sche schal arryve.

470 Men mighten aske why sche was nou*gh*t slayn,
     Ek at the fest who might hir body save?   also
     And I answered to that, demaunde agayn –
     Who saved Daniel in thoribble cave,[41]
     That every wight **sauf** he, mayste or knave,   except
     Was with the lioun **frete** or he asterte?   eaten
     No wight but God, that he **bar** in his herte.   carried

     God **lust** to schewe his wondurful miracle   desired
     In hir, for sche schuld seen his mighty werkes.
     Crist, which that is to every harm **triacle**   medicine
480 By **certeyn** menes ofte, as knowen clerkes,   particular
     Doth thing for certeyn ende that ful derk is
     To man's witt, that for our ignoraunce
     Ne can nought knowe his prudent **purvyaunce**.   provision

     Now **sith** sche was nat at the fest **y-slawe**,   since; slain
     Who kepte hir fro **drenching** in the see?   drowning
     Who kepte Jonas in the fisches mawe,[42]
     Til he was spouted up at Ninive?
     Wel may men know, it was no wight but he
     That kept the pepul Ebrayk fro her drenchyng,
490 With drye feet thurghout the see passyng.[43]

41 Daniel and his companions refused to sacrifice to Babylonian gods, and was put
   into a den of lions, where God saved him
42 Jonah disobeyed God, and was swallowed by a huge fish. God kept him alive,
   and he was fetched up again.
43 Moses and the Israelites crossed the Red Sea dry-shod through the intervention
   of God, who caused the waters to part.

Who badde foure spirits of tempest,
That power han to **noyen** land and see,   harm
Bothe north and south, and also west and est,
Anoyeth neyther londe, see, ne tree?
Sothly, the Comaunder of that was He
That fro the tempest ay this womman kepte,
As wel when sche awok as when sche slepte.

Wher might this womman mete and drinke have
Thre yer and more? How lasteth her vitaille?
Who fedde the Egipcien Marie in the cave,[44]   500
Or in desert? No wight but Crist, **sauns** faile.   without
Fyf thousand folk – it was a gret mervaile –
With **loves** fyf and fissches tuo to feede;   loaves
God sent his **foysoun** at her grete neede.[45]   plenty

Sche dryveth forth into **oure Occean**,   North Sea
Thurghout oure wilde see, til atte last
Under an **holte** that men **nempne** can,   castle; name
Fer in Northumberland the **wawe** hir cast;   wave
And in the sand the schip styked so fast
That thennes wold it noug*h*t, **in al a tyde**.   in one tide's length (of time)   510
The wille of Crist was that sche schold abyde.

The constabil of the castel doun is **fare**   gone
To se this **wrak**, and al the schip he sought,   wreck
And **fond** this wery womman, ful of care –   found
He fand also the tresour that sche brought.
In hir langage, 'Mercy!' sche **bisought**,   begged
The lif out of hir body for to **twynne**,   separate
Hir to **delyver of** woo that sche was inne.   free from

A maner **latyn corupt** was hir speche,   vulgar Latin
But **algates** therby sche was understonde.   nevertheless   520
The constabil, whan him lust no lenger **seche**,   seek
This woful womman broughte he to londe.

44 A fifth-century desert saint.
45 At the prayer of Christ, God fed five thousand people with five loaves and two
   fishes.

Sche kneleth doun and thanketh God's **sonde** –   provision
But what sche was, sche wolde no man seye
For foul ne faire, though sche scholde deye.   for good or ill

Sche was, sche seyd, so **mased** in the see   confused
That sche forgat hir mynde, **by hire trowthe**.   on her word
The constable had of hir so gret pitee,
And eek his wyf; they **wepeden** for **routhe**.   wept for pity
530 Sche was so diligent, withouten **slouthe**,   laziness
To serve and plese ever in that place,
That alle hir loven that loken on hir face.

The constable and Dame Hermegyld his wyf,
To telle you playne, in **peynes** bothe were;   of pagan faith
But Hermegyld loved Constance as hir lyf,
And Constance hath so long **herberwed** there   lodged
In orisoun, with many a bitter teere,
Til Jhesu converted, thurgh his grace,
Dame Hermegyld, the constable's wif of the place.

540 In al the lond no cristen men durst **route**;   meet together
Al cristen men ben fled from that contre
Thurgh **payen**, that conquered al aboute   pagans
The places of the north by land and see.
To Wales fled the Cristianite
Of olde Britouns dwellyng in this yle;
Ther was hir **refut** for the mene while.   refuge

But yit **nere** Cristen Britouns so exiled   were not
That ther nere some in here **pryvite**   secret
Honoured Crist, and hethen men **bygiled**.   tricked
550 And neigh the castel such ther dwellid thre,
That oon of hem was blynd and might nat se,
But if it were with eyen of his mynde,
With which men seen after that they ben blynde.

Bright was the sonne as in somer's day,
For which the constable and his wif also
And Constaunce had take the **righte** way   quickest
Toward the see, a forlong wey or two,

To pleyen and to romen to and fro;
And in that walk the blynde men they mette,
Croked and olde, with eyen **fast y-schette**. tightly shut 560

'In name of Crist!' cryed this old britoun,
'Dame Hermegyld, gif me my sight ageyn!'
This lady **wax affrayed** of the soun, grew afraid
Lest that hir houseband, schortly to sayn,
Wold hir for Jhesu Crist's love have slayn;
Til Constaunce made hir bold, and bad hir **werche** work/do
The wil of crist, as dou*g*hter of holy chirche.

The constable **wax abaisshed** of that sight, troubled
And sayde, '**What amounteth al this fare?**' what's all this about
Constaunce answered, 'Sir, it is Crist's might, 570
That helpeth folk out of the feend's snare.'
And **so ferforth** sche gan hir **lay** declare, to such an extent; faith
That sche the constable, or that it was **eve**, evening
Converted, and on Crist made him bileve.

This constable was no thing lord of the place
Of which I speke, ther he Constance fond;
But kept it strongly many a wynter space
Under **Alla**, kyng of Northumberlond, Aella
That was ful wys and worthy **of his hond** in fighting
Agein the Scottes, as men may wel heere – 580
But tourne agein I wil to my mateere.

Satan, that ever us wayteth to begile,
Sawe of Constaunce the perfeccioun,
And cast anoon how he might **quyt** hir while, get his own back
And made a yong knight that dwelt in the toun
Love hir so hoot of foul affeccioun,
That verrayly him thou*g*ht he schulde **spille** die
But he of hire oones had his wille.

He **wowith** hir, but it avayleth nought. woos
Sche wolde do no synne by no weye, 590
And for despyt he **compassed** in his thought imagined
To maken hir a schamful deth to deye.

He wayteth whan the constable was aweye,
And pryvyly upon a nyght he crepte
In Hermyngyldes chambre, whil sche slepte.

Wery, **forwaked in here orisoun**,   tired out by praying
Slepeth Constaunce, and Hermyngyld also.
This knight, thurgh Satanas temptacioun,
Al softely is to the bed y-go,
600 And kutte the throte of Hermegild **a-two**,   in two
And leyd the bloody knyf by Dame Constaunce,
And went his way, that God geve him **meschaunce**!   ill luck

Sone after comth this constable hom agayn,
And eek Alla, that kyng was of that lond,
And say his wyf dispitously y-slayn,
For which ful ofte he wept and wrong his hond;
And in the bed the blody knyf he fond
By Dame Custaunce – allas! What might he say?
For verray woo **hir witt was al away**.   she'd lost her mind

610 To king Alla was told al this meschaunce,
And eek the tyme, and wher and eek the **wyse**   manner
That in a schip was founden this Constaunce,
As here bifore ye have herd me devyse.
The king's hert of pite gan **agrise**,   trouble
Whan he saugh so benigne a creature
Falle in **disese**, and in mysaventure.   unhappiness

For as the lomb toward his deth is brought,
So stant this innocent bifore the kyng.
This false knight, that hath this tresoun wrought,
620 **Bereth hir an hand** that sche hath don this thing.   told secretly
But nevertheles ther was gret mornyng
Among the poeple, and **seyn** they can not **gesse**   they say; contemplate
That sche had doon so gret a wikkednesse.

For they han seyen hir so vertuous,
And lovyng Hermegyld right as hir lyf –
Of this bar witnesse **everich** in that hous,   everyone
Save he that slow*gh* Hermegyld with his knyf.

This gentil kyng **hath caught a gret motyf**   was greatly moved
Of his witnesse, and thought he wold enquere
Deppere in this cas, a trouth to **lere**.   deeper; learn   630

Allas, Constaunce! Thou ne has no champioun!
Ne fighte canstow nat, so welaway!
But He that for oure redempcioun
Bonde Sathan and yit lith ther he lay,[46]
So be thy stronge champioun this day!
For but Crist upon the miracle **kythe**,   reveal
Withouten gilt thou schalt be slayn, **as swithe**.   immediately

Sche set hir doun on knees and than sche sayde,
'Immortal God, that savedest Susanne[47]
For false blame, and thou mercyful mayde   640
Mary; I mene, doughter of Seint Anne,
Bifore whos child aungeles syng Osanne![48]
If I be gultles of this felonye,
My **socour** be; for elles schal I dye!'   help

Have ye not seye somtyme a pale face
Among a **prees** of him that hath be **lad**   crowd; led
Toward his deth, wher him **geyneth no grace**,   get no mercy
And such a colour in his face hath had,
Men mighte knowe his face was so **bystad**?   troubled
Among all the faces in that **route**   company   650
So stant Constance, and loketh hire aboute.

O queenes, lyvyng in prosperite!
Duchesses, and ye ladies everychon –
Haveth som **reuthe** on hir adversite;   pity
An emperoure's dou**ght**er stond allon;
Sche nath no wight to make hir **moon**.   complaint
O blod ryal, that stondest in this **drede**,   danger
Ferre be thy frendes at thy grete neede!   far

46 Christ bound Satan by his death on the Cross.
47 Susanna was brought before the elders under a false accusation in the Book of
   Susannah (Apocrypha).
48 The Virgin Mary, daughter of St Anne.

This Alla kyng hath such compassioun,
660   As gentil hert is fulfild of pite,
      That from his eyen ran the water doun:
      'Now hastily do fech a book,' quod he,
      'And if this knight wil swere how that sche
      This womman slow*gh*, yet wol we us **avyse**   consider
      Whom that we wille schal be oure justise.'

      A britoun book y-write with Evaungiles[49]
      Was fette, and on this book he swor anoon
      Sche **gultif** was, and in the menewhiles   guilty
      An hond him smot upon the nekke **boon**,   bone
670   That doun he fel anon, right at a stoon,
      And bothe his **yen** brast out of his face,   eyes
      In sight of every body in that place.

      A vois was herd in general audience
      And seist, 'Thou hast **disclaundred** gulteles   slandered
      The doughter of holy chirche; in hire presence
      Thus hastow doon, & yit I holde my pees.'
      Of this mervaile agast was al the **prees**:   crowd
      As **mased** folk they stooden everychon   amazed
      For drede of **wreche**, save Custaunce alone.   vengeance

680   Gret was the drede, and eek the repentaunce
      Of hem that hadden gret **suspeccioun**   suspicion
      Upon the sely innocent Custaunce;
      And for this miracle, in conclusioun,
      And by Custaunce's mediacioun,
      The kyng and many other in the place
      Converted was, thanked by Crist's grace.

      This false knight was slayn for his untrouthe
      By juggement of Alla, hastyly,
      And yit Custaunce hath of his deth gret routhe;
690   And after this, Jhesus of his mercy
      Made Alla wedde, fule solempnely,

49 A celtic gospel-book.

This holy mayde that is bright and schene;
And thus hath Crist y-maad Constance a queene.

But who was woful – if I schal not lye –
Of this weddyng but Domegild, and no mo:
The kyng's mooder, ful of **tyrannye**,   evil
Hir thought hir cursed herte **brast** a-two.   burst
Sche wolde nat hir sone had y-do so;
Hir thought despyte that he schulde take
So straunge a creature unto his **make**.   mate   700

Me lust not of the **caf**, ne of the **stree**,   chaff; straw
Make so long a tale, as of the corn:
What schuld I telle of the **realte**   royalty
Of mariage, or which cours goth biforn;
Who bloweth in a trompe, or in an horn?[50]
The fruyt of every tale is for to seye –
They ete & drynk, and daunce, and synge, and pleye.

They gon to bed, as it was **skile** & right –   reasonable
For though that wyfes be ful holy thinges,
They moste take in pacience a-night   710
Such maner necessaries as be plesynges
To folk that han y-wedded hem with rynges;
And **halvendel** her holynesse ley aside –   for a while
And for the tyme, it may non other betyde.

On hire he gat a **knave** child anoon,   boy
And to a bisschope & a constable **eeke**   also
He took his wyf, to kepe whan he is goon
To **Scotlondward**, his **foomen** for to seeke.   towards Scotland; enemies
Now, faire Custaunce, that is so humble & meke,
So long is goon with childe til that stille   720
Sche **held** hir chambre, **abidyng** God's wille.   stayed in; awaiting

The tyme is come, a knave child sche bere;
Maurius **atte funtstoun** men him calle.   at the font (baptism)

50 Each course at the feast was introduced by music.

This constabil **doth** come forth a messager,   orders
And wrot to his kyng, that cleped was Alle,
How that this blisful tydyng is bifalle,
And other thinges; **spedful** for to seye,   quickly
He taketh the lettre, and forth he goth his weye.

This messanger, to **doon his avauntage**,   advance himself
730 Unto the kynges moder he goth ful **swithe**,   quickly
And salveth hire fair in his langage:
'Madame,' quod he, 'ye may be glad and **blithe**,   happy
And thanke god an hundred thousand **sithe**!   times
My lady queen hath child, withouten doute,
To joye and blis of al the reame aboute.

Lo! Heer the lettres sealed of this thing,
That I mot bere with al the hast I may.
If ye wole ought unto youre sone the kyng,
I am youre servaunt both night and day.'
740 Doungyld answerde, 'As now this tyme, nay,[51]
But here al nyght I wol thou take thy rest;
To morwen I wil say the what me **lest**.'   tomorrow; likes

This messanger drank **sadly** ale and wyn,   assiduously
And stolen were his lettres pryvely
Out of his box, whil he sleep **as a swyn**,   like a pig
And countrefeet they were subtily.
Another sche him wroot ful synfully
Unto the kyng direct, of this matiere,
Fro his constable – as ye schul after heere.

750 The lettre spak the queen delyvered was
Of so orryble and feendly creature,
That in the castel noon so **hardy** was   bold
That eny while dorste therin endure:
The mooder was an elf, by **aventure**   chance
Bycome, by charmes, or by sorcerie,
And every man hatith hir companye.

51 'not right now'

Wo was this kyng whan he this letter had **sein**,   seen
But to no wight he told his sorwes sore,
But of his own hand he wrot agayn,
'Welcome the **sond** of Crist for everemore   commandment   760
To me, that am now lerned in this lore.
Lord, welcome be thy **lust** and thy **plesaunce** –   desire; pleasure
My lust I putte al **in thyn ordinaunce**.   at your disposal

Kepeth this child, al be it **foul** or fair,   ugly
And eek my wyf unto myn hom comyng,
Crist whan him lust may sende me an **hair**   heir
More agreable than this to my likyng.'
The lettre he seleth, pryvyly wepyng,
Which to the messager he took ful sone;
And forth he goth – ther nys no more to done.   770

O messager, fulfiled of dronkenesse!
Strong is thy breth, thy lymes **faltren** ay,   falter
And thou **bywreyest** all **sykernesse**.   betrayest; sureness
Thy mynde is **lorn**, thou **janglest** as a jay,   lost; chatter
Thy face is torned al in a newe array.
Ther drunkenesse regneth in eny route,   wherever
Ther is no counseil hid, withouten doute.

O Domegyld, I have non Englisch digne
Unto thy malice and thy tyrannye!
And therfor to the feend I the resigne;   780
Let him **endyten** of thi treccherie.   write
Fy, **mannyssch**! Fy! O nay, be God, I lye!   man-like/human
Fy, feendly spirit! For I dar wel telle
Though thou here walke, thy spirit is in helle.

This messanger comth fro the kyng agayn,
And at the king's modre's court he **light**;   alighted (from his horse)
And sche was of this messenger ful **fayn**,   welcoming/glad
And pleseth him in al that ever sche might.
He drank, and wel **his gurdel underpight**;   filled his belly
He slepeth and he fareth in his gyse   790
Al nyght, unto the sonne gan arise.

Eft were his lettres stolen everichon,
And countrefeted lettres in this wise:
The kyng comaundeth his constable anon,
Up peyne of hangyng of an heigh justise,
That he ne schulde suffre in no maner wyse
Constaunce in his regne for to abyde
Thre dayes and a quarter of a tyde.

But in the same schip as he hir fond,
800   Hire and hir yonge sone, and al hire gere
He schulde putte, and **crowde** fro the londe,   push
And charge hire that sche never **eft** come there.   afterwards
O, my Constaunce, wel may thy **goost** have fere,   spirit
And, slepyng, in thy drem ben in penaunce,
Whan Domegyl **cast al this ordynaunce**!   made all these things happen

This messanger, a-morwe whan he awook,
Unto the castel held the **nexte** way,   closest
And to the constable he the lettre took,
And whan that he the pitous lettre say,
810   Ful ofte he seyd, 'Allas, and welaway!
Lord Crist!' quod he, 'how may this world endure?
So ful of synne is many a creature.

O mighty God, if that it be thy wille,
Seth thou art rightful jugge – how may this be,
That thou wolt suffre innocents to **spille**,   die
And wikked folk regne in prosperite?
O good Constance, allas, so wo is me
That I moot be thy tormentour, or deye
On schamful deth – ther is non other weye!'

820   Wepyng, both yong & olde in al that place,
Whan that the kyng this corsed lettre sent,
And Constance, with a dedly pale face,
The fayre day toward hir schip sche went.
But nevertheles, sche taketh in good entent
The wil of Crist and, knelyng on the grounde,
Sche sayde, 'Lord, **ay** welcome be thy sonde.   always

He that me kepte fro the false blame
Whil I was on the lond amonges you,
He can me kepe from harm, & eek fro schame
In see, although I se nat how.   830
As strong as ever he was, he is right now –
In him trust I, & in his mooder deere,
That is to me my sayl and eek my **steere**.'   steersman

Hir litel child lay wepyng in hir arm,
And knelyng pitously, to him sche sayde,
'Pees, litel sone, I wol do the noon harm.'
With that hir kerchef of hir hed sche **brayde**,   took
And over his litel **yyen** sche it layde,   eyes
And in hir arm sche **lullith** it wel faste,   cradles
And unto heven hir eyyen up sche caste.   840

'Moder,' quod sche, 'and mayde, bright Marie,
Soth is that thurgh womman's **eggement**   incitement ('egging on')
Mankynde was lorn, and dampned ay to dye;
For which thy child was on a cros to-rent.
Thyn blisful eyyen sawh al this torment;
Then nys ther noon comparisoun bitwene
Thy wo, and any woo may nat sustene.[52]

Thow saugh thy child **y-slaw byfor thyn yen**,   killed before your eyes
And yit now lyveth my litel child, **par fay**.   by my faith
Now, lady bright, to whom all woful cryen,   850
Thou glory of wommanhod, thou faire **may**;   maid (virgin)
Thou heven of **refute**, bright sterre of day,   refuge
Rewe on my child, that of thyn gentilnesse   have pity
Rewest on every synful in destresse.

O litel child, allas! What is thi gilt,
That never **wroughtest** synne as yet, **parde**?   did; by God
Why wil thyn harde fader han the spilt?
O mercy deere, and constable,' seyde sche,

---

52 Here the scribe of the manuscript has erred – the line should read 'any woo man
   may sustene', which makes sense.

'And let my litel child here dwelle with the;
860   And if thou darst not saven him for blame,
So kys him oones, in his fadre's name.'

Therwith sche loked bakward to the lond,
And seyde, 'Farwel, housbond **rewtheles**.'   pitiless
And up sche **rist** and walketh doun the **stronde**   rises; beach
Toward the schip; hir folweth al the prees.
And ever sche preyeth hir child to hold his pees,
And took hir leve, and with an holy entent
Sche **blesseth hire**, and to the schip sche went.   crosses herself

Vytailled was the schip, it is no drede,
870   Abundauntly for hire a ful longe space,
And other necessaries that schulde nede
Sche had ynou*gh*, **heryed** be Crist's grace;   blessed
For wynd and water Almighty God **purchace**   provide
And bryng hir hom, I can no bettre say,
But in the see sche **dryveth** forth hir way.   goes

Alla the kyng comth hom soon after this,
Unto the castel of the which I tolde,
And asketh wher his wyf and his child ys.
The constable **gan** about his herte colde,   became
880   And playnly al the maner he him tolde
As ye han herd – I can telle it no better –
And schewed the kyng's seal and his letter.

And seyde, 'Lord, as ye comaunded me
Up peyne of deth, so have I do certayn.'
This messager **tormented** was til he   tortured
Moste **biknowe**, and telle it **plat** and playn   reveal; blunt
Fro nyght to night in what place he had layn;
And thus by witt and subtil enqueryng,
Ymagined was by wham this gan to spryng.

890   The hand was knowen that the lettre wroot,
And al the venym of this cursed dede,
But in what wyse certeynly I **noot**.   do not know
Theffect is this; that Alla, out of drede,

His moder **slough**, as men may pleynly reede;   killed
For that sche traytour was to hir **ligeaunce**,   allegiance
Thus endeth olde Domegild, with meschaunce.

The sorwe that this Alla night and day
maketh for his wyf, and for his child also,
Ther is no tonge that it telle may;
But now I wol unto Custaunce go,   900
That **fleeteth** in the see, in peyne and wo,   floats
V yeer and more, as liketh Crist's **sonde**,   five; providence
Er that hir schip approched unto londe.

Under an hethen castel atte last,
Of which the name in my text nou**g**ht I fynde,
Constaunce and eek hir child the see upcast.
Almighty God, that saveth al mankynde,
Have on Constaunce and on hir child som mynde,
That fallen is in hethen hond **eftsone**,   once more
In poynt to spille – as I schal telle you soone.   910

Doun fro the castel cometh many a wight
To **gawren** on this schip, and on Constaunce,   gaze
But schortly fro the castel on a night
The lord's styward – God give him meschaunce! –
A theef that had **reneyed** oure **creaunce**,   abandoned; faith
Com into schip alone, and seyd he scholde
Hir **lemman** be, whethir sche wold or nolde.   lover

Wo was this wrecched womman tho **bigoon**!   come upon
Hire childe crieth, and sche, pytously;
But blisful Mary **hilp** hir right anoon,   helped   920
For with hir strengthe wel and mightily
The theef fel overboord al sodeinly,
And in the see he drenched for vengaunce,
And thus hath crist **unwemmed** kept Constance.   Untouched

O foule lust! O **luxurie**! Lo, thin ende!   lechery (concupiscence)
Nought oonly that thou **feyntest** man's **mynde**,   weaken; reason
But verrayly thou wold his body **schende**.   destroy
The ende of thyn werk or of thy lustes blynde

Is compleynyng – how many may men fynde
930 That nought for **werk** som tyme, but for thentent   the doing
To doon his synne, ben **eyther** slayn or schent?   either

How may this **weyke** womman han the strengthe   weak
Hir to defende agein the **renegat**?   renegade
O Golias, unmesurable of lengthe
How mighte David make the so mate,[53]
So yong and of armure so **desolate**?   lacking
How dorst he loke upon thyn dredful face?
Wel may men seyn, it nas but God's grace.

Who gaf Judith corage or hardynesse,
940 To slen him Olefernes in his tent,[54]
And to delyveren out the wrecchednes
The peple of God? I say in this entent,
That right as God spiryte and vigor sent
To hem, and saved hem out of meschaunce,
So sent he might and vigor to Constaunce.

Forth goth hir schip thurghout the **narwe** mouth   narrow
Of **Jubalt[er]** and Septe, dryvyng ay,[55]   Gibraltar
Somtyme west, and som tyme north and south,
And som tyme est, ful many a wery day;
950 Til Crist's mooder, blessed be sche ay,
Hath schapen, thurgh hir endeles goodnesse,
To make and ende of hir hevynesse.

Now let us stynt of Constance but a **throwe**,   while
And speke we of the Romayn emperour,
That out of Surrye hath by lettres knowe
The slaughter of cristen folk, and deshonour
Doon to his doughter by a fals traytour –
I mene the cursed and wikked sowdenesse,
That at the fest **leet** slee bothe more and lesse.   commanded

53 The boy David killed the giant Philistine Goliath with stones from a sling.
54 Judith saved her city from the general Holofernes by going to his tent and cutting
off his head whilst he slept
55 The boat passes through the Straits of Gibraltar into the Mediterranean (Gibraltar
is on the north side, Septe on the south).

For which this emperour hath sent anoon   960
His senatours, with **real ordynaunce**,   royal ordinance (artillery)
And other lordes, God wot, many oon,
On **Surriens** to take high vengeaunce.   Syrians
They **brenne**, sleen, and bringen hem to meschaunce   burn
Ful many a day, but schortly this is thende;
Homward to Rome they schapen hem to wende.

This senatour **repayreth** with victorie   returns
To Romeward, saylyng ful really,
And mette the schip dryvyng, as seth the story,
In which Constance sitteth ful pitously.   970
Nothing ne new he what sche was, ne why
Sche was in such **aray**; sche nolde seye   a state
Of hire **astaat**, although sche scholde deye.   status

He bryngeth hir to Rome and to his wyf
He gaf hir, and hir yonge sone also,
And with the senatour lad sche hir lyf.
Thus can our lady bryngen out of woo
Woful Constance and many another moo;
And longe tyme dwelled sche in that place
In holy werkes, as ever was hir grace.   980

The senatour's wif hir aunte was,
But for al that sche knew hir never more.
I wol no lenger taryen in this cas,[56]
But to Kyng Alla, which I spak of **yore**,   long ago
That for his wyf wepeth and **siketh** sore   sighs
I wol retorne, and **lete** I wol Constaunce   leave
Under the senatour's governaunce.

Kyng Alla, which had his mooder slayn,
Upon a day fel in such repentaunce,
That if I shortly telle schal playn –   990
To Rome he cometh, to receyve his penaunce,
And putte him in the pope's **ordynaunce**   guidance

56 'I won't talk about this any longer'

In heigh and lowe, and Jhesu Crist bysought
Forgef his wikked werkes that he wrought.

The fame anon thurgh Rome toun is born
How Alla kyng schal come in pilgrymage,
By **herberiurs** that wenten him biforn,   harbingers
For which the senatour, as was usage,
Rood **him agein**, and many of his lynage,   to meet him
1000   As wel to schewen his magnificence
As to doon eny kyng a reverence.

Gret cheere doth this noble senatour
To kyng Alla, and he to him also;
Everich of hem doth other gret honour,
And so bifel that, on a day or two,
This senatour is to kyng Alla go
To fest, and – schortly, if I schal not lye –
Constance's sone went in his companye.

Som men wold seyn at request of Custaunce
1010   This senatour hath lad this child to feste,
I may not telle every circumstaunce –
Be as be may, theer was he, atte leste,
But soth it is right – at his modre's heste,
Byforn hem alle **duryng the mete's space**,   whilst the meal lasted
The child stood lokyng in the kyng's face.

This Alla kyng hath of the child gret wonder,
And to the senatour he seyd anoon,
'Whos is that faire child that stondeth yonder?'
'**I not**' quod he, 'by God and by Seynt John –   do not know
1020   A moder he hath, but fader hath he non.'
That I of woot, and schortly, **in a stounde**,   in a short while
He told Alla how that thus child was founde.

'But, God woot,' quod this senatour also,
'So vertuous a lyver in my lyf
Ne saugh I never such as sche; **nomo**   no more
Of worldly womman, mayden or of wyf –
I dar wel say sche hadde lever a knyf

Thurghout hir brest, than ben a womman wikke.
Ther is no man can bryng hir to that **prikke**   point

Now was this child as lik unto Constaunce   1030
As possible is a creature to be;
This Alla hath the face in remembraunce
Of Dame Custance, and theron **mused** he,   contemplated
If that the child's mooder **were ought sche**   might not be she
That is his wyf, and pryvely he **sight**,   sighed
And sped him fro the table, **that he might**.   when he could

'Parfay,' thought he, '**fantom** is in myn heed –   illusion
I ought to **deme** of rightful juggement   judge
That in the salte see my wyf is deed.'
And afterward he made this argument: 1040
'What **woot** I wher Crist hath hider sent   know
My wyf by see, as wel as he hir sent
To my contre, fro thennes that sche went?'

And after noon home with the senatour
Goth Alla, for to see this wonder chaunce.
This senatour doth Alla gret honour,
And hastely he sent after Custaunce,
But trusteth wel, hir luste nat to daunce
Whan that sche wiste whefore was that sonde –
Unnethes on hir feet sche mighte stonde.   hardly 1050

Whan Alla saugh his wyf, fayre he hire **grette**,   greeted
And wepte that it was rewthe to se;
For at the firste look he on hir sette
He knew wel verrely that it was sche,
And for sorwe as domb sche stant as **tre**,   tree
So was hire herte **schett** in his distresse,   shut
Whan sche remembred his unkyndenesse.

Twies sche swowned in his owen sight;
He wept, and him excuseth pitously:
'Now God,' quod he, 'and alle his **halwes** bright   saints 1060
So wisly on my soule have mercy,
That of youre harm as gulteles am I

As is Maurice my sone so lyk youre face –
Elles the feend me **fecche** out of this place!'   seize

Long was the sobbyng and the bitter peyne
Or that here woful herte mighte cesse;   before
Gret was the pite, for to here hem **pleyne**,   complain/bemoan
Thurgh whiche playnt gan here wo **encresse**.   grow greater
I pray you all my labour to relesse –[57]
1070 I may not telle al here sorwe unto morwe,
I am so wery for to speke of the sorwe.

But fynally, whan that **the soth is wist**   the truth is known
That Alla gilteles was of hir woo,
I trowe an hundred tymes they ben kist,
And such a blys if ther bitwix hem tuo
That, save the joye that lasteth eveermo,
Ther is noon lyk that eny creature
Hath **seyn**, or schal whil that the world may **dure**.   seen; endure

Then prayde sche hir housbond meekely
1080 **In the relees** of hir pytous **pyne**,   to relieve; pain/suffering
Thet he wold **preye** hir fader specially,   beg
That of his majeste he wold **enclyne**   stoop
To vouchesauf somtyme with him to dyne.
Sche preyeth him eek he schulde by no weye
Unto hir fader no word of hir seye.

Som men wold seye that hir child Maurice
Doth his message unto the emperour,
But as I gesse Alla was nat so **nyce**   ill-mannered/ill-advised
To him that is soverayn of honour,
1090 As he that is of Crist's folk the flour,
Sent eny child; but it is best to **deeme**   consider
He went himsilf – and so it may wel seme.

This emperour hath graunted gentilly
To come to dyner, as he him bysought,

57 'let me stop telling this story (release my labour)'

And wel **reded** I, he loked **besily**   read; intently
Upon the child, and on his doughter thought.
Alla goth to his **in**, and as him ought   house (where he was staying)
Arrayed for this fest in every wyse,
As **ferforth** as his **connyng** may suffise.   far; ingenuity/knowledge

The morwe cam, and Alla gan him dresse,   1100
And eek his wyf, the emperour for to meete;
And for they ryde in joye and in gladnesse,
And whan sche saugh hir fader in the streete
Sche light adoun, and falleth **him to feete**.   at his feet
'Fader,' quod sche, 'your yonge child Constance
Is now **ful clene** out of your remembraunce.   entirely

I am your doughter Custance,' quod sche,
'That whilom ye have sent unto Surrye.
It am I, fader, that in the salte see
Was put alloon, and dampned for to dye.   1110
Now, goode fader, mercy I you crye –
Send me no more unto noon hethenesse,
But thanke my lord her of his kyndenesse.'

Who can the pytous joye telle al
Bitwix hem thre, **sith** they be thus y-mette?   since
But of my tale make an ende I schal:
The day goth fast, I wol no lenger **lette**   delay
This glade folk – to dyner they ben sette.
In joye and blys at mete I let hem dwelle,
A thousandfold wel more than I can telle.   1120

This child Maurice was **siththen** Emperour   afterwards
Y-maad by the pope, and lyved cristenly.
To Crist's chirche dede he gret honour;
But I let al his story passen by –
Of Custaunce is my tale specially.
In olde Romayn **gestes** men may fynde   histories
Maurice's lyf – I bere it nought in mynde.

This kyng Alla, whan he his tyme **say**,   saw
With his Constaunce, his holy wyf so swete,
1130 To Engelond they com the **righte** way,   shortes
Wheras they lyve in joye and in quyete –
But litel whil it last, I you **biheete**:   assure
Joy of this world for tyme wol not abyde,
For day to night it changeth as the tyde.

Who lyved ever in such delyt a day,
That him ne **meved** eyther his conscience,   troubled
Or ire, or talent, or som maner affray;
Envy, or pride, or passioun, or offence?
I ne say but for this ende, this sentence:
1140 But litel whil in joye or in plesaunce
Lasteth the blis of Alla with Constaunce.

For deth, that taketh of heigh & low his rent,
Whan passed was a yeere, as I gesse,
Out of this worlde kyng Alla he **hent**,   took/seized
For whom Custauns hath ful gret hevynesse.
Now let us pray that God his soule blesse.
And Dame Custaunce, fynally to say,
Toward the toun of Rome goth hir way.

To Rome is come this nobil creature,
1150 And **fynt** hir freendes ther, bothe hool & sound.   found
Now is sche **skaped** al hir aventure,   escaped
And whanne sche hir fader had y-founde,
Doun on hir knees falleth sche to grounde,
Wepyng for tendirnes, in herte blithe,
Sche **heried** god an hundred thousand **sithe**.   blessed; times

In vertu and in holy almesdede
They lyven all, and never **asondre wende**:   apart; went
Til deth departe hem this lyf they lede.
And far now wel, my tale is at an ende;
1160 Now Jhesu Crist that of his might may sende
Joy after wo, governe us in his grace,
And keep ous alle that ben in this place.'

❦ Our **ost** upoon his **styrops** stood anoon   host; stirrups
And seyde, 'Good men, **herkneth everychoon**!   listen, each one of you
This was a **thrifty** tale for the noones!   useful
Sir parissh prest,' quod he, 'for God's boones!
Tel out a tale, as was thy **forward** yore!   agreement
I see wel that ye **lered** men in **lore**   learned; learning
Can moche good, by God's **dignete**!'   knows a thing or two
The parsoun him answerde, '**Benedicite**!   God bless us 1170
What **eyleth** the man, so synfully to swere?'   is wrong with
Our ost answerd, 'O Jankyn, be ye there?
I smel a **loller** in the wynd!' quod he.   lollard (heretic)
'Now, good men,' quod our oste, 'herkneth me,
Abydeth, for Goddes **digne** passioun, wait a bit;   worthy
For we schal have a **predicacioun** –   sermon
This loller wolde **prechen us** heer somwhat.'   preach to us
'Nay, by my fader soule, that schal ne that!'
Sayde the sompnour, 'He schal heer nought preche;
He schal no gospel preche here, ne teche.
We **levyn** all in the grete God,' quod he,   believe 1180
'He wolde **schewen** som difficulte,   reveal
Or **springen cokkil** in our clene corn;   corn cockle will spring up
And therfor oft I warne the byforn –
My joly body schal a tale telle,
And I schal clynken you so mery a belle
That I schal waken al this companye,
But it schal nat ben of philosophie,
Ne phylyas, ne termes queynte of lawe,[58]
Ther is but litel Latyn in my **mawe**!'   mouth

Here endith the man of lawe his tale   1190

---

58 'nor files (word unknown, probably a technical term from the summoner's court experience: could possibly also mean 'cases' or 'legal formulae'), nor peculiar terms used by lawyers (or 'in court').

THE WIFE OF BATH'S PROLOGUE AND TALE

The wife says that she will tell all about her experiences of marriage. She proceeds to talk about her five husbands. She lists the authorities who tell of the woes of married life, and the evil natures of women, then demolishes these arguments with her own, practical, logic. She admits that she is a liar, and describes how she put her first four husbands through purgatory while they were alive. She used her sexuality to gain financial profit, and nagged her husbands ceaselessly, and yet they loved her, because she was such a good companion. Her fourth husband was a lecher, who made her jealous, and yet she committed adultery with her friend's lodger, a 'hende' clerk named Jankin. When her husband died, she married him. Jankin would not allow her to do anything she liked, he beat her and read to her from a book of 'wikked wives', until she, literally, tore a leaf out of his book. He hit her so hard that she fell down as if dead. Thinking he had killed her, Jankin swore to let her have sovereignty ('maistrie') over him. She 'miraculously' recovered, and made him burn his book, but from then on they had an ideal marriage, although the incident left her 'somdeel' deaf. She is now looking for her sixth husband.

A young knight at the court of King Arthur meets a young girl on his travels, and rapes her. Although he should die for his crime, the king allows the queen to decide his fate. The queen tells him that he must find out what women most desire within a year and a day, or he will be beheaded. The knight travels for a year, but cannot find the answer. On his way home, he comes upon some fairies dancing in a forest clearing. When he approaches, he finds only an ugly old hag. She says that she can give him the answer he seeks, but he must grant her the first request that she makes of him. He agrees, and she accompanies him back to court. He gives the answer – women most desire to have sovereignty over their husbands and lovers – and nobody can argue against it, so his life is granted. The old hag then steps forward and asks the knight to marry her. He begs her to change her mind, to take his goods and let his body alone, but she will not. They are married and go to bed, but the knight is miserable. She gives him a lecture on true nobility. She offers to be either ugly and faithful, or beautiful and possibly untrue. He gives her the authority to make the decision on his behalf. In return for this correct answer, she gives him the reward – that she will be both beautiful and true. They live happily ever after.

The goodwife of Bath, taking up the theme of correct/perfect female behaviour introduced by the previous speaker (in some anthologies, the clerk's tale is given immediately before the wife's, but this is a similar story about a perfect woman, so the theme is the same). Alison (which she reveals to be her name) attacks the idea of women being 'glossed' by men; that is, the idea that written authorities ('auctoritee' – male and religious) should be able to dictate what women are and should be. She opposes the authority of clerkly writers with her 'experience', an authority which women, who have no higher education, can and do possess. In her prologue, she offers the wisdom she has gained from the 'university of life' as a viable, and preferable (from a female point of view) alternative to philosophy and book-learning. This applies whether she is discussing the lawyer's tale of a passive heroine, or the clerk's tale of a woman who is stripped and re-clothed, similarly silent and obedient. The wife takes the language of misogynist writers and turns it against them. She claims that her own experience is the universal experience of all women (hence her name, Alison, is 'everywoman') in a world shaped and ruled by men. Women must fight for control of their marriages, and for control of the language with which they are themselves enclosed. Her body is her text, and she will not be glossed, as glossing is a form of containment. She understands the economy of marriage, and has used what is available to her, her body, to make a profit in terms of money and power. When she cannot use her body any longer, she can use her money to attract even young men, as she proves with Jankin. The wife knows that language is gendered (an instrument of male power), and that male discourse always encloses the feminine, just as the male always controls the female in society and in law. Language is an instrument of male power, over women as well as over the poor and the illiterate.

Alison herself is constructed from a variety of different literary sources depicting dominant women, and 'anti-marriage' literature, a very powerful tradition in the later Middle Ages. The character of the wife is very close to that of La Vieille in *The Romance of the Rose*. This is an allegorical love-poem begun *c.*1237 by Guillaume de Lorris, and continued later in the same century by Jean de Meun. La Vieille, an old woman who tells the hermaphroditic Bel Acceuil how to attract and manage men, is drawn from the later part of the work. There has been considerable debate about whether the wife manages successfully to appropriate misogynist language, or whether she ends up by proving all of their assertions. It may be that both are true, as she cannot escape from the fact that the only language available to her is that of her male enemies.

As a skilled clothworker and entrepreneur, who wears her wealth in the form of expensive red cloth, Alison is a woman of affairs and thus the equal of the lawyer and the doctor, and wealthy in her own right. Like Constance, her origins are less important than her journey. It is not who she is which is important, but how she has reacted to the world as she has experienced it. Like the real-life wife, traveller and otherwise independent merchant's spouse Margery Kempe, she not only refuses to be told 'who she is', or 'what she should be', she understands the relationship between money and independence. Unlike Margery, who took the path of saintly mysticism, Alison advocates embracing the joy of sex and the pleasures of the married life.

Like Alison's fifth husband Jankin, the knight in the tale deals with his own insecurity by violently abusing a woman. Consequently, he loses control of his own body, and his own fate. The knight has to take on the powerlessness of a woman. The old hag completes this female domination when she forces him to marry her. He is then in the same position as the young girl he raped – 'take my good and let my body go'. Unlike the girl, however, his position is not irreparable. The wife allows the knight to escape by giving sovereignty to the hag, who then becomes his ideal wife. However, she is still the hag underneath. Shape-shifting denies the man the ability to control or 'gloss' the woman. The wife would like to imagine herself in this way, and perhaps she really seeks a romance like the one with which she ends the tale; she would like to be young again.

The tale the wife tells is relevant for an aspirational member of the urban middle classes, who formed an important part of the audience for Arthurian romance in the fifteenth century. The story forms part of a tradition of romances concerning Sir Gawain, which includes *The Wedding of Sir Gawain and Dame Ragnell* (its closest analogue), *Sir Gawain and the Carl of Carlisle* and *Sir Gawain and the Green Knight*. The old hag may be a version of the 'loathly lady' of Arthurian romance, she may be the elf queen herself, or maybe an avatar of the arch-fairy, Morgan le Fay. The slippage between this woman and the wife herself is obvious. Her sermon on the nature of nobility – it is an inner quality, not a result of birth – offers a challenge to the noble dominance of society which has been open to question ever since the knight first told his tale.

Alison's prologue is part confession, part sermon, part exemplum, part autobiography, and its themes carry on into her tale. It has been suggested that Alison is a romantic at heart, and is motivated in part by the fact that she seems to have no children, despite her five marriages. This cannot be assumed, however. It may be that Chaucer does not tell his audience about Alison's family because it is not important for his story. Although she stands up for herself, putting in a sidelong insult to friars in retaliation at the friar's interruption of her story, there *is* a submissive streak in Alison, despite her protestations. She remains with a husband who 'batters' her, saying that he could entice her into bed again, even after he had bruised every bone in her body, because he was so good at making love. At least this is suffering in which she herself is complicit, and the idea of a 'trade-off' suits her character. She appears to be implying that male-dominated society is much more culpably violent towards women, and that the marriage of a twelve-year-old girl to an old man is a rape in which both society and the Church collude. This, in the end, is her justification for her life and her attitudes.

Key Questions

What is the evidence for the truth (or not) of what the wife says about women in medieval English society? What is her own position, as a merchant's wife and then widow? Does her class impact on her prologue and tale?

Does the nature and content of Alison's tale suit her character and experience as given in the prologue/general prologue?

Does Alison prove her point about 'experience' and 'authority'?

Topic Keywords

Medieval marriage and family/ crafts and trades/ misogynist literature in the Middle Ages/ female pilgrims/ clerical attitudes to women/ popular Gawain romances/ Arthurian literature and its audiences/ medieval Bath and the West Country

Further Reading

John A. Alford, 'The Wife of Bath versus the Clerk of Oxford: What their Rivalry Means', *Chaucer Review*, 21, 1986, pp. 108–32

Peter Beidler (ed.), *Geoffrey Chaucer: The Wife of Bath* – Complete, Authoritative Text with Biographical and Historical Contexts, Critical History, and Essays from Five Contemporary Critical Perpectives, Boston, St Martin's Press, 1996

Alcuin Blamires, 'The Wife of Bath and Lollardy', *Medium Ævum*, 58, 1989, pp. 224–42

Carole Koepke Brown, 'Episodic Patterns and the Perpetrator: The Structure and Meaning of Chaucer's Wife of Bath's Tale', *Chaucer Review*, 31, 1996, pp. 18–35

Mary Carruthers, 'The Wife of Bath and the Painting of Lions', *Publications of the Modern Language Association of America*, 94, 1979, pp. 209–22

Susan Carter, 'Coupling the Beastly Bride and the Hunter Hunted: What Lies Behind Chaucer's Wife of Bath's Tale', *Chaucer Review*, 37, 2003, pp. 329–45

Catherine S. Cox, 'Holy Erotica and the Virgin Word: Promiscuous Glossing in The Wife of Bath's Prologue', *Exemplaria*, 5, 1993, pp. 207–37

Susan Crane, 'Alison's Incapacity and Poetic Instability in the Wife of Bath's Tale', *Publications of the Modern Language Association of America*, 102, 1987, pp. 20–8

Sheila Delany, 'Strategies of Silence in the Wife of Bath's Recital', *Exemplaria*, 2, 1990, pp. 49–69

Louise O. Fradenburg, 'The Wife of Bath's Passing Fancy', *Studies in the Age of Chaucer*, 8, 1986, pp. 31–58

Barbara Gottfried, 'Conflict and Relationship, Sovereignty and Survival: Parables of Power in The Wife of Bath's Prologue', *Chaucer Review*, 19, 1985, pp. 202–24

Marc Glasser, ' "He nedes moste hire wedde": The Forced Marriage in The Wife of Bath's Tale and its Middle English analogues', *Neuphilologische Mitteilungen*, 85, 1984, pp. 239–41

Charles Henebry, 'Apprentice Janekyn/Clerk Jankyn: Discrete Phases in Chaucer's Developing Conception of The Wife of Bath', *Chaucer Review*, 32, 1997, pp. 146–61

Laura F. Hodges, 'The Wife of Bath's Costumes: Reading the Subtexts', *Chaucer Review*, 27, 1993, pp. 359–76

Patricia Clare Ingham, 'Pastoral Histories: Utopia, Conquest, and The Wife of Bath's Tale', *Texas Studies in Literature and Language*, 44, 2002, pp. 34–46

Stewart Justman, 'Trade as Pudendum: Chaucer's Wife of Bath', *Chaucer Review*, 28, 1994, pp. 344–52

Edgar Laird, 'The Astronomer Ptolemy and the Morality of The Wife of Bath's Tale', *Chaucer Review*, 34, 2000, pp. 289–99

Robert Longsworth, 'The Wife of Bath and the Samaritan Woman', *Chaucer Review*, 34, 2000, pp. 372–87

Kathryn McKinley, 'The Silenced Knight: Questions of Power and Reciprocity in The Wife of Bath's Tale', *Chaucer Review*, 30, 1996, pp. 359–78

Marjorie M. Malvern, ' "Who peyntede the leon, tel me who?": Rhetorical and Didactic Roles Played by an Aesopic Fable in The Wife of Bath's Prologue', *Studies in Philology*, 80, 1983, pp. 238–52

Ann B. Murphy, 'The Process of Personality in Chaucer's Wife of Bath's Tale', *Centennial Review*, 28, 1984, pp. 204–22

Shawn Normandin, 'The Wife of Bath's Urinary Imagination', *Exemplaria*, 20, 2008, pp. 244–63

Carter Revard, 'The Wife of Bath's Grandmother; or, How Gilote Showed her Friend Johane that the Wages of Sin is Worldly Pleasure, and how Both then Preached this Gospel throughout England and Ireland', *Chaucer Review*, 39, 2004, pp. 117–36

S. H. Rigby, 'The Wife of Bath, Christine de Pizan, and the Medieval Case for Women', *Chaucer Review*, 35, 2000, pp. 133–65

D. W. Robertson Jr., ' "And for my land thus hastow mordred me?": Land Tenure, the Cloth Industry, and The Wife of Bath', *Chaucer Review*, 14, 1980, pp. 403–20

Jerry Root, ' "Space to speke": The Wife of Bath and the Discourse of Confession', *Chaucer Review*, 28, 1994, pp. 252–74

Warren Smith, 'The Wife of Bath Debates Jerome', *Chaucer Review*, 32, 1997, pp. 129–45

Mel Storm, 'Speech, Circumspection, and Orthodontics in the Manciple's Prologue and Tale and The Wife of Bath's Portrait', *Studies in Philology*, 96, 1999, pp. 109–26

Barrie Ruth Strauss, 'The Subversive Discourse of the Wife of Bath: Phallocentric Discourse and the Imprisonment of Criticism', *English Literary History*, 55, 1988, pp. 527–54

Susanne Thomas, 'What the Man of Law Can't Say: The Buried Legal Argument of The Wife of Bath's Prologue', *Chaucer Review*, 31, 1997, pp. 256–71

Thomas A. Van, 'False Texts and Disappearing Women in the Wife of Bath's Prologue and Tale', *Chaucer Review*, 29, 1994, pp. 179–93

Here bygynneth the prologue of the Wyf of Bathe

❦ 'Experiens, though noon **auctorite**   (learned) authority
Were in this world, it were ynough for me
To speke of wo that is in mariage;
For lordyngs, syns I twelf yer was of age –
I thank it God that is **eterne** of lyve –   eternal
Housbondes atte chirch dore I have had fyve,[1]
For I so ofte might have weddid be;
And all were worthy men in here **degre**.   station (in life)
But me was taught, nought longe tyme **goon** is,   ago   10
That **synnes** Crist went never but **onys**   since; once
To weddyng, in the Cane of Galile,[2]
That by the same **ensampul** taught he me   example
That I ne weddid schulde be but **ones**.   once
Herken, such a scharp word for the nones!
Biside a welle Jhesus, god and man,
Spak in **reproef** of the Samaritan:[3]   reproof
'Thow hast y-had fyve housbondes,' quod he,
'And that **ilk** man which that now hath the   same
Is nought thin housbond.' Thus he sayd certayn;   20
What that he ment therby I cannot sayn,
But that I **axe** why the fyfte man   ask
Was nought housbond to the Samaritan?
How many might sche have in mariage?
Yit herd I never tellen **in myn age**   in my time
Uppon this noumbre **diffinicioun**.   definition
Men may **divine**, and **glosen** up and doun,   consider; interpret/gloss
But wel I **wot**, withouten eny lye,   know

---

1 The first part of the wedding service (betrothal) took place in the church porch. This was regarded as binding, although the solemnisation of the wedding took place, in the church, at a later date.

2 In St John's gospel, Christ attended a wedding at Cana in Galilee, where he turned water into wine.

3 Again in St John's gospel, Jesus met and disputed with a Samaritan woman, who was fetching water from a well.

God bad us for to **wax** and multiplie: increase (numbers)
30   That **gentil tixt** can I wel understonde.   pleasant text
Ek wel I wot he sayd myn housebonde
Schuld **lete** fader and moder and **folwe** me,   leave; follow
But of no noumber mencioun made he,
Of Bygamye of of Octogamye;[4]
Why schuld men speken of that **vilonye**?   evil
Lo! Hier the wise kyng, Daun Salamon;
I **trow** he haddde wifes **mo** than **oon** –   believe; more; one
As wold God it were **leful** unto me   lawful
To be **refreisshed** half so oft as he!   refreshed (sexually)
40   **Which** gift of God had he for alle his wyves –   what
No man hath such that in the world **on lyve** is –   alive
God wot, this nobil king, as to my **wit**   knowledge
The first night had many a mery fit
With ech of hem, so wel was him on lyve!
Y-blessid be God that I have weddid fyve!
Welcome the sixte, whan that ever he schal!
Forsothe, I **nyl** not kepe me **chast** in al;   will not (ne will); chaste
Whan myn housbond is fro the world y-gon,
Som Cristen man schal wedde me **anoon**,   immediately
50   For than thapostil saith that I am fre
To wedde, **a Goddis half**, wher so it be.[5]   by God's side
He saith that to be weddid is no synne –
Bet is to be weddid than to brynne[6]
What **recchith** me what folk sayn vilonye   care
Of **schrewith** Lameth and of his Bigamye?   cursed
I wot wel Abram was an holy man,
And Jacob eek, as **ferforth** as I can,   far
And ech of hem had wyves mo than tuo –
And many another holy man also.[7]
60   Whan sawe ye in eny maner age

---

4 Bigamy – having two spouses at the same time; octogamy – having eight spouses
   at the same time.
5 The apostle of whom the Wife is speaking is St Paul, whose letters were the
   source of many misogynistic doctrines.
6 'It is better to marry than to burn (with lust)'
7 The Wife is making the point that the Old Testament patriarchs all had more
   than one wife at the same time.

That highe God **defendid** mariage?   forbad
By **expres** word I pray yow, tellith me –   definite
Or wher commaunded he virginite?
I wot as wel as ye, it is no drede.[8]
Thapostil, whan he speketh of **maydenhede**,   virginity
He sayd that precept therof had he noon.[9]
Men may **counseil** a womman to be **oon**,   advise; single
But counselyng nys no comaundement –
He put it in our owne juggement;
For hadde God comaundid maydenhede,   70
Than had he dampnyd weddyng with the dede.
And certes, if ther wer no seed y-sowe,
Virginite, wheron schuld it growe?
Poul ne dorst not comaunde, atte lest,
A thing of which his maister gaf non **hest**.   commandment
The dart is set upon virginite –
Cach who so may, who rennith best let se.[10]
But this work is not taken of every **wight**,   person
But ther as God **list** give it of his might.   wants to
I wot wel that thapostil was a **mayde** –   virgin   80
But natheles, though that he wrot or sayde
He wolde that every wight were such as he,
Al **nys but** counseil unto virginite;   is only
And for to ben a wyf he gaf me leve
Of **indigence**, so nys it to repreve   indulgence
To wedde me if that my make deye[11]
Withoute **excepcioun** of bigamye.   exception
Al were it good no womman for to touche –   although
He mente in his bed or in his couche;
For peril is bothe **fuyr** and **tow** to assemble –   fire; flax   90
Ye knowe what this ensample wold resemble.[12]
This is **al and som**, he holdith virginite   all there is
More parfit than weddyng in **frelte** –   frailty
Frelte **clepe I but if** that he and sche   I call it; unless

---

8 'it is not in doubt'
9 'he couldn't find any precedent which covered the question'
10 'a prize is offered for virginity: catch it who can, let's see who runs fastest'
11 'it's no sin to marry me if my mate dies'
12 'you know what the meaning of this example is'

Wold leden al ther lif in chastite.
I graunt it wel; I have noon envye,
Though maidenhede **preferre** bygamye;   is better than
It liketh hem to be clene in body and **gost**.   spirit
Of myn estate I nyl make no **bost**,   boast
100 For wel ye wot a lord in his houshold
He nath not every vessel ful of gold
Som ben of **tre**, and don her lord servise.   wood
God **clepeth** folk to him in **sondry wise**,   calls; various ways
And **every** hath of God a **propre** gifte;   each; their own
Som this, som that, as him likith to **schifte**.   bestow
Virginite is gret perfeccioun,
And **continens** eek, with gret devocioun: abstention
But Christ, that of perfeccioun is **welle**,   the well
Bad nought every **wight** schuld go and selle   person
110 Al that he had, and give it to the pore,
And in such wise folwe him and his **fore**.   footsteps
He spak to hem that wolde lyve parfytly –
But lordyngs, by your leve, that am not I.
I wol **bystowe** the flour of myn age   give
In the actes and in the fruytes of mariage.
Tel me also, to what conclusioun
Were **membres** maad of generacioun,   organs/body parts
And in what wise was a wight **y-wrought**?   made
Trustith right wel, thay were nou*g*ht maad for **nought**!   nothing
120 **Glose** whoso wol, and say bothe up and doun,   interpret
That thay were made for **purgacioun**   ejection
Of **uryn**, and oure bothe thinges smale   urine
Was eek to knowe a femel fro a male,
And for non other cause? Say ye no?
Thexperiens wot wel it is not so.
So that these clerkes ben not with me **wrothe**[13]   angry
I say this, that thay makid ben for bothe;
That is to say, for office and for **ease**   pleasure
Of **engendrure**, ther we god nou*g*ht displease.   conception
130 Why schuld men elles in her bokes sette
That man schal **yelde** to his wif his **dette**?   yield/give up; debt

13 Here the Wife is probably addressing the clerics in the pilgrim group.

Now wherwith schuld he paye his payement,

If he ne used his **sely** instrument?   happy/nice/sweet

Than were thay **maad up** a creature   made; upon

To purge uryn, and eek for engendrure.

By I say not that every wight is **holde**,   bound

That hath such **harneys** as I to yow tolde,   equipment

To gon and usen hem in engendrure –

Than schuld men take of chastite no **cure**.   care/value

Crist was a mayde, and **schapen** as a man,   mad   140

And many a seynt, **sin** that the world bygan,   since

Yet lyved thay ever in parfyt chastite –

I nyl envye no virginite.

Let hem be **bred** of pured whete seed,   bread

And let us wyves eten **barly** breed;   barley

And yet with barly bred, men telle can,

Oure Lord Jhesu refreisschid many a man.[14]

In such astaat as God hath **cleped ous**   called us

I wil persever, I am not **precious**.   fastidious

In wyfhode I wil use myn instrument   150

Als frely as my maker hath me it sent.

If I be **daungerous**, God give me **sorwe**!   unwilling; sorrow

Myn housbond schal **han** it at eve and **at morwe** –   have; in the morning

Whan that him list com forth and pay his dette –

An housbond wol I have, I wol not **lette**,   give up

Which schal be bothe my **dettour** and my **thral**,   debtor; servant

And have his tribulacioun withal

Upon his **fleissch**, whil that I am his wyf.   body

I have the power duryng al my lif

Upon his **propre** body, and not he –   own   160

Right thus thapostil told it unto me,

And bad oure housbondes for to love us wel –

Al this sentence me likith every **del**.'   bit

Up **start** the pardoner, and that anoon,   jumped

'Now, Dame,' quod he, 'by God and by Seint John!

Ye ben a noble prechour **in this caas**!   on this subject

I was aboute to wedde a wif – allaas,

---

14 A reference to the feeding of five thousand (and in some gospel stories four
    thousand) men with five loaves and two fishes, after Christ had blessed them.

What schal I buy it on my fleisch so deere?

Yit had I **lever** wedde no wyf **to yere**.'   rather; this year

170 'Abyd,' quod sche, 'my tale is not bygonne!

Nay, thou schalt drinke of another **tonne**   barrel

Er that I go, schal **savere wors** than ale: taste worse

And whan that I have told the forth my tale

Of tribulacioun in mariage,

In which I am expert in al myn age –

This is to say, myself hath ben the whippe –

Than might thou **chese** whethir thou wilt sippe   choose

Of thilke **tonne** that I schal **abroche**.   barrel; broach

Bewar of it, er thou to **neigh** approche,   near

180 For I schal telle ensamples mo than ten:

'Whoso that nyl be war by other men,

By him schal other men corrected be,'

The same wordes writes Ptholome;[15]

Rede in his *Almagest*, and **tak** it there.'   find

'Dame, I wold pray you, if that youre wille were,'

Sayde this pardoner, '**as ye bigan** –

Tel forth youre tale, sparith for no man.

Teche us yonge men of youre **practike**.'   practice

'Gladly,' quod sche, 'syns it may yow like.[16]

190 But that I pray to al this companye,

If that I speke after my **fantasie**,   whim

As taketh nought **agreef** of that I say,   offence

For myn entente is nought but to play.'

Narrat

she tells (her story)

❦ 'Now sires, now wol I telle forth my tale.

As ever **mote** I drinke wyn or ale,   may

I schal say soth of housbondes that I hadde,

As thre of hem were goode and tuo were badde;

Tuo of hem were goode, riche, and olde;

200 **Unnethes** mighte thay the statute holde   hardly

---

15 Ptolemy, the Greek writer whose Almagest was the foundation of medieval astrology.
16 'since you would like to hear it'

In which that that were bounden unto me – [17]
Ye wot wel what I mene of this, **parde**!   by; by God
As help me God, I laugh whan that I thinke   so
How pitously on night I made hem **swynke**!   work
But, by my **fay, I told of it no stoor** –   faith; I set no value on it
Thay had me give her lond and her tresor –
Me **nedith not** no lenger **doon diligence**   didn't need to; exert myself
To wynne her love, or doon hem reverence.
Thay loved me so wel, by God above,
That I tolde no **deynte** of her love.   value   210
A wys womman wol **bysi hir** ever in oon,   be busy
To gete hir love ther sche hath noon –
Buy synnes I had hem **holly** in myn hond,   wholly
And synnes thay had me geven al her lond,
What schuld I **take keep** hem for to please,   bother
But it were for my profyt or myn **ease**?   unless; pleasure
I sette hem so on werke, by my fay,[18]
That many a night thay songen, 'Weylaway!'
The bacoun was nought fet for hem, I **trowe**,   believe
That som men fecche in Essex at Donmowe.[19]   220
I governed hem so wel after my lawe,
That ech of hem ful **blisful** was, and **fawe**,   happy; eager
To bringe me gaye thinges fro the faire –
They were ful glad whan I spak to hem faire,
For, God it woot, I **chidde hem spitously**!   nagged them spitefully
Now herkeneth how I **bar me** proprely –   behaved
Ye wise wyves that can understonde –
Thus scholde ye speke and **bere hem wrong on honde**;

                                                                       wrongly accuse them
For half so boldely can ther no man
Swere and lye, as can a womman.   230
I say not by wyves that ben wise,
But if it be whan thay ben mysavise.
Y-wis, a wif, if that sche can hir good[20]

17 They found it difficult to satisfy her sexual appetite.
18 'I made them work so hard'
19 The Dunmow Flitch: a side of bacon awarded each year to a husband and wife
   who can prove they have not had a cross word for a year and a day.
20 'if she knows what's good for her'

Schal **beren him on hond** the cow is wood,[21]   *convince him*
And take witnes on hire **oughne mayde**   *own maid*
Of hire assent; but herkenith how I sayde:
'See, olde **caynard**, is this thin **array**?   *dotard; clothing*
Why is my neighebor's wif so gay?
Sche is honoured over **al ther** sche goth –   *everywhere*
240   I sitte at hom; I have no **thrifty cloth**.   *nice clothes to wear*
What **dostow** at my neighebores hous?   *are you doing*
Is sche so fair? What, **artow** amorous?   *are you*
What **roune** ye with hir maydenes? Benedicite!   *whisper*
Sir olde lecchour, let thi **japes** be!   *tricks*
And if I have a **gossib** or a frend   *female (gossiping) companion*
Withouten gilt, thou chidest as a **fend**   *devil*
If that I walk or play unto his hous.
Thou comest hom as dronken as a **mous**[22]
And prechist on thy bench, with **evel preef**!   *ill fortune*
250   Thou saist to me it is a gret **meschief**   *trouble*
To wedde a **pouer** womman, for **costage**   *poor; expense*
And if that sche be riche and of **parage**,   *high status parentage*
Thanne saist thou that it is a **tormentrie**   *torment*
To suffre hir pride and hir malencolie;
And if that sche be fair, thou verray knave,
Thou saist that every **holour** wol hir have;   *lecher*
Sche may no while in chastite abyde,
That is **assayled** thus on eche syde.   *beseiged*
Thou saist that som folk desire us for riches,
260   Som for our **schap**, and som for our fairnes,   *figure*
And some for that sche can synge and daunce,
And some for gentilesse or **daliaunce**;   *social skills*
Som for hir handes and hir armes smale –
Thus goth al to the devel, by thi tale.
Thou saist men may nought kepe a castel wal,
It may so be biseged over al.
And if sche be foul, thanne thou saist that sche
Coveitith every man that sche may se,

---

21 The chough: possibly a reference, like the manciple's, to a bird which tells the
   husband of an unfaithful wife
22 'as drunk as a mouse' – one of the recognised medieval degrees of drunkenness.
   It was also possible to be 'as drunk as an ape'.

For as a **spaynel** sche wol on him **lepe**,	spaniel; leap
Til that sche fynde som man hire to **chepe**;	do business with 270
Ne noon so gray a **goos** goth in the lake	goose
As, sayest thou, wol be withouten make;	
And saist it is an hard thing for to **wolde**	control
Thing that no man wol, **his willes**, holde.	by his own will
Thus **seistow**, **lorel** whan thou gost to bedde,	you say; scoundrel
And that no wys man nedith for to wedde,	
Ne no man that **entendith** unto hevene.	hopes
With wilde thunder **dynt** and fuyry **levene**	clap; lightening
Mote thi wicked necke be to-broke!	
Thou saist that **dropping** hous and eek smoke,	dripping 280
And chydyng wyves, maken men to fle	
Out of here oughne hous, a **bendicite**!	God bless us!
What **eylith** such an old man for to chyde!	is wrong with
Thou seist we wyves **woln** oure vices hide	will
Til we ben weddid, and than we wil hem **schewe** –	show
Wel may that be a proverbe of a **schrewe**!	wicked person
Thou saist that assen, oxe and houndes,	
Thay ben **assayed** at divers **stoundes** –	tried; times
Basyns, **lavours** eek, er men hem bye;	basins; bowls (for washing)
Spones, stooles, and al such **housbondrie**,	household goods 290
Also pottes, clothes and **array**;	clothing
But folk of wyves maken non assay	
Til thay ben weddid, old dotard schrewe!	
And thanne, saistow, we woln oure vices schewe.	
Thou saist also that it displesith me	
But if that thou wilt praysen my beaute,	unless
And but thou **pore** always in my face,	gaze
And clepe me, 'Faire dame', in every place;	
And but thou make a **fest** on **thilke** day	feast; same
That I was born, and make me freisch and gay;	300
And to my **chamberer** withinne thy **boure**,	chambermaid; bedroom
And to my fadres folk and myn **allies** –	relatives
Thus saistow, olde barel ful of lies!	
And yit of oure **apprentys** Jankyn,	apprentice
For his crisp **her** schynyng as gold so fyn,	hair
And for he **squiereth** me up and doun,	accompanies
Yet hastow caught a fals **suspeccioun**.	suspicion
I **nyl** him nought, though thou were deed tomorwe!	don't want

But tel me, wherfor **hydestow**, with sorwe,   do you hide
310   Thy keyes of thy **chist** away fro me?   chest
It is my **good** as wel as thin, parde!   possessions
What! **Wenest thou** make an ydiot of oure dame?   do you think you can
Now, by that lord that **cleped** is Seint Jame,   called
Thow schalt not bothe, though thou were **wood**,   mad
Be **maister** of my body and of my **good**;   master; possessions
That oon thou schalt forgo, **maugre** thin **yen**.   despite; eyes (angry looks)
What helpeth it on me **tenqueren** or **espien**?   to enquire; to spy
I trowe thou woldest lokke me in thy chist!
Thou scholdist say, 'Wif, go wher **the lest** –   you like
320   Take youre disport, I **nyl lieve no talis**.   I won't believe any gossip
I know yow for a trewe wif, Dame Alis.'
We loveth no man that takith keep or charge
Wher that we goon – we love to be at large.
Of alle men y-blessed most he be,
The wise **astrologien**, Daun Ptholomie,   astrologer
That saith this proverbe in his *Almagest*:
'Of alle men his wisedom is highest
That rekkith not **who hath the world in honde**.'   who controls the world
By this proverbe thou schalt understonde:
330   'Have thou ynough, what thar the **recch of care**   care about
How merily that other folks fare.'
For certes, olde dotard, with your leve,
Ye schul have **queynte** right ynough at eve.   (my) genitals
He is to gret a **nygard** that wol **werne**   miser; refus
A man to light a candel at his lanterne.
He schal have never the lasse light, parde –
Have thou ynough, **the thar not pleyne the**!   don't complain
Thou saist also that if we make us gay
With clothing, and with precious array,
340   That it is peril of our chastite.
And yit, with sorwe, thou most **enforce the**,   be masterful
And say these wordes, in thapostle's name:
'In **abyt** maad with chastite and schame   clothing
Ye wommen schuld apparyl yow,' quod he,
'And nought with **tressed** her and gay **perre**   arranged; precious stones
As perles, ne with golden clothis riche.'   such as
After thy text, ne after thin **rubriche**,   heading
I wol nou*g*ht wirche as moche as a gnat!

Thow saist thus, that I was lik a cat;

For who so wolde **senge** the cat's skyn,   singe   350

Than wold the catte **duellen in his in**;   stay at home

And if the cat's skyn be **slyk** and gay,   smooth/shiny

Sche wol not **duelle** in house half a day,   stay

But forth sche wil, er eny day be **dawet**,   dawned

To schewe hir skyn and goon a **caterwrawet**.   caterwauling

This is to say, if I be gay – Sir Schrewe!

I wol **renne** out my **borel** for to schewe –   run; (poor) clothing

Sir Olde Fool, what **helpith the** to aspien?   good does it do you

Though thou prayedest Argus, with his hundrid **yen**,[23]   eyes

To be my **warde corps**, as he can best,   personal guard   360

In faith, he schuld not kepe me but **if me lest**;   if I wanted him to

Yit couthe I **make his berd**, though **queynte** he be!   trick him; clever

Thou saydest eek that ther **ben** thinges thre,   are

The whiche thinges troublen al this erthe,

And that no wight may endure the **ferthe**.   fourth

O, leve Sire Schrewe! Jhesu **schorte** thy lif!   shorten

Yit **prechestow**, and saist an hateful wif   you preach

Y-rekened is for oon of these meschaunces.

Ben ther noon other of thy **resemblaunces**   examples

That ye may liken youre parables unto,   370

But if a cely wyf be oon of tho?

Thow likenest womman's love to helle,

To bareyn lond, ther water may not duelle.

Thou likenest it also to wilde fuyr –[24]

The more it **brenneth**, the more it hath desir   burns

To consume everything that brent wol be.

Thou saist, right as wormes **schenden** a tre,   destroy

Right so a wif schendith hir housebonde;

This knowen tho that ben to wyves **bonde**.   bound

Lordynges, right thus, as ye han understonde,   380

Bar I styf myn housebondes **on honde**,   soundly swore

That thus thay sayde in here dronkenesse –

And al was fals, but that I took witnesse

On Jankyn, and upon my nece also.

O Lord, the peyne I dede hem, and the wo –

23 In Greek mythology, Argus had a hundred eyes.
24 Greek fire, the medieval form of napalm.

Ful **gulteles**, by God's swete **pyne**;   guiltless; passion
For as an hors I couthe bothe bite and **whyne**;   whinny
I couthe **pleyne**, and yet I was in the gilt,   complain
Or elles I hadde often tyme be **spilt**.   lost
390 Whoso first cometh to the mylle, first grynt!²⁵
I pleyned first, so was oure **were stynt**.   quarrel; stopped
Thay were ful glad to excuse hem ful **blyve**,   quickly
Of thing that thay never agilt in her lyve;
And wenches wold I beren hem on honde,
Whan that for seek thay might unnethes stond.²⁶
Yit tykeled I his herte, for that companionship.²⁷
Wende that I hadde of him so greet **chiertee**.   affection
I swor that al my walking out a-nyght
Was for to **aspie** wenches that he **dight**;   see; slept with
400 Under that colour had I many a mirthe,
For al such witte is geven us of birthe –
Decipt, wepyng, **spynnyng**, God hath give   deceipt; spinning (a yarn)
To wymmen **kyndely**, whil thay may lyve;   as part of their nature
And thus of o thing I **avaunte** me,   boast
And thende I had the bet in ech degree,²⁸
By **sleight**, or **fors**, or of som maner thing   cunning; strength
As by continuel murmur or chidyng;
Namly on bedde hadden thay meschaunce –
Ther wold I chide, and **do hem no plesaunce**.   not please them
410 I wold no lenger in the bed abyde,
If that I felt his arm over my side,
Til he had maad his raunsoun unto me;²⁹
Than wold I suffer him doon his **nycete**.   pleasure
And therfor every man this tale telle:
Wynne whoso may, for al is for to selle –
With empty hond men may noon **haukes** lure.   hawks
For **wynnyng** wold I al his lust endure,   making a profit
And make me a **feyned** appetyt –   pretended
And yit in **bacoun** had I never delyt.   old, smoked flesh

25 'who comes to the mill first, grinds first'
26 'I said they had whores when they were so sick they could hardly stand'
27 'tickled his heart', ie amused him.
28 'in the end I got the better of them in every way'
29 The Wife is saying here that she made her husbands pay her for sex.

That made me that ever I wold hem **chyde**;   *nag*   420
For, though the pope had seten hem bisyde,
I nold not spare hem at her oughne **bord**.   *table*
For, by my trouthe, I **quyt** hem word for word;   *paid back*
Als help me verray God omnipotent,   *so*
Though I right now schuld make my **testament**,   *will*
I owe hem nought a word that it nys quitte.
I brought it so aboute by my **witte**   *cunning*
That they most geve it up, as for the best,[30]
Or ellis had we never ben in rest;
For though he loked as a grym lyoun,   430
Yit schuld he fayl of his **conclusioun**.   *intention*
Than wold I say, 'Now, goode **leef**, tak **keep**   *love; notice*
How meekly lokith Wilkyn our scheep!
Com ner, my spouse, let me **ba** thy cheke!   *kiss*
Ye schulde be al pacient and meke,
And have a swete spiced consciens,
Siththen ye preche so of Job's paciens.   *since*
Suffreth alway, syns ye so wel can preche –
And but ye do, certeyn we schul yow teche
That it is fair to have a wyf in pees: 440
On of us tuo mot bowe, douteles,
And siththen man is more reasonable
Than womman is, ye moste be **suffrable**.   *back down*
What **aylith** yow for to **grucche** and grone –   *ails; grumble*
Is it **for** ye wold have my **queynt** alone?   *because; genitals*
Why, tak it al! Lo, have it every del!
Peter, I **schrewe** yow, but ye love it wel;   *nag/hen-peck*
For if I wolde selle my **bele chose**,   *'pretty thing'*
I couthe walk as freisch as eny rose;
But I wol kepe it for youre owne **toth** –   *tooth*   450
Ye ben to blame: by God, I say yow soth!'
Such maner wordes hadde we on honde:
Now wol I speke of my fourth housbonde.
My fourthe housbond was a **revelour**;   *reveller*
This is to say, he had a **paramour**.   *lover/mistress*
I was yong and ful of **ragerie**,   *spirit*

30 'the best thing they could do was give in'

Stiborn and strong, and joly as a **pye**.   magpie
How couthe I daunce to an harpe smale,
And synge, y-wys, as eny nightingale,
460   Whan I had dronk a draught of swete wyn!
Metillius, the foule cherl, the swyn,
That with a staf byraft his wyf hir lyf
For sche drank wyn, though I had ben his wif
Ne schuld nou*gh*t have **daunted** me fro drink!   scared
And after wyn, on Venus most I think;
For also **siker** as cold **engendrith hayl**,   surely; gives rise to hail
A **likorous** mouth most have a licorous tail.   lecherous
In wymmen **vinolent** is no defens –   drunk
This knowen lecchours by experiens.
470   But, lor Crist! Whan that it remembrith me
Upon my youthe, and on my jolite,
It tikelith me about myn herte roote.
Unto this day it doth myn herte **boote**   good
That I have had my world as in my tyme;
But age, allas, that al wol **envenyme**,   poison
Hath me **bireft** my beaute and my **pith** –   taken from; vigour
Let go, far wel! The devyl go therwith!
The flour is goon, ther this no more to telle;
The bran, as best I can, now **mot** I selle.   must
480   But yit to be mery wol I **fonde**:   attempt
Now wol I telle of my fourth housbonde.
I say, I had in herte gret **despyt**   anger
That he of eny other had delit;
But he was quit, by God and by Seint **Joce** –   Judocus
I made him of the same woode a **croce**.   cross
Nought of my body, in no foul manere,
But certeynly I made folk such chere,
That in his owne **grees** I made him **frie**   fat; fry
For anger and for jalousie.
490   By God, in erthe I was his purgatory,
For which I hope his soule be in glory;
For, **God it wot**, he sat ful stille and **song**   God knows; 'sang'
Whan that his **scho** ful bitterly him **wrong**.   shoe; wrung
Ther was no wight, **sauf** God and he, that **wist**   except; knew

In many wyse how sore I him **twist**.   tormented
He deyde whan I cam fro Jerusalem,
And lith y-grave under the roode bem[31]
Al is his tombe nought so curious
As was the sepulcre of him Darius,
Which that Appellus wrought so **subtily**;   skilfully   500
It nys but **wast** to burie him **preciously**.   wasteful; expensively
Let him farwel, God give his soule rest!
He is now in his grave and in his **chest**.   coffin
Now of my fifte housbond wol I telle –
God let his soule never come in helle!
And yit was he to me the moste **schrewe** –   badly-behaved
That fele I on my ribbes all **on rewe**,   in a row
And ever schal unto myn ending day;
But in oure bed he was so freisch and gay,
And therwithal so wel he couthe me **glose**   'sweet-talk'   510
Whan that he wold have my 'bele chose',
That though he had me **bete** on every **boon**,   beaten; bone
He couthe wynne my love **right anoon**.   Immediately
I trowe, I loved him beste, for that he
Was of his love **daungerous** to me.   difficult
We wymmen han, if that I schal nou*gh*t lye,
In this matier a queynte fantasie.
Wayte what thyng we may not lightly have,   whatever
Ther after wol we sonnest crie and crave.
Forbeed us thing, and that desire we;   520
Pres on us fast, and thanne wol we fle.[32]
With daunger outen alle we oure ware –   unwillingly
Greet pres at market makith deer chaffare,[33]
And **to greet chep** is holden at litel pris;   too much available
This knowith every woman that is wys.
My fyfth housbond, God his soule blesse,

---

31 Rood beam – the beam which traversed the crossing arch between the chancel
   and nave of a church, so named because of the Rood, or cross with Christ
   crucified, which stood upon it.
32 'keep offering us something'
33 'we're unwilling to show all our wares at once; when there are lots of buyers at
   the market, the price goes up. If there's too much on sale it fetches a smaller
   price'.

Which that I took for love, and no richesse,
He somtyme was a clerk of Oxenford,
And had left scole, and went at hoom to **borde**   lodge
530 With my gossib, duelling in oure toun –
God have hir soule! Hir name was Alisoun.
Sche knew myn herte and my **privete**   secrets
Bet than oure parisch prest, so mot I the!
To hir **bywreyed** I my counseil al;   gave away
For had myn housbond pissed on a wal,
Or don a thing that schulde have cost his lif,
To hir, and to another worthy wyf,
An to my neece, which I loved wel,
I wold have told his counseil every del –
540 And so I did ful ofte, God it **woot**,   knows
That made his face ofte reed and hoot
For very schame, and blamyd himself that he
Had told to me so gret a privete.
And so byfel that oones in a lent³⁴
So ofte tyme to my gossib I went –
For ever yit I loved to be gay,
And for to walk in March, Averil and May
From hous to hous, to here sondry **talis** –   stories
That Jankyn clerk and my gossib, dame Alis,
550 And I myself, into the **feldes** went;   fields
Myn housbond was at Londoun al that Lent.
I had the betir **leysir** for to pleye,   leisure
And for to see and eek for to be **seye**   seen
Of lusty folk. What wist I wher my **grace**   destiny
Was **schapen** for to be, or in what place?   ordained
Therefore I made my visitaciouns,
To vigils and to processiouns,
To prechings eek, and to this pilgrimages,
To **pleyes miracles** and mariages,   miracle plays
560 And wered upon my scarlet **gytes**.   robes
These wormes, these **moughtes**, ne these mytes   moths
Upon my **perel fretith** hem never a deel.   clothing; feasted
And **wostow** why? For thay were used wel.   do you know

---

34 Lent – the four weeks before Easter.

Now wol I telle forth what **happid** me: happened to
I say, that in the **feldes** walkid we,   fields
Til trewely we had such **daliaunce**,   flirting
This clerk and I, that of my **purvyaunce**   forethought
I spak to him, and seide how that he,
If I were wydow, schulde wedde me;
For certynly, I say for no **bobaunce**,   boasting
Yit was I never withouten purveyaunce   570
Of marriage, ne of no thinges eek.
I hold a mouse's hert not worth a leek
That hath but oon hole to **sterte** to;   bolt
And if that faile, than is al **y-do**.   lost
But now, sir, let me se; what I schal sayn?
A-ha! By God, I have my tale again.
Whan that my fourthe housbond was **on bere**   on his bier (funeral)
I wept algate, and made a **sory cheere** –   miserable countenance
As wyves **mooten**, for it is **usage** –   must; custom
And with my **kerchief** covered my **visage**;   headcloth; face   580
But **for that** I was **purveyed** of a make,   because; provided with
I wept but small, and that I undertake.
To chirche was myn housbond brought **on morwe**,   in the morning
With neighebors that for him made sorwe,
And Jankyn oure clerk was oon of tho.
As help me God, whan that I saugh him go
After the beere, me thought he had a paire
Of legges and of feet so clene and faire
That al myn **hert I gaf** unto his hold.   heart; gave
He was, I trowe, twenty winter old,   590
And I was fourty – I schal say the **sothe** –   truth
But yit I had always a colt's **tothe**;   tooth
Gattothid I was, and that bycom me wel –   gap-toothed
I had the prynte of Seynt Venus sel.[35]
Myn ascent was Taur, and Mars therinne.[36]
Allas! Alas, that ever love was synne!
I folwed **ay** myn **inclinacioun**   always; feelings
By vertu of my constillacioun,
That made me that I couthe nought withdrawe

35 'imprint of St Venus's seal' – possibly a birthmark.
36 When the Wife was born, Taurus was in the ascendent, and Mars was in Taurus.

600 My chambre of Venus from a good felawe.[37]
What schuld I say, but at the month's ende
This joly clerk, Jankyn, that was so heende,
Hath weddid me with gret solempnitee,
And to him gaf I al the lond and **fee**   rents
That ever was me give therbifore;
But aftirward repented me ful sore –
He nolde suffre nothing of **my list**.   my will
By God, he **smot** me oones with his fist   hit
For I rent oones out of his book a **lef**,   leaf
610 That of that strok myn eere **wax** al **deef**.   became; deaf
Styborn I was, as is a **leones**,   lioness
And of my tonge a verray **iangleres**;   chatterer
And walk I wold, as I had don biforn,
Fro hous to hous, although he had it **sworn**;   forbidden
For which he ofte tyme wolde preche,
And me of olde Romayn **gestes** teche;   histories
How he Simplicius Gallus left his wyf,[38]
And hir forsok for term of al his lyf,
Nought but for **open heedid** he hir **say**   bareheaded; saw
620 Lokyng out at his dore upon a day.
Another Romayn told he me by name,
That for his wyf was at a somer game
Without his **wityng**, he forsok hir **eeke**,   knowing; also
And thanne wold he upon his book seeke
That ilke proverbe of Ecclesiaste,[39]
Wher he commaundith and forbedith faste
Man schal not suffre his wyf go **roule** aboute.   roam
Than wold he say right thus, withouten doute:
'Who that buyldith his hous al of **salwes**,   twigs
630 And priketh his blynde hors over the **falwes**,   fallow (so muddy) land
And suffrith his wyf to go seken **halwes**,   holy places
Is worthy to ben honged on the **galwes**.'   gallows
But al for nought, I sette nought an **hawe**   haw (berry)
Of his proverbe, ne of his olde **sawe**;   saying
Ne I wold not of him **corretted** be.   corrected

37 Possibly astrological, but also possibly a metaphor for the vagina.
38 Both stories from Roman writer Valerius Maximus.
39 Ecclesiasticus; also in the Book of Proverbs.

I hate him that vices tellith me,
And so **doon mo**, God it wot, than I.   do more
This made him with me **wood** al **outerly**;   mad; utterly
I nolde not **forbere** him in no cas.   obey
Now wol I say yow soth, by Seint Nicholas,   640
Why that I rent out of the book a leef,
For which he smot me that I was al deef.
He had a book that gladly, night and day,
For his **desport** he wolde rede always;   amusement
He clepyd it Valerye and Theofrast,[40]
At which book he **lough** always ful fast.   laughed
And eek thay say ther was somtyme at Rome
A clerk, a cardynal, that **heet** Seint Jerome,   was called
That made a book agens Jovynyan,
650In which book eek ther was Terculan,   650
Crisippus, Tortula, and eek Helewys,
That was **abbas** not fer fro Paris,[41]   abbess
And eek the **parablis** of Salamon,   parables (Proverbs)
Ovydes Art, and boukes many oon,[42]
And all these were bounde in oo volume;
And every night and day was his custume,
Whan he had **leysir** and **vacacioun**   rest and free time
From other world's occupacioun,
To reden on this book of wikked wyves.
He knew of hem mo legendes and lyves   660
Than ben of goode wyves in the Bible –
For trustith wel, it is an **inpossible**   impossibility
That any clerk schal speke good of wyves,
But if if be of holy seintes' lyves,
Ne of noon other wyfes never the mo –
Who peyntid the leoun, tel me who?[43]
By God, if wommen hadde writen stories

---

40 Valerius' letter of advice to Theofrastus not to marry, and Theofrastus' misogynistic
   treatise on marriage. The letter against Jovinian was written by St Jerome, fourth-
   century saint and aesthete. The Wife also mentions the Roman writer Tertullian,
   the proverbs of Solomon (Book of Proverbs), and Ovid's Ars Amatoria.
41 Heloise, the lover of Peter Abelard.
42 Ovid's Ars Amatoria (The Art of Love).
43 'If the lion painted the picture of a man killing a lion, the man wouldn't look so
   heroic'

As clerkes have, withinne her **oratories**,   cells
Thay wold have write of men more wickidnes
670   Than al the mark of Adam may redres.
These children of Mercury and of Venus
Ben in her werkyng ful contrarious;
Mercury lovith wisdom and **science**,   learning
And Venus loveth **ryot** and **dispense**,   debauchery; expense
And for her **divers** disposicioun,   differing
Ech fallith in other's exaltacioun,[44]
And thus, God wot, Mercury is **desolate**   impotent
In **Pisses**, wher Venus is **exaltate**;   Pisces; most powerful
And Venus faylith wher Mercury is reysed;[45]
680   Therfor no womman of clerkes is preised.
The clerk, whan he is old and may nought do
Of Venus werkis, is not worth a **scho**.   shoe
Than sit he doun, and writ in his dotage
That wommen can nought kepe here mariage.[46]
But now to purpos: why I tolde the
That I was beten for a leef, **parde**.   by God
Upon a night Jankyn, that was oure **sire**,   lord (head of household)
Rad on his book, as he sat by the fyr,
Of Eva first, that for hir wikkidnes
690   Was al mankynde brought to wrecchednes.[47]
Tho rad he me how Sampson left his **heris**;   hair
Slepyng, his **lemman** kut it with hir **scheris**,   lover; scissors
Thurgh which tresoun lost he bothe his **yen**.[48]   eyes
Tho rad he me, if that I schal not lyen,
Of Ercules and of his Deianyre,[49]
That caused him to sette himself on fuyre.
No thing forgat he the care and wo

---

44 'each falls when the other rises'
45 Mercury is associated with clerks, and is the opposite in the heavens to Venus –
    so clerks can never say anything good about women.
46 'women can't be faithful in their marriages'
47 A reference to how Eve, tempted by Satan, gave the forbidden fruit to Adam, and
    thereby caused the Fall of humankind.
48 Samson's hair, the source of his strength, was cut by his lover Delilah whilst he
    slept. He was taken by his enemies, the Philistines, and his eyes were put out.
49 Deianire gave Hercules a poisoned shirt; to hasten his death and ease the pain,
    he burned himself to death.

That Socrates had with his wyves tuo;
How **Exantia** cast pisse upon his heed: Xantippa
This seely man sat stille, as he were deed.   700
He wyped his heed, no more durst he sayn
But, 'Er thunder stynte, ther cometh rayn.'[50]
Of Phasipha, that was the queen of Creete –[51]
For schrewednes him thought the tale sweete –
Fy, spek no more! It is a grisly thing,
For her horribil lust and her **likyng**.   lechery
Of Clydemystra, for hir leccherie[52]
That falsly made hir housbond for to dye,
He rad it **with ful good devocioun**.   religiously
He told me eek for what occasioun   710
Amphiores at Thebes lest his lif;
Myn housbond had a legend of his lyf.
Exiphilem, that for an **ouche** of gold   brooch
Hath prively unto the Grekes told
Wher that hir housbond hyd him in a place,
For which he had at Thebes sory grace.
Of Lyvia told he me, and of Lucye;
Thay bothe made her housbondes for to dye –
That oon for love, that other was for hate –
Lyvia hir housbond, on an **even** late,   evening   720
Empoysond hath, for that sche was his **fo**;   enemy
Lucia, **licorous**, loved hir housbond so,   lecherous
For that he schuld always upon hir think,
Sche gaf him such a maner love drink
That he was deed er it was by the morwe;
And thus **algates** housbondes had sorwe.   in all ways
Than told he me how oon Latumyus
Compleigned unto his felaw Arrious,
That in his gardyn growed such a tre
On which, he sayde how that his wyves thre   730
Honged hemselfe, for herte **despitous**.   full of spite

---

50 'Before thunder ends, the rain comes'. Socrates was a Greek philosopher,
   Xantippa his wife.
51 Copulated with a bull to produce the minotaur.
52 She and her lover Agabus slaughtered her husband Agamemnon on his return
   from Troy.

'O **leve** brother,' quod this Arrious,   dear
'*G*if me a **plont** of thilke blessid tre,   cutting
And in my gardyn schal it plantid be!'
Of latter date, of wyves hath he red,
That some han slayn her housbondes in her bed,
And let her lecchour **dighten** al the night,   have sex
Wil that the corps lay in the flor **upright**;   flat out
And some han dryven nayles in her brayn
740   Whiles thay sleepe, and thus thay han hem slain.
Some have hem give poysoun in her drink –
He spak more harm than herte may bythynk –
And ther withal he knew mo proverbes
Than in this world ther growen **gres** or herbes.   grass
'Better is,' quod he, 'thyn habitacioun
Be with a leoun, or a foul dragoun,
Than with a womman **usyng** for to **chyde**.   used to; nag
Better is,' quod he, '**hihe** in the roof abyde,   high
Than with a wikked womman doun in a hous;
750   They ben so wicked and so contrarious,
Thay haten that her housbondes loven ay.'
He sayd, a womman cast hir schame away
Whan sche cast of hir **smok**; and forthermo   petticoat
A fair womman, **but** sche be chast also,   unless
Is lik a gold ryng in a sow's nose.
Who wolde wene, or who wolde suppose[53]
The wo that in myn herte was, and **pyne**?   suffering
And whan I saugh he **nolde** never **fyne**   would not; finish
To reden on this cursed book al night,
760   Al sodeinly thre **leves** have I **plight**   leaves/pages; pulled
Out of this booke that he had, and eeke
I with my fist so took him on the cheeke,
That in oure fuyr he fel bakward adoun;
And he **upstert** as doth a **wood** leoun,   jumped up; crazed
And with his fist he smot me on the hed,
That in the floor I lay as I were deed.
And whan he saugh so stille that I lay
He was **agast**, and wold have fled away;   astonished

---

53 'who could imagine'

Til atte last out of my swown I **brayde**.   woke
'O, hastow slayn me, false **thef**?' I sayde,   thief   770
'And for my lond thus hastow **mourdrid** me?   murdered
Er I be deed, yit wol I kisse the!'   before
And ner he cam, and knelith faire adoun,
And sayde, 'Deere suster Alisoun,
As help me God, I schal the never smyte;
That I have doon, it is thiself to **wite**.   blame
Forgive it me, and that I the **biseke**!'   beg
And yet **eftsones** I hyt him on the cheke   right away
And sayde, 'Thef! Thus **mekil** I me **wreke**!   much; avenge
Now wol I dye, I may no lenger speke.'   780
But atte last, with **mochil** care and wo,   much
We **fyl accordid** by oureselven tuo.   'made it up'
He gaf me al the bridil in myn hand,
To have the governaunce of hous and land,
And of his tonge and of his hond also;
And made him **brenne** his book **anoon** right tho.   burn; immediately
And whan I hadde geten unto me
By **maistry**, al the sovereynete,   overcoming
And that he sayde, 'Myn owne trewe wif,
Do as the list in term of al thy lif.[54]   790
Kepe thyn honour, and kep eek myn **estat**.'   social standing/reputation
And after that day we never had **debat**.   argument
God help me, so I was to him as kynde
As eny wyf from Denmark unto Inde,
And also trewe was he unto me.
I pray to God, that sitte in mageste,
So blesse his soule, for his mercy deere.
Now wol I say my tale, if ye wol heere.

Here makith the frere an interpretacion of the Wyf's tale

❦ The Frere **lough** whan he had herd al this,   laughed   800
'Now, Dame,' quod he, 'so have I joye or blis,
This is a long **preambel** of a tale.'   prologue
And whan the Sompnour herd the Frere **gale**,   shout out

---

54 'Do as you like for the rest of your life'

'Lo!' quod the Sompnour, 'for God's armes tuo!
A frer wol **entremet him** evermo!   interfere
Lo, goode men, a **flie** and eek a frere   fly
Woln falle in every dissche and matiere!
What spekst thou of perambulacioun?[55]
What! Ambil, or trot, or pees, or go sit doun!
810 Thou **lettest** oure disport in this matere.'   hinder
'Ye, woltow so, Sir Sompnour,' quod the Frere,
'Now by my fay, I schal, er that I go,
Telle of a sompnour such a tale or tuo
That all the folk schuln laughen in this place.'
'Now ellis, Frere, I **byschrew** thy face,'   curse
Quod this Sompnour, 'and I byschrewe me,
But if I telle tales tuo or thre
Of freres, er I come to **Sydingborne**,   Sittingbourne (Kent)
That I schal make thin herte for to **morne**,   mourn/grieve
820 For wel I wot, thi paciens is goon.'
Oure hoste cride, 'pees! And that **anoon**!   right away
And sayde, 'let the womman telle hir tale!
Ye **fare** as folkes that dronken ben of ale.   behave
Do, Dame, tel forth your tale, and that is best.'
'Al redy, sir,' quod sche, 'right as you lest,
If I have licence of this worthy frere.'
'Yis, Dame,' quod he, 'tel forth, and I schal heere.'

Narrat

she tells (her story)

❦ In olde dayes of the kyng Arthour,
830 Of which that Britouns speken gret honour,
Al was this lond fulfilled of **fayrie**;   fairies
The elf queen with hir joly compaignye
Daunced fuloft in many a grene **mede**.   meadow
This was the old **oppynyoun**, as I **rede** –   belief; understand
I speke of many hundrid yer ago:
But now can no man see noon elves mo,

---

55 Chaucer is punning here; the Friar means 'perambulation' in a literary and
   philosophical sense, but the Summoner interprets it literally, that is, to walk
   about.

For now the grete charite and prayeres
Of **lymytours**, and other holy freres,   friars with licence to beg
That sechen every lond and every streem
As thik as **motis** in the sonne beem,   rays   840
Blessynge halles, chambres, kichenes, **boures**,   bedrooms
Citees, **burghes**, castels hihe, and toures;   towns
Thropes, bernes, **shepnes**, and **dayeries**,   villages; stables; dairies
That makith that ther ben no fayeries.
For ther as wont was to walken an elf,
Ther walkith noon but the lymytour himself,
In **undermeles** and in morwenynges, [56]   late mornings
And saith his matyns and his holy thinges
As he goth in his lymytacioun.
Wommen may go **saufly** up and doun;   safely   850
In every bussch and under every tre
Ther is non other incumbent but he, [57]
And he wol but doon hem dishonour.
And so bifel it that this king Arthour
Had in his hous a lusty **bacheler**,   young knight
That on a day com rydyng fro ryver,
And **happed**, al alone as sche was born,   it happened that
He saugh a mayde walkyng him byforn;
Of which mayden anoon, **maugre** hir **heed**,   despite; struggle
By **verray fors** he **byraft** hir **maydenhed**.   brute force; took; virginity   860
For such oppressioun was such clamour,   because of
And such **pursuyte** unto Kyng Arthour,   pleading
That **dampned** was the knight, and schuld be ded   condemned
By cours of lawe, and schuld have lost his heed –
Paraventure such was the statut **tho** –   then
But that the queen, and other ladys mo,
So longe preyeden [thay] the kyng **of grace**,   for mercy
Til he his lif hath graunted in the place,
And gaf him to the queen al at hir wille,
To chese wethur sche wold him save or **spille**.   kill   870
The queen thanked the kyng with al hir might,
And after, thus sche spak unto the knight,

56 After prime, so from nine o'clock until midday.
57 Other manuscripts have 'incubus' (evil spirit) instead of 'incumbent', which
   implies a priest with an ecclesiastical living. Either makes sense.

Whan that sche saugh hir tyme upon a day:
'Thow stondest yet,' quod she, 'in such **array**   condition
That of thy lyf hastow no **sewerte**.   certainty
I graunte thy lif, if thou canst telle me
What thing is it that wommen most desiren;
Be **war**, and keep thy nekbon fro the **iren**.   careful; iron (axe or sword)
And if thou canst not tellen it anoon,
880   Yet wol I give the leve for to goon
A twelf month and a day, it for to **lere**   learn
An answar suffisaunt in this matiere;
And **seurte** wol I have, er that thou **pace**,   pledge; go away
Thy body for to yelden in this place.'
Wo was this knight, and sorwfully he **siked**,   sighed
But what? He may not doon al as him liked.
And atte last he **ches** him for to **wende**,   chose; go
And cam agein, right at the yere's ende,
With swich answer as God him wolde **purveye**;   provide
890   And takith his leve, and **wendith** forth his weye.   goes
He **sekith** every hous and every place   searches
Wherso he hopith for to fynde grace
To lerne what thing wommen loven most,
But he ne couthe arryven **in no cost**   at no place
Wheras he mighte fynde this matiere
To these thinges accordyng **in fere**:   together
Somme sayden wommen loven best richesse,
Somme sayde honour, and some sayde jolynesse,
Somme sayde riche **array**, some sayden lust on bedde,   clothing
900   And ofte tyme to be widwe and wedde.
Somme sayden, 'Owre herte is most **y-eased**   made happy
Whan we ben y-flaterid and y-pleased.'
He goth ful neigh the **soth**, I wil not lye –   truth
A man schal wynne us best with flaterye,
And with attendaunce and busynesse
Ben we **y-limed**, bothe **more** and lesse –   caught; greater
And somme sayen that we loven best
For to be fre, and to doon as us **lest**,   like
And that no man repreve us of our vice,
910   But say that we be wys, and no thing nyce;
For trewely, ther is noon of us alle,
If eny **wight** wold **claw us on the galle**,   person; scratch a sore spot

That we nyl like, for he saith us **soth** –   truth
Assay, and he schal fynd it that so doth;
For be we never so **vicious** withinne,   ful of vices
We schuln be holde wys, and clene of synne.
And somme sayen that gret delit han we
For to be holden **stabil** and **secre**,   reliable; discreet
And in oon purpos stedfastly to duelle,
And nought **bywreye** thing that men us telle.   betray/give away 920
But that tale is not worth a **rake's stele** –   rake's handle
Pardy, we wymmen can right no thing **hele**:   hold
Witnes on **Mida**, wil ye here the tale?   Midas
Ovyd, among his other thinges smale,
Sayde Mida had under his **lange heris**,   long hairs
Growyng upon his heed, tuo ass's **eeris**,   ears
The whiche vice he hid, as he best might,
Ful subtilly fro every man's sight,
That save his wyf, ther wist of that nomo;
He loved hir most, and trusted hir also.   930
He prayed hir that to no creature
Sche schulde tellen of his disfigure.
Sche swor him, nay, for al this world to wynne,
Sche nolde do that vilonye or synne,
To make hir housband have so foul a name.
Sche wold not tel it, for hir **oughne** schame.   own
But natheles, hir thoughte that sche **dyde**   died
That sche so long a counseil scholde hyde;
Hir thought it **swal** so sore about hir **hert**   swelled; heart
That **needely** som word hir most astert;   of necessity 940
And sins sche dorst not tel it unto man,
Doun to a **marreys** fastby sche ran.   marsh
Til sche cam ther hir herte was on **fuyre**,   fire
And as a **bytoure bumblith** in the **myre**,   bittern booms; mere/lake
Sche layd hir mouth unto the water doun:
'**Bywreye** me not, thou watir, with thi **soun**!'
Quod sche, 'To the I telle it, and nomo –
Myn housbond hath long asse eeris tuo!
Now is myn hert **al hool**, now is it oute;   feels better
I might no lenger kepe it, **out of doute**.'   doubtless/for sure 950
Her may ye se, **theigh** we a tyme **abyde**,   though; wait
Yet out it **moot**; we can no **counseil** hyde.   must; secret

The remenaunt of the tale, if ye wil here,
Redith Ovid; and ther ye **mow** it **leere**.   may; learn
This knight, of which my tale is specially,
Whan that he saugh he might nou*g*ht come therby;
This is to say, what wommen loven most,
Withinne his brest ful sorwful was the **gost**,   spirit
But hom he goth; he might no lenger **sojourne**.   stay
960 The day was come that homward most he torne;
And in his way it hapnyd him to ride
In al his care, under a forest side,[58]
Wheras he saugh upon a daunce go
Of ladys four and twenty, and yit mo.
Toward this ilke daunce **y-drough** ful **yerne**,   he came; eagerly
In hope that som wisdom schuld y-lerne,
But certeynly, er he com fully there,
Vanysshid was this daunce, he **nyste** where.   did not know
No creature saugh he that **bar lif**,   was alive
970 **Sauf** on the greene he saugh sittyng a **wyf**;   except; woman
A **fouler** wight ther no may no man **devyse**.   uglier; imagine
Agens the knight this olde wyf gan ryse,   to greet
And sayde, 'Sir Knight, heer forth lith no way;
Tel me what ye seekyn, by your **fay**.   faith
Paradventure it may the better be –   perhaps
Thise olde folk **con mochil** thing,' quod sche.   know many
'My lieve modir,' quod this knight, 'certayn
I am but ded, but if that I can sayn
What thing is it that wommen most desire.
980 Couthe ye me wisse, I wold wel quyt your huyre.'[59]
'**Plight me thy trouth** her in myn hond,' quod sche,   give me your word
'The nexte thing that I require the
Thou schalt it doo, if it be in thy might,
And I wol telle it the **er** it be night.'   before
'Have her my trouthe,' quod the knight, 'I graunte.'
'Thanne,' quod sche, 'I dar me wel **avaunte**   boast
Thy lif is **sauf**, for I wol stonde therby –   safe
Upon my lif, the queen wol say as I.
Let se which is the proudest of hem alle

58 'beside a forest'
59 'if you let me know I'll make it worth your while'

That werith on a coverchief or a **calle**,   headdress   990
That dar say nay of thing I schal the teche;
Let us go forth, withouten more speche.'
Tho **rowned** sche a **pistil** in his eere,   whispered; message
And bad him to be glad, and have no fere.
Whan thay ben comen to the court, this knight
Sayd he had holde that day that he **hight**.   promised
Al redy was his answer, as he sayde.
Ful many a noble wyf and many a mayde,
And many a wydow, for that thay ben wyse,
The queen hirself sittyng as a justise,   1000
Assemblid ben, his answer for to **hiere**;   hear
And afterward, this knight was **bode appiere**;   ordered to appear
To every wight comaundid was silence,
And that the knight schuld telle in audience
What thing that worldly wommen loven best.
The knight ne stood not stille, as doth a best,[60]
But to the questioun answerde
With manly voys, that al the court it herde:
'My liege lady, generally,' quod he,
'Wommen desiren to have **soveraynte**,   rule   1010
As wel over hir housbond as over hir **love**,   lover
And for to be in **maystry** him above.   power/authority
This is the most desir, though ye me kille;
Doth as yow list, I am heer **at your wille**.'   in your power
In al the court ne was ther wyf ne mayde,
Ne wydow, that **contraried** that he sayde,   argued against
But sayden he was worthy have his lif;
And with that word, up start that olde wif
Which that the knight saugh sittyng on the grene:
'Mercy,' quod sche, 'my soveraign lady queene!   1020
Er that your court departe, doth me right;
I taughte this answer unto the knight,
For which he plighte me his trouthe there,
The first thing that I wold him requere
He wold it do, if it lay in his might.
Bifore the court then, pray I the, Sir Knight,'

60 'shuffled about like a beast'

Quod sche, 'that thou me take unto thy wif,

For wel thou **wost** that I have **kept** thy lif.   know; saved

If I say fals, sey nay, **upon thy fey**.'   upon your faith

1030 This knight answerd, 'Allas, and waylawey!

I wot right wel that such was my **byhest** –   promise

For God's love, as **chese** a new request: choose

Tak al my **good**, and let my body go!'   possessions

'Nay,' quod sche, 'than I schrew us bothe tuo;

For though that I be foule, old, and pore,

I nolde for al the metal, ne for the **oure**   ore

That under erthe is **grave**, or **lith** above,   buried; lies

But I thy wife were, and eek thy love.'

'My love!' quod he, 'Nay, nay! My dampnacioun!

1040 Allas, that any of my nacioun

Schuld ever so foule **disparagid** be!'   married beneath themselves

But al for nought, the ende is this; that he

Constreigned was, he needes most hir wedde;   forced

And takith his wif, and goth with hir to bedde.

Now wolden som men say, paradventure,

That for my negligence I **do no cure**   don't bother

To telle yow the joye and tharray

That at that fest was maad that **ilke** day.   same

To which thing schortly answeren I schal,

1050 And say, ther nas fest ne joy at al;

Ther nas but hevynesse and muche sorwe,

For **prively** he weddyd hir in a morwe,   secretly

And alday **hudde** him, as doth an **oule**,   hid; owl

So wo was him, his wyf loked so foule.

Gret was the wo the knight had in his thought,

Whan he was with his wyf on bedde brought;

He **walwith**, and he torneth to and fro;   tosses

His olde wyf lay smylyng ever mo,

And sayd, 'O deere housbond, **benedicite**!   God bless us

1060 Fareth every knight with his wyf as ye?

Is this the lawe of King Arthur's hous?

Is every knight of his love thus daungerous?

I am your oughne love, and your wyf;

I am sche that hath savyd your lyf,

And certes ne dede I yow never **unright**.   wrong

Why **fare** ye thus with me the first night?   behave

Ye fare lik a man that had left his wit.
What is my **gult**? For God's love, tel me it,   guilt
And it schal be **amendid**, if that I may.'   put right
'Amendid?' quod this knight, 'Allas! Nay, nay!   1070
It wol nought be amendid never mo;
Thow art so **lothly**, and so old also,   ugly
And therto comen of so **lowh a kynde**   low birth
That litil wonder is though I **walwe and wynde**;   toss and turn
So wolde God, myn herte wolde brest!'[61]
'Is this,' quod sche, 'the cause of your unrest?'
'Ye, certeynly,' quod he, 'no wonder is.'
'Now sire,' quod sche, 'I couthe amende al this,
If that me list, **er it were dayes thre**;   before three days have passed
So wel ye mighte **bere** yow to me.   behave towards 1080
But **for** ye speken of such **gentilesse**   because; nobility
As is descendit out of old richesse,
Therfor schuld ye ben holden gentil men –
Such arrogaunce is not worth an hen!
Lok who that is most vertuous always,
Prive and **pert**, and most **entendith ay**   publicly; tries always
To do the gentil dedes that he can,
Tak him for the grettist gentilman.
Crist wol we **clayme of** him oure gentilesse,   derive from
Nou**g**ht of oure eldres, for her olde richesse;   1090
For though thay give us al her heritage,
For which we claime to be of high **parage**,   lineage/descent
Yit may thay not biquethe for no thing
To noon of us, so vertuous lyvyng
That made hem gentilmen y-callid be,
And bad us folwe hem in such **degre**.   quality/status
Wel can the wyse poet of Florence
That **hatte Dannt**, speke of this sentence.   is called; Dante
Lo, in such maner of rym is Dannt's tale,[62]
Ful **seeld** uprisith by his braunchis smale   seldom   1100
Prowes of man; for God of his prowesse
Wol that we clayme of him our gentilesse;
For of our auncestres we nothing clayme

61 'So help me God, my heart is bursting'
62 'this is the meaning of Dante's tale'

But temporal thing, that men may hurt and **mayme**.   harm
Ek every wight wot this as wel as I;
If gentiles were plaunted naturelly
Unto a certeyn lignage, doun the line,
Prive ne apert thay wolde never **fine**   privately nor publicly; stop
To don of gentilesce the fair office;
1110 Thay might nought doon no vileny or vice.
Tak fuyr, and **ber** it in the derkest hous   carry
Bitwixe this and the **mount Caukasous**,   Caucasus mountains
And let men **shit** the dores and go **thenne**;   shut; away
Yit wol the fuyr as fair and lighte brenne
As twenty thousand men might it biholde;[63]
His office naturel ay wol it holde,[64]
Up peril on my lif, til that it dye.
Her may ye se wel how that genterye
Is nought **annexid** to **possessioun**,   joined; earthly possessions
1120 Sithins folk ne doon her operacioun[65]
Always, as doth the fuyr, lo, **in his kynde**,   according to its nature
For, God it wot, men may ful often fynde
A lord's sone do schame and vilonye,
And he that wol have **pris** of his gentrie   respect
For he was boren of a gentil hous,
And had his eldres noble and vertuous,
And nyl himselve doo no gentil dedes,
Ne folw his gentil **aunceter** that deed is –   ancestor
He is nought gentil, be he duk or erl,
1130 For vileyn synful deedes maketh a cherl;[66]
For gentilnesse nys but **renome**   renown
Of thin auncestres, for her heigh bounte,
Which is a straunge thing to thy persone;[67]
Thy gentilesce cometh fro God alloone.
Than comth oure **verray** gentilesse of grace;   true
It was no thing biquethe us with oure place.
Thinketh how nobil, as saith Valerius,

---

63 'as if twenty thousand men were looking at it'
64 'it will always do what it is naturally supposed to'
65 'gentlefolk aren't always 'gentle' in what they do'
66 'for low-born sinful deeds make a man a churl'
67 'which doesn't belong to you personally'

Was thilke Tullius Hostilius,
That out of povert ros to high noblesse;[68]
Redith Senek, and redith eek Boece:[69]   1140
Ther schuln ye se **expresse** that no dred is   explicitly
That he is gentil that doth gentil **dedis**.   deeds
And therfor, **lieve** housbond, I conclude,   dear
Al were it that myn aunectres wer **rude**,   although; rough/poor
Yit may the highe God, and so hope I,
Graunte me grace to live vertuously;
Than am I gentil, whan that I bygynne
To lyve vertuously, and **weyven** synne;   avoid
And theras ye of povert me **repreve**,   reprove/blame
The heighe God, on whom that we bilieve,   1150
In **wilful** povert **ches** to leve his lif;   voluntary; chose
And certes, every man, mayden or wif,
May understonde that Jhesus, heven king,
Ne wold not chese a vicious lyvyng.
Glad povert is an honest thing, certayn;
This wol Senek and other clerkes sayn.
Who that holt him payd of his povert,[70]
I hold him riche, al had he nou*gh*t a **schert**.   shirt
He that **coveitith** is a pore wight,   is envious
For he wold have that is not in his might;   1160
But he that nou*gh*t hath, ne coveyteth nou*gh*t to have,
Is riche, although ye hold him but a knave;
Verray povert, it syngeth proprely.   true
Juvenal saith of povert, 'Merily
The pore man, whan he goth by the way,
Bifore the theves he may synge and play.'
Povert is hateful, and, as I gesse,
A ful gret brynger out of **busynesse**,   hard work
A gret **amender** eek of **sapiens**,   increaser; wisdom
To him that takith it in paciens.   1170
Povert is this, although it seme **elenge**,   miserable
Possessioun that no wight wil chalenge.
Povert ful often, whan a man is lowe,

68 Tullius Hostilius was a farm worker who became emperor of Rome.
69 Seneca and Boethius.
70 'whoever is happy with his poverty'

Makith him his God and eek himself to knowe.

Povert a **spectacle** is, as thinketh me,   mirror

Thurgh which he may his **verray** frendes se;   true

And therfor, sir, syth that I yow nought greve,

Of my povert no more ye me repreve.

Now, sir, of **elde** ye repreve me;   old age

1180 And certes, sir, though noon auctorite

Were in no book, ye gentils of honour

Sayn that men schold an old wight **doon favour**,   defer to

And **clepe** him, 'fader,' for your gentilesse,   call

And certes I schal fynden, as I gesse.[71]

Now ther that ye sayn I am foul and old,

Than drede yow nought to ben a **cokewold**;   cuckold

For **filthe** and **elde**, also mot I the,   dirt; old age

Ben grete **wardeyns** upon chastite.   guardians

But natheles, sith I knowe your **delyt**,   pleasure

1190 I schal fulfille youre worldly appetyt.

'**Chese** now,' quod sche, 'oon of these thinges tweye: choose

To have me foul and old til that I deye,

And be to yow a trewe humble wyf,

And never yow displease in al my lyf,

Or elles ye wold have me yong and fair,

And take your **aventure** of the **repair**   chance; callers

That schal be to your hous bycause of me,

Or in som other place may wel be.

Now chese yourselven, **whethir** that yow liketh.'   which

1200 This knight **avysith him**, and sore **sikith**,   considers; sighs

But atte last he sayd in this manere:

' 'My lady and my love, and my wif so deere,

I putte me in your wyse governaunce;

Chesith yourself which may be most pleasaunce

And most honour to yow, and me also –

I do no fors the whether of the tuo,   I don't care

For as yow likith, **it suffisith me**.'   it's good enough for me

'Than have I gete of yow the maystry,' quod sche,

'Sith I may govern and chese as me list.'

1210 'Ye, certis, wyf,' quod he, 'I hold it best.'

'Kys me,' quod sche, 'we ben no lenger **wrothe**,   angry

71 'I shall find such authorities'

For, by my trouthe, I wol be to yow bothe;
This is to say, ye, bothe fair and good;
I pray to god that I mot **sterve wood**   die mad
But I be to yow also good and trewe
As ever was wyf, **siththen** the world was newe: since
And but I be tomorow as fair to seen
As eny lady, emperesse, or queen
That is bitwixe **thest** and eek the west,   the east
Doth by my lyf right even as yow lest.   1220
Cast up the curtyn and see how that it is.'
And whan the knyght saugh verrayly al this,
That sche so fair was, and so yong therto,
For joye he **hent** hir in his armes tuo,   seized
His herte bathid in a bath of blisse –
A thousand tyme on rowe he **gan** hir kisse,   began
And sche obeyed him in everything
That mighte doon him pleisauns or likyng.
And thus thay lyve unto her lyves' ende
In parfyt joye, and Jhesu Crist us sende   1230
Housbondes meke, yonge, and freissche on bedde,
And grace to overbyde hem that we wedde.   outlive
And eek I pray to Jhesu, **schort** her lyves   shorten
That wil nought be governed after her wyves;
And old and angry **nygardes of despense**,   misers about expenditure
God send hem sone verray pestilence!

Here endith the Wif of Bathe hire tale

THE FRIAR'S PROLOGUE AND TALE

Despite the host's best efforts, the friar and the summoner insist on having a loud argument, based on whose profession is the most abusive. In the friar's tale, a summoner goes out to make some money from a poor old widow. On the way, he meets a handsome stranger dressed in green. The man says he is a bailiff, and the summoner says that he is a bailiff too, as he is too ashamed to say that he is really a summoner. The stranger tells the summoner about himself, eventually revealing that he is a devil from hell, but the summoner either is not listening, or he does not believe or care. Despite this knowledge, he swears to hold fellowship with the other man, and they will make a profit together. He is proud to show the devil his methods of extortion, but the other man says that he only takes what is genuinely offered to him. They meet a carter whose cart is stuck in the mud. The carter swears that the devil should take his horses, but the devil refuses to do so on the grounds that the carter did not mean it. When the cart is out of the mud and the carter praises his horses for a job well done, this is proved correct. The summoner goes to the old woman's house, and threatens to summon her to court if she does not pay him twelve pence. She refuses, and swears at him, consigning him and her pan to the devil. The devil asks her if she really meant it. She says she did, and so the devil takes both the pan and the summoner's soul to hell.

The sweet-voiced, slightly effeminate friar and the loud, scabby summoner, who children fear like the devil, are not only abusers of their respective positions. Their argument is particularly disrespectful to the wife of Bath, whose story they interrupt. As it continues, they seem to forget everyone else. As their quarrel reveals them as the individuals they really are, it can be seen that there is very little difference, in moral terms, between them. Both are dedicated to the making of profit by any means. It becomes clear that, whatever the host may say, the summoner is going to follow the reeve's precedent and tell a story against the friar, and that the friar will tell a story against the summoner, so they begin a literary duel: death by narrative.

The Friar's Tale relies for its effect on irony. Much of its humour is generated, as in Chaucer's other comic tales, by the distance between the knowledge of the audience and that of the main character, in this case, of course, a summoner. The handsome stranger drops plenty of hints about his identity, all of which would be familiar to the audience; his shape-changing, his home in the north (the domain of the devil), his occupation. When it is finally revealed that the stranger is a devil, the audience can hardly be surprised. He exists on the margins of the world, which is where the summoner works. His dress, like that of a forester, emphasises the stranger's marginality, and his ability to move 'between worlds'. However, the wilful ignorance of the summoner, who actually at one point says that he will hold with the stranger even if he is the devil, creates the humour. The audience may laugh at the summoner in all good conscience, as they have already been told what a complete scoundrel he is. He deserves his fate.

The other main irony, which is central to the tale's comedy, is the fact that the devil is a far more moral man than the summoner. He is courteous, and unlike the summoner, he is certainly not a liar. Outlaw characters in medieval literature deliver moral tests to those who hold positions of power in society (like the sheriff in Gamelyn and in the Robin Hood stories), and punish them on behalf of all if they fail. The stranger in green performs this function in the friar's tale, and the summoner is punished for failing the moral test. The devil always gives the summoner a truthful answer, even telling the summoner bluntly that he *is* a devil. Again, unlike the summoner, he takes only what is freely given to him. He will not take the carter's horses because the carter does not really mean what he says, although he does take the summoner's soul when the old woman genuinely consigns it to the devil. The devil has parameters within which he must remain, according to medieval beliefs concerning demons, which the story outlines in some fascinating detail. The summoner in the tale is, of course, just like the friar himself, so in another, elegant irony, the friar, as well as insulting summoners, is actually telling a tale against himself. The tale leaves an unanswered question about the venality of those who employ summoners to bring people to court, or to pay fines, on charges of immorality. Who is more guilty, the summoner or the bishop who employs him?

Key Questions

Who is morally right, or wrong, in this story? Has the friar successfully attacked the summoner?

What does the story tell us about medieval beliefs concerning devils and demons?

How venal are the friar and the summoner, and how venal is the Church they serve?

Topic Keywords

Medieval Church/ Church courts/ medieval popular religion/ the medieval countryside

Further Reading

Gail Berlin, 'Speaking to the Devil: A New Context for The Friar's Tale', *Philological Quarterly*, 69, 1990, pp. 1–12

Morton Bloomfield, 'The Friar's Tale as a Liminal Tale', *Chaucer Review*, 17, 1985, pp. 286–91

Nathaniel Brody, 'The Fiend and the Summoner, Statius and Dante: A Possible Source for The Friar's Tale', *Chaucer Review*, 32, 1997, pp. 175–82

Carole K. Brown and Marion F. Egge, 'The Friar's Tale and The Wife of Bath's Tale', *Publications of the Modern Language Association of America*, 91, 1976, pp. 291–2

Brantley L. Bryant, ' "By extorcions I lyve": Chaucer's Friar's Tale and Corrupt Officials", *Chaucer Review*, 42, 2007, pp. 180–95

John Finlayson, 'Art and Morality in Chaucer's Friar's Tale and *The Decameron* – Day One, Story One', *Neophilologus*, 89, 2005, pp. 139–52

Mary Godfrey, 'Only Words: Cursing and the Authority of Language in Chaucer's Friar's Tale', *Exemplaria*, 10, 1998, pp. 307–28

Thomas Hahn, 'Text and Context: Chaucer's Friar's Tale', *Studies in the Age of Chaucer*, 5, 1983, pp. 67–101

Edward Jacobs and Robert E. Jungman, 'His Mother's Curse: Kinship in The Friar's Tale', *Philological Quarterly*, 64, 1985, pp. 256–9

Daniel Kline, ' "Myne by Right": Oath-Making and Intent in The Friar's Tale', *Philological Quarterly*, 77, 1998, pp. 271–93

V. Kolve, 'Man in the Middle: Art and Religion in Chaucer's Friar's Tale', *Studies in the Age of Chaucer*, 12, 1990, pp. 3–46

H. Marshall Leicester, ' "No vileyns word": Social Context and Performance in Chaucer's Friar's Tale', *Chaucer Review*, 17, 1982, pp. 21–39

R. T. Leneghan, 'The Irony of the Friar's Tale', *Chaucer Review*, 7, 1973, pp. 281–94

Daniel M. Murtaugh, 'Riming Justice in The Friar's Tale', *Neuphilologische Mitteilungen*, 74, 1973, pp. 107–12

Peter Nicholson, 'The Analogues of Chaucer's Friar's Tale', *English Language Notes*, 17, 1979, pp. 93–8

Richard H. Passon, ' "Entente" in Chaucer's Friar's Tale', *Chaucer Review*, 2, 1968, pp. 166–71

Helen Phillips, ' "A gay yeman, under a forest side": The Friar's Tale and the Robin Hood Tradition', in *Medieval Cultural Studies: Essays in Honour of Stephen Knight*, edited by Ruth Evans, Helen Fulton and David Matthews, Cardiff, University Press of Wales, 2006, pp. 123–37

Penn R. Szittya, 'The Friar's Tale and The Wife of Bath's Tale', *Publications of the Modern Language Association of America*, 91, 1976, pp. 292–3

Here bygynneth the prologe of the Frere's tale

❦ This worthy lymytour, this noble frere,
He made always a **lourynge** cheere   *frowning*
Upon the Sompnour, but for **honeste**   *good manners*
No **vileyn's worde** yit to him spak he,   *bad language*
But atte last he sayd unto the wyf,
'Dame,' quod he, "God give yow good lyf!
Ye han her **touchid**, al so mot I the,   *mentioned*
In **scole matier** gret difficulte;   *matter for academics*
Ye han sayd **mochel** thing right wel, I say,   *many*
But, Dame, right as we ryden by the way   10
Us needeth nought but for to speke of **game**,   *entertainment*
And **lete auctorites**, in Goddes name,   *leave (learned) authorities*
To preching and to **scoles** of clergie.   *colleges*
But if it like to this companye,
I wil yow of a sompnour telle a game –
Parde, ye may wel knowe by the name
That of a sompnour may no good be sayd –
Pray yow that noon of yow be **evel apayd**!   *treated badly*
A sompnour is a **renner** up and doun,   *runner*
With **maundements** for **fornicacioun**,   *summonses; sexual sin* 20
And is **y-bete** at every toune's eende.'   *beaten*
Our **oste** spak: 'A, Sir, ye schold been **heende**   *host; polite*
And **curteys**, as a man of your **estaat**;   *courteous; station (in life)*
In company we wol have no **debaat**.   *argument*
Telleth your tale, and let the Sompnour be.'
'Nay,' quoth the Sompnour, 'let him say to me
What so him **list**: whan it cometh to my lot   *likes*
By God, I schal him **quyten** every **grot**!   *pay him back; groat (coin)*
I schal him telle which a gret honour
Is to ben a fals flateryng **lymytour**,   *friar with licence to beg* 30
And his **offis** I schal him telle, y-wis!'   *job/duty/religious service*
Oure host answerd and sayd the Sompnour, 'Pees!'
And after this he sayd unto the Frere,
'Telleth forth your tale, my maister deere.'[1]

1 'my good man'

Narrat

he tells (his story)

❦ **Whilom** ther was dwellyng in my countre[2]   *some time ago*
An **erchedeken**, a man of gret **degre**,[3]   *archdeacon; rank*
That boldely **did execucioun**   *carried out*
In punyschyng of fornicacioun,
40   Of wicchecraft, and eek of **bauderye**,   *pimping*
Of diffamacioun and **avoutrie**,   *adultery*
Of **chirchreves** and of **testamentes**,   *theft from churches; wills*
Of contractes and of **lak of sacraments**,   *missing the sacraments*
And **eek** of many another cryme,   *also*
Which needith not to **reherse** at this tyme,   *tell*
Of **usur** and of **symony** also;[4]   *usury; simony*
But certes, lecchours did he grettest woo.
Thay schulde synge, if thay were **hent**,   *seized*
And **smale tythers**, thay were fouly **schent**[5]   *small tithers; ruined*
50   If eny persoun wold upon hem **pleyne** –   *accuse*
Ther might **astert** him no **pecunial** peyne.   *escape; financial*
For smale tythes and for smal offrynge
He made the people pitously to synge,
For **er** the bisschop caught him in his **hook**,[6]
Thay weren in the archedekene's book,
And hadde thurgh his **jurediccioun**   *jurisdiction*
Power to have of hem **correccioun**.   *punishment*
He had a sompnour redy to his hond,
A slyer boy was noon in Engelond;
60   Ful prively he had his **espiaile**,   *spy network*
That taughte him wher he might **avayle**.   *take his opportunity*
He couthe spare of lecchours oon or tuo,
And **techen** him to four and twenty mo.   *lead*
For though this Sompnour **wood** were as an hare,   *mad*
To telle his harlottry I wol not spare;

---

2 'country' at this time means not 'nation' but 'region' or 'extended community'
3 Officer (responsible for moral discipline) under the bishop in a diocese.
4 Usury is the sin of lending money for the payment of interest, simony the payment of money in return for ecclesiastical preferment.
5 Those who did not pay their tithes (one tenth of their income, to the Church) in full at the appointed time.
6 before; crook (curved staff).

For we ben out of here correccioun –
Thay have of us no jurediccioun,
Ne never schul to terme of alle her lyves[7]
'**Peter**! So been the wommen of the styues –[8]   by St Peter
Thay beth y-put al out of oure cures!'[9]   70
'Pees, with **meschaunce** and with **mesaventures**!'   ill luck; misfortune
Thus sayd our host, "And let him telle his tale!
Now telleth forth, although the Sompnour **gale**;   complain
Ne spareth nought, myn owne maister deere.'
This false theef, the sompnour, quoth the frere,
Had always **bawdes** redy to his hond,   whores
As eny **hauk** to lure in Engelond,   hawk
that told him al the secre that thay knewe,
For here acqueintaunce was not **come of newe**;   only just come by
Thay were his **approwours**; prively   agents provocateurs   80
He took himself a gret profyt therby –
His maister knew nat always what he **wan**.   gained
Withoute **maundement**, a **lewed** man,   unlearned
He couthe sompne up **peyne** of Crist's **curs**,   threat; curse
And thay were glad to fille wel his purs,
And make him grete festis **atte nale**;   in the town
And right as Judas hadde purses smale
And was a theef, right such a theef was he;
His maister had not half his **duete**.   amount owing
He was, if I schal give him his **laude**,   deserts   90
A theef, a sompnour, and eek a **baude**;   pimp
And he had **wenches** at his **retenue**,   whores; hired band
That whethir that Sir Robert or Sir Hughe,
Or Jak, or Rauf, or whoso that it were
That lay by hem, they told it in his eere.
Thus was the wenche and he of oon assent,
And he wold fecche a **feyned maundement**,   false summons
And sompne hem to **chapitre**, bothe tuo,   chapter (court)
And **pyle** the man and let the wenche go.   rob
Than wold he sayn, 'I schal, frend, for thy sake   100
Don strike the out of oure **lettres blake**;   record of wrongdoers

7 'as long as they live'
8 Stews, or bath-houses. They were the haunt of prostitutes.
9 Here the Summoner is interjecting.

The thar nomore as in this cas **travayle**.   trouble
I am thy frend, ther I the may **avayle**.'   benefit
Certeynly he knew of **bribours** mo   bribers
Than possible is to telle in yeres tuo,
For in this world **nys dogge for the bowe**[10]
That can an hurt deer from an **hol** y-knowe   fit
Bet than this sompnour knew a leccheour,
Or avoutier, or ellis a **paramour**;   (illicit) lover
110 And for that was the **fruyt of al his rent**,   best part of his income
Therfore theron he set al his entent.
And so bifel that **oones in a day**   one day
This sompnour, ever **waytyng on** his pray,   lying in wait for
Rod forth to sompne a widew, an old ribibe,[11]
Feynyng a cause, for he wolde bribe.   pretending
It happed that he **say** bifore him ryde   saw
A gay **yeman under a forest syde**.   yeoman; beside a forest
A bow he bar, and arwes bright and **kene**;   sharp
He had upon a **courtepy** of grene,   jacket
120 An hat upon his heed, with **frenges** blake,   fringes
'Sir,' quod this sompnour, 'heyl and wel overtake!'
Welcome,' quod he, 'and every good felawe!'
'Whider **ridestow** under this grene **schawe**?'   are you riding; wood
Sayde this yiman, 'Wiltow fer to day?'
This sompnour answerd and sayde, 'Nay.
Her **faste** by,' quod he, 'is myn entent;   close
To ryden for to reysen up a rent
That longith to my lord's duete.'[12]
'Artow than a **bayely**?' quod he.   bailiff
130 He durste not, for verray filth and schame
Sayn that he was a sompnour, for the name.
'**De par dieux**!' quod the yeman, '**Lieve** brother,   by God; dear
Thou art a bayly, and I am another!
I am unknowen as in this contre –
Of thin acqueyntance I wol praye the,
And eek of brotherheed, if it yow **lest**   likes

10 'is not an archer's hunting dog'
11 Stringed instrument: related to the use of the same in the saying 'there's many a
    good tune played on an old fiddle'.
12 'that is owing to my lord by right'

I have gold and silver in my chest;

If that the **happe** come in to oure schire,   happen

Al schal be thin, right as thou wolt desire.'

'**Graunt mercy**,' quod this sompnour, 'by my faith.'   many thanks   140

Everich in otheres hond his **trouthe** laith,   each; pledge

For to be sworne bretheren til thay **deyen** –   died

In **daliaunce** forth thay ride and pleyen;   gay banter

This sompnour, which that was as ful of **jangles**   gossip

As ful of venym ben these **wery angles**,   shrike

And ever enquering upon everything.

'Brother,' quod he, 'Wher is now your dwelling,

Another day if I sholde yow seeke?'

This yeman hym answerede in softe speche,

'Brother,' quod he, 'fer in the north contre,   150

Wheras I hope somtyme I schal the se,

Er we depart, I schal the so wel **wisse**,   know

That of myn hous ne schaltow never misse.'

'Now brother,' quod this sompnour, 'I yow pray,

Teche me, whil that we ryden by the way,

Syn that ye ben a baily, as am I,

Som **subtilte** as tel me faithfully,   craft

In myn office how that I may wynne,

And spare not for consciens or for synne,

But as my brother tel me how do ye.'   160

'Now by my trouthe, brothir myn,' sayd he,

'As I schal telle the a faithful tale,

My wages ben ful **streyt**, and eek ful **smale**.   pinched; meagre

My lord to me is hard and **daungerous**,   demanding

And myn office is ful **laborous**;   hard work

And therfor by extorciouns I lyve –

Forsoth, I take al that men wil give,

Algate by sleighte or by violence,   in any way

Fro yer to yer I wynne my **despence**;   outgoings

I can no better telle faithfully.'   170

'Now certes,' quod this sompnour, 'so fare I;

I spare not to take, God it woot,

But if it be to **hevy** or to **hoot**,   unless; difficult; onerous

What I may gete in counseil prively,

No more consciens of that have I.

Nere myn extorcions I might not lyven,   if it were not for

No of such **japes** I wil not be **schriven**.[13]
Stomak ne conscience know I noon;
I **schrew** thes **schriftefadres** everychoon!   curse; confessors
180 Wel be we met, by God and by **Seint Jame**;   St James
But, **leve** brother, telle me thy name,'   dear
Quod this sompnour. In this menewhile
This yeman gan a litel for to smyle –
'Brothir,' quod he, '**woltow** that I the telle?   Do you wish
I am a **feend**, my dwellyng is in helle,   fiend/demon
And her I ryde about my **purchasyng**,   making a profit
To wite wher men wol give me eny thing.
My purchas is th'effect of al my rent;[14]
Loke how thou ridest for the same entent –
190 To wynne good, thou **rekkist** never how;   understand
Right so fare I, for ryde I wolde now
Unto the world's ende for a pray.'
'A!' quod the sompnour, '**Benedicite**, what ye say!   God bless (us)
I **wende** ye were a yeman, trewely,   understood
Ye han a mannes **schap** as wel as I.   figure
Have ye a figure than **determinate**   definite
In helle, ther ye ben in your estate?'
'Nay, certeynly,' quod he, 'ther have we non,
But whan us likith we can take us **on**,   one
200 Or ellis make yow seme that we be **schape**   shaped
Somtyme like a man, or like an ape,
Or lik an aungel can I ryde or go;
It is no wonder thing, though it be so.
A lousy **iogelour** can deceyve the,   juggler/conjurer
And parfay, yit **can** I more craft than he.'   know
'Why,' quod this sompnour, 'ryde ye than or goon
In **sondry** wyse, and nou*ght* alway in oon?'   different
'For,' quod he, 'we wol us in such forme make
As most abil is oure pray to take.'[15]
210 'What makith yow to have al this labour?'
'Ful many a cause, lieve Sir Sompnour,'
Sayde this feend, 'but al thing hath a tyme –

13 tricks; forgiven (on confession).
14 'My profit is the substance of all my income . . .'
15 'as will help us best to take our prey . . . '

The day is schort, and it is passed **prime**,   *after nine o'clock*
And yit ne wan I nothing in this day.
I wol **entent** to wynnyng, if I may,   *set myself to*
And not entende oure **thinges** to declare;   *business*
For, brother myn, thy wit is al to **bare**   *inadequate*
To understond, although I told hem the.
For, but thou **axid** whi laboure we –   *asked*
For somtyme we ben God's **instrumentes**,   **220**
And menes to don his comaundements
Whan that him list, upon his creatures,
In **divers** act and in divers figures.   *various*
Withouten him we have no might, certeyn,
If that him **liste** stonde **ther-agayn**.   *wants; against it*
And somtyme at our prayer have we leeve,
Only the body, and not the soule greve:
Witness on **Jope**, whom we did ful wo.[16]   *Job*
And somtyme have we might of bothe tuo,
This is to say, of body and soule eeke,   **230**
And som tyme be we suffred for to **seeke**   *inflict trouble*
Upon a man, and doon his soule unrest,
And not his body, and al is for the best
Whan he withstondith oure temptacioun.
Al be it so, it was nought oure **entent**   *intention*
He schuld be **sauf**, but that we wold him **hent**.   *safe; seize*
And somtyme we ben servaunt unto man,
As to th'erchebisshop Seynt Dunstan,[17]
And to **th'apostolis** servaunt was I.'   *the apostles*
'Yit tel me,' quod the sompnour, 'faithfully –   **240**
Make ye yow newe bodies always
Of elements?' The fend answerde, 'Nay,
Somtyme we **feyne** and somtyme we ryse   *pretend*
With dede bodies, in ful wonder wyse,[18]
And speke **renably** and as fair and wel   *readily*
As to the Phitonissa dede Samuel;[19]

16 God allowed Job to be tempted by the devil, who caused unbearable suffering to
    be inflicted upon him.
17 Saint Dunstan, Archbishop of Canterbury, had several encounters with devils.
18 'In the physical guise of the dead'
19 Saul had the Witch of Endor raise the spirit of Samuel from the dead to advise him.

And yit wol somme say it was not he:

I **do no fors** of your divinite.   *don't care about*

But oon thing warne I the, I wol not **jape**;   *joke*

250 Thou wilt algates **wite** how we ben schape.   *know*

Thow schalt herafterward, my brother deere,

Come wher the nedith nothing for to **leere**,   *learn*

For thou schalt by thin **oughne** experience   *own*

Conne in a **chayer** reden of this sentence,   *(professorial) chair*

Bet than Virgile, whils he was **on lyve**   *alive*

Or Dannt also – now let us ryde **blyve**,[20]   *speedily*

For I wol holde company with the,

Til it be so that thou forsake me.'

'Nay' quod the sompnour, 'that schal nought **betyde**;   *happen*

260 I am a yiman that knowen is **ful wyde**,   *well known*

My trouthe wol I hold as in this caas;   *I'll keep my word*

For though thou be the devyl **Sathanas**,   *Satan*

My trouthe wol I holde to the, my brother,

As I am swore, and ech of us to other,

For to be trewe bretheren in this caas,

For bothe we goon abouten oure **purchas**.   *profit-making*

Tak thou thi part, and that men wil the gyven,

And I schal myn; thus may we bothe lyven,

And if eny of us have more than other,

270 Let him be trewe, and part it with his brother.'

'I graunte,' quod the devel, 'by my fay.'

And with that word thay riden forth her way,

And right at th'entryng of a town's ende,

To which this sompnour **schope** him for to **wende**,   *readied; go*

Thay **seigh** a cart that **chargid** was with hay   *saw; loaded*

Which that a carter drof forth in his way;

Deep was the way, **for** which the carte **stood**.   *because of; was stuck*

This carter **smoot**, and cryde as he wer wood,   *hit*

'Hayt, brok! Hayt stot,! **What spare ye** for the stoones?

     why do you hold back

280 The **fend**,' quod he, 'yow **fech**, body and bones,   *devil; take*

As **ferforthly** as ever wer ye **folid**,   *surely; foaled*

So moche wo as I have with yow **tholid** –   *suffered*

The devyl have al, bothe cart and hors and hay!'

20 Virgil describes Aeneas' visit to hell in the Aeneid, and Dante in Inferno.

This sompnour sayde, 'Her schal we se play!'
And ner the feend he drough **as nought ne were**,[21]
Ful prively, and **rouned** in his eere: whispered

❦ 'Herke, my brother! Herke, by thi faith!
Ne herest nought thou what the carter saith?
Hent it anoon, for he hath given it the,   seize
Bothe hay and **caples**, and eek his cart, **parde**!'   horses; by God   290
'Nay,' quod the devyl, 'God wot, **never a del**.   not a bit
It is nought his **entente**, trustith wel.   intention
Ask it thiself, if thou not **trowist** me,   believe
Or ellis **stint** awhile, and thou schalt se.'   hold back
This carter **thakketh** his hors upon the **croupe**,   whacks; backside
And thay bygon to **drawen** and to **stowpe**.   pull; strain
'Hayt, now,' quod he, 'ther Jhesu Crist yow blesse,
And al his **hondwerk**, bothe more and lesse!   handiwork
That was wel **twight**, myn oughne Lyard, boy!   pulled
I pray God save thy body, and Seint Loy –   300
Now is my cart out of the **sloo**, parde!'   mud
'Lo, brother,' quod the feend, 'what told I the –
Her may ye seen, myn owne deere brother,
The carter spak oon thing, and thought another.
Let us go forth abouten our **viage**;   journey
Hier wynne I nothing upon cariage.'[22]
Whan that thay comen somwhat out of toune,
This sompnour to his brothir gan to **roune**.   whisper
'Brothir,' quod he, 'her **wonyth** an old rebekke,   lives
That had almost **as lief to leese** hir necke   rather; lose   310
As for to give a peny of hir good.
I **wolt pens**, though that sche go **wood**,   want some money; mad
Or I wol somone hir to oure office –
And yit, God wot, I know of hir no vice.
But for thou canst not, as in this contre,
Wynne thy cost; tak her **ensample** of me.'   example
This sompnour **clapped** at the widow's gate;   knocked
'Com out,' quod he, 'thou olde **viritrate**!   hag
I trowe thou hast som frere or prest with the!'

21 'as if nothing had happened'
22 cariage – the lord's right to use a feudal tenant's horses.

320 'Who clappith ther?' sayde this widow, '**Benedicite**!   God bless (us)
    God save yow, Sir, what is your swete wille?'
    'I have,' quod he, 'a somonaunce of a bille.²³
    Up payne of cursyng, loke that thou be
    Tomorwe biforn our erchedekne's kne,
    To answer to the court of certeyn thinges.'
    'Now,' quod sche, 'Jhesu, Crist and King of Kinges,
    So wisly helpe me, as **I ne may**.   I cannot
    I have ben **seek**, and that ful many a day;   sick
    I may not goon so fer,' quod sche, 'ne ryde,
330 But I be deed, so **prikith** it in my syde.   hurts
    May I nat aske a **lybel**, Sir Sompnour,   libel (written copy)
    And answer ther by my **procuratour**   representative
    To suche thing as men wold **oppose** me?'   bring against
    '*Yis*,'quod this sompnour, 'pay **anoon** – let se –   immediately
    Twelf pens to me, and I the wil acquite;
    I schal no profyt have therby but **lite** –   a little
    My mayster hath the profyt and not I;
    Com of, and let me ryden hastily.   hurry up
    Gif me my twelf pens – I may no lenger tary.'
340 'Twelf pens!' quod sche, 'Now Lady, Seinte Mary,
    So wisly help me out of care and synne,
    This wyde world though that I schulde wynne
    Ne have I not **xii** pens withinne myn **hold**!   twelve; possession
    Ye knowen wel that I am pore and old;
    Kith youre almes on me, pore wrecche.'   show your charity
    'Nay than,' quod he, 'the foule fend me fecche
    If I the excuse, though thou schalt be **spilt**.'   ruined
    'Allas!' quod sche, 'God wot, I have no **gilt**.'   guilt
    'Pay me,' quod he, 'or by the swet Seint Anne,
350 As I wol bere away thy newe panne,
    For dette which thou owest me of old,
    Whan that thou madest thin housbond **cokewold**,   cuckold
    I payd at hom for thi correccioun.'
    'Thou **lixt**!' quod sche, 'By my savacioun,   liest
    Ne was I never er now, wydow ne wyf,
    Somound unto your court in al my lyf.

---

23 A bill is, technically speaking, a plea or request.

Ne never I was but of my body trewe –
Unto the devel, rough and blak of hiewe,
Give I thy body and the panne also.'
And whan the devyl herd hir curse so,   360
Upon his knees he sayd, in this manere,
'Now, Mabely, myn owne modir deere;
Is this your wil in ernest that ye seye?'
'The devel,' quod she, 'fecche him er he deye;
And panne and al, but he wol him repente!'
'Nay, olde **stot**! That is not myn entente,'   nag
Quod this sompnour, 'to repente me
For eny thing that I have had of the.
I wold I had thy **smok** and every cloth.'   petticoat (undergarment)
'Now brothir,' quod the devyl, 'be not **wroth**;   angry   370
Thy body and this panne is myn by right –
Thow schalt with me to helle yit tonight,
Wher thou schalt knowen of oure **privete**   secrets
More than a maister of divinite.'
And with that word the foule fend him hente;
Body and soule, he with the devyl wente
Wheras the sompnours han her **heritage** –   inheritance
And God, that maked after his ymage
Mankynde, save and gyde us all and some,
And **leeve** this sompnour good man to bycome.   grant   380
Lordyngs I couth han told yow,' quod the frere,
'Had I had leysir for this Sompnour here,
After the text of Crist, **Powel**, and Jon,   St Paul
And of other doctours many oon,
Such peynes that our herte might **agrise**,   trouble
Al be it so no tonge may devyse,
Though that I might a thousand wynter telle
The peyn of thilke cursed hous of helle.
But for to kepe us from that cursed place,
Wakith and prayeth Jhesu for his grace.   390
So kepe us fro the temptour Sathanas;
Herknith this word, beth **war** as in this cas – listen; wary/careful
The lyoun syt in his **awayt** alway,   ambush
To slen the innocent, if that he may.
Disposith youre hertes to withstonde
The fend, that wolde make yow **thral** and **bonde**: slave; bondsman/woman

He may not tempte yow **over** your **might**,   beyond; power
For Crist wol be your champioun and knight;
And prayeth that oure Sompnour him repent
Of his mysdede, er that the fend him hente.

Here endith the frere his tale

THE SUMMONER'S PROLOGUE AND TALE

A friar is taken to hell. Because he cannot see any friars there, he assumes that there are no friars in hell, thus demonstrating their moral value. His angel-guide then commands Satan to lift up his tail, and the friar sees thousands of friars, running up and down under the devil's tail.

A corrupt friar visits a husbandman, Thomas, who has fallen sick. He knows the man and his wife well, and has had many donations from them. He sits down on the bench, cuddling and flirting with Thomas's wife. She says that her husband is neglecting her, and asks why the friar has not been to see her for so long, since her child has recently died. To placate her, the friar concocts a story about how the friars in his convent saw a vision of the dead child being taken to heaven. The friar offers Thomas, the husband, confession, but he says that he has already confessed to his parish priest. The friar offers Thomas a sermon on the evils of anger, and then asks for a donation, telling Thomas that he is ill because he hasn't given enough to the friars. The convent has only just completed the tiled pavement in its new church, and they need money to build a cloister. Thomas says that he has something hidden in his bed which he will donate, and Friar John will find it if he gropes underneath his backside. The friar does so, and Thomas lets out a back-breaking fart. Friar John is overwhelmed with anger, and goes to the local lord, a knight, demanding retribution for the insult done to Holy Church. The knight wonders how a fart may be divided in twelve, as the gift was for the whole convent. In return for a gown-cloth the squire Jankin – a young man with an eye for the main chance – arrives at an answer. The friars must stand around a cartwheel with twelve spokes, one at each spoke, with Friar John at the hub, and Thomas will be fetched to repeat his fart. Then each friar will get a little, and John will get the most. And so it is done . . .

The summoner's tale succeeds as well, if not better, than the friar's, in making its object a figure of fun. Its humour is differently constructed, relying partly on punning and partly on sheer coarseness for its effects. The major pun centres on the relationship between 'air' and 'speech'. The friar's sweet words and his courteous attitude are enough to fool the lady of the house, although it is obvious that the friar is only interested in his own belly, and in obtaining money. (His courtesy does not extend to the cat, which he unceremoniously pushes off the bench, in order to

take its place, offering a comparison between a friar and a fat cat.)
Thomas and his wife have an obviously comfortable peasant lifestyle and
a good diet, indicating that he is one of the 'upwardly mobile' peasants
who featured in English society in the aftermath of the Black Death. The
friar, it is implied, would not bother with a poor man. This is an attack
on the essence of the friars' calling, which required them to own no
possessions, and to beg for their living (mendicancy).

The friar's words, as with *cor meum eructavit*, are compared with
belching, which is literally, hot air. By extension, this highlights a
question which was current in Chaucer's day (particularly with Lollard
heretics) – does a priest's ability to impart God's grace or preach God's
word depend on his interior worth? Wycliffites would say yes, whilst
the Church officially said (a qualified) no. Thomas has made these
connections for himself, and produces his own 'offertory' for the friar –
a fart, also hot air. The friar is prepared, for a financial reward, to grope
around, literally, in shit. The entire episode then descends into farce, as
the friar goes to the knight, his local lord, demanding reparation for the
insult to his house. Encouraged by the cunning squire Jankin, who is
better than the friar at spotting an opportunity, the knight decides to
see the whole thing as a philosophical, mathematical problem of 'ars-
metrike' (itself, of course, another pun), and takes Jankin's advice on
how to divide the fart equally. The churchman is subjected to the
secular power, and made to suffer the fate of a complete idiot.

The two tales reveal the clergy as rogues, using their supposedly
superior education, together with the esteem due to their exalted position,
in order to fill their bellies and make a personal, financial, profit. In
both cases they are depicted as far inferior to lay people: the devil, the
old woman, the knight, the squire and Thomas make the friar and the
summoner appear corrupt and foolish. By attempting to make fools of
one another, the friar and the summoner succeed in making fools of
themselves. The final scene, with the friars gathered around the wheel,
is a parody of Pentecost, when Christ's disciples received the Holy
Spirit in the form of tongues of fire. The venom of the situation is
relieved by humour, however, as 'ernest' again gives way to 'game'.

Key Questions

Do the friar and the summoner manage successfully to 'quit' one another by storytelling?

What do these stories tell us about the medieval Church, if anything? There was a strong anti-fraternal literature (attacks on friars) in the later Middle Ages . . . what does this story tell us about how friars were regarded, and how does this relate to their function in society?

Topic Keywords

Medieval friars/ popular religion/ Church art and drama/ mathematics and science/ comic tales and blasphemy/ medieval society

Further Reading

David G. Allen, 'Death and Staleness in the "Son-less" World of The Summoner's Tale', *Studies in Short Fiction*, 24, 1987, pp. 1–8

James Andreas, ' "Newe science" from "olde bokes": A Bakhtinian Approach to The Summoner's Tale', *Chaucer Review*, 25, 1990, pp. 138–51

Catherine Cox, ' "Grope wel bihynde": The Subversive Erotics of Chaucer's Summoner's Tale, *Exemplaria*, 7, 1995, pp. 145–77

R. D. Eaton, 'More "Groping" in The Summoner's Tale', *Neophilologus*, 88, 2004, pp. 615–21

John Finlayson, 'Chaucer's Summoner's Tale: Flatulence, Blasphemy and the Emperor's Clothes', *Studies in Philology*, 104, 2007, pp. 455–70

Robert Finnegan, 'The Wife's Dead Child and Friar John: Parallels and Oppositions in The Summoner's Tale', *Neuphilologische Mitteilungen*, 92, 1991, pp. 457–62

Patrick Gallacher, 'The Summoner's Tale and Medieval Attitudes Towards Sickness', *Chaucer Review*, 20, 1986, pp. 200–12

Linda Georgianna, 'Lords, Churls and Friars: The Return to Social Order in The Summoner's Tale', *Studies in Medieval Culture*, 29, 1991, pp. 149–72

Britton J. Harwood, 'Chaucer on "Speche": House of Fame, The Friar's Tale and The Summoner's Tale', *Chaucer Review*, 26, 1992, pp. 343–9

Robert Hasenfratz, 'The Science of Flatulence: Possible Sources for The Summoner's Tale', *Chaucer Review*, 30, 1996, pp. 241–61

Anne Haskell, 'St Simon in The Summoner's Tale', *Chaucer Review*, 5, 1971, pp. 218–24

Mary Hayes, 'Privy Speech: Sacred Silence, Dirty Secrets in The Summoner's Tale', *Chaucer Review*, 40, 2006, pp. 263–88

Erik Hertog, ' "To parte that wol not departed be": A Plot-Analysis of The Summoner's Tale and its Analogues', in *This Noble Craft: Proceedings of the Xth Research Symposium of the Dutch and Belgian Teachers of Old and Middle English and Historical Linguistics, Utrecht, 19–20 January 1989*, edited by Erik Kooper, Amsterdam, Rodopi, 1991, pp. 200–21

Ian Lancashire, 'Moses, Elijah and the Back Parts of God: Satiric Scatology in Chaucer's Summoner's Tale', *Mosaic*, 14, 1981, pp. 17–30

Alan Levitan, 'The Parody of Pentecost in Chaucer's Summoner's Tale, *University of Toronto Quarterly*, 40, 1971, pp. 236–46

Timothy O'Brien, ' "Ars-Metrik": Science, Satire and Chaucer's Summoner', *Mosaic*, 23, 1990, pp. 1–22

Glending Olson, 'On the Significance of St Simon in The Summoner's Tale', *Chaucer Review*, 33, 1998, pp. 60–5

—— 'The End of The Summoner's Tale and the Uses of Pentecost', *Studies in the Age of Chaucer*, 21, 1999, pp. 209–45

Phillip Pulsiano, 'The Twelve-Spoked Wheel of the Summoner's Tale', *Chaucer Review*, 29, 1995, pp. 382–9

Jay Ruud, ' "My spirit hath his fostryng in the Bible": The Summoner's Tale and the Holy Spirit', *Studies in Medieval Culture*, 29, 1991, pp. 125–48

Fiona Somerset, ' "As just as is a squyre": The Politics of "Lewed Translacion" in Chaucer's Summoner's Tale', *Studies in the Age of Chaucer*, 21, 1999, pp. 187–207

Penn R. Szittya, 'The Friar as False Apostle: Antifraternal Exegesis and The Summoner's Tale', *Studies in Philology*, 71, 1974, pp. 19–46

Peter W. Travis, 'Thirteen Ways of Listening to a Fart: Noise in Chaucer's Summoner's Tale', *Exemplaria*, 16, 2004, pp. 323–48

And here bygynneth the Sompnour his prologe

❦ This Sompnour, in his **styrop** up he stood,   stirrup
Upon the frere his herte was so **wood**   angry
That lyk an **aspen leef** he **quok** for **ire**.   ash leaf; quaked; anger
'Lordyngs,' quod he, 'but oon thing I desire;
I yow **biseke** that of your curtesye,   beseech/beg
Syn ye han herd this fals frere lye,
As **suffrith** me I may my tale telle.   let
This frere bosteth that he knowith helle,
And, **God it wot**, that is litil wonder –   God knows
Freres and **feendes** been but litel **asonder** –   devils; different   10
For **pardy**, ye han often tyme herd telle,   by God
How that a frere **revyscht** was to helle   carried off
In spirit **ones**, by a visioun,   once
And as an aungel lad him up and doun,
To schewen him the peynes that ther were,
In al the place saugh he not a frere.
Of other folk he saugh **ynowe** in wo;   enough
Unto this aungel spak this frere **tho**,   then
'Now, Sire,' quod he, 'han freres such a grace
That noon of hem schal comen in this place?'   20
'Yis,' quod this aungil, 'many a **mylioun**.'
And unto Sathanas he **lad** him doun;   led
'And now hath Sathanas,' saith he, 'a tayl
Broder than of a **carrik** is the sayl.   a large ship

❦ Hold up thy tayl, thou Sathanas!' quod he,
'Schew forth thyn **ars**, and let the frere se   arse
Wher is the nest of freres in this place!'
And er than half a furlong way of space,
Right so as bees swarmen out of an hyve,
Out of the devel's ers thay gonne **dryve** –   move   30
Twenty thousand freres **on a route**,   in a company
And thoroughout helle swarmed al about;
And comen as fast as thay may goon,
And in his ers thay crepen **everichoon**.   every one

He **clappid** his tayl agayn, and lay ful stille.   shut
This frere, whan he loked had **his fille**   as much as he wanted
Upon the torment of this sory place,
His spirit God restored of his grace
Unto his body agayn, and he awook.
40 But **natheles**, for fere yit he **quook**,   nevertheless; quaked
So was the devel's ers yit in his mynde;
That is his heritage of **verray kynde**.   because of his true nature
God save yow alle, **save** this cursed frere!   except
My proloug wol I ende in this manere.

Narrat

he tells (his story)

❦ Lordyngs ther is in Engelond, I gesse,
A **mersschly** lond called Holdernesse,[1]   marshy
In which ther went a **lymytour** aboute,   friar with licence to beg
To preche, and eek to begge, it is no doute.
50 And so bifel it, **on a day** this frere   one day
Had preched at a chirch in his manere,
And specially, aboven every thing,
Excited he the poepul in his preching
To trentals, and to give for God's sake[2]
Wher that men mighten holy soules make;
Ther as divine servys is honoured,
Nought ther as it is wasted and devoured.
Neither it needeth not for to be give
As to possessioneres, that **mow** lyve,[3]   may
60 Thanked be God, in **wele** and abundaunce –   prosperity
Hir freendes soules, as wel old as yonge,
Ye, whanne that they hastily ben songe;[4]

1 An area in South-East Yorkshire, comprising the Spurn peninsula and the area
  immediately behind it.
2 Masses for the soul in purgatory – the intermediate stage between earth and
  heaven where the soul was to be cleansed. The friar would be paid for this
  service.
3 Members of religious orders which owned property, such as monks and nuns:
  there was continual tension between these and the friars. The summoner is here
  giving the friar's 'opinion'.
4 'not when they finish singing so quickly'

Nought for to **hold** a prest jolif and gay –   maintain
He syngith not but oon masse in a day.
'Delyverith out,' quod he, 'the soules!
Ful hard it is, with **fleischhok** or with **oules**[5]   meathook; awls
To ben **y-clawed** or **brend** or y-bake –   torn to pieces; burned
Now speed yow hastily, for Crist's sake.'
And whan this frere had sayd **al his entent**,   everything he wanted
With, '**Qui cum patre**,' forth he went.   final blessing   70
Whan folk in chirch had give him what hem **lest**,   wanted
He went his way – no lenger wold he rest;
With **scrip** and pyked staf, **y-touked** hye,   bag; skirt tucked up
In every hous he gan to **pore** and prye,   peek
And begged mele, or chese, or ellis corn.
His felaw had a staf typped with horn,
A payr of **tablis**, al of yvory,   tablets
And a **pyntel** y-polischt **fetisly**,   pointed stylus; well
And wroot the names always as he stood
Of alle folk that gaf him eny good,   80
Ascaunce that he wolde for hem preye.   as if
'**Gif** us a busshel whet, or malt, or **reye**,   rye
A **goddes kichil** or a **trip** of chese,   small cake/biscuit; piece
Or elles what yow list, we may not **chese**;   be choosy
A God's halpeny or a masse peny,[6]
Or **gíf** us of youre **braune**, if ye have eny;   brawn (jellied meat)
A **dagoun** of your blanket, **leeve** Dame,   snippet; dear
Oure **suster** deer – lo, her I write your name;   sister
Bacoun or beef, or such thing as we fynde.'
A stourdy **harlot ay** went hem byhynde,   knave; always   90
That was her host's man, and **bar** a sak,   carried
And what men gaf hem, layd it on his bak;
And whan that he was out atte door, anoon
He **planed** out the names everychoon   rubbed
That he biforn had writen in his tablis –
He served hem with **nyfles** and with fablis.'   trifles
'Nay, ther **thou lixt**, thou Sompnour,' sayd the frere.   you lie
'Pees!' quod our host, 'for Crist's moder deere –

5 Tools used in carpentry.
6 Two forms of monetary offering given to priests.

Tel forth thy tale, and spare it not at al.'
100 'So thrive I,' quod the Sompnour, 'so I schal.
So long he wente, hous by hous, til he
Cam **til** an hous ther he was wont to be   to
Refresshid mor than in an hundrid placis.
Syk lay the housbondman whos that the place is; [7]
Bedred upon a **couche**, lowe he lay: bedridden; bed
'**Deus hic**,' quod he, 'O Thomas, frend, good day,'[8]
Sayde this frere, al curteysly and softe:
'O Thomas, God yeld it yow, ful ofte
Have I upon this bench **y-fare ful wel** –   done very well
110 Her have I eten many a mery mel!'
And fro the bench he drof away the cat,
And layd adoun his **potent** and his hat,   stick
And **eek** his scrip, and set him soft adoun.   also
His **felaw** was go walkid in the toun,   companion
Forth with his **knave** to the **ostelrye**,   manservant; inn
Wher as he **schop him** thilke night to lye.   intended
'O deere maister,' quod the seeke man,
'How have ye fare **siththe** March bygan?   since
I saygh yow nou*g*ht this fourtenight or more.'
'God wot,' quod he, 'labord have I ful **sore**,   hard
120 And specially for thy salvacioun
Have I sayd many a precious **orisoun**,   prayer
And for myn other frendes, God hem blesse,
I have to day be at your chirche at messe,
And sayd a sermoun after my simple **wit** –   understanding
Nought al after the text of holy wryt,
For it is hard for yow, as I suppose,
And therfor wil I teche yow ay the glose.   interpretation
Glosyng is a glorious thing, certayn,
130 For letter **sleth**, so as we clerkes sayn.[9]
Ther have I taught hem to be charitable,
And spend her good ther it is resonable;
And ther I **seigh** our dame – wher is she?'   saw
'**Yond** in the yerd I trowe that sche be,'   over there

---

7 A peasant, in this case a relatively prosperous one.
8 Literally, 'God is here' or 'May God be here': a greeting.
9 'the letter (of the Law) kills'

Sayde this man, 'and sche wil come anoon.
'Ey mayster, welcome be ye, by Seint John.'
The frere ariseth up ful curteysly,
And her embracith in his armes **narwe**,   tightly
And kist hir swete, and **chirkith** as a **sparwe**   chatters; sparrow
With his lippes. 'Dame,' quod he, 'right wel   140
As he that is your servaunt **everydel**,   entirel
Thankyd be God that yow gaf soule and lif –
Yit saugh I not this day so fair a wyf
In al the chirche, God so save me!'
'Ye, God amend **defautes**, Sir,' quod sche,   (my) failings
'Algates welcome be ye, by my fay!'
'**Graunt mercy**, Dame, this have I found always;   many thanks
But of your grete goodnes, by youre leve,
I wolde pray yow that ye yow not greeve –
I wil with Thomas speke a litel **throwe**;   while   150
These curates ben ful negligent and slowe[10]
To **grope** tendurly a conscience;   interrogate/examine
In **schrift** and preching is my diligence,   forgiving (sins)
Study in Peter's wordes and in **Poul's**,   Peter; Paul
And walk and fissche Cristen men's soules,
To yelde Jhesu Crist his **propre** rent –   own
To spreden his word is al myn entent.'
'Now by your leve, O Deere Sir,' quod sche,
Chyd him right wel, for **Seinte Trinite** –   chide; the Holy Trinity
He is as angry as a **pissemyre**,   ant   160
Though that he have al that he can desire,
Though I him **wrye** on night and make him warm,   cover
And over him lay my leg **other** myn arm,   or
He groneth lik our boor that lith in sty –
Othir **disport** of him right noon have I;   pleasure
I may please him in no maner **caas**.'   event
'O Thomas, **jeo vous dy** – Thomas! Thomas!   I tell you
This makth the feend; this most ben amendid!   the devil is doing this
Ire is a thing that highe God **defendid**,   forbade
And therof wold I speke a word or tuo.'   170
'Now maister,' quod the wyf, 'er that I go –

10 A clergyman: a vicar or rector's deputy.

What wil ye dyne; **I wil go theraboute**.' I'll see to it
'Now Dame,' quod he, '**jeo vous dy sauns doute**,

I tell you without a doubt

Have I not of a capoun but the **lyvere**, liver
And of your softe brede but a **schivere**, sliver
And after that a rostyd pig's heed –
But that I wold for me no **best** were deed – beast
Than had I with yow homly **suffisaunce**. homely satisfaction
I am a man of **litel sustinaunce**; few (gastronomic) needs
180 My spirit hath his **fostryng** on the Bible. nourishment
The body is ay so redy and **penyble** at pain
To wake, that my stomak is destroyed.
I pray yow Dame, that ye be not anoyed,
For I so frendly yow my **counseil** schewe: secret
By God, I **nold** not telle it but a fewe.' would not
'Now Sir,' quod sche, 'but **o** word er I go; one
My child is deed withinne this wyke's tuo,
Soon after that ye went out of this toun.'
'His deth saugh I by revelacioun,'
190 Sayde this frere, 'at hoom in oure dortour.[11]
I dar wel sayn, er that half an hour
After his deth I seigh him born to blisse
In myn **avysioun**, so God me **wisse**; vision; know/advise
So did our **sextein** and our **fermerere**, sexton; infirmerer
That han ben trewe freres many a yere.
Thay may now, God be thanked of his **bone**, gift
Maken her **jubile** and walk alloone;[12] jubilee
But up I **roos** and al our covent **eeke**, rose; also
With many a teere **trilling on** my cheeke. trickling down
200 'Te Deum' was our song, and nothing ellis,[13]
Withouten noys or **clateryng** of bellis,
Save that to Crist I sayd an **orisoun**, prayer
Thankyng him of my revelacioun –
For, Sire and Dame, trustith me right wel,
Our orisouns ben more effectuel,
And more we se of God's secre thinges

---

11 Room in a convent or monastery set aside for sleeping accommodation.
12 A celebration of fifty years of life/existence; in this case, of the friars' convent
13 'To you, God . . . '; a celebration.

Than **borel** folk, although that thay ben kinges.   lay
We lyve in povert and in abstinence,
And borel folk in riches and **dispence**   expenditure
Of mete and drink, and in her ful delyt.
We han al this world's delit in despyt: 210
Lazar and Dives lyveden diversely,[14]
And divers **guerdoun** hadde thay therby.   reward
Who so wol praye, he must faste and be **clene**,   pure
And fatte his soule and make his body lene.
We faren as saith thapostil; cloth and foode
Sufficeth us, though thay ben not goode.
The **clennes** and the fastyng of us freres   purity
Makith that Crist acceptith oure prayeres.
Lo! Moyses fourty dayes and fourty night   220
Fasted, er that the highe God of might
Spak with him in the mount of Synay;[15]
With empty **wombe**, fastyng many a day,   belly
Receyved he the lawe that was writen
With God's fynger; and Eli holy, wel ye witen,
In Mount Oreb, or he had any speche
With highe God that is oure lyve's **leche**,   physician
He fastid and was in contemplacioun,
And eek the other prestes everychoon.
Into the temple whan thay schulden goon   230
To preye for the people and doon servise,
Thay nolden drinken in no maner wise
No drynke which that dronke might hem make,
But ther in abstinence prey and wake,
Lest that thay **deydin** – tak heed what I say –   died
But thay ben sobre that for the pepul pray.
War that I say – no mor, for it **suffisith** –   is enough
Oure Lord Jhesu, as oure **lore devysith**,   teaching tells
Gaf us **ensampil** of fastyng and prayeres,   example
Therfore we **mendinaunts**, we sely freres,   mendicants   240
Ben wedded to povert and to continence,
To charite, humblesse, and abstinence,
To persecucioun for **rightwisnesse**,   righteousness

14 Dives and Lazarus; the rich Dives went to hell, the poor Lazarus to heaven.
15 Receiving the Ten Commandments.

To wepyng, **misericord**, and clennesse; mercy
And therfor may ye seen that oure prayeres –
I speke of us, we mendeaunts, we freres,
Ben to the hihe God more acceptable
Than youres, with your **festis** at your table: feasts
Fro Paradis first, if I schal not lye,
250 Was man out chaced for his glotonye,
And chast was man in Paradis, certeyn.
But now herk, Thomas, what I schal the seyn –
I ne have no **tixt** of it, as I suppose, text
But I schal fynd it in a maner glose,
That specially our swete Lord Jhesus
Spak this by freres, whan he sayde thus:
'Blessed be thay that **pover** in spirit ben.'[16] poor
And so forth, in the gospel ye may seen
Whether it be **likir** oure professioun – more like
260 Fy on her pomp, and on her glotenye!
And on her leweydnesse – I hem defye!
Me thinkith thay ben lik Jovynian,
Fat as a whal and **walken** as a swan, waddling
Al **vinolent** as botel in the **spence**; wine-soaked; wine-store
Her prayer is of ful gret reverence
Whan thay for soules sayn the Psalm of David –
'Lo, boef!' thay say, 'Cor meum eructavit!'[17]
Who folwith Crist's gospel and his **lore**, teaching
But we that humble ben, and chast, and pore,
270 Workers of God's word and **auditours**? listeners
Therfor, right as an **hauk** upon a **sours** hawk; soa
Upspringeth in to **thaer**, right so prayeres the air
Of charitabil and chaste, busy, freres
Maken her sours to God's eeres tuo.
Thomas, Thomas! So **mote** I ryde or go; may
And by that lord that **clepid** is **seint Ive**, called; St Ive
Ner thou oure brother, schuldestow never thrive! if you were not (ne were)
In oure chapitre pray we day and night
To Crist, that he the sende **hele** and might, health

16 From the Sermon on the Mount.
17 'My heart has uttered . . . ' after the sound of a belch ('boef'); Psalm 45.

Thy body for to **welden hastily**.'   speedily get up and move   280
'God wot,' quod he, 'therof nought feele I!
As help me Crist, as I in fewe yeeres
Have spendid upon many **divers** freres   various
Ful many a pound, yit fare I never the **bet**!   better
Certeyn, my good have I almost **byset** –   spent/lost
Farwel my gold, for it is almost ago.'
The frere answerd, 'O Thomas! Dostow so?
What needith yow dyverse freres **seche**?   seek out
What needith him that hath a parfyt **leche**   doctor
To sechen othir leches in the toun?   290
Youre **inconstance** is youre confusioun.   faithlessness/infidelit
Hold ye than me or oure covent
To praye for yow insufficient?
Thomas, that **iape** is not worth a **myte**!   trick; mite
Youre malady is **for** we have to **lite**!   because; little
A, give that covent half a quarter otes!
A, give that covent four and twenty grotes!¹⁸
A, give that frere a peny, and let him go!
Nay, nay, Thomas! It may nought be so!
What is a ferthing worth **depart** in twelve?   divided   300
Lo! Ech thing that is **ooned** in himselve   united/concentrate
Is more strong than whan it is **toskatrid**!   scattered/divided up
Thomas, of me thou schalt not be **y-flatrid**!   flattered
Thow woldist have our labour al for nought –
The hihe God, that al this world hath wrought,
Saith that a werkman is worthy of his hyre.
Thomas, nou*g*ht of your tresor I desire
For myself, but for that oure covent –
To pray for yow is ay so diligent –
And for to **bylden** Crist's holy chirche.   build   310
Thomas, if ye wil lerne for to **wirche**   wor
Of buyldyng up on chirches, may ye fynde
If it be good, in **Thomas's lyf of Ynde**:   St Thomas of India
Ye lye her ful of anger and of ire,
With which the devel set your hert on fuyre,
And chyden her the holy innocent,

18 A coin, worth four pence.

Your wyf, that is so meke and pacient;

And therfor **trow** me, Thomas, if thou list,   believe

Ne stryve nought with thy wyf, as for **thi best**,   what's best for you

320   And ber this word away now, by thy faith,

Touchinge such thing – lo, the wise man saith:

'Withinne thin hous be thou no lyoun;

To thy subiects do noon oppressioun,

Ne make thyn **acqueyntis** fro the fle.'   acquaintances

And yit, Thomas, **eftsons** I charge the –   again

Bewar for hir that in thy bosom slepith,

War for the serpent, that so slely crepith

Under the gras, and styngith prively.

Bewar, mi sone, and werk paciently;

330   For twenty thousend men han lost her lyves

For stryvyng with her **lemmans** and her wyves.   lover

Now syns ye han so holy and meeke a wif,

What nedith yow, Thomas, to make strif?

Ther nys, I wis, no serpent so cruel

When men trede on his tail, ne half so **fel**   dreadful

As womman is whan sche hath **caught an ire**.   grown angry

Vengeans is thanne al that thay desire;

Schortly may no man by **rym** and vers   rhyme

Tellen her thoughtes, thay ben so dyvers.

340   Ire is a thing, oon the grete of sevene,[19]

Abhominable to the God of hevene,

And to himself it is destruccioun –

This every lewed **vicory** or parsoun   vicar

Can say how ire **engendrith** homicide.   gives birth to

Ire is, in **soth**, executour of pride;[20]   truth

I couthe of ire seyn so moche sorwe

My tale schulde laste til tomorwe!

Ire is the grate of synne, as saith the wise,

To fle therfro ech man schuld him **devyse**,   take care

350   And therfor pray I God bothe day and night.

An irous man, God send him litil might –

It is greet harm and also gret pite

19 One of the seven deadly sins; anger, sloth, gluttony, lust, envy.
20 One who carries out another's wishes, for example, the executor of a will.

To set an irous man in high **degre**.   rank/status
Whilom ther was an irous **potestate**,   potentate
As seith Senek, that duryng his **estaat**[21]   term of office
Upon a day out riden knightes tuo
And, as fortune wolde, right as it were so
That oon of hem cam home, that other nou*gh*t.
Anoon the knight bifore the **juge** is brou*gh*t   judge
That sayde, 'Thus thou has thy **felaw** slayn,   companion   360
For which I **deme** the to deth, certayn.'   Judg
And to anothir knight comaundid he
To lede him to the deth, I charge the;
And happed as they wente by the weye
Toward the place ther he schulde deye,
The knight com which men **wend** had be deed.   believed
Than thoughten thay it were the beste **reed**   advice
To lede hem bothe to the juge agayn.
Thay sayden, 'Lord, the knight hath not slayn
His felaw – lo, heer he stont **hool, on lyve!**'   fit and alive 370
'Ye schal be deed,' quod he, 'so **mote** I thrive,   ma
That is to sayn bothe – oon, tuo and thre!'
And to the first kni*gh*t right thus spak he;
'I deme the thou most algate be deed.'
Than thought thay it were the beste rede
To lede him forth into a fair **mede**.   meadow
'And,' quod the juge, 'also thou most **lese** thin heed,   lose
For thou art cause why thy felaw deyth.'
And to the thridde felaw thus he seith:
'Thou has nought doon that I comaundid the.'   380
And thus he **let don** sle hem alle thre.   ordered
Irous Cambises was eek **dronkelewe**,   drunken
And ay delited him to ben a **schrewe**.   evil-tempered
And so bifel a lord of his **meigne**,   household
That loved vertues and eek moralite,
Sayd on a day bitwix hem tuo right thus:
'A lord is lost if he be **vicious**;   full of vices
An irous man is lik a **frentik best**,   crazy beast
In which ther is of wisdom noon arrest,

21 Seneca, from his book De Ira.

390 And dronkenes is eek a foul record
    Of any man, and namly of a lord.
    Ther is ful many an eyye and many an eere
    Awaytand on a lord, and he **not** where.   fixed upon;does not know
    For God's love, drynk more **attemperely** –   moderately
    Wyn makith man to lese wrecchedly
    His mynde, and eek his lymes **everichoon**.'   every one
    'The **revers** schaltow seen,' quod he anoon,   opposite
    'And prove it by thin own experience,
    That wyn ne doth to folk non such offence.
400 Ther is no wyn **byreveth** me my wit   takes away from
    Of hond, of foot, ne of myn eyyesight.'
    And for despyt he dronke moche more,
    An hundrid part than he had doon byfore,
    And right anoon this irous cursid wrecche
    Let this knighte's sone anoon biforn him **fecche**,   ordered; brought
    Comaundyng hem thay schulde biforn him stonde,
    And sodeinly he took his bowe on honde,
    And up the streng he pulled to his eere,
    And with an **arwe** he slough the child right there.   arrow
410 'Now, whethir have I a **sikur** hond or noon,'   steady
    Quod he, 'is al my mynde, and might agoon?
    Hath wyn byreved me myn eyesight?'
    What schuld I telle the answer of the knight?
    His sone was slayn, ther is no more to say –
    Bewar, therfor, with lordes how ye play –
    Syngith, '*Placebo*', and I schal if I can,[22]
    But if it be unto a pore man.   unless
    To a pore man men schuld his vices telle,
    But not to a lord, **they** he schuld go to helle.   though
420 Lo, irous **Cirus**, **thilke Percien**,   Cyrus (king of Persia)
    For that an hors of his was **dreynt** therinne,   drowned
    Whan that he wente **Bebiloyne** to wynne,   Babilon
    He made that the ryver was so smal
    That wommen mighte wade it over al.
    Lo, what sayde he that so wel teche can,
    Ne be no felaw to an irous man,

22 Literally, 'I shall please . . . '; always say what pleases the lord.

Ne with no **wood** man walke by the way,   mad
Lest the repent – I wol no lenger say.
Now Thomas, **leve** brother, leve thin ire;   dear
Thow schalt me fyde as just as is a squire.   430
Thyn anger doth the al to sore **smerte** –   hurt
Hald not the devel's knyf ay at thyn herte,   hold
But schewe to me al thy confessioun.'
'Nay.' quod this syke man, 'by Seynt Symoun,[23]
I have ben **schriven** this day of my curate;   forgiven, after confession
I have him told holly al myn **estate**.   the state of my sins
'Nedith no more to speken of it,' saith he,
'but if me **list**, of myn humilite.'   like
'**Gif** me than of thy good to make our cloyster,'
Quod he, 'for many a **muscle** and many an oyster   mussel   440
Hath ben our foode, our cloyster to **arreyse**,   erec
Whan other men han be ful wel at eyse.
And yit, God wot, **unnethe** the **foundement**   hardly; foundation
Parformed is ne of oure pavyment.[24]   constructed
Is nought a **tyle** yit withinne our **wones** –   tile; place
By God, we owe yit fourty pound for stones!
Now help, Thomas, for him that harewed helle,[25]
Or elles moote we oure bookes selle;
And yif yow lakke oure **predicacioun**,   intercessory prayers
Thanne goth the world al to destruccioun;   450
For who so wold us fro the world **byreve**,   take away
He wolde byreve out of this world the sonne –
For who can teche and werken as we conne?
And this is not of litel tyme,' quod he,
'But siththen **Elye** was her, or **Ele**,   Elijah; Elisha
Han freres ben, fynde I **of record**,   record (written)
In charite, y-thanked be Oure Lord!
Now Thomas, help, for **Seynte Charite**!'   Holy charity
Adoun he sette him anoon on his kne.
This sike man wex wel neigh **wood** for **ire** –   mad; anger   460

23 May be a reference to Simon Magus, or to St Peter (Simon Peter), the apostle.
24 The tiled area in front of the high altar.
25 The harrowing of hell was the supposed descent of Christ into hell after his
   crucifixion, before his resurrection, to free the souls of those (including the Old
   Testament prophets) who had died in faith before his birth.

He **wolde** that the frere had ben on fuyre,   wished
With his fals dissimulacioun.
'Such thing as is in my possessioun,'
Quod he, 'that may I geve yow and noon other –
Ye sayn me thus how that I am your brother.'
'Ye **certes**,' quod the frere, 'trusteth wel,   indeed
I took **our dame** the letter under oure **sel**.'   your wife; seal
'Now wel,' quod he, 'and somwhat schal I give
Unto your holy covent whils that I lyve,
470   And in thyn hond thou schalt it have anoon,
On this condicioun, and other noon,
That thou **depart** it so, my deere brother,   divide
That every frere have as moche as other –
This schaltow swere on thy professioun,
Withouten fraude or **cavillacioun**.'   argument
'I swere it,' quod this frere, 'upon my faith.'
And therwith his hond in his he laith:
'Lo here myn hond – in me schal be no lak.'
'Now thanne, put thyn hond doun at my bak,'
480   Sayde this man, 'and grope wel byhynde;
Bynethe my buttok there schaltow fynde
A thing that I haue **hud** in privete.'   hidden
'A!' thought this frere, 'that schal go with me.'
And doun his hond he launched to the **clifte**,[26]
In hope for to fynde ther a gifte;
And whan this syke man felte this frere
Aboute his **tuel** grope, ther and heere,   tool/genitals
Amyd his hond he leet the freere a fart.
There is no **capul** drawyng in a cart   horse
490   That might have let a fart of such a soun.
The frere upstart as doth a wood lyoun –
'A, false cherl!' quod he, 'For God's bones!
This hastow in despit don, for the noones,
Thou schalt **abye** this fart, if that I may!'   regret
His **meyne**, which that herd of this affray,   household servants
Com **lepand** in and chased out the frere,   springing
And forth he goth, with a foul angry cheere,

26 cleft (between the buttocks).

And **fet** his felaw, ther lay his **stoor**;   fetched; 'takings'
He lokid as it were a wylde boor,
And grynte with his teeth, so was he wroth.   500
A **stordy paas** doun to the court he goth,   strong pace
Wher as ther **wonyd** a man of gret honour,   lived
To whom that he was always confessour;
This worthy man was lord of that village.
This frere com, as he were in a rage,
Wher that this lord sat etyng at his **bord**.   table
Unnethe might the frere speke a word,   hardly
Til atte last he sayde, '**God yow se**.'   God keep you
This lord gan loke, and sayde, 'Benedicite!
What, Frere John, what maner world is this!   510
I se wel that somthing is amys –
Ye loke as though the woode were ful of **thevys**!   thieves
Sit doun anoon, and tel me what your gref is,
And it schal ben amendit, if that I may.'
'I have,' quod he, 'had a **despit** to day –   insult
God yelde yow adoun in youre vilage,
That in this world is noon so pore a page
That he nold have abhominacioun,
Of that I have receyved in youre toun;
And yet ne grevith me no thing so sore   520
As that this **elde** cherl, with lokkes **hore**,   old; grey
Blasphemed hath our holy covent eeke!'
'Now maister,' quod this lord, 'I yow biseke . . . '
'No maister sir,' quod he, 'but servitour;
Though I have had in **scole** such honour,   college/university
God likith not that **Raby** men us calle,   rabbi
Neither in market, neyther in your large halle.'
'No fors,' quod he, 'tellith me al your greef.'
This frere sayd, 'Sire, an odious meschief
This day bytid is to myn ordre, and to me,   530
And so, **par consequens**, to ech **degre**   in consequence; level
Of holy chirche – God amend it soone.'
'Sir,' quod the lord, 'ye wot what is to doone.
Distrempre yow nought, ye ben my confessour –   upset
Ye ben the salt of th'erthe, and savyour;
For God's love, youre pacience ye holde –
Tel me your greef.' And he anoon him tolde

As ye han herd bifore – ye wot wel what –
The lady of that hous ay stille sat,
540   Til sche had herd what the frere sayde.
'Ey, God's Moodir!'quod sche, 'Blisful Mayde!
Is ther ought elles, tel me faithfully?'
'**Ma dame**,' quod he, 'y-wis I schal not lye,   my lady
But I in othir wise may be **wreke**;   avenged
I schal defame him over al wher I speke,
The false blasfememour that chargid me
To parten that wil not departed be
To every man **y-liche**, with **meschaunce**.'   alike; ill-luck
The lord sat stille, as he were in a traunce,
550   And in his hert he rollid up and doun,
'How had this cherl **ymaginacioun**   wit
To schewe such a probleme to the frere?
Never eft er now herd I of such matiere[27]
I **trowe**, the devel put it in his mynde –   believe
In **ars metrik** schal ther no man fynde   arithmetic
Biforn this day of such a question!
Who schulde make a demonstracioun
That every man schuld have alyk his part,
As of a soun or of a savour of a fart?
560   O nyce, proude cherl, I **schrew** his face!'   curse
'Lo sires,' quod the lord, 'with **harde grace**,   hard chance
Whoever herde of such a thing er now –
To every man y-like, tel me how?
It is impossible, it may not be!
Ey, nyce cherl, God let him never the!
The romblyng of a fart, and every soun,
Nis but of **aier** reverberacioun,   air
And ever it wastith **lyte and lyte** away –   little by little
Ther nys no man can **deme**, by my fay,   judge
570   If that it were departed equally!
What! Lo, my cherl! What! Lo, how schreewedly
Unto my confessour today he spak!
I hold him certeinly **demoniak**!   possessed
Now etith your mete, and let the cherl go play –

27 'I've never heard of such a thing until now'

Let him go honge himself, **on devel way**!'	in the devil's name
Now stood the lord's squier at the **bord**,	table
That **carf** his mete and herde word by word,	carved
Of al this thing which that I of have sayd:	
'My lord,'quod he, 'be ye nou**g**ht **evel payd** –	displeased
I couthe telle, for a **gowne cloth**,	cloth for making a gown 580
To yow, Sir Frere, so that ye be not wroth,	
How that this fart even departed schuld be	
Among your covent, if I comaunded be.'	
'Tel,' quod the lord, 'and thou schalt have anoon	
A goune cloth, by God and by Seint John!'	
'My lord,' quod he, 'whan that the **wedir** is fair,	weather
Withoute wynd or **pertourbyng** of ayr,	disturbance
Let bring a large **whel** into this halle;	wheel
But that it have his spokes alle –	
Twelf spokes hath a cart whel **comunly** –	usually 590
And bring me **xii** freres – wit ye why?	twelve
For **threttene** is a covent, as I gesse:	thirteen
Your noble confessour her, God him blesse,	
Schal **parfourn** up the nombre of this covent,	make up
Thanne schal thay knele doun, by oon assent,	
And to every spokes ende in this manere	
Ful **sadly** lay his nose schal a frere.	carefully
Your noble confessour, ther God him save,	
Schal hold his nose upright under the **nave**;	hub (centre)
Than schal this churl, with bely stif and tought	600
As eny **tabor**, hider ben y-brought,	tabor (drum)
And sette him on the whele of this cart,	
Upon the nave, and make him lete a fart;	
And ye schul seen, up peril of my lif,	
By verray proef that is **demonstratif**,	empirical (to be seen)
That equally the soun of it wol wende –	
And eek the stynk – unto the spokes' ende;	
Save that this worthy man, your confessour,	
Bycause he is a man of gret honour,	
Schal have the firste fruyt, as resoun is.[28]	610
The noble **usage** of freres is this;	custom

28 The first offering: traditionally also the best.

The worthy men of hem first schal be served,
And certeynly he hath it wel deserved;
He hath today taught us so **mochil** good,   much
With preching in the pulpit ther he stood,
That I may **vouche sauf**, I say for me,   grant
He hadde the firste smel of fartes thre –
And so wold al his covent, hardily –
He berith him so fair and holily.'
620   The lord, the lady, and ech man **sauf** the frere,   except
Sayde that Jankyn spak in this matiere
As wel as Euclide or elles Phtolome.[29]
Touchand the cherl, thay sayd that **subtilte**   mental agility
And high wyt made him speken as he spak;
He nas no fool, ne no **demoniak**.   demon-possessed person
And Jankyn hath y-wonne a newe goune –
My tale is don; we ben almost at toune."

Here endith the Sompnour's tale

29 Euclid, the ancient Greek mathematician, and Ptolemy, 'father' of astronomical/
astrological calculation.

THE CLERK'S PROLOGUE AND TALE

The host turns to the clerk of Oxford, gently making fun of his shy demeanour and his silence, coaxing him to join in the storytelling. The clerk accepts the host's 'rule', announcing that he will tell a tale, originally from Petrarch, which he himself learned from a clerk at Pavia.

A wealthy marquis named Walter, ruling in the north of Italy, is pressed by his loyal people to marry. He consents, on condition that they allow him to marry whomsoever he chooses. He decides to marry Griselda, a poor girl from a local village, on account of her remarkable qualities of temperance and patience. On their wedding day, he has her stripped of her poor, ragged clothing and re-clothed in the gown of a ruler's wife. Griselda proves to be an excellent wife and ruler, and her reputation spreads far and wide. When she and Walter have a daughter, he decides to test her patience. He has one of his confidential servants take the girl and pretend to kill her, but Griselda does not complain or change her demeanour. When they have a son, he does the same, and still Griselda does not change. Then he tells her that he has demeaned himself by marrying a poor woman; for the good of his people he must set her aside, in order to take a new wife from a noble family. He sends Griselda back to her father in her original rags. When Walter compounds Griselda's agony by suggesting that she should prepare the reception for his new bride, she is not only uncomplaining, but she cheerfully does so. He then reveals that the 'bride' is their own daughter, and her brother their son, who have been kept by his sister since their faked abduction and murder. All are reconciled, and live happily. Walter never 'tests' Griselda again.

The story of Griselda is very similar to a story told by Boccaccio in *The Decameron*, and resembles the story of Constance in that it presents a suffering heroine, in the power of others, who bears her trials and is rewarded, eventually, with a happy life. However, Griselda's trials are not orchestrated by God for a divine purpose, but are contrived by her husband in order fulfil his wish to find out how 'patient' she is. The story resembles the lawyer's tale, in its presentation of the virtues essential for a 'good woman', as demonstrated by a series of almost unbearable trials heaped upon her. Even more than Constance, Griselda reveals nothing of her inner self, nothing, either by speech or demeanour, of what she really thinks or feels, because this is of no account in society. Like the

Virgin Mary, and some other romance heroes (for example, the hero and his wife in *Amis and Amiloun*) she sacrifices herself and her children without demur, in order to keep her sworn word. She actively resists her husband's cruel testing by her passivity.

In this tale, Chaucer uses his usual five-stress line, but divides it into stanzas, each of seven lines. Chaucer assigns this form, which became known as 'rhyme royal', to those of his storytellers who are attempting to develop pathos. In this case, the clerk is employing this 'affective' form of poetry in order to encourage an emotional response to the heroine's sufferings in his audience, in addition to demonstrating his skill as a speaker and a 'maker' of narrative poems. This is a response to the host's urging that he should put aside his skills in the use of classical, rhetorical 'colours' in order to make his story accessible to a mixed audience of what might now be termed 'general readers'.

Although he obviously wishes to use the story, Chaucer appears to struggle, as does the clerk himself, with its content. The theme of trial, whether by a deity or by another person, can usually be shown to have some noble purpose in literature, but Walter's treatment of his wife cannot. Chaucer's clerk does not disguise this difficulty, but brings it to the audience's attention, foregrounding the problems inherent in the subject matter. Should a man behave like this towards his wife? The answer, surely, even in the misogynist world of the fourteenth century, is no. Griselda's loyalty and her patience and obedience are already well-established facts, and Walter has proved them in his own experience of their marriage (after all, this was why he married her in the first place), so there is really no need to test them further. The means employed go beyond all reason. What the story does reveal is the power of men, and the powerlessness of women and children. It may be that Walter is being shown as an Italian tyrant in the likeness of Visconti, whose power Chaucer had witnessed in person. Unlike Theseus in the knight's tale, Walter is torturing the powerless, rather than defending their interests. The clerk says that Walter was 'loved and drad', implying that he was a good ruler. His people loved him for his humanity, although when Walter besmirches his reputation by his evil treatment of Griselda, his people are obliged to remain loyal. They accept his new 'wife' as being good for the region and its people. This is the reality of power.

Griselda is stripped, re-clothed, and stripped and re-clothed again, indicating her change of status, and her movement from one world to another. This has been interpreted as Christian allegory, with Walter representing God, who permits the Christian to be tried sorely in this world before he receives the heavenly reward. If this is so, there is no reason given for Walter's temptation of Griselda, other than his own personal whim. The clerk offers the tale as a matter of debate for the 'common profit' of all his listeners. From his position as a recluse and an outsider, he offers challenges to the basis of gender relations, and the rules by which society operates. It seems unlikely that this would be put forward as God's motivation. In fact, the tale raises many questions that would have engaged Chaucer's audience, and that have, indeed, engaged his readers ever since.

Key Questions

Is the clerk's questioning the true function of a university education? What challenges does he pose?

How would this story relate to the 'common profit' of all?

Is Walter a good, or a bad, ruler? Are he and Griselda stereotypes?

How does this story relate to issues of gender and/ or class, and power?

Topic Keywords

Women in society/ rulership/ class/ medieval universities/ medieval children/ female saints/ romance heroines

Further Reading

Laura Ashe, 'Reading Like a Clerk in The Clerk's Tale', *Modern Language Review*, 101, 2006, pp. 935–44

Gail Ashton, 'Patient Mimesis: Griselda and The Clerk's Tale', *Chaucer Review*, 32, 1998, pp. 232–8

Diane Bornstein, 'An Analogue to Chaucer's Clerk's Tale', *Chaucer Review*, 15, 1981, pp. 322–31

Howell Chickering, 'Form and Interpretation in the Envoy to The Clerk's Tale', *Chaucer Review*, 29, 1995, pp. 352–72

Rodney Delasanta, 'Nominalism and The Clerk's Tale Revisited', *Chaucer Review*, 31, 1997, pp. 209–31

Valerie Edden, 'Sacred and Secular in The Clerk's Tale', *Chaucer Review*, 26, 1992, pp. 369–76

Lars Engle, 'Chaucer, Bakhtin and Griselda', *Exemplaria*, 1, 1989, pp. 429–59

Thomas J. Farrell, 'The Style of The Clerk's Tale and the Functions of its Glosses', *Studies in Philology*, 86, 1989, pp. 286–309

—— 'Source or Hard Analogue? *Decameron*, x, 10 and The Clerk's Tale', *Chaucer Review*, 37, 2003, pp. 346–64

John Finlayson, 'Petrarch, Boccaccio and Chaucer's Clerk's Tale', *Studies in Philology*, 97, 2000, pp. 255–75

John M. Ganim, 'Carnival Voices and the Envoy to The Clerk's Tale', *Chaucer Review*, 22, 1987, pp. 112–27

Linda Georgianna, 'The Clerk's Tale and the Grammar of Assent', *Speculum*, 70, 1995, pp. 793–821

Kristine Gilmartin, 'Array in The Clerk's Tale', *Chaucer Review*, 13, 1979, pp. 234–46

Michaela Grudin, 'Chaucer's Clerk's Tale as Political Paradox', *Studies in the Age of Chaucer*, 11, 1989, pp. 63–92

Michael Hanrahan, ' "A strange succesour sholde take youre heritage": The Clerk's Tale and the Crisis of Ricardian Rule', *Chaucer Review*, 35, 2001, pp. 335–50

Carol Falvo Heffernan, 'Tyranny and "Commune Profit" in The Clerk's Tale', *Chaucer Review*, 17, 1983, pp. 332–40

Laura F. Hodges, 'Reading Griselda's Smocks in The Clerk's Tale', *Chaucer Review*, 44, 2009, pp. 84–109

Lynn Staley Johnson, 'The Prince and his People: A Study of the Two Covenants in The Clerk's Tale', *Chaucer Review*, 10, 1975, pp. 17–29

William McClellan, 'Bakhtin's Theory of Dialogic Discourse, Medieval Rhetorical Theory, and the Multi-Voiced Structure of The Clerk's Tale', *Exemplaria*, 1, 1989, pp. 461–497

—— ' "Ful pale face": Agamben's Biopolitical Theory and the Sovereign Subject in Chaucer's Clerk's Tale', *Exemplaria*, 17, 2005, pp. 103–34

Kathryn McKinley, 'The Clerk's Tale: Hagiography and the Problematics of Lay Sanctity', *Chaucer Review*, 33, 1998, pp. 90–111

J. Allan Mitchell, 'Chaucer's Clerk's Tale and the Question of Ethical Monstrosity', *Studies in Philology*, 102, 2005, pp. 1–26

Gerald Morgan, 'The Logic of The Clerk's Tale', *Modern Language Review*, 104, 2009, pp. 1–25

Allyson Newton, 'The Occlusion of Maternity in Chaucer's Clerk's Tale', in *Medieval Mothering*, edited and introduced by John Carmi Parsons and Bonnie Wheeler, New York, Garland, 1996, pp. 63–75

Larry Scanlon, 'What's the Pope got to do with it? Forgery, Didacticism and Desire in The Clerk's Tale', *New Medieval Literatures*, 6, 2003, pp. 129–65

Andrew Sprung, ' "If it youre wille be": Coercion and Compliance in Chaucer's Clerk's Tale', *Exemplaria*, 7, 1995, pp. 345–69

Sarah Stanbury, 'Regimes of the Visual in Premodern England: Gaze, Body, and Chaucer's Clerk's Tale', *New Literary History*, 28, 1997, pp. 261–89

David C. Steinmetz, 'Late Medieval Nominalism and The Clerk's Tale', *Chaucer Review*, 12, 1977, pp. 38–54

N. S. Thompson, 'Man's Flesh and Woman's Spirit in *The Decameron* and *The Canterbury Tales*', in *The Body and the Soul in Medieval Literature*, edited and prefaced by Piero Boitani and Anna Torti, Cambridge, D. S. Brewer, 1999, pp. 17–29

Thomas A. Van, 'Walter at the Stake: A Reading of Chaucer's Clerk's Tale', *Chaucer Review*, 22, 1988, pp. 214–24

Robin Waugh, 'A Woman in the Mind's Eye (and Not), Narrators and Gazes in Chaucer's Clerk's Tale and in Two Analogues', *Philological Quarterly*, 79, 2000, pp. 1–18

And here bygynneth the Clerk of Oxenford's prolog

❦ 'Sir Clerk of Oxenford,' our hoste sayde,
'Ye ryde as stille and coy as doth a mayde
Were newe **spoused**, sittyng at a **bord**;   married; table
This day ne herd I of your mouth a word.
I **trowe** ye study aboute som **sophime** – believe; argument
But Salomon saith everything hath tyme;
For God's sake **as beth** of better cheere –   be
It is no tyme for to stody hiere.
Tel us som mery tale, by your **fay**,   faith 10
For what man is entred unto play,
He moot nedes unto that play assent – [1]
But prechith not, as freres doon in Lent,
To make us for our **olde** synnes wepe,   past
Ne that thy tale make us for to slepe.
Tel us som mery thing of aventures;
Youre termes, your colours, and your figures, [2]
Keep hem in stoor til so be that ye **endite**   write/speak
High style, as whan that men to kynges write: [3]
Spekith so playn at this tyme, I yow pray,   20
That we may understonde that ye say.'
This worthy Clerk **benignely** answerde,   kindly
'Sir host,' quod he, 'I am **under your yerde**. under your authority
Ye have of us as now the governaunce,
And therfor wol I do yow obeissaunce   obey you
Als fer as resoun askith, hardily.
I wil yow telle a tale which that I
Lerned at **Padowe** of a worthy clerk,   Padua
As proved by his wordes and his werk.
He is now deed and nayled in his **chest** –   coffin 30
Now God give his soule wel good rest!

---

1 'if you agree to the game then you must abide by the rules and be more cheerful'
2 technical terms, rhetorical colours (or 'fancy literary devices') and allegorical examples.
3 'keep your high style for when you need it and speak plainly'

Fraunces Petrark, the laureat poete	Francis Petrarch
Highte this clerk, whos rethoriques swete[4]	was called
Enlumynd al **Ytail** of poetrie,	illumined; Italy
As Linian did of philosophie,[5]	
Or lawe, or other art **particulere**;	particular/specialised
But deth, that wol not suffre us duellen heere	
But as it were a **twyncling** of an **ye**,	twinkling; eye
Hem bothe hath slayn, and all schul dye –	

40   But forth to telle of this worthy man,

That taughte me this tale, as I first bigan,	
I say that he first with heigh **stile** enditith,	style
Er he the body of his tale writith,	
A **proheme** in which **descrivith** he	prologue; describes
The **mounde** and of **Saluces** the contre,	mountain; Saluzzo
And spekith of **Appenyne** the **hulles hye**	Apennines; hills; high
That ben the boundes of al west Lombardye,	
And of mount Vesulus in special,[6]	
Wheras the **Poo**, out of a welle smal,	Po (river)

50   Takith his first springyng and his **sours**,   source

That estward **ay encresceth** in his cours,	ever grows
To Emyl-ward, to Ferare and to Venise,[7]	
The which a long thing were to **devyse**;	recount
And trewely, as to my juggement,	
Me thinketh it a thing **impertinent**,	irrelevant
Save that he wold **conveyen** his matiere –	introduce
But this is the tale, which that ye schuln heere.'	

Explicit Prohemium

the prologue ends

Incipit narare [8]

60   ❧ Ther is at the west ende of Ytaile,

Doun at the **root** of Vesulus the colde,	foot

---

4 Rhetoric, originally the classical art of public speaking, became applied to the techniques of 'creative writing'.

5 John of Lignano.

6 Monte Viso, in the Italian Alps.

7 Emilia, Ferrara, Venice. The action takes place in northern Italy.

8 'he begins to tell (his story)'

A **lusty** playn, abundaunt of **vitaile**,   vigorous; food and drink
Wher many a tour and toun thou maist byholde,
That foundid were in tyme of fadres olde;
And many anothir **delitable** sight,   delightful
And Saluces this noble contray **hight**.[9]   is called

A marquys **whilom** duellid in that lond,   formerly
As were his worthy **eldris** him bifore,   elders/ancestors
And obeisaunt, **ay redy to his hond**,   ready to obey him
Were alle his **liegis**, bothe lesse and more.   subjects   70
Thus in delyt he lyveth and hath don **yore**,   for some time
Biloved and **drad**, thurgh favour of fortune,   feared
Both of his lordes and of his **comune**.   'common' people

Therwith he was, as to speke of lynage,
The **gentileste** born of Lumbardye;   noblest
A fair persone, and strong, and yong of age,
And ful of honour and of curtesie,
Discret ynough his contre for to **gye** –   lead
Savyng in som thing he was to blame –
And **Wautier** was this yonge lord's name.   Walter   80

I blame him thus, that he considered nought
In tyme comyng what mighte **bityde**,   happen
But on his **lust present** was al his thought,   present desire
As for to hauke and hunte on every syde.
Wel neigh al othir **cures** let he slyde,   cares
And eek he **nolde** – that was the worst of al –   would not
Wedde no wyf, for nothing that might bifal.

Only that poynt his people bar so sore[10]
That **flokmel** on a day to him thay went,   in small gatherings
And oon of hem that wisest was of **lore**,   custom   90
Or elles that the lord wolde best assent,[11]
That he schuld telle him what his people ment,
Or ellis **couthe he** schewe wel such matiere.   he knew how to

---

9 Saluzzo, in Piedmont, northern Italy.
10 'were so worried/grieved about'
11 'he was most likely to get the lord's agreement'

He to the marquys sayd, as ye **schuln** hiere: shall

'O noble marquys, youre humanite
Assureth us, and giveth us **hardynesse**,   boldness
As ofte as tyme is of necessite,
That we to yow may telle oure hevynesse.
Acceptith lord now, of your necessite,
100 That we with **pitous** hert unto yow **playne**   sorrowful; complain
And let youre eeris my **vois** not disdeyne.   voice

Al have I nought to doon in this matere
More than another man hath in this place[12]
Yit for as moche as ye, my lord so deere,
Han always schewed me favour and grace,
I dar the better ask of yow a **space**   time
And audience to asken oure request,
And ye, my lord, to doon right as yow **lest**   like/wish

For certes, lord, so wel us likith yow
110 And al your werk – and ever han doon – that we
Ne couthen not **devysen** how   work out
We mighte lyve more in **felicite**.   happiness
Save oon thing, lord, if that your wille be;
That for to be a weddid man yow list –
Than were your peple in sovereign herte's rest.[13]

Bowith your neck undir that blisful yok
Of sovereignete, nought of servis,
Which that men clepe spousail or wedlok,
And thenketh, lord, among your thoughtes wise,
120 How that our dayes passe, in sondry wyse;
For though we slepe, or wake, or rome aboute,
Ay **fleth** the tyme; it wil not man **abyde**.   goes; wait for

And though your grene youthe floure as yit,
In crepith age, always as stille as stoon;

---

12 'this has no more to do with me than with any other man in this place'
13 'would rest well content'

And deth **manasith** every age, and **smyt**   threatens; strikes down
In ech **estat**, for ther ascapith noon;   social rank
And as certeyn as we knowe everychoon
That we schuln deye, as uncerteyn we alle
Ben of that day that deth schal on us falle.

Acceptith thanne of us the trewe entent,   130
That never yit refusid youre **hest**,   order
And we wil, lord, if that ye wil assent,
Chese yow a wyf **in schort tyme** atte lest,   quickly
Born of the gentilest and the heighest
Of al this lond, so that it oughte seme
Honour to God and yow, as we can **deme**.   judge

Deliver us out of al this **busy drede**,   'nagging' anxiety
And take a wyf, for hihe God's sake;
For if it so bifel, as God forbede,
That thurgh your deth your lignage schuld **aslake**,   fail   140
And that a straunge successour schuld take
Your heritage, O wo were us on lyve!
Wherfor we pray yow hastily to **wyve**.'   get married

Her meeke prayer and **her** pitous chere   their
Made the marquys for to han pite:
'Ye wolde,' quod he, 'myn owne people deere,
To that I never erst thought **constreigne** me;[14]   restrict
I me **rejoysid** of my liberte,   rejoiced
That **selden** tyme is founde in mariage –   seldom
Ther I was fre; I mot ben in **servage**.   servitude 150

But **natheles**, I se of yow the trewe entent,   nevertheless
And trust upon your **witt**, and have doon **ay**,   knowledge; always
Wherfor of my fre wil I wil assent
To wedde me, as soon as ever I may,
But ther as ye have **profred** me to day   offered
To chese me a wyf – I wol **relese**   release you from

14 'you want me to do that . . . '

That choys, and pray yow of that profre **cesse**.   cease

For God it woot that **childer** ofte been   children
Unlik her worthy eldris hem bifore;
160 Bounte cometh al of God, nought of the **streen**   bloodline
Of which thay ben **engendrid and y-bore**.   conceived and born
I trust in God's **bounte**, and therfore   provision
My mariage and myn estat and rest
I him **bytake** – he may doon as him lest.   entrust

Let me alloon in **chesyng** of my wif;   choosing
That charge upon my bak I wil endure.
But I yow pray, and charge upon your lyf,
That wyf that I take, ye me assure
To worship whil that hir lif may endure,
170 In word and werk, bothe heer and everywhere,
As sche an emperour's doughter were.

And forthermor, thus schul ye swer, that ye
Ageins my chois schuln never **grucche** ne stryve;   complain
For **sins** I schal forgo my liberte   since
At your request, as ever mot I thrive,
Ther as myn hert is set, ther wil I wyve;
And **but** ye wil assent in such manere,   unless
I pray spek no more of this matiere.'

With **hertly** wil thay sworen and **assentyn**   good/strong; agreed
180 To al this thing – ther sayde no wight nay –
Bysechyng him of grace, **er** that thay wentyn,   praying; before
That he wol graunten hem a certeyn day
Of his **spousail**, as soone as ever he may;   marriage
For yit always the peple somwhat dredde
Lest that the marquys wolde no wyf wedde.

He graunted hem a day, such as him lest,
On which he wolde be weddid, **sicurly**,   definitely
And sayd he ded al this at her requeste.
And thay, with humble hert, ful **buxomly**   obediently
190 Knelyng upon her knees, ful reverently
Him thanken alle, and thus thay have an ende

Of her **entent**, and hom agein thay wende.   *intention*

And herupon he to his officeris
Comaundith for the fest to **purveye**;   *make ready*
And to his **prive** knightes and squyeres   *household*
Swich charge gaf as him list on hem leye;[15]
And thay to his comaundement obeye,
And ech of hem doth his **diligence**   *care*
To doon unto the feste reverence.

Explicit prima pars   200

                           the first part ends

❦ Nought **fer** fro thilke **palys honurable**   *far; palace; noble*
Wheras this marquys **schop** his mariage,   *prepared*
Ther stood a **throp** of sighte delitable,   *village*
In which that pore folk of that vilage
Hadden her **bestes** and her **herburgage**,   *animals; housing*
And **after** her labour took her **sustienaunce**   *by means of; living*
After the erth gaf hem **abundaunce**   *plenty*

Among this pore folk ther duelt a man
Which that was holden porest of hem alle;
But heighe God somtyme sende can   210
His grace unto a litel oxe stalle.
Janicula men of that throop him calle;
A doughter had he, fair ynough to sight,
And **Grisildes** this yonge doughter **hight**.   *Griselda; was called*

But for to speke of hir vertuous beaute,
Than was sche oon the fayrest under sonne.
For porely **y-fostred** up was sche,   *because; brought*
No **licorous** lust was in hir body ronne;   *lecherous*
Wel ofter of the welle than of the **tonne**   *barrel*
Sche dronk, and for sche wolde vertu please,   220
Sche knew wel labour, but noon **ydel** ease.   *idle*

But though this mayden tender were of age,

15 'he gave such orders as he wanted to give them'

Yet in the brest of hir virginite
Ther was enclosed **rype** and **sad corrage**,   mature; serious; spirit
And in gret reverence and charite
Hir olde **poer** fader **fostred** sche.   poor; cared for
A fewe scheep, **spynyng**, on the feld sche kept;   as she span
Sche nold not be ydel til sche slept.

And whan sche com hom sche wolde brynge
230 **Wortis** or other herbis, tymes ofte,   cabbages
The which sche schred and **seth** for hir lyvyng,   boiled
And made hir bed ful hard, and no thing softe.
And ay sche kept hir fadre's lif **on lofte**,   'holding up'
With every **obeissance** and diligence,   obedience
That child may doon to fadres reverence.

Upon Grisildes, the pore creature,
Ful ofte **sithes** this marquys set his **ye**   times; eye
As he on huntyng **rood**, **peraventure**;   rode; perhaps
And whan it fel he mighte hir **espye**   see
240 He, not with **wantoun** lokyng of folye   lecherous
His eyyen cast upon hir, but in **sad** wyse   sober
Upon hir cheer he wold him oft **avise**,   notice

Comendyng in his hert hir wommanhede,
And **eek** hir vertu, passyng any other **wight**   also; person
Of so yong age, as wel in **cheer** as ded;   temperament
For though the people have no gret insight
In vertu, he considereth aright
Hir bounte, and **desposed** that he wolde   purposed
Wedde hir oonly, if ever he wedde scholde.

250 The day of weddyng cam, but no wight can
Telle what womman it schulde be,
For which mervayle wondrith many a man,
And sayden whan thay were in **privete**,   private
'Wol nought our lord yit leve his vanite?
Wol he not wedde? Allas, allas, the while!
Why wol he thus himself and us **bigyle**?'   trick

But natheles, this marquys hath **doon make**   had made

Of gemmes set in gold, and in **asure**,   blue
Broches and rynges for Griside's sake,
And of hir clothing took he the **mesure**   size   260
By a mayde y-lik to hir of stature,
And eek of other ornamentes alle
That unto such a weddyng schulde falle.

The tyme of **undern** of the same day   mid morning
Approchith, that this weddyng schulde be,
And al the palys **put was in array**,   was decorated
Bothe halle and chambur y-lik here degre;
Houses of office stuffid with plente.   outbuildings
Ther **maystow** se of **deynteuous vitayle**   you may; delicious food
That may be founde as fer as lastith Itaile.[16]   270

This **real** marquys, really arrayd,   royal
(Lords and ladyes in his compaignye)
The which unto the feste were **prayed**,   invited
And of his **retenu** the **bachelerie**,   following; knights
With many a soun of sondry melodye,
Unto the vilage of which I tolde,
In this array the **right** way han thay holde.   most direct

Grysild of this, God **wot**, ful innocent,   knows
That for hir schapen was al this array,
To fecche water at a welle is went,   280
And cometh hom as soone as sche may,
For wel sche had herd say that **ilke** day   same
The marquys schulde wedde; and if sche might
Sche wolde have seyen somwhat of that sight.

Sche sayd, 'I wol with other maydenes stonde
That be my felawes, in oure **dore**, and see   doorway
The marquys; and therfore wol I **fonde**   make an effort
To **don** at hom, as soone as it may be,   finish
The labour which that **longeth** unto me;   belongs
And thanne may I at leysir hir byholde,   290

16 'from one end of Italy to the other'

And sche this way into the castel **holde.'**   if; takes

And as sche wold over the **threisshfold** goon,   threshold
The marquys cam and gan hir for to calle;
And sche set doun hir water pot **anoon**   immediately
Bisides the threischfold of this oxe stalle,
And doun upon hir knees sche gan falle,
And with **sad** countenaunce knelith stille,   sober
Til sche had herd what was the lord's wille.

This thoughtful marquys spak unto this mayde,
300   Ful sobrely and seyde in this manere:
'Wher is your fader, Grisildis?' he sayde,
And sche with reverence and humble cheere
Sayde, 'Lord, he is alredy heere.'
And in sche goth, withouten lenger **let**,   delay
And to the marquys sche hir fader **fet**.   fetched

He by the hond than takith this olde man
And sayde thus, whan he him had **on syde**:   aside
'Janicula, I neither may ne can
Lenger the **plesauns** of myn herte hyde.   desire/pleasure
310   If that ye **vouchsauf**, **what so bytyde**,   grant; whatever happens
Thy doughter wil I take er that I wende
As for my wyf, unto hir lyve's ende.

Thow lovest me, I wot it wel certeyn,
And art my faithful leige man **y-bore**,   born
And al that likith me, I dar wel say
It likith the, and specially therfore
Tel me that poynt as ye have herd bifore,[17]
If that thou wolt unto that purpos **drawe**,   assent
To take me as for thy sone in lawe.'

320   The sodeyn **caas** the man **astoneyd tho**   situation; astonished then
That **reed** he **wax** – **abaischt** and al quakyng   red; grew; taken aback

17 That is, the arrangements and conditions for the marquis's wedding.

He stood: **unnethe** sayd he wordes mo   hardly
But oonly this, 'Lord,' quod he, 'my willyng
Is as ye wol; agenst youre **likyng**   wish
I wol no thing, ye be my lord so deere.
Right as yow list governith this matiere.'

'Yit wol I,' quod this markys softely,
'That in thy chambre I, and thou, and sche,
Have a **collacioun** – and **wostow** why?   talk; do you know
For I wol aske if it hir wille be   330
To be my wyf, and **reule hir after me**.   do as I tell her
And al this schal ben doon in thy presence –
I wol nought speke out of thyn **audience**.'   hearing

And in the chamber, whil thay were aboute
Her **tretys**, which as ye schul after hiere,   discussion
The people cam unto the hous withoute,
And **wondrid** hem in how honest manere   wondered
And tendurly sche kept hir fader deere;
But **outerly** Grisildes wonder might,   utterly/completely
For never **erst** ne saugh sche such a sight.   before   340

No wonder is though, that sche were **astoned**   astonished
To seen so gret a gest come into that place;
Sche never was to suche gestes **woned**,   used
For which sche loked with ful pale face.
But schortly, this matiere forth to **chace**,   move forward
These arn the wordes that the marquys sayde
To this benigne verray faithful mayde:

'Grisyld,' he sayde, 'ye schul wel understonde
It liketh to your fader and to me
That I yow wedde, and eek it may so stonde,   350
As I suppose ye wil that it so be;
But these demaundes aske I first,'quod he,
'That, **sith** it schal be doon in hasty wyse,   since
Wol ye assent, or elles yow **avyse**.   think about it

I say this – be ye redy with good hert
To al my lust, and that I frely may

As me best liste, **do** yow laughe or **smert**,   make; cry
And never ye to **gruch** it night ne day,   complain about
And eek whan I say, 'ye,' ye say not, 'nay',
360   Neyther by word, ne frownyng countenaunce –
Swer this, and here swer I oure alliaunce.'

Wondryng upon this word, quakyng for drede,
Sche sayde, 'Lord **undigne** and unworthy   unsuitable
I am to thilk honour that ye me **bede**,   offer
But as ye wil yourself, right so wol I,
And here I swere that never **wityngly**   knowingly
In werk ne thought, I nyl yow disobeye
For to be deed; though me were loth to deye.'   upon my life

'This is ynough, Grisilde myn!' quod he,
370   And forth goth he with a ful sobre chere
Out at the dore, and after that cam sche,
And to the pepul he sayd in this manere:
'This is my wyf,' quod he, 'that stondith here.
Honoureth hir and loveth hir, I yow pray,
Whoso me loveth, ther is no more to say.'

And for that nothing of hir olde **gere**   clothing
Sche schulde brynge unto his hous, he bad
That wommen schuld **despoilen** hir right there –   strip
Of which these ladyes were noght ful glad
380   To handle hir clothes wherin sche was clad –
But natheles this mayde, bright of **hew**,   colour
Fro foot to heed thay **schredde** han al newe.   clothe

Hir heeres han thay **kempt**, that lay **untressed**   combed; unkempt
Ful **rudely**, and with hir fyngres smale   coarsely
A **coroun** on hir heed thay than **y-dressed**'   crown; placed
And set hir ful of **nowches** gret and smale.   brooches
Of hir array, what schuld I make a tale?
Unnethe the people hir knew, for hir fairnesse,   hardly
Whan sche translated was in such richesse.

390   This marquis hath hir spoused with a ryng
Brought for the same cause, and than hir sette

Upon an hors, snow whyt and **wel amblyng**,   *going slowly along*
And to his palays, er he lenger **lette**,   *delayed*
With joyful people that hir ladde and mette,
Conveyed hire; and thus the day thay spende
In **revel** til the sonne gan descende.   *celebration*

And schortly, this tale for to **chace**,   *follow/speed up*
I say that to this newe marquisesse
God hath schewed favour, and sent hir of his grace
That it ne **semyd not by liklynesse**   *it was not possible to tell*   400
That sche was born and fed in **rudenesse**,   *poverty*
As in a **cote** or in an oxe stalle,   *cot/ hut*
But **norischt** in an emperour's halle.   *brought up*

To every wight sche waxen is so deere
And worschipful, that folk ther sche was born
And from hir burthe knew hir yer by yere,
Unneth **trowed** thay, but dorst han sworn,   *believed*
That to Janicle, of which I spak biforn,
Sche doughter were; for as by **coniecture**   *guesswork*
Hem thought sche was another creature.   410

For though that ever vertuous was sche
Sche was **encresed** in such excellence,   *increased/grew*
Of **thewes** good y-set in high bounte,   *traits*
And so discret and fair of eloquence,
So **benigne**, and so **digne** of reverence,   *kind; worthy*
And couthe so the poeple's hert embrace,
That ech hir loveth that lokith in hir face.

Nought oonly of Saluce, in the toun,
Publissched was the bounte of hir name,
But eek byside in many a regioun.   420
If oon sayd wel, another sayd the same;
So sprad of hire heigh bounte the fame
That men and wommen, as wel yong as olde,
Gon to Saluce, upon hir to byholde.

Thus Walter lowly, nay, but **really**,   *royally*
Weddid with fortunat honestete,

In God's pees lyveth ful esily
At home, and outward grace ynough hath he;
And for he saugh that under low **degre**   status
430   Was ofte vertu y-hid, the people him helde
A prudent man, and that is seyn ful **selde**.   seldom

Nought oonly this, Grisildis thurgh hir witte
Couthe al the **feet of wifly homlynesse**;[18]
But eek whan that the tyme required it
The comun profyt couthe sche redresse:[19]
Ther nas discord, rancour, ne hevynesse
In al that lond that sche ne couthe **appese**,   settle
And wisly bryng hem all in rest and ese.

Though that hir housbond absent were anoon,
440   If gentilmen or other of hir contre
Were **wroth**, sche wolde brynge hem **at oon**,   in dispute; together
So wyse and **rype** wordes hadde sche,   suitable
And juggement of so gret **equite**,   fairness
That sche from heven sent was, as men **wende**,   believed
People to save and every wrong to amende.

Nought longe tyme after that this Grisilde
Was wedded, sche a doughter hath y-bore.
Al had hir **lever** han had a **knave** childe,   rather; boy
Glad was this marquis, and the folk therfore;
450   For though a mayden child come al byfore,
Sche may unto a knave child atteigne
By liklihed, **sith** sche nys not **bareigne**.[20]   since; barren

Incipit tertia pars

the third part begins

❧ Ther **fel**, as fallith many times mo,   happened
Whan that this child hath souked but a **throwe**,   short time
This marquys in his herte longith so

18 'homely tasks of being a wife'
19 'she could address herself to the welfare of the people'
20 'she'd be likely to have a boy next time'

Tempte his wyf, hir **sadnesse** for to knowe,   faithfulness
That he ne might out of his herte throwe
This mervaylous desir his wyf **t'assaye**;   to test
Now, God wot, he thought hir to **affraye**.   make her afraid   460

He had assayed hir ynough bifore,
And fond hir ever good – what needith it
Hire to tempte, and always more and more?
Though som men prayse it for a subtil wit,
But as for me, I say that evel it sit
T'assay a wyf whan that is no neede,
And putte hir in anguysch and in **dreede**.   fear

For which this marquis **wrought** in this manere: did
He com aloone a-night ther as sche lay,
With sterne face and with ful trouble **cheere**   manner   470
And sayde this: 'Grisild,' quod he, 'that day
that I yow took out of your pore array
And putte yow in estat of heigh noblesse
Ye have not that forgeten, as I gesse.

I say, Grisild, this present **dignite**   honour
In which that I have put yow, as I trowe,
Makith yow not forgetful for to be
That I yow took in pore estat, ful lowe.
For eny **wele** ye **moot** yourselve knowe,   prosperity; may
Tak heed of every word that I yow say;   480
Ther is no wight that herith it, but we tway.

Ye wot your self how ye comen heere
Into this hous; it is nought long ago.
And though to me that ye be **leef** and deere,   beloved
Unto my **gentils** ye be nothing so;   aristocracy
Thay seyn to hem it is gret schame and wo
For to ben subject, and ben in **servage**   servitude
To the, that born art of a smal village.

And namely, syn thy doughter was y-bore,
These wordes han thay spoken, douteles;   490
But I desire, as I have doon byfore,

To lyve my lif with hem in rest and pees.
I may not in this caas be **reccheles**;   reckless
I moot do with thy doughter for the best –
Not as I wolde, but as my pepul **lest**.   wish

And yit, God wot, this is ful **loth** to me,   hateful
But natheles, withoute youre **witynge**   knowing
Wol I not doon, but this wol I,' quod he,
'That ye to me assent as in this thing.
500   Schew now your paciens in your **wirching**   behaviour
That thou me **hightest** and swor in yon village,   promised
That day that maked was oure mariage.'

Whan sche had herd al this sche nou*gh*t **ameevyd**,   changed
Neyther in word, or **cheer**, or **countenaunce**,   manner; facial expression
For as it semed sche was nought agreeved.
Sche sayde, 'Lord, al lith in your plesaunce;
My child and I, with **hertly obeisaunce**,   heartfelt obedience
Ben youres al, and ye may save or **spille**   kill
Your oughne thing – werkith after your wille.

510   Ther may nothing, God my soule save,
Liken to yow that may displesen me,
Ne I desire nothing for to have
Ne drede for to lese, save oonly ye.
This wil is in myn hert, and ay schal be;
No length of tyme or deth may this deface,
Ne chaunge my **corrage** to other place.'   intention

Glad was this marquis of hir answeryng,
But yit he **fayned** as he were not so;   pretended
Al **dreery** was his **cheer** and his **lokyng**,   sad; mood; expression
520   Whan that he schold out of the chambre go.
Soon after this, a forlong way or tuo,
He prively hath told al his **entent**   intention
Unto a man, and unto his wyf him sent.

A maner sergeant was this **prive** man,   close personal servant
The which that faithful ofte he founden hadde
In thinges grete; and eek such folk wel can

Don execucioun in thinges badde.	carry out
The lord knew wel that he him loved and **dradde**,	feared
And whan this sergeant wist his lordes wille,	
Into the chamber he stalked him ful stille.	530

'Madame,' he sayd, 'ye most forgive it me,	
Though I do thing to which I am **constreynit**;	forced
Ye ben so wys that ful wel knowe ye	
That lord's **hestes** mow not be **y-feynit** –	orders; disobeyed
They mowe wel be biwaylit or compleynit,²¹	
But men moot neede unto her **lust** obeye,	desire
And so wol I; ther is no more to seye.	

This child I am comaundid for to take.'	
And spak no more, but out the child he **hent**	seized
Dispitously, and gan a **chiere** make	appearance 540
As though he wold han slayn it er he went.	
Grisild **moot** al suffer and al consent,	must
And as a lamb sche sitteth meeke and stille,	
And let this cruel sergeant doon his wille.	

Suspecious was the **defame** of this man,	reputation
Suspect his face, suspect his word also;	
Suspect the tyme in which he this bigan.	
Allas, hir doughter that sche loved so!	
Sche **wend** he wold han slayen it right **tho**,	thought; then
But natheles sche neyther weep ne **siked**,	sighed 550
Conformyng hir to that the marquis liked.	

But atte last speke sche bigan,	
And mekely sche to the sergeant preyde,	
So as he was a worthy gentilman,	
That sche most kisse hir child er that it deyde.	
And on hir arm this litel child sche leyde	
With ful sad face, and gan the child to **blesse**	made the sign of the cross
And **lullyd** it, and after gan it **kesse**.	cuddled; kiss

And thus sche sayd, in hir benigne vois:

21 'they may be wept over or complained about'

560 'Farwel, my child – I schal the never see,
But sith I the have marked with the croys,
Of thilke fader blessed mot thou be
That for us deyde upon a cros of tre.[22]
Thy soule, litel child, I him **bytake**,   commend
For this night schaltow deyen for my sake.'

I trowe that to a **norice** in this **caas**   nurse; situation
It had ben hard this **rewthe** for to see;   pity
Wel might a moder than have cryed, 'Allas!'
But natheles so sad, stedefast, was sche
570 That sche endured al adversite,
And to the sergeant mekely sche sayde,
'Have her agayn, your litel yonge mayde.

Goth now,' quod sche, 'and doth my lord's heste;
But o thing wil I pray yow of your grace –
That **but** my lord forbede yow, atte leste   unless
Burieth this litel body in som place
That bestes ne no briddes it **to race**.'   tear it to pieces
But he no word wil to the purpos say,
But took the child, and went upon his way.

580 This sergeant com unto this lord agayn,
And of Grisildes wordes and hir cheere
He tolde, poynt for poynt, in schort and playn,
And him presentith with his doughter deere.
Somwhat this lord had **rewthe** in his manere,   pity
But natheles his purpos **huld** he stille –   held to
As lordes doon, whan thay woln have her wille.

And bad the sergeaunt that he **prively**   secretly
Scholde this childe softe wynde and wrappe,
With alle circumstaunces tendurly,
590 And cary it in a **cofre**, or in his lappe,   cradle
Upon peyne his heed of for to **swappe**,   swipe
That no man schulde knowe of this entent,
Ne whens he com, ne whider that he went.

22 Christ/ God the Father.

But at Boloygne, to his suster deere,
That **thilke tyme** of Panik was countesse,[23]   *at that time*
He schuld it take, and **schewe** this **matiere**,   *reveal; story/plan*
Byseching hir to doon hir **busynesse**   *do the best she can*
This child to fostre in alle gentilesse,
And whos child that it was he bad hir hyde
From every **wight**, for ought that might **bytyde**.   *person; happen*   **600**

The sergeant goth and hath fulfild this thing,
But to this marquys now retourne we;
For now goth he, ful fast ymaginyng[24]
If by his wyve's cher he mighte se
Or by hir word apparceyve, that sche
Wer chaunged; but he hir never couthe fynde
But ever in oon ylike, sad and kynde,[25]

As glad, as humble, as busy in servise,
And eek in love as sche was wont to be
Was sche to him, in every maner wyse;   **610**
Ne of hir doughter nought o word spak sche,
Non accident, for noon adversite   *not accidentally*
Was seyn in hir, ne never hir doughter name
Ne **nempnyd** sche, in ernest ne in game.   *named*

Incipit Quarta pars

the fourth part begins

❦ In this estaat ther passed ben foure yer
Er sche with childe was; but as God wolde,
A knave child sche bar by this Waltier,
Ful gracious and fair for to biholde;
And whan that folk to his fader tolde   **620**
Nought oonly he, but al his contre, merye
Was for this child, and God thay thank and **herie**.   *praise*

Whan it was tuo yer old, and fro the brest
Departed fro his **noris**, upon a day   *nurse*

23 Panico.
24 'trying to find out'
25 'she was always the same'

This markys caughte yit another **lest**   desire
To tempt his wif yit **after**, if he may.   again
O! Needles was sche tempted in assay!
But weddid men ne knowen no **mesure**,   restraint
Whan that thay fynde a pacient creature.

630 'Wyf,' quod this marquys, 'ye han herd er this
My peple **sekly** berith our mariage,   badly
And namly, syn my sone y-boren is,
Now is it wors than ever in **al our age**;   these times
The murmur **sleth** myn hert and my corrage,   kills
For to myn eeris cometh the vois so **smerte**,   painful
That it wel neigh destroyed hath myn herte.

Now say thay thus: 'Whan Wauter is **agoon**,   dead
Than schal the blood of Janicula succede
And ben our lord, for other have we noon.'
640 Such wordes saith my people out of **drede**;   fear
Wel ought I of such murmur taken heede,
For certeynly I drede such **sentence**,   talking
Though thay not pleynly speke in my **audience**.   hearing

I wolde lyve in **pees**, if that I might,   peace
Wherfor I am disposid **outrely**,   entirely
As I his suster **servede** by night,   treated
Right so thynk I to serve him prively.
This warn I you; that ye not sodeinly
Out of your self for nothing schuld **outraye**;   become hysterical
650 Beth pacient, and therof I yow pray.'

'I have,' quod sche, 'sayd thus and ever schal:
I **wol** nothing ne **nil nothing**, certayn,   will; don't want anything
But as yow list; nought greveth me at al
Though that my doughter and my sone be slayn
At your comaundement; this is to sayn
I have no had no part of children twayne,
But first **syknes**, and after **wo** and payne.   sickness; sorrow

Ye ben oure lord; doth with your owne thing
Right as yow list; **axith** no **red** of me.   ask; advice

For as I left at hom al my clothing   660
Whan I first com to yow, right so,' quod sche,
'Left I my wille and my liberte,
And took your clothing; wherfor I yow preye,
Doth youre **plesaunce** – I wil youre **lust** obeye.   pleasure; desire

And certes, if I hadde **prescience**   foreknowledge
Your wil to knowe er ye youre lust me tolde,
I wold it doon withoute negligence.
But now I wot your lust and what ye wolde,
At your plesaunce ferm and stable I holde,
For **wist** I that my deth wold doon yow **ease**,   knew; comfort   670
Right gladly wold I deye yow to please;

Deth may make no comparisoun
Unto your love.' And whan this marquys **say**   saw
The **constance** of his wyf, he cast adoun   constancy
His eyyen tuo, and wondrith that sche may
In pacience suffre al this array;
And forth he goth, with **drery** countenaunce –   unhappy
But to his hert it was ful gret plesaunce.

This ugly sergeaunt, in the same wise
That he hir doughter **fette**, right so he –   fetched   680
Or worse, if men worse can devyse –
Hath **hent** hir sone, that ful was of beaute,   seized
And ever in oon so pacient was sche,
That sche no cheere made of hevynesse,
But kist hir sone, and after gan him blesse.

Save this: sche prayed him if that he mighte
Hir litel sone he wold in eorthe **grave**,   bury
His tendre **lymes**, delicate to sight,   limbs
From foules and from bestes him to save.
But sche noon answer of him mighte have;   690
He went his way as him no thing ne **rought**,   cared
But to Bolyne he tenderly it brought.[26]

26 Bologna.

This marquis wondreth ever **the lenger the more**   more and more
Upon hir pacience, and if that he
Ne hadde **sothly** knowen ther bifore   truly
That **parfytly** hir children loved sche,   perfectly
He wold have **wend** that of som subtilte   believed
And malice, or of cruel **corrage**,   nature
That sche had suffred this with sad visage.

700   But wel he knew that next himself, certeyn,
Sche loved hir children best in every wise:
But now of wommen wold I aske **fayn**   gladly
If these **assayes** mighten not suffice;   tests
What couthe a **stourdy** housebonde more devyse   hard
To prove hir wyfholde and hir stedefastnesse,
And he contynnyng ever in **stourdynesse**?   cruelty

But ther ben folk of such condicioun
That whan thay have a certeyn purpos take,
Thay can nought **stynt** of her **entencioun**;   give up; intention
710   But right **as** thay were bounden to a stake,   as if
Thay wil not of her firste purpos **slake**;   weaken
Right so this marquys fullich hath purposed
To tempt his wyf, as he was first disposed.

He **wayteth** if by word or countenaunce   waited to see
That sche to him was chaunged, or corage,
But never couthe he fynde variaunce.
Sche was ay **oon** in hert and in visage;   one
And **ay** the **ferther** that sche was in age   always; older
The more trewe, if that were possible,
720   Sche was to him, and more **penyble**.   dutiful

For which it semyd this; that of hem tuo
Ther nas but oo wil, for as Walter lest
The same plesaunce was hir lust also;
And God be thanked, al **fel** for the best –   happened
Sche schewed wel, for no worldly **unrest**,   trouble
A wyf as of hirself nothing ne scholde
Wylne, in effect, but as hir housbond wolde.

The sclaunder of Walter ofte and wyde spradde,
That of a cruel hert he wikkedly,
For he a pore womman weddid hadde,   730
Hath **morthrid** bothe his children prively.   murdered
Such murmur was among hem **comuly**   commonly held
No wonder is, for to the peple's eere
Ther com no word, but that thay mortherid were.

For which, wheras his peple therbyfore
Had loved him wel, the sclaunder of his **diffame**   infamy
Made hem that thay him hatede therfore;
To ben a mordrer is an hateful name,
But natheles, for ernest or for **game**,   sport
He of his cruel purpos **nolde** stente –   would not   740
To tempt his wyf was set al his entente.

Whan that his doughter twelf yer was of age
He to the court of Rome in suche wise,
Enformed of his wille, sent his message,
Comaundyng hem such bulles to devyse[27]
As to his cruel purpos may suffise;
How that the pope, as for his peple's reste,
Bad him to wedde another, if him leste.

I say, he bad thay schulde countrefete
The pope's bulles, makyng mencioun   750
That he hath leve his firste wyf to **lete**   leave
As by the popes dispensacioun,
To **stynte rancour** and **discencioun**   end; bitterness; dissent
Bitwix his peple and him, thus sayd the bulle,
The which thay han publisshid **atte fulle**.   in full

The rude people, as it no wonder is,
Wende ful wel that it had be right so;   believed
But whan these tydynges come to Grisildis,
I **deeme** that hir herte was ful wo,   judge
But sche, **ylike sad** for evermo,   continually sober   760

27 Papal documents.

Disposid was this humble creature
Th'adversite of fortun al **t'endure**,   to endure

Abydyng ever his lust and his plesaunce,
To whom that sche was give, hert and al,
As to hir verray worldly suffisaunce.[28]
But schortly, if I this story telle schal,
This marquys writen hath in special
A letter, in which he schewith his entent,
And secrely he to Boloyne it sent.

770   To therl of Panyk, which that hadde tho
Weddid his suster, prayd he specially
To bryng hom agein his children tuo
In honurable estaat, al openly;
But oon thing he him prayde outerly,
That he to no **wight**, though men wold enquere,   person
Schuld not tellen whos children thay were,

But say the mayde schuld y-weddid be
Unto the markys of Saluce anoon;
And as this eorl was prayd, so dede he,
780   For at day-set he on his way is goon
Toward Saluce, and lordes many oon,
In riche array this mayden for to guyde,
Hir yonge brother rydyng by hire syde.

Arrayed was toward hir mariage
This freissche **may**, al ful of gemmes **clere**   maiden; bright
Hir brother, which that seven yer was of age,
Arrayed eek ful freissh in his manere.
And thus in gret noblesse, and with glad chere,
Toward Saluces **schapyng** her journay,   making
790   Fro day to day thay ryden in her way.

28 'with regard to everything that she humanly needed'

Incipit pars Quinta

part five begins

❦ Among al this, after his wikked **usage**,   custom
This marquis yit his wif to tempte more
To the **uttrest** proef of hir corrage,   uttermost
Fully to han experiens and **lore**   knowledge
If that sche were as stedefast as byfore,
He on a day, in open audience,
Ful **boystrously** hath sayd hir this **sentence**:   loudly; speech

'Certes, Grisildes, I had ynough pleasaunce
To have yow to my wif, for your goodnesse,   800
And for youre trouthe, and for your obeissaunce,
Nought for your lignage, ne for your richesse,
But now know I in verray **sothfastnesse**   truthfulness
That in gret lordschip, if I wel **avyse**,   consider
Ther is gret servise, in **sondry** wyse.   many different

I may not do as every ploughman may;
My people me **constreignith** for to take   force
Another wyf, and certeyn day by day,
And eek the pope's rancour for to **slake**,   end
Consentith it, that dar I undertake,   agree to it   810
And trewely thus moche I wol yow say –
My newe wif is comyng by the way.

Be strong of hert, and **voyde** anoon hir place,   make empty
And thilke dower that ye broughten me,
Tak it agayn; I graunt it of my grace –
Retourneth to your fadres hous,' quod he,
'No man may always have prosperite;
With even hert I **rede** yow endure   advise
The strok of fortune, or of **adventure**.'   chance

And sche agayn answerd in pacience: 820
'My lord,' quod sche, 'I wot and wist always
How that **bitwixe** your magnificence   between
And my poverte no wight can, ne may,
Make comparisoun, it is **no nay**;   without doubt

I ne held me never **digne** in no manere   suitable/worthy
To ben your wyf, ne yit your **chamberere**,   chambermaid

And in this hous ther ye me lady made,
The highe God take I for my witnesse,
And als so wisly he my soule glade,
830   I never huld me lady, ne maistresse,
But humble servaunt to your worthinesse,
And ever schal, whil that my lyf may **dure**.   last
Aboven every worldly creature

That ye so longe of your benignite
Han holden me, in honour and nobleye,
Wheras I was not worthy for to be,
That thonk I God and yow, to whom I preye –
For, yeld it yow, ther is no more to seye –
Unto my fader gladly wil I wende,
840   And with him duelle unto my lyve's ende.

Ther I was fostred as a child ful smal;
Til I be deed my lyf ther wil I lede,
A widow clene in body, hert and al,
For **sith** I yaf to yow my maydenhede   since
And am your trewe wyf – it is no drede.
God schilde such a lord's wyf to take
Another man to housbond, or to **make**.   mate

And of your newe wif god of his grace
So graunte yow wele and prosperite,
850   For I wol gladly yelden hir my place,
In which that I was **blisful** wont to be.   happy
For sith it liketh yow, my lord,' quod sche,
'That whilom were al myn herte's reste,
That I schal gon – I wil go whan yow leste.

But theras ye **profre** me such **dowayre**   offer; dowry
As I ferst brought, it is wel in my mynde
It were my wrecchid clothes, no thing faire,
The which to me were hard now for to fynde.
O, goode God! How gentil and how kynde

Ye semed, by your speche and your visage,   860
The day that maked was our mariage!

But soth is sayd; **algate** I fynd it trewe,   entirely
For in effect it proved is on me,
Love is nought old as whan that it is newe;²⁹
But certes, lord, for noon adversite
To deyen in the caas, it schal not be   if I died
That evere in word or werk I schal repente
That I yow gaf myn hert in **hol entente**   in complete willingness

My lord, ye wot that in my fadre's place
Ye dede me stripp out of my pore **wede**,   clothes   870
And richly me **cladden** of youre grace: dressed
To *yow* brought I nought elles, out of drede,
But faith and mekenes and **maydenhede**;   virginity
And her agayn my clothyng I restore,
And eek my weddyng ryng, for evermore.

The **remenant** of your jewels redy be   remainder
Within your chambur dore, dar I saufly sayn;
Naked out of my fadre's hous,' quod sche,
'I com; and naked moot I **torne** agayn.   return
Al your **pleisauns** wold I fulfille **fayn**;   pleasure; gladly   880
But yit I hope it be not youre entent
That I **smocles** out of your chambre went.   without a petticoat

Ye couthe not doon so dishonest a thing,
That **thilke** wombe in which your children leye   the same
Schulde byforn the people in my walkyng
Be seye al bare; wherfore I yow pray,
Let me not lik a worm go by the way –
Remembre yow, myn oughne lord so deere –
I was your wyf, though I unworthy were.

Wherfor in **guerdoun of** my maydenhede,   exchange for   890
Which that I brought and nought agayn I bere,

29 'when love grows old it isn't like when it was new'

As vouchethsauf as geve me to my **meede**   reward
Such a smok as I was wont to were,
That I therwith may **wrye** the wombe of here   wrap
That was your wif, and here take I my leve
Of yow, myn **oughne** lord, lest I yow greve.'   own

'The smok,' quod he, 'that thou hast on thy bak,
Let it be stille, and ber it forth with the.'
But wel **unnethes** thilke word he spak,   hardly
900 But went his way for **routhe** and for pite.   pity
Byforn the folk hirselven strippith sche,
And in hir smok, with heed and foot al bare,
Toward hir fader's house forth is sche fare.

The folk hir folwen, wepyng in hir weye,
And fortune ay thay cursen as thay goon;
But sche fro wepyng kept hir **eyen dreye**,   eyes dry
Ne in this tyme word ne spak sche noon.
Hir fader, that this tyding herd anoon,
Cursed the day and tyme that nature
910 Schoop him to be a **lyve's** creature.   living

For out of doute, this olde pore man
Was ever in suspect of hir mariage;
For ever he **deemed sith** that it bigan,   judged; since
That whan the lord fulfilled had his corrage,
Him wolde think that it were **disparage**   beneath
To his estate so lowe for to light,
And **voyden hire** as sone as ever he might.   get rid of her

Agayns his doughter hastily goth he,   to meet
For he by noyse of folk knew hir comyng,
920 And with hir olde cote, as it might be,
He covered hir, ful sorwfully wepyng;
But on hir body might he it nou*ght* **bringe**,   put
For **rude** was the cloth, and sche mor of age   coarse
By dayes **fele** than at hir mariage.   many

Thus with hir fader, for a certayn space
Dwellith this flour of wifly pacience,
That neyther by her wordes, ne by hir face,
Byforn the folk, nor eek in her absence,
Ne schewed sche that hir was doon offence,
Ne of hir highe **astaat** no remembraunce   status   930
Ne hadde sche, as by hir **countenaunce**.   appearance

No wonder is, for in hir gret estate
Hir gost was ever in playn humilite;
Ne tender mouth, noon herte delicate,
Ne pompe, ne **semblant** of **realte**;   outward show; royalty
But ful of pacient **benignite**,   kindness
Discrete and prideles, ay honurable,
And to hir housbond ever meke and **stable**.   trustworthy

Men speke of Job, and **most** for his **humblesse**   mostly; humility
As clerkes whan hem lust can wel **endite**,   tell/recount   940
Namely of men; but as in sothfastnesse
Though clerkes prayse wommen but a **lite**,   little
Ther can no man in humblesse him acquyte
As wommen can, ne can be half so trewe
As wommen ben, but it **be falle of newe**.   sudden/recent

Fro Boloyne is this erl of Panik y-come,
Of which the fame up sprong to **more and lasse**   greater and lesser (people)
And to the poeple's eeres all and some
Was **couth** eek that a newe marquisesse   known
He with him brought, in such pomp and richesse,   950
That never was ther seyn with man's **ye**   eye
So noble array in al West Lombardye.

The marquys, which that schoop and knew al this,
For that this erl was come, sent his message
For thilke cely, pore, Grisildis,
And sche, with humble hert and good visage,
Not with no swollen hert in hir corrage,
Cam at his **hest** and on hir knees hir sette,   order
And reverently and wyfly sche him **grette**.   greeted

960 'Grisild,' quod he, 'my wil is outrely
This mayden that schal weddid be to me,
Receyved be tomorwe as really
As it possible is in myn hous to be,
And eek that every wight **in his degre**   according to his station
Have his estaat in **sittyng** and **servyse**[30]
In high plesaunce, as I can devyse.

I have no womman **suffisant**, certeyne,   good enough
The chambres for **t'array in ordinance**   to set in order
After my lust, and therfor wold I feyne   as I like them
970 That thin were al such maner governaunce[31]
Thow knowest eek of al my plesaunce;
Though thyn **array** be badde and ille **byseye**   clothing; to look at
Do thou thy **dever**, atte leste weye.'   duty

'Nought oonly, lord, that I am glad,' quod sche,
'To don your lust, but I desire also
Yow to serve, and plese in my degre
Withoute **feynyng**, and schal evermo;   pretending/lying
Ne never for no wele, ne for no wo,
Ne schal the **gost** withinne myn herte **stente**   spirit; cease
980 To love yow best, with al my trewe entent.'

And with that word sche gan the hous to **dight**,   make ready
And tables for to sette and beddes make,
And peyned hir to doon al that sche might,
Preying the **chamberers**, for God's sake,   chambermaids
To hasten hem, and faste swepe and schake.
And sche, the most **servisable** of alle,   hardworking
Hath every chamber **arrayed**, and his halle.   got ready

Abouten **undern** gan this erl alight,   late morning
That with him brought these noble children tweye,
990 For which the peple ran to se that sight,
Of her array so richely **biseye**;   to be seen

30 'seating and serving arrangements'
31 'that all these things were under your control'

And than at erst amonges hem thay seye
That Walter was no fool, though that him lest
To chaunge his wyf, for it was for the best.

'For sche is fairer,' as thay **demen** alle,   judge
'Than is Grisild, and more tender of age,
And fairer **fruyt** bitwen hem schulde falle,   children/offspring
And more plesaunt, for hir high lynage.
Hir brother eek so fair was of visage,
That hem to seen the peple hath **caught plesaunce**,   were pleased 1000
Comending now the marquys' **governaunce**.'   handling (of affairs)

'O stormy people, unsad and ever untrewe,
Ay undiscret, and chaungyng as a **fane**!   (weather) vane
Desyryng ever in **rombel** that is newe,   rumour
For lik the moone ay wax ye and wane!
Ay ful of **clappyng** dere ynough a jane,[32]   loud chatter
Youre **doom** is fals, your **constaunce** yvel previth!   judgement; constancy
A ful gret fool is he that on yow **leevith**!'   believes

Thus sayde saad folk in that citee,
Whan that the people **gased** up and doun,   gazed 1010
For thay were glad right of the novelte,
To han a newe lady of her toun.
No more of this now make I mencioun,
But to Grisildes agayn wol I me **dresse**,   turn my attention
And tell hir constance and hir bisyness.

Ful busy was Grisild in everything
That to the fest was **appertinent**;   belonging
Right nought was sche **abaissht** of hir clothing,   ashamed
Though it were **ruyde** and somdel eek **to rent**,   poor; torn
But with glad cheer to the gate is sche went,   1020
With other folk, to griete the marquisesse,
And after that doth forth her **busynesse**.   duties

32 'of very little worth'

With so glad chier his gestes sche receyveth,
And so **connyngly** everich in his degre,   appropriately
That no defaute no man **aparceyveth**,   perceives
But ay thay wondren what sche mighte be,
That in so pover array was for to se,
And **couthe** such honour and reverence,   knew
And worthily thay prayse hir prudence.

1030   In all this menewhile sche ne **stent**   ceased
This mayde and eek hir brother to comende
With al hir hert, in ful **buxom** entent,   submissive
So wel that no man couthe hir **pris** amende;   praise
But atte last, whan that these lordes wende
To sitte doun to mete, he gan to calle
Grisild, as sche was busy in his halle.

'Grisyld,' quod he as it were **in his play**,   jokingly
'How likith the my wif and hir beaute?'
'Right wel my lord,' quod sche, 'for in good **fay**,   faith
1040   A fairer saugh I never noon than sche.
I pray to God give hir prosperite,
And so hope I that he wol to yow sende
Plesaunce ynough unto your lyves' ende.   pleasure

On thing warn I yow, and **biseke** also;   beg
That ye ne **prike** with no tormentynge   trouble
This tendre mayden, as ye have do **mo**,   me
For sche is **fostrid** in hir **norischinge**   raised; upbringing
More tendrely, and to my supposynge,
Sche couthe not adversite endure
1050   As couthe a pore-fostrid creature.'

And whan this Walter saugh hir pacience,
Hir glade cheer and no malice at al,
And he so oft had doon to hir **offence**,   wrong
And sche ay **sad** and constant as a wal,   sober
Continuyng ever hir innocence overal,
This sturdy marquys gan his herte **dresse**   move
To **rewen** upon hir wyfly stedefastnesse.   have pity

'This is ynough, Grisilde myn,' quod he,
Be now no more **agast**, ne **yvel apayed**;   frightened; feel badly
I have thy faith and thy benignite,   1060
As wel as ever womman was **assayed**   tried/tested
In gret estate, and **porliche arrayed**;   poorly dressed
Now knowe I, dere wyf, thy sedefastnesse.'
And hir in armes took and **gan hir kesse**.   began; kiss

And sche for wonder took of it no **keepe** –   notice
Sche herde not what thing he to hir sayde;
Sche ferd as sche had stert out of a sleepe[33]
Til sche out of hir **masidnesse abrayde**.   amazement; recovered
'Grisild,' quod he, 'by God that for us deyde,
Thou art my wyf, ne noon other I have,   1070
Ne never had, as God my soule save.

This is my doughter, which thou hast supposed
To be my wif, that other faithfully
Schal be myn heir, as I have **ay purposed**;   always intended
Thow **bar** hem in thy body trewely –   carried
At Boloyne have I kept them **prively**.   secretly
Tak hem agayn, for now maistow seye
That thou has **lorn** noon of thy children tweye.   lost

And folk that otherweyes han seyd of me,
I warn hem wel that I have doon this deede   1080
For no malice, ne for no cruelte,
But for t'assaye in the thy wommanhede;
And not to slen my children – God forbede! –
But to kepe hem prively and stille
Til I thy purpos knewe, and al thy will.'

Whan sche this herd, **aswoned** doun sche fallith   in a faint
For pitous joy, and after hir swownyng,
Sche bothe hir yonge children to hir callith,
And in hir armes, pitously wepyng,
Embraseth hem, and tenderly kissyng,   embraces   1090

---

33 'she feared that she had woken suddenly out of a sleep'

Ful lik a moder, with hir salte **teris**,   tears
Sche **bathis** bothe hir **visage** and hir eeris.   bathes; face

O, such a pitous thing it was to see
Hir swownyng, and hir humble vois to heere!
'**Graunt mercy**, Lord God, thank it yow,' quod sche,   many thanks
'That ye han kept my children so deere!
Now rek I never to be deed right heere,[34]
Sith I stond in your love and in your grace;   since
No fors of deth, ne whan my spirit **pace**!   no matter; leaves

1100   O tender, deere yonge children myne,
Youre woful moder **wende stedefastly**   truly believed
That cruel houndes and som foul **vermyne**   vermin
Had **eten** yow, but God of his mercy   eaten
And your benigne Fader tenderly,
Hath doon yow kept.' And in that same **stounde**   moment
Al sodeinly sche **swapped** doun to grounde.   down

And in hir **swough** so sadly holdith sche   swoon
Hir children tuo, whan sche gan hem t'embrace,
That with gret **sleight** and gret **difficulte**   craft; difficulty
1110   The children from her arm thay gonne **arace**.   break away
O many a teer, on many a pitous face,
Doun ran of hem that stooden hir **bisyde**!   beside
Unnethe aboute hir mighte thay **abyde**.   hardly; stay

Waltier hir **gladith** and hir sorwe **slakith**;   cheers; subsided
Sche rysith up **abaisshed** from hir traunce,   embarassed
And every wight hir joy and **feste** makith,   rejoicing
Til sche hath **caught** agayn hir **continaunce**.   regained; composure
Wautier hir doth so faithfully plesaunce
That it was **daynte** for to see the cheere   pleasant
1120   Bitwix hem tuo, now thay be met **in feere**.   together

These ladys, whan that thay her tyme say,
Han taken hir and into chambre goon,

34 'I don't care if I die right here'

And strippen hir out of hir rude array,
And in a cloth of gold that brighte schon,
With a coroun of many a riche **stoon**   stone
Upon hir heed, that into halle hir broughte,
And ther sche was honoured as **hir ought**.   she should be

Thus hath this pitous day a **blisful** ende,   happy
For every man and womman doth his might
This day in mirth and revel to **despende**,   spend 1130
Til on the **welken** schon the sterres bright;   heaven
For more solempne in every man's sight
This feste was, and **gretter of costage**,   more expensive
Than was the **revel** of hir mariage.   celebration

Ful many a yer, in heigh prosperite,
Lyven these tuo in concord and in rest,
And richeliche his doughter maried he
Unto a lord, on of the worthiest
Of al Ytaile; and thanne in pees and rest
His wyve's fader in his court he kepith,   1140
Til that the soule out of his body crepith.

His sone succedith in his heritage
In rest and pees, after his fader day,
And fortunat was eek in mariage –
Al put he not his wyf in gret assay.
This world is not so strong, it is no nay,
As it hath ben in olde tymes **yore**;   long ago
And herknith what this auctor saith, therfore:

This story is sayd not for that wyves scholde
Folwe Gisild, as in in humilite,   1150
For it were **importable** though they wolde,   unacceptable
But for that every **wight** in his degre   person
Schulde be constant in adversite,
As was Grisild; therefore Petrark writeth
This story, which with high **stile** he enditeth.   style

For swich a womman was so pacient
Unto a mortal man, wel more us oughte

Recyven al **in gre** that God us sent,   with grace
For gret skil is he prove that he wroughte;[35]
1160 But he ne temptith no man that he boughte,
As saith Seint Jame, if he his **pistil** rede: epistle
He provith folk al day, it is no drede,

And suffrith us, as for our exercise,
With scharpe **scourges** of adversite   whips
Ful ofte to be **bete**, in **sondry** wise;   beaten; various
Nought for to knowe oure wille, for certes he
Er we were born knew al our **frelte**,   frailty
And for oure best is al his governaunce;[36]
Leet us thanne lyve in vertuous **suffraunce**.   endurance

1170 But oo word, lordes, herkneth er I go;
It were ful hard to fynde nowadayes
As Grisildes, in al a toun thre or tuo[37]
For if that thay were put to such assayes,
The gold of hem hath now so badde **alayes**   alloys
With bras, that though the coyn be fair at ye,[38]
Hit wolde rather **brest** in tuo than **plye**.   burst; bend

For which heer, for the wyve's love of Bathe,
Whos lyf, and all of hir **secte** God **meyntene**   like; keep
In high **maistry**, and elles were it **scathe**.   sovereignty; a shame
1180 I wil with lusty herte, freisch and grene,
Say yow a song to glade yow, I wene,
And lat us stynt of **ernestful** matiere –   serious
Herknith my song, that saith in this manere:

Lenvoy de Chaucer

Chaucer's envoy

---

35 'it is reasonable that he make trial of that which he made'
36 'in our best interests'
37 'it would be hard to find two or three Griselda's in a town nowadays'
38 'although the coin is pretty to look at'

❦ Grisild is deed, and **eek** hir pacience,   also
And bothe at oones buried in Itayle;
For whiche I crye, in open audience,
No weddid man so hardy be to assayle
His wyve's pacience in hope to fynde   1190
Grisildes, for in certeyn he schal fayle.

O noble wyves, ful of heigh prudence!
Let noon humilite your tonges **nayle**,   nail down
Ne lat no clerk have cause or diligence
To write of yow a story of such mervaile
As of Grisildes, pacient and kynde,
Lest Chichivach yow **swolwe** in hir **entraile**!³⁹   swallow; guts

Folwith Ecco, that holdith no silence,⁴⁰
But ever answereth at the **countretayle**;   in echo
Beth no**u**ght **bydaffed** for your innocence,   fooled   1200
But scharply tak on yow the **governayle**.   mastery
Empryntith wel this lessoun in your mynde   imprint
For comun profyt, **sith** it may **avayle**.   since; be helpful

Ye archweyves, stondith **at defens**,   on guard
Syn ye ben strong as is a greet **chamayle**,   camel
Ne suffre not that men yow don offens;
And **sclendre** wydewes, **felle** as in batayle,   slender; deadly
Beth **egre** as is a tyger, yond in Inde,   fierce
Ay **clappith** as a mylle, I yow counsaile.   sound your tongue

Ne **drede** hem not, do hem no **reverence**,   fear; respect   1210
For though thin housbond armed be in **mayle**,   mail
The **arwes** of thy crabbid eloquence   arrows
Schal **perse** his brest and eek his adventayle;⁴¹   pierce
In gelousy I **rede** eek thou him bynde,   advise
And thou schalt make him **couche** as doth a quayle.   lie down (in fear)

If thou be fair ther folk ben in presence,
Schew thou thy **visage** and thin **apparaile**;   face; clothing

39 The cow, in popular contemporary literature, who ate good wives.
40 The nymph who faded away to just a voice.
41 A 'curtain' of mail covering the back of the neck.

If thou be **foul** be **fre** of thy **despense**,[42]
To gete the frendes do ay thy **travayle**.   work
1220 Be ay of chier as light as **lef** on **lynde**,   leaf; linden tree
And let hem **care**, and wepe, and wryng, and wayle.   worry

Explicit

                                                                   it ends

42 ugly; generous; expenditure

THE MERCHANT'S PROLOGUE AND TALE

The merchant says he knows about the woes of marriage, although he has only been married for two months. Far from the patience of Griselda, his wife's cruelty would make her a match for the devil himself. The host remarks that, since the merchant knows so much about this, he might like to expound upon it. The merchant accepts this invitation.

An elderly knight, who has lived his life in lechery, decides he will get married in order to save his soul, beget an heir, and to legitimise his sexual activities. He thinks that he must have a young wife, no more than sixteen, to fulfil his appetites. His brother Justinus argues against this course, but Placebo agrees with everything that January says, on the grounds that he, as a courtier, believes that one's lord must always be told that he is right, whether one agrees with him or not. A bride, May, is found and married to January. She is forced to cope with his vigorous sexuality and his disgusting old body, although she actually considers his lovemaking worthless. January's squire Damian falls in love with May, and, pretending to be sick, he manages to give her a letter declaring his love. She disposes of the letter, and writes back agreeing to commit adultery with him. Their situation becomes difficult when January becomes blind, and always keeps his hand on May to prevent her from cuckolding him. January has a garden in which he and May perform sexual activities, which the merchant does not disclose, but which he intimates are such as may not be done in bed. May steals the key to the gate, and Damian makes a copy. On a designated day, Damian hides in the garden. May coaxes her husband into the garden, indicating by a sign to Damian that he should climb into the pear tree. She then makes groaning noises and tells her husband that she may be pregnant. Claiming to be craving pears, she climbs on her husband's back into the tree. In the meantime, the god Pluto and his wife Proserpine have been sitting in the garden arguing about this situation. Pluto says that if May cuckolds January, he will give January his sight back, whilst Proserpine says that women have a bad experience of marriage anyway, and everything is always blamed on them, so she will give May the wit to make a quick reply. As May and Damian have sex in the tree, Pluto gives January his sight back, and he sees them. Proserpine then gives May a quick reply – she says that she was told to wrestle with a man in the tree, so that January's sight could be restored. He should be grateful, not angry. January believes his wife's explanation, and everyone is happy.

This is a fabliau story about youth and age, an old husband, a young wife and a young lover, in which the husband is tricked and cuckolded. The names of the husband and wife are suggestive; January represents the saturnine and crabbed, and May represents the young, vernal and Venusian. January resembles the reeve in his exaggerated sexual vigour and relentless sexual appetite, and the horror of his perverted lust for May, regardless of her feelings, contributes a deeper, darker level to what is essentially a comic tale of trickery. It is what the narrator carefully does not say which enhances the hideousness of the old man's lustful desire. What happens in the garden can only be guessed, as can May's disgust for her husband's physical appearance. The presence of Proserpine in the garden suggests rape. In classical legend, Proserpine was abducted by Pluto, and was forced to remain with him for six months of every year. Here she and Pluto, in the manner of the gods of the knight's tale, are represented as a bickering husband and wife, who susequently find a means of consensus, and a resolution to their differences, as human couples have to do.

January's physical blindness, which is outside his control, is compatible with his inner blindness, which blinds him to the truth of his situation. When this is stated for him by Justinus, he does not wish to listen, preferring the sycophantic agreement of Placebo. January manages to twist both holy writ and the prompting of his conscience to fit the framework of his desires. The generalised names of January and May suggest that this is the human condition in general; man is predatory and woman is the victim, and always to blame. This is the allegation made by Proserpine to her husband in the garden, the reason why she gives May her answer to January's accusation. May is able, with the goddess's help, to save herself from retribution, but she must return to her life with January, who has now had his sight restored. She will be able to continue her relationship with Damian, so everything and nothing is concluded. Everyone finds a way of dealing with the unsatisfactory details of life.

January is a knight, a member of the ruling class, epitomised by the knight of the pilgrimage. Whilst the knight has spent his life in the pursuit of chivalric ideals, January has wasted his life in peaceful idleness, sexual sin and a life of pleasure. As a member of the ruling class, he epitomises the tyrant; his own will is his law, he listens only to flatterers and he spends his wealth on the pursuit of his own pleasures, the fulfilment of his whims, the achievement of which is more important to him than his (clearly expendable) God. He might just as well be a 'stock' eastern potentate of epic romance. His life, unlike that of Chaucer's knight, is sterile. As he has not produced good works so he has failed to produce good 'fruit' from his illicit liaisons. The knight has a handsome, chivalric son and heir, but January has no heir to succeed him. He may be able to graft himself to the fruitfulness of young May and the pear tree, but the only fruit he is likely to get from it will be bastard fruit, whether by means of Damian or of another.

The garden, a *hortus conclusus*, lies at the heart of this story. A parody of the garden in *The Romance of the Rose*, it represents January's inability to see beyond the world of his imagination. He is an older man, so this may be a result of his 'romance' view of the world, once socially valid but now 'old fashioned', like the world-view of The Squire's Tale and Sir Thopas. As the wife of Bath says, the fairies have all gone from the woods. In January's romance garden Damian is the maggot boring – literally – into his rose, who is actually a pear, ripe and receptive, rather than the chaste rose awaiting her lover. The centre of the garden is occupied not by the rose bush, but by a pear tree. In the end, January continues to live his dream, which continues outwardly, although the reality is somewhat different.

Key Questions

What is the relationship between fabliau and romance in this story?

How are gender relations depicted? Who desires what, and do they achieve their desires?

What is the function of the gods in the story? What does the tale have to say about relationships between the sexes and/or ages?

Topic Keywords

Romance and fabliau as genres/ classical gods and romance/ romance and medieval society/ rulership/ medieval marriage/ medieval gardens

Further Reading

Malcolm Andrew, 'January's Knife: Sexual Morality and Proverbial Wisdom in The Merchant's Tale', *English Language Notes*, 16, 1979, pp. 273–7

Leigh A. Arrathoon, 'Antinomic Cluster Analysis and the Boethian Verbal Structure of Chaucer's Merchant's Tale', *Language and Style*, 17, 1984, pp. 92–120

Joan Baker and Susan Signe Morrison, 'The Luxury of Gender: *Piers Plowman* and The Merchant's Tale', *Yearbook of Langland Studies*, 12, 1998, pp. 31–63

Peter G. Beidler, 'Chaucer's Merchant's Tale and *The Decameron*', *Italica*, 50, 1973, pp. 266–84

Peter G. Beidler and Therese Decker, 'Lippijn: A Middle Dutch Source for The Merchant's Tale?' *Chaucer Review*, 23, 1989, pp. 236–50

Donald R. Benson, 'The Marriage "Encomium" in The Merchant's Tale: A Chaucerian Crux', *Chaucer Review*, 14, 1980, pp. 48–60

Kenneth Bleeth, 'Joseph's Doubting of Mary and the Conclusion of The Merchant's Tale', *Chaucer Review*, 21, 1986, pp. 58–66

Morton W. Bloomfield, 'The Merchant's Tale: A Tragicomedy of the Neglect of Counsel; The Limits of Art', in *Medieval and Renaissance Studies: Proceedings of the Southeastern Institute of Medieval and Renaissance Studies*, 1975, edited Siegfried Wenzel, Chapel Hill, North Carolina University Press, 1978, pp. 37–50

M. C. Bodden, 'Via erotica/via mystica: A Tour de Force in The Merchant's Tale', in *Intersections of Sexuality and the Divine in Medieval Culture: The Word Made Flesh*, edited by Susannah Mary Chewning, Aldershot, Ashgate, 2005, pp. 51–73

Emerson Brown Jr, 'Biblical Women in The Merchant's Tale: Feminism, Antifeminism, and Beyond', *Viator*, 5, 1974, pp. 387–412

Peter Brown, 'An Optical Theme in The Merchant's Tale', *Studies in the Age of Chaucer*, 1, 1985, pp. 231–43

Michael A. Calabrese, 'May Devoid of all Delight: January, The Merchant's Tale and *The Romance of the Rose*', *Studies in Philology*, 87, 1990, pp. 261–184

Holly A. Crocker, 'Performative Passivity and Fantasies of Masculinity in The Merchant's Tale', *Chaucer Review*, 38, 2003, pp. 178–98

Marcia A. Dalby, 'The Devil in the Garden: Pluto and Proserpine in Chaucer's Merchant's Tale', *Neuphilologische Mitteilungen*, 75, 1974, pp. 408–15

Robert R. Edwards, 'Narration and Doctrine in The Merchant's Tale', *Speculum*, 66, 1991, pp. 342–67

Marta Powell Harley, 'Chaucer's Use of the Proserpina Myth in The Knight's Tale and The Merchant's Tale', in *Images of Persephone*: Feminist Readings in Western Literature, edited by Elizabeth T. Hayes, Gainesville, Florida University Press, 1994, pp. 20–31

Carol F. Heffernan, 'Contraception and the Pear Tree Episode of Chaucer's Merchant's Tale', *Journal of English and Germanic Philology*, 94, 1995, pp. 31–41

—— 'Two 'English "Fabliaux": Chaucer's Merchant's Tale and Shipman's Tale, and Italian Novelle', *Neophilologus*, 90, 2006, pp. 333–49

Michelle Kohler, 'Vision, Logic, and the Comic Production of Reality in the Merchant's Tale and Two French Fabliaux', *Chaucer Review*, 39, 2004, pp. 137–50

Richard Neuse, 'Marriage and the Question of Allegory in The Merchant's Tale', *Chaucer Review*, 24, 1989, pp. 115–31

Joseph D. Parry, 'Interpreting Female Agency and Responsibility in the Miller's Tale and The Merchant's Tale', *Philological Quarterly*, 80, 2001, pp. 133–67

Roy J. Pearcy, 'Anglo-Norman Fabliaux and Chaucer's Merchant's Tale', *Medium Ævum*, 69, 2000, pp. 227–60

Christine Rose, 'Woman's Pryvete, May, and the Privy: Fissures in the Narrative Voice in The Merchant's Tale', *Chaucer Yearbook*, 4, 1997, pp. 61–77

Wolfgang E. H. Rudat, 'Chaucer's Spring of Comedy: The Merchant's Tale and Other 'Games' with Augustinian theology', *Annuale mediaevale*, 21, 1981, pp. 111–20

Christian Sheridan, 'May in the Marketplace: Commodificaton and Textuality in The Merchant's Tale', *Studies in Philology*, 102, 2005, pp. 27–44

Here bygynneth the prologe of the marchaund's tale

❧ 'Wepyng and wailyng, care and other **sorwe**   sorrow/grief
I knowe ynough bothe on **even** & on **morwe**,'   evening; morning
Quod the marchaund, "and so doon other mo
That weddid ben; I **trowe** that it be so,   believe
For wel I **woot**, it fareth so with me.   know
I have a wyf, the worste that may be –
For though the **feend** to hir **y-coupled** were,   devil; married
Sche wold him **over macche**, I dar wel **swere**.   overbear; swear
What schuld I yow reherse in special   10
Hir **high** malice? Sche is a schrewe **at al**.   exceptional; in every way
Ther is a long and a large difference
Bewix Grisilde's grete pacience
And of my wyf the **passyng** cruelte.   great
Were I **unbounden**, also mot I the,[1]   unmarried
I wolde never **eft** come in the snare.   after
We weddid men lyve in sorwe and care;
Assay whoso wil, and he schal fynde   test
That I say sothe, by seint Thomas of Inde![2]
As for the more part, I say not alle –   20
God schilde that it schulde so byfalle![3]
A, good Sir Host, I have y-weddid be
Thise monthes tuo, and **more not, parde** –   no longer, by God
And yit I trowe, he that al his lyve
Wyfles hath ben, though that men wold him **rive**   pierce
Unto the hert, ne **couthe** in no **manere**   could not; way
Tellen so moche sorwe as I now heere
Couthe telle of my wyfe's cursednesse.'
'No,' quod our ost, 'marchaunt, so God yow blesse –
Sin ye so moche knowen of that **art**,   subject   30
Ful hertily tellith us a part.'
'Gladly,' quod he, 'but of myn **oughne sore**,   own pain
For sory hert, I telle may **na** more.'   no

1 'so may I thrive'
2 St Thomas the apostle, who allegedly carried the Christian faith to India.
3 'I'm not talking about everyone – God forbid that that should be the case!'

Narrat

he tells (his story)

❦ 'Whilom ther was dwellyng in Lombardy[4]   *once upon a time*
A worthy knight, that born was of Pavy,
In which he lyved in gret prosperite,
And fourty **yer** a wifles man was he,   *years*
And folowed ay his **bodily delyt**   *carnal desires*
40 On wommen, theras was his appetyt,
As doon these fooles that ben **seculere**;   *laymen*
And whan that he was **passed fourty yere** – *over forty years old*
Were it for holyness or for **dotage**   *senility*
I cannot say – but such a gret **corrage**   *will/desire*
Hadde this knight to ben a weddid man,
That day and night he doth al that he can
Taspye wher that he mighte weddid be,   *to see*
Praying our lord to graunte him, that he
Might **oones** knowen of that blisful lif   *once*
50 That is bitwix an housbond and his wyf,
And for to lyve under that holy bond
With which god first man to womman bond.[5]
'Noon other lif,' sayd he, 'is worth a **bene**, *bean*
For wedlok is so holy and so **clene**,   *pure*
That in this world it is a paradis.'
Thus sayd this olde knight, that was so wys,
'And certeinly, as **soth** as God is king,   *truly*
To take a wyf is a glorious thing;
60 And namely, whan a man is old and **hoor**, *white-haired*
Than is a wyf the **fruyt** of his **tresor**. *choicest; treasure*
Than schuld he take a yong wif and a fair,
On which he might **engendre** him an **hair**, *beget; heir*
And lede his lyf in **mirthe** and in **solace** *happiness; ease/pleasure*
Wheras these bachileres synge, "Allas!"
Whan thay fynde eny adversite
In love, which is but child's vanite;

---

4 Lombardy, a region in Northern Italy, whose regional capital is Milan. The town
 of Pavia, where the knight was born, is to the south of Milan, also in Lombardy.
5 A reference to the presentation of the newly-created Eve to Adam in the Garden
 of Eden, in the Book of Genesis.

And trewely, it sit wel to be so,[6]
That bachilers have ofte peyne and wo –
On **brutil** ground thay **bulde**, and brutelnesse   brittle; build   70
Thay fynde whan thay **wene sikernesse**.   expect security
Thay lyve but as a **brid, other** as a **best**,   bird; or; beast
In liberte, and under noon **arrest**,   restraint
Theras a weddid man in his **estate**   whereas; station in life
Lyvith his lif busily and **ordinate**,   ordered
Under the yok of mariage y-bounde –
Wel may his herte in joye and blisse abounde,
For who can be so **buxom** as a wyf,   obedient
Who is so trewe, and eek so **ententyf**,   attentive
To kepe him **seek** and **hool** as is his **make** –   sick; well; mate   80
For **wele** or woo, sche wol him not forsake;   prosperity
Sche is not **wery** him to love and serve,   tired
Theigh that he lay **bedred** til that he **sterve**;   bedridden; die
And yet som clerkes seyn it is not so,
Of whiche Theofrast is oon of tho.[7]
What fors though Theofrast **liste** lye?[8]
'Ne take no wif,' quod he, 'for **housbondrye**,   economy/housekeeping
As for to spare in houshold thy **despense**.   expense/ 'outgoings'
A trewe servant doth more **diligence**   care
Thy good to kepe, than thin oughne wif,   90
For sche wol **clayme** half part in al hir lif,   lay claim to
And if that thou be seek, so God me save,
Thyne verray frendes, or a trewe **knave**   manservant
Wol **kepe the bet**, than sche that waytith ay   look after you better
After thy good, and hath doon many day;
And if that thou take a wif, bewar
Of oon peril which declare I ne **dar**.   dare
This entent, and an hundrid **sithe wors**   times; worse
Writith this man, ther God his bones curs![9]
But take no keep of al such vanite,   100
Deffy Theofrast, and **herkne** me.   defy; listen to

6 'it is deservedly so'
7 See what the Wife of Bath says about Theophrastus, author of a misogynistic
  treatise advising men against marriage.
8 what does it matter; likes to lie
9 'may god curse his bones!'

A wyf is God's gifte **verrayly** –   truly
Al other maner giftes, hardily,
As landes, rentes, pasture, or comune,
Or other **moeblis**, ben giftes of fortune,   property
That passen as a schadow on a wal –
But **dred** not if I playnly telle schal –   fear
A wyf wil last, and in thin hous endure
Wel lenger than the lust, **peradventure**.   perhaps
110 Mariage is a ful gret sacrament;
He which hath no wif, I hold him **schent**.   ruined
He lyveth helples and is al desolate –
I speke of folk in seculer estate –
And herken why – I say not this for nought –
The womman is for man's help **y-wrought**.   made
The heighe God, whan he had Adam maked,
And saugh him al aloone, body naked,
God of his grete goodnes sayde thanne,
'Let us now make an helpe to this manne,
120 Lyk to himself.' And than he made Eve.
Her may ye see, and here may ye **preve**,   have proof
That wyf is man's help and his comfort,
His paradis **terrestre** and his **desport**;   earthly; pleasure
So buxom and so vertuous is sche,
Thay mosten neede lyve in unite.
O **fleisch** thay ben, and on blood, as I gesse;   one flesh
Have but oon **hert**, in wele and in distresse.   heart
A wyf, A! Seinte Mary benedicite![10]
How might a man have eny adversite
130 That hath a wyf? Certes, I cannot say
The joye that is betwixen hem **tway**!   two
Ther may no tonge telle, ne herte think –
If he be pore, sche helpith him to **swynk**;   labour
Sche kepith his good and wastith never a **del**,   bit
And al that her housbond **list**, sche likith it wel;   wishes/likes
Sche saith nought oones, "Nay," whan he saith, "Ye,"
'Do this,' saith he; 'al redy, sir,' saith sche.
O blisful order! O wedlock precious!

10 'May St Mary bless us!'

Thou art so mery, and **ek** so vertuous,   also
And so comendid and approved eek,   140
That every man that holt him worth a leek,
Upon his bare knees ought al his lyf
Thanken his God that him hath sent a wif,
Or pray to God oon him for to sende,
To be with him unto his lyve's ende;
For than his lyf is set in **sikernesse** –   security
He may not be **decyved**, as I gesse –   deceived
So that he worche after his wyfes **red**,   advice
Than may he boldely bere up his **heed**,   head
Thay ben so trewe, and also so wyse;   150
For whiche, if thou wolt do as the wyse,
Do alway so as the womman wol the **rede**.   advise
Lo! How that Jacob, as the clerkes rede,
By good counseil of his moder Rebecke[11]
Band the kyd's skyn about his son's nekke,
For which his fader **benesoun** he wan.   blessing
Lo, Judith, as the story telle can,
By wys counseil sche God's poepel **kept**,   saved
And **slough** him Oliphernus whil he slept.[12]   killed
Lo, Abygaille, by good counseil how sche   160
Savyd hir housbond Nabal, whan that he
Schold han ben slayn, and loke Ester also
By good counseil delivered out of wo
the people of God, and made him Mardoche
Of Assuere **enhaunsed** for to be.[13]   exalted
Ther nys nothing in **gre superlatif**   highest degree
As seith **Senek**, above a humble wyf   Seneca
Suffre thy wyve's tonge, as Catoun **byt** – [14]   bad
Sche schal comaunde, and thou schalt suffre it,
And yit sche wil obeye of curtesye.   170
A wif is keper of thin housbondrye;
Wel may the sike man wayle and wepe

11 Rebecca helped Jacob to steal the birthright of his brother Esau, by diguising
   himself with hair.
12 Judith killed Holofernes by cutting off his head whilst he was in a drunken sleep.
13 Esther saved her people, and her uncle Mordecai was both saved and promoted
   by her husband King Ahasuerus.
14 Cato.

Theras ther is no wyf the hous to kepe.
I warne the, if wisly thou wilt **wirche**,   do
Love wel thy wyf, as Crist doth his chirch.
If thou lovest thiself, thou lovest thy wyf;
No man hatith his fleissche, but in his lif
He **fostrith** it, and therfore warne I the,
Cherissch thy wif, or thou shalt **never the**   never prosper

180 Housband and wif, what men **iape** or pleye
Of worldly folk, **holden** the righte weye;   keep to
Thay ben so **knyt** ther may noon harm bytyde,   joined
And nameliche upon the wyve's syde.'
For which this January, of which I tolde,
Considered hath **inwith his dayes olde**,   in his old age
The **lusty** lif, the vertuous quiete   sexually boisterous
That is in mariage honey swete,
And for his frendes on a day he sent,
To tellen hem **theffect** of his **entent**.   result; will

190 With face **sad** he hath hem this tale told: serious
He sayde, 'Frendes, I am hoor and old,
And almost, God woot, at my **pittes brinke**;   edge of the grave
Upon my soule somwhat most I thynke.
I have my body **folily dispendid** –   used foolishly
Blessed be God that it schal be **amendid**!   put right
For I wil be, certeyn, a weddid man,
And that **anoon**, in al the hast I can,   immediately
Unto som mayde fair and tender of age.
I pray yow, helpith for my mariage

200 **Al sodeynly**, for I wil not **abyde** –   as soon as possible; wait
I wil **fonde tespien** on my syde   take steps to find out
To whom I may be weddid **hastily**,   without delay
But for als moche as ye ben **mo** than I,   more (in number)
Ye schul rather such a thing aspien
Than I, and wher me lust best to **allien**.   ally
But oo thing warne I yow, my frendes deere,
I wol noon old wyf have in no manere;
Sche schal not passe sixtene yer, certayn –
Old fleisch and yong fleisch, that wold I have ful fayn.

210 Bet is,' quod he, 'a **pyk** than a **pikerell**,[15]

15 mature pike; immature pike

And bet than old **boef** is tendre **vel**.   beef; veal
I wil no womman twenty yer of age;
It nys but **bene strew** and gret forage.   bean straw
And eek, these olde wydewes, God it woot,
Thay **can** so moche craft of **Wade's boot**,[16]   know; Woden's boat
So moche **borken harm** whan that hem **list**   cause harm; like
That with hem schuld I never lyven in rest;
For **sondry scolis** maken **subtil** clerkes.   various colleges; cunning
Womman of many a skile half a clerk is,
But certeyn a yong thing may men **gye**,   shape   220
Right as men may worm wax with hondes plye;
Wherfor I say yow **plenerly**, in a clause,   plainly
I wil noon old wyf **han**, right for that cause.   have
For if so were I hadde so **meschaunce**   bad luck
That I in hir couthe have no **plesaunce**,   pleasure
Than schuld I lede my lyf in **advoutrie**,   adultery
And go streight to the devel whan I dye,
Ne children schuld I noon upon hir geten –[17]
Yet were me **lever** houndes had me eten   rather
Than that myn heritage schulde falle   230
In straunge hond – and thus I telle yow alle.
I doute not I **wot** the cause why   know
Men scholde wedde, and forthermor woot I
Ther spekith many man of mariage
That wot nomore of it than wot my page,
For whiche causes man schuld take a wyf;
If he ne may not chast be by his lif,
Take him a wif with gret devocioun,
Bycause of lawful **procreacion**   conception
Of children, to th'honour of God above,   240
And not oonly for **paramour** and for love,   passion
And for thay schulde leccherye **eschiewe**,   avoid
And yeld oure dettes whan that it is due,
Or for that **ilk** man schulde helpen other   each
In **meschief**, as suster schal to brother,   bad times
And lyve in chastite ful holily –
But Sires, by your leve, that am not I;

16 This expression, possibly proverbial, is obscure.
17 The medieval view was that adulterous wives were barren.

For God by thanked, I dar make **avaunt**,   boast
I fele my **lemys stark** and **suffisaunt**   limbs; strong; sufficient
250 To doon al that a man bilongeth unto;
I wot myselve best wat I may do.
Though I be hoor, I fare as doth a tree,
That blossemith er that the fruyt **y-waxe** be.   grow
A blossemy tre is neither drye ne deed;
I fele me nowher hoor but on myn heed –
Myn herte and al my lymes ben as greene
As **laurer thurgh** the yeer is for to seene,   laurel; through
And **synnes** ye han herd al myn entent,   since
I pray yow to my wille ye assent.'
260 **Diverse** men diversly him tolde   various
Of mariage many **ensamples** olde;   examples
Some blamed him, some praised it certayn,
But atte laste, schortly for to sayn,
As al day **fallith altercacioun**   an argument goes on
Bitwixe frendes in **disputesoun**,   disputation
Ther fel a strif bitwen his bretheren tuo,
Of which that oon was **clepid** Placebo;   called
Justinus **sothly** cleped was that other.   truly
Placebo sayde, 'O January, brother,
270 Ful litel need had ye, my lord so deere,
Counseil to **axe** of eny that is here,   ask
But that ye ben so ful of **sapience**,   wisdom
That yow ne likith, for your heigh prudence,
To wyve; fro the word of **Salamon**,   Solomon
This word said he unto us **everychoon**,   every one
'Werk al thing by counsail,' thus sayd he,
'And thanne schaltow nought repente the.'
But though that Salamon speke such a word,
Myn owne deere brother and my lord,
280 So wisly, God bring my soule at ese and rest,
I holde your oughne counseil is the best.
For, brother myn, of me tak this **motif**;   advice
I have now ben a **court man** al my lyf,   courtier
And, God wot, though that I unworthy be,
I have standen in ful gret **degre**   estate
Abouten lordes in ful gret estat,
Yit had I never with noon of hem debaat;

I never hem **contraried**, trewely   spoke against
I wot wel that my lord **can** more than I.   knows
What that he saith, I hold it ferm and stable –   290
I say the same, or elles thing **sembable**.   similar
A ful gret fool is eny counselour
That servith any lord of high honour,
That dar presume, or oones **thenken** it,   think
That his counseil schuld passe his lordes **wit**.   knowledge
Nay lordes, ben no fooles, by my fay –
Ye have yourself y-spoken heer today
So heigh sentens, so holly and so wel,
That I consente and conferme every del
Youre wordes all, and youre oppinioun.   300
By God, ther is no man in al this toun,
Ne in **Ytaile**, couthe better have sayd –   Italy
Crist holdith him of this ful wel **apayd** –   rewarded
And trewely it is an **heigh corrage**   courageous act
Of any man that **stopen** is in age   stooping
To take a yong wyf, by my fader kyn –
Your herte **hongith on a ioly pyn**!   hangs on a merry pin
Doth now in this matier right as yow **lest**;   like
For fynally, I hold it for the best.'
Justinus, that **ay** stille sat and herde,   ever   310
Right in this wise he to Placebo answerde;
'Now, brother myn, be pacient, I yow pray –
Syns ye have sayd, and **herknith** what I say.   listen
Senec, amonges other wordes wyse,
Saith that a man aught him wel **avyse**   consider
To whom he giveth his lond or his **catel**;   possessions
And syns I **aught** avyse me right wel   ought to
To whom I give my good away from me,
Wel more I aught avised for to be
To whom I give my body for **alwey**.   ever   320
I warn yow wel, it is no child's pley
To take a wyf withoute avisement;
Men most enquere – this is myn assent –
Wher sche be wys, or sobre, or **dronkelewe**,   drunken
Or proud, or other way a schrewe;
A chyder, or a wastour of thy good,
Or riche, or pore, or elles man is **wood**.   crazy/mad

Al be so that no man fynde schal
Noon in this world that **trottith hool** in al,   is perfectly happy
330 Neyther man ne best such as man can devyse,
But natheles it aught ynough suffise
With any wyf, if so were that sche hadde
Mo goode **thewes** than hir vices badde.   qualities
And al this **askith leyser** to enquere;   takes time
For, God woot, I have weped many a tere
Ful prively, syns I have had a wyf.
Prayse whoso wil a weddid man's lif –
Certes, I fynd in it but **cost** and care,   expense
And **observaunce** of alle **blisses** bare;   duties; happinesses
340 And yit, God woot, myn neighboures aboute,
And namely of wommen many a **route**,   crowd
Sayn that I have the moste stedefast wyf,
And eek the mekeste oon that berith lyf –
But I woot best **wher wryngith me my scho**.[18]
Ye may for me right as yow liste do;
Avysith yow, ye ben a man of age,   be careful
How that ye entren into mariage,
And namly with a yong wif and a fair.
By him that made water, eorthe, and air,
350 The yongest man that is in al this route
Is busy ynough to bring it wel aboute   finds it hard enough
To have his wif **alloone**; trustith me,   to himself
Ye schul not please hir fully yeres thre –
This is to say, to doon hir ful plesaunce –
A wyf axith ful many an observaunce.
I pray yow that ye be not evel apayd.'
'Wel,' quod this January, 'and **hastow** sayd!   you have
Straw for thy Senec, and for thy proverbis!
I coveyte nought a **panyer** ful of herbes   basket
360 Of scole termes; wiser men than thow,
As I have sayd, assenten here right now
Unto my purpose – Placebo, what say ye?'
'I say it is a cursed man,' quod he,
'That **lettith** matrimoigne, **sicurly**.'   hinders; certainly

18 'where my shoe pinches me'

And with that word, thay risen up sodeinly,
And be assentid fully that he scholde
Be weddid, whan him lust and wher he wolde.
The fantasy and the curious busynesse
Fro day to day gan in the soule impresse
Of January aboute his mariage; [19]   370
Many a fair **schap** and many a fair **visage**   figure; face
Ther passith thorough his herte, night by night,
As whoso took a mirrour, polissched bright,
And set it in a comun market place,
Than schuld he se many a figure pace
By his mirrour; and in the same wise
Gan January in his thought **devyse**   imagine
Of maydens, which that dwellid **him bisyde**.   in his neighbourhood
He wist not where that he might **abyde**,   make his choice
For though that oon have a beaute in hir face,   380
Another stant so in the peoples **grace**   good opinion
For hir **sadnesse** and hir **benignite**,   steadfastness; kindness
That of the people grettest vois hath sche;
And som were riche, and hadde badde name,
But natheles, bitwix ernest and game,
He atte last **appoynted** him an oon,   chose
And let al other from his herte goon;
And ches hir **of his oughne auctorite**,   by his own opinion
For love is blynd al day, and may not se.
And whan he was into bedde brought,   390
He **purtrayed** in his hert and in his thought   pictured
Hir freische beaute and hir age tendre,
Hir **myddel** smal, hir armes long and sclendre,   waist
Hir wise governaunce, hir gentilesse,
Hir wommanly beryng and hir sadnesse,
And whan that he on hir was **condescendid**,   decided
Him thought his chois mighte nought ben **amendid**,   made better
For whan that he himself concludid hadde,
Him thought ech other man's wyf so badde
That impossible it were to **repplie**   argue   400

19 'The fantasy and the careful business of his marriage began from day to day to
   impress itself upon January's imagination'

Agayn his choys, this was his fantasie.
His frendes sent he to at his instaunce,
And prayed hem to doon him that plesaunce
That hastily thay wolde to him come;
He wold **abrigge** her labour, alle an some.   shorten
Nedith no more for him to gon ne ryde;
He was appoynted, ther he wold abyde.[20]
Placebo cam, and eek his frendes soone,
And **altherfirst** he bad hem all a **boone**,   first of all; favour
410   That noon of hem noon argumentis make
Agayn the purpos which that he had take;
Which purpos was **plesaunt** to God, sayd he,   pleasing
And verray ground of his prosperite.
He sayd ther was a mayden in the toun
Which that of beaute hadde gret renoun,
Al were it so sche were of **smal degre**,   low status
Suffisith him hir trouthe and hir beaute;
Which mayde he sayd he wold have to his wyf,
To lede in ease and holinesse his lyf;
420   And thanked God that he might have hir al,
That no **wight** with his blisse **parten** schal;   person; share
And prayed hem to laboure in this neede,
And **schapen** that he faile not to **speede**,   make it be; succeed
For than, he sayd, his spirit was at ease –
'Than is,' quod he, 'no thing may me displease;
Save oon thing **prikkith** in my conscience,   nags
The which I wil **reherse** in your presence.   tell
I have herd sayd,' quod he, '**ful yore ago**,   a long time ago
Ther may no man have parfyt blisses tuo;
430   This is to say, in erthe and eek in hevene,
For though he kepe him fro the synnes sevene,
And eek from ylk a braunche of thilke tre,[21]
Yit is ther so **parfyt felicite**   perfect; happiness
And so gret ease and lust in mariage,
That ever I am **agast** now in myn age,   fearful
That I schal lede now so mery a lyf,
So **delicat**, withoute wo and stryf,   delightful

20 'He had made his choice, and he would stick to it.'
21 'and also from every branch of that same tree (of the Seven Deadly Sins)'

That I schal have myn heven in erthe heere;

For **sith** that verray heven is brought so deere,   since

With tribulacioun and gret penaunce,   440

How schuld I thanne, that live in such **plesaunce** –   pleasure

As alle weddid men doon with her wyves –

Come to blisse, ther Crist **eterne** on lyve is?   eternal

This is my **drede**, and ye, my bretheren tweye,   fear

Assoilith me this questioun, I yow preye.'   answer

Justinus, which that hated his folye,

Answerd anoon right **in his japerie**,   mockingly

And for he wold his longe tale **abrigge**,   shorten

He wolde noon auctorite **alegge**,   cite

But sayde, 'Sir, so ther be noon obstacle   450

Other than this, God of his **high miracle**   great wonder

And of his mercy, may so for yow wirche

That er ye have your rightes of holy chirche

Ye may repente of weddid man's lyf,

In which ye sayn ther is no wo ne stryf,

And ellis, God forbede but he sente

A weddid man grace him to repente

Wel ofte, rather than a sengle man;

And therfor, Sire, the beste **reed** I can –   advice

Dispaire yow nought, but have in youre memorie   460

Paradventure sche may be your purgatorie – [22]   perhaps

Sche may be God's mene and God's **whippe**;

Than schal your soule up to heven skippe

Swyfter than doth an **arwe** out of a bowe;   arrow

I hope to God herafter ye shuln knowe

That ther nys noon so gret felicite

In mariage, ne nevermor schal be,

That yow schal **lett** of your savacioun;   hinder/deprive

So that ye use, as **skile** is and **resoun**,   fitting; reasonable

The lustes of your wyf **attemperely**,   in moderation   470

And that ye plese hir not to amorously,

And that ye kepe yow eek from other synne.

My tale is doon, for my witt is thynne –

Beth not agast herof, my brother deere,

---

22 Purgatory: the place between earth and heaven where souls were purged of their
  sins before they could be fit to enter God's presence.

But let us **waden** out of this **matiere**.   wade; subject
The Wif of Bathe, if ye han understonde,
Of mariage – which ye han now on honde –
Declared hath ful wel in litel space.
Fareth now well, God have yow in his grace.'
480 And with that word Justinus and his brother
Han take her leve, and ech of hem of other;
For whan thay saugh that it must needis be,
Thay wroughten so by **sleight** and wys **trete**,   cunning; negotiation
That sche, this mayden which that **Mayus hight**,   was called May
As hastily as ever sche might,
Schal weddid be unto this Januarie.
I **trow** it were to longe yow to **tarie**   believe; slow down
If I yow tolde of every scrit and bond
By which that sche was feoffed in his lond,[23]
490 Or for to herken of hir riche array,
But finally y-comen is that day
That to the chirche bothe ben thay **went**   gone
For to receyve the holy sacrament.
Forth comth the preost, with stoole aboute his necke,[24]
And bad hir be lik Sarra and Rebecke[25]
In wisdom and in trouth of mariage,
And sayd his **orisouns**, **as is usage**,[26]
And **crouched hem**, and bad God schuld hem blesse,
                                        made the sign of the cross
And made al **secur** ynowh, with holinesse.   sure
500 Thus ben thay weddid, with solempnite,
And atte fest sittith he and sche,
With othir worthy folk, upon the deys.[27]
Al ful of joy and blis is that paleys,
And ful of instruments and of **vitaile**,   food
The moste **deinteuous** of Ytaile.   delicate/delicious
Biforn hem stood such intruments of soun,

23 She received entitlement to part of his landed wealth.
24 Stole: the coloured scarf worn by a priest around his neck.
25 Sarah and Rebecca – the wives of Old Testament patriarchs Abraham and Isaac.
26 prayers; according to custom
27 Dais: a raised area at the end of the hall where the host and most honoured
   guests sat.

That Orpheus, ne of Thebes Amphioun,[28]
Ne maden never such a melodye.
At every cours ther cam loud menstralcye,
That never tromped Joab for to heere,   510
Ne he Theodomas yit half so cleere
At Thebes, whan the cite was **in doute**.[29]   in danger
Bechus the wyn hem **schenchith** al aboute,[30]   pours
And Venus laughith upon every wight,
For January was bycome hir knight,
And wolde both **assayen** his corrage   test
In liberte, and eek in mariage,
And with hir **fuyrbrond** in hir hond aboute,   firebrand
Daunceth bifore the bryde and al the **route**;   company
And certeynly I dar right wel say this –   520
Imeneus, that god of weddyng is,[31]
Seigh never his lif so mery a weddid man.
Holde thy pees, thow poete Marcian,
That writest us that ilke weddyng merye
Of hir Philologie and he Mercurie,
And of the songes that the Muses songe –
To smal is bothe thy penne, and eek thy tonge,
For to **descrive** of this mariage,   describe
Whan tender youthe hath weddid stoupyng age;
Ther is such mirthe that it may not be write –   530
Assaieth it yourself, than may ye **wyte**   try; understand
If that I lye or noon in this mateere.
Mayus, that sit with so **benigne a cheere**,   gracious countenance
Hir to bihold it semed **fayerye**.   magic
Queen Ester loked never with such an **ye**   eye
On Assure, so meke a look hath sche,[32]
I may not yow devyse al hir beaute;
But thus moche of hir beaute telle I may,

28 Great musicians of classical legend.
29 Two army leaders of the ancient world – Joab from the Old Testament, and
   Theodomas from Greek legend.
30 Bacchus, Roman god of wine and revelry – also associated with orgies and sexual
   licence.
31 Hymen.
32 Esther saved the Jews by seducing and marrying the king; see the biblical Book of
   Esther.

That sche was lyk the bright **morw** of May,   morning
540 Fulfild of alle beaute and plesaunce.
This January is **ravyscht** in a traunce   caught up
At every tyme he lokith in hir face,
But in his hert he gan hir to **manace**,   threaten
That he that night in armes wold hir **streyne**   hold tightly
Harder than ever Paris did Eleyne;[33]
But natheles, yit had he gret pite
That thilke night offenden hir most he,
And thought, 'Alas1 O tendre creature!
Now wolde God ye mighte wel endure
550 Al my **corage**, it is so scharp and keene.   lust/libido
I am **agast** ye schul it not **susteene**;   afraid; endure
For God forbede that I dede al my might!
Now wolde God that it were **woxe** night,   become
And that the night wold **stonden evermo**!   last for ever
I wold that al this peple were **a-go**!'   gone
And fynally, he doth al his labour[34]
As he best mighte, **savyng** his honour,   whilst preserving
To **hast** hem from the **mete** in **subtil** wise.   hurry; food; cunning
The tyme cam that **resoun was** to ryse,   reason said it was
560 And after that men daunce and drynke **fast**,   heartily
An spices about the hous they cast,
And ful of joy and blis is every man,
Al but a squier that **hight** Damyan,   was called
Which **karf tofor** the knight ful many a day.   carved before
He was so ravyssht on his lady May,
That for the verray peyne he was nigh **wood**;   mad
Almost he **swelt** and **swowned** as he stood,   fainted; swooned
So sore hath Venus hurt him with hir brond,
As that sche bare it, daunsyng, in hir hond.
570 And to his bed he wente him hastily,
No more of him at this tyme telle I,
But ther I lete him now his wo **compleyne**,   bemoan
Til freisshe May wol **rewen on** his payne.   takes pity on
O perilous fuyr, that in the bed-straw **bredith**!   breeds/grows
O **famuler fo**, that his service **bedith**!   enemy in the house; offers

33 Paris, lover of Helen of Troy in Homer's Iliad.
34 'tried his hardest'

O servaunt traitour! False **homly** hewe!   domestic
Lyk to the **nedder**, in bosom untrewe!   adder
God schild us alle from your acqueintance!
O January, dronken in **plesaunce**   pleasure
In mariage! Se how thy Damyan,   580
Thyn oughne squier and thy **borne man**,   household servant
Entendith for to do the **vilonye**!   intends; harm/evil
God graunte the thin homly fo espye,
For in this world nys worse pestilence
Than homly foo, al day in thy presence!
Parfourmed hath the sonne his ark diourne
No lenger may the body of him soiourne
On th'orisonte as in latitude.[35]
Night with his **mantel**, that is derk and rude   cloak/coat
Gan oversprede th'hemesperie aboute,[36]   590
For which departed is the route
Fro January, with thank on every side;
Hoom to her houses lustily thay ryde,
Wheras thay doon her thinges as hem leste[37]
And whan thay seigh her tyme, thay goon to reste.
Soone after that, this hasty Januarie
Wold go to bed; he wold no lenger **tarie**.   wait
He drinkith **ypocras**, **clarre** and **vernage**,[38]
Of spices hote to encres his corrage,
And many a **letuary** had he ful fyn,   potion   600
Such as the cursed monk daun Constantin
Hath writen in his book, *de Coitu* –[39]
To ete hem alle he nas no thing eschieu –[40]
And to his prive frendes thus sayd he,
'For God's love, as soone as it may be,
Let **voyden** al this hous **in curteys wise**.'   empty; politely
And thay han doon right as he wold devyse –
Men drinken and the **travers** drawe anoon;   curtain/partition

35 'The sun has journeyed along his daily arc; his body may no longer remain above
      the level horizon'
36 the hemisphere – the sky above the horizon.
37 'they do the things they want to do'
38 hippocras (a sweet medieval wine); claret; sweet wine
39 De coitu : on sexual intercourse.
40 'there's nothing he won't eat'

The **bruyd** was brought abedde as stille as stoon,   bride
610   And whan the bed was with the prest y-blessid,
Out of the chambre hath every wight him dressed,
And January hath fast in armes take
His freissche May, his paradys, his **make**.   mate
He **lullith** hir, he kissith hir ful ofte;   cuddles
With thikke **bristlis** on his berd unsofte,   bristles
Lik to the skyn of houndfisch, scharp as brere,[41]
For he was **schave** al newe, in his manere.   shaved
He rubbith hir about hir tendre face,
And sayde thus, 'Allas! I **mot** trespace   must
620   To yow, my spouse, and yow gretly offende,
Or tyme come that I wol doun descende;   before
But natheles, considerith this,' quod he,
'Ther nys no werkman, whatsoever he be,
That may bothe werke wel and **hastily**.   quickly
This wol be doon at leysir, parfitly,
It is no fors how longe that we pleye –[42]
In trewe wedlock coupled be we tweye,
And blessed be the **yok** that we ben inne,   yoke
For in actes we **mow** do no synne.   may
630   A man may do no synne with his wif,
Ne hurt himselven with his oughne knyf,   own
For we han leve to play us by the lawe.'
Thus laborith he til that the day **gan dawe**,   began to dawn
And than he takith a **sop** in fyn **clarre**,   piece of bread; claret
And upright in his bed than sittith he,
And after that he song ful lowd and clere,
And kissed his wyf, and made **wantoun** cheere.   wanton/lecherous
He was al **coltissch**, ful of **ragerye**;   frisky; liveliness
And ful of **jargon** like a **flekked pye**:   chatter; speckled magpie
640   The slakke skin about his nekke **slaketh**   hung loosely
Whil that he song, so chaunteth he and **craketh**;   croaks
But God wot what that May thought in her hert,
Whan sche him saugh up sittyng in his schert,
In his night cappe, and with his nekke lene –

41 Preserved fish.
42 'It doesn't matter how long we take having sex'

Sche praysith nought his **pleying** worth a bene.   lovemaking
Than sayd he thus, 'My reste wol I take
Now day is come; I may no lenger wake.'
And doun he layd his heed, and sleep til **prime**;   about six o'clock
And afterward, whan that he saugh his tyme,
Up riseth January, but freissche May   650
Holdith hir chamber unto the fourthe day,   stayed in
As usage is of wyves, for the best;
For every labour somtyme **moot** have rest,   must
Or elles longe may he not endure –
This is to say, no **lyves** creature –   living
Be it fissch, or brid, or best, or man.
Now wol I speke of woful Damyan,
That languyssh for love, as ye schuln here;
Therefore I speke to him in this manere –
I say, 'O sely Damyan, allas!   660
Answere to my demaunde as in this caas!
How schaltow thy lady, freissche May,
Telle thy woo? Sche wol always say, "Nay".
Eek if thou speke, sche wol thy woo **bywreye**.   also; betray
God be thin help; I can no better seye.'
This **seke** Damyan, in Venus fuyr   sick
So **brennith** that he deyeth for desir,   burns
For which he put his lyf **in aventure**.   in hasard
No lenger might he in this wo endure,
But prively a **penner** gan he borwe,   writing implement   670
And in a letter wrot he al his sorwe,
In maner of a **compleynt** or of a **lay**,   love-poem; song
Unto his faire, freissche, lady May,
And in a purs of silk **heng** on his schert   hanging
He hath it put, and layd it **at** his **hert**.   over; heart
The moone, that anoon was thilke day
That January hath weddid freissche May,
In tuo of Taure was into Cancre gliden,[43]
So long hath Mayus in hir chambre abiden
As custom is unto these nobles alle –   680

43 The moon had moved from the second degree of Taurus (the Bull) into the sign
   of Cancer (the Crab) – it was the beginning of the month of May.

A bryde schal not eten in the halle
Til dayes foure or thre dayes atte lest
Y-passed ben, than let hir go to the fest.
The fourthe day complet from noon to noon,[44]
Whan that the **heighe masse** was y-doon,   High Mass
In halle sitte this January and May,
As freissch as is the brighte somer's day;
And so **bifelle** that this goode man   it happened
Remembrid him upon this Damyan,
690 And sayde, 'Seinte Mary! How may this be,
That Damyan **entendith** not to me?   attends
Is he ay seek, or how may this bityde?'
His squiers, which that stoode ther bisyde,
Excusid him bycause of his syk* nesse,
Which **letted** him to doon his **subynesse**.   hindered; service
'Noon other cause mighte make him tarie
That me for thinketh,' quod this Januarie.[45]
'He is a gentil squyer, by my trouthe –
If that he deyde it were harm and **routhe**.   pity
700 He is as wys, discret, and eek **secre**   trustworthy
As any man, I wot, of his degre,
And therto manly and **servysable**,   happy to serve
And for to be a **thrifty** man right able.   successful
But after mete, as soon as ever I may,
I wol myself visit him, and eek May,
To doon him al the confort that I can.'
And for that word him blessed every man,
That of his **bounte** and his **gentilesse**   generosity; nobility
He wolde so comfort in seekenesse
710 His squyer, for it was a gentil deede.
'Dame,' quod this January, 'tak good heede
At **after-mete** ye with your wommen alle,   after the meal
Whan ye han ben in chambre, out of this halle
That alle ye goo to se this Damyan –
Doth him desport, he is a gentil man,   entertain him
And tellith him that I wil him visite
Have I not thing but rested me a lyte,   after I have

44 'the fourth complete day'
45 'I can't think of any other reason why he would stay away'

And spedith yow faste, for I wol **abyde**   stay awake
Til that ye slepe faste by my syde.'
And with that word he gan unto him calle   720
A squier, that was marchal of his halle,
And told him certeyn thinges what he wolde.
This freissche May hath streight hir wey **y-holde**,   taken
With alle hir wommen, unto Damyan.
Doun by the bed's syde sat sche than,
Comfortyng him as goodly as sche may.
This Damyan, whan that his tyme he **say**,   saw
In secre wise his purs and eek his **bille**,   plea
In which that he y-writen had his wille,
Hath put into hir hond, withouten more,   730
Save that he **siketh** wonder deepe and sore,   sighs
And softely to hir right thus sayd he;
'Mercy, and that ye not **discover me**,   give me away
For I am deed if that this thing discovered be!'
This purs in hir bosom **hud** had sche,   hid
And went hir way – ye gete no more of me –
But unto January comen is sche,
That on his bed's syde sit ful softe.
He takith hir, and kissith hir ful ofte,
And layd him doun to slepe and that anoon.   740
Sche **feyned** hir as that sche moste goon   pretended
Theras ye woot that every wight moot neede,
And whan sche of this bille hath taken heede,
Sche rent it al to **cloutes** atte laste,   pieces
And into the **privy** softely it cast.   toilet
Who **studieth** now but faire freissche May?   thinks deeply
A-doun by olde January sche lay,
That slepith til that the coughe hath him awaked;
Anoon he prayde stripen hir al naked –
He wold of hir, he sayd, have some plesaunce;   750
Hir clothis dede him, he sayde, som grevaunce –
And sche obeieth, **be hir lief or loth**;   whether she likes it or not
But lest that **precious** folk be with me **wroth**,   decent; angry
How that he **wroughte** I dar not telle,   did
Or whethir it semed him paradys or helle,
But here I lete hem **werken** in her wise,   carry on
Til **evensong rong**, and than thay most arise.   the bell for evening service

Whethir it be by desteny or **adventure**,   chance
Were it by influence or by nature,
760 Or by constellacioun, that in such estate
The heven stood that tyme fortunate,[46]
As for to putte a bulle of Venus werkis;[47]
For alle thing hath tyme, as seyn these clerkis,
To eny womman, for to gete hir love –
I cannot say, but grete God above,
That knowith that noon acte is causeles,
He **deme** of al, for I wil holde my pees;   judges
But soth is this – how that this freissche May
Hath take such impressioun that day,
770 Of pite of this sike Damyan,
That from hir herte sche ne dryve can
The remebraunce, for to doon him ease.
'Certeyn,' thought sche, 'whom that this thing displease
I **rekke** not, for **her** I him assure   care; here
To love him best of eny creature,
Though he no more hadde than his scherte.
Lo! Pite renneth soone in gentil herte!
Heer may ye see how excellent **fraunchise**   generosity (of spirit)
In womman is, whan thay **narow** hem **avyse**.   carefully; consider
780 Som tyraunt is, as ther ben many oon,
That hath an hert as hard as is a stoon,
Which wold han lete **sterven** in the place   die
Wel rather than han graunted him her grace,
And hem rejoysen in her cruel pride,
And rekken nou*gh*t to ben an homicide.[48]
This gentil May, fulfillid of pite,
Right of hir hond a letter maked sche,
In which sche grauntith him hir verray grace;
Ther **lakkid** nought, but oonly day and place   lacked
790 Wher that sche might unto his lust **suffise**,   meet
For it schal be right as he wold **devyse** –   like it to be
And whan sche saugh hir tyme upon a day,

---

46 The merchant wonders whether it was the configuration of the heavens which
      made this a fortunate time to give a woman a letter, begging for her love.
47 A love-letter.
48 'and don't consider themselves a homicide'

To visite this Damyan goth May,
And subtilly this lettre doun sche thruste
Under his **pylow**, rede it if him luste.   pillow
Sche takith him by the hond, and hard him **twiste**,   squeezed
So secrely that no wight of hit **wiste**,   knew
And bad him be al **hool**, and forth sche wente   well
To January, whan that he for hir sente.
Up ryseth Damyan the nexte morwe;   810 ← 800
Al passed was his siknes and his sorwe.
He **kembith** him, he pruneth him and **pyketh**;   combs; 'preens'
He doth al that unto his lady likith,
And eek to January he goth as lowe
As ever did a dogge for the bowe.[49]
He is so plesaunt unto every man –
For craft, if al whoso that do it can –
That every wight is **fayn** to speke him good,   glad
And fully in his lady's grace he stood.
Thus **lete** I Damyan about his neede,   leave   810
And in my tale forth I wol procede.
Some clerkes holden that **felicite**   happiness
Stant in **delit**, and therfor certeyn he   pleasure
This noble January, with al his might,
In honest wise, as **longith** to a knight   is suitable for
Schop him to lyve ful **deliciously**;   delightfully
His housyng, his **array**, as honestly   clothing
To his degre was maked as a kynges –
Amonges other of his honest thinges
He mad a gardyn, walled al with stoon;   820
So fair a gardyn **wot** I **not wher** noon,   know; nowhere
For **out of doute**, I verrely suppose,   doubtless
That he that **wroot** the Romauns of the Rose[50]   wrote
Ne couthe of hit the beaute wel **devyse**,   recount
Ne Pirapus might not wel **suffise**,[51]   be sufficient
Though he be god of gardyns, for to telle

---

49 A dog, specially trained to hunt with an archer.
50 The Romance of the Rose was a love allegory, where the lover enters the garden
   and picks the rose (makes love to his lady).
51 Priapus was the god of open sexuality: here he is associated with the garden, a
   clue to its true purpose.

The beaute of the gardyn and the welle,
That stood under a **laurer**, always greene.   laurel tree
Ful ofte tyme he Pluto, and his queene
830 Preserpina, and al the **fayerie**   fairies
Desporten hem, and maken melodye   play
Aboute that welle, and daunced, as men tolde.
This noble knight, this January the olde,
Such **deynte** hath in it to walk and pleye   delight
That he wold no wight suffre bere the keye
Save he himself; for of the smale **wyket**   gate
He bar always of silver a smal **cliket**,   key
With which whan that him list he it **unschette**;   undo
And whan he wolde pay his wyf hir dette,[52]
840 In somer sesoun thider wold he go,
And May his wyf, and no wight but thay tuo;
And thinges which that weren not doon in bedde
He in the gardyn parformed hem, and spedde;
And in this wise many a mery day
Lyved this January and freische May,
But wordly joye may not alway endure
To January, ne to no creature.
O sodeyn **hap**! O thou fortune unstable!   happening
Lyk to the scorpioun **desceyvable**,   deceiptful
850 That flaterest with thin heed whan thou wilt stynge;
Thy tayl is deth, thurgh thin **envenymynge**!   poisoning
O **britel** joye! O sweete venym queynte![53]   fleeting
O monster, that so subtily canst **peynte**   cover
Thyn giftes under **hiew** of stedfastnesse,   colour
That thou desceyvest bothe **more and lesse**!   greater and lesser
Why hastow January thus desceyved,
That haddist him for thy fulle frend receyved?
And now thou hast **byreft** him bothe his **yen**,   taken from; eyes
For sorw of which desireth he to dyen.
860 Allas! This noble January fre,
Amyd his lust and his prosperite,
Is **woxe** blynd, and that al sodeynly.   become

52 'pay her debt' – have sexual intercourse with her.
53 'queynte' can mean cunning, clever, unfathomable, but also refers to the
   genitalia and to sexual activity.

He wepith and he wayleth pitously,
And therwithal the fuyr of jalousye,
Lest that his wif schuld falle in som folye;
So **brent** his herte that he wold **fayn**   burnt; be glad
That som man bothe hir and him had slayn,
For neyther after his deth nor in his lyf
Ne wold he that sche were love ne wyf,
But ever lyve as wydow, in clothes blake,   870
Soul, as the **turtil** that lost hath hir make;   alone; turtledove
But atte last, after a moneth or **tweye**,   two
His sorwe gan **aswage**, **soth** to **seye**;   grow less; truth; tell
For whan he **wist** it may noon other be,   knew
He paciently took his adversite,
Save out of doute – he may not forgoon –
That he nas jalous evermore in oon,[54]
Which jalousie it was so outrageous
That neyther in halle, ne in noon other hous,
Ne in noon other place, never the mo,   880
He nolde suffre hir to ryde or go
But if that he had hond on hir alway,
For which ful ofte wepeth freissche May,
That loveth Damyan so benignely
That sche moot **outher** deyen sodeinly,   either
Or elles sche moot han him as hir lest –
She waytith whan hir herte wolde brest.[55]
Upon that other syde, Damyan
Bicomen is the sorwfulleste man
That ever was; for neyther night ne day   890
Ne might he speke a word with freissche May
As to his p[ur]pos, of no such matiere,
But if that January most it heere,
That had an hond upon hir evermo;
But **natheles**, by writyng to and fro,   nevertheless
And **prive signes** wist he what sche ment,   secret signals
And sche knew **eek** the **fyn** of his entent.   also; object
O January! What might it the **availe**,   help
If thou might see as fer as schippes saile!

54 He couldn't stop being jealous.
55 'she thought her heart was going to burst'

900	For as good is blynd deceyved be,	
	As to be deceyved whan a man may see.	
	Lo, Argus which that had an hundred **eyen**,	eyes
	For al that ever he couthe **poure** or **prien**,	peer; pry
	Yet was he **blent** as, God wot, so ben moo	deceived
	That **weneth wisly** that it be nought so –[56]	truly believe
	Passe over is an ease, I say no more.	'turn a blind eye'
	This freissche May that I spak of so **yore**,	long ago
	In warm wex hath **emprynted** the cliket	made an impression of
	That January bar, of the smale wiket,	
910	With which into his gardyn ofte he went,	
	And Damyan, that knew al his entent,	
	The cliket **counterfeted** prively.	copied
	Ther nys no more to say, but **hastily**	very soon
	Som wonder by this cliket schal **betyde**,	take place
	Which ye schal heeren, if ye wol abyde.	
	O noble Ovyde! Wel **soth** saistow, **God woot**,	truth; God knows
	What **sleight** is it, though it be long & hoot,	trick
	That love nyl fynd it out in some manere!	
	By Piramus and Thesbe may men leere –[57]	
920	Though thay were kept ful longe streyt over al,[58]	
	Thay ben accorded **rownyng** thurgh a wal –	whispering
	Ther no wight couthe han found out **swich** a sleight!	such
	For now to purpos – er that dayes eyght	
	Were passid, er the moneth of Juyl **bifille**,	came
	That January hath caught so gret a wille,	
	Thorugh **eggyng** of his wyf him for to pleye	urging
	In his gardyn, and, 'no wight but we tweye,'	
	That in a morwe unto this May saith he,	
	'Rys up, my wif, my love, my lady fre;	
930	The **turtlis** vois is herd, my **douve** swete –	turtledove; dove
	The wynter is goon with his **raynes** wete –	rain
	Come forth now, with thin eyyen **columbine**;	dovelike
	How fairer ben thy brestes than is the wyne!	
	The gardyn is enclosed al aboute;	

56 Argus was set to guard the goddess Juno, but fell asleep, after which his hundred eyes were put into a peacock's tail as punishment.

57 Pyramus and Thisbe spoke to one another through a hole in the wall.

58 'they were very closely confined'

Com forth, my swete spouse, out of doute
Thow hast me wounded in myn hert, O wyf!
No **spot** in the knew I in al my lif!   stain
Com forth and let us take oure desport;
I **ches** the for my wyf and my comfort!'   chose
Such olde lewed wordes used he.   940
On Damyan a signe made sche,
That he schuld go **biforn** with his **cliket**.   ahead; key
This Damyan than hath opened the wiket,
And in he **stert**, and that in such manere   leapt
That no wight it mighte see nor heere,
And stille he **seet** under a bussch anoon.   sat
This January is blynd as is a stoon;
With Mays in his hond, and no wight mo,
Into his freische gardyn is ago,
And **clappid** to the wiket sodeinly.   shut   950
'Now, wyf,' quod he, 'her nys but ye and I,
That art the creature that I best love;
For by that lord that sit in heven above,
Lever ich had to dyen on a knyf   I had rather
Than the offende, deere trewe wyf!
For God's sake thenk how I the chees,
Nought for no **coveytise** douteles,   covetousness
But oonly for the love I had to the;
And though that I be old and may not se,
Beeth trewe to me – and I wol telle yow why: 960
Thre thinges, certes, schul ye wynne therby.
First, love of Crist and to your self honour,
And al myn **heritage**, toun and tour,   inheritance
I give it yow; makith **chartres** as yow **leste**;   charters; like
This schal ben doon tomorw **er sonne reste**.   before sunset
So wisly God my soule bring in blisse,   as
I pray yow first in **covenaunt** ye me kisse,   agreement/promise
And though that I be jalous, **wyt** me nought –   blame
Ye ben so deep emprinted in my thought,
That whan that I considre your beaute,   970
And therwithal the unlikely **eelde** of me,   old age
I may nought certes, though I schulde dye,
Forbere to ben out of your companye,
For **verray** love this is withouten doute.   true

Now kisse me, wyf, and let us **rome** aboute.'   wander
This freissche May, whan sche his worde herde,
Benignely to January answerde;   kindly
But first and forward sche bigan to wepe –
'I have,' quod sche, 'a soule for to **kepe**   guard
980 As wel as ye, and also myn honour,
And of my wifhod **thilke** tendre flour   the same
Which that I have **ensured in** your hond,   entrusted to
Whan that the prest to yow my body bond;
Wherfor I wil answer in this manere:
By the leve of yow,my lord so deere,
I pray to God that never **dawe** the day,   dawn
That I ne sterve as foule as womman may,
If ever I do unto my **kyn** that schame,   family
Or elles I **empaire** so my name,   besmirch
990 That I be fals – and if I do that **lak**,   offence
Doth **strepe** me and put me in a sak,   strip
And in the nexte ryver do me **drenche** –   drown
I am a gentil womman, and no **wenche**.   whore
Why speke ye thus? But men ben ever untrewe,
And wommen han reproef of yow ever newe.[59]
Ye have noon other contenaunce, I **leve**,   believe
But speke to us as of untrust and **repreve**.'   blame
And with that word, sche saugh wher Damyan
Sat in the **buissh**, and coughen sche bigan,   bush
1000 And with hir fyngres signes made sche
That Damyan schuld clymb upon a tre
That **charged** was with fruyt, and up he went,   full
For verrayly he knew al hir **entent**,   intention
And every signe that sche couthe make,
Wel bet than January, hir oughne make;
For in a letter sche had told him al
Of this matier, how he **worche** schal.   behave
And thus I lete him sitte upon the **pirie**,   pear tree
And January and May romynge mirye.
1010 Bright was the day and **bliew** the **firmament**;   blue; heavens
Phebus hath of gold his stremes doun y-sent[60]

59 'women are always getting the blame from you'
60 'Phoebus (the sun) had sent down his streams (rays) of gold'

To gladen every flour with his warmnesse.
He was that tyme in **Gemmes**, as I gesse,   *Gemini*
But litel fro his declinacioun
Of **Canker**, Joves exaltacioun;[61]   *Cancer*
And so bifel that brighte morwen tyde,
That in that gardyn, in the **ferther** syde,   *farther*
Pluto, that is kyng of fayerye,
And many a lady in his compaignie,
Folwyng his wif, the queene Preserpine,   **1020**
Ech after other as **right** as a lyne,   *straight*
Whil that sche gadred floures in the **mede** –   *meadow*
In Claudian ye may the story rede –[62]
How in this grisly carte he hir **fette**,   *carried off*
This king of fayry, than adoun him sette
Upon a bench of **turves**, freissh and greene,   *turf*
And right anoon thus sayd he to his queene;
'My wyf,' quod he, 'ther may no wight say nay,
Th'experiens so **preveth** every day   *proves*
The **tresoun** which that womman doth to man;   *betrayal* **1030**
Ten hundrid thousand tellen I can,
Notable of your untrouth and **brutelnesse**.   *inconstancy*
O Salamon! Wys and richest of richesse,
Fulfild of **sapiens** and of worldly glorie,   *wisdom*
Ful worthy ben thy wordes to **memorie**   *remember*
To every wight that wit and resoun **can**!   *knows*
Thus praysith he yit the bounte of man:
Among a thousand men yit fond I oon,
But of wommen alle, fond I noon.
Thus saith the king that knoweth your wikkednesse,   **1040**
That Jhesus, **filius** Sirac, as I gesse,[63]   *son of*
Ne spekith of yow but **selde** reverence –   *seldom*
A wilde fuyr and corrupt pestilence
So falle upon your bodies yit tonight –
Ne see ye not this honurable knight?
Bycause, allas, that he is blynd and old,

---

61 Jupiter (Jove) was high in the sign of Cancer (it was 'high summer').
62 Roman writer Claudian told the story of the rape of Proserpine.
63 The writer of the apocryphal book of Ecclesiasticus.

His owne man schal make him **cokewold**!   cuckold
Loo, wher he sitt, the lechour, in the tre!
Now wol I graunten of my majeste
1050 Unto this olde, blinde, worthy knight,
That he schal have agein his eyyen sight
Whan that his wyf wol do him vilonye;
Than schal he knowe al her harlotrye,
Bothe in reproef of hir and **other mo**!'   others besides
'Ye schal,' quod Preserpine, 'and wol ye so?
Now, by my **modre's sire's** soule I swere   mother's father's
That I schal give hir **suffisaunt** answere,   good enough
And alle wommen after, for hir sake,
That though thay be in any **gult** y-take,   guilt
1060 With face bold thay schul hemself excuse,
And bere hem doun that wolde hem acccuse.
For lak of answer noon of hem schal dyen –
Al had a man **seyn** a thing with both his **yen**,   seen; eyes
Yit schul we wymmen **visage it hardily**,   face it out boldly
And wepe, and swere, and chide subtilly,
So that ye men schul ben as **lewed as gees**;
What rekkith me of your auctoritees!   what do I care about
I **wot** wel that this Jew, this Salamon,   know
Fond of us wommen fooles many oon;
1070 But though he ne fond no good womman,
Ye hath ther founde many another man
Wommen ful trewe, ful good and vertuous.
Witnesse on hem that dwelle in Crist's hous –
With martirdom thay proved hir **constaunce**.   constancy
The Romayn **gestes** eek make remembraunce   histories
Of many a verray trewe wyf also;
But Sire, be nought wrath – al be it so
Though that he sayd he fond no good womman,
I pray yow tak the **sentens** of the man.   meaning
1080 He mente thus: that in sovereign bounte
Nis noon but God, that sit in Trinite –
Ey, for **verrey God**, that nys but oon.   God himself
What make ye so moche of Salamon?
What though he made a temple, God's hous?
What though he were riche and glorious?
So made he **eek** a temple of fals godis;   also

How might he do a thing that more **forbod** is?   forbidden
Parde! Als fair as ye his name **emplastre**,   cover over
He was a lecchour and an **idolastre**,   idolater
And in his **eelde** he verraily God forsook,   old age   1090
And if God ne had – as saith the book –
Y-spared him for his fadre's sake, he scholde
Have lest his **regne rather** than he wolde.   kingdom; sooner
I **sette** right nought of the vilonye   value
That ye of wommen write, a **boterflie**!'   butterfly
I am a womman, needes most I speke,
Or elles swelle til myn herte breke!
For syn so he sayd, that we ben **jangleresses**,   chatterers
As ever hool I moote **brouke my tresses**,   have hair (live)
I schal not spare for no curtesye   1100
To speke him harm that wold us vilonye!'
'Dame,' quod this Pluto, 'be no lenger **wroth**!   angry
I give it up; but **sith** I **swere** myn **oth**   since; swore; oath
That I wil graunte him his sight agein,
My word schal stonde, I warne yow certeyn;
I am a kyng – it sit me nought to lye.'[64]
'And I,' quod sche, 'a queen of faierie!
Hir answer schal sche have, I undertake –
Let us no mo wordes herof make.
Forsoth, I wol no lenger yow **contrarie**.'   argue against 1110
Now let us turne agayn to Januarye,
That in this gardyn with this faire May
Syngeth ful merier than the **papinjay**;   parrot
'Yow love I best, and schal, and other noon!'
So long about the **aleys** is he goon,   paths
Til he was com **ageyn** thilke **pirie**   up to; pear tree
Wheras this Damyan sittith ful mirye
On heigh, among the freissche **levyes** greene.   leaves
This freissche May, that is so bright and **scheene**,   shining
Gan for to **syke**, and sayd, 'Allas, my syde!   sigh   1120
Now Sir,' quod sche, 'for ought that may bityde,
I most han of the **peres** that I see,   pears
Or I moot dye, so sore longith me

64 'it doesn't become me to lie'

To eten of the smale peris greene!
Help, for hir love that is of heven queene!
I telle yow, wel a womman in my **plyt**   condition
May have to fruyt so gret an appetyt,
that sche may deyen but sche it have!'
'Allas,' quod he, 'that I nad heer a **knave**   manservant
1130 That couthe climbe! Allas, allas,' quod he,
'For I am blynd!' 'Ye, Sire, **no fors**,' quod sche,   no problem
'But wolde ye **vouchesauf** for God's sake,   grant
The piry **inwith** your armes for to take –   in
For wel I woot that ye mystruste me –
Thanne sholde I climb wel ynough,' quod she,
So I my foot might set upon your bak.'
'**Certes**,' quod he, 'theron schal be no lak.   yes indeed
Might I yow helpe with myn herte blood!'
He stoupith doun, and on his bak sche stood,
1140 And caught hir by a **twist**, and up sche goth.   branch
Ladys, I pray yow that ye be not wroth –
I can not **glose**, I am a **rude** man –   gloss; plain
And sodienly anoon this Damyan
Gan pullen up the **smok**, and in he **throng**;   petticoat; thrust
And whan that Pluto saugh this grete wrong
To January he gaf his sight agayn –
Ne was ther never man of thing so **fayn**,   glad
But on his wyf his thought was evermo;
Up to the tree he **kest** his eyyen tuo,   cast
1150 And seigh that Damyan his wyf had **dressid**   treated
In which maner it may not ben expressid,
But if I wolde speke uncurteisly –
And up he gaf a roryng and a cry,
As doth the moder whan the child schal dye;
'Out! Help! Allas! Harrow!' he gan to crie,
'O **stronge** lady **stoure**, what dos thow?'   bold; crude
And sche answerith, 'Sire, what eylith yow?
Have paciens and resoun in your mynde;
I have yow **holpen** on bothe your eyen blynde!   helped
1160 Up peril of my soule, I schal not lyen,
As me was taught to **hele** with your **yen**,   heal; eyes
Was nothing **bet** for to make yow see,   better
Than stroggle with a man upon a tree!

God woot, I ded it in ful good entent!'
'Stroggle?' quod he, 'Ye, **algat** in it went! — at all events
God give yow bothe **on schames** deth to dyen! — one shameful
He **swyved** the! I saugh it with myn yen, — fucked
And elles be I honged by the **hals**!' — neck
'Than is,' quod sche, 'medicine fals,
For certeynly, if that ye mighten see, — 1170
Ye wold not say tho wordes unto me.
Ye han som **glymsyng**, and no parfyt sight.' — glimpsing
'I se,' quod he, 'as wel as ever I might,
Thankid be God, with bothe myn yen tuo –
And by my trouth, me thought he did the so!'
'Ye **mase**, **mase**, goode Sir,' quod sche, — are confused
'This thank have I, **for** I have maad yow see. — because
Allas,' quod sche, 'that ever I was so kynde!'
'Now Dame,' quod he, 'let al passe out of mynde!
Com doun, my **leef**, and if I have myssayd, — love 1180
God help me, so as I am evel appayd![65]
But by my fader's soule, I **wende** have seyn — believed
How that this Damyan had by the **leyn**, — lain
And that thy smok had layn upon thy brest!'
'Ye, Sire,' quod sche, 'ye may **wene** as yow lest; — believe
But Sire, a man that wakith out of his slep,
He may not sodeynly wel **take keep** — focus
Upon a thing, ne seen it parfytly,
Til that he be **adawed** verrayly. — woken up
Right so a man that long hath blynd **y-be**, — been 1190
He may not sodeynly so wel y-se
First whan the sight is newe comen agayn,
As he that hath a day or tuo **y-sayn**. — seen
Til that your sight **y-stablid** be a while, — settled down
Ther may ful many a sighte yow **bigile**. — deceive
Beth war, I pray yow, for by heven king,
Ful many man wenith for to se a thing,
And it is al another than it semeth –
He that mysconceyveth, he **mysdemeth**.' — misjudges
And with that word sche leep doun fro the tre; — 1200

65 'God let me be badly rewarded' The Squire's Prologue and Tale (Footnotes)

This January, who is glad but he?

He kissith hire, and **clippith** hir ful ofte,   cuddles

And on hir wombe he strokith hir ful ofte,

And to his paleys hom he hath hir lad –

Now, goode man, I pray yow to be glad.

Thus endith her my tale of Januarye;

God blesse us, and his moder Seinte Marie. Amen"

Here endith the marchaunt's tale

THE SQUIRE'S PROLOGUE AND TALE

In response to the merchant's tale, the host reveals some of his own wife's unpleasant traits. Conjecturing that the squire, being married, must also know something of these 'truths' about women, the host suggests that he might like to tell a tale. The squire excuses himself from the argument, claiming that his wife is good, so he will tell a story about something else.

Cambyuskan (Genghis Khan), King of Tartary, has two sons and a daughter called Canace. One day an exotic visitor rides into the king's hall bearing gifts – a brass horse (on which he is riding), a mirror and a ring. He explains that the horse will take the king wherever he wants to go and back. The mirror will show the holder who is a friend or an enemy; or if held by a woman will reveal the identity of her future husband. The ring will enable the wearer to hear and understand the language of birds. The ring is given to Canace. She rises early and goes out into the woods, where she meets a hawk lamenting her unfaithful lover. Canace is filled with pity for the bird, which she takes up and cares for. The story then returns to the king, but the franklin intervenes, and politely but firmly silences the squire.

The squire is very well aware of his story as a construction, and tries too hard to construct it. He says that he does not have the ability to paint his words in rhetorical colours. On several occasions he speaks of the need to get back to the 'knotte' or 'knub' of the tale, but he never does this. Unfortunately he fails to knit together his own material, and the two aspect of his story, initially very loosely connected, drift further apart.

The squire's story is, like January's garden, a romance 'vision' of an ideal, fantasy world in which the real and the surreal, the magic and the supernatural, exist side-by-side. It contains elements of a *chanson d'aventure* or a romance epic. The rider entering the hall is the prelude to many Arthurian adventures, as in *Le Morte Darthur* and *Sir Gawain and the Green Knight*. The presentation of exotic gifts with magical properties, linking the mortal present to the prophetic, the eternal and the divine, is another feature of Arthurian and other romance epics; magic horses, rings, mirrors and swords abound in such tales. These are the stories on which, presumably, the chivalrous squire has been raised, and which inform his own life of fighting, singing and love-longing.

The story of Canace and the bird is connected to the gifts somewhat loosely; she uses the mirror, and then she can understand the bird because of the ring. The bird story is about *gentil* pity and tenderness, as is underlined by the narrator and the bird. In fact, there is little else in the story apart from its self-conscious affectiveness. Apart from the magical element of the ring, the bird has little to do with exotic strangers and brass horses. The tale's alchemy leads, like that of the canon's yeoman, to nothing but failure and another attempt, as the squire piles images upon images and tropes upon tropes. This is carried even further in 'Geoffrey's' tale of Sir Thopas. There is plenty of interest and movement, but the storyteller's craft of 'making' is absent. The squire, being only a 'trainee' knight, does not have his father's ability to construct a story, or the experience and learning to compete with the knight's tale. His story arouses expectations, which it then utterly fails to fulfil. It may be that, like January, he is clinging to an outdated philosophy and an irrelevant lifestyle. In addition to this, the squire has an imperfect understanding of his subject matter; he touches on the incest at its heart without seeming to understand that he is doing so. There are, therefore, several possible reasons for the franklin's prompt action – to save the squire from embarrassment?

Topic Keywords

Romance as genre/ chivalry and knighthood/ courtly love/ alchemy/ magic and experimental science

Further Reading

Alan S. Ambrisco, ' "It lyth nat in my tonge": Occupatio and Otherness in The Squire's Tale', *Chaucer Review*, 38, 2004, pp. 205–28

Craig A. Berry, 'Flying Sources: Classical Authority in Chaucer's Squire's Tale', *Journal of English Literary History*, 68, 2001, pp. 287–313

Joseph A. Dane, ' "Tyl Mercurius house he flye": Early Printed Texts and Critical Readings of The Squire's Tale', *Chaucer Review*, 34, 2000, pp. 309–16

Vincent DiMarco, 'Supposed Satiric Pointers in Chaucer's Squire's Tale', *English Studies*, 78, 1997, pp. 330–4

John M. Fyler, 'Domesticating the Exotic in The Squire's Tale', *Journal of English Literary History*, 55, 1988, pp. 1–26

Karl Goller, 'Chaucer's Squire's Tale: The Knotte of the Tale', in
  Chaucer und seine Zeit: symposion fur Walter S. Schirmer, edited by
  Arno Esch, Tubingen, Niemeyer, 1968, pp. 163–88

Carol Heffernan, 'Chaucer's Squire's Tale: The Poetics of Interlace or the
  Well of English Undefiled', *Chaucer Review*, 32, 1997, pp. 32–45

Patricia Clare Ingham, 'Little Nothings: The Squire's Tale and the
  Ambition of Gadgets', *Studies in the Age of Chaucer*, 31, 2009, pp.
  53–80

Lindsey M. Jones, 'Chaucer's Anxiety of Poetic Craft: The Squire's
  Tale', *Style*, 41, 2007, pp. 300–18

Stanley Kahrl, 'Chaucer's Squire's Tale and the Decline of Chivalry',
  Chaucer Review, 7, 1973, pp. 194–209

William Kamowski, 'Trading the Knotte for Loose Ends: The Squire's
  Tale and the Poetics of Chaucerian Fragments', *Style*, 31, 1997, pp.
  391–412

Lesley Kordecki, 'Chaucer's Squire's Tale: Animal Discourse, Women,
  and Subjectivity', *Chaucer Review*, 36, 2002, pp. 277–97

Robert Miller, 'Chaucer's Rhetorical Rendition of Mind: The Squire's
  Tale', in *Chaucer and the Craft of Fiction*, edited by Leigh Arrathoon,
  Rochester, MI, Solaris, 1986, pp. 219–40

Charles A. Owen Jr, 'The Falcon's Complaint in The Squire's Tale',
  Studies in Medieval Culture, 29, 1991, pp. 173–88

Shirley Sharon-Zisser, 'The Squire's Tale and the Limits of Non-
  Mimetic Fiction', *Chaucer Review*, 26, 1992, pp. 377–94

❦ 'Ey, God's mercy,' sayd our hoste **tho**,   *then*
'Now such a wyf I pray God keep me fro!
Lo, whiche **sleightes** and **subtiltees**   *tricks; slyness*
In wommen ben! For, ay as busy as bees
Ben thay, us seely men for to desceyve,
And from a **soth** ever wol thay **weyve** –   *truth; waiver*
By this marchaund's tale it proveth wel –
But douteles, as trewe as eny steel,
I have a wyf, though that sche pore be,
But of hir tonge a **labbyng** schrewe is sche;   *gabbing*   10
And yit sche hath an heep of vices mo.
Therof **no fors** – let all such thinges go –   *no matter*
But **wite** ye what in **counseil** be it seyd;   *know; secret*
Me **rewith** sore I am unto hir **teyd**,   *regret; tied*
And if I scholde **reken** every vice   *count*
Which that sche hath, y-wis I were to nyce.
And cause why? It schuld reported be,
And told to hir **of** som of this **meyne**   *by; group*
Of whom, it needith not for to declare,
Syn wommen connen **oute** such **chaffare**;   *take out; merchandise*   20
And eek my witte suffisith nought therto,
To tellen al – wherfor my tale is do.
Sir Squier, com **forth**, if that your wille be,   *forward*
And say us a tale, for certes ye
Connen theron as moche as ony man.'   *know*
'Nay Sire,' quod he, 'but I wil say as I can
With herty wil, for I wil not rebelle
Against your wille; a tale wil I telle.
Have me excused if that I speke amys –
My wil is good, and therto my tale is this.'   30

Her endith the prolog

And her bygynneth the squyer's tale

❦ At Sarray, in the lond of Tartary[1]

Ther dwelled a kyng that **werryed Russy**,   waged war on; Russia

Thurgh which ther **deyed** many a **doughty** man.   died; bold

This nobil kyng was **cleped** Cambynskan,[2]   called

Which in his tyme was of so gret **renoun**   fame

That ther nas nowher, in no regioun,

So excellent a lord in alle thing;

40 Him lakked nought that **longed** to a kyng.   belonged

As of the **secte** of which that he was born   religious faith

He kept his lawe, to which he was sworn;

And therto he was **hardy**, wys, and riche,   bold

And pitous and just, alway **y-liche**;   the same

Soth of his word, benign and honurable,   honest

Of his **corage** as eny centre stable;   will

Yong, freisch, and strong, in armes desirous

As eny **bachiler** of al his hous.   knight

A fair person he was, and fortunat,

50 And kepte so wel his **real astat**   royal status

That ther was nowher such a **ryal** man.   royal

This noble kyng, this **Tartre**, this Cambynskan,   Tartar

Hadde tuo sones by Elcheta his wyf,

Of which the eldest highte Algaryf;

That other was **y-cleped** Samballo.   called

A doughter had this worthi king also

That yongest was, and **highte** Canace;   was called

But for to telle yow al hir beaute

It lith not on my tonge, ne my **connyng**;   understanding

60 I dar nou*g*ht undertake so heigh a thing.

Myn Englisshe **eek** is insufficient –   also

He moste be a **rethor** excellent,   rhetor (public speaker)

That couth his colours **longyng** for that art,[3]   belonging

If he schold hir **discryve** in eny part –   describe

I am non such; I mot speke as I can.

And so bifel it that this Cambynskan

Hath twenty wynter born his **dyademe**.   diadem (crown)

1 Probably a place in modern Russia; the land of the Tartars in central/eastern Europe.
2 Genghis Khan.
3 Rhetorical 'colours': the devices used to make speech and writing more interesting.

As he was wont fro yer to yer, I **deme**,	judge
He **leet** the fest of his **netivite**	ordered; birth
Don cryen thurgh Sarray, his cite,	70
The last Idus of March[4] after the yeer[5]	
Phebus the sonne was joly and cleer,	
For he was neigh his exaltacioun	
In Mars's face, and in his mansioun	
In Aries, the colerik the hote signe,	
Ful lusty was the wedir and benigne;[6]	
For which the **foules** agein the sonne **scheene**,	birds; bright
What for the sesoun & for the **yonge greene**,	new green shoots
Ful lowde song in here **affecciouns**,	feelings
Hem semed have geten hem **protecciouns**	protection 80
Agens the swerd of wynter, **kene** and cold.	sharp
This Cambynskan, of which I have told,	
In royal vesture sittyng on his **deys**	dais (raised platform)
With dyadem, ful heigh in his paleys,	
And held his fest, solmpne and so riche,	
That in this worlde was ther noon it **liche**;	like
Of which, if I schal tellen al th'**array**,	riches
Than wold it occupie a somer's day;	
And eek it needeth nou*g*ht for to **devyse**	recount
At every cours the **ordre** and the servyse –	order 90
Ne of her swannes nor of her heronsewes.	
I wol nat tellen of her straunge stewes.	
Ek in that lond, as tellen knightes olde,	
Ther is som **mete** that is ful **deynte** holde,	food; precious
That in this lond men **recch** of it but smal –	reckon/value
Ther is no man it may reporten al.	
I wol not tarien you, for it is pryme;	
And for it is no **fruyt**, but los of tyme,	benefit
Unto my purpos I wol have my recours.	
That so bifelle after the **thridde** cours,	third 100
Whil that the kyng sit thus in his **nobleye**,	estate

4 15th March, after the classical Roman calendar.

5 'as the year goes'

6 The sun is high in the sign of Aries, in the mansion – or house – of Mars, thus indicating the position of the stars and planets in the sky at this time of year, and suggesting a possible astrological interpretation.

Herkyng his mynstrales her **thinges** pleye   repertoire
Byforn him atte boord, **deliciously**.   delightfully
In atte halle dore, al sodeynly,
Ther com a knight upon a **steed** of **bras**,   horse; brass
And in his hond a brod myrour of glas.
Upon his thomb he had of gold a ryng,
And by his side a naked swerd hangyng;
And up he rideth to the hey*g*he bord – [7]
110   In al the halle ne was ther spoke a word –
For **mervayl** of this knight, him to byholde,   wonder
Ful **besily** they **wayten**, yong and olde.   attentively; await
This straunge knight, that cam thus sodeynly,
Al armed **sauf** his **heed** ful richely,   except; head
Salved the kyng and queen, and lordes alle,   greeted/hailed
By ordre as they seten into halle,
With so heigh reverens and observaunce,
As wel in speche as in contynaunce,
That **Eawen** with his olde curtesye,   Gawain
120   **They** he were come agein out of **fayrye**,   though; fairyland
Ne couthe him nou*g*ht **amende** with no word;   do better
And after this, **biforn** the highe bord,   before/in front of
He with a manly vois sayd his message
After the forme used in his langage,
Withouten **vice** of syllabil or letter;   getting wrong
And for his tale schulde seme the better,
Accordaunt to his wordes was his cheere – [8]
As techeth art of **speche** ham that it **leere** –   speaking; learn
Albeit that I can sowne his style,
130   Ne can nat clymben over so heigh a style,[9]
Yit say I this, as to comun entent,
Thus moche amounteth al that ever he ment,
If it so be that I **have it in mynde**.   remember it
He sayd, 'The kyng of Arraby and Ynde,[10]

7   The knight rode up the interior of the hall to the high table, on the dais at the
     end. It was customary for the king of England's champion to do this at the
     coronation banquet.
8   'his manner was in accordance with his words'
9   'I cannot speak in his style, nor climb over so high a stile (punning reference to
     attaining such mastery of the art of speaking in public)'.
10 Arabia and India.

My liege lord, on this solempne day
Saluteth you as he best can or may,
And sendeth you, in honour of your feste,
By me that am redy at al his heste,
This steede of bras, that esily and wel,
That can in the space of o day naturel–   one   140
This is to say, in four an twenty houres –
Wher so yow **lust**, in **droughthe** or in **schoures**,   like; drought; rain
Beren your body into every place   carry
To which your herte **wilneth** for to **pace**   wants; go
Withouten **wem** of you, thurgh foul and fair;   harm
Or if you lust, to flee as hei*gh* **in th'air**   into the air
As doth an egle whan him list to **sore**.   soar
This same steede schal bere you evermore
Withoute harm, til ye be ther you **leste**,   like
Though that ye slepen on his bak, or reste,   150
And torne agein, with **wrything** of a pyn;   turning
He that it wrought, he **cowthe** ful many a **gyn**.   knew; craft
He wayted many a constellacioun[11]
Er he had do this operacioun,
And knew ful many a seal and many a bond.
This mirour eek, that I have in myn hond,
Hath such a mighte that men may in it see
When ther schal falle eny adversite
Unto your **regne**, unto yourself also,   kingdom
And openly who is your frend or **fo**;   foe/enemy   160
And over al this, if eny lady bright
Hath set hir hert on eny maner **wight**,   man
I he be fals, sche schal his tresoun see,
His newe love, and his **subtilite**   cunning
So openly that ther schal nothing hyde.
Wherfor, ageins this lusty somer **tyde**,   time
This mirour and this ryng that ye may see,
He hath send to my lady Canacee,
Your excellente doughter, that is heere,
The **vertu** of this ryng, and ye wol heere,   properties   170
Is this – that whoso lust it for to **were**   wear

11 He had consulted the heavens using his astronomical/astrological calculations, to
   find the most auspicious time to do his work.

Upon hir thomb, or in hir purs to bere,
Ther is no **foul** that **fleeth** under the heven   bird; flies
That sche ne schal understonden his **steven**,   speech
And know his menyng openly and pleyn,
And answer him in his langage ageyn;
And every gras that groweth upon roote,
Sche schal eek know to who it wol do **boote**,   remedy
Al be his woundes never so deep and wyde.

180 This **naked** swerd, that hangeth by my syde,   unsheathed
Such vertu hath, that what man that it **smyte**,   strikes with it
Thurghout his armur it wol **kerve** and byte,   carve
Were it as thikke as a braunched **ook**;   oak
And what man is y-wounded with the strook
Schal never be **hool**, til that you lust of grace   healed
To strok him with the **plat** in thilke place   flat side
Ther his is hurt – this is as moche to seyn,
Ye moote with the platte swerd agein
Stroke him in the wound, and it wol close –

190 This is the verray **soth**, withouten glose –   truth
It failleth nought whil it is in your **hold**.'   Possession
And whan this knight thus had his tale told,
He **rit** out of the hall, and doun he **light**.   rode; alighted
His steede, which that schon as sonne bright,
Stant in the court as stille as eny stoon.   stood
This knight is to his **chambre lad** anoon;   room; led
He is **unarmed**, and to mete **y-sett**.   disarmed; sat down
This presents ben ful richely **y-fett** –   fetched
This is to sayn, the swerd and the myrrour –

200 And born anon unto the highe tour,
With certein officers **ordeynd** therfore,   appointed
And unto Canace the ryng is bore
Solempnely, ther sche syt atte table;
But **sikerly**, withouten eny fable,   surely
The hors of bras, that may nat be **remewed**,   moved
It stant as it were to the ground y-glewed;
Ther may no man out of the place it dryve,
For noon engyn of wyndyng or **polyve**,   pulley
And cause why? For **thay can nought the craft**,[12]

12 'they don't have the skill to do it'

And therfor in the place thei have it laft   210
Til that the knight hath taught hem the manere
To **voyden** him, as ye schul after heere.   move him away
Greet was the **pres** that swarmed to and fro,   crowd
To **gauren** on this hors that stondeth so,   gaze
For it so **wyl** was, and so brod and long,   wild
So wel proporcioned to be strong,
Right as it were a sted of Lumbardye,
Therto so **horsly** and so quyk of **ye**   like a horse; eye
As it a gentil **Poyleys** courser were;   Apulian
For certes, fro his tayl unto his eere,   220
Nature ne art ne couthe him nought **amende**   improve
In no degre, as al the poeple **wende**;   understood
But evermore her **moste** wonder was   greatest
How that it couthe goon, and was of bras.
It was of **fayry**, as the people semed;   magic
Diverse peple diversly they **demed**.   various; judged
As many hedes as many **wittes** been –   ideas
They murmured as doth a swarm of **been**,   bees
And made **skiles** after her fantasies,   arguments
Rehersyng of the olde poetries,   telling   230
And seyden it was y-like the Pagase,[13]
The hors that hadde wynges for to **fle**,   fly
Or elles it was the Grekissche hors Synon,[14]
That broughte Troye to destruccioun,
As men may in the olde **gestes** rede.   histories
'Myn hert,' quod oon, 'is evermore **in drede**;   fearful
I **trow** som **men of armes** ben therinne,   believe; armed men
That **schapen hem** this cite for to wynne;   plan
It were good that such thing were knowe.'
Another **rowned** to his **falaw** lowe,   whispered; companion   240
And sayde, 'It lyth for it is rather lik
An apparence maad by som magyk
As jogelours playen at thise festes greet.'
Of sondry doutes thus they **jangle** and **trete**,   gossip; discuss
As lewed poeple demeth comunly

13 Pegasus, the flying horse of Greek mythology.
14 The wooden horse left by the Greeks as a gift-offering at Troy, full of armed men
   who opened the city gates and let the Greeks back inside to sack the city.

Of thynges that ben maad more subtily
Than they can in her **lewednes** comprehende;   ignorance
They deemen gladly to the badder ende.[15]
And som of hem wondred of the mirrour,
250 That born was up into the maister tour,
How men might in it suche thinges se.
Another answerd, and sayd it might wel be
Naturelly, by **composiciouns**   arrangements
Of angels, and of heigh reflexiouns,
And sayde that in Rome was such oon.
They speeke of Alceyt and Vitilyon,
Of Aristotle, that writen in her lyves[16]
Of queynte morrours and **prospectyves**   lenses
As knowen they that han her bokes herd;
260 And other folk have wondred on the swerd
That wolde passe thorughout everything,
And fel in speche of Telophus the kyng,
And of Achilles, for his queynte spere,
For he couthe with hit bothe hele and **dere**,[17]   harm
Right in such **wise** as men may with the swerd   a way
Of which right now ye have yourselven herd.
They speeken of sondry **hardyng** of metal,   hardening
And speken of medicines therwithal,
And how and whan it schulde harded be –
270 Which is unknowe **algat** unto me –   entirely
Tho speeken they of Canace's ryng,
And seyden all that such a wonder thing
Of craft of rynges herd they never noon,
Sauf that he Moyses and Kyng Salamon   except
Had a name of **connyng** in such art.   knowledge/skill
Thus seyen the peple on every part;
But natheles som seiden that it was
Wonder thing to make of ferne glas
And yit is glas nou**g**ht like **aisschen** of **ferne**,   ashes; ferns
280 But for they han y-knowen it so **ferne**.   from long ago

15 'they gladly think the worst'
16 Three writers on optics and the science of seeing.
17 In Greek mythology, Achilles' spear could heal the wound it made: with this
   spear he wounded Telophus.

Therfor cesseth her **ianglyng** and her wonder,	chattering
And sore wondred som of cause of thonder,	
On ebbe and flood, on **gossomer** and on myst,	gossamer/web
And on all thing, til that the cause is **wist**.	known
Thus janglen they, and **demen** and devyse,	consider
Til that the kyng gan fro his **bord** arise.	table

❧ Phebus hath loft the angel merydyonal,		
And yit ascendyng was a best roial		
The gentil Lyoun, with his Adryan,[18]		
Whan that this gentil kyng, this Cambynskan,		290
Ros fro his bord theras he sat ful hye.		
Biforn him goth ful lowde menstralcye		
Til he cam to his chambre of **parements**,	counsel chamber	
Theras ther were divers instruments,		
That is y-like an heven for to heere.		
Now dauncen lusty Venus' children deere		
For in the fissch her lady sat ful hey*ghe*,[19]		
And loketh on hem with a frendly eyye.		
This noble kyng is set upon his **trone**;	throne	
This straunge knight is **fet** to him ful sone,	fetched	300
And in the daunce he gan with Canace.		
Her is the revel and the jolyte,		
That is not able a dul man to devyse;		
He most have knowe love, and his servise,		
And ben a **festly** man, as freisch as May,	gay, as at festivals	
That schulde you **devyse** such array.	recount	
Who couthe telle you the forme of daunce		
So **uncouth**, and such a freische countinaunce,	unknown	
Such subtil lokyng of **dissimilynges**,	dissimulations	
For drede of jalous folk **apparceyvynges**?	perceptions	310
No man but Launcelet – and he is deed;[20]		
Therfore I passe over al this **lustyheed**.	virility	
I say no more, but in this jolynesse		

---

18 The sun has passed into the meridional angle (sector) of the sky, with Leo in the
  ascendant.
19 Those born under the sign of Venus dance because their zodiacal sign is high in
  the sign of Pisces (the fishes).
20 Lancelot, the lover of Guinevere in the Arthurian romances.

I **lete** hem til men to soper hem **dresse**;   leave; go
The styward **byt** the spices for to **hye**,   told; bring
And eek the wyn, in al this melodye.
These usschers and thes squyers ben agon;
The spices and the wyn is come anoon.
They **eet** and drank, and whan this had an ende,   ate
320   Unto the temple, as resoun was, they **wende**.   went
The servise doon, they soupen al by day;
What needeth you to rehersen her array?
Ech man **wot** wel that a kyng's feste   knew
Hath plente to the **lest** and to the **meste**,   least; greatest
And deyntees mo than ben in my knowyng.
At after-souper goth this noble kyng
To see this hors of bras, with al his **route**   company
Of lordes and of ladyes al aboute;
Swich wondryng was ther on this hors of bras
330   That **seth** this grete siege of Troye was,   since
Theras men wondred on an hors also –
Ne was ther such a wondryng as was **tho**.   then
But fynally the kyng asked the knight
The vertu of this courser, and the might,
And prayd him tellen of his **governaunce**.   how to control him
The hors anoon **gan** for to trippe and daunce   began
Whan the knight leyd hand upon his **rayne**,   rein
And sayde, 'Sir, ther is nomore to **sayne**,   say
But whan you lust to ryde anywhere,
340   Ye moote **trille a pyn stant in his ere**,   turn a pin in his ear
Which I schal telle you bitwen us two.
Ye moste **nempne** him to what place also,   tell
Or what countre you luste for to ryde,
And whan ye come **ther** you lust **abyde**,   where; stop
Bid him descende, and trille another pynne,
For therin lith th'efet of al the **gynne**,   mechanism
And he wol doun descend and do your wille,
And in that place he wol abyde stille.
Though al the world had the contrary swore,
350   He schal nat thennes be **y-throwe** ne **bore**.   thrown out; carried
Or if you lust to bid him **thennes** goon,   from there
Trill this pyn, and he wol vanyssh **anoon**   immediately
Out of the sight of every maner **wight**,   person

And come agein, be it by day or night,
Whan that you lust to **clepen** him agayn   call
In such a **gyse** as I schal yow sayn   manner
Betwixe you and me, and therfor soone;
Byd whan you lust, ther nys nomor to doone.'
Enformed when the kyng was of the knight,
And had **conceyved in his wit** aright   understood in his mind   360
The maner of the forme, and al this thing,
Ful glad and **blith** this noble, doughty, kyng,   happy
Repeyryng to his revel as biforn,   going back
The bridel is unto the tour y-born,
And kept among his jewels **leef** and deere.   beloved
The hors vanyscht – **I not in what menere** –   I don't know how
Out of her sight; ye get nomore of me,
But thus I **lete** him in his jolite,   leave
This Cambiskan, his lordes festyng,
Til wel neigh the day bigan to spryng.   370

Explicit prima pars

                                                    the first part ends

The **norice** of digestioun, the sleep,   nurse
Gan to him wynk, and bad of him take **keep**   care
That merthe and labour wol have his rest.
A **galpyng** mouth he him **keste**,   yawning; kissed
And sayd that it was tyme to lye doun,
For blood was in his dominacioun.[21]
'Cherischeth blood, nature's dame,' quod he.
They thankyn him, galpyng by two and thre,
And every wight gan drawe him to his rest,   380
As sleep hem bad; they took it for the best.
Her dremes schul not now be told for me;
Ful were here **heedes** of fumosite,[22]   heads
That causeth **drem** of which ther is no **charge**;   dreams; significance
They sleepen til it was **prime large**   nine o'clock (morning)
The moste part, **but it were** Canace;   except
Sche was ful **mesurable**, as wommen be,   moderate

---

21 A medical condition of the humours which had this drowsy effect.
22 Fumes (from the drink): they were bleary-eyed with the effects of much drinking.

For of hir fader hath sche take hir leve,
To go to reste, soon after it was eve.
390   Hir luste not **appalled** for to be,   pale
Ne on the morwe **unfestly** for to se;   cheerless
And kept hir firste sleep, and than awook,[23]
And such a joye sche in herte took
Bothe of her queynte ryng and hir myrrour,
That twenty tyme chaunged hir colour,
And in hir sleep, right for impressioun
Of hir myrrour, sche had a visioun;
Wherfor, **er** that the sonne up gan glyde,   before
Sche cleped upon hir **maistresse** beside,   governess
400   And sayde that hir **luste** for to **ryse**.   wanted; get up
These olde wommen that ben gladly wyse,
As is here maystresse, answered her anoon
And sayde, 'Madame, whider wold ye goon
Thus erly, for folk ben all in reste.'
'I wil,' quod sche, 'aryse, for me leste
No lenger for to slepe, and walke aboute.'
Hir maistres clepeth wommen, a gret route,
And up they risen, a ten **other** a twelve.   or
Up ryseth fresshe Canace hirselve,
410   As **rody** and bright as is the yonge sonne,   red(-cheeked)
That in the Ram is ten degrees y-ronne.[24]
No heiher was he, whan sche redy was,
And forth sche walked esily **a pas**,   slowly
Arayed after the lusty sesoun **soote**,   dressed for; sweet
Lightly for to play and walke on foote,
Nought but with fyve or six of hir **meyne**,   household
And in a **trench** fer in the park goth sche.   sunken path
The vapour which that of the erthe **glod**,   rose
Maketh the sonne seme **rody** and brood;   red
420   But natheles, it was so fair a sight
That it made all here hertes for to light,
What for the sesoun, what for the mornyng,
And for the **foules** that sche herde syng;   birds

23 Probably refers to the now-defunct habit of sleeping once, waking for a short
   time, then sleeping again – a 'second' sleep.
24 The sun has risen ten degrees in Aries (the Ram).

For right anoon sche **wiste** what they ment   knew
Right by here song, and knew al here entent.
The **knotte** why that every tale is told,   point
If that it be taryed til lust be cold
Of hem that han it after herkned yore,[25]
The **savour** passeth ever lenger the more   taste
For fulsomnes of the **prolixite**;   prolixity (precious speech)   430
And by this same resoun thinketh me
I schulde to the knotte condescende,[26]
And make of hir walkyng sone an ende.
Amyddes a tree, for **druye** as whit as chalk,   dryness
As Canace was pleyyng in hir walk,
Ther sat a **faukoun** over hir heed ful hye,   falcon
That al the woode **resowned of** hire cry,   resounded with
Beten hadde sche hirself so pitously
With bothe hir wynges, **to** the reede blood   till
Ran **endelong** the tree theras sche stood,   the length of   440
And ever in oon sche cried and sche **schryght**,   shrieked
And with hir **bek** hirselve so sche **pight**,   beak; pricked
That ther nys tigre non, ne cruel beste,
That dwelleth eyther in wood or in foreste,
That nold han wept if that he cowde
For sorw of hir, sche schright alwey so lowde;
For ther nas never yit no man **on lyve**,   alive
If that he couthe a faukoun **descrive**,   describe
That herd of such another of fairnesse,
As wel of plumage as of gentillesse,   450
Of schap, of al that might **y-rekened** be.   considered
A faukoun **peregryn** than semed sche   peregrine
Of **fremde** lond, and ever as sche stood   foreign
Sche swowned **now and now**, for lak of blood,   now and again
Til wel neigh sche falleth fro the tre.
This faire kyng's doughter, Canace,
That on hir fynger bar the queynte ryng,
Thurgh wich sche understood wel everything
That eny foul may in his **lydne** sayn,   language

25 'If the point of the story is delayed until everyone's desire to hear it has grown
   cold'
26 'I should get to the point'

460 And couthe answer him in his lydne agayn,
Hath understonde what the faukoun seyde,
And wel neigh almost for **rewthe** sche deyde,   pity
And to the tree sche goth ful hastily,
And on this faukoun loketh **pitously**,   full of pity
And held hir lappe abrod, for wel sche wist[27]
The faukoun moste falle fro the **twist**   branch
Whan that it swowned next, for lak of blood.
A long while to **wayten** hir sche stood,   wait for
Til atte last sche spak in this manere
470 Unto the hauk, as ye schul after heere:
'What is the cause, if it be for to telle,
That ye ben in that **furyall** peyne of helle?'   terrible
Quod Canace unto this hauk above,
'Is this for sorwe of deth, or elles love?
For, as I trowe, this ben causes tuo
That causen most a gentil herte wo.
Of other harm it needeth nou*gh*t to speke,
For ye yourself upon your elf **awreke**;   revenge
Which that **preveth** wel that either **ire** or **drede**   demonstrates; anger; fear
480 **Motte** ben **enchesoun** of your cruel dede,   must; reason
Sith that I se noon other wight you chace.
For love of God, so doth yourselve grace
Or what ben your helpe, for west ner est
Ne saugh I never er now no bryd ne beste
That **ferde with him self** so pitously –   treated himself
Ye sle me with your sorwe so. Verrily,
I have of you so gret compassioun –
For God's love, come fro the tree adoun,
And as I am a kyng's doughter trewe,
490 If that I verrayly the cause knewe
Of your **disese**, if it lay in my might,   unhappiness
I wold amenden it if that I might
Als wisly help me grete God of kynde,
And herbes schal I right y-nowe fynde
To helen with your hurtes hastyly.'
Tho schright this faukoun more pitously   then; shreiked
Than ever sche did, and fil to ground anoon,

27 She spread out her skirt to catch the bird in case it fell.

And lay **aswowne**, **deed** as eny stoon,	unconscious; dead
Til Canace hath in hir lap y-take	
Unto that tyme sche gan of swowne **slake**;	abate 500
And after that sche gan of swown **abreyde**,	recover
Right in hir hauk's **lydne** thus sche sayde,	language
'That pite renneth sone in gentil hert,	
Felyng his **similitude** in peynes smerte,	like
Y-proved alday as men may see	
As wel by werk as by **auctorite**;	(written) authority
For gentil herte **kepeth** gentillesse,	cares for
I see wel that ye have on my distresse	
Compassioun, my faire Canace,	
Of verray wommanly **benignite**,	kindness 510
That nature in your **principles** hath set;	nature
But for noon hope for to fare the bet,[28]	
But for to **obeye** unto your herte fre,	answer
And for to make other **war** by me,	beware
As by the whelp chastised in the lyoun,	
And for that cause and that conclusioun,	
Whiles that I have a **leyser** and a space,	leisure
Myn harm I wil confessen, er I **pace**.'	go
And whil sche ever of hir sorwe told,	
That other wept as sche to water wolde,	520
Til that the faucoun bad hir to be stille,	
And with a sighe thus sche sayd hir **tille**:	to
'Ther I was, allas! That ilke day,	
And fostred in a **roch** of marble gray,	rock
So tendrely that nothing **eyeld** me;	ailed
I **wiste not** what was adversite,	did not know
Til I couthe **flee** ful heigh under the sky.	fly
Tho dwelled a **tercelet** me **faste** by,	male falcon; close
That semed well of all gentillesse,	
Al were he ful of tresoun and falsnesse;	530
It was **y-wrapped** under humble cheere	covered
And under heewe of trouthe, in such manere,	
Under plesaunce and under besty peyne,	
That no wight **wende** that he couthe **feyne**,	knew; pretend

28 'Not in the hope of making things better . . . '

So deep in greyn he deyed his colours.
Right as a serpent **hut** him under floures   hides
Til he may see his tyme for to byte,
Right so this god of love, this ypocrite,
Doth so his **sermonys** and his observaunce,   speeches/sermons
540 Under subtil colour and aqueyntaunce
That **sowneth unto** gentilesse of love,   seems to be
As in a **thombe** is al the faire above,   tomb
And under is the **corps** – whiche that ye wot –   dead body
Such was this ipocrite bothe cold and hot,
And in this wise he served his entent,
That **sauf** the **feend** noon wiste what he ment;   except; devil
Til he so long had weped and compleyned,
And many a yeer his service to me feyned,
Til that myn hert to pitous and to nyce,
550 Al innocent of his crouned malice
For fered of his deth, as thoughte me
Upon his othes and his **sewerte**,   security
Graunted him love on this condicioun,
That evermo myn honour and my renoun
Were saved, both **privy and apert**;   in private and in public
That is to sayn, that after his **desert**   deserving
I gaf him al myn hert and al my thought
God woot and he; that other wyse nought –
And took his hert in chaunge of myn for **ay**;   ever
560 But soth is sayd, go sithens many a day,[29]
'A trew wight and a theef thenketh no*ugh*t oon'.
And when he saugh the thyng so fer y-goon,
That graunted him fully my love,
In such a wyse as I have sayd above,
And geven him my trewe hert as fre
As he swor that he yaf his herte to me,
Anon this tigre, ful of **doublenesse**,   deceit
Fil on his knees with so gret devoutenesse,
With so high reverence, and as by his **chere**   manner
570 So lyk a gentil lover of manere,
So ravysched as it semeded for joye

29 'and has been many a day'

That never Jason ne Parys of Troye – [30]
Jason, certes, ne noon other man
Sith Lameth was, that **altherfrist** bygan   at first
To loven two, as writen folk biforn –
Ne never sith the firste man was born,
Ne couthe man by twenty thousand part
Contrefete the **sophemes** of his art;   learned arguments
Ne were worthy to unbokel his **galoche**,   boot
Ther doublenes of **feynyng** schold approche.   pretence   580
Ne so couthe thankyn a knight as he did me;
His maner was an heven for to see
To eny womman, were sche never so wys,
So **peynteth** he, and **kembeth poynt devys**[31]
As wel his wordes as his **continaunce**,   face
And I so loved him for his obeisaunce,
And for the trouthe I **demed** in his herte;   thought to be
That is so were that eny thing him smerte[32]
Al were it never so litel, and I it wist,
Me thought I felte deth at myn hert twist.   590
And schortly, **so ferforth this thing went**,   as this thing went on
That my wil was his will's instrument;
This is to say, my wille obeyed his wille
In all thing, as fer as resoun **fille**,   allowed
Kepyng the **boundes** of my worschip ever.   boundaries
Ne never had I thing so leef ne **lever**   more loved
As him, God woot, ne never schal nomo.
This **laste** lenger than a yeer or two,   lasted
That I supposed of him nought but good;
But fynally atte laste thus it stood   600
That fortune wolde that he moste **twynne**   depart
Out of the place which that I was inne.
Wher me was wo, it is no questioun –
I can nat make of it descripcioun –
For **o** thing dar I telle boldely;   one

30 Famous lovers of Greek mythology. Jason was helped by Medea to win the
   Golden Fleece for love, Paris's love for Helen led to the destruction of Troy.
   Lameth had two wives, in Genesis 4:19–23.
31 painted; combed/groomed very carefully
32 'if anything caused him pain'

I know what is the peyne of deth therby.
Which harm I felt; for he ne mighte **byleve**.   stay
So on a day of me he took his leve
So sorwful eek, that I **went** verrayly   believed
610 That he had feled als moche as I,
Whan that I herd him speke and saugh his **hewe**;   colour
But **natheles**, I thought he was untrewe,   nevertheless
And eek that he schulde **repeire** ageyn   come back
Withinne a litel while, **soth to seyn**,   truth to tell
And resoun **wold** eek that he moste go,   dictated
For his honour, as oft **happeth** so.   happens
Than I made vertu of necessite
And took it wel, **sethens** it moste be,   since
As I best might, I had for him my sorwe,
620 And took him by the hand, Seint John **to borwe**,   as surety
And sayde thus: 'Lo, I am your al.
Beth such as I have be to you, and schal.'
What he answerd, it needeth nat to reherse;
Who can best say than he who can do werse?
Whan he hath al wel sayd, than hath he doon –
Therfor **bihoveth** him a ful long spoon   needs
That schal ete with a **feend**, thus herd I say.   devil
So atte last he moste forth his way,
And forth he fleeth til he cam ther him **leste**.   wanted
630 Whan it cam him to purpos for to reste,
I **trow** he hadde **thilke** text in mynde,   believe; that same
That alle thing, **repeyryg** to his **kynde**   returning; nature
Gladeth himself; thus seyn men, as I gesse –
Men loven **of kynde newefangilnesse**,   by nature; novelties
As **briddes** doon that men in cage feede;   birds
For **theigh** thou night and day take of hem **heede**   though; care
And straw her cage faire, and soft as silk,
And geve hem sugre, hony, breed and mylk;
Ye, right anoon as his dore is uppe,
640 He with his feet wil **sporne** doun his cuppe . . .   kick
And to the wode he **wole** and wormes ete   wishes (to go)
So **newfangel** be they of hir mete   liking new things
And loven **novelrie** of **propre kynde**,   new things; of their very nature
No gentillesse of blood may hem bynde.
So ferde this tercelet, allas the day!

Tho he were gentil born, fressh and gay,
And goodlich for to seen, humble and free,
He saugh upon a tyme a kyte flee,   fly
And sodeynly he loved this kyte so
That al his love is clene from me ago,   650
And hath his trouth falsed in this wyse:
Thus hath the kyte my love in hir servyse,
And I am lorn, withouten remedye.   lost
And with that word this faucon gan to crie,
And swowned eft in Canace's barm.   often; lap
Greet was the sorwe for the haukes harm,
That Canacee and all hir women made;
They wist how they myghte the faucon glade,   wondered
But Canacee hom bereth hir in hir lappe   home
And softely in plastres gan hir wrappe.   bandages   660
Theras she with hir beek hadde hurt herselve
Now kan nat Canacee but herbes delve
Out of the grounde, and make salves newe
Of herbes preciouse and fyne of hewe.   colour
To heelen with this fro day to nyght
She dooth hir bisynesse and hire fulle myght,   work/best
And by hir beddes heed she made a mewe,   bird cage/enclosure
And covered it with velvetes blewe,   velvet
In signe of trouthe that is in women sene
And al withoute the mewe is peynted grene,
In which there were ypeynted all thise false fowles,   670
As beth thise tidyves, tercelettes and owles,   small birds; male falcons
Right for despit were peynted hem bisyde
And pyes, on hem for to crie and chyde.   magpies
Thus lete I Canace hir hauk kepying   leave
I wol namoore as now speke of hir ryng,
Til it come eft to purpos for to seyn,
How that this faucon gat hir love ageyn,
Repentant, as the storie telleth us,
By mediacion of Cambalus,
The kynges son of which I yow tolde,   680
But hennesforth I wol my proces hold,
To speken of aventures and of batailles,
That never yet was herd so grete mervailles.
First wol I telle yow of Cambyuskan,

That in his tyme many a citee wan
And after wol I speke of Algarsif,
How that he wan Theodera to his wif,
For whom ful often in greet peril he was,
Ne had he be helpen by the steede of bras.
690 And after wol I speke of Cambalo,
That faughte in lystes with the bretheren two
For Canacee er that he myghte hir wynne,
An **ther** I lefte I wol ageyn bigynne   where

Explicit seconda pars

Incipit pars tertia

❦ Appollo whirleth up his **chaar** so hye   chariot
Til that the god Mercurius hous, the slye
. . .

Heer Folwen the wordes of the Frankelyn to the aquier – and the Wordes of the hoost to the Frankeleyn

700 ❦ 'In feith, Squier, thow hast thee wel yquit,
and gentilly I preise wel thy wit,'
Quod the frenkeleyn, 'consideryng thy yowthe,
So feelyngly thou spekest, sire, I allowethe.
As to my **doom**, ther is noon that is heere,   judgement
Of eloquence that shal be thy **peere**.   equal
If that thou lyve, god yeve thee good chaunce,
And in vertu sende thee coninuance;
For of thy speche I have greet **deyntee** . . .   pleasure
I have a sone, and by the trinitee,
710 I hadde **lever** than twenty pound worth lond   rather
Though it right now were fallen in myn hond,
He were a man of swich discrecion,
As that ye been, fy on possession!
But if a man be vertuous withal,
I have my sone **snybbed**, and yet shal,   chided/told off
For he to vertu listeth nat entende,
But but for to pleye at **dees**, and to **despende**,   dice; spend
And lese al that he hath is his **usage**,   custom

And he hath lever talken with a page
Than to commune with any gentil **wight**,   person/man   720
Where he mighe lerne gentillesse aright.'
'Straw for your gentillesse!' quod oure hoost,
'What, frankeleyn, pardee, sire! Well thou **woost**,   know
That ech of yow **moot** tellen at leste   must
A tale or two, or breken his biheste.'
'That know I wel sire,' quod the frankeleyn,
'I prey yow haveth me nat in desdeyn,
Though to this man I speke a word or two.'
'Telle on thy tale, withouten wordes mo.'
'Gladly, sire hoost,' quod he, 'I wole obeye   730
Unto youre wyl, now herkeneth what I seye.
I wol yow nat **contrarien** in no wyse.   gainsay
As fer as that my wittes wol suffyse,
I prey to god that it may plesen yow,
Than **woot** I wel that it is good **ynow**.'   know; enough

THE FRANKLIN'S PROLOGUE AND TALE

The franklin says that his tale will be a Breton lay. He excuses himself for his 'rude'speech and for his lack of knowledge of rhetorical devices.

Arveragus, a knight, marries Dorigen, a lady of higher status than himself, for love. They agree that their marriage will be an equal partnership, but in public Dorigen will appear to defer to Arveragus (in order to be socially acceptable and agreeable). They are very happy, but after a while, Arveragus goes away on campaign to prove his worth, leaving Dorigen alone and distraught. In her fear and anguish, she imagines accidents which could happen to Arveragus's ship when he returns, and wishes the rocks on the Breton coast did not exist. Her friends, in order to 'take her mind off' these forebodings, persuade her to go to a dance with them. Here Dorigen's neighbour, the noble knight Aurelius, declares his love for her. She rejects his suit, saying that she could only accept him if he could make the rocks on the coast disappear. Aurelius's brother, seeing Aurelius in despair, takes him to meet a clerk he knows at Orleans, who is expert in all kinds of illusory magic. The clerk offers to make the rocks seem to disappear in return for a thousand pounds, and Aurelius agrees. The clerk does his magic, and the rocks appear to have gone. Dorigen is hysterical, as she must now keep her word, and she considers suicide. When Arveragus returns, he says that Dorigen must keep her word, but must never tell anyone of it. She goes to meet Aurelius, but filled with pity for her, and with admiration for Arveragus's selflessness, he releases her from her bargain. The clerk then releases Aurelius from his payment. The franklin asks, 'Who was the most generous?'

Breton 'lais' were popular in English translations from at least the early fourteenth century, although they were read in French before this, and were transmitted both orally and in written form. Some, for example the early fourteenth-century English *Sir Orfeo*, claim to have been originally produced and delivered by minstrels. They are tales of love and adventure, often with a Celtic background of mystery and/or magic. One of the characteristic themes of the Breton lay is that of 'trewthe'. In legal terms, this was not evidential truth, but the value of a person's word on oath. Another theme is that of marriage and relationships, especially within families. This story hinges on the nature of marriage and the keeping of one's word.

The story opens with a description of the nature of the marriage between Dorigen and Arveragus. Both agree that this will be a partnership, in which both will have equal status. This is, in effect, the ideal marriage, which is then tested to the uttermost by Dorigen's rash promise. It may be questioned whether this ideal marriage can exist at all, but its (fated) collapse is mirrored by Dorigen's loss of her sanity and composure. She is distraught at the absence of her husband (he is the one in motion, she must remain behind), and she is reduced to near madness by the fulfilment of her conditions and the knowledge that she must surrender her body to Aurelius or be accused of breaking her word. This puts her entirely into the power of her husband, a reversal of the position at the beginning of the tale, where she lowered herself to marry him. The partnership no longer exists by the end of the story; the power has all been surrendered to the man. Arveragus sends Dorigen to be raped by a man she does not want to touch her, and it is Aurelius's generosity, at his own expense, which saves her from her fate. Why did she give the promise at all?

There are no unsympathetic characters in this story, because they all act out of the best of motives. Even Aurelius, who could be portrayed as a villain, is actually a noble squire, of the same social status as Dorigen, and although he does not have the maturity of Arveragus, he is arguably more worthy (in social terms) of her affection than the upstart Arveragus. He follows the rules of courtly love implicitly, his only questionable act being his reliance on the dubious practices of the clerk of Orleans. His brother acts out of pity for Aurelius's condition, and the clerk also is simply making a living while trying to be of service to a friend. Arveragus, like the pilgrimage knight, pursues the ideals of his knightly class, and tries to enhance his reputation. It could be argued that he is blameworthy in leaving Dorigen alone, although the knightly ideal itself could also be seen to be at fault here.

On being apprised of the situation, Arveragus's first concern is with the effect on his reputation, rather than his wife's predicament. He sends her to meet her fate, from which Aurelius, not Arveragus, frees her. They then live happily ever after. Aurelius, Arveragus and Dorigen are trapped within the ethos of chivalry and courtly love, which decrees that a woman who says no is simply being 'daungerous', so the lover must try harder. In other words, 'no' actually means 'perhaps'. Under these conditions, it is impossible for Dorigen to say 'no' and be believed. This may be why she feels the need to add another, seemingly impossible condition, to underline the fact that she really does *not* want to commit adultery with

Aurelius. He is bound not to accept the negative, and so the impossible is made to happen. Dorigen is then trapped by the code of chivalry and courtly love, which dictates that one's word must never be broken. It is Aurelius who breaks the stranglehold by releasing her, which then prompts the clerk to release him. In other words, the characters are all trapped within the nature of their own narrative. Dorigen and Arveragus resemble January in that they are living in a romance 'dreamworld' of love, and fail to see how this affects others in the 'real' world. Courtly love is stripped down and revealed for what it is, a fiction, which hides less attractive desires and acts. The happy couple are forced to consider their relationship in 'ernest', rather than as 'game', and in doing so they see its true worth.

At the end of the story, the franklin poses a question for his audience, and Chaucer's audience, to discuss. Who was the more generous? The problem for Dorigen is that generosity requires freedom, and she has none. It is only the men who have the power to exercise generosity, while the woman is reduced to the status of object.

Key Questions

What does this story have to say about relations between the sexes? What does it reveal, or claim, about chivalry and courtly love? Is anyone to blame for the situation in which the characters find themselves?

What is the function of magic and fantasy in the tale?

Does the franklin's undefined social status, wealthy and gentil but not noble, help him in this situation, and does his tale reveal anything of this?

Topic Keywords

Romance as genre/ breton lais/ knighthood and chivalry/ courtly love/ magic and experimental science/ medieval society and the franklin

Further Reading

Elizabeth Archibald, 'The Breton Lay in Middle English Genre: Transmission and The Franklin's Tale', in *Medieval Insular Romance: Translation and Innovation*, edited and introduced by Judith Weiss, edited by Jennifer Fellows and Morgan Dickson, Cambridge, D. S. Brewer, 2000, pp. 55–70

Dominique Battles, 'Chaucer's Franklin's Tale and Boccaccio's *Filocolo* Reconsidered', *Chaucer Review*, 34, 1999, pp. 38–59

Paul Battles, 'Magic and Metafiction in The Franklin's Tale: Chaucer's Clerk of Orléans as Double of the Franklin', in *Marvels, Monsters, and Miracles: Studies in the Medieval and Early Modern Imaginations*, edited by Timothy S. Jones and David A. Sprunger, Kalamazoo, MI, Medieval Institute Publications, 2002, pp. 243–66

Mary Bowman, 'Half As She Were Mad: Dorigen in the Male World of The Franklin's Tale', *Chaucer Review*, 27, 1993, pp. 239–51

Carole Koepke Brown, ' "It is true art to conceal art": The Episodic Structure of Chaucer's Franklin's Tale', *Chaucer Review*, 27, 1992, pp. 162–85

Neil Cartlidge, ' "Nat that I chalange any thyng of right": Love, Loyalty, and Legality in The Franklin's Tale', in *Writings on Love in the English Middle Ages*, edited by Helen Cooney, Basingstoke and New York, Palgrave Macmillan, 2006, pp. 115–30

Carolyn Collette, 'Seeing and Believing in the Franklin's Tale', *Chaucer Review*, 26, 1992, pp. 395–410

Susan Crane, 'The Franklin as Dorigen', *Chaucer Review*, 24, 1990, pp. 236–52

Craig R. Davis, 'A Perfect Marriage on the Rocks: Geoffrey and Philippa Chaucer, and The Franklin's Tale', *Chaucer Review*, 37, 2002, pp. 129–44

Sheila Delany, 'Difference and the Difference it Makes: Sex and Gender in Chaucer's Poetry', in *A Wyf Ther Was: Essays in Honour of Paule Mertens-Fonck*, edited by Juliette Dor, Liège, Univérsite de Liège, 1992, pp. 103–11

Robert R. Edwards, 'Rewriting Menedon's Story: *Decameron* x, 5 and The Franklin's Tale', in *The Decameron and the Canterbury Tales*, edited by Leonard Michael Koff and Brenda Deen Schildgen, Madison, NJ, Fairleigh Dickinson University Press; London and Toronto, Associated University Presses, 2000, pp. 226–46

John Finlayson, 'Invention and Disjunction: Chaucer's Rewriting of Boccaccio in The Franklin's Tale', *English Studies (The Netherlands)*, 89, 2008, pp. 385–402

Timothy Flake, 'Love, Troth and the Happy Ending of The Franklin's Tale', *English Studies*, 77, 1996, pp. 209–26

Cynthia Gravlee, 'Presence, Absence and Difference: Reception and Deception in The Franklin's Tale', in *Desiring Discourse: The Literature of Love, Ovid through Chaucer*, edited and introduced by James Paxson and edited by Cynthia Gravlee, Selinsgrove, PA, Susquehanna University Press, 1998, pp. 177–87

Nina Manasan Greenberg, 'Dorigen as Enigma: The Production of Meaning and The Franklin's Tale', *Chaucer Review*, 33, 1999, pp. 329–49

Kurtis B. Haas, 'The Franklin's Tale and the Medieval Trivium: A Call for Critical Thinking', *Journal of English and Germanic Philology*, 106, 2007, pp. 45–63

Cathy Hume, ' "The name of Soveraynetee": The Private and Public Faces of Marriage in The Franklin's Tale', *Studies in Philology*, 105, 2008, pp. 284–303

Angela M. Lucas, ' "But if a man be vertuous withal": Has Aurelius in Chaucer's Franklin's Tale "lerned gentillesse aright"?', in *Studies in Late Medieval and Early Renaissance Texts in Honour of John Scattergood: 'The Key of all Good Remembrance'*, edited by Anne Marie D'Arcy and Alan J. Fletcher, Dublin and Portland, OR, Four Courts Press, 2005, pp. 181–200

Sandra McEntire, 'Illusions and Interpretation in The Franklin's Tale', *Chaucer Review*, 31, 1996, pp. 145–63

Francine McGregor, 'What of Dorigen? Agency and Ambivalence in The Franklin's Tale', *Chaucer Review*, 31, 1997, pp. 365–78

Steele Nowlin, 'Between Precedent and Possibility: Liminality, Historicity and Narrative in Chaucer's The Franklin's Tale', *Studies in Philology*, 103, 2006, pp. 47–67

Carol Pulham, 'Promises, Premises: Dorigen's Dilemma Revisited', *Chaucer Review*, 31, 1996, pp. 76–86

Anne Scott, ' "Considerynge the beste on every syde": Ethics, Empathy and Epistemology in The Franklin's Tale', *Chaucer Review*, 29, 1995, pp. 390–415

Barrie Strauss, 'Truth and Woman in Chaucer's Franklin's Tale', *Exemplaria*, 4, 1992, pp. 135–68

Mark N. Taylor, 'Servant and Lord/Lady and Wife: The Franklin's Tale and Traditions of Courtly and Conjugal Love', *Chaucer Review*, 32, 1997, pp. 64–81

Warren S. Walker, 'Extant Analogues of The Franklin's Tale in the Turkish Oral Tradition', *Chaucer Review*, 33, 1999, pp. 432–7

Colin Wilcockson, 'Thou and Tears: The Advice of Arveragus and Dorigen in Chaucer's Franklin's Tale', *Review of English Studies*, 54, 2003, pp. 308–12

❦ Olde **gentil Britons**, in hir dayes,   noble; Bretons
Of **diverse aventures** maden layes,[1]   various happenings
Rymeyed in hir firste Briton tonge;   rhymed
Whiche layes, with hir instruments, they songe,
Or ellis **redden** hem for hire **plesaunce**;   read; pleasure
And oon of hem have I in remembraunce,
Which I shal seyn with good wyl, as I kan;
But, sires, bycause I am a **burel** man,   unlettered
At my bigynnyng first I yow **biseche**,   beg
Have excused of my **rude** speche;   unlearned   10
I lerned nevere rethorik, certeyn –[2]
Thyng that I speke, it **moot** be **bare** and pleyn –   must; unadorned
I sleepe nevere in the Mount of Parnaso,[3]
Ne lerned Marcus Tullius Scithero;[4]
Colours ne knowe I none, withouten drede,   rhetorical 'tricks'
But **swiche** colours as growen in the **mede**,   such; meadow
Or ellis swiche as men dye or peynte;
Colours of rethoryk, they ben too **queynte** –   devices; skilful
My spirit feeleth nat of swich matere,
But if yow **list** my tale shul ye heere.   like   20

❦ In **Armorik**, that called is **Britayne**,   Armorica; Brittany
Ther was a knyght that lovede, and dide his payne
To serve a lady in his beste wise,
And many a labour, many a gret **emprise**,   enterprise
He for his lady wroghte **er** she were wonne;   before
For she was oon the faireste under sonne,
And eek therto come of so **heigh kynrede**   noble family
That wel **unnethes** dorste this knyght for **drede**   hardly; fear
Telle hire his wo, his peyne, and his distresse;
But atte laste she, **for** his worthynesse,   because of   30

---

1 The lai – a form of poetic, romance narrative, originally oral in transmission
   (sung or spoken by minstrels).
2 Rhetoric; the art of public speaking – and of writing poetry.
3 Parnassus, the mountain of the Muses.
4 Wrote books on rhetoric.

And namely for his meke **obeysance**,   obedience
Hath **swich** a pitee caught of his penance   such
That prively she **fel of his acord**,   agreed with him
To taken hym for hir housbonde and hir lord.
Of swich lordshipe as men han over hir wyves,
And for to lede the moore in blisse hir lyves,
Of his fre wyl he swoor hire as a knyght
That nevere in al his lyf he, day ne nyght,
Ne sholde upon hym take no **maistrye**   superiority/sovreignty
40 Agayn hir wyl, ne **kithe** hire jalousye,   show
But hire obeye and folwe hir wyl in al,
As any lovere to his lady shal,
Save that the name of soveraynetee,
That wolde he have, for shame of his **degree**.   station (in life)
She thonked hym, and with ful gret humblesse
She seyde, 'Sire, **sith** of youre gentilesse   since
Ye **profre** me to have so large a reyne,[5]   offer
Ne wolde nevere God **bitwix** us **tweyne**   between; two
As in my gilt, were **outher** werre or stryf.[6]   either
50 Sire, I wol be youre humble, trewe, wyf.
Have heer my **trouthe**, til that myn herte breste.   word
Thus been they bothe in quiete and in reste;
For **o** thyng, Sires, **saufly** dar I seye,   one; safely
That freendes **everich** oother **moote** obeye   each; must
If they wol longe holden compaignye –
Love wol nat be **constreyned** by maistrye.   restricted
Whan maistrie comth, the god of love anon
Beteth his wynges and, 'Farwel!' he is gon.
Love is a thyng, as any spirit free;
60 Wommen **of kynde** desiren libertee,   by nature
And nat to been constreyned as a **thral** –   servant
And so doon men, if I **sooth** seyn shal.   truth
Looke who that moost is pacient in love,
He is at his avantage al above.
Pacience is an heigh vertu, certeyn,
For it **venquysseth**, as thise clerkes seyn,   overcomes
Thynges that **rigour** sholde nevere atteyne;   might

5 'so wide a scope'
6 'if I betrayed you'

For every word men may nat chide or pleyne –
Lerneth to suffre or ellis, so moot I gon,
Ye shul it lerne, **wherso** ye **wole** or non.   whether; will   70
For in this world certeyn ther no **wight** is,   person
That he ne dooth or seith som tyme **amys**;   wrong
Ire, siknesse or **constellacioun**,   working of the heavens
Wyn, wo, or chaungyng of **complexioun**   wine; temperament
Causeth ful ofte to doon amys, or speken –
On every wrong a man may nat be **wreken**.   avenged
After the tyme moste be temperaunce,   as befits the time
To every wight that **kan on** governaunce;   knows about
And therfore hath this wise, worthy knyght
To lyve in ese, **suffraunce** hire **bihight**,   tolerance; promised   80
And she to hym ful wisly **gan** to swere   began
That nevere sholde ther be **defaute** in here.   fault

Here may men seen an humble, wys **acord**;   agreement
Thus hath she take hir servant and hir lord –
Servant in love, and lord in mariage;
Thanne was he bothe in lordshipe and servage.
Servage, nay – but in lordshipe above,
Sith he hath bothe his lady and his love.
His lady, certes, and his wyf also,
The which that lawe of love acordeth to;   90
And whan he was in this prosperitee,
Hom with his wyf he gooth to his contree.
Nat fer fro Pedmark, ther his dwellyng was,[7]
Wheras he lyveth in blisse and in solas.
Who koude telle, but he hadde wedded be,
The joye, the ese, and the prosperitee
That is bitwix an housbonde and his wyf?
A yeer and moore lasted this blisful lyf,
Til that the knyght of which I speke of thus,
That of Kairrud was **clepid** Arveragus,[8]   called   100
Shoope hym to goon and dwelle a yeer or twayne
In Engelond, that **clepid was ek** Britayne,   was also called
To seke in armes worshipe and honour,

7 Pedmarch, an area on the Breton coast.
8 'Kairrud' is meant to be a Breton place-name.

For al his **lust** he sette in swich labour,   desire
And dwelled ther two yeer; the book seith thus.
Now wol I **stynte** of this Arveragus,   stop (talking about)
And speke I wole of Dorigene, his wyf,
That loveth hir housbonde as hir hert's lyf.
For his absence wepeth she and **siketh**,   sighs
110 As doon thise noble wyves, whan hem liketh.
She moorneth, waketh, waileth, fasteth, **pleyneth**;   complains
Desir of his presence hir so **destreyneth**   weighs heavy on
That al this wide world she set at noght.
Hir freendes, whiche that knowe hir hevy thoght,
Conforten hire in al that ever they may.
They **prechen** hire, they telle hire nyght and day   preach to
That causelees she sleeth hirself, allas!
And every confort possible in this cas
They doon to hire, with al hir bisynesse,[9]
120 Al for to make hire leve hir hevynesse.
By **proces**, as ye knowen **everichoon**,   degrees; everyone
Men may so longe **graven** in a stoon   carve
Til som figure therinne **emprinted** be;   carved
So longe han they conforted hire, til she
Receyved hath, by hope and by resoun,
The emprintyng of hir consolacioun;
Thurgh which hir grete sorwe gan **aswage**;   lessen
She may nat alwey **duren** in swich rage.   last/carry on
And eek Arveragus, in al this care,
130 Hath sent hire lettres hom of his welfare,
And that he wole come hastily agayn,
Or ellis hadde this sorwe hir herte slayn.
Hire freendes sawe hir sorwe gan to **slake**,   abate
And preyde hire on knees, for God's sake,
To come and romen hire in compaignye,
Awey to dryve hir derke fantasye;
And finally she graunted that requeste,
For wel she saw that it was for the beste.
Now stood hir castel faste by the see,
140 And often with hir freendes walketh she,

9 'as best they can'

Hir to disporte up on the bank an heigh,
Wheras she many a shipe and barge **seigh**,   saw
Seillynge hir cours, wheras hem **liste** go;   sailing; want to
But thanne was that a parcel of hir wo,
For of hirself ful ofte, 'Allas!' seith she,
'Is ther no shipe, of so manye as I se,
Wol bryngen hom my lord? Thanne were myn herte
Al **warisshed** of hise bittre peynes smerte.'   cured
Another tyme there wolde she sitte and thynke,
And caste hir eyen downward fro the **brynke**;   cliff edge   150
But whan she seigh the grisly rokkes blake,
For verray fere so wolde hir herte quake
That on hir feet she myghte hir noght **sustene**.   keep
Thanne wolde she sitte adoun upon the grene,
And pitously into the see biholde,
And seyn right thus, with sorweful **sikes** colde: sighs
'Eterne God, that thurgh thy **purveiance**   providence
Ledest the world, by certeyn governance –
In ydel, as men seyn, ye nothyng make –   for no useful purpose
But Lord, thise grisly, feendly rokkes blake,   160
That semen rather a foul confusioun
Of werk, than any fair creacioun
Of swich a parfit, wys God and a stable –
Why han ye wroght this werk **unresonable**?   irrational
For by this werk south, north, ne west, ne est,
Ther nys **yfostred** man, ne bryd, ne beest.   benefited
It doth no good to my wit, but anoyeth.
Se ye nat, Lord, how mankynde it destroyeth?
An hundred thousand bodies of mankynde
Han rokkes slayn, al be they nat **in mynde**;   remembered   170
Which mankynde is so fair part of thy werk,
That thow it madest lyk to thyn owen **merk**.   image
Thanne semed it ye hadde a greet **chiertee**   benevolence
Toward mankynde, but how thanne may it be
That ye swiche **menes** make it to destroyen,   means
Whiche menes do no good, but evere anoyen?
 I woot wel clerkes wol seyn as hem leste,
By arguments, that al is for the beste;
Thogh I ne kan the causes nat y-knowe,
But thilke God that made wynd to blowe,   180

As kepe my lord, this my conclusioun –
To clerkes **lete** I al **disputisoun** – [10]
But wolde God that alle thise rokkes blake
Were sonken into helle for his sake;
Thise rokkes sleen myn herte for the feere!'
Thus wolde she seyn, with many a pitous teere.
Hir freendes sawe that it was no **disport**   entertainment/fun
To romen by the see, but disconfort,
And **shopen** for to pleyen somwher ellys.   decided
190   They leden hire by ryvers and by wellys,
And eek in othere places **delitables**;   pleasant
They dauncen and they pleyen at **ches** and **tables**.   chess; backgammon
So on a day, right in the **morwe tyde**,   morning time
Unto a gardyn that was ther bisyde,
In which that they hadde **maad hir ordinance**   arranged
Of **vitaille** and of oother **purveiance**,   food and drink; needs
They goon and pleye hem al the longe day –
And this was on the sixte morwe of May,
Which May hadde peynted with his softe **shoures**,   showers
200   This gardyn ful of leves and of floures,
And craft of man's hond so curiously
Arrayed hadde this gardyn, trewely,
That nevere was ther gardyn of swich **prys**,   value
But if it were the verray paradys.
The odour of floures and the fresshe sighte
Wolde han maked any herte lighte
 That evere was born, but if to greet siknesse
Or to greet sorwe helde it in destresse –
So ful it was of beautee, with plesaunce.
210   At after dyner gonne they to daunce
And synge also, save Dorigen allone,
Which made alwey hir compleynt and hir mone,
For she ne saugh hym on the daunce go,
That was hir housbonde and hir love also;
But **nathelees** she moste a tyme **abyde**,   nevertheless; wait
And with good hope lete hir sorwe **slyde**.   subside
Upon this daunce, amonges othere men,
Daunced a squier bifore Dorigen,

10 leave; scholarly disputation

That fressher was and jolier of **array**   appearance
As to my **doom**, than is the monthe of May.   judgement   220
He syngeth, daunceth, **passyng** any man   surpassing
That is or was, sith that the world bigan.
Therwith he was, if men sholde hym **discryve**,   describe
Oon of the **beste farynge** man on lyve;   best looking
Yong, strong, right vertuous, and riche and wys,
And wel biloved, and **holden in gret prys**;   highly valued
And shortly, if the **sothe** I tellen shal,   truth
Unwityng of this Dorigen at al,   unknown to
This lusty squier, servant to Venus,
Which that **y-clepid** was Aurelius,   called   230
Hadde loved hire best of any creature
Two yeer and moore, as was his aventure;
But nevere dorste he tellen hire his grevance.
Withouten coppe he drank al his penance – [11]
He was **despeyred**, no thyng **dorste** he seye,   in despair; dare
Save in his songes somwhat wolde he **wreye**   except; let slip
His wo, as in a general compleynyng.
He seyde he lovede and was biloved nothyng;
Of which matere made he many layes,
Songes, compleyntes, roundels, vyrelayes,[12]   240
How that he dorste nat his sorwe telle,
But langwissheth as a furye dooth in helle;
And dye he moste, he seyde, as dide Ekko,[13]
For Narcisus that dorste nat telle hir wo.
In oother manere than ye heere me seye,
Ne dorste he nat to hire his wo **biwreye**,   reveal
Save that **paraventure** somtyme at daunces,   perhaps
Ther yong folk kepen hir observaunces,
It may wel be he looked on hir face
In swich a wise as man that asketh grace –   250
But nothyng **wiste** she of his entente.   knew
Nathelees it happed, er they **thennes** wente,   nevertheless; from there
Bycause that he was hir neghebour,

11 'he drank all his misery without a cup', that is, he was in great pain.
12 songs complaining about love (compleyntes), songs with refrains/choruses
   (roundels), and more of the same (virelayes).
13 Echo wasted away for love of Narcissus, who loved himself.

And was a man of worshipe and honour,
And hadde y-knowen hym of tyme yoore,[14]
They fille in speche, and forth moore and moore
Unto this purpos drough Aurelius,
And whan he saugh his tyme he seyde thus:
'Madame,' quod he, 'by God that this world made,
260 So that I wiste it myghte youre herte glade,
I wolde that day that youre Arveragus
Wente over the see, that I Aurelius
Hadde went ther – nevere I sholde have come agayn,
For well woot my servyce is in vayn;
My **gerdon** is but **brestyng** of myn herte –   reward; bursting
Madame, **reweth** upon my peynes **smerte**,   have pity; intense
For with a word ye may me **sle** or save –   kill
Here at youre feet, God wolde that I were grave.
I ne have as now no **leyser** moore to seye;   opportunity
270 Have mercy, swete, or ye wol **do me deye**!'   cause my death
She gan to looke upon Aurelius:
'Is this youre wil?' quod she, 'and sey ye thus?'
'Nevere **erst**,' quod she, 'ne **wiste** I what ye mente – before; knew
But now, Aurelie, I knowe youre entente.
By thilke God that yaf me soule and lyf,
Ne shal I nevere been untrewe a wyf
In word, ne werk – as fer as I have wyt
I wol been hys to whom þat I am knyt;
Taak this for fynal as of me.'[15]
280 But after that, **in pleye**, thus seyde she: jokingly
'Aurelie,' quod she, 'by heighe God above,
Yet wolde I graunte yow to been youre love,
Syn I yow se so pitously complayne:
Looke what day that **endelong** Britayne   the length and breadth of
Ye remoeve alle the rokkes, stoon by stoon,
That they ne **lette** shipe ne boot to goon.   hinder
 I seye, whan ye han maad the coost so clene
Of rokkes that ther nys no stoon **y-sene**,   to be seen
Thanne wol I love yow best of any man –
290 Have heer my trouthe, in al that evere I kan.'

14 'she'd known him for a long time'
15 'this is my last word on the matter'

'ls ther noon oother grace in yow?' quod he.
'No, by that lord,' quod she, 'that maked me.
For wel I woot that it shal nevere **bityde**.   happen
Lat swiche folies out of youre herte slyde.'
What deyntee sholde a man han his lyf
For to love another man's wyf,
That hath hir body whan so that hym liketh?'
Aurelius ful ofte soore siketh.
Wo was Aurelie, whan that he this herde,
And with a sorweful herte he thus answerde: 300
'Madame,' quod he, 'this were an **inpossible**!   impossibility
Thanne moot I dye of sodeyn deth horrible!'
And with that word, he turned hym **anon**.   straight away
Tho coome hir othere freendes, many oon,
And in the **aleyes** romeden up and doun,   paths
And nothyng wiste of this conclusioun,
But sodeynly bigonne revel newe,
Til that the brighte sonne loste his hewe;
For **thorisonte** hath **reft** the sonne his light –   horizon; taken
This is as muche to seye as it was nyght –   310
And hom they goon, in joye and in solas,
Save oonly wrecched Aurelius, allas!
He to his hous is goon with sorweful herte;
He seeth he may nat from his deeth **asterte**.   escape
Him semed that he felte his herte colde –
Up to the hevene hise hondes he gan holde,
And on his **knowes** bare he sette hym doun,   knees
And in his ravynge seyde his **orisoun**.   prayer
For verray wo out of his wit he **breyde**;   went
He **nyste** what he spak, but thus he seyde.   did not know   320
With pitous herte his **pleynt** hath he bigonne   complaint
Unto the goddes, and first unto the sonne
He seyde, 'Apollo, god and governour
Of every plaunte, herbe, tree and flour,
That gevest after thy **declynacioun**   position in the sky
To ech of hem his tyme and his sesoun,
As thyn **herberwe** chaungeth, lowe or heighe;   lodging
Lord Phebus, cast thy merciable **eighe**   eye
On wrecche Aurelie, which that am but **lorn**.   forlorn
Lo, Lord! My lady hath my deeth y-sworn   330

Withouten gilt, but thy **benygnytee**   kindness
Upon my **dedly** herte have som pitee.   dying
For wel I woot, Lord Phebus, if yow lest,
Ye may me helpen save my lady best.
Now **voucheth sauf** that I may yow devyse   grant
How that I may been **holpe**, and in what wyse   helped
Youre blisful suster Lucina the **shene**,   bright
That of the see is chief goddesse and queene,[16]
Thogh Neptunus have **deitee** in the see,   status of god
340   Yet empiresse aboven hym is she.
Ye knowen wel, Lord, that right as hir desir
Is to be **quyked** and lighted of youre fyr,   quickened
For which she folweth yow ful bisily;
Right so the see desireth naturelly
To folwen hire, as she that is goddesse
Bothe in the see and ryvers, moore and lesse;
Wherfore, Lord Phebus, this is my requeste:
Do this myracle, or do myn herte breste,
That now next at this opposicioun,[17]
350   Which in the signe shal be of the lioun,[18]
As preyeth hire so greet a flood to brynge
That fyve **fadme** at the leeste it **over-sprynge**   fathoms; overwhelms
The hyeste rok in Armoryk Britayne,
And lat this flood endure yeris twayne;
Thanne certes to my lady may I seye,
'Holdeth youre heste – the rokkes been aweye!'[19]
Lord Phebus, dooth this myracle for me;
Pray hire she go no faster cours than ye.
I seye this: prayeth youre suster that she go
360   No faster cours than ye thise yeris two,
Thanne shal she been evene at the fulle alway,[20]
And spryng flood lasten bothe nyght and day;
And but she **vouche sauf** in **swich** manere   grant; such
To graunte me my soverayn lady deere,
Pray hire to synken every rok adown

16 Lucina, the moon.
17 Opposition of sun and moon.
18 The sign of Leo.
19 'keep your promise – the rocks have gone'
20 'at the full of the moon'

Into hir owene **dirke** regioun   dark
Under the ground, ther Pluto dwelleth inne,
Or nevere mo shal I my lady wynne.
Thy temple in Delphos wol I barfoot seke –
Lord Phebus, se the teerys on my cheke,   370
And of my peyne have som compassioun!'
And with that word **in swowne** he fil adoun,   in a swoon
And longe tyme he lay forth in a traunce.
His brother, which that knew of his **penaunce**,   pain
Up caughte hym, and to bedde he hath hym broght,
Despeired in this torment and this thoght.
Lete I this woful creature lye –
Chese he for me when he wol lyve or dye.   let him choose
Arveragus, with **heele** and greet honour,   health
As he that was of chivalrie the flour,   380
Is comen hom, and othere worthy men.
O, blisful artow now, thow Dorigen!
That hast thy lusty housbonde in thyn armes,
The fresshe knyght, the worthy **man of armes**,   knight
That loveth thee as his owene hert's lyf;
Nothyng list hym to **been ymagynatyf**   think about
If any wight hadde spoke whil he was oute
To hire of love – he ne hadde of it no doute.
He noght **entendeth** to no swich matere,   bother about
But **daunceth**, **justeth**, maketh hire good cheere;   jousts   390
And thus in joye and blisse I lete hem dwelle,
And of the syke Aurelius wol I telle.
In langour and in torment furyus,
Two yeer and moore lay wrecche Aurelius,
Er any foot he myghte on erthe gon,
Ne confort in this tyme hadde he non,
Save of his brother, which that was a clerk.
He knew of al this wo and al this werk,
For to noon oother creature certeyn
Of this matere he dorste no word seyn.   400
Under his **brist** he baar it moore secree   breast
Than evere dide Panfilus for Galathee.[21]
His brist was hool withoute for to sene,

---

21 Lovers Pamphilius and Galathea.

But in his herte ay was the **arwe kene**;   sharp arrow
And wel ye knowe that of a **sursanure**   surface cure
In surgerye is perilous the cure.
But men myghte touche the arwe, or come therby,   so that nobody
His brother weepe and wayled pryvely,
Til at the laste hym **fil in remembrance**   remembered
410 That whils he was at Orliens in France,[22]
As yonge clerkes that been **lykerous**   desirous
To reden arts that been curious,
Seken in every **halke** and every **herne**   every hole and corner

Particuler sciences for to lerne;   specialised knowledge
He hym remembred that upon a day
At Orliens, in **studie**, a book he **say**   in college; saw
Of magyk naturel, which his **felawe**   companion/friend
That was that tyme a bachiler of lawe –
Al were he ther to lerne another craft –
420 Hadde prively upon his desk **ylaft**;   left
Which book spak **muchel** of the operaciouns   much
Touchynge the **xxviij** mansiouns   twenty-eight
That longen to the moone, and swich folye
As in oure dayes is nat worth a flye;
For holy chirch's feith, in oure **bileve**,   belief
Ne suffreth noon illusioun us to greve.
And whan this book was in his remembraunce,
Anon for joye his herte gan to daunce,
And to hymself he seyde pryvely,
430 'My brother shal be **warisshed** hastily,   relieved
For I am **siker** that ther be sciences   sure
By whiche men make diverse apparences,
Swiche as thise subtile **tregettours** pleye;   illusionists
For ofte at festes have I wel herd seye
That tregettours withinne an halle large
Have maad come in a water and a barge,
And in the hall rowen up and doun.
Sorntyme hath semed come a grym leoun,
And somtyme floures **sprynge** as in a **mede**;   spring up; meadow
440 Somtyme a vyne, and grapes white and rede,

22 Orleans had a reputation for experimental science.

Somtyme a castel, al of **lym** and stoon,   lime
And whan hem lyked, **voyded** it anoon.   disappeared
Thus semed it to every man's sighte –
Now thanne, conclude I thus: that if I myghte
At Orliens som old felawe y-fynde,
That hadde this moon's mansions in mynde,
Or oother magyk naturel above,
He sholde wel make my brother han his love;
For with an apparence a clerk may make
To man's sighte that alle the rokkes blake   450
Of Britaigne were **y-voyded** everichon,   vanished
And shippes by the **brynke** comen and gon,   shore
And in swich forme enduren a day or two,
Thanne were my brother warisshed of his wo.
Thanne moste she nedes **holden hir biheste**,   keep her promise
Or ellis he shal shame hire, at the leeste.'
What sholde I make a lenger tale of this?
Unto his brotheres bed he comen is,
And swich confort he gaf hym for to gon
To Orliens, that he up **stirte** anon,   leapt   460
And on his wey forthward thanne he is **fare**,   gone
In hope for to been **lissed** of his care.   released
Whan they were come almoost to that citee,
But if it were a two furlong or thre,
A yong clerk, romynge by hymself they mette,
Which that in latyn **thriftily** hem **grette**;   politely; greeted
And after that he seyde a wonder thyng.
'I knowe,' quod he, 'the cause of youre comyng.'
And er they ferther any foote wente,
He tolde hem al that was in him entente.   470
This Britoun clerk hym asked of felawes
The whiche that he hadde knowe in olde **dawes**,   days
And he answerde hym that they dede were,
For which he weepe ful ofte many a teere.
Doun of his hors Aurelius lighte anon,
And with this magicien forth he is gon
Hom to his hous, and maden hem wel at ese;
Hem lakked no **vitaille** that myghte hem plese.   food and drink
So wel arrayed hous as ther was oon,
Aurelius in his lyf saw nevere noon.   480

He shewed hym er he wente to soper
Foreste parkes ful of wilde deer;
Ther saw he **hertes** with hir hornes hye,   harts (male deer)
The gretteste that evere were seyn with eye.
He say of hem an hundred slayn with houndes,
And somme with arwes **blede** of bittre woundes.   bleed
He saw whan voyded were thise wilde deer,
Thise fawconers upon a fair ryver,
That with him hawkes han the heron slayn.
490   **Tho** saugh he knyghtes **justyng** in a playn,   then; jousting
And after this he dide hym this plesaunce
That he hym shewed his lady on a daunce,
On which hymself he daunced, as hym thoughte;
And whan this maister, that this magyk wroughte
Saugh it was tyme, he clapte his handes two,
And, 'Farwel, al!' oure revel was **ago**;   gone
And yet **remoeved** they nevere out of the hous,   moved
Whil they sawe al this sighte merveillous,
But in his studie theras his bookes be
500   They sitten stille, and no wight but they thre.
To hym this maister called his squyer,
And seide hym thus, 'Is redy oure soper?
Almoost an houre it is, I undertake,
Sith I yow **bad** oure soper for to make,   since; told
Whan that thise worthy men wenten with me
Into my studie, theras my bookes be.'
'Sire,' quod this squyer, 'whan it liketh yow
It is al redy, thogh ye wol right now.'
'Gowe thanne soupe,' quod he, 'as for the beste.
510   This amorous folk somtyme mote han hir reste.'
At after soper fille they in **tretee**   and; discussion
What somme sholde this maistre's **gerdoun** be   reward
To remoeven alle the rokkes of Britayne,
And eek from Gemounde to the mouth of Sayne.[23]
He **made it straunge**, and swoor, so God hym save,   was difficult
Lasse than a thousand pound he wolde nought have;

23 Between the Gironde and the Seine.

Ne gladly for that somme he wolde not goon.[24]
Aurilius, with blisful hert, anoon
Answerde thus, 'Fy on a thousand pound!
This wyde world, which that men say is round,   520
I wold it give, if I were lord of it!
This bargeyn is ful **dryve**, for we ben **knyt**.   driven; agreed
Ye schal be payed, trewly, by my trouthe.
But loketh now, for necligence or slouthe
Ye **tarie** us heer no lenger than tomorwe.'   keep
'Nay,' quod this clerk, 'have her my faith **to borwe**.'   in pledge
To bed is goon Aurilius whan him leste,
And wel neigh al night he had his reste,
What for his labour and his hope of blisse,
His woful hert of penaunce had a **lisse**.   break/pause   530
Upon the morwe, whan that it was day,
To Bretiegn take thei the **righte** way,   shortest
Aurilius and this magicien bisyde,
And ben descendid ther thay wol abyde;
And this was, as these bookes me remembre,
The colde, frosty seisoun of Decembre.
Phebus **wax** old and **hewed lyk latoun**,[25]   grew; coloured like latten (bronze)
That in his hoote declinacioun
Schon as the burned gold, with **stremes** bright;   rays
But now in Capricorn adoun he light,[26]   540
Wheras he schon ful pale, I dar wel sayn.
The bitter frostes, with the sleet and rayn,
Destroyed hath the grene in every **yerd**.   garden (enclosed)
Janus sit by the fuyr with double berd,[27]
And drynketh of his bugle horn the wyn;
Biforn him **stont** the **braun** of **toskid** swyn,   stands; jellied meat; tusked
And '**Nowel**!' crieth every lusty man.   Nowell (Christmas)
Aurilius, in al that ever he can
Doth to his maister chier and reverence,
And peyneth him to doon his diligence   550
To bringen him out of his peynes smerte,

24 'he wouldn't be happy to do it for anything less'
25 grew; coloured like latten (bronze)
26 The sun is in Capricorn, a sign of winter (ie January, the month of Janus).
27 Janus, the god of endings and beginnings, had two faces, one facing in each
    direction.

Or with a swerd that he wold slytte his herte.
This subtil clerk such **routhe** had of this man,   pity
That night and day he spedeth him that he can,[28]
To **wayte** a tyme of his conclusioun,   await
This is to say to make illusioun
By such an apparence of **jogelrie** –   magic
I **can** no termes of astrologie –   know
That sche and every wight schold **wene** and saye   believe
560   That of Breteygn the rokkes were awaye,
Or elles they sonken were under the grounde;
So atte last he hath a tyme y-founde
To make his **japes** and his wrecchednesse   tricks
Of such a supersticious cursednesse.
His tables Tollitanes forth he brought,[29]
Ful wel corrected; ne ther lakked nought
Neither his collect, ne his expans yeeres,[30]
Ne his rootes, ne his other geeres,
As ben his centris & his argumentis,
570   And his proporcionels convenientis,
For her equaciouns in every thing;
And by his thre speeres in his worching
He knew ful wel how fer Allnath was schove,
For the heed of thilke fixe Aries above,
That in the fourthe **speere** considred is;   sphere
Ful subtilly he **calkiled** al this.   calculated
Whan he had founde his firste **mancioun**,   house (of the moon)
He knew the **remenaunt** by proporcioun,   rest
And knew the arisyng of this moone wel,
580   And in whos face and terme, and every del,
And knew ful wel the moon's mancioun,
Acordaunt to his operacioun,   in accordance with
And knew also his other observaunces,
For suche illusiouns and suche **meschaunces**   bad luck

28 'works as quickly as he can'
29 Tables of sun, moon, tides etc used by astrologers/astronomers.
30 This explains how the clerk used his tables, with its expanses and collects
   (groupings of years), his instruments (argumentis), his tables of space (centris)
   and of the motion of planets ((proporcionels conuenientis) and the positions of
   the stars and planets in the sky (mansions, spheres) to create his illusion that the
   rocks had gone. Alnath is a star in Aries.

As hethen folk used in thilke dayes;
For which no lenger maked he delayes,
But thurgh his magik, for a **wike** or tweye,   week
It semed that the rokes were aweye.
Aurilius, which yet dispayred is
Wher he schal have his love, or fare **amys**,   badly   590
Awayteth night and day on this miracle,
And whan he knew that ther was noon obstacle,
That **voyded** were these rokkes everichoon,   disappeared
Doun to his **maistre's** feet he fel anoon,   master's
And sayd, 'I wrecched, woful Aurilius,
Thanke you, Lord, and my Lady Venus,
That me han holpe fro my cares colde.'
And to the temple his way forth he hath holde,
Wheras he knew he schold his lady se;
And whan he saugh his tyme, anoon right he   600
With **dredful** hert, and with ful humble cheere,   fearful
Salued hath his owne lady deere.   greeted
'My soverayn lady,' quod this woful man,
'Whom I most drede and love as I can,
And lothest were of al this world displese;
Nere it that I for you have such **desese**   if it were not; suffering
That I most deye her at youre foot anoon,
Nought wold I telle how me is wo bygoon.
But certes **outher** most I dye or pleyne –   either
Ye sleen me gulteles, for verrey peyne –   610
But of my deth, though that ye have no **routhe**   pity
Avyseth yow, er that ye breke your **trouthe**.   consider; word
Repenteth yow, for thilke God above;
Ye me **sleen** bycause that I you love.   kill
For Madame, wel ye **woot** what ye han **hight**;   know; promised
Nat that I chalenge eny thing of right
Of yow, my soverayn lady, but youre grace;
But in a gardyn **yonde**, at such a place   yonder
Ye wot right wel what ye **byhighte** me,   promised
And in myn hond **your trouthe plighte ye**   you gave me your word   620
To love me best, God woot, ye sayde so,
Al be that I unworthy am therto.
Madame, I speke it for th'honour of yow,   my lady
More than to save myn hert's lif right now.

I have do so as ye comaunded me,
And if ye vouchesauf, ye may go see.
Doth as you list – have youre **byheste in mynde** –   promise; remember
For quyk or deed, right ther ye schul me fynde.
In yow lith al to do me lyve or deye,
630   But wel I wot the rokkes ben aweye.'
He taketh his leve and he **astoned** stood;   dumbfounded
In all hir face **nas** oon drop of blood –   was not
Sche wende never have be in such a trappe.
'Allas!' quod sche, 'That ever this schulde happe!
For wend I never by possibilite,
That such a monstre or merveyl mighte be;
It is agayns the **proces** of nature!'   course
And hom sche goth, a sorwful creature –
For verray fere **unnethe** may sche go –   hardly
640   Sche wepeth, wayleth, al a day or tuo,
And swowneth that it routhe was to see.
But why it was, to no **wight** tolde sche,   person
For out of toune was goon Arviragus;
But to hirself sche spak and sayde thus,
With face pale and with ful sorwful **chiere**,   countenance
In hir compleignt, as ye schul after hiere.
'Allas!' quod sche, 'On the, Fortune, I pleyne,
That **unwar** wrapped me hast in thy **cheyne**,   unwary; chain
Fro which t'escape **woot I no socour**   I know no help
650   Save oonly deth, or elles dishonour.
Oon of these tuo **bihoveth me** to **chese**;   I have to; choose
But natheles, yet have I **lever leese**   rather; lose
My lif than of my body to have schame,
Or knowe myselve fals, or **lese my name**,   lose my reputacion
And with my deth I may be quyt, y-wys.   I think
Hath ther not many a noble wyf er this,
And many a mayden, slayn hirself, allas!,
Rather than with her body doon trespas.
Yis certeynly – lo, stories beren witnes[31]
660   Whan **thritty tiraunts**, ful of cursednes,   thirty tyrants

---

31 These examples are all taken from St Jerome's book, Adversus Jovinianum
(Against Jovinian). Jerome was a writer of the late fourth and early fifth century
(he died in AD 420).

Hadde slayn Phidon in Athenes atte fest,
Thay comaunded his doughtres to **arest**   be arrested
And bryngen hem biforn hem in **despit**,   insult
And naked, to fulfille her foule **delyt**,   lust
And in her fadre's blood they made hem daunce
Upon the **pavyment**, God geve hem **meschaunce**!   tiled floor; ill luck
For which these woful maydens, ful of drede,
Rather than they wolde lese her **maydenhede**,   virginity
They prively ben **stert** into a welle,   threw themselves
And **drenched** hem selfen, as the bookes telle.   drowned   670
They of **Mecene leet enquere** and seeke   Messene; ordered; ask
Of **Lacidomye** fifty maydenes eeke,   Lacidemon
On which thay wolden doon her leccherie;
But was ther noon of al that companye
Was slayn, and with a good entente,
Chees rather for to die than assente
To be oppressed of hir meydenhede – [32]
Why schuld I than to deyen ben **in drede**?   in dread
Lo! Eek the tyraunt Aristoclides,
That loved a mayden **heet** Stimphalides,   called   680
Whan that hir father slayn was on a night,
Unto Dyane's temple goth sche right,
And **hent** the ymage in hir hondes tuo,   seized
Fro which ymage wold sche never go.
No wight might of it hir hondes **race**,   tear
Til sche was slayn right in the **selve** place.   same
Now, sith that maydens hadde such despit
To be defouled with mannes foul delit,
Wel aught a wyf rather hirself to sle
Than be defouled, as it thenketh me.   690
What schal I seyn of **Hasdrubalde's** wyf   Hasdrubal's
That at **Cartage byraft** hirself the lyf;   Carthage; took from
For whan sche saugh that Romayns wan the toun,
Sche took hir children all and skipte adoun
Into the fuyr, and **ches** rather to deye   chose
Than eny Romayn dide hir vilonye.
Hath nought **Lucresse** slayn hirself, allas!,   Lucrece
At Rome, whanne sche **oppressid** was   raped

32 'the whole group were happy to be slain in order to keep their virginity'

Of Tarquyn, for hir thought it was a schame

700 To lyven whan sche hadde lost hir name?
The seven maydens of **Milisie** also   Miletus
Han slayn hemself, for verray drede and wo,
Rather than folk of **Gawle** hem schulde oppresse.   Gaul
Mo than a thousand stories, as I gesse,
Couthe I now telle as touching this matiere:
Whan **Habradace** was slayn, his wif so deere   Abradates
Hirselven slough, and leet hir blood to glyde
In Habradace's woundes, depe and wyde,
And seyde, 'My body, **atte leste way**,   at the very least

710 Ther schal no wight defoulen, if I may.'
What schold I mo ensamples herof sayn,
Seththen so many han hemselven slayn,   since
Wel rather than they wolde defouled be?
I wol conclude that it is best for me
To slen myself than be defouled thus.
I wol be trewe unto Arvegarius,
Or rather sle myself in som manere,
As dede Democion's doughter deere,
Bycause sche wolde nought defouled be.

720 O **Cedasus**! It is ful gret pite   Scedasus
To reden how thy doughteren dyed, allas,
That slowe hemself for suche maner caas!
As gret a pite was it, or wel more
The Theban mayden that for Nichonor
Hirselven slough. Right for such maner wo
Another Theban mayden dede right so,
For oon of Macidone had hir oppressed –
Sche with hire deth hire maydenhede redressed.
What schal I sayn of Niceratus's wif,

730 That for such caas biraft hirself hir lyf;
How trewe eek was sche to Alcebiades,
His love, that rather to dyen ches
Than for to suffre his body unburied be.
Lo, which a wif was Alceste,' quod sche,
'What saith Omer of good Penolope – [33]

33 Homer, the Greek historian of the Trojan wars. Penelope remained faithful to
   Odysseus during his long absence, despite the pressure of many suitors.

Al Grece knoweth of hir chastite.

Pardi, of Laodomya is writen thus,   by God
That whan out of Troye was Protheselaus,
No lenger wol sche lyve after his day;
The same of noble Porcia telle I may –   740
Withoute Brutus kynde sche my*ght* not lyve,
To whom sche had al hool hir herte gyve.
The parfyt wyfhod of **Artemesye**   Artemisia
Honoured is thurgh al the Barbarie.
O, **Thena** queen! thy wifly chastite   Athens's
To alle wyves may a mirour be!'
Thus playned Dorigen a day or tweye,
Purposyng ever that sche wolde deye;
But natheles, upon the thridde night,
Hom cam Arveragus, this worthy knight,   750
And asked hir why that sche wept so sore,
And sche gan wepe **ever lenger the more**.   more and more
'Allas,' quod sche, 'that ever was I born!
Thus have I sayd,' quod sche, 'thus have I sworn.'
And told him al, as ye han herd biforn –
It nedith nought **reherse** it you no more.   recount
This housbond with glad **chiere**, in good wise   expression
Answerd, and sayde as I schal you devyse.
'Is ther aught elles Dorigen, but this?'
'Nay, nay,' quod sche, '**God me so rede** & wis.   so help me God   760
This is to moche, and it were God's wille!'
'Ye, wyf,' quod he, '**let slepe that may be stille**.   'let sleeping dogs lie'
It may be wel **peraunter** – yet today   perhaps
Ye schal **your trouthe holden**, by my fay;   keep your word
For, God so wisly have mercy on me,
I hadde wel lever **y-stekid** for to be,   sticked/killed
For verray love which I to you have,
But if ye scholde your trouthe kepe and save.'
Trouthe is the **hyeste** thing that man may kepe   noblest/best
But with that word he gan anoon to wepe,   770
And sayde, 'I yow forbede, **up peyne of deth**   on pain of death
That never whil the lasteth lyf or breth,
To no **wight** telle thou of this aventure –   person
As I may best, I wil my woo endure.
Ne make no contenaunce of hevynesse,   don't look troubled

That folk of you may **deme harm**, or gesse.'   judge anything wrong
And forth he **cleped** a squyer and a mayde;   called
'Goth forth anoon with Dorigen,' he sayde,
'And bryngeth hir to such a place anoon.'
780 Thay take her leve and on her wey they gon,
But thay ne **wiste** why sche thider went;   know
He nolde no wight tellen his entent.
This squyer, which that hight Aurelius,
On Dorigen that was so **amerous**,   in love
Of aventure happed hire to mete   by chance
Amyd the toun, right in the **quyke** strete,   busy
As sche was **boun** to goon the wey forth right   prepared
Toward the gardyn, theras sche had **hight**;   promised
And he was to the gardynward also,
790 For wel he spyed whan sche wolde go
Out of hir hous to eny maner place;
But thus thay mette of **adventure**, or grace,   chance
And he **salueth** hir with glad entent,   greeted
And askith hire whiderward sche went,
And sche anwswered, half as sche were mad,
'Unto the gardyn, as myn housbond bad,
My trouthe for to holde, allas, allas!'
Aurilius gan wondren on this **caas**,   situation
And in his hert had gret compassioun
800 Of hire, and of hir lamentacioun,
And of Arveragus, the worthy knight,
That bad hir hold al that sche hadde **hight**,   promised
So loth him was his wif schuld breke hir **trouthe**.   word
And in hir hert he caught of this gret routhe.
Consideryng the best on every syde,
That fro his lust yet were him **lever** abyde   rather
Than doon so high a **cheerlissch** wrecchednesse,   unworthy
Agayns fraunchis of alle gentilesce;[34]
For which in fewe wordes sayd he thus:
810 'Madame, saith to your lord Arveragus
That sith I se his grete gentilesse

34 Fraunchise and gentilesse are chivalric qualities, roughly translated 'generosity,
   openness of heart, mind and hand', and 'the quality of being gentle or noble in
   upbringing, mind and spirit'.

To you, and **eek** I se wel your distresse,   also
That him were lever have schame – and that were routhe –
Than ye to me schulde breke your trouthe;
I have wel lever ever to suffre woo,
Than I **departe** the love **bytix** yow tuo.   break; between
I yow **relesse**, madame into your hond,   release
Quyt every **seurement** and every **bond**   quit; surety; pledge
That ye han maad to me, as her biforn,
Sith thilke tyme which that ye were born.   820
My trouthe.I plight, I schal yow never repreve
Of no byhest, and her I take my leve,[35]
As of the trewest and the beste wif
That ever yit I knew in al my lyf;
But every wyf be war of hir byhest –
On Dorigen remembreth, atte lest.
Thus can a squyer doon a gentil dede
As wel as can a knyght, withouten drede.'
Sche thanketh him upon hir knees al bare,
And hoom unto hir housbond is sche fare,   830
And told him al, as ye han herd me sayd;
And – be ye **siker** – he was so wel **apayd**   sure; satisfied
That it were impossible me to write.
What schuld I lenger **of this caas endite**?   tell you about this
Arveragus and Dorigen his wif
In sovereyn blisse **leden forth** here lyf;   carried on
Never **eft** ne was ther anger hem bytwen.   after
He cherisscheth hir as though sche were a queen,
And sche was to him trewe for evermore –
Of these tuo folk ye gete from me nomore.   840
Aurilius, that his **cost** hath al **forlorn**,   outlay; lost
Curseth the tyme that ever he was born.
'Allas!' quod he, 'Allas, that I byhight
Of pured gold a thousand pound of **wight**   weight
Unto this **philosophre**, how schal I doo?   learned man
I se no more, but that I am **fordoo**.   ruined
Myn **heritage** moot I **needes** selle,   inheritance; of necessity
And ben a begger; her may I not duelle,

35 'I give you my word that I shall never hold you to any promise'

And schamen al my **kynrede** in this place;   family
850 **But** I of him may gete better **grace**.   unless; time to pay
But natheles, I wol of him **assay**   ask
At certeyn dayes yeer by yer to pay,
And thanke him of his grete curtesye –
My **trouthe** wol I kepe, I wol nou*g*ht lye.'   word
With herte soor he goth unto unto his **coffre**,   chest (for valuables)
And broughte gold unto this philosophre
The value of fyf hundred pound I gesse,
And him bysecheth of his gentilesce
To graunte him dayes of the **remenaunt**,[36]   remainder
860 And sayde, 'Maister, I dar wel make **avaunt**   boast
I fayled never of my trouthe as yit,
For **sikerly** my dettes schal be **quyt**   surely; paid
Towardes yow, how that ever I fare,
To goon a-begge in my **kurtil** bare –   tunic
But wolde ye **vouchesauf** upon **seurte**   grant; surety
Tuo yer, or thre, for to respite me?
Than were I wel, for elles most I selle
Myn heritage; ther is nomore to telle.'
'This philosophre sobrely answered
870 And seyde, whan he these wordes herde,
'Have I not **holden covenaunt** unto the?'   kept my bargain
'*Y*is, certes, wel and trewely,' quod he.
'Hastow nou*g*ht had thy lady as the liketh?'
'No, no,' quod he, and sorwfully he **siketh**.   sighs
'What was the cause? Tel me, if thou can.'
Aurilius his tale anoon bygan,
And told him al as ye han herd bifore –
It needeth nat to you reherse it more.
He sayde Arveragus, of gentilesse,
880 Had lever dye in sorwe and in distresse
Than that his wyf were of hir trouthe fals.
The sorwe of Dorigen he tolde him als,
How loth hir was to ben a wikked wikked wyf,
And that sche **lever** had han lost hir lyf,   rather
And that hir trouthe sche swor thurgh innocence –
Sche never **erst** hadde herd speke of **apparence** –   before; illusion

36 Give him days to pay, that is, by installments.

That made me han of hir so gret pyte,
Bycause hir housebond sente hir to me;
And right as frely sent I hir to him agayn –
This is **al and som**; ther is no more to sayn.'   all there is   890
This philosopher answerde, 'Leve brother,
Everich of yow dede **gentilly** to other.   each; nobly
Thow art a squyer and he is a knight,
But God forbede for his blisful might,
But if a clerk couthe doon as gentil dede   that
As wel as eny of you, it is no drede.
Sire, I relesse the thy thousand pound,
As thou right now were **crope** out of the ground,   crept
Ne never **er** now ne haddest knowen me;   before
For, Sire, I wil not take a peny of the   900
For al my **creat**, ne nought for my **travayle**.   creations; work/effort
Thou hast y-payed wel for my **vitayle**;   food
It is ynough, and farwel, have good day!'
And took his hors, and forth he goth his way.
Lordynges, this questioun wolde I **axe** now –   ask
Which was the moste **free**, as thinketh yow?   generous
Now telleth me, er that I ferthere wende –
I can no more, my tale is at an ende.

here endeth the Frankeleyn's tale

THE SHIPMAN'S TALE

A French merchant has a beautiful, sociable wife, but he has to pay for her extravagance. He has a friend, a monk who claims kinship with him because they were born in the same village. The merchant enjoys the monk's company, as do the rest of his household, and he does not gainsay this. One day the monk is walking in the merchant's garden, when the merchant's wife waylays him. She says that her husband is a miser, and she needs to borrow a hundred francs to buy clothes, or her public reputation will be ruined. The monk tells her that he is not really the merchant's relative, but only pretended this in order to see her. He will lend her the money in exchange for sex. She agrees, so the monk goes to her husband and borrows the hundred francs, telling the merchant that it is for buying animals for his abbey. The husband lends him the money, and he gives it to the wife. The merchant goes away to do business at a fair in Bruges, so the monk is able to spend the night in bed with with his wife. When her husband returns, the monk tells him that he has already given the money to repay the merchant's loan to his wife, on the understanding that she will give it to him on the monk's behalf. The monk then makes a hasty retreat to his abbey. As his wife has not mentioned anything about the money, the merchant rebukes her. She remains calm, and curses the monk for not saying that it was the repayment for a loan. As she didn't know, she has already spent the money on clothes for herself. She says that he can have the equivalent in sex, so the merchant 'cuts his losses' and accepts her offer.

Like The Man of Law's Tale, this also has an analogue in *The Decameron* (Day 8). It is a simple fabliau, which centres on the relationship, seen in the wife of Bath's prologue, between sex and money. Its focus is a bargain, which is basically prostitution; the wife sells her body to the monk in return for a hundred franks. The fabliau was probably widely known. Being set in France, the original may have been French, but a version of it was obviously known to Boccaccio in Italy. It seems to tell, purely and simply, of the extravagance and moral culpability of women. That the wife is a stereotype for other married women is implicit in the fact that she is not named, and neither is her, equally stereotypical, husband. The husband is a rich merchant oligarch, with a beautiful 'trophy' wife, who is obviously paraded in public as a sign of her husband's wealth, power and virility. This vanity means that the merchant is easily duped by the intelligent, opportunistic, monk. The laughter is once again at the expense of the victim of a bourgeios and a clergyman, although no-one really seems unduly harmed by the whole affair, of which the husband is mostly ignorant anyway. Like January in The Merchant's Tale, he remains in the fantasy world created by his own vanity and self-deceit.

Seen in the context of the ongoing debate about marriage among the pilgrims, this tale is simply a revelation of the sufferings of being a husband. The wife cannot be excused for her behaviour, because it is she who initiates the whole affair by accosting the monk in the garden; he does not solicit her attention in any way, as far as the narrative tells. This may be an allusion to the temptation of Adam in the Garden of Eden, although, in the manner of fabliaux, this is simply a passing blasphemy; the bargain hardly costs the monk anything at all. Perhaps the husband values his gold too much, but there is only a faint hint (such as when he goes into his counting house) of this possibility. He may not have deserved to be cuckolded in this way, but his failings make him an obvious butt for the shipman's joke. A hundred francs seems a paltry sum to offer for the wife's sexual favours, given her husband's riches. However, she is used to being spoiled, and is prepared to sell herself for a small sum in order to have the clothes that she wants. Her only excuse seems to be that she simply cannot help herself . . . she just lives this way. The monk is a 'chancer', another clergyman more concerned with his personal gain (in this case, his pleasure and perhaps the 'frisson' of conquering a society beauty, as he hardly needs the money) than with his calling. The immoral bargain is made after swearing on the monk's breviary, a brilliantly blasphemous detail. The light-hearted ending, with its pun on 'talying' (i.e. linking tally sticks with the genitalia, or tail) suggests that the story should not be taken too seriously. Unlike the other fabliaux in The Canterbury Tales, this story is more concerned with stratagems and manoeuvres than with characterisation or philosophy. The only moral seems to be 'if you are vain enough to marry a woman like this, she will 'cost' you – you know what to expect.'

Key Questions

What can this story tell us about the construction of fabliaux? How stereotypical are the characters? Do they represent character types, gender types, occupational types?

Do the characters deserve any sympathy, or are they all as bad as one another? Is the wife simply a good entrepreneur? A quick-witted woman, like the wife of Bath or May in The Merchant's Tale?

Why might the shipman tell a tale such as this?

Topic Keywords

Medieval commerce/ urban life/ urban monasteries and monks/ fabliau as genre/ ships and the sea/ the medieval Low Countries/Flanders/ medieval women

Further Reading

Robert Adams, 'The Concept of Debt in The Shipman's Tale', *Studies in the Age of Chaucer*, 6, 1984, pp. 85–102

Peter G. Beidler, 'The Price of Sex in Chaucer's Shipman's Tale', *Chaucer Review*, 31, 1996, pp. 5–17

—— 'Just Say Yes, Chaucer knew *The Decameron*; or, Bringing The Shipman's Tale out of Limbo', in *The Decameron and The Canterbury Tales*, edited by Leonard Michael Koff and Brenda Deen Schildgen, Madison, NJ, Fairleigh Dickinson University Press; London and Toronto, Associated University Presses, 2000, pp. 25–46

Mary Flowers Braswell, 'Chaucer's "queinte termes of lawe": A Legal View of The Shipman's Tale', *Chaucer Review*, 22, 1988, pp. 295–304

Theresa Coletti, 'The Mulier Fortis and Chaucer's Shipman's Tale', *Chaucer Review*, 15, 1981, pp. 236–49

Holly A. Crocker, 'Wifely Eye for the Manly Guy: Trading the Masculine Image in The Shipman's Tale', in *'Seyd in Forme and Reverence': Essays on Chaucer and Chaucerians in Memory of Emerson Brown Jr*, edited by T. L. Burton and John F. Plummer, Provo, UT, Chaucer Studio Press, 2005, pp. 59–73

Robert Easting, 'Credit in Chaucer's Shipman's Tale', in *Still Shines When You Think of It: A Festschrift for Vincent O'Sullivan*, edited by Bill Manhire and Peter Whiteford, Wellington, Victoria University Press, 2007, pp. 48–63

John Finlayson, 'Chaucer's Shipman's Tale, Boccaccio and the "Civilizing" of Fabliau', *Chaucer Review*, 36, 2002, pp. 336–51

Helen Fulton, 'Mercantile Ideology in Chaucer's Shipman's Tale', *Chaucer Review*, 36, 2002, pp. 311–28

Thomas Hahn, 'Money, Sexuality, Wordplay and Context in The Shipman's Tale', in *Chaucer in the Eighties*, edited by Robert Blanch and Julian Wasserman, Syracuse, Syracuse University Press, 1986, pp. 235–49

Carol F. Heffernan, 'Two "English Fabliaux", Chaucer's Merchant's Tale and Shipman's Tale, and Italian Novelle', *Neophilologus*, 90, 2006, pp. 333–49

John Hermann, 'Dismemberment, Dissemination, Discourse: Sign and Symbol in The Shipman's Tale', *Chaucer Review*, 19, 1985, pp. 302–37

Cathy Hume, 'Domestic Opportunities: The Social Comedy of The Shipman's Tale', *Chaucer Review*, 41, 2006, pp. 138–62

John M.Ganim, 'Double Entry in Chaucer's Shipman's Tale: Chaucer and Bookkeeping before Pacioli', *Chaucer Review*, 30, 1996, pp. 294–305

Gerhard Joseph, 'Chaucer's Coinage: Foreign Exchange and the Puns of The Shipman's Tale', *Chaucer Review*, 17, 1983, pp. 341–57

George Keiser, 'Language and Meaning in Chaucer's Shipman's Tale', *Chaucer Review*, 12, 1977, pp. 147–61

Elliot Kendall, 'The Great Household in the City: The Shipman's Tale', in *Chaucer and the City*, edited by Ardis Butterfield, Woodbridge, D. S. Brewer, 2006, pp. 145–61

Peter Nicholson, 'The Shipman's Tale and the Fabliaux', *Journal of English Literary History*, 45, 1978, pp. 583–96

Lorraine Kochanske Stock, 'La Vieille and The Merchant's Wife in Chaucer's Shipman's Tale', *Southern Humanities Review*, 16, 1982, pp. 333–9

Karla Taylor, 'Social Aesthetics and the Emergence of Civic Discourse from The Shipman's Tale to Melibee', *Chaucer Review*, 39, 2005, pp. 298–322

William Woods, 'A Professional Thyng: The Wife as Merchant's Apprentice in The Shipman's Tale,' *Chaucer Review*, 24, 1989, pp. 139–49

here bygynneth the schipman his tale

❦ A marchaunt **whilom** dwelled at Seint Denys[1]   once
That rich was, for which men **hild him** wys.   believed him to be
A wyf he had, of excellent beaute,
And **companable** and reverent was sche;   sociable
Which is a thing that causeth more **despence**   expenditure
Than worth is al the **cher** and reverence   good manners
That men doon hem at festes, or at daunces –
Such salutaciouns and **continaunces**   courtesies
Passeth as doth the schadow on a wal –   10
But wo is him that paye **moot** for al.   must
The sely housbond **algat** most pay;   at all events
He most us clothe in ful good array,
Al for his oughne **worschip**, richely,   honour
In which **array** we daunce jolily;   clothing
And if that he may not, **paraventure**,   perhaps
Or elles wil not such dispens endure,
But thynketh it is wasted and y-lost,
Than moot another paye for oure cost,
Or **lene** us gold that is perilous.   lend   20
The worthy marchaunt **huld a noble hous**,[2]
For which he hadde alday gret repair[3]
For his **largesce**, and for his wyf was fair.   because of; generosity
What wonder is? But **herkneth** to my tale.   listen
Amonges al these gestes, **gret and smale**,   important and not ..
Ther was a monk, a fair man and a bold;
I trowe **thritty** wynter he was old,   thirty
That **ever in oon** was drawyng to that place.   always
This yonge monk, that was so fair of face,
Aqueynted was so with the good man   30
Sith that her firste **knowleche** bygan,   acquaintance
That in his hous as familier was he

---

1 Saint-Denis, now a suburb of Paris.
2 'maintained a great household'
3 'many people came to visit him'

As it is possibil is a frend to be,
And for as mochil as this goode man
And eek this monk, of which that I bygan,
Were bothe tuo y-born in oon village,
The monk him claymeth as for **cosynage**,   as a relative
And he agein him **saith nat oones nay**,   doesn't deny it
But was as glad therof as **foul** of day;   bird
40   For to his hert it was a gret **plesaunce**.   pleasure
Thus ben thay **knyt** with eterne alliaunce,   joined
And **ilk** of hem gan other to assure   each
Of brotherhed, whil that her lif may **dure**.   endure
Fre was daun John, and **manely** of despence,[4]   generous
As in that hous, and ful of diligence
To do plesaunce and also gret costage.
He nought forgat to geve the leste page
In al that hous, but **after her degre**   according to their status
He gaf the lord and **siththen** the **meyne**   afterwards; household
50   Whan that he com, som maner honest thing;
For which thay were as glad of his comyng
As **foul** is **fayn** whan that the sonne upriseth.   bird; glad
No mor of this as now, for it suffiseth –
But **so bifel** this marchaunt on a day   it so happened
Schop him to make redy his array   planned
Toward the toun of Bruges for to fare,
To **byen** ther a porcioun of **ware**;   buy; goods
For which he hath to Paris sent anoon
A messanger, and prayed had Dan John
60   That he schuld come to Seint Denys and play
With him, and with his wyf, a day or **tway**   two
Er he to Brigges went, in alle wise.
This nobil monk, of which I yow **devyse**,   tell
Hath of his abbot as him **list**, licence,   liked
Bycause he was a man of heih **prudence**,   wisdom/judgement
And eek an officer out for to ryde
To se her **granges** and her **bernes** wyde;   farms; barns
And unto Seint Denys he cometh anoon.
Who was so welcome as my lord, Dan John?

4 'as a man should be where expenditure is concerned'

Oure deere cosyn, ful of curtesie, 70
With him brought he a **jubbe of Malvesie**, jug of Malmsey (wine)
And eek another, ful of **wyn vernage**, Italian wine
And **volantyn**, as **ay** was his **usage**. game; always; custom
And thus I lete hem ete and drynk and play,
This marchaunt and this monk, a day or tway.
The thridde day this marchaund up he riseth,
And on his needes **sadly him avyseth**, he prepared diligently
And up into his **countour hous** goth he,[5] counting house
To **rekyn with himself**, as wel may be, do his accounts
Of thilke yer, how that it with him stood, 80
And how that he **dispended** had his good, spent
And if that he **encresced were** or noon. had made a profit
His bookes and his bagges many oon
He hath byforn him on his counter bord,[6]
For riche was his tresor and his hord,
For which ful fast his countour dore he **schette**, shut
And eek he wolde no man schold him **lette** hinder
Of his accomptes, for the mene tyme;[7]
And thus he sat, til it was **passed prime**. after 9am
Dan John was risen in the morn also, 90
And in the gardyn walkith to and fro,
And hath his **thinges** said ful curteisly. devotions
This good wyf com walkyng, ful **prively**, secretly
Into a gardyn ther he walketh softe,
And him **salveth**, as sche hath doon ful ofte; greeted
A **mayde child** com in hir compaignie, virgin/young girl
Which as hir list sche may governe and **gye**, bring up
For yit **under the yerde** was the mayde. under (adult) authority
'O dere cosyn myn, Dan John,' sche sayde,
'What **ayleth** yow, so **rathe** to arise?' ails; early 100
'Nece,' quod he, 'it aught ynough suffise
Fyve houres for to slepe upon a night,
But it were for eny old **palled** wight, pallid

---

5 This was usually a room adjoining the owner's private rooms, where his treasure
  was kept.
6 An exchequer board, a table with a chequered cloth on which coin could be
  counted, as on an abacus.
7 'whilst he was busy'

As ben these weddid men, that lye and **dare**,   doze
As in a **forme** lith a **wery** hare   grassy hollow; weary
Were al **forstraught** with houndes gret and smale –   distressed/worried
But, dere nece, why be ye so pale?
I trowe certis that oure goode man
Hath on yow **laborid** sith the night bygan,   worked
110   That yow were nede to resten hastiliche.'[8]
And with that word he **lowgh** ful meriliche,   laughed
And of his owne thought he was al **reed**.   red/blushed
This faire wyf bygan to schake hir heed,
And sayde thus: 'Ye, God wot al,' quod sche,
'Nay, cosyn myn, it stant no so with me;
For by that God that gaf me soule and lif,
In al the **reme** of Fraunce is ther no wyf   kingdom
That **lasse lust** hath to that sory play,   less desire
For I may synge, allas and waylaway
120   That I was born; but to no **wight**,' quod sche,   person
'Dar I not telle how it stont with me.
Wherfor I think out of this londe to **wende**   go
Or elles of myself to make an ende,
So ful am I of **drede**, and eek of **care**.'   fear; sorrow
This monk bygan upon this wif to stare,
And sayd, 'Allas, my nece! God forbede
That ye for eny sorw or eny drede
Fordo yourself; but telleth me your greef.   harm yourself
Paraventure I may in youre **mescheef**   perhaps; trouble
130   Councel or help, and therfor telleth me
Al your **annoy**, for it schal be secre;   trouble
For on my **portos** I make an oth,   breviary
That never in my lif, for lief ne loth,[9]
Schal I of no counseil you **bywray**.'   disclose
'The same agein,' quod sche, 'to yow I say –
By God and by this portos wil I swere,
Though men me wolde al in peces tere,
Ne schal I never, for to go to helle,
Bywreye word of thing that ye me telle,
140   Not for no **cosynage**, ne alliaunce,   relationship

8 'so that you would need a good rest'
9 'for love nor hate'

But verrayly for love and **affiaunce**.'   friendship
Thus ben thay sworn, and herupon **y-kist**,   exchanged kisses
And ilk of hem told other what hem list.
'Cosyn,' quod sche, 'if that I had a space –
As I have noon, and namly in this place – [10]
Then wold I telle a legend of my lyf,
What I have suffred sith I was a wyf
With my housbond, though he be your **cosyn**.'   relative
'Nay,' quod this monk, 'by God and Seint Martyn!
He is no more cosyn unto me   150
Than is this **leef** that hangeth on the tre!   leaf
I **cleped** him so, by Seint Denis of Fraunce,   called
To have the more cause of acquyntaunce
Of yow, which I have loved specially
Aboven alle wommen, **sikerly**.   truly/surely
This swere I yow on my **professioun**;   monk's oath
Tellith youre greef, lest that he come adoun,
And **hasteth yow**, and goth your way anoon.'   be quick
'My deere **louw**,' quod sche, O Dan John!   love
Ful leef me were this counseil to hyde –   I had rather   160
But out it moot, I may no more abyde!
Myn housbond is to me the worste man
That ever was **siththe** the world bigan,   since
But sith I am a wif, it **sit nought me**   I shouldn't
To telle eny wight of oure **privete**,   private business
Neyther abedde ne in noon other place –
God **schilde** I scholde telle it, for his grace!   forbid
A wyf ne schal no say of hir housbonde
But al honour, as I can understonde;
Save unto yow thus moche telle I schal –   170
As help me God, he is ought worth at al
In no degre the valieu of a flie,[11]
But yit me greveth most his **nigardye**;   miserliness
And wel ye wot that wymmen **naturelly**   by their nature
Desiren sixe thinges as wel as I:
They wolde that here housbondes scholde be
Hardy, and wys, and riche, and **fre**,   strong; generous

10 'and especially not here'
11 'he isn't worth a fly'

And **buxom** to his wyf, and freisch on bedde–   obedient
But by the Lord that for us alle bledde,
180 For his honour, myselven to **array**   clothe
A-Sonday next comyng, yit most I pay
And hundred frank, or elles I am **lorn** –   lost
Yit were me **lever** that I were unborn,   rather
Than me were doon a sclaunder or vilenye;
And if myn housbond eek might it espie,
I ner but lost; and therfor I yow pray
Lene me this somme, or elles moot I deye.
Dan John, I seye, lene me thise hundred franks –
Parde, I wol nat faille yow my thankes,
190 If that yow list to doon that I yow praye.
For at a certein day I wol yow pay,
And do yow what pleasaunce and service
That I may do, right as you list devyse;[12]
And **but** I do, God take on me vengeaunce   unless
As foul as hadde Ganeloun of Fraunce.'[13]
This gentil monk answard in this manere:
'Now trewely, myn owne lady deere,
I have on yow so gret pite and **reuthe**,   pity
That I yow swere and **plighte yow my treuthe**,   give you my word
200 Than whan your housbond is to **Flaundres fare**,   Flanders; gone
I schal deliver yow out of youre care,
For I wol bringe yow an hundred frankes.'
And with that word he caught hir by the **schankes**   legs
And hir **embraced hard**, and kist hir ofte.   held her tightly
'Goth now your way,' quod he, al **stille** and softe,   quietly
'And let us dyne as sone as ye may;
For by my chilindre it is prime of day.[14]
Goth now, and beth as trew as I schal be.'
'Now elles God forbede, Sire,' quod sche,
210 And forth sche goth, as joly as a **pye**,   magpie
And bad the cookes that **thai scholde hem hye**   'jump to it'
So that men myghte dyne, and that anoon.

12 'I'll be good to you and do what you what you want of me'
13 Ganelon betrayed the French romance hero, Roland.
14 A cylinder; a cylindrical, portable form of the astrolabe. It could be used for
  telling the time.

Up to hir housbond this wif is goon,
And knokketh at his dore boldely.
'Qy la?' quod he. 'Peter, it am I!'   who's there
Quod sche, 'How longe, Sire, wol ye **fast**?   go without food
How longe tyme wol ye **reken** and cast   count
Your sommes and your bokes and your thinges?
The devel have part of all such rekenynges!
Ye have ynough **pardy**, **of God's sonde**!   by God's command   220
Com doun today, and let your bagges stonde!
Ne be ye not aschamed that Daun John
Schal al day fastyng thus **elenge** goon?   long
What! Let us hiere masse and gowe dyne!'[15]
'Wif,'quod this man, 'litel canstow **divine**   understand
The **curious** beynesse that we have;   singular
For of us **chapmen** al, so God me save,   merchants
And by that lord that **cleped** is Seint Ive,   called
Scarsly among twelve two **schuln** thrive,   shall
Continuelly lastyng into her **age**.   old age   230
We may wel make cheer and **good visage**,   put on a happy face
And **dryve forth** the world as it may be,   make our way in
And kepen our estat in privete[16]
Til we be **deed**, or elles that we play   dead
A pilgrimage, or goon out of the way.
And therfor have I gret necessite
Upon this queynte world to avyse me,
For evermor we moste stond in drede
Of **hap** and fortun in our **chapmanhede**.[17]
To Flaundres wol I go tomorw at day,   240
And come agayn as soone as I may;
For which, my deere wif, I the **byseek**,   beg
And be to every wight buxom and meeke,
And for to kepe our good be **curious**,   careful
And honestly governe wel our hous.
Thou hast ynough, in every maner wise,
That to a thrifty housbond may **suffise**.   be sufficient

---

15 A private mass celebrated in the house chapel by a privately-hired priest (in this
   case, probably Sir John).
16 'keep ourselves to ourselves'
17 chance; merchant's occupation

The lakketh noon array, ne no vitaile;
Of silver in thy purs thou mayst not faile.'

250 And with that word his countour dore he **schitte**,   shut
And doun he goth; no lenger wold he **lette**.   stay
And hastily a masse was ther sayd,
And spedily the tables were y-layd,
And to the dyner fast thay hem spedde,
And rychely this chapman the monk fedde.
And after dyner Daun John, sobrely,
This chapman took **on part**, and prively   on one side
Sayd him thus: 'Cosyn, it stondeth so
That wel I se to Brigges wol ye go.

260 God and Seint Austyn spede you and gyde;
I pray yow cosyn, wisly that ye ryde.
Governeth yow also of your diete   take care
Attemperelly, and namely in this hete;   with moderation
Bitwix us tuo nedeth no **straunge fare** –   elaborate farewells
Far wel, cosyn! God schilde you fro care!
If eny thing ther be, by day or night,
If it lay in my power and my might
That ye wil me comaunde in eny wise,
It schal be doon right as ye wol **devyse**.   wish

270 O thing er that ye goon, if it might be –
I wolde pray yow for to **lene** me   lend
An hundred frankes for a **wyke** or tweye,   week
For certeyn **bestis** that I moste **beye**   beasts; buy
To store with a place that is oures – [18]   to stock therewith
God help me so, I wolde it were youres –
I schal not faile seurly of my day, [19]
Nought for a thousand frankes a myle way.
But let this thing be secre, I yow pray,
For for the bestis this night most I pay.

280 And fare now wel, myn owne cosyn deere;
Graunt mercy of your cost and of your cheere.'[20]
This noble merchaunt gentilly anoon
Answerd, and sayde, 'O cosyn myn, Daun John!

18 It belongs to the monk's community.
19 'I won't fail to pay you back at the due time'
20 'many thanks for your expense and your hospitality'

Now **sikerly** this is a smal request;   surely
My gold is youres, whanne that yow lest;
And nought oonly my gold, but my **chaffare**.   merchandise
Tak what yow liste, God schilde ye spare!²¹
But oon thing is – ye know it wel ynough
Of chapmen – that her money is here plough.
We may **creaunce**, whils we have a **name**,   get credit; reputation   290
But goldles for to be, it is no game.²²
Pay it agayn whan it lith in your ese;
After my might ful **fayn** wold I yow plese.'²³
This hundred frankes he **fet** forth anoon,   fetched
And prively he took hem to Daun John.
No wight in al this world wist of this **loone**,   loan
Savyng the marchaund and Daun John alloone.
Thay drynke, & speke, and rome a while, and play,
Til that Dan John rydeth to his abbay.
The morwe cam, and forth the marchaund rideth   300
To Flaundresward; his **prentis** wel him gydeth   apprentice
Til that he cam to **Brigges**, merily.   Bruges (in Flanders)
Now goth this marchaund faste and busily
Aboute his neede, and **bieth** and **creaunceth**;   buys; gets credit
He neither pleyeth atte dys ne daunceth,
But as a marchaund, schortly for to telle,
He lad his lyf – and ther I let him dwelle.
The Sonday next the marchaund is agoon,
To Seint Denys y-com is Daun John,
With **croune** and berd al freisch and newe y-schave;   crown (of his head) 310
In al the hous ther nas so litel a knave
Ne no wight elles, that he nas ful **fayn**   glad
For that my lord Dan John was come agayn.
And schortly to the poynte for to gon,
This faire wif **acordith** with Dan John,   made an agreement
That for these hundred frank he schuld al night
Have hir in his armes bolt upright;²⁴

---

21 'God forbid you don't take enough'
22 'it is no laughing matter to be without money'
23 'pay it back when you can comfortably do so; I would do all in my power to
   please you'
24 'flat on her back (underneath him)'

And this **acord** parformed was in **dede** –   agreement; deed
In mirth al night a bisy lif thay lede –
320 Til it was day, that Dan John went his way,
And bad the **meigne**, 'Far wel, have good day!'   household
For noon of hem, ne no wight in the toun,
Hath of Dan John right noon **suspeccioun**.   suspicion
And forth he rideth, hom to his abbay,
Or wher him list – no more of him I say.
This marchaund, whan that ended was the faire,
To Seynt Denys he gan to repeire,
And with his wif he maketh fest and cheere,
And tellith hir that **chaffare** is so deere   merchandise
330 That needes most he make a **chevisaunce**,   loan
For he was bounde in a **reconisaunce**   pledge
To paye twenty thousand scheldes anoon,[25]
For which this marchaund is to Paris goon,
To borwe of certeyn frendes that he hadde
A **certein** frankes, and some with him he **ladde**.   certain sum of; brought
And whan that he was come into the toun,
For gret **chiertee** and gret affeccioun,   friendliness
Unto Dan John he first goth him to play –
Nought for to borwe of him no **kyn** monay,   sum of
340 But for to **wite** and se of his welfare,   find out
And for to telle him of his chaffare,
As frendes doon whan thay ben met **in fere**.   together
Dan John maketh fest and mery cheere,
And he him told agayn ful specially
How he had bought right wel and graciously,
Thanked be God, al his marchaundise;
Save that he most in alle manere wise
Maken a chevyssauns, as for his best,
And than he schulde be in joye and rest.
350 Dan John answerde, 'Certis, I am **fayn**   glad
That ye in **hele** are comen hom agayn.   health
And if that I were riche, as have I blisse,
Of twenty thousand scheld schuld ye not **mysse**,   go without

25 Shields; a unit of currency.

For ye so kyndely this other day
Lente me gold, and as I can and may
I thanke you, by God and by Seint Jame;
But natheles, I took it to our Dame
Youre wif the same gold agein,
Upon your bench – sche wot it wel, certeyn,
By certein **toknes** that I can hir telle.   proofs 360
Now by your leve, I may no lenger **duelle**;   remain
Oure abbot wol out of toun anoon,
And in his compaignye moot I goon.
Grete wel oure Dame, myn nece swete,
And fare wel, dere cosyn, til that we meete!'
This marchaund, which that was bothe **war** and wys,   careful
Creaunced hath, and payed eek in Parys
To certeyn Lombardes, redy in hir hond,
This somme of gold, and took of hem his bond;[26]
And hom he goth, as mery as a **popiniay**,   parrot 370
For wel he knew he stood in such **array**   a state
That needes most he wynne in such **viage**   journey
A thousand frenkes above al his costage.[27]
His wyf redy mette him at the gate,
As sche was wont of old **usage** algate;   custom
And al that night in mirthe thay ben sette,
For he was riche and clerly out of dette.
Whan it was day, this marchaund gan embrace
His wyf al newe, and kist hir on hir face;
And up he goth, and maketh it ful tough.[28]   380
'No more!' quod sche, 'By God! Ye have ynough!'
And wantounly with hem sche lay and playde,
Til atte laste thus this marchaund sayde:
'By God!' quod he, 'I am a litel **wroth**   annoyed
With yow my wyf, although **it be me loth**.   I don't want to
And wite ye why? By God, as that I gesse,
Ye han y-maad a maner **straungenesse**   distance
Bitwixe me and my cosyn, Dan John –
Ye schold have warned me, er I had goon,

26 'took assurances from him'
27 'above his expenses'
28 'and up he went, and gave her a hard time (sexually)'

390	That he yow had an hundred frankes payd
	By redy token, and huld him evel appayd[29]
	For that I to him spak of **chevysaunce**. — credit
	Me semed so, as by his countenaunce,
	But natheles, by God, of heven king,
	I thoughte nought to **axe** him nothing. — ask
	I pray the, wif, do no more so –
	Tel me alway, **er** that I fro the go, — before
	If eny **dettour** have in myn absence — debtor
	Y-payed the; lest in thy necgligence
400	I may him axe a thing that he hath payed.'
	This wyf was not **affered**, ne **affrayed**; — fearful; flustered
	But **holly** sche sayde, and that anoon, — boldly
	'Mary! I diffy that false monk, Dan John!
	I kepe not of his tokenes never a del![30]
	He took me a certeyn gold, that wot I wel –
	What evel **thedom** on his monk's snowte! — ill luck
	For, God it wot, I **wende** withoute doute — believed
	That he had geve it me bycause of yow,
	To do therwith myn honour and my **prow**, — profit
410	For **cosynage** and eek for **bele cheer** — kinship; good cheer
	That he hath had ful ofte tyme heer;
	But **synnes** that I stonde in this **disioynt** — since; difficulty
	I wol anwer yow schortly, to the poynt.
	Ye han mo **slakke** dettours than am I, — slow
	For I wol pay yow wel and redily
	Fro day to day, and if so be I faile;
	I am your wif – score it upon my taile,[31]
	And I schal paye it as soone as I may,
	For by my trouthe, I have on myn array –
420	And nought on **wast** – **bistowed** it every del; — rubbish; spent
	And for I have bistowed it so wel
	To youre honour, for God's sake I say,
	As beth nought wroth, but let us laugh and play. — don't be angry
	Ye schul my joly body have **to wedde**; — as a pledge/surety
	By God, I wol not pay yow but on bedde!

29 'in ready cash; and considered himself hard done by'
30 'I haven't got any of his cash at all'
31 'chalk it up on my tally' but also 'I will pay you back with sex (tail)'

Forgeve it me, myn owne spouse deere –
Turne **hiderward**, and make better cheere!'   *this way*
This marchaund saugh noon other remedy,
And for to chide it nas but foly,
Sith that the thing may not **amendid** be.   *put right*   430
'Wif,' he sayde, 'and I forgive it the;
But by thi lif, ne be no more so **large**.   *generous*
Keep better my good – this give I the in charge.'
Thus endeth now my tale, and God us send
Talyng ynough, unto our lyves' ende.[32]   *enough credit*

32 But also has a sexual meaning 'enough tail-ing'

THE PRIORESS'S PROLOGUE AND TALE

After laughing at the shipman's story, and lightheartedly cursing all monks, the host, very respectfully, asks the prioress to tell a tale. She begins by praising God and the Virgin Mary as Mother of God, and calls upon the Blessed Virgin to help her in telling her story.

In Asia Minor there is a city with a Jewish ghetto. The city has a Christian community, which has a school for little children. These children have to pass through the Jewish ghetto to reach the school. In the school there is a seven-year-old scholar, a young boy who is especially devoted to the Virgin Mary. One day he hears a song called 'Alma Redemptoris Mater', a hymn to the virgin, and asks an older boy to explain it. When he knows it praises Mary, the boy sings it all the way to and from school. The devil persuades the Jews to have a contract killer murder the boy on his way through the ghetto. This done, the killer throws the boy's body into a cesspit. The boy's distraught mother searches all over for him, and eventually he is found by the sound of his singing, although he is dead. Taken to the abbey for burial, the boy tells the abbot that the Virgin came to him in the pit and put a grain in his mouth. As long as the grain is there, he will continue to sing, but when it is removed the Virgin will come and take him to heaven. The abbot removes the grain, and the boy is taken (that is, he finally dies). The provost of the city has all the Jews in the ghetto killed. The prioress is reminded by this story of another boy martyr, Hugh of Lincoln, allegedly killed by Jews.

There has been much debate concerning this story's anti-Semitism. On one side are those who perceive that the story is only seemingly anti-Semitic, because the teller is a woman presented as something of an impostor by Chaucer. The fact that the prioress is described as ignorant of biblical knowledge and addicted to courtly romance, means that the tale is intended to be ironic, and its anti-Jewish sentiments cannot therefore be meant to be taken seriously; nor can they be Chaucer's own views. On the other side are those who say that this is pure anti-Semitism, and that Chaucer was a conventional medieval Christian, who intended these views to be taken seriously. Although both views have some foundation, the latter appears, unfortunately, to be the most likely. The writer does seem to take this story seriously – the host accords every respect to the 'lady prioresse', and there is no indication that this tale is told by her out of ignorance, nor is there any hint of ironic intent.

The tale is, however, more than a piece of anit-Semitic invective. It is also a tale about a child told by a woman who has no children, but who might perhaps have wanted some had her circumstances been different. She identifies herself with the little child of twelve months old 'souking'. The little clergeoun has not reached puberty, nor will he, as he dies before he can become a 'real man'. The power in the story belongs to a woman, the Virgin, who has the power of life and death, even over men. However, it is the abbot who takes the grain from the boy, and thereby silences him. The Virgin was particularly associated in medieval times with women, children and Jewish or Saracen converts. There is a relationship between women, children and Jews configured within this story, which was perceived by Chaucer, but within the structures of the tale and the Christian beliefs he held, he was unable fully to articulate it, and therefore the tale fails. These groups, for different reasons, were all marginalised in medieval society, which was run by (qualified) men for men. The Jews choose a child-victim, the woman looks for her child, but none of this has any influence at all on society. It is the abbot who performs the ritual by which the boy becomes a 'saint' and a holy martyr, part of institutionalised faith, and the provost who takes society's revenge on the Jews. The boy's mother is not mentioned again after his funeral. In fact, the Jews were placed in an impossible bind because the provost permitted them to live in the city in the first place, to perform the necessary usury which allowed trade to flourish (as had been their function in England until their expulsion in 1290), but which was itself a condemned and therefore marginalised practice.

Although the prioress is a well-brought-up lady, from a comfortable background, and holds the highest office in the Church open to a woman, she cannot perform the Mass for her convent, but is reliant upon the priest, simply because he is a man. It is unsurprising that her heroine is the Virgin Mary, a woman who has divine power, although of course that power is only conveyed by her function as the mother of a man who is also God, Jesus Christ. It may be that she finds little children so appealing because she is a woman of 'sensibilities' and emotion, but her 'calling' denies her the opportunity to have children of her own. The prioress appears to lack the ability of her 'chapeleyne' to articulate her desire for inclusion and for power in a world where almost all authority is male.

Key Questions

Why does the prioress tell a story with such violent content? Why is it concerned with child martyrs and evil Jews?

The setting is Asia Minor, where Christians lived under Muslim control in Chaucer's time. What does this story reveal about how the Holy Land/non-Christians were viewed?

Is the prioress frustrated by her 'calling' as a nun?

Topic Keywords

Child saints/ nuns and female religious/ medieval children and families/ the exotic/ non-Christian 'others', especially Jews/ Marian devotion/ singing and the medieval liturgy/ popular religion

Further Reading

Robert Adams, 'Chaucer's New Rachel and the Theological Roots of Medieval Anti-Semitism', *Bulletin of the John Rylands Library*, 77, 1995, pp. 9–18

Laurence Besserman, 'Ideology, Anti-Semitism, and Chaucer's Prioress's Tale', *Chaucer Review*, 36, 2001, pp. 48–72

Michael Calabrese, 'Performing the Prioress: "Conscience" and Responsibility in Studies of Chaucer's Prioress's Tale', *Texas Studies in Literature and Language*, 44, 2002, pp. 66–91

Carolyn P. Collette, 'Sense and Sensibility in The Prioress's Tale', *Chaucer Review*, 15, 1980, pp. 138–50

Roger Dahood, 'English Historical Narratives of Jewish Child-Murder, Chaucer's Prioress's Tale, and the Date of Chaucer's Unknown Source', *Studies in the Age of Chaucer*, 31, 2009, pp. 125–40

Sheila Delany, 'Chaucer's Prioress, the Jews and the Muslims', *Medieval Encounters*, 5, 1999, pp. 199–213

Denise Despres, 'Cultic Anti-Judaism and Chaucer's Litel Clergeoun', *Modern Philology*, 91, 1994, pp. 413–27

Sumner Ferris, 'Chaucer at Lincoln (1387): The Prioress's Tale as a Political Poem', *Chaucer Review*, 15, 1981, pp. 295–321

Louise O. Fradenberg, 'Criticism, Anti-Semitism and The Prioress's Tale', *Exemplaria*, 1, 1989, pp. 69–115

Hardy Frank, 'Seeing the Prioress Whole', *Chaucer Review*, 25, 1991, pp. 229–37

Kathleen Hobbs, 'Blood and Rosaries: Virginity, Violence and Desire in Chaucer's Prioress's Tale', in *Constructions of Widowhood and Virginity in the Middle Ages*, edited by Cindy Carlson, edited and introduced by Angela Weisl, New York, St Martin's Press, 1999, pp. 181–98.

Bruce Holsinger, 'Pedagogy, Violence and the Subject of Music: Chaucer's Prioress's Tale and the Ideologies of Song', *New Medieval Literatures*, 4, 1997, pp. 157–92

Allen Koretsky, 'Dangerous Innocence: Chaucer's Prioress and her Tale', in *Jewish Presences in English Literature*, edited by Derek Cohen and Deborah Heller, Montreal, McGill-Queen's University Press, 1990, pp. 10–24

Lee Patterson, ' "The Living Witnesses of our Redemption": Martyrdom and Imitation in Chaucer's Prioress's Tale', *Journal of Medieval and Early Modern Studies*, 31, 2001, pp. 507–60

Richard Rambuss, 'Devotion and Defilement: The Blessed Virgin Mary and the Corporeal Hagiographics of Chaucer's Prioress's Tale', in *Textual Bodies: Changing Boundaries of Literary Representation*, edited by Lori Hope Lefkovitz, Albany, NY, State University of New York Press, 1997, pp. 75–99

Stefan Russell, 'Song and the Ineffable in The Prioress's Tale', *Chaucer Review*, 33, 1998, pp. 176–89

Stephen Spector, 'Empathy and Enmity in The Prioress's Tale', in *The Olde Daunce: Love, Friendship, Sex and Marriage in the Medieval World*, edited by Robert Edwards and Stephen Spector, Albany, NY, State University of New York Press, 1991, pp. 211–28

Greg Wilsbacher, 'Lumiansky's Paradox: Ethics, Aesthetics and Chaucer's Prioress's Tale', *College Literature*, 32, 2005, pp. 1–28

Emmy Stark Zitter, 'Anti-Semitism in The Prioress's Tale', *Chaucer Review*, 25, 1991, pp. 277–84

Proemium

prologue

❦ Wel sayd, **by corpus boones**! quod oure host,   *by Christ's bones*
'Now longe **mot** thou sayle by the **cost**,   *may; coast*
Sir gentil maister, gentil mariner!
God give the monk a thousand **last quadeyer**!   *cartloads of bad luck*
Ha!ha! Felaws, bewar for such a **iape**;   *joke*
The monk put in the man's hood an ape,
And in his wyve's eek, by Seint Austyn!
Draweth no monkes more unto your **in** –   *house (in town)*
But now **pasover** and let us loke aboute;   *pass on*   10
Who schal telle first of al this **route**   *company*
Another tale?' And with that word he sayde,
As curteisly as it had ben a mayde,
'My Lady Prioresse, by your leve,
So that I wist I scholde yow not greve –
I wolde **deme** that ye telle scholde   *judge*
A tale next, if so were that ye wolde.[1]
Now wol ye **vouche sauf**, my lady deere?'   *grant*
'Gladly,' quod sche, and sayd in this manere:

Benedicite dominus noster   20

may Our Lord bless us

❦ 'O Lord, Our Lord, thy name how merveylous[2]
Is in this large world y-sprad,' quod sche,
'For nought oonly thy **laude precious**   *worthy praise*
Parformed is by men of **heih degre**,   *high status*
But by mouthes of children thy **bounte**   *goodness*
Parformed is, on oure brest **soukyng**;   *sucking*
Somtyme schewe thay thin **heriyng**.   *worship*

Wherfore, in **laude**, as I best can or may,   *praise*
Of the and of thy white lily **flour**   *flower (the Virgin Mary)*

1 'If you would like to'
2 Psalm 8

30	Which that the **bar**, and is a **mayde** alway,	bore; virgin
	To telle a story I wil **do my labour**;	try (hard)
	Nought that I may **encresce** youre honour –	increase
	For sche hirsilf is honur and roote	
	Of bounte next hir sone, and soul's **boote**.	benefit

	O Modir, **Mayde**! O Mayde, Mooder fre!	virgin
	O bussh **undrent** brennyng in Moises sight,[3]	unconsumed
	That ravysshedest doun fro the deite!	
	Thurgh thin humblesse the **gost** that in the alight,	(Holy) spirit
	Of whos **vertu**, when he in thin herte **light**,	power; alighted
40	Conceyved was the Fadre's **sapience**;	wisdom
	Help me to telle it in thy reverence.	

	Lady, thi bounte and thy magnificence,	
	Thy **vertus** and thi gret humilite,	virtue
	Ther may no tonge expres in no **science**;	knowledge
	For somtyme, Lady, er men pray to the,	
	Thow gost **biforn**, of thy **benignite**,	before; kindness
	And getist us the light, thurgh thy prayere,	
	To gyden us the way to thy Sone so deere.	

	My **connyng** is to **weyk**, O blisful Queene,	knowledge; weak
50	For to declare thy grete worthinesse,	
	That I may not this in my wyt susteene,[4]	
	But as a child of twelf month old, or lesse,	except like
	That can **unnethes** eny word expresse;	hardly
	Right so fare I, and therfore I you pray,	
	Endith my song that I schal of yow say.	

	Ther was in **Acy**, in a greet cite	Asia
	Amonges Cristen folk, a **Jewerye**,	Jewish ghetto
	Susteyned by a lord of that contre	
	For foul **usure** and **lucre** of felonye,	usury; profit
60	Hateful to Crist and to his compaignye;	
	And thurgh the strete men might ride and **wende**,	go
	For it was **fre**, and open at **everich** ende.	accessible; each

3 The burning bush w as seen to prefigure the impregnation of Mary.
4 'I cannot deal with this material by my own intellectual capacity alone'

A litel scole of Cristen folk ther stood
Doun at the forther ende, in which ther were
Children an **heep**, **y-comen of Crist's blood**,   pile; Christians
That **lered** in that scole yer by yere   studied
Such maner doctrine as men used there;
This is to say, to synge and to rede,
As smale childer doon in her childhede.

Among these children was a widow's sone,   70
A litel **clergeoun**, that seven yer was of age,   boy in church school
That day by day to scole was his **wone**,   custom
And eek also, **wherso** he saugh **thymage**   wherever; the image
Of Crist's Moder **had he in usage**   it was his custom
As him was taught, to knele adoun and say
His **Ave Maria**, as he goth by the way.   Hail Mary

Thus hath this widow her litel child y-taught
Oure blisful Lady, Crist's Moder deere,
To worship **ay**, and he **foryat** it nought;   always; forgot
For **cely** child wil alway soone **leere** –   happy/sweet; learn   80
But ay whan I remembre of this matiere,
Seint Nicholas **stont ever in my presence**,[5]
For he so yong to Crist dede reverence.

This litel child, his litel book lernynge,
As he sat in the scole, in his **primere**,   first reading book
He, '*O alma redemptoris*' herde synge,[6]
As children lerned her **antiphonere**;   hymn-book
And as he durst he **drough** him **ner and neere**,   drew; nearer and nearer
And herkned ever the wordes and the note,
Til he the firste vers **couthe al by rote**.   knew by heart   90

Nought wist he what this Latyn **was to say**,   meant
For he so yong and tender was of age;
But on a day his **felaw** gan he pray   companion
To **expoune** him the song in his **langage**,   explain; language

5 'always comes into my mind'
6 'O Mother of the Redeemer'; a hymn to the Virgin, in Latin.

Or telle him **what** this song **was in usage**.   how .. was used
This prayd he him to **construe** and declare   explain
Ful often tyme, upon his knees bare.

His felaw, which that **elder** was than he,   older
100   Answerd him thus, 'This song, I have herd seye,
Was maked of Our blisful Lady fre,
Hire to **salven**, and eek hire to preye,   greet
To ben our help and socour whan we **deye**.   die
I can no more expoune in this matere –
I lerne song; I **can** no more **gramer**.'   know; grammar

'And is this song y-maad in reverence
Of Cristes Moder?' sayde this innocent,
'Now certes, I wol do my **diligence**   very best
To **conne** it al, er Cristemasse be went,   learn
110   Though that I for my primer schal be **schent**,   punished
And schal be **betyn thries** in an hour;   beaten three times
I wol it conne, Oure Lady to honoure.'

His felaw taught him **homward**, prively,   on the way home
From day to day, til he couthe it by rote;
And than he song it wel and boldely –
Twyes on the day it passed thurgh his throte,
From word to word, accordyng to the note.
To scoleward and homward, whan he went,
On Crist's Moder was set al his entent.

120   As I have sayd, thurghout the Jewrye
This litel child, as he cam to and fro,
Ful merily than wold he synge and crie,
'*O alma redemptoris*,' evermo.
The swetnes hath his herte **persed** so   pierced
Of Crist's Moder, that to hir to pray,
He cannot **stynt** of syngyng by the way.   stop

Oure firste **foo**, the serpent **Sathanas**,   foe/enemy; Satan
That hath in Jewes' hert his waspis nest,
Upswal and sayde, 'O **Ebreik** peple, allas!   rose up; Hebrew
130   Is this a thing to yow that is honest,

That such a boy schal walken **as him lest**   just as he likes
In youre despyt, and synge of such sentence
Which is ayens your lawe's reverence?'

Fro thennesforth the Jewes han conspired
This innocent out of this world to **enchace**;   chase/despatch
An homicide therto han thay hired,
That in an **aley** had a **prive** place;   alley/side-road; secret
And as the childe gan forth by to pace,
This false Jewe him **hent** and **huld** ful faste,   seized; held
And kut his throte and threw him in atte laste –   140

I say, in a **wardrobe** thay him threw,   cess pit
Wher as the Jewes **purgen her entraile**.   empty their bowels
O cursed folk! O Herodes al newe!
What may your evyl entente you **availe**?   help
Morther wol out – certeyn, it wil nought faile –   murder
And namly **ther** th'honour of God schuld sprede,   where
The blood out crieth on your cursed dede.

O martir, **sondit** to virginite!   in union with
Now maystow synge, folwyng **ever in oon**   for ever
The white Lomb Celestial,' quod sche,   150
Of which the grete evaungelist, Seint John,[7]
In Pathmos wroot, which seith that thay goon
Bifore the Lamb, and synge a song al newe,
That never **fleischly** wommen thay knewe.   carnally/sexually

This pore widowe **wayteth** al this night   awaited
After this litel child, but he cometh nought;
For which, as soone as it was day's light,
With face pale, in drede and busy thought,[8]
Sche hath at scole and elleswher him sought,
Til fynally sche gan of hem **aspye**   find out 160
That he was last seyn in the Jewerie.

7 The lamb of God, from the Revelation of St John. The lamb, representing the
  crucified and resurrected Christ, sits at the heart of God's throne.
8 'thoughts running through her head'

With moodre's pite in hir brest enclosed,
Sche goth as sche were half out of hir mynde,
To every place wher sche hath supposed
By liklihede hir child for to fynde,
And ever on Crist's Mooder, meke and kynde,
Sche cried; and atte laste thus sche wrought –
Among the cursed Jewes sche him sought.

Sche **freyned**, and sche prayed pitously   asked
170   To every Jew that dwelled in that place,
To telle hir if hir child wente ther by.
Thay sayden, 'Nay,' but Jhesu of his grace
yaf in hir thought withinne a litel space,   put into her mind
That in that place after hir sone sche cryde,   so that
Wheras he was cast in a **put** bysyde.   pit

O grete God, that parformedist thin **laude**   praise
By mouth of innocents! Lo, here thy might!
This gemme of chastite, this **emeraude**,   emerald
And eek of martirdom the ruby bright;
180   **Ther** he with throte y-kut lay **upright**,   where; flat out
He, 'Alma redemptoris,' gan to synge,
So lowde that al the place bigan to rynge.

The Cristen folk that thurgh the strete went
In comen, for to wonder upon this thing;
And hastily for the provost thay sent.[9]
He cam **anoon**, withoute tarying,   immediately
And **heriede** Crist, that is of heven king,   worshipped
And eek his Moder, Honour of mankynde –
And after that, the Jewes **let** he bynde.   commanded

190   This child, with pitous lamentacioun,
Up-taken was, syngyng his song alway
And with honour of gret processioun
Thay caried him unto the next abbay.
His modir **swownyng** by the **beere** lay;   swooning; bier

9 An official, in charge of the maintenance of law and order.

Unnethe might the poeple that was there   hardly
This newe Rachel bringe fro the beere.[10]

With torment, and with schamful deth **echon**,   every one
This provost **doth** these Jewes for to **sterve**   made; kill
That of this moerder **wist**, and that anoon.   knew
He wolde no such cursednesse observe –   200
Evel schal have that evyl wol deserve –
Therfore with wilde hors he dede hem **drawe**,   pull along the ground
And after that he **heng** hem, **by** the lawe.   hanged; according to

Upon his beere ay **lith** this innocent,   lay
Biforn the chief **auter**, whiles the masse last,   altar
And after that th'abbot with his **covent**   community of monks
Hath sped him for to burie him ful fast;
And whan thay **halywater** on him cast,   holy (blessed) water
Yet spak this child, whan **spreynde** was the water,   sprinkled
And song, '*O alma redemptoris mater.*'   210

This abbot, which that was an holy man
As monkes ben – or elles oughte be –
This yonge child to **conjure** he bigan,   ask
And sayd, 'O deere child, I **halse** the,   beseech
In vertu of the Holy Trinite,
Tel me what is thy cause for to synge,
Sith that thy throte is kit, **at my semynge**?'   it seems to me

'My throte is kit unto my nekke boon,'
Sayde this child, 'and as **by way of kynde**   as nature is
I schulde han ben deed long tyme agoon;   220
But Jhesu Crist, as ye in bookes fynde,
Wol that his glorie laste and be **in mynde**;   remembered
And for the worship of his Moder deere,
Yet may I synge, 'O alma,' lowde and cleere.

This welle of mercy, Crist's Moder swete
I loved alway, as after my **connynge**;   understanding
And whan that I my lyf schulde **leete**,   leave

10 A reference to Herod's Massacre of the Innocents.

To me sche cam and bad me for to synge
This **antym**, verraily, in my **deyinge**,   anthem; dying
230   As ye have herd; and whan that I had songe,
Me thought sche layde a **grayn** under my tonge.   grain

Wherfor I synge, and synge **moot** certeyne   must
In honour of that blisful Mayden fre,
Til fro my tonge taken is the greyn;
And after that, thus saide sche to me:
'My litil child, now wil I **fecche** the,   fetch
Whan that the grayn is fro thi tonge y-take.
Be nought **agast** – I wol the nought forsake.'   afraid

This holy monk, this abbot – him mene I –
240   His tonge out caught, and took awey the greyn,
And he **yaf up the gost** ful softely.   gave up the ghost (died)
And whan the abbot hath this wonder **seyn**,   seen
His salte teres **striken** doun as **reyn**   fell; rain
And **gruf** he fel adoun unto the grounde,   prostrate
And stille he lay, as he had ben y-bounde.

The covent eek lay on the **pavyment**,   tiled floor
Wepyng and **herying** Crist's Moder deere;   praising
And after that thay rise and forth thay went,
And took away this martir fro his **beere**;   bier
250   And in a tombe of marble stoones cleere
Enclosed thay this litil body sweete;
Ther he is now, God lene us for to meete.[11]

O yonge Hughe of Lyncoln, slayn also[12]
With cursed Jewes, as it is notable –
For it **nys** but a litel while ago –   is not
Pray eek for us, we synful folk **unstable**,   inconstant
That of his mercy God so **merciable**   merciful
On us his grete mercy multiplie,
For reverence of his Modir Marie. **Amen**.

11 May God make us fit to go where he is now...
12 Hugh of Lincoln, a supposed child martyr killed by Jews in 1255

'GEOFFREY'S' TALES: SIR THOPAS AND
THE TALE OF MELIBEE

The Tale of Sir Thopas

The pilgrims are quiet and serious after this, so the host begins gently to tease 'Geoffrey', remarking on how 'cute' he is, and how attractive he must be to women. The host asks for a happy story, and 'Geoffrey' agrees, on the condition that he only knows one story, which he learned long ago.

A knight named Sir Thopas lives beyond the sea, in Flanders. He is chivalrous, a fighter and a hunter, and he is chaste, although women sigh for him. One day he is riding through a forest, which enchants him so that he lies down and longs for the love of a fairy, an elf queen. He goes to seek one of these, and meets a Saracen giant, named Olifaunt, and agrees to fight him. Thopas arms himself, and 'Geoffrey' begins to describe his armour in detail, when the host breaks in and demands that he stops this dreadful rhyming . . .

The host asks 'Geoffrey' to tell a tale, thinking from his physical appearance that it will be a good one. In fact, only a brilliant poet could have written a tale so self-consciously dreadful as that of Sir Thopas. 'Geoffrey' introduces an amalgam of romance tropes and subject matter, including the device of the mortal who has a faery lover. There are full descriptions of Sir Thopas's ideal appearance, his armour and the wild nature through which he travels. The trope of the faery lover is common to thirteenth- and fourteenth-century romances such as *Sir Launfal,* and *Partenope of Blois.* Thomas of Erceldoune is kidnapped by a faery woman and kept inside a mountain for a year and a day. The 'plot', such as it is, wanders nonchalantly along and goes nowhere. The form used is the four-stress line of popular, often orally-transmitted, romances such as the Robin Hood stories. Alongside Chaucer's more flexible five-stress lines, this type of poetry appears ridiculously old-fashioned, not sophisticated enough for his discerning audience. The host bursts in to stop 'Geoffrey', telling him that his dreadful poetry is not worth a turd. 'Geoffrey' says that this is an 'old' story, further indicating that this type of romance literature was seen as old-fashioned, along with the lifestyle which inspired, and was inspired by, it.

Key Questions

What is wrong with Sir Thopas? Why does the host intervene to stop it? Why would Chaucer present his own 'alter ego' as such a dreadful poet?

Does Sir Thopas have anything in common with The Squire's Tale, which was also interrupted?

Topic Keywords

Chivalry and knighthood/ romance as genre/ magic and fairies/ giants and monsters/ plants, forests and nature

Further Reading

William Askins, 'All that Glisters: The Historical Setting of The Tale of Sir Thopas', in *Reading Medieval Culture: Essays in Honor of Robert W. Hanning*, edited by Robert M. Prior and Sandra Pearson, Notre Dame, IN, Notre Dame University Press, 2005, pp. 271–89

Marianne Borch, 'Writing Remembering Orality: Geoffrey Chaucer's Sir Thopas', *European Journal of English Studies*, 10, 2006, pp. 131–48

Celia Daileader, 'The Thopas–Melibee Sequence and the Defeat of Antifeminism', *Chaucer Review*, 29, 1994, pp. 26–39

Alan T. Gaylord, 'Chaucer's Dainty "Dogerel": The "Elvyssh" Prosody of Sir Thopas', *Studies in the Age of Chaucer*, 1, 1979, pp. 83–104

—— 'The Miracle of Sir Thopas', *Studies in the Age of Chaucer*, 6, 1984, pp. 65–84

Ann S. Haskell, 'Sir Thopas: The Puppet's Puppet', *Chaucer Review*, 9, 1975, pp. 253–61

Erik Kooper, 'Inverted Images in Chaucer's Tale of Sir Thopas', *Studia Neophilologica*, 56, 1984, pp. 147–54

Seth Lerer, 'Now Holde Youre Mouth: The Romance of Orality in the Thopas–Melibee Section of *The Canterbury Tales*', in *Oral Poetics in Middle English Poetry*, edited by Mark Amodio and Sarah Miller, New York, Garland, 1994, pp. 181–205

Lee Patterson, ' "What Man Artow?": Authorial Self-Definition in The Tale of Sir Thopas and The Tale of Melibee', *Studies in the Age of Chaucer*, 11, 1989, pp. 117–75

Victor Scattergood, 'Chaucer and the French War: Sir Thopas and Melibee', in *Court and Poet: Selected Proceedings of the Third Congress of the International Courtly Literature Society*, edited by Glyn Burgess, A. Deyermond, W. Jackson, A. Mills and T. P. Ricketts, Liverpool, Cairns, 1981, pp. 287–96

Paul Beekman Taylor, 'Triadic Contexts and Structures of Chaucer's Sir Thopas', *English Language Notes*, 37, 1999, pp. 1–13

Glenn Wright, 'Modern Inconveniences: Rethinking Parody in The Tale of Sir Thopas', *Genre*, 30, 1997, pp. 167–94

THE TALE OF MELIBEE

Having been stopped from finishing his tale of Sir Thopas, 'Geoffrey' says that he will give a little treatise on more serious subjects, and begs the pilgrims not to stop him again, before he has finished.

Melibee is a 'gentil' man whose wife and daughter are attacked while he is away. On his return, he is very angry and wants revenge on his enemies. He summons all his friends and neighbours for their advice. The younger ones advise him to summon his strength and make war on the perpetrators, whilst he interprets the more sage advice of his older friends in the same vein. His wife, Prudence, offers her own wisdom. At first Melibee says that he will not be counselled by a woman, as people will think him a fool, but she explains that women can be both good and wise, summoning examples from the Bible (the Virgin Mary, Rebecca, Judith, Abigail, Esther) in support. As a result, Melibee agrees to be advised by her. Prudence tells him you do not think reasonably when you are angry; you should listen to your real friends; you should keep your own counsel, and share it only with a few friends you trust; don't listen to flattery; don't act hastily; two 'wrongs' do not make a 'right'; it is better to be loved by your dependants than to have a garrison and supplies; it is stupid to act alone against those who are much stronger than yourself – leave vengeance to the judges; avoid idleness, be moderate in getting and in spending; consider your own faults first; rule yourself if you want to rule others.

She tells Melibee that his troubles are sent by God in order to show him how fortunate he has been, to help him to understand that he must learn how to deal with reversals, too.

Melibee agrees that this is really good advice, and he will be ruled by it. He allows Prudence to act as a go-between to broker a peace deal between himself and his enemies.

Having been told to change his story or be quiet, 'Geoffrey' offers something in prose, a form traditionally used for historical and didactic works. The Tale of Melibee is a translation of a French translation by Reynaud de Louens from the *Liber consolationis et consilii* ('Book of Consolation and Counsel') by the thirteenth-century writer Albertanus of Brescia. It is a stylised debate between the husband, Melibee, and his wife Prudence. Melibee's daughter Sophie has been wounded five times by enemies who have burst into his house. The debate is allegorical: Sophie's wounds are the senses, Prudence is a personification of an abstract virtue, and Melibee, whose name, as Prudence explains, means, 'one who eats honey', or 'one who takes in wise/sweet counsel', can be seen as representative of the human lord, or ruler; one who wields a position of wealth and authority. Given this, the tale can be seen to be a treatise on good lordship. Melibee wishes to exact violent revenge by waging war on his enemies, but Prudence gradually dissuades him, countering all his arguments one by one. In the end, Melibee and his enemies are reconciled, when he exercises good, prudent and merciful lordship.

The treatise was written independently of *The Canterbury Tales*, and included later, although how much later is not certain. It has been suggested that it was written for Richard II, to encourage him to show mercy and good judgement. Helen Cooper has suggested that Chaucer's additions to the lines

> the litel wesele wol slee the grete bole and the wilde hert. And the book seith
> 'A litel thorn may prikke a kyng ful soore . . .

indicate a date after Richard's assumption of the white hart badge in 1390. In fact, they may indicate a date later than this, as Henry Bolingbroke's badge was the hawthorn. Henry was back in England after his crusading adventures by 1397. As the main character in the treatise is not Melibee but Prudence, and she fulfils the role not only of a wife but a ruler and guide, a political role, it may be that Chaucer compiled the treatise not for Richard, but for Richard and his wife, in this case his new wife Isabelle, daughter of the King of France, the child-queen whose marriage cemented the twenty-year truce Richard signed with her father Charles VI in 1396. Prudence is not simply a wife, but a ruler's wife, making this an ideal gift for a queen.

Key Questions

Can Prudence be related to any of the women in other tales, in particular the wise Constance and Griselda? Does she compare to the Lady Philosophy in *Boece*?

How does Prudence's advice compare with the 'good rulership' advice in stories such as the knight's?

How does this advice compare with the parson's tale, the other 'prose treatise' in *The Canterbury Tales*?

Can the setting of the tale, and the advice it offers, be related to history/society in the late fourteenth and early fifteenth century in England?

Topic Keywords

Medieval philosophy/ rulership/ women in society/ society and history/ instructional (didactic) literature

Further Reading

William Askins, 'The Tale of Melibee and the Crisis at Westminster, November 1387', *Studies in the Age of Chaucer*, 2, 1986, pp. 102–12

Diane Bornstein, 'Chaucer's Tale of Melibee as an Example of the Style Clergial', *Chaucer Review*, 12, 1978, pp. 236–54

Carolyn Collette, 'Heeding the Counsel of Prudence: A Context for the Melibee', *Chaucer Review*, 29, 1995, pp. 416–33

Patricia DeMarco, 'Violence, Law, and Ciceronian Ethics in Chaucer's Tale of Melibee', *Studies in the Age of Chaucer*, 30, 2008, pp. 125–69

Thomas Farrell, 'Chaucer's Little Treatise, the Melibee', *Chaucer Review*, 20, 1985, pp. 61–7

Judith Ferster, 'Chaucer's Tale of Melibee: Contradictions and Context', in *Inscribing the Hundred Years' War in French and English Cultures*, edited by Denise N. Baker, Albany, New York State University Press, 2000, pp. 73–89

James Flynn, 'The Art of Telling and the Prudence of Interpreting: The Tale of Melibee and its Context', *Medieval Perspectives*, 7, 1992, pp. 53–63

Dominick Grace, 'Telling Differences: Chaucer's Tale of Melibee and Renaud de Louens' Livre de Mellibee et Prudence', *Philological Quarterly*, 82, 2003, pp. 367–400

Ronald Hartman, 'Boethian Parallels in The Tale of Melibee', *English Studies (The Netherlands)*, 79, 1998, pp. 166–70

Lynn Staley Johnson, 'Inverse Counsel: Contexts for the Melibee', *Studies in Philology*, 87, 1990, pp. 137–55

Kathleen E. Kennedy, 'Maintaining Love through Accord in The Tale of Melibee', *Chaucer Review*, 39, 2004, pp. 165–76

Stephen G. Moore, 'Apply Yourself: Learning while Reading The Tale of Melibee', *Chaucer Review*, 38, 2003, pp. 83–97

Mari Pakkala-Weckström, 'Prudence and the Power of Persuasion: Language and Maistrie in The Tale of Melibee', *Chaucer Review*, 35:4, 2001, pp. 399–412

Jamie Taylor, 'Chaucer's Tale of Melibee and the Failure of Allegory', *Exemplaria*, 21, 2009, pp. 83–101

Amanda Walling, ' "In hir tellyng difference": Gender, Authority and Interpretation in The Tale of Melibee', *Chaucer Review*, 40, 2005, pp. 163–81

❧ Whan sayd was this miracle, every man
As sober was that wonder was to se;
Til that oure host to **jape** bigan,   joke
And than **at erst** he loked upon me,   for the first time
And sayde thus, 'What man art thou?' quod he,
'Thou lokest as thou woldest fynde an hare,[2]
For ever upon the ground I se the stare!
Approche ner, and loke merily!
Now **ware you**, Sires, and let this man have space!   pay attention
He in the **wast** is schape as well as I;   waist   10
This were a **popet**, in an arm to embrace   little doll
For any womman, smal and fair of face!
He semeth **elvisch** by his countenaunce,   faery
For unto no wight doth he daliaunce.[3]
Say now somwhat, **sins** other folk han said.   since
Telle us a tale, and that of mirthe anoon.'
'Host,' quod I, 'ne beth nought **evel apayd**,   displeased
For other tale, certes, **can** I noon,   know
But of a rym I lerned **yore agoon**.'   a long time ago
'Ye, that is good,' quod he, 'now schul we heere   20
Som **deynte** thing, me thinketh by his **cheere**.'   fine; appearance
Lesteneth, Lordyngs, in good entent,[4]
And I wol telle **verrayment**   truly
Of myrthe and **solas**,   amusement/leisure
Of a knyght was fair and **gent**   gentle
In batail and in tornament;
His name was Sir Thopas.
Y-bore he was in **fer contre**,   born; far country
In Flaundres al byyond the se,
At Poperyng, in the place;   30
His fader was a man ful fre,
And lord he was of that contre,

1 Helen Cooper, *The Canterbury Tales*, Clarendon Press, Oxford, 1989, p. 312
2 'you look as if you're looking for a hare'
3 'he passes the time with nobody'
4 'with good will'

As it was God's grace.
Sir Thopas **wax** a doughty **swayn**   grew; young man
Whyt was his face as **payndemayn**,   white (hand) bread
His lippes reed as Rose,
His **rode** is lik scarlet **en grayn**;   complexion; dyed
And I yow telle in good certayn,
He had a **semly** nose.   good-looking
His **heer**, his berd, was lik **safroun**,   yellow (dye)
That to his girdil **raught** adoun,   reached
His **schoon** of **cordewane**.⁵
Of **Brigges** were his **hosen broun**,   Bruges; brown hose
His robe was of **sicladoun**,   silk
That coste many a **jane**.   coin
He **couthe** hunt at wilde deer   knew how to
And ride on haukyng for ryver,
With gray goshauk on honde.⁶
Therto he was a good archeer;
Of wrastelyng was noon his peer,
Ther eny Ram schal stonde.⁷
Ful many mayde, bright in **bour**,   bower/bedroom
Thay mourne for him **paramour**   for passionate love
Whan hem were **bet** to slepe;   better
But he was chast and no lecchour,
And sweet as is the **bembre** flour   dogrose
That bereth the reede **heepe**.   hip/berry
And so it fel upon a day,
For **soth** as I yow telle may,   truth
Sir Thopas wold out ryde.
He **worth** upon his steede gray,   mounts
And in his hond a **launcegay**,   light lance
A long sword by his syde.
He **priketh** thurgh a fair forest,   rides
Therin is many a wilde best;
Ye, bothe **buk** and hare.   buck (rabbit)
And as he priketh, north and est,

40
50
60

---

5 shoes; (fine) Cordovan leather
6 He went down to the river to hawk with a grey goshawk sitting on his gloved hand.
7 The ram is a traditional prize for a wrestling contest in this type of romance.

I tel it yow, hym had **almest**   almost
Bityd a **sory care**.   happened; sad event
Ther springen herbes greet and smale,   70
The licorys and the cetewale,[8]
And many a **clow gilofre**;   clove; gillyflower
And **notemuge** to put in ale,   nutmeg
Whethir it be moist or stale,
Or for to lay in **cofre**.   chest (to sweeten linen)
The briddes synge, it is no nay,
The **sperhauk** and the **popinjay**,   sparrowhawk; parrot
That ioye it was to heere.
The **throstilcok** maad **eek** his **lay**,   male thrush; also; song
The woode **dowve** upon the **spray**   dove/pigeon; branch   80
So song ful lowde and cleere.
Sir Thopas fel in love-longing
Whan that he herde the briddes synge,
And **priked** as he were **wood**.   spurred; mad
His faire steede, **in** his prikynge,   because
So **swette** that men might him **wrynge**;   sweated; wring out
His sydes were al blood.
Sir Thopas eek so wery was,
For priking on the softe gras –
So **feers** was his **corrage** –   strong; lustfulness   90
That doun he layd him in the place,
To make his steede som **solace**,   rest
And gaf him good **forage**.   grazing
'O Seinte Mary, **benedicite**!   bless us
What eylith this love at me,[9]
To bynde me so sore?
Me dremed al this night, **parde**,   by God
An **elf** queen schal my **lemman** be,   fairy; lover/mistress
And slepe under my **gore**.   skirt
An elf queen wol I have, y-wis,   100
For in this world no womman is
Worthy tho be my make **in toune**.   anywhere
Alle othir wommen I forsake,

8 A form of spice.
9 'why does this love have a grievance against me?'

And to an elf queen I me take,
By **dale** and eek by **doune**.'   valley; hill
Into his sadil he clomb anoon,
And priked over stile and stoon,
An elf queen for to spye;
Til he so longe hath ryden and goon,
110   That he fond in a prive **woon**   place
The contre of fairye so wylde,
For in that contre was ther noon,
Neither wif ne childe,
Til that ther cam a greet **geaunt** –   giant
His name was Sir Olifaunt –
A perilous man of dede.[10]
He swar, 'Child, 'by Termagaunt,[11]
For if thou prike out of myn haunt,
Anon I slee the with my mace.
120   Heer is the queen of fayerie,
With harp, and lute, and symphonye,
Dwellyng in this place.'
The child sayd, 'Al so mote I the,
Tomorwe wil I meete with the,
Whan I have myn **armure**;   armour
And yit I hope, **par ma fay**,   by my faith
That thou schalt with this **launcegay**   light lance
Abyen it **ful sore**.   regret; very badly
Schal I **persyn**, if that I may,   pierce
130   Er it be fully **prime** of day?   about 9 am.
For heer schalt thou be slawe.'
Sir Thopas drough abak ful fast;
This geaunt at him stoones cast
Out of a **staf** slynge;   staff-mounted
But faire **eschapeth** child Thopas,   escaped
And al it was thurgh God's **gras**,   grace
And thurgh his berynge.
Yet lesteneth, Lordynges, to my tale,
Merier than the nightyngale

10 'a man dangerous in his deeds'
11 One of the 'gods' of Muslims in medieval romance.

I wol yow **roune**	whisper	140
How Sir Thopas, with sides **smale**,	slender	
Prikyng over hul and dale,		
Is come ageyn to toune.		
His mery men comaunded he,		
To make him bothe **game** and **gle**,	fun and merriment	
For needes most he fight		
With a geaunt with heedes thre,		
For paramours and jolite		
Of oon that schon ful bright.		
'Do come,' he sayd, 'my mynstrales		150
And **gestours**, for to telle tales	storytellers	
Anoon, in myn armynge,[12]		
Of Romaunces that ben **reales**,	royal	
Of popes and of cardinales,		
And eek of love-likynge.'		
Thay **y-fet** him first the swete wyn,	fetched	
And made him eek in a **maselyn**	pan	
A real **spicerye**	sweetmeats	
Of **gyngebred** that was so fyn,	gingerbread	
And licorys, and eek **comyn**,	cumin	160
With sugre that is **trye**.	fine	
He dede next his white **leere**,	skin	
Of cloth of **lake** whyt and cleere	linen	
A **brech** and eek a **schert**;	breeches; shirt	
And next his schert an **aketoun**,	quilted shirt	
And over that an **haberioun**,	mail shirt	
For persyng of his hert;[13]		
And over that a fyn **hauberk**	breast plate	
Was al y-wrought of Jewes' werk,		
Ful strong it was of plate;		170
And over that his **cote armour**,	coat of arms	
As whyt as is a lily flour,		
In which he wold **debate**.	fight	
His scheld was al of gold so red,		
And theronne was a **bore's heed**,	boar's head	

12 'to tell stories whilst I put my armour on'
13 To prevent his heart from being pierced.

A **charbocle** by his syde.   carbuncle
And ther he swor on ale and bred,
How that the geaunt schal be deed,
Bytyde what betyde.
180 His **iambeux** were of **quirboily**,   leg-guards; boiled leather
His swerdes **schethe** of **yvory**,   sheath; ivory
His helm of **latoun** bright.   latten
His sadel was of **rowel boon**,   ivory
His bridel as the sonne schon,
Or as the moonelight.
His spere was of **cipres**,   cypress
That **bodeth** werre, and no thing pees,   foretells
The heed ful scharp y-grounde.
His steede was al dappul gray;
190 Hit goth an **ambel** in the way,   amble
Ful softely and **rounde** in londe.   easily
Lo, Lordes! Heer is a fyt,
If ye wil eny more of it –
To telle it wold I **fonde**.   attempt

❦ 'Now hold your mouth, **for charite**,   for charity's sake
Bothe knight and lady fre,
And herkneth to my **spelle**   story
Of batail and of chivalry,
And of ladys love **drewery**,   passionate
200 Anoon I wol yow telle.
Men speken of Romauns of **pris**,   excellence
Of Horn child and of Ypotis,
Of Bevys and sir Gy,
Of Sir Libeaux and Pleyndamour,[14]
But Sir Thopas bereth the flour
Of real chivalry.[15]
His goode steede he bistrood,
And forth upon his way he **glood**,   glid
As spark out of the **bronde**.   firebrand

14 Heroes of medieval romances: King Horn, Sir Bevis of Hamtoun, Guy of
   Warwick, Lybaeus Desconus.
15 'Sir Thopas is the epitome of royal chivalry'

Upon his crest he bar a **tour**,   tower   210
And therin stiked a lily flour –
God schilde his corps fro **schonde**!   harm
And **for** he was a kny*ght* **auntrous**,[16]   because; errant
He **nolde** slepen in noon hous,   would not
But **liggen** in his hood.   lay down
His brighte helm was his **wonger**,   pillow
And by him **bytith** his **destrer**   eats; warhorse
Of herbes fyne and goode.
Him self drank water of the welle,
As ded the knight of Pertinelle,[17]   220
So worthy under wede . . .

❦ 'No more of this, for God's dignite!'
Quod our hoste, 'for thou makest me
So wery of thy verray **lewednesse**   lack of learning
That – al so wisly God my soule blesse –
Myn eeres **aken** for thy **drasty** speche!   ache; rubbishy
Now, such a rym the devel I **byteche**!   give
This may wel be rym dogerel,' quoth he.
'Why so?' quod I, 'Why wilt thou **lette** me   stop
More of my tale than another man,   230
Syn that it is the beste rym that I can?'
'By God!' quod he, "For pleinly, at o word,
Yhy drasty rymyng is not worth a **tord**!   turd
Thou dost nought elles, but **despendist** tyme!   waste
Sir – at o word – thou schalt no lenger ryme!
Let se wher thou canst tellen ought in gest,
Or telle in prose somwhat, atte lest
In which ther be some merthe or doctrine.'
'Gladly,' quod I, 'by God's swete **pyne**,   suffering
I wol yow telle a litel thing in prose   240
That oughte like yow, as I suppose;   that you should like
Or elles, certes, ye be to **daungerous**.   choosy
It is a moral tale vertuous,
Albeit told somtyme in sondry wise

16 A knight errant is one who wanders in search of adventures.
17 Sir Perceval, one of the knights who found the Holy Grail in Arthurian legend.

Of sondry folk, as I schal yow devyse;
As thus ye woot that every **evaungelist**   *preacher*
That telleth us the peyne of Jhesu Crist
Ne saith all thing as his felawes doth,
But natheles here sentence is al **soth**,   *truth*
250   And all accorden as in here sentence,[18]
Al be ther in her tellyng difference;
For some of hem sayn more, and some lesse,
Whan thay his pitous passioun expresse –
I mene of Mark, Mathew, Luk and John –
But douteles, her sentence is al oon.
Therfore, Lordynges, all I yow **biseche**,   *beg*
If yow think that I varye as in my speche,
As thus – though that I telle somwhat more
Of proverbes than I have herd bifore
260   Comprehended in this litel tretys here,
To **enforcen with** th'effect of my matiere,   *reinforce*
And though I not the same wordes say
As ye have herd, yit to yow alle I pray,
Blameth me nought; for in my sentence
Schul ye nowher fynde difference
Fro the sentence of this tretys **lite**,   *little*
After the which this litel tale I wryte;
And therfor herkeneth what I schal say,
And let me tellen al my tale, I pray.'

❦ A yong man called Melibeus, mighty and riche, bygat upon his wif, that called was Prudens, a doughter, which that called was Sophie.

Upon a day byfel that for his desport he is went into the feldes him to play. His wif, and his doughter eek, hath he laft in-with his hous, of which the dores were fast y-schitte. Thre of his olde foos han it espyed, and setten laddres to the walles of his hous, and by the wyndowes ben entred and beetyn his wyf, and woundid his doughter with fyve mortal wounds in fyve sondry places; that is to sayn, in here feet, in here hondes, in here eeres. in here nose and in here mouth, and lafte her for deed and went away.

18 'they all agree in basic content although they all tell the story in a different way'

Whan Melibeus retourned was into his hous and seigh al this meschief, he lik a man mad, rendyng his clothes, gan wepe and crie. Prudens his wyf, as ferforth as sche dorste, bysought him of his wepyng to stynte. But not forthi, he gan to crie ever lenger the more.

This noble wyf Prudence remembred hire upon the sentens of Ovide, in his book that cleped is *The Remedy of Love*, wheras he seith:[19]

He is a fool that destourbeth the moder to wepe in the deth of hir childe, til sche have y-wept hir fille as for a certeyn tyme, and than schal man doon his diligence, as with amyable wordes hire to recomforte, and praye hire of hire wepyng to stinte.

For which resoun this noble wif Prudens suffred hir housbonde for to wepe and crie as for a certeyn space, and whan sche seigh hir tyme, sche sayd him in this wise: 'Allas, my lord,'quod sche, 'why make ye youreself for to be lik a fool? Forsothe, it apperteyneth not to a wys man to make such sorwe. Youre doughter, with the grace of God, schal warischt[20] be and eschape. And al were it so that sche right now were deed, ye ne oughte nought as for hir deth youresilf destroye. Senec saith, 'The wise man schal not take too gret discomfort for the deth of his children; but certes he schulde suffren it in pacience, as wel as he abydeth[21] the deth of his owne persone.'

This Melibeus answerde anoon, & sayde, 'What man,' quod he, 'schuld of his wepyng stynte that hath a cause for to wepe? Jhesu Crist oure Lord himself wepte for the deth of Lazarus, his frend.' Prudens answerde, 'Certes wel I wot attemperel[22] wepyng is no thing defended to him that sorwful is amonges a folk in sorwe, but it is rather graunted him to wepe. The apostel Puole unto the Romayns writeth: 'A man schal rejoyce with hem that maken joye, and wepe with such folk as wepen.'[23] But though attempered wepyng be graunted, outrageous wepyng certes is defended. Mesure of wepyng be conserved, after the lore of Crist, that

---

19 Ovid, Remedia Amorum (Remedies of Love). Prudence's other chief sources are the Roman writers Cicero (Tullius) and Seneca, with selections from a variety of their works (perhaps from a compendium), and Publius Syrius, from his Sententia. There are some references to the Distichs of Cato, which were used in the teaching of grammar. Also cited is the De Disciplina Clericalis of the early twelfth century writer Peter Alphonse (Petrus Alphonsus), and the Variarum of the early sixth century writer Cassiodorus.

20 recovered

21 'waits for'

22 moderate

23 Romans 12:15

techeth us Senec: 'Whan that thi frend is deed,' quod he, 'let nought thin yen too moyste ben of teres, ne to moche drye. Although the teeres come out of thine eyyen, let hem not falle, and whan thou hast forgon thy frend, do diligence to gete another frend; and this is more wisedom than to wepe for thy frend which that thou hast lorn, for therin is no boote.[24] And therfore, if ye governe yow by sapience,[25] put away sorwe out of youre hert. Remembreth yow that Jhesus Sirac saith, 'A man that is joyous and glad in herte it him conserveth, florisching in his age, but sothly sorweful herte maketh his boones drye.' He saith eek thus, that sorwe in herte sleth ful meny a man. Salamon saith that, right as motthes in schep's flees annoyeth the clothes, and the smale wormes to the tre; right so annoyeth sorwe to the herte. Wherfore us oughte, as wel in the deth of oure children as in the losse of oure goodes temporales, have pacience. Remembreth yow upon the pacient Job – whan he hadde lost his children and his temporal substance, and in his body endured and receyved ful many a grevous tribulacioun, yit sayde he thus: 'Oure Lord it sent unto me; oure Lord it hath raft fro me: Right so as oure Lord wil, right so be it doon. Y-blessed be the name of Oure Lord!'[26]

To these forsayde thinges anwerith Melibeus unto his wif Prudens, 'Alle thine wordes ben soth,' quod he, 'and therto profytable, but sothly myn herte is so troubled with this sorwe that I noot what to doone.' 'Let calle,' quod Prudence, 'thy trewe frendes alle and thy linage[27] whiche that be trewe & wise; telleth hem youre grevaunce, and herken what thay say in counseilynge, and yow govern after here sentence. Salamon saith, 'Werke al thi thing by counseil, and the thar never rewe.'[28]

Than, by the counseil of his wyf Prudens, this Melibeus let calle a gret congregacioun of peple; as surgiens, phisiciens, olde and yonge, and some of his olde enemyes recounsiled – as by her semblaunt[29] – to his loue and to his grace; and therwithal ther come some of his neighebours that deden him reverence more for drede than for love, as happeth ofte. Ther comen also ful many subtil flaterers, and wise advoketes, lerned in the lawe.

And whan these folk togidere assemblid were, this Melibeus in sorwful wyse schewed hem his caas[30], and by the maner of his speche it semed

24 'this is wiser than to weep for the friend you have lost, for in that there is no remedy'
25 wisdom
26 Job 1:21
27 family
28 'do all things by taking advice and you'll never be sorry'
29 seeming
30 situation

that in herte he bar a cruel ire, redy to do vengeance upon his foos, and sodeynly desirede that the werre schulde bygynne; but natheles, yit axed he her counseil in this matier. A Sirurgien, by licens and assent of suche as were wyse, up ros, and to Melibeus sayde as ye may hiere:

'Sire,'quod he, 'as to us Sirurgiens appertieneth that we do to every wight the beste that we can, wheras we ben with-holde, and to oure pacient that we do no damage; wherfore it happeth many tyme and ofte that whan tweye han everich wounded other oo same surgien heleth hem bothe,[31] where unto our art it is not perteyned to norische werre, ne parties to supporte; but certes, as to warisching of youre doughter, albeit so that sche perilously be woundid, we schullen do so tentyf besynes[32] fro day to night that, with the grace of God, sche schal be hool and sound als soone as it is possible.' Almost right in the same wise the phisiciens answerden, save that thay sayden a fewe wordes more; that ryght as maladies ben cured by her contraries,[33] right so schal man warissch werre by vengeaunce.

His neygheboures ful of envy, his feyned freendes that semede recounsiled, his flatereres, maden semblaunt of wepyng, and appaired and aggregged moche of this matiere,[34] inpreisyng gretly Melibe of might, of power, of riches, and of frendes, despisinge the power of his adversaries, and sayden outerly that he anoon schulde wreke him on his adversaries be bygynnynge of werre.

Up roos thane an advocate that was wys, by leve and by counseil of othere that were wise, and sayde, 'Lordynges, the needes for whiche we ben assemblit in this place is ful hevy thing, and an heigh matier, bycause of the wrong of the wikkednes that hath ben doon, and eek of the grete damages that in tyme comyng ben possible to falle for the same, and eek bycause of the grete richesse and power of the partes bothe; for the whiche resouns it were a ful gret peril to erren in these materes.

Wherfore, Melibeus, this is oure sentence: We conseile yow, aboven all thinges, that right anoon thou do diligence in kepyng of thy body in such a wyse that thou ne wante noon espye, ne wacche, thy body for to save.[35] And after that, we conseile that in thin hous thou sette suffisaunt garnisoun[36] so that in thin hous thou sette suffcaunt garnisoun, so that

---

31 'where two people have wounded one another, the same surgeon heals them both'
32 'we'll do our very best'
33 opposites
34 'pretended to weep, and made things worse and fuelled the matter'
35 'that you lack no spy or watchman to guard your person'
36 garrison/guard

thay may as wel thy body as thin hous defende; but certes, for to moeve
wer, ne sodeynly for to doo vengeaunce, we may not deme in so litel
tyme that it were profitable. Wherfore we axen leysir and a space in this
caas to demen,[37] for the comune proverbe saith this: 'He that soone
demeth, soone schal repente.' And eek men sayn that, 'thilke juge is wys
that soone understondeth a matier, and juggeth by leysir, for albeit so
that alle taryinge is anoyful, algates it is no reproef in gevyng of juggement,
ne of vengaunce takyng, whan it is suffisaunt and resonable, and that
schewed oure Lord Jhesu Crist by ensample, for whan that the womman
that was y-take in advoutrie[38] was brought in his presence to knowen
what schulde be doon of hir persone, albeit that he wist himself what
that he wolde answere, yit wolde he not answere sodeynly, but he wolde
have deliberacioun, and in the ground hem wrot twyes; and by these
causes we axe deliberacioun, and we schul thanne by the grace of God
counseile the thing that schal be profytable.'

Upstarten thenne the yonge folkes anoon at oones, and the moste
parte of that companye han skorned these olde wise men, and bygonne
to make noyse and sayden, 'Right so as whil that iren is hoot men
scholden smyte, right so schulde men wreke here wronges whil that thay
ben freische and newe.' And with lowde vois thay cryde, 'Werre, werre!'

Uproos tho oon of these olde wise, and with his hond made counten-
aunce that men schulde holde hem stille, and given him audience.
'Lordyngs,' quod he, 'ther is ful many a man that crieth, 'Werre, werre!'
wot ful litel what werre amounteth. Werre at his bygynnyng hath so
greet an entre and so large, that euery wight may entre whan him liketh,
and lightly fynde werre; but certes, what ende schal falle therof it is not
lightly to knowe. For sothly, whan that werre is oones bygonne ther is
ful many a child unbore of his mooder that schal sterve yong bycause of
thilke werre, or elles lyve in sorwe and deye in wrecchidnes; & therfore
er that eny werre be bygonne men moste have gret counseil and gret
deliberacioun.' And whan this olde man wende to enforce his tale by
resouns, wel neigh all at oones bygonne thay to rise for to breke his tale,
and beden him fulofte his wordes to abrigge.[39] For sothly, he that
precheth to hem that liste not to heere his wordes, his sermoun hem
anoyeth. For Jhesus Sirac saith that wepyng in musik is a noyous thing;

---

37 'we ask for time and space to judge in this matter'
38 adultery
39 'they began to rise to interrupt his speech, and frequently asked him to cut it
   short'

this is to say as moche avayleth to speke tofore folk to whiche his speche annoyeth, as it is to synge byfore hem which that wepith. And whan this wise man saugh him wanted audience, al schamefast he sette him doun agayn. For Salamon saith, 'Theras thou may have noon audience, enforce the not to speke.' 'I se wel,' quod this wise man, 'that the comune proverbe is soth, that 'good counseil wantith whan it is most neede'.[40]

Yit hadde this Melibeus in his counseil many folk that prively in his eere han counseled him certein thinges, and counseled him the contrarie in general audience. Whan Melibeus hadde herd that the grettest party of his counseil were accorded that he schulde make werre, anoon he consented to here counseilyng, and fully affermed here sentence.[41]

Thanne Dame Prudence, whan that sche saugh that hir housbonde schop him to wreke him of his enemyes and to begynne werre, sche in ful humble wise, whan sche saugh hire tyme, sayde him these wordes: 'My lord,' quod sche, 'I yow biseche as hertily as I dar and kan; ne haste yow nought too faste, and for all guerdouns as geue me audience, for Peres Alfons saith, 'Who that doth to thee outher good or harm, haste the nought to quyten him, for in this wise thy freend wil abyde and thin enemy schal the lenger lyve in drede.' The proverbe saith, 'He hastith wel, that wisly can abyde', and, 'In wikked haste is no profyt'.

This Melibeus answerde unto his wyf Prudens, 'I purpose not,' quod he, 'to werke by thy counseil, for many causes and resouns, for certes, euery wight wolde holde me thanne a fool. This is to sayn; if I for thy counseil wolde chaunge thinges that affermed ben by so many wise, I say that all wommen be wikked and noon good of hem alle, for, 'Of a thousand men, sith Salamon, 'I fond oon good man, but certes of alle wommen, good womman fond I never noon.' And also, certes, if I governede me by thy counseil it schulde seme that I hadde given to the over me the maistry – an God forbeede er it so were – for Jhesus Syrac saith that if a wif have maistrie, sche is contrarious to hir housbond. And Salamon saith, 'Never in thy lif to thy wyf, ne to thy child, ne to thy freend, ne geve no power over thiself, for better it were that thy children axen of thy persone thinges that been needful to hem, than thou set thiself in the hondes of thy children. And also, if I wolde werke by thy counselynge, certes it most somtyme be secre, til it were tyme that it most be knowe – and this ne may not be.'

40 'good counsel is lacking when it is needed most'
41 judgement

Whan Dame Prudence, ful debonerly and with gret pacience, hadde herd al that hir housbonde liked for to seye, thanne axed sche of him licence for to speke, and sayde in this wise: 'My lord,' quod sche, 'as to youre firste resoun; certes, it may lightly be answered, for I say it is no foly to chaunge counsel whan the thing is chaungid. For elles, whan the thing semeth otherwise than it was biforn, and moreover I say, though that ye han sworn and y-hight to parforme youre emprise, and natheles ye wayve to parforme thilke same emprise, by juste cause men schulde not say therfore that ye were a lyere, ne forsworn. For the book seith that the wise man maketh no lesyng whan he torneth his corrage to the better. And albeit so that youre emprise be establid and ordeyned by gret multitude of poeple, yit can ye not accomplise thilke same ordinaunce but you like; for the trouthe of thing and the profyt ben rather founde in fewe folk that ben wise and ful of resoun, than by gret multitude of folk that euery man crieth and clatereth what that him liketh – sothly, such multitude is not honest.

And to the secounde resoun; wheras ye sayn that all wommen ben wikke, save youre grace. Certis, ye despise all wommen in this wise, and 'he that all despysith, al displeseth,' saith the book. And Senec saith, 'Whoso wil have sapience schal no man desprayse, but he schal gladly teche the science that he can,[42] withoute presumpcioun of pryde; and suche thinges as he nought can, he schal not be aschemed to lerne hem, and enquere of lasse folk than himself .' And, Sire, that ther hath be ful many a good womman, may lightly be preved. For, certes, Sire, Our Lord Jhesu Crist wolde never have descendid to be born of a womman, if all wommen hadde ben wikke. And after that, for the grete bountee that is in wommen, Our Lord Jhesu Crist, whan he was risen from deth to lyve, appeered rather to a womman than to his aposteles. And though that Salamon say he fond never good womman, it folwith nought therfore that alle wommen ben wikke; for though that he fonde noone goode wommen, certes many another man hath founden many a womman ful goode and trewe. Or elles paraventure th'entent of Salamon was this: as in sovereyn bountee he fond no womman, this is to say that, 'Ther is no wight that hath soverein bounte, save God aloone,' as he himself recordeth in his Euauungelie.[43] For ther nys no creature so good that him wantith somwhat of the perfeccioun of God, that is his makere.

Youre thridde resoun is this: ye seyn that if ye governed yow by counsel of me, it schulde seme that ye hadde geve me the maystry and the

<hr/>

42 knows
43 Gospel

lordschipe over youre persone. Sire, save youre grace, it is not so; for if so were that no man schulde be counseiled but by hem that hadde maystrie and lordschipe of his persone, men wolde nought be counseiled so ofte, for sothly, thilke man that axeth counseil of a purpos, yet hath he fre chois whether he wil werke by that purpos or noon.

And so to youre ferthe resoun, ther ye sayn that the janglerie of wommen can hyde thinges that thay wot not of, as who saith that a womman can nought hyde that sche woot. Sire, these wordes ben understonde of wommen that ben jangelers, and wikke, of whiche wommen men sayn that, 'Thre thinges dryven a man out of his oughne hous; that is to say smoke, droppyng of reyn, and wikked wyfes'. Of suche wommen saith Salamon that it were better to a man to dwelle in desert than with a womman that is riotous – and sche, by youre leve, am not I, for ye han ful ofte assayed my grete silence and my grete pacience, and eek how wel that I can hyde and hele thinges that ben secrely to hyde.

And sothly, as to youre fyfte resoun; wheras ye sayn that in wikkede counseil wommen venquisscheth men. God wot, thilke resoun stont here in no stede, for understondith now ye agein counseil to do wickidnes, and if ye wil wirke wickidnes and youre wyf restryne thilke wicked purpos, and overcome you by resoun and by good counseil; certes, youre wyf oweth rather be preised than y-blamed. Thus schulde ye understonde the philosopher that seith, 'In wicked counseil wommen venquyschen her housbondes'. And theras ye blame alle wymmen and here resouns, I schal schewe by many resouns[44] and ensamples that many a womman hath ben ful good, and yit been; and here counseiles ful holsome and profitable. Eke, some men han sayd that the counseilyng of wommen is outher to dere or to litel of pris. But albeit so that ful many a womman is badde, and hir counseil vile and not worth, yet han men founde many a ful good womman, and ful discret and wys in counseilyng.

Lo Jacob, by counseil of his moder Rebecca, wan the blessyng of his fader Isaac, and the lordschipe of alle his bretheren. Judith by hire good counseil delyvered the citee of Bethulie, in which sche dwellid, out of the hond of Olophernus, that had it byseged and wolde it al destroye. Abigayl delivered Nabal hir housbond fro Dauid the king, that wolde have y-slayn him, and appesed the ire of the king by hire witte and by hir good counseilynge. Hester by good counseil enhaunsed gretly the poeple of God in the regne of Assuerus the kyng.[45] And the same bounte in good

44 reasonings
45 Genesis 27; Judith 8; 1 Samuel 25; Esther 7.

counseilyng of many a good womman may men rede and telle. And moreover, whan Oure Lord had creat Adam, oure forme fader, he sayde in this wise: 'It is not good to be a man aloone; make we to him an help, semblable to himself.' Here may ye se that if that a womman were not good, and hir counseil good and profytable, oure Lord God of heven wolde neither have wrought hem, ne called hem help of man, but rather confusioun to man. And ther saide oones a clerk in tuo versus, 'What is better than gold? Jasper. And what is better than jasper? Wisedom. And what is better than wisedom? Womman. And what is better than good womman? Nothing. And Sire, by many other resouns may ye se that many wommen ben goode and profitable. And therfore, if ye wil truste to my counseil, I schal restore you youre doughter, hool and sound, and eek I wil doon you so moche, that ye schul have honour in this cause.'

Whan Melibe had herd these wordes of his wif Prudens, he seide thus, 'I see wel that the word of Salomon is soth; he seith that the wordes that ben spoken discretly by ordinaunce been hony-combes, for thay geven swetnes to the soule and to the body. And wyf, bycause of thy swete wordes, and eek for I have assayed and proved thi grete sapiens & thi grete trouthe, I wil governe me by thy counseil in all thinges.'

'Now, Sire,' quod Dame Prudens, 'and syn ye vouchen sauf [46] to be governed by my counseilyng, I wil enform you how ye schul governe youreself in chesyng of youre conseil. Ye schul first, in all youre werkes, mekely biseche to the hihe God that he wol be your counseilour, schape you to that entent, that he give you counseil and confort, as taughte Toby his sone: 'At alle tymes thou schalt blesse God and pray him to dresse thy wayes, and loke that all thi counseiles be in him for evermore.' Seint Jame eek saith: 'If eny of yow have neede of sapiens, axe it of God'. And aftirward thanne schul ye take counseil in yourself, and examine wel youre thoughtes of suche thinges as you thinkith that is best for youre profyt, and thanne schul ye dryve fro youre hertes tho that ben contrarie to good counseil; that is to say ire, coveytise and hastynes. First, he that axeth counseil of himself, certes he moste be withoute ire for many cause:

The first is this: He that hath gret ire and wrathe in himself, he weneth alwey he may do thing that he may not doo; and secoundly, he that is irous and wroth he may not wel deme,[47] and he that may not wel deme may nought wel counseile. The thridde is this: that he that is irous and

46 grant
47 judge

wroth, as saith Senec, may not speke but blameful thinges, and with his vicious wordes he stireth other folk to anger and to ire. And eek, Sire, ye most dryve coveitise out of youre herte, for th'apostil saith that coveytise is roote of all harmes; and trusteth wel that a coveitous man ne cannot deme ne thinke, but oonly to fulfille the ende of his coveitise,[48] and certes, that may never ben accomplised, for ever the more abundaunce that he hath of riches, the more he desireth. And Sire, ye moste also dryve out of your herte hastynes, for certes, ye may nought deme for the beste a sodein thought that falleth in youre herte, but ye moste avyse you on it ful ofte; for, as ye herde here biforn, the comune proverbe is this, 'that somtyme semeth to yow that it is good for to doo, another tyme it semeth to you the contrarie'.

Whan ye han taken counseil in yourselven and han demed by good deliberacioun such thing as yow semeth best, thanne rede I you that ye kepe it secre. Bywreye nought youre counseil to no persone but it so be that ye wene sicurly that thurgh youre bywreyinge,[49] youre condicioun schal be to yow the more profytable, for Jhesus Syrac saith, 'Neither to thi foo, ne to thi freend, discovere not thy secre ne thy foly, for they wil give you audience and lokyng and supportacioun in thi presence, and scorn in thin absence'. Another clerk saith that skarsly schal thou fynde eny persone that may kepe counseil secreely. The book saith, 'Whil thou kepist thi counsail in thin herte, thou kepest it in thi prisoun, and whan thou bywreyest thi counseil to any wight, he holdeth the in his snare'. And therfore yow is better hyde youre counseil in youre herte, than prayen him to whom ye have bywryed youre counseil that he wol kepe it close and stille; for Seneca seith, 'If so be that thou ne maist not thin owne counsel hyde, how darst thou preyen any other wight thi counseil secreely to kepe?'

But natheles, if thou wene securly that thy condicioun stonde in the better plite, thanne schalt thou telle him thy counsel in this wise:[50] first; thou schalt make no semblaunt wher the were lever werre or pees, or this or that, ne schewe him not thi wille and thin entent, for truste wel that comunly these counseilours ben flaterers, and namely the counselours of grete lordes, for thay enforcen hem alway rather to speke plesaunt wordes, enclynyng to the lorde's lust, than wordes that been trewe and

---

48 1 Timothy 6:10
49 revelation
50 'if you truly believe that your situation is the better for it, than you should tell him your counsel like this:'

profytable; and therfore men say that the riche man hath selden good counseil, but if he have it of himself. And after that, thou schalt consider thy frendes and thine enemyes. And as touching thy frendes, thou schalt considere which of hem beth most faithful and most wise, and eldest, and most approvyd in counsaylinge, and of hem schalt thou axe thy counsail, as the caas[51] requireth.

I say that first ye schul clepe to youre counseil youre frendes that ben trewe, for Salamon saith, 'For right as the hert of a man delitith in savour that is soote,[52] right so the counseil of trewe frendes geveth swetnes to the soule'. He saith also, 'Ther may nothing be likened to the trewe freend, for certes gold ne silver beth nought so moche worth as the goode wil of a trewe freend'. And eek he sayde that 'a trewe frend is a strong defens; who that it fyndeth, certes he fyndeth a gret tresour'. Thanne schul ye eek considere if that youre trewe frendes ben discrete and wyse, for the book saith, 'Axe thi counseil alwey of hem that ben wyse'. And by this same resoun schul ye clepe to youre counseil of youre frendes that ben of age suche as have y-seye sightes, and ben expert in many thinges, and ben approvyd in counseylinges; for the book saith that 'in olde men is the sapience, and in longe tyme the prudence'. And Tullius saith that grete thinges ben not ay accompliced by strengthe, ne by delyvernes[53] of body, but by good counseil, by auctorite of persones, and by science,[54] the whiche thre thinges ne been not feble by age, but certis thay enforsen and encresen day by day.

And thanne schul ye kepe this for a general reule. First schul ye clepe to youre counseil a fewe of youre frendes that ben especial, for Salamon saith, 'Many frendes have thou, but among a thousand chese the oon to be thy counseilour, for albeit so that thou first ne telle thy counseil but to a fewe, thou mayst afterward telle it to mo folk if it be neede. But loke alwey that thy counseilours have thilke thre condiciouns that I have sayd bifore; that is to say, that thay ben trewe and olde, and of wys experiens. And werke nought alwey in every neede by oon counseilour alloone, for somtyme byhoveth it be counseiled by many. For Salamon saith 'Salvacioun of thinges is wher as ther beth many counseilours'.

Now, sith that I have told yow of whiche folk ye schul be counseiled, now wil I telle yow which counsel ye ought eschiewe.[55] First, ye schal

51 situation
52 sweet
53 agility
54 knowledge
55 avoid

espie the counseil of fooles, for Salomon seith, 'Take no counseil of a fool, for he ne cannot counseile but after his oughne lust, and his affeccioun. The book seith that the proprete of a fool is this; he troweth lightly[56] harm of every wight, & lightly troweth all bounte in himself. Thow schalt eschiewe eek the counseil of all flaterers suche as enforcen hem rathere to prayse youre persone by flaterie, than for to telle yow the sothfastnesse of thinges.[57] Wherfore Tullius saith, 'Amonges all pestilences that ben in frendschipe, that is the grettest flaterie', and therfore is it more neede that thou eschiewe and drede flaterers more than eny other peple. The book saith, 'Thou schalt rather drede and flee fro the swete wordes of flateres then fro the egre[58] wordes of thy frend that saith the thi sothes'. Salamon saith that the wordes of a flaterer is a snare to cacche in innocents. He saith also, 'He that speketh to his frend wordes of swetnesse and of plesaunce setteth a nette byfore his feet to cacche him', and therfore saith Tullius, 'Encline not thin eeres to flateres, ne take no confort of the wordes of flaterers', and Catoun saith, 'Avyse the wel, and eschiewe wordes of swetnes and of plesaunce'.

And eek thou schalt eschiewe the counselyng of thin olde enemys that ben recounsiled. The book saith that a wight retorneth soone into the grace of his olde enemyes, and Ysope saith, 'Ne truste not to hem with which thou hast had somtyme werre or enmyte, ne telle not hem thy counseil',[59] and Seneca telleth the cause why it may not be – saith he that wher as a greet fuyr hath longe tyme endured, that there ne leveth som vapour of hete. And therfore saith Salamon, 'In thine old enemy truste thou nevere, for sicurly, though thin enemy be reconsiled and make the cheer of humilite, and lowteth to the his heed, ne trist him never; for certes he makith thilke feyned humilite more for his profyt than for eny love of thi persone, bycause he demyth to have victorie over thi persone by such feyned countynaunce, the which victorie he might nought have by stryf and werre. And Petir Alphons saith, 'Make no felaschipe with thine olde enemyes, for if thou do hem bounte they wil perverten it into wikkednes; & eek thou most eschiewe the counseilynge of hem that ben thy servaunts, and beren the gret reverence, for paraventure[60] thai say it more for drede than for love. And therfore saith a philosophre in this

56 easily
57 'the truth about things'
58 'sharp'
59 Aesop, writer of the Fables.
60 perhaps

wise, 'Ther is no wight parfytly trewe to him that he so sore dredeth, and Tullius saith, 'Ther is no wight so gret of any emperour, that longe may endure but if he have more love of the peple than drede.

Thow also eschiewe the counseil of folk that be dronkelewe,[61] for thay ne can no counsel hyde; for Salomon saith, 'Ther regneth no privete ther as is dronkenesse'. Ye schul also have in suspect the counseil of such folk as counseileth you on thing prrively, and counseile yow the contrarie openly', for Cassiodorie saith, 'It is a maner sleighte to hindre, whan he schewith to doon oon thing openly, and werkith prively the contrarie'. Thou schalt also eschiewe the counseil of wikked folkes, for the book saith, 'The counselyng of wikked folk is alway ful of fraude', and David saith, 'Blisful is that man that hath not folwed the counseilyng of wikked men or schrewes'. Thow schalt also eschiewe the counseilnge of yonge folk, for here counseil is nought rype.

Now Sire, syn I have schewe yow of what folk ye schul take youre counsail and of which folk ye schullen folwe the counseil, now schal I teche yow how ye schul examyne youre counseil, after the doctrine of Tullius. In the examynyng of youre counseiloures ye schul considre many thinges: Althirfirst[62] ye schul considre that in thilke thing that thou proposist, and up what thing thou wilt have counseil, that verray trouthe be sayd and considerid; this is to sayn, telle trewely thy tale; for he that saith fals may not wel be counseled in that cas of which he lyeth. And after this thou schalt considere the thinges that accorden to that purpos for to do by thy counseil, if resoun accorde therto, and eek if thy might may accorde therto, and if the more part and the better part of thy counseilours accorde therto, or noon. Thanne schalt thou considere what thing schal folwe of that consailynge, as hate, pees, werre, grace, profyt, or damage, and many other thinges; and in alle these thinges thou schalt chese the beste and weyve alle other thinges. Thanne schalt thou considre of what roote engendred is thy matier of thy counseil, and what fruyt it may conserve and engendre. Thow schalt also consider al these causes from whens thai ben sprongen.

And whan ye hauv examined youre counseil, as I have said, and which party is the better and more profitable, and han approved by many wise folkes and olde. Than schalt thow considre if thou maist parforme it, and make of it a good ende. For resoun wol nought that any man schuld bygynne a thing, but if he mighte parforme it and make therof a good

61 drunkards
62 first of all

ende, ne no wight schulde take upon him so hevy a charge that he might not bere it. For the proverbe seith, 'He that moche embrasith, destroyeth litel'. And if so be that thou be in doute wher thou maist performe a thing or noon, chese rather to suffre than bygynne. And Petre Alfons saith, 'If thou hast might to doon a thing of which thou most repente, it is better nay than yee; this is to sayn, that the is better holde thy tonge stille than to speke, than may ye understonde by strenger resouns that if thou hast power to performe a werk of which thou schalt repente, thanne is it better that thou suffre than bigynne'. Wel sayn thay that defenden every wight to assaie thing of which he is in doute whethur he may performe it or noon. And after whan ye han examyned youre counseil as I have sayd biforn, and knowen wel ye may performe youre emprise, conferme it thanne sadly til it be at an ende.[63]

Now is it tyme and resoun that I schewe yow whanne and wherfore that ye may chaunge youre counseil withouten reproef. Sothly, a man may chaunge his purpos and his counseil if the cause cesseth, or whan a newe cause bytydeth, for the lawe seith upon thinges that newely bitydeth, bihoveth newe counseil, and Seneca seith, 'If thy counseil be comen to the eeres of thin enemy, chaunge thy counsail'. Thow maist also chaunge thy counseil if so be that thou fynde that by errour or by other processe harm or damage may bytyde. Also, thou chaunge thy counseil if thay be dishonest, or elles comuneth of dishoneste, for the lawes sayn that alle the hestes that ben dishoneste ben of no valieu, and eek if it so be that it be impossible, or may not goodly be performed or kept, and take this for a general reule; that every counseil that is affermed or strengthed so strongly that it may not be chaunged for no condicioun that may bitide, I say that thilke counseil is wikked.'

This Melibeus, whan he had herd the doctrine of his wyf Dame Prudens, answerde in this wise: 'Dame,' quod he, 'yit as unto this tyme ye han wel and covenabely taught me as in general how I schal governe me in chesynge and in withholdynge of my counseiloures, but now wold I fayn ye wolde condescende as in especial telleth me what semeth, or how liketh yow by oure counseiloures that we han chosen in oure present neede?' 'My lord,' quod sche, 'I byseke yow in al humblesce that ye wil not wilfully repplye ageinst my resouns ne, distempre youre herte, though I say or speke thing that yow displesith, for God woot that as in myn entent I speke it for youre beste, for youre honour, and for your profyt eek, and sothly I hope that youre benignite wol take it into pacience; for trusteth me wel,' quod sche,

63 'follow it dutifully until it is finished'

'that youre counseil as in this caas ne schulde not, as for to speke, propurly be called a counseilyng, but a mocioun or a moevyng of foly – in which counseil ye han erred in many a sondry wise.'

First and forward, ye han erred in the gaderyng of youre counseillours, for ye schulde first han cleped a fewe folkes, if it hadde be neede; but certes, ye han sodeinly cleped to your counseil a gret multitude of poeple ful chargeous[64] and ful anoyous for to hiere. Also ye han erred, for ther as ye schulde oonly have clepid to youre counseil youre trewe frendes, olde and wise, ye have y-cleped straunge folk, yonge folk, false flatereres, and enemyes reconsiled, and folk that doon yow reverence withoute love. Eek also ye han erred, for ye han brought with yow to youre counseil ire, coveitise and hastynes, the whiche thre things ben contrarious to every counsail honest and profitable; the whiche thre thinges ye have nought anentissched[65] or destroyed, neyther in yourself, ne in youre counseiloures, as ye oughte. Also ye have erred, for ye have schewed to youre counseilours youre talent and youre affeccioun to make werre, and for to doon vengeaunce anoon. Thay han espyed by youre wordes to what thing ye ben enclined, and therfore have thay counseiled yow rather to youre talent than to youre profyt. Ye have erred also, for it semeth that yow sufficeth to have been counseiled by these counseilours only, and with litel avys; wheras in so gret and so heigh a neede it hadde be necessarious mo counseilours and more deliberacioun to performe youre emprise. Ye have erred also, for ye have maked no divisioun bytiwixe youre counsailours; this is to sayn, bitwix youre frendes and youre feyned counseilours ne ye ne have nought y-knowe the wille of youre frendes olde and wise, but ye have cast all here wordes in an hochepoche,[66] and enclyned youre herte to the more part and to the gretter nombre, and there be ye condescendid. And syn ye wot wel men schal alway fynde a gretter nombre of fooles than of wyse men, and therfore the counsailes that be at congregaciouns and multitudes of folk ther as men taken more reward to the nombre than to the sapience[67] of persones, ye se wel that in suche counseilynges fooles have maystrie.'

Melibeus answerde agayn and seyde, 'I graunte wel that I have erred, but there as thou hast told me toforn that he is nought to blame that chaungeth his counseilours in certeyn caas and for certeyn juste causes, I am al redy to chaunge my counseilours right as thou wilt devyse. The

64 burdensome
65 wiped out/annihilated
66 a mixed stew
67 wisdom

proverbe saith that for to do synne is mannysche,[68] but certes, for to persevere long in synne is werk of the devyl.' To this sentence anoon answerde Dame Prudens and saide: 'Examineth,' quod sche, 'youre counsail and let us se which of hem hath spoke most resonably, and taught you best counsail. And for as moche as the examinacioun is necessarie, let us bygynne at the surgiens and at the phisiciens, that first speken in this matiere.

I say you, that the surgiens and the phisiciens han sayd yow in youre counseil discretly as hem ought, and in here speche sayden ful wisely that to the office of hem appendith to doon to euery wight honour and profyt, and no wight to annoye, and after here craft to do gret diligence unto the cure of hem whiche that thay have in here governaunce. And Sire, right as thay answerde wisely and discretly, right so rede I that thay be heighly and soveraignly guerdoned for here noble speche, and eek for they schullen do the more ententyf besynes in the curyng of youre doughter dere; for al be it so that thai be youre frendes, therfore schul ye nought suffre that thay schul serve yow for nought, but ye oughte the rathere to guerdoune[69] hem, and schewe hem youre largesse; & as touchyng the proposiciouns which the phisiciens han schewed you in this caas, this is to sayn that in maladyes oon contrarie is warisshed by another contrarie, I wolde fayn knowe thilke text and how thay understonde it, and what is youre entent.'

'Certes' quod Melibeus, 'undertonden it in this wise; that right as thay han do me a contrarie, right so schold I do hem another; for right as thai han venged hem on me and doon me wrong, right so schal I venge me upon hem and doon hem wrong, and thanne have I cured oon contrarie by another.' 'Lo, lo,' quod Dame Prudence, 'how lightly is every man enclyned to his oughne plesaunce, and to his oughne desir. Certes,' quod sche, 'the wordes of the phisiciens ne schulde nought have ben understonde sone in that wise, for certes, wikkednesse is no contrarie to wickednesse, ne vengauns to vengeaunce, ne wrong to wrong, but thai ben semblable. And therfore a vengeaunce is nought warisshed by another vengeaunce, ne oon wrong by another wrong, but everych of hem encreseth and engreggith[70] other; but certes, the wordes of the phisiciens schul ben understonde in this wise, for good and wikkednesse ben tuo contraries, and pees and werre, vengeaunce & sufferaunce, discord and

68 human
69 reward
70 aggravates

accord, and many other thinges. But certes, wikkednes schal be warrisshed by goodnesse, discord by accord, werre by pees, and so forth of other thinges, and herto accordith Seint Paul the apostil in many places.[71] He saith, 'Ne yeldith nought harm for harm, ne wikked speche for wikked speche, but do wel to him that doth the harm, and blesse him that doth the harme', and in many other places he amonesteth pees and accord.

But now wil I speke to yow of the counseil which was give to yow by the men of lawe & the wise folk, that sayde all by oon accord as ye have herd byfore; that over alle thinges ye schal do youre diligence to kepe youre persone and to warmstore youre house, and seyden also that in this yow aughte for to wirche ful avysily, and with gret deliberacioun. And Sire, as to the firste poynt that touched to the kepinge of youre persone; ye schul understonde that he that hath werre schal evermore devoutly and mekely prayen biforn alle thinges that Jhesu Crist wil of his mercy have him in his proteccioun and ben his soverayn, helpyng at his neede; for certes, in this world ther nys no wight that may be counseiled, or kept sufficauntly, withoute the kepinge of Oure Lord Jhesu Crist. To this sentence accordeth the prophete David, that seith,[72] 'If God ne kepe not the citee, in ydel wakith he that kepith hit.'

Now Sire, thanne schul ye committe the keping of youre p[r]sone to your trewe frendes that ben approved and y-knowe, and of hem schul ye axen help youre persone to kepe; for Catoun saith, 'If thou haue neede of help, axe it of thy freendes, for ther is noon so good a phisicien at neede as is a trewe frend'. And after this, than schal ye kepe you fro all straunge folkes, and fro lyeres, and have alway in suspect here compaignye; for Pieres Alfons saith, 'Ne take no compaignye by the way of a straunge man, but so be that thou knowe him of a lenger tyme, and if so be he falle into thy compaignye paraventure, withouten his assent enquere thanne as subtilly as thou maist of his conversacioun and of his lyf bifore, and feyne thy way, and say that thou wilt go thider as thou wolt nought goon; and if he bere a swerd, holde the on the lyft syde. And so after this, thanne schul ye kepe you wisely from al such peple – as I have sayd bifore – and hem and here counseil eschiewe. And after this thanne schul ye kepe yow in such manere, that for eny presumpcioun of youre strengthe that ye despise not the might of youre adversarie so lite, that ye lete the kepinge of youre persone for your presumpcioun: for every wis man dredeth his enemy. And Salomon saith, 'Weleful is he that of alle hath

71 for example, Romans 12:17; 1 Corinthians 4:12
72 Psalm 126

drede, for certes, he that thurgh hardynes of his herte and thurgh the hardinesse of himself hath to gret presumpcioun, him schal evyl bitide'.

Thanne schal ye evermore counterwayte enbusshements and alle espiall.[73] For Senec saith that the wise man that dredith harmes eschiewith harmes, ne he ne fallith into noone perils, that perils eschieweth. And albeit so that the seme that thou art in sikur[74] place, yit schaltow alway do thy diligence in kepyng of thy persone; this is to say, be not necgligent to kepe thy persone, nought oonly for thy gretteste enemyes but fro thy lest enemyes. Senec saith, 'A man that is wel avysed, he dredith his lest enemy'. Ovide seith that the litel wesil wol sle the grete bole[75] and the wilde hert, and the book saith, 'A litel thorn wol prikke a thing ful sore, and an hound wol holde the wilde boore'; but natheles, I say not that ye schul be so moche a coward that ye doute where is no neede or drede. The book saith that som folk have gret lust to disceyve, but yit thay dreden hem to be deceyved. Yet schal ye drede to ben empoisoned, and kepe the fro the companye of scorners; for the book saith, 'With scorners make no compaignye, but flee hem and here wordes as venym'.

Now as to the secounde poynt: wheras youre wise counseilours warnede yow to warmstore youre hous with gret diligence, I wolde fayn wite how that ye understoode thilke wordes. What is your sentence?' Melibeus answerde and saide,' 'Certes, I understonde it in this wise; that I schal warmstore myn hous with toures suche as han castiles and other maner edifices, and armure, and artilries; by such thinges I may my persone & myn hous so kepen, and edifien, and defenden that myn enemyes schul be in drede myn hous to approche.' To this sentence answerde Dame Prudence, 'Warmstorynge,' quod sche 'of heihe toures and grete edifices, with grete costages and grete travaile, and whan that thay ben accomplised, yit beth thay nought worth a straw but if they be defended by trewe frendes that beth olde and wise. And understondeth that the grettest strength or garnisoun[76] that the riche man may have, as wel to kepe his persone as his goodes, is that he be biloved with his subgites, and with his neighebours; for thus saith Tullius, that ther is a maner garnisoun that no man may venquisshe, ne discomfite, and that is a lord to be biloved with his citezeins and of his peple.

Now thanne, as to youre thridde poynt; whereas youre olde and wyse

73 'you may guard against ambushes and spies'
74 safe/secure
75 bull
76 garrison (fighting men who keep a castle, town etc).

counseillours sayde ye oughte nought sodeinly ne hastily procede in this neede, but that ye oughte purveyen yow, and apparaile yow,[77] in this caas with greet diligence and gret deliberacioun – trewely, I trowe that thay sayden soth, and right wisely. Tullius saith, 'In every nede, er thou bigynne it, apparaile the with gret diligence'. Thanne say I, that in vengeaunce takinge, in werre, in bataile, and in warmstoringe of thin hous; er thou bygynne I rede that thou apparaille the therto, and do it with gret deliberacioun. For Tullius saith, that long apparaylyng byfore the bataille maketh schort victorie, and Cassidorus saith, 'The garnisoun is strenger whan it is long tyme avysed'.

But now let us speke of the counseil that was accorded by youre neighbours suche as doon you reverence withoute love, youre olde enemyes recounsiled that counseile yow certeyn thinges pryvely, and openly counseile yow the contrarie; the yonge also, that counsaile yow to make werre and venge yow anoon. And certes, Sire, as I have sayd byforn, ye have gretly erred to have cleped such maner folk to youre counsei, whiche be now repreved by the resouns byfore sayd; but natheles, let us now descende to the purpos especial[78] Ye schul first procede after the doctrine of Tullius: certes, the trouthe of this or this counseil nedeth nought diligently enquerre, for it is wel wist whiche it ben that doon to yow this trespas and vilonye, & how many trespasoures, and in what maner thay han to yow doon al this wrong and al this vilonye. And after that schul ye examyne the secounde condicioun which Tullius addith therto in this matier. Tullius put a thing which that he clepeth covetyng; this is to sayn, who ben thay, and which ben thay, and how many, that consentid to this matiere, and to thy counsail in thy wilfulnesse to do hasty vengeaunces? And let us considere also who ben tho, and how many ben tho, that ben counseilours to youre adversaries; and certes, as to the first poynt, it is wel knowen whiche folk ben thay that consentid to youre first wilfulnes, for trewely, alle tho that consailled yow to make sodeyn werre beth nought youre frendes. Let us considre whiche ben tho that ye holde so gretly youre frendes as to youre persone; for albeit so that ye be mighty and riche, certes ye been alloone; for certes, ye have no childe but a doughter, ne ye have no bretheren, ne cosins germayns,[79] ne noon other neigh kynrede wherfore that youre enemyes for drede schulden stynte for to plede with you, and struye[80] youre persone. Ye

---

77 'supply and prepare yourself'
78 the matter in hand
79 first cousins

knowe also that youre richesses mooten in divers parties be departed, and whan every wight hath his part, thay wol take but litel reward to venge thy deth, but thyne enemyes ben thre, and have many children, bretheren, cosynes, and othere neigh kynrede; and though it so were ye hadde slayn of hem tuo or thre, yet dwellen there ynowe to wreke[81] here deth, and sle thi persone. And though so were that youre kynrede were more sekir and stedefast than the kynrede of youre adversaries, yit natheles, youre kynrede nis but a litel kinrede, and litel sib[82] to yow, and the kyn of youre enemyes ben neigh sibbe to hem; and certes, as in that here condicioun is bet than youres.

Thanne let us considere also if the counseilynge of hem that counseiled yow to take sodein vengeaunce: whethir it accorde to resoun, & certes, ye knowe wel nay. For as by right and resoun ther may no man take vengeaunce upon no wight but the jugge that hath jurediccioun of it, whan it is y-graunted him to take thilke vengeaunce, hastily or attemperely as the lawe requireth; and yit moreover of thilke word that Tullius clepith consentynge; thou schalt considre if thy might and thy power may consente and suffice to thy wilfulnes, and to thy counseilours', and certes, thou maist wel say that nay. For sicurly, as for to speke properly, we may doo nothing but oonly oon thing which we may do rightfully. And certes, rightfully may ye take no vengeaunce as of your owne auctorite. Than may ye se that youre power consentith not, ne accordith not, with youre wilfulnesse. Let us now examyne the thridde poynt that Tullius clepeth consequente: thou schalt understonde that the vengeance that thou purposiddest for to take is consequent, and therof folweth another vengeaunce, peril and werre, and other damages withoute nombre, of whiche we be not war[83] as at this tyme. And as touching the fourthe poynt that Tullius clepeth engendrynge: thou schalt considre that this wrong which that is doon to the is engendred of the hate of thin enemyes, and of the vengeaunce takinge up that wolde engendre another vengeaunce, & moche sorwe and wastyng of riches, as I sayde.

Now Sire, as to the poynt that Tullius clepith causes: which that the laste poynt thou schalt understonde that the wrong that thou hast receyved hath certeyn causes whiche that clerkes calle prience and officience, and *causa longinqua* and *causa propinqua*; this is to say, the fer

---

80 destroy
81 avenge
82 relation
83 aware

cause and the neigh cause. For the fer cause is Almighty God, that is cause of alle thing; the nere cause is the thre enemyes. The cause accidental was hate; the causes materiales been the fyve woundes of thy doughter; the cause formal is the maner of here werkyng that brought in laddres and clombe in at thin wyndowes; the cause final was for to sle thy doughter hit letted nought, inasmoche as was in hem. But for to speke of the fer cause, as to what ende thay schal come or what schal finally betyde of hem in this cause can I not deme, but by comittyng and by supposyng; for we schul suppose that thay schul come to a wikked ende, bycause that the Book of Degrees saith,[84] 'Seelden or with gret peyne ben causes y-brought to a good ende whan thay ben evyl bygonne'.

Now Sire, if men wolde axe me why that ye suffrede men to do yow this wrong and vilonye; yet certes, I can not wel answere, as for no sothfastnes, for the apostil saith that the sciences and the juggementes of oure Lord God Almyghty ben ful deepe,[85] ther may no man comprehende ne serchen hem sufficiauntly. Natheles, by certeyn presumpciouns and conjectinges I holde and bilieve that God, which that is ful of justice and of rightwisnesse, hath suffred this to betyde, by juste cause resonable. Thy name, Melibe, is to say 'a man that drynketh hony'. Thou hast y-dronke so moche hony of sweete temperel richesses, and delices and honours of this world that thou art dronke, and hast forgete Jhesu Crist thy creatour; thou hast not doon him such honour and reverence as the oughte to doone, ne thou hast nought wel taken keep to the wordes of Ovide, that saith, 'Under the hony of thy goodes of thy body is hid the venym that sleeth thi soule'. And Salomon saith, 'If thou have founde hony, ete of it that sufficeth, for if thou ete of it out of mesure thou schalt spewe, and be nedy and pouere. And peraventure Crist hath the in despit, and hath torned away fro the his face and his eeres of misericorde,[86] and also he hath suffred that thou hast ben punysshed in the maner that thou hast y-trespassed. Thou hast doon synne ageinst oure Lord Crist; for certes thi thre enemyes of mankynde, that is to say thy flessche, the feend and the world, thou hast y-suffred hem to entre into thin herte wilfully by the wyndow of thy body, and hast nought defended thiself sufficiently agayns here ascentis an here temptaciouns, so that thay have woundid thi soule in fyve places, this is to sayn the dedly synnes that ben entred into thin herte by thy fyve windowes. And

84 Book of the Decrees of the Roman emperor Gratian.
85 A vague reference to Paul's Epistles, possibly 1Corinthians 4:55
86 mercy

in the same maner Oure Lord Crist hath wolde and suffred that thy thre enemyes ben entred into thin hous by the wyndowes, and have y-woundid thi doughter in the forsayde maner.'

'Certes,' quod Melibeus, 'I se wel that ye enforce yow moche by wordes to overcome me, in such manere that I schal not venge me on myn enemyes, schewynge me the perils and the yveles that mighten falle of this vengeaunce. But whoso wolde considre in alle vengeaunces the periles and the yveles that mighten folwe of vengeaunces takynge, a man wolde never take vengeaunce – and that were harm; for by vengeaunce takynge be wikked men destruyed and dissevered fro the goode men, and thay that have wille to wikkednes restreignen here wikked purpos whan thay seen the punysshyng and the chastisyng of trespasours.'

And to this answered Dame Prudence, 'Certis,' sayde sche, 'I graunte wel that of vengeaunce cometh muchel yvel and muchel good; but vengeaunce takinge aperteneth nat unto everichoon, but oonly unto juges and unto hem that han jurisdiccioun upon the trespasours. And yit say I more; that right so as a sengle persone synneth in taking of vengeaunce, right so the jugge synneth if he doo no vengeaunce of him that it hath deserved. For Senec saith thus, 'He that maister is, he doth good to reprove schrewes', and as Cassoder saith, 'A man dredeth to doon outrage whan he woot and knoweth that it displeseth to the jugges and the soveraynes', and another saith, 'The jugge that dredeth to demen right maketh schrewes'. And Seint Poul th'appostil saith in his epistil, whan he writeth to the Romayns,[87] 'The jugges bere not the spere withoute cause, but they beren it to punysshe the schrewes and mysdoers, and for to defende with the goode men'. If ye wol take vengeaunce on youre enemyes ye schul retourne or have recours to the jugges that have jurediccioun upon hem, and he schl punissche hem as the lawe axeth and requireth.'

'A' quod Melibeus 'this vengeaunce liketh me nothing. I bythenke me now and take heed how Fortune hath norissched me fro my childhode, and hath holpe me to passen many a strayt passage. Now wol I aske her that sche schal, with God's help, helpe me my schame for to venge.'

'Certes' quod Prudence, 'if ye wil wirche by my counseil ye schul not assaye Fortune by no maner way, ne schul not lene ne bowe unto hire, after the word of Senec: 'For thinges that beth folye and that beth in hope of Fortune schul never come to good ende'. And as the same Senec saith, 'The more cleer and the more schynynge that Fortune is, the more brutil and the sonner breketh sche'. So trusteth nought in hire, for sche is

87 Romans 13:4

nought stedefast ne stable; for whan thou wenest or trowest to be most seur of hir help, sche wol fayle the and deceyue the. And wheras ye say that Fortune hath norisshed yow fro youre childhode, I say that in so mochel ye schul the lasse truste in hire and in hire witte. For Senek saith, 'What man that is norissched by Fortune, sche maketh him to gret a fool'. Now sithe[88] ye desire and axe vengeaunce, and the vengeaunce that is doon in hope of Fortune is perilous and uncerteyn, thanne haveth noon other remedye but for to have recours unto the soverayne jugge that vengith alle vilonies and wronges, and he schal venge yow after that himself witnesseth, where as he saith, 'Leveth the vengeaunce to me, and I schal yelde it''.

Melibeus answerd, 'If I ne venge me nought of the vilonye that men have doon unto me, I schal soun or warne hem that han doon to me that vilonye, and all othere, to doo me another vilonye. For it is writen, 'Tak no vengeaunce of an old vilonye, thou suffrest thin adversarie do the a newe vilonye. And also, for my suffraunce men wolde do me so moche vilonye that I mighte neither bere it ne susteyne it, and so schulde I be put over-lowe. For men say, 'In moche sufferynge schal many thinges falle unto the which thou schalt nought nowe suffre'.

'Certes,' quod Prudence, 'I graunte yow wel that over-mochil suffraunce is nought good, but yit folwith it nought therof that every persone to whom men doon vilonye take of it vengeaunce. For it apperteneth and longeth al oonly to the jugges, for thay schul venge the vilonyes and the injuries; and therfore the auctoritees that ye have sayd above been oonly understonden in the jugges. For whan thay suffre to mochil the wronges and the vilonyes that ben doon withoute punysshyng, thay soune not a man oonly to doo newe wronges, but thay comaunde hit. Also the wise man saith, 'The jugge that correcteth not the synnere comaundith him and byddith him doon another synne'; and the jugges and sovereignes mighten in here lond so mochil suffren of the schrewes and mysdoeres, that thay schulde by such suffraunce, by proces of tyme, wexen of such power and might that thay schulde put out the jugges and the sovereignes from here places, & atte laste do hem lese here lordschipes.

But lete us now putte that ye han leve to venge yow; I say ye ben nought of might ne power as now to venge you. For if ye wolde make comparisoun as to the might of youre adversaries, ye shulde fynde in many thinges that I haue y-schewed yow er this, that here condicioun is bettre than youres; and therfore say I that it is good as now that ye suffre and be pacient.

88 since

Forthermore, ye know that after the comune sawe it is a woodnesse[89] a man to stryve with a stenger or a more mighty man than himselven is, and for to stryve with a man of evene strengthe; that is to say, with as strong a man as he is, it is peril; and for to stryve with a weykere it is folye, and therfore schulde a man fle stryvyng as moche as he mighte. For Salomon seith, 'It is a gret worschipe a man to kepe him fro noyse and stryf'. And if it so bifall or happe that a man of gretter might and strengthe than thou art do the grevaunce, stude and busye the rather to stille the same grevaunce than for to venge the. For Senec saith, 'He putteth him in a gret peril that stryveth with a gretter man than he himselven is', and Catoun saith, 'If a man of heiher estat or degre, or more mighty then thou, do the another greuaunce, suffre him; for he that hath oones don the a grievaunce may another tyme relieve the and helpe the'.

Yit sette I a caas ye have both might and licence for to venge yow; I say ther ben ful many thinges that schulde restreigne yow of vengeaunce takynge, and make yow to encline to suffre and to have pacience of the wronges than han ben doon to yow. First and forward, ye wol considre the defautes that been in youre owne persone, for which defautes God hath suffred yow to have this tribulacioun, as I have sayd yow her byfore. For the poete saith, 'We oughten paciently to suffre the tribulacioun that cometh to us, whan that we thenken and consideren that we han deserved to have hem'. And Seint Poul saith that whan a man considereth wel the nombre of his defautes, and of his synnes, the peynes and the tribulaciouns that he suffreth semen the lasse unto him;[90] and inasmoche as him thenkith his synnes the more hevy and grevous, in so moche his peyne is the lighter and the more esier unto him. Also, ye oughten to encline and bowe youre herte to take the pacience of Oure Lord Jhesu Crist, as seith Seint Peteer in his epistles,[91] 'Jhesu Crist,' he seith, 'hath suffred for us, and given ensample unto every man to folwe and sewe him, for he dede never synne, ne never cam vileyn's worde out of his mouth. Whan men cursed him he cursed hem not, and whan men beete him he manased hem not'. Also, the grete pacience which that seintes that been in Paradys han had in tribulaciouns that thay have had and suffred withoute desert or fult, oughte moche stire yow to pacience. Forthermore, ye schuld enforce yow to have pacience, consideringe that the tribulaciouns of this world but litel while enduren, & soon passed

89 madness
90 Unknown: attributed in some manuscripts to St Gregory the Great.
91 1Peter 2:21

ben and goon, and the joye that a man secheth to have by pacience in tribulaciouns is perdurable,[92] after that th'apostil seith in his epistil: 'The joye of god,' he saith, 'is perdurable; that is to say, evermore lastynge'. Also troweth, and believeth stedefastly, that he is not wel norisched and taught that can nought have pacience, or wil nought receyve pacience. For Salomon saith that the doctrine and the witte of a man is y-knowe by pacience; and in another place he seith, ' He that hath pacience governeth him by gret prudence'. And the same Salamon seith that the wrathful and the angry man maketh noyses, and the pacient man attempereth and stilleth him. He seith also, 'It is more worth to be pacient than for to be right strong'. And he that may have his lordschipe of his oughne herte is more worth, and more to preise, than he that by his force & by his strengthe taketh grete citees. And therfore saith Seint Jame in his epistil that pacience is a gret vertu of perfeccioun.'

'But euery man may not have the perfeccioun that ye sekyn, ne I am not of the nombre of right parfyte men, for myn herte may never be in pees unto the tyme it be venged; and albeit so that it was a gret peril to myne enemyes to don me a vilonye in takinge vengeaunce upon me, yit tooken thay noon heede of the peril, but filden here wikked desir and her corrage; and therfore me thenkith men oughten nought repreve me, though I putte me in a litel peril for to venge me, and though I do a gret excesse; that is to say, that I venge oon outrage by another.'

'A,' quod Dame Prudence, 'ye say youre wille and as yow likith, but in noon caas in the world a man ne schulde nought doon outrage ne excesse for to venge him. For Cassidore saith, 'As evel doth he that avengith him by outrage, as he that doth the outrage', and therfore ye schul venge yow after the ordre of right; that is to sayn, by the lawe, and nought by excesse ne by outrage. And also, if ye wil venge yow of the outrage of your adversaries in other maner than right comaundeth, ye synnen. And therfore saith Senec that a man schal never venge schrewednes by schrewednes. And if ye say that right axeth a man to defende violence by vyolence and fightyng by fightyng, certes, ye say soth, whan the defence is doon anoon, withouten intervalle or withouten taryinge or dilay, for to defenden him, and nought for to venge him. And it bihoveth a man putte such attemperaunce in his defence that men have no cause ne matiere to repreven him that defendith him of excesse and outrage. Parde, ye knowe wel that ye make no defence as now for to defende yow, but for to venge yow; and so semeth it that ye have no wille to do youre wille attemperelly,

92 eternal

& therfore me thenkith that pacience is good; for Salamon saith that he
that is not pacient schal have gret harm.

'Certes,' quod Melibeus, 'I graunte you wel, that whan a man is
impacient and wroth, of that that toucheth him noght and that aperteneth
nat unto him, though it harme him, it is no wonder, for the lawe saith
that he is coupable that entremettith him or mellith him with such thing
as aperteyneth not unto him.[93] Dan Salamon saith, 'He that entremetteth
him of the noyse or stryf of another man is lik him that takith the hound
by the eeres; for right as he that takith the hound by the eeres is other
while biten with the hound, right in the same wise it is resoun that he
have harm that by his impacience melleth him of the noise of another
man, where it aperteyneth not to him'. But ye schal knowe wel that this
dede, that is to sayn myn disease and my grief, toucheth me right neigh.
And therfore, though I be wroth, it is no mervayle; and savynge your
grace, I cannot see that it mighte gretly harme me, though I toke
vengeaunce, for I am richer and more mighty than myn enemyes been;
and wel knowe ye that by money and by havyng of grete possessiouns ben
alle the thinges of this world governede. And Salamon saith that all
thinges obeyen to moneye, dispraisyng the power of his adversaries.'

Tho sche spak, and sayde in this wyse: 'Certes, deere Sire, I graunte
yow that ye ben riche and mighty, and that richesse is good to hem that
wel have geten it and that wel conne use it; for right as the body of a man
may not be withoute the soule, no more may a man lyve withoute
temperel goodes, and by richesse may a man get him greet frendschipe.
And therfore saith Pamphilles, 'If a neet hurdes[94] doughter,' he saith, 'be
riche, sche may cheese of a thousand men which sche wol take to hir
housbonde, for of a thousand men oon wil not forsake hir ne refuse hir';
and this Pamphilles seith also, 'If thou be right happy, that is to sayn, if
thou be right riche, thanne schale thou fynde a gret nombre of felawes
and frendes; and if thy fortune chaunge, that thou waxe pore, farewel
frendschipe; for thou schalt be aloone withouten eny companye, but if it
be the compaignye of pore folk'. And yit saith this Pamphillus, moreover,
fhat they that ben thral and bonde of linage, schullen ben maad worthy
and noble by richesse. And right so as by richesse ther come many
goodes, right so by povert comen ther many harmes. And therfore clepeth
Cassidore povert, ruyne; that is to sayn, the moder of overthrowyng or

93 'the man is blameworthy who gets involved in, or meddles in such things as are
   nothing to do with him'
94 cowherd's

fallynge doun. Therfore saith Pieres Alphons, 'Oon of the grettest adversites of this world is whan a free man, by kyn or burthe, is constreigned by povert to eten the almes of his enemyes', and the same seith Innocent in oon of his bookes, that sorweful & unhappy is the condicioun of a pouere begger; For if he axe nou*ght* his mete, he deyeth for hongir, and if he axe he deyeth for schame; and algates the necessite constreigneth hym to axe. And therfore saith Salamon that bettre is it to dey than to have such pouert. And as the same Salamon saith, ' Bettir is to deye on bitter deth than for to lyve in such a wyse'.

By these resouns that I have sayd unto yow, and by many another resoun that I know and couthe say, I graunte yow that richesses ben goode to hem that gete hem wel, & to hem that hem wel usen. And therfore wol I schewe yow how ye schulde bere yow in getyng of riches, and in what maner ye schulde use hem. First, ye schulde gete hem withoute gret desir, by good leysir sokyngly,[95] and nought over-hastily; for a man that is to desirynge for to gete riches abandoneth him first to thefte, and to alle othere yveles. And therfore saith Salamon, 'He that hastith him to bisyly to wax riche schal ben noon innocent'. He saith also that the riches that hastily cometh to a man soone & lightly goth and passeth fro a man, but that richesse that cometh alway litel and litel, waxeth alway and multiplieth. And Sire, ye schal gete richesse by youre witte and by youre travayle unto youre profyt, and that withoute wrong or harm doyng to eny other persone, for the lawe saith that no man maketh himself riche that doth harm to another wight; this is to say, that nature defendeth and forbedith by right that no mn make him self riche unto the harm of another persone. Tullius saith that no sorwe ne drede of deth, ne thought that may falle to a man, is so moche ageinst nature as a man to encresce his oughne profyt to the harm of another man; and though the grete men and the riche men gete richesse more lightly than thou, yit schalt thou not be ydil, ne slowe to thy profyt, for thou schalt in all wise flee ydilnes. For Salamon saith that ydelnesse techith a man to do many yveles, and the same Salamon saith that he that travaileth and besieth him to tilye the lond schal ete the breed, but he that is ydil and casteth him to no busynesse ne occupacioun schal falle into povert, and deye for hunger. And he that is ydel and slough can never fynde him tyme for to do his profyt, for ther is a versifiour saith the ydel man excuseth him in wynter bycause of the grete colde, and in somer by enchesoun of the grete hete. For these causes saith Catoun, 'Waketh, and eclineth yow nought

95 gradually/carefully

over-moche for to slepe, For over-moche reste norischeth and causeth many vices. And therfore saith Seint Jerom, 'Doth some goode deedes, that the devel, which that is oure enemy, ne fynde yow unoccupied', for the deuel ne takith not lightly unto his werkes suche as he fyndeth occupied in goode werkes. Thanne, thus, in getyng of riches ye moot flee ydelnesse. And afterward ye schul use the richesses the whiche ye han geten by youre witte and by youre travaile in such a maner that men holde yow not skarce, ne to sparynge, ne to fool large;[96] that is to say, over large a spender; for right as men blamen an averous man bycause of his skarsete and chyncherie,[97] in the same manere is he to blame that spendeth over largely. And therfore saith Catoun, 'Use,' he saith, 'thi richesses that thou hast y-geten in such a manere that thay have no matier ne cause to calle the neither wrecche ne chynche, for it is a gret schame to a man to haue a pouer herte and a riche purse'. He saith also, 'The goodes that thou hast y-geten, use hem by mesure; that is to say, spende hem mesurably; for thay that folily wasten and spenden the goodes that thay have, whan thay haue, whan thay haue no more propre of here oughne, thay schape hem to take the goodes of another man'. I say, thanne, ye schul flee avarice, usynge youre richesse in such manere that men say nat that your richesses been y-buried, but that ye have them in youre might and in youre weldyng. For the wise man reproveth the averous man, and saith thus in tuo versus: 'Wherto and why burieth a man his goodes by his avarice, and knowith wel that needes most he deye, for deth is the ende of every man as in this present lif? And for what cause or enchesoun joyneth he him or knetteth him so fast unto his goodes, that alle his wittes mowe nought dissever him or departe him fro his goodes, & knowith wel – or oughte knowe wel – that whan he is deed he schal nothing bere with him out of this world?' And therfore seith Seint Austyn that the averous[98] man is likned unto helle, that the more that it swolwith, the more it desireth to swolwe and devoure. And as wel as ye wolde eschwe to be cleped an averous man or chinche, as wel schulde ye kepe yow and governe yow in such a wise that men clepe yow nought fool large. Therfore saith Tullius, 'The goodes,' he saith, 'of thin hous schulde nought be hidde, ne kepte so clos but that thay might ben opened by pite and by bonairete;[99] that is

96 'not too niggardly, nor mean, nor foolishly generous'
97 miserliness/avarice
98 avaricious
99 generosity

to sayn, to give hem part that han gret neede, ne thy goodes schul not be so open to be every man's goodes'.

Aftirward, in getynge of youre richesses and in usyng hem, ye schul alway have thre thinges in youre herte; that is to say, oure Lord God, conscience and good name. First, ye schul have God in youre herte, and for no riches ye schul in no manere doo no thing which might displese God, that is your creatour and youre maker. For after the word of Salamon, it is better to have litil good with love of God, than to have mochil good and tresor, and lese the love of his Lord God. And the prophete saith, 'Better is to ben a good man and have litel good and tresore, than to be holden a schrewe and have gret riches'. And yit say I forthermore that ye shuln alway doon youre businesse to gete yow riches, so that ye gete hem with good conscience. And the apostil seith, 'Ther nys thing in this world of which we schuln have so gret joye as whan oure conscience bereth us good witnes'. And the wise man saith, 'Substaunce of a man is ful good whan synne is not in his conscience'. Afterward, in getynge of youre richesses and in usynge of hem thou most have gret busynesse & gret diligence that youre good name be alway kept and conserved, for Salamon saith, 'Better it is and more it availleth a man for to have a good name than for to have gret riches'. And therfore he saith in another place, 'Do gret diligence,' saith Salamon, 'in kepynge of thy frend and of thy good name, for it schal lenger abyde with the than eny tresor, be it never so precious'. And certes, he schulde nought be cleped a gentil man that after God and good conscience, alle thinges left, ne doth his diligence and busynesse to kepe his good name. And Cassidore saith that it is a signe of a good man & a gentil, or of a gentil herte, whan a man loveth or desireth to have a good name. And therfore saith Seint Augustyn that ther ben tuo thinges that ben necessarie and needful, and that is good conscience and good loos;[100] that is to sayn, good conscience in thin oughne persone inward, and good loos of thin neghbor outward. And he that trusteth him so moche in his good conscience that he displeseth and settith at nought his good name or loos, and rekketh nought though he kepe not his good name, nys but a cruel churl.

Sire, now have I schewed yow how ye schulde doon in getyng of good and riches and how ye schulde use hem, I see wel that for the trust that ye have in youre riches ye wolde meve werre and bataile. I counseile yow that ye bygynne no werre in trust of youre riches, for thay suffisen not werres to mayntene. And therfore saith a philosophre, that man that

100 name

desireth and wol algate have werre schal never have sufficeaunce, for the richere that he is, the gretter dispense[101] most he make if he wol have worschipe or victorie. And Salamon saith, 'The gretter riches that a man hath the moo despendours[102] he hath'. And, deere Sire, albeit so that for youre riches ye mowe have moche folk, yit byhoveth it not, ne it is not good to bygynne werre, theras ye may in other maner have pees, unto youre worschipe and profyt; for the victorie of batailles that ben in this world lith not in gret nombre or multitude of poeple, ne in vertu of man, but it lith in the wille & in the hond of oure Lord God Almighty. And Judas Machabeus,[103] which was God's knight, whan he schulde fight ageinst his adversaries that hadde a gretter nombre & a gretter multitude of folk and strengere than was the poeple of this Machabe, yit he reconforted his litel poeple and sayde ryght in this wise: 'As lightly,' quod he, 'may oure Lord God Almighty give victory to fewe folk, for the victorie of batailles cometh nought by the grete nombre of poeple, but it cometh fro oure Lord God of heven'. And dere Sire, for as moche as ther is no man certeyn if it be worthi that God give him victorie or nought, after that that Salamon saith, 'Therfore every man schulde gretly drede werres to bygynne'. And bycause that in batailles falle many mervayles and perils, and happeth other while that as soone is the grete man slayn as the litel man, and as it is writen in the Secounde Book of Kynges, the deedes of batayles be aventurous and no thing certeyn, for as lightly is oon hurt with a spere as another, and therfore is gret peril in werre. Therfore schulde a man flee and eschewe werre, inasmoche as a man may, goodly. For Salamon saith, 'He that loveth peril schal falle in peril'.'

After that Dame Prudens hadde spoke in this maner, Melibe answerde and sayde, 'I se wel, Dame, that by youre faire wordes and by youre resouns that ye have schewed me, that the werre liketh yow nothing; but I have not yit herd youre counseil how I schall doo in this neede.'

'Certes,' quod sche, 'I counseile yow that ye accorde with youre adversaries and that ye haue pees with hem, for Seint Jame saith in his Epistles that by concord and pees the smale ryches wexen grete, and by debaat and discord the gret richesses fallen doun. And ye knowe wel that oon of the most grettest and soveraign thing that is in this world is unite & pees, and therfore saith Oure Lord Jhesu Crist to his aposteles in this

---

101 expenditure
102 distributors of money
103 Judas Maccabeus, who led the Jews against the forces of Rome. His deeds are
     told in the apocryphal Book of Maccabees. In the Middle Ages, he was one of
     the 'Nine Worthies' of history.

wise:[104] 'Wel happy and blessed be thay that loven and purchacen pees, for thay ben called children of Crist'.'

'A!' quod Melibe, 'Now se I wel that ye loven not myn honour, ne my worschipe, and knoweth wel that myne adversaries han bygonne this debate and brige[105] by here outrage, and ye see wel that thay require ne praye me not of pees, ne thay askyn nought to be recounseild. Wol ye thanne that I goo & meke me unto hem and crie hem mercy? Forsothe, that were not my worschipe, for right as men seyn that ouer-gret pryde engendreth dispisyng, so fareth it by to gret humblete or mekenes.'

Thanne bygan Dame Prudence to make semblant of wrathe[106] and sayde, 'Certes Sire, save youre grace, I love youre honour and youre profyt as I doo myn owne, and euer have doon – ye ne mowe noon other seyn. And yit if I hadde sayd ye scholde have purchaced pees and the reconciliacioun I ne hadde not moche mystake me ne seyd amys. For the wise man saith, 'The discencioun bigynneth by another man, and the reconsilyng bygynneth by thyself . And the prophete saith, 'Flee schame and schrewednesse, and doo goodnesse; seeke pees and folwe it as moche as in the is'. Yet seith he not that ye schul rather pursewe to youre adversaries for pees than thei schul to yow, for I knowe wel that ye be so hard-herted that ye wil doo nothing for me. And Salamon saith, 'He that is over hard-herted, atte laste he schal myshappe and mystyde'.'

Whan Melibe had seyn Dame Prudence make semblaunce of wrathe, he sayde in this wise: 'Dame, I pray yow that ye be not displesed of thinges that I say, for ye knoweth wel that I am angry and wroth, and that is no wonder; and thay that be wroth wot not wel what thay doon, ne what thay say. Therfore the prophete saith that troublit eyen have no cleer sight. But sayeth and counsaileth me forth as yow liketh, for I am redy to doo right as ye wol desire. And if ye reprove me of my folye, I am the more holde to yow, and to prayse yow, for Salamon saith that he that repreveth him that doth folie, he schal fynde gretter grace than he that decyveth him by swete wordes.'

Thanne sayde Dame Prudence, 'I make no semblant of wrathe, ne of anger, but for youre grete profyt; for Salamon saith, 'He is more worth that reproveth or chydeth a fool for his folie, schewynge him semblant of wrathe, than he that supporteth him and prayseth him in his mysdoyng,

104 Matthew 5:9; part of the Sermon on the Mount.
105 struggle/strife
106 'to pretend to be angry'

and laugheth at his folie'. And this same Salamon saith afterward, that by
the sorweful visage of a man; that is to sayn, by sory and hevy counten-
aunce of a man, the fool corretteth himself and amendeth.'

Thanne sayde Melibeus, 'I schal not conne answere to so many resouns
as ye putten to me and schewen; sayeth schortly youre wille and youre
counseil, and I am al redy to fulfille and perfourme it.'

Thanne Dame Prudence discovered[107] al hire counsail and hire wille
unto him, and sayde, 'I counseile yow,' quod sche, 'above all thinges that
ye make pees bitwen God and yow, and beth reconsiled unto him and to
his grace, for I have sayd yow herbiforn God hath suffred yow have this
disease for youre synnes, and if ye do as I say yow, God wol sende youre
adversaries unto yow and make hem falle at youre feet, al redy to doo
youre wille and youre comaundment. For Salamon saith, 'Whan the
condicioun of man is plesant, and likyng to God, he chaungeth the
hertes of the man's adversaries and constreigneth hem to biseke him of
pees & of grace. And I pray yow, let me speke with youre adversaires in
prive place, for thay schul not knowe it by youre wille or youre assent;
and thanne, whan I knowe here wille and here assent, I may counseile
yow the more seurly.' 'Dame,' quod Melibeus, 'doth youre wille and
youre likyng, for I putte me holly in youre dispocioun and ordinaunce.'

Thanne Dame Prudence, whan sche seih the good wille of hire hous-
bond, sche deliuered and took avis by hirself, thenkynge how sche mighte
bringe this neede unto good conclusioun and to a good ende. And whan
sche saugh hire tyme, sche sente for these adversaries to come unto hire
into a prive place, and schewed wysly unto hem the grete goodes that
comen of pees, and the grete harmes and perils that ben in werre, and
sayde to hem in goodly manere how that hem aughte to have gret
repentaunce of the injurie & wrong that thay hadde doon to Melibe, hire
lord, and unto hire and hur doughter. And whan thay herden the goodly
wordes of Dame Prudence they were tho surprised and ravyssched, and
hadden so gret joye of hire, that wonder was to telle. 'A, lady!' quod thay,
'Ye have schewed unto us the blessyng of swetenes after the sawe[108] of
David the prophete, for the recounsilyng which we be nought worthy to
have in no manere, but we oughten require it with gret contricioun and
humilite, ye of youre grete goodnes have presented unto us. Now we se
wel that the science of Salamon is ful trewe. He saith that swete wordes

107 revealed
108 saying

multiplien and encrescen frendes and maken schrewes to ben debonaire
and meke. Certes,' quod thay, 'we putten oure deed and al oure matier
and cause al holly in youre good wille, and ben redy to obeye to the
speche, and to the comaundement of my lord Melibe. And therfore,
deere & benigne lady, we pray yow and byseke yow as meekely as we
conne and may, that it like to yowre grete goodnes to fulfille in deede
youre goodliche wordes; for we considere and knowleche wel that we
have offended and greved my lord Melibe, out of resoun and out of
mesure, so ferforth that we ben nought of power to make his amendes;
and therfore we oblie us and bynde us and oure frendes for to doo al his
wille and his comaundements. But peraventure he hath such hevynes &
such wrathe to us-ward bycause of oure offence, that he wol enioyne us
such peyne as we mow not bere ne susteyn. And therfore, noble lady, we
biseke to youre wommanly pite to take such avysement in this neede that
we, ne oure frendes, ben not disherited and destroyed thurgh oure folye.'

'Certes' quod Dame Prudence, 'it is an hard thing and right a perilous
that a man put him al outrely in the arbitracioun and juggement, and the
might and power, of his enemyes. For Salamon saith, 'Leeveth and giveth
credence to that that I schal say: I say,' quod he, 'geve poeple and
governours of holy chirche – to thy sone, to thi wyf, and to thy frend, ne
to thy brother, ne geve thou never might ne maystry of thy body, whil
thou lyvest'. Now sith he defendith[109] a man schulde not give to his
brother, ne to his frend, the might of his body, by a strenger resoun he
defendeth and forbedith a man to give his body to his enemye; but
natheles, I counseile yow that ye mystruste nought my lord, for I wot wel
and knowe verraily that he is debonaire and meke, large, curteys, and
nothing desirous ne coveytous of good, ne richesse. For ther nys nothing
in this world that he desireth, save oonly worschipe and honour. Forther-
more, I knowe and am right seure that he wol nothing doo in this neede
withoute counsail of me, and I schal so worche in this cause that by the
grace of oure Lord God ye schul be recounsiled unto us.'

Thanne sayde thay with oon voys, 'Worschipful lady, we putte us and
oure goodes al fully in youre wille and disposicioun, and ben redy to
come what day that it like yow, and unto youre noblesse, to limite us or
assigne us, for to make oure obligacioun and bond as strong as it liketh
to youre goodnes, that we mowe fulfille the wille of yow and of my lord
Melibe.'

Whan Dame Prudence had herd the answeres of thise men, sche bad

109 forbids

hem go agayn pryvely, and sche retourned to hire lord Melibe, and tolde him how sche fond his adversaries ful repentant, knowlechinge ful lowely here synnes and trespasses, and how thay were redy to suffre alle peyne, requiring and praying him of mercy and pite. Thanne saide Melibeus, 'He is wel worthy to have pardoun and forgevenes of his synne that excusith not his synne, but knowlecheth and repentith him, axinge indulgence; for Senek saith, 'Ther is the remissioun and for-gevenesse wheras the confessioun is, for confessioun is neighbor to innocence'. And he saith in another place, 'He that hath schame of his synne, knowlechith it'. And therfore I assente and conferme me to have pees; but it is good that we doo it nought withoute assent & the wille of oure frendes.'

Thanne was Prudence right glad & jolyf, and sayde, 'Certes Sire,' quod sche, 'ye ben wel & goodly avysed; for right as by the counsail and assent and help of youre frendes ye have be stired to venge yow & make werre, right so withoute here counseil schul ye nought acorde yow, ne have pees with youre adversaries. For the lawe saith, 'Ther nys nothing so good, by way of kinde, as thing to be unbounde by him that it was bounde.'. And thanne Dame Prudence, withoute delay or tarying, sent anoon messageres for here kyn and for here olde frendes, whiche that were trewe and wyse, and tolde hem by ordre, in the presence of Melibe, of this matier as it is above expressed, and declared and praide hem that thay wolde give here avys and counseil what best were to doon in this matiere. And whan Melibeus' frendes hadde take here avys and deliberacioun of the forsayde matier, and hadden examyned it by greet besynes and gret diligence, thay gafe him ful counsail to have pees and reste, and that Melibeus schulde with good hert resceyve his adversaires, to forgivenes and mercy.

And whan Dame Prudence had herd th'assent of hir lord Melibeus, and counseil of his frendes, accorde with hire wille & hire entencioun, sche was wonderly glad in herte and sayde, 'Ther is a noble proverbe that saith, 'The goodnesse that thou maist do this day, abyde not ne delaye it, nought unto tomorwe', and therfore I counseile yow ye sende youre messageres, which that ben discrete and wise, unto youre adversaries, tellynge hem on youre bihalve that if thay wol trete of pees and of accord, that thay schape hem withoute dilay or taryinge to come to us.' Which thing was parformed in dede, and whan these trespasours and repentynge folk of here folies; that is to sayn, the adversaries of Melibe, hadden herd what the messangeres sayden unto hem, thay were right glad and jolif, and answerden ful mekely and benignly, yeldynge graces & thankinges to here lord Melibe and to al his compaignye, and schope hem withoute delay to go with the messangeres, and obeye hem to the comaundement of here lord Melibe. And right anoon thay token here way to the court of Melibe, and token with hem some of here trewe frendes to make faith for hem, and for to ben here borwes.[110]

And whan thay were comen to the presence of Melibeus, he sayde hem thise wordes: 'It stondith thus,' quod Melibeus, 'and soth it is, that ye causeles and withouten skile and resoun, have doon gret injuries and wronges to me and to my wyf Prudence, and to my doughter also; for ye have entred into myn hous by violence, and have doon such outrage that all men knowe wel that ye have deserved the deth; and therfore wil I knowe and wite of yow whether ye wol putte the punyschment and the chastisement, and the vengeaunce, of this outrage in the wille of me and of my wif Dame Prudence, or ye wil not.'

Thanne the wisest of hem thre answerde for hem alle, & sayde, 'Sire,' quod he, 'we knowe wel that we be unworthy to come to the court of so gret a lord and so worthy as ye be, for we han so gretly mystake us, and have offendid and giltid in such a wise ageins youre heighe lordschipe, that trewely we have deserved the deth; but yit for the greet goodnes and debonairete that al the world witnesseth of youre persone, we submitten us to thin excellence and benignite of youre gracious lordschipe, and ben redy to obeye to alle youre comaundements, bisekyng yow that of youre merciable pite ye wol considre oure grete repentaunce and lowe submissioun, and graunte us forgiveness of oure outrage, trespas, and offence. For wel we knowen that youre liberal grace and mercy strechen forthere into goddnesse than doth oure outrage, gilt and trespas into wikkednes, albeit that cursedly & dampnably we have agilt ageinst youre heighe lordschipe.' Thanne Melibe took hem up fro the ground ful benignely, and resceyved her obligaciouns and here londes by here othes, upon certeyn day to retourne unto his court for to accepte and receyve the sentence and juggement that Melibe wolde comaunde to be doon on hem, by these causes aforn sayde, which thing ordeyned, every man retourned home to his hous.

And whan that Dame Prudence saugh hire tyme, sche feyned, and axed hire lord Melibe what vengeance he thoughte to take upon his adversaries. To which Melibeus answerd, and saide, 'Certes,' quod he, 'I thenke and purpos me fully to desherite hem of al that ever thay have, and for to putte hem in exil for evermore.'

'Certes,' quod Dame Prudence, 'this were a cruel sentence, and mochil

110 pledges

ageinst resoun, for ye ben riche ynough, & have noon neede of other men's good; and ye mighte lightly gete yow a coveitous name, which is vicious thing, and oughte to ben eschewed of every man; for after the sawe of the word of th'apostil, 'Covetise is roote of alle harmes'. And therfore it were bettre for yow to lese so moche good of youre oughne, than for to take of here good in this manere. For bettir it is to lese good with worschipe, than it is to wynne good with vilonye and schame. And ever a man oughte to do his diligence and his busynesse to get him a good name, but he schulde enforce him alway to do somthing by which he may renovele[111] his good name; for it is writen that the olde goode loos of a man is soone doon, or goon and passed, whan it is not newed ne renoveled. And as touchinge that ye sayn that ye wol exile youre adversaries; that thinketh me mochil ageinst resoun and out of mesure. Considerith the power that thay han gyve to yow upon here body and on hemself; and it is writen that he is worthy to lese his privelege that mysuseth the might and the power that is geve to him. And yit I sette the caas: ye mighte enjoyne hem that peyne by right and lawe which I trowe ye mow nought do; I say ye mighte nought putte it to execucioun per-aventure, and thanne were it likly to torne to the werre, as it was biforn. And therfore, if ye wol that men do yow obeissaunce, ye moste deme more curteisly; this is to sayn, ye moste give more esyere sentence & juggment. For it is writen, 'He that most curteysly comaundeth, to him men most obeyen', and therfore I pray yow that in this necessite and in this neede, ye caste yow to overcome youre herte. For Senek saith, 'He that overcometh his herte, overcometh twyes', and Thullius saith, 'Ther is nothing so comendable in a gret lord, as whan he is debonaire and meeke, and appesith him lightly'. And I pray yow that ye wol forbere now to do vengaunce, in such a manere that youre goode name may be kept & conserved, and that men mowe have cause and matiere to prayse yow of pite and of mercy, and that ye have noon cause to repente yow of thing that ye doon. For Senec saith, 'He overcometh in an evel manere that repenteth him of his victorie'. Wherfore I pray yow, let mercy be in youre herte, to th'effect and th'entent that God Almighty have mercy and pite upon yow in his laste juggement; for Seint Jame saith in his epistil, 'Juggement withoute mercy schal be doon to him that hath no mercy upon another wight'.'

Whan Melibe had herd the grete skiles and resouns of Dame Prudens, and wys informacioun and techynge, his herte gan enclyne to the wille of

111 renew

his wyf, consideryng hir trewe entent; and confermed him anoon, and consented fully to werke after hir reed[112] and counseil; and thankid God, of whom procedth al goodnes, that him sente a wif of so gret discrecioun. And whan the day cam that his adversaries schulden appere in his presence, he spak ful goodly, and sayde in this wise:

'Al be it so that of youre pryde and heigh presumpcioun and folye, and of youre negligence and unconnynge, ye have mysbore yow and trespassed unto me, yit forasmoche as I se and biholde youre humilite, that ye ben sory and repentaunt of youre giltes, hit constreigneth me to do yow grace and mercy. Wherfore I receyve yow to my grace, and forgeve yow outerly alle the offenses, injuries and wronges that ye have don to me, and agayns me and myne. This is th'effect, & to this ende that God of his endles mercy wole, at the tyme of oure deyinge, forgive us oure giltes that we have trespased to him in this wrecched world. For douteles, & we ben sory & repentaunt of the synnes & giltes which we have trespassed inne, in the sight of oure Lord God, he is so free and so merciable that he wil forgive us oure gultes, and bringe us to the blisse that never hath ende. Amen.'

here endith Chaucer his tale of Melibe

112 advice

THE MONK'S PROLOGUE AND TALE

When 'Geoffrey' has finished, the host seizes upon the idea of the wise and helpful wife, giving the other pilgrims some bits of information about his own wife. She is, apparently, a nag and a virago, and he wishes she could have heard the story of Prudence and Melibee. The host then turns to the monk, playfully remarking on his vigour and masculinity, regretting that such good 'breeding stock' should be wasted in a celibate monastic order. The monk accepts this teasing with a good grace, and announces that he could tell a story about St Edward the Confessor (is he a monk of Westminster Abbey, site of St Edward's shrine?), but he will leave that for later. Instead, he will tell a story, in hexameters, about the tragic fall of powerful people. He begins with biblical examples, then classical, then more recent examples such as Pedro the Cruel of Spain and Peter of Cyprus. However, he then reverts to biblical and classical examples. The knight breaks in before the monk can go any further . . .

The monk's tale is not really a tale at all, in the same sense as most of the other stories in *The Canterbury Tales*. It is a didactic work within the genre classifed as *De casibus illustrium virorum* (on the fall of illustrious men), which was popular in the later Middle Ages, and for which Chaucer's immediate source is, again, Boccaccio. This is really a series of short *exempla* concerning men and women who have held great power and/or wealth, but have fallen from their exalted positions, and come to non-illustrious ends. Like Melibee, they may have been largely written as independent works, and added into *The Canterbury Tales* later. The monk's overall moral is that nobody should trust in Fortune, because she is fickle. (Fortune was often depicted as a woman holding a wheel, which turns at her will, those at the top falling to the bottom.) This is one of the themes taken up by Prudence in The Tale of Melibee, and derives ultimately from Boethius. It does, therefore, follow on from the essential subject matter of the previous tale. The religious conclusion of the collection is that only the power of God can be relied upon but, strangely for a learned cleric, the monk fails to point to this conclusion. He is simply concerned to pile up examples, and, of course, he is himself the epitome of the rich, powerful men whose fates he is retelling.

The use of a didactic form of poetry gives educational authority ('auctoritee' as the wife of Bath would say) to the monk's stories, and reflects the seriousness of his subject-matter. He is also, like the tellers of the other stanzaic tales, attempting to arouse the audience's emotions in response to the victims' sufferings. The pathos is gradually built up, with stories of starving children and the rich Croesus ending his life as a swaying corpse, despite the warnings of his child. The irony is that the monk himself is entirely detached from the emotional content of his stories. He says that he has hundreds of these things in his cell, an attitude which implies a certain contempt, and some of his examples are obviously (and this would have been obvious to a fourteenth-century audience) ill-chosen; for example, the tyrant Barnabo Visconti is hardly a sympathetic figure. The thought that there are hundreds more may be what finally prompts the knight to intervene. As the highest-ranking secular pilgrim, he may be the only one who dares.

The monk's wish to retain his position of authority over the other pilgrims is confirmed by his choice of material. Although he outwardly agrees to the rules of the 'game', he will not submit to the host's authority, unlike the nun's priest, who does so cheerfully. He is conscious of his rank, and wants to appear as 'clever' as little 'Geoffrey', but succeeds in being pompous and annoying. Because the monk will only be part of the fellowship on his own terms, he proves himself unworthy of the host's unqualified admiration. In appearance the 'best', he has proved himself to be one of the least of the pilgrims.

Key Questions

How appropriate is the monk's tale for a monk? Why does he select it, and how does it reflect his personality?

What do the examples show about rulership and wisdom? Are the reasons given for their 'fall' the whole story? Can they be interpreted in other ways?

How representative is the monk of the monastic life as a whole? How does he compare with the nun's priest?

Topic Keywords

Monasticism/ rulership/ de casibus as genre and the represetation of great men and women/ medieval education/ philosophy/ medieval ideas of history

Further Reading

Piero Boitani, 'The Monk's Tale: Dante and Boccaccio', *Medium Ævum*, 15, 1976, pp. 50–69

Anna Czarnowus, ' "My cours, that hath so wyde for to turn,/Hath moore power than woot any man": The Children of Saturn in Chaucer's Monk's Tale', *Studia Anglica Posnaniensia*, 40, 2004, pp. 299–310

Vincent DiMarco, 'Nero's Nets and Seneca's Veins: A New Source for The Monk's Tale?', *Chaucer Review*, 28, 1994, pp. 384–92

Donald K. Fry, 'The Ending of The Monk's Tale', *Journal of English and Germanic Philology*, 71, 1972, pp. 355–68

Keiko Hamaguchi, 'Transgressing the Borderline of Gender: Zenobia in The Monk's Tale', *Chaucer Review*, 40, 2005, pp. 183–205

Amanda Holton, 'Which Bible did Chaucer Use? The Biblical Tragedies in The Monk's Tale', *Notes and Queries*, 55, 2008, pp. 13–17

Emily Jensen, 'Winkers and Janglers: Teller/Listener/Reader Response in The Monk's Tale, The Link and The Nun's Priest's Tale', *Chaucer Review*, 32, 1997, pp. 183–95

Henry Ansgar Kelly, 'The Evolution of The Monk's Tale: Tragical to Farcical', *Studies in the Age of Chaucer*, 22, 2000, pp. 407–14

Scott Norsworthy, 'Hard Lords and Bad Food Service in The Monk's Tale', *Journal of English and Germanic Philology*, 100, 2001, pp. 313–32

Daniel Pinti, 'The Comedy of The Monk's Tale: Chaucer's Hugelyn and Early Commentary on Dante's *Ugolino*', *Comparative Literature Studies*, 37, 2000, pp. 277–97

Jahan Ramazani, 'Chaucer's Monk: The Poetics of Abbreviation, Aggression and Tragedy', *Chaucer Review*, 27, 1993, pp. 260–76

Jay Ruud, ' "In meetre in many a sondry wyse": Fortune's Wheel and The Monk's Tale', *English Language Notes*, 26, 1989, pp. 6–11

Jane Zatta, 'Chaucer's Monk: A Mighty Hunter before the Lord', *Chaucer Review*, 29, 1994, pp. 111–33

And here bygynneth the prologe of the Monk's tale

❦ Whan ended was my tale of Melibe,
And of Prudence and hire benignite,
Oure hoste sayde, 'As I am **faithful** man,   full of faith
And by the precious corpus Madryan,[1]
I hadde **lever** than a barel ale   rather
That Godeleef, my wyf, had herd this tale,[2]
For sche is nothing of such pacience
As was this Melibeus' wyf, Dame Prudence!
By God's boones! Whan I bete my **knaves**,   menservants 10
Sche bringeth me forth the grete **clobbet** staves,   clubbed
And crieth, '**Slee** the dogges everychon,   slay
And breke of hem bothe bak and bon!'
And if that eny neghebour of myne
Wol noght to my wyf in chirche **enclyne**,   bow
Or be so hardy to hir to trespace,[3]
Whan sche comth hom, sche **rampeth** in my face,   shakes her fist
And crieth, 'False coward, **wreke** thy wyf!   avenge
By **corpes bones**! I wil have thy knyf,   God's/Christ's bones
And thou schalt have my distaf and go spynne!'[4]   20
Fro day to night, right thus sche wil bygynne.
'Allas,' sche saith, 'that every I was **y-schape**   made
To wedde a mylksop, or a coward ape
That wil be **over-lad with** every wight!   overborne by
Thou darst nought stonde by thy wyve's right!'
This is my lif, **but if that** I wil fight;   unless
And out atte dore anoon I most me **dight**,   hurry
And ellis I am lost but if that I
Be lik a wilde leoun, foolhardy.

---

1 'by the precious body of St Madrian' (no St Madrian is known to have existed).
2 Godeleef – a proper name, meaning 'well-beloved'.
3 'to upset her'
4 The distaff was a long staff, on the top of which was placed a lump of unspun
 wool. This was held in one hand, whilst the holder teased out and twisted the
 wool into strands, with the other hand. The work was associated with women.

30	I wot wel sche wol **do me** sle som day	make me
	Some neighebor, and thanne **renne** away –	run
	For I am **perilous** with knyf in honde,	dangerous
	Al be it that I dar not hir withstonde –	
	For sche is **big in armes**, by my faith;	strong-armed
	That schal he fynde that hire mysdoth or saith –	
	But let us passe away fro this **matiere**.	subject
	My lord the monk,' quod he, 'be mery of chere,	
	For ye schul telle a tale, trewely.	
	Lo, **Rowchestre** stant heer faste by!⁵	Rochester
40	Ryde forth, myn oughne lord, **brek** nought oure game –	spoil
	But, by my trouthe, I **can** not youre name,	know
	Whether schal I calle yow, my Lord Dan John,	
	Or Daun Thomas, or elles Dan Albon.	
	Of what hous be ye, by your fader kyn?	
	I vow to God, thou hast a ful fair skyn.	
	It is a gentil pasture **ther thou gost**;	in which you walk
	Thow art not lik a **penaunt** or a goost.	penitent
	Upon my faith, thou art an officer;	
	Som worthy **sexteyn** or some celerer–	sexton; cellarer
50	For, by my fader soule, **as to my doome**	by my judgement
	Thou art an officer whan thou art at home,	
	No pover cloysterer ne non novys,⁶	
	But a governour, bothe wily and wys,	
	And therwithal of **brawne** and of bones;	muscle
	A **wel faryng** persone, for the noones.	good-looking
	I praye God give him confusioun	
	That first the brought to religioun!⁷	
	Thow woldist han be a **trede foul** aright,	cock (sexual metaphor)
	Haddist thou as gret a **leve** as might	permission/opportunity
60	To performe al thi wil in **engendrure**;	begetting of children
	Thow haddist bigeten many a creature!	
	Allas, why werest thou so wyd a cope?	
	God gif me sorwe, and I were a pope,	
	Nought only thou but every mighty man,	

---

5 Rochester, a town in Northern Kent. The pilgrims might have broken their journey to see the cross there.

6 'no poor, ordinary monk or a novice, but one with authority'

7 'I pray God confound the person who first made you become a religious'

Though he were **schore** brode upon his **pan**,   shorn; skull
Schuld han a wif, for al this world is **lorn**;   lost
Religioun hath take up al the corn[8]
Of tredyng, and we burel men ben schrympes.
Of feble trees ther cometh feble ympes;
This makith that oure wyfes wol **assaye**   try   70
Religious folk, for thay may bettre paye
Of Venus' payementes than may we –
God **woot**, no **lusscheburghes** paye ye!   knows; cheap coins
Beth nou3t **wroth**, my Lorde, though I play,   angry
For oft in game a **soth** I have herd say.'   truth
This worthy monk took al in pacience,
And saide, 'I wol doon al my diligence
Als fer as souneth into honeste,[9]
To telle yow a tale, or tuo or thre;
And if yow lust to **herken hiderward**,   listen to me   80
I will yow say the lif of Seint Edward[10]
Or elles first **tredes**[11] wil I yow telle,
Of which I have an hundred in my **celle**.   monk's room
Tregedis is to sayn, a certeyn storie
As olde bookes **maken us memorie**,   remind us
Of hem that stood in greet prosperite,
And is y-fallen out of heigh **degre**   estate
Into miserie, and endith wrecchedly;
And thay ben versifyed comunly
Of six feet, which men clepe **exametron**.[12]   hexameter   90
In prose ben eek **endited** many oon,   written/constructed
And in metre eek, and in **sondry wise**.   various ways
Lo, this declaryng ought ynough suffise!
Now herkneth, if yow likith for to heere;
But first I yow **biseche** in this matiere,   beg
Though I **by ordre** telle not thise thinges –   in order
Be it of popes, emperours, or kynges –
After her age, as men may write fynde,   in chronological order

---

8 'religion has taken all the manly men'
9 'as far as is compatible with decency'
10 St Edward the Confessor, the royal saint associated with Westminster Abbey.
11 'tregedes' (tragedies)
12 A form of Latin poetry, often used in didactic poetry.

But telle hem som bifore and som byhynde,
100   As it cometh now to my remembraunce,
Haveth me excused, **of** myn ignoraunce.   because of

  ❧ I wol bywaile, in maner of tregedye,
The harm of hem that stood in heigh degre,
And fallen so ther is no remedye
To bring hem out of her adversite;
For certeynly, whan Fortune lust to flee,
Ther may no man the cours of hir whiel holde.[13]
Let no man truste in blynd prosperite –
Beth war by these ensamples, trewe and old.

110   *Lucifer*
  ❧ At Lucifer, though he an aungil were
And no man; at him wil I bygynne,
For though fortune may non aungel **dere**,   harm
From heigh degre yit fel he, for his synne,
Doun into helle, wher he yet is inne.
O Lucifer, brightest of aungels alle!
Now art thou **Sathanas**, that maist nou*ght* **twynne**   Satan; depart
Out of miserie in which thou art falle!

Adam
120   ❧ Lo Adam, in the feld of Damassene[14]
With God's **oughne** fynger wrought was he,   own
And nought **bigeten** of man's sperma unclene;   conceived
And **welt** al paradys, savyng oon tre.   ruled
Had never worldly man suche degre
As Adam, til he for **mysgovernance**   misconduct
Was dryven out of heigh prosperite,
To labour, and to helle, and to **meschaunce**.   bad fortune

13 The wheel of fortune; fortune was often shown as a woman holding a wheel,
   upon which humans were moved up and down.
14 In the Middle Ages it was believed that Damascus grew up on the site of Adam's
   creation.

Sampson

🐦 Lo, Sampson that was **annunciate**   announced
By th'angel, long **er** his **nativite**,   before; birth   130
And was to God Almighty **consecrate**,   consecrated
And stood in **nobles** whil that he might se – [15]   nobility
Was never such another as was he
To speke of strength, and therto hardynesse –
But to his wyfe tolde he his secre,
Thurgh which he **slough** himselfe for wrecchidnesse.   killed

Thre hundred foxis tok Sampson, for **ire**,   anger
And alle her tayles he togider **bond**,   tied
And sette the foxes tailes alle on fuyre,
For he in every tail hath **knyt** a brond,   woven   140
And thay **brent** alle the cornes of that lond,   burnt
And all her **olyvers** and **vynes** eeke.   olive trees; vines
A thousand men he slough eek with his hond,
And hadde no wepen but an ass's **cheeke**   jawbone

Whan thay were slayn, so thursted him, that he
Was wel ner **lorn**, for which he **gan** to preye   lost; began
That God wolde of his payne have som pite,
And send him drynk, and elles most he deye;
And out of this ass's cheke, that was so dreye,
Out of a **woung toth** sprong anon a welle,   molar   150
Of which he dronk ynough, schortly to seye;
Thus **halp** him God, as **Judicum** can telle.   helped; Judges (book of)

By verray fors of **Algason** on a night,   Gaza
Maugre the **Philistiens** of that cite,   despite; Philistines
The gates of the toun he hath up-**plight**,   pulled
And on his bak caried hem hath he
Heigh upon an hil, wher men might hem se.
O noble, almighty Sampson, **leef** and **deere**!   beloved
Haddest thou nought to wommen told thy secre,
In al the world ne hadde be thy **peere**!   equal   160

15 'whilst he had his eyesight'

This Sampson neyther **siser** dronk ne wyn,   strong drink
Ne on his heed com **rasour** ne **schere**,   razor; scissors
By **precept** of the messager **divyn**,   precept; divine
For all his strengthes in his **heres** were;   hair
And fully twenty wynter, yer by yere,
He hadde of Jerusalem the governaunce –
But soone he schal wepe many a teere,
For wymmen schuln him bringe to **meschaunce**.   misfortune

Unto his **lamman Dalida** he tolde   mistress; Delilah
170 That in here heres al his strengthe lay,
And falsly to his foomen sche him solde;
And, slepyng in hire **barm** upon a day,   arms/lap
Sche made to clippe or schere his heres away,
And made his foomen al his **craft espien**   ability; see
And whan thay fonde him in this **array**   state
They bound him fast, and put out bothe his yen.[16]

But er his heer clipped was or y-schave,
Ther was no bond with which men might him bynde;
But now is he in prisoun in a cave,
180 Theras thay made him at the **querne** grynde.   millstone
O noble Sampson, strengest of al mankynde!
O **whilom jugge**, in glory and in richesse!   former judge
Now **maystow** wepe with thine eyyen blynde,   you may
Sith thou fro **wele** art falle to wrecchednesse!   since; good fortune

Th'end of this **caytif** was as I schal say –   wretch
His **foomen** made a **fest** upon a day,   enemies; feast
And made him as here fool **biforn** hem **play**,   before; perform
And this was in a temple of gret array;
But atte last he made a **foul affray**,   terrible assault
190 For he two **pilers** schook, and made hem falle,   pillars
And doun fel temple and al, and ther it lay,
And slough himsilf and **eek** his fomen alle.   also

16 'gouged out both his eyes'

This is to sayn, the princes **everichon**,   every one
And eek thre thousand bodies were ther slayn
With fallyng of the grete temple of stoon.
Of Sampson wil I no more sayn;
Be war by these ensamples, olde and playn,
That no man telle his counseil to his wyf
Of such thing as he wold have secre, fayn,
If that it touche him lymes or his lif.[17]   200

De Ercule

❧ Of **Ercules**, the sovereyn conquerour,   Hercules
Singing his werkes, **laude**, and heigh **renoun**;   praise; reputation
For in his tyme of strength he bar the flour.[18]
He slough, and **rafte** the skyn fro the leoun;   tore
He of Centaures leyde the bost adoun,[19]
He Arpies slough, the cruel briddes felle;[20]
The gold appul he **raft** fro the dragoun;[21]   took
He drof out Cerbures, the fend of helle.[22]

He slough the cruel tyrant Buserus[23]   210
And made his hors to ete him, fleisch and boon.
He slough the verray serpent **venencus**;   venomous
Of Adiloyus' tuo hornes he **raft oon**.   took one
He slough Catus in a cave of stoon,
He slough the geaunt Adeus the stronge,
He slough the grisly leoun, and that anoon,
And bar the hevene upon his necke longe.[24]

17 'if it is a matter of life and limb'
18 'he was the greatest'
19 'he brought down the pride of the Centaurs (mythical beings, half man, half
   horse). The Monk goes on to mention the so-called 'labours' of Hercules, from
   Greek legend.
20 The predatory Harpies; half bird, half woman.
21 The golden apple of the Hesperides, which was guarded by a dragon.
22 Cerberus, the three-headed dog which guarded Hades, kingdom of the dead.
23 Busirus of Egypt killed all foreign visitors; Diomedes of Thrace fed human flesh
   to his horses; Hercules also killed the Lernean hydra, Achiloys, Cacus, Antheus,
   and the Erymanthean boar
24 With his superhuman strength, Hercules was able to relieve the giant Atlas by
   holding the world on his own shoulders for a while.

Was never wight, **siththen** the world bigan   since
That slough so many monstres as dede he;
220 Thurghout the wide world his name ran,
What for his strengthe, and for his bounte;
And every **roialme** went he for to se.   kingdom
He was so strong, ther might no man him **lette**.   stop
At bothe the world's endes, as saith **Trophe**,   Trophimus
In stede of **boundes**, he a piler sette.[25]   boundaries

A **lemman** hadde this noble champioun   lover/mistress
That highte Dianire, freissh as May;
And, as these clerkes maken **mensioun**,   mention
Sche hath him sent a **schurte**, fresch and gay.   shirt
230 Alas! This schirt, allas a wailaway!
Envenymed was **suthly**, withalle,   poisoned; truly
That er he hadde wered it half a day,
It made his fleisch al fro his bones falle.

But **natheles**, som clerkes hir excusen   nevertheless
By oon that highte Nessus, that it maked;[26]
Be as be may, I wil nought hir **accusyn** –   accuse
But on his bak he wered this schirt al naked,
Til that his fleisch was for the venym **blaked**;   blackened
And whan he saugh noon other remedye,
240 In hote colis he hath himself y-raked,
For with no venym deyned him to dye.[27]

Thus **starf** this mighty and worthy Ercules.   died
Lo, who may truste fortune **eny throwe**!   at all
For him that folweth al this world of **pres**,   troubles
Er he be war, is oft y-layd ful lowe.   unless he be wary
Ful wys is he that can himselven knowe.
Be war, for whom that fortune **lust** to **glose**,   likes; deceive
Than waytith sche hir man to overthrowe,
By such way as he wolde **lest** suppose.   Least

25 The 'Pillars of Hercules'.
26 'because of one called Nessus, who made it (ie the shirt)'
27 'he raked hot coals over himself, because he was too proud to die of poison'

De rege Nabugodonosor[28]   of King Nebuchadnezzar   250
The mighty trone, the precious tresor,
The glorious **ceptre**, and **real mageste**   sceptre; royal majesty
That had the king Nabugodonosore,
With tonge **unnethes** may **descryved** be.   hardly; described
He **twyes wan** Jerusalem, that cite.   twice; conquered
The vessel out of the temple he with him **ladde**.   took
At Babiloyne was his **sovereyn see**,   capital city
In which his glorie and his **delyt** he ladde.   pleasure

The fairest children of the blood **roial**   royal
Of Israel he ded **gelde** anoon,   castrate   260
And made **ylk** of hem to ben his **thral**.   each; servant
Amonges othre Daniel was oon,
That was the wisest child of **everychoon**;   them all
For he the **dremes** of the king **expouned**,   dreams; interpreted
Ther as in **Caldeyn** was ther clerkes noon   Chaldea/Babylon
That wiste to what **fyn** his dremes **souned**.   end; tended

This proud king **let** make a statu of gold,   ordered
Sixty cubites long and seven in **brede**;   breadth
To which ymage bothe yonge and olde
Comaunded he to love, and have in **drede**,   fear   270
Or in a fornays, ful of flames rede,
He schulde be brent that wolde not obeye –
But never wolde assente to that dede
Danyel, ne his felawes tweye.

This king of kinges proud was and **elate**;   haughty
He **wende** God, that sit in mageste,   believed
Ne might him nought **bireve of** his estate;   take away
But sodeynly he left his dignite –
Y-lik a **best** him semed for to be,   beast
And eet hay as an oxe, and lay **theroute**.   Outside   280
In rayn with wilde bestes walkyd he,
Til certein tyme was y-come aboute.

28 Book of Daniel; 2 Kings:24

And lik an **egle's** fetheres were his **heres**,	eagle's; hairs
His hondes like a bridde's **clowes** were,	claws
Til God relessed him, **a certeyn yeres**,	after a certain time
And gaf him **witte**; and thanne with many a tere	understanding
He thanked God; and ever he is **afere**	afraid
To doon **amys**, or more to trespace;	wrong
And er that tyme he layd was **on bere**,	on his bier (died)

290 He knew wel God was ful of might and grace.

His sone, which that **highte** Balthasar,[29]	was called
That huld the **regne** after his fader day,	kingdom
He by his fader **couthe nought** be war,	had not learned to
For proud he was of hert and of **array**,	bearing
And eek an **ydolaster** was he **ay**.	idolater; always
His heigh astate **assured him** in pryde,	reassured him
But Fortune cast him doun, and ther he lay;	
And sodeynly his regne **gan divide**.	was divided

A fest he made unto his lordes alle

300 Upon a tyme; he made hem **blithe** be,	happy/cheerful
And than than his officers gan he calle,	
'**Goth**, bringeth forth the **vessealx**,' quod he,	go; vessels
The which my fader, in his prosperite,	
Out of the temple of Jerusalem **byraft**;	took
And to oure hihe goddis thanke we,	
Of honours that oure **eldres** with us laft.'	honours; elders/ancestors

His wif, his lordes, and his concubines	
Ay dronken, whiles her **arriont** last,	appetites
Out of this noble vesseals **sondry** wynes;	various
310 And on a wal this king his **yhen** cast,	eyes
And saugh an hond, armles, that **wroot** fast,	wrote
For fere of which he quook and **siked sore**.	sighed deeply
This hond, that Balthasar made so sore **agast**,	afraid
Wrot, 'Mene, techel, phares,' and no more.	

---

29 Belshazzar

In al the lond magicien was noon
That couthe expounde what this lettre ment,
But Daniel expoundith it anoon,
And sayde, 'King, God thy fader sent
Glori and honour, regne, tresor and rent,
And he was proud and nothing God ne dredde;   320
And therfore God gret **wreche** upon him sent,   misery
And him **biraft** the regne that he hadde.   took away

He was out-cast of man's compaignye;
With asses was his habitacioun,
And ete hay in wet, and eek in drye
Til that he knew, by grace and by resoun,
That God of heven had dominacioun
Over every regne and every creature;
And than had God of him compassioun,
And him restored to his regne and his **figure**.   standing   330

Eke thou that art his sone art proud also,
And knowest al this thing so **verrayly**,   truly
And art rebel to God and art his fo.
Thou dronk eek of his vessel bodily,
Thy wyf eek, and thy **wenche**, sinfully   whore
Dronke of the same vessel sondry wynes,
And **heriest** false goddes cursedly;   worship
Therfore to the schapen ful gret pyne es.[30]

This hond was send fro God, that on the wal
Wrot, 'Mane, techel, phares' – truste me;   340
Thy regne is doon, thou **wenist** nou*gh*t at al.   know/expect
Divided is thy regne, and it schal be
To **Meedes** and to **Perses** *g*even,' quod he.   Medes; Persians
And thilke same night the king was **slawe**,   slain
And Darius occupied his **degre**,   place/kingship
Though therto neyther had he right, ne lawe.

30 'great misery has been fore-ordained for you'

Lordynges, ensample herby may ye take,
How that in lordschip is no **sikernesse**;   security
For whan Fortune wil a man forsake,
350 Sche bereth away his regne and his richesse
And eek his frendes, bothe more and lesse;
And what man hath of frendes the Fortune,
Mishap wil make hem enemyes, I gesse –
This proverbe is ful **sothe & ful comune**.   true and well-known

Cenobia, of Plamire the queene,[31]
As writen Perciens of hir noblesse,
So worthy was in armes and so **keene**   fierce
That no wight passed hir in **hardynesse**,   boldness
Ne in **lynage** ne in other **gentilesse**.   descent; nobility
360 Of the kinges' blood of Pers sche is descendid;
I say that sche had not most fairnesse,
But of hir **schap** sche might not ben **amendid**.   figure; improved

Fro hir childhod I fynde that sche fledde
Office of wommen, and to woode sche went,
And many a wilde **hert's** blood sche schedde,   hart (deer)
With arwes brode that sche to hem sent;
Sche was so swyft that sche **anoon** hem **hent**,   swiftly; seized
And whan that sche was **elder** sche wolde kille   older
Leouns, **lebardes** and beres **alto rent**,   leopards; torn to bits
370 And in hire armes **weld** hem at hir wille.   Wielded

Sche dorste wilde bestes' dennes seke,
And renne in the mounteyns al the night,
And slepe under a bussh, and sche couthe eeke
Wrastil by verray fors and verray might   wrestle
With eny yong man, were he never so **wight**;   vigorous
Ther mighte nothing in hir armes stonde.
Sche kept hir **maydenhed** from every **wight**;   virginity; man
To no man deyned hire to be bonde.

31 Zenophobia of Palmyra.

But atte last hir frendes han hir maried
To Odenake, prince of that citee;   380
Al were it so that sche him longe taried –[32]
And ye schul understonde how that he
Had suche fantasies as hadde sche –
But natheles, whan thay were knyt in fere,   together
Thay lyved in joye and in felicite,   happiness
For ech of hem had other leef and deere.   beloved

Save oon thing – sche wolde never assent
By no way that he schulde by hir lye
But oones, for it was hir playn entent
To have a child, the world to multiplie;   390
And also, soone as sche might aspye
That sche was not with child yit in dede,
Than wold sche suffre him doon his fantasie
Eftsones; and nought but oones, out of drede   again; doubtless

And if sche were with child at thilke cast,   by the same deed
No more schuld he playe thilke game   the same
Til fully fourty dayes were y-past,
Than wold sche suffre him to do the same.
Al were this Odenake wilde or tame,
He gat no more of hir; for thus sche sayde: 400
Hit nas but wyve's lecchery and schame,
In other caas if that men with hem playde.   for other reasons

Tuo sones by this Odenake had sche,
The whiche sche kept in vertu and lettrure;   education
But now unto our purpos torne we –
I say, so worschipful a creature,   praiseworthy
And wys, worthy, and large with mesure,   generous
So penyble in the werre and curteys eeke,   tireless
Ne more labour might in werre endure
Was nowher noon, in al this world to seeke.[33]   410

32 'she kept him waiting'
33 'could not be found anywhere' – referring to 'so praiseworthy a creature'

Hir riche array ne might be told,
As wel in vessel as in hir clothing;
Sche was al clothed in **perre** and gold,   precious stones
And eek sche **lafte nought**, for hir huntyng,   didn't neglect
To have of sondry tonges ful knowing,
Whan sche had **leyse** and might therto entent.   leisure
To lerne bookes was al hir **likyng**,   enjoyment
How sche in **vertu** might hir lif **despent**   virtue; spend

And schortly of this story for to trete,
420   So doughty was hir housbond, and eek sche,
That thay conquered many regnes grete
In th'Orient, with many a fair citee
Appurtienant unto that mageste   belonging
Of Rome, and with strong hond hulden hem fast;
Ne never might her fomen **doon hem fle**   make them run away
Ay while Odenake's dayes last.[34]

Her batails, whoso **lust** hem for to **rede**,   wants; read
Agayn Sapor the king, and other mo,[35]
And how that this processe fel in dede,[36]
430   Why sche conquered, and what title had therto;
And after of hir meschief and hir woo,
How that sche was deceyved and y-take,
Let hem unto my mayster Perark go,[37]
That writeth of this ynough, I undertake.

Whan Odenake was deed, sche mightily
The regnes huld, and with hir **propre** hond   own
Ageins hir foos sche faught ful trewely,
That ther nas king ne prince in that lond
That he **nas** glad, if he that **grace** fond,   was not; favour
440   That sche ne wold upon his lond **werraye**.   wage war
With hir thay made alliaunce by bond,
To ben in **peese**, and let hir ryde and play.   peace

34 'whilst Odenake's life lasted'
35 Sapor, king of Persia.
36 'how all of this actually happened'
37 Francis Petrarch, poet laureate.

The emperour of Rome, Claudius,
Ne him biforn the Romayn Galiene
Ne dorste never be so **corrageous**,   daring
Ne noon Ermine ne Egipciene,
No Surrien ne noon Arrabiene,[38]
Withinne the **feld** that durste with hir fight,   (battle)field
Lest that sche wold hem with her hondes sleen,
Or with hir **meyne** putten hem to flight.   army (own soldiers)   450

In kinges **abyt** went hir sones tuo,   clothing
As heires of her fadres regnes alle,
And Hermanno and Themaleo
Here names were, and **Parciens** men hem calle;   Persians
But ay Fortune hath in hir hony **galle**.   bitterness
This mighty queene may no while endure;
Fortune out of hir regne made hir falle
To wrecchednesse and to mysadventure

Aurilian, whan that the **governaunce**   Aurelian; rule
Of Rome cam into his hondes tway,   460
He **schop** him of this queen to do vengeaunce,   planned
And with his legiouns he took the way
Toward **Cenoby**; and schortly to say,   Zenobia
He made hir flee, and atte last hir hent,
And **feterid** hir, and eek hir children tweye   fettered
And wan the lond, and home to Rome he went.

Amonges other thinges that he wan,
Hir **chaar**, that was with gold wrought and **perre**,   chariot; precious stones
This grete Romayn, this Aurilian,
Hath with him lad, for that men schulde se;   470
Bifore this **triumphe** walkith sche,   triumphant procession
And **gilte cheynes** in hir necke hongynge.   golden chains
Corouned sche was, as aftir hir **degre**,   crowned; station
And ful of perre chargid hir clothyng.

38 Arminian, Egyptian, Syrian, Arabian.

Allas, Fortune! Sche that **whilom** was — formerly
Dredful to kinges and to emperoures,
Now **gaulith** al the pepul on hir, alas! — stare
And sche that helmyd was in **starke stoures**, — violent battles
And wan bifore **tones** stronge and toures, — towns
480   Schal on heed now were a **wyntermyte**, — woman's headdress
And sche that bar the **cepter** ful of floures, — sceptre
Schal bere a distaf **hirself for to quyte**. — to make her way

De Petro Hispanie rege[39]   of Peter, king of Spain

  ❦ O noble Petro, the glori of Spayne!
Whom Fortune held so heigh in mageste,
Wel oughte men thy pitous deth complayne;
Thy bastard brother made the to fle,
And after, at a sege by **subtilte**, — stealth
Thow were bytrayed and lad to his tent,
490   Wheras he with his oughne hond slough the,
Succedyng in thy lond and in thy **rent**. — possessions

The feld of snow with th'**egel** of blak therinne, — eagle
Caught with the leoun **reed**-coloured as is the **gleede**,[40] — fire
He brewede the cursednesse and synne,
The wikked nest-werker of this neede;
Nought Oliver, ne Charles, that ay took heede
Of trouthe and honour, but of Armoryk
Geniloun Oliver, corruptid for nede,[41]
Broughte this worthy king in such a **bryk**. — dire strait

---

39 Assassinated by his brother Enrique in 1369, supported by the Black Prince in
   1367.
40 A white shield, with a black eagle and a red lion on a baton were the arms of
   Pedro's betrayer, the French military leader Bertrand du Guesclin.
41 A reference to the 'Charlemagne' series of crusade romances; Oliver was the best
   friend of the crusading hero Roland, Charlemagne's war leader. Ganelon was the
   traitor who rose against Charlemagne whilst he was away on crusade.

De Petro Cipre rege[42]   of Peter, king of Cyprus   500
❧ O worthy Petro, king of Cipres also,
That **Alisaunder** wan by heigh maistrye;   Alexandria
Ful many an hethen wroughtest thou ful wo,
Of which thin oughne **lieges** had envye,   followers/liegemen
And for nothing but for thy chivalrie
Thay in thy bed han slayn the by the **morwe**.   morning
Thus can Fortune the **whel** governe and **gye**,   wheel; turn
And out of joye bringe men into **sorwe**.   sorrow

De Barnabo comite Mediolano[43]
❧ Of Melayn, grete Barnabo Viscount,   510
God of delyt and strength of Lumbardye;
Why schuld thyn **infortune** I nought **accounte**,   misfortune; recount
Syn in astaat thou clombe were so hye?
Thy brother sone, that was thy double allie –
For he thy **nevew** was and sone in lawe –   nephew
Withinne his prisoun made the to dye,
But why ne how not I that thou were **slawe**.   slain

De Hugilino comite Pise[44]   of Hugilin count of Pisa
❧ Of the erl Hugilin of Pise the **langour**   suffering
Ther may no tonge telle the pite;   520
But **litil** out of Pise stant a tour,   a little way
In whiche tour in prisoun put was he,
And with him been his litil children thre.
Th'eldest skarsly fyf yer was of age –
Allas, Fortune, it was gret cruelte
Suche **briddes** to put in such a cage!

42 Pierre de Lusignan, assassinated 1369.
43 Bernarbo Visconti, tyrant of Milan, met Chaucer in 1378.
44 Died 1289.

Dampnyd he was to deye in that prisoun,
For Roger, which that bischop was of Pise
Had on him maad a fals **suggestioun**,   accusation
530 Thurgh which the peple gan on him arise,
And putte him in prisoun in such wise
As ye han herd, and mete and drynk he hadde
So smal that wel **unnethe** it may suffise,   hardly
And therwithal it was ful pore and badde.

And on a day bifel that in that hour
Whan that his mete was wont to be brought,
The **gayler schet** the **dores** of that tour.   jailer; shut; doors
He herd it wel, but he saugh it nought,
And in his hert anoon ther fel a thought
540 That thay for hungir wolde **doon him dyen**.   cause him to die
'Alas'quod he 'allas that I was **wrought**'   made
Therwith the teeres fel fro his eyen

His yongest sone, that thre yer was of age,
Unto him sayde, 'Fader, why do ye wepe?
Whan wil the gayler bringen oure **potage**?   thin soup
Is ther no morsel bred that ye **doon kepe**?   are keeping
I am so hongry that I may not slepe.
Now wolde God that I mighte slepe ever,
Than schuld not hunger in my **wombe** crepe;   belly
550 Ther is no thing save bred that me were lever.'[45]

Thus day by day this child bigan to crie,
Til in his fadres **barm** adoun he lay,   lap
And sayde, 'Farwel, fader, I moot dye!'
And kist his fader, and dyde the same day;
And whan the woful fader deed it say,
For wo his armes tuo he gan to byte
And sayde, 'Fortune, alas and waylaway!
Thin false **whel** al my woo I wyte!'   wheel

45 'there is nothing I would rather have than bread'

His **childer wende** that it for hongir was	children; believed
That he his armes **gnew**, and nought for wo,	gnawed 560
And sayden, 'Fader, do nought so, allas!	
But rather **et** the fleisch upon us tuo –	eat
Oure fleisch thou gave us, oure fleissh thou take us fro,	
And ete ynough!' right thus thay to him seyde;	
And after that, withinne a day or two,	
Thay layde hem in his lappe adoun, and deyde.	

Himself, **despeired**, eek for honger **starf**,	in despair; starved
Thus ended is this myghty Erl of Pize	
For his estate Fortune fro him **carf**;	cut away
Of this **tegrede** it ought ynough suffise –	tragedy 570
Whoso wil it hiere in lenger wise,	
Rede the gret poet of Itaile	
That highte Dannt, for he can it devise[46]	
Fro poynt to poynt; nat oon word wil he fayle.	

De Nerone
	of Nero
☙ Although Nero were als **vicious**	full of vice
As any **fend** that lith ful lowe adoun,	devil/demon
Yit he, as tellith us Swethoneus,[47]	
This wyde world had in subieccioun,	
Bothe est and west and **septemtrioun**;	north 580
Of rubies, **safers**, and of perles white	sapphires
Were all his clothes **embroudid**, up and doun,	embroidered
For he in **gemmis** gretly gan delite.	gems

More delyt, more pomp of **array**,	display
More proud was never emperour than he;	
That **ylke** cloth that he had wered **a day**,	same; for a day
After that tyme he **nolde** it never se.	did not want to
Nettis of gold thred had he gret plente,	nets
To fissche in **Tyber** whan him lust to pleye.	(river) Tiber
His willes were as lawe in his degre,	590
For Fortune as his frend wold him obeye.	

46 Ugolino appears in Dante's *Inferno*.
47 Suetonius, *De Vita Caesarum* (Lives of the Caesars), tells the story of the emperor Nero.

He Rome **brent** for his **delicacie**;   burnt; delight
The senatours he slough upon a day,
To here how men wolde wepe and crye;
And slough his brother, and by his suster lay.
His modir made he in **pitous array**,   terrible state
For hire wombe slyte he, to byholde
Wher he conceyved was – so waylaway,
That he so litel of his moodir **tolde**.   valued

600 No teer out of his eyen for that sight
Ne cam, but sayde, 'A fair womman was sche.'
Gret wonder is, that he couthe or might
Be **domesman** on hir beaute.   judge
The wyn to bringen him comaundid he,
And drank anoon; noon other **wo** he made.   mourning
Whan might is torned unto cruelte,
Allas, to deepe wil the venym **wade**!   penetrate

In youthe a maister had this emperour,
To teche him **letterure** and curtesye;   letters
610 For of moralite he was the flour,
As in his tyme, but if the book lye.
And whil his maister had of him **maistrie**   sovreignty
He made him so **connyng** and so **souple**,   clever; pliant
That long tyme it was **or** tyrannye,   before
Or ony vice, dorst on him **uncouple**.   set upon

Senaca

❦ This **Senaca** of which that I devyse,   Seneca
Bycause Nero had of him such drede,
For fro vices he wol him chastise
620 Discretly, as by word and nought by dede;
'Sir,' wold he sayn, 'an emperour mot neede
Be vertuous, and hate tyrannye.'
For which he in a bath made him to bleede
On bothe his armes, til he moste dye.

The Nero hadde eek a **custumance**   custom
In youthe, agein his maister for to ryse;
Which afterward him thought a gret **grevaunce**,   grievance
Therfor he made him deye in this wise.
But natheles, this Seneca the wise
Ches in a bath to deye in this manere,   630
Rather than to have another tyrranye;
And thus hath Nero slayn his maister deere.

Now fel it so that Fortune lust no lenger
The highe pride of Nero to **cherice**;   cherish
For though he were strong, yit was sche strenger;
Sche thoughte thus, 'By God! I am to **nyce**   discerning/'fussy'
To set a man that is ful **sad of** vice   grounded in
In high degre, and emperour him calle.
By God, out of his cite I wil him **trice**!   take
Whan he lest weneth, sonnest schal byfalle.'[48]   640

The poeple ros on him upon a night
For heigh **defaute**, and whan he it **aspyed**   evil-doing; saw
Out of his dores anoon he hath him **dight**   taken himself
Aloone, and ther he wende have **ben allyed**;   found support
He knokked fast, and ay the more he cried
The faster schette thay the dores alle;
Than wist he wel he had himself **mysgyed**,   misguided
And went his way; no lenger **durst** he calle.   dared

The peple cried, and **rumbled** up and doun,   murmured
That with his **eris** herd he how thay sayde: ears   650
'Her is this fals traitour, this Neroun!'
For fere almost out of his witte he **brayde**,   went
And to his goddes pitously he prayde
For socour, but it mighte nought **betyde**.   happen
For drede of this him thoughte that he dyde,
And ran into a gardyn him to hyde.

48 'this will happen just when he least expects it'

And in this gardyn fond he **cherlis twaye**   two churls
Sittynge by a fuyr ful greet and reed,
And to these cherles tuo he gan to praye
660 To sleen him, and to **girden** of his heed,   cut
That **to** his body, whan he were **deed**   lest that...; dead
Were no **despyt** y-doon for his defame.   insult
Himself he slough, he **couthe** no better **reed**;   knew; advice
Of which Fortune thai **lough** and **hadde game**.   laughed; made fun

De Olipherno   of Holophernes

❦ Was never capitaigne under a king
That regnes mo put in subjeccioun,
Ne strenger was **in feld** of alle thing,   in battle
As in his tyme ne gretter of **renoun**,   fame
670 Ne more pompous, in heih presumpcioun,
Than Oliphern, which that Fortune ay kist
So **licorously**, and ladde him up and doun   lecherously
Til that his heed was **of er he it wist**.   off; before he knew it

Nought oonly that the world had of him awe,
For **lesyng** of riches and liberte,   losing
But made every man **reneye his lawe**   renounce his faith
Nabugodonosor was lord, sayde he –
Noon other god schuld honoured be.
Ageinst his **heste** dar no wight trespace,   will
680 Save in Betholia, a strong cite,
Wher Eliachim was **prest** of that place.   priest

But tak keep of that day of Oliphernus;[49]
Amyd his ost he dronke lay on night
Withinne his tent, large as is a **berne**,   barn
And yit for all his pomp and al his might
Judith, a womman, as he lay **upright**   flat out
Slepyng, his heed **of smot** – and fro his tent   cut off
Ful prively sche **stal** from every wight,   stole away
And with his heed unto hir toun sche went.

49 Told in the apocryphal Book of Judith.

De rege Antiochie illustri[50]   690

❦ What needith it of king Antiochus[51]

To telle his **heye real mageste**,   high royal majesty

His heyhe pride, his werke **venemous**,   poisonous

For such another was ther noon as he;

Redeth which that he was in Machabe,[52]

And redith the proude wordes that he sayde,

And why he fel fro his prosperite,

And in an hil how wrecchidly he deyde.

Fortune him hath **enhaunced** so in pryde   raised up

That verraily he **wend** he might han **teyned**   thought; reached   700

Unto the sterris upon every syde,

And in a **balaunce weyen** what ech mounteyne,   scale; weigh

And all the **floodes** of the see **restreyne**,   tides; hold back

And God's peple had he most in hate;

Hem wold he slee, in torment and in peyne,

Wenyng that God ne might his pride abate.   believing

And **for that** Nichosor and Thimothe[53]   because

With Jewes were **venquist** mightily,   vanquished

Unto the Jewes such an hate had he

That he bad **graithe** his **chaar** hastily,   prepare; chariot   710

And swor, and sayde ful despitously

Unto Jerusalem he wold **eftsoone**,   very soon

To **wreke** his **ire** on it full cruelly,   visit; anger

But of his purpos he was **let** ful soone.   hindered

God for his **manace** him so sore smoot   threatening

With invisible wounde incurable,

That in his guttes **carf** so and **bot**   cut; bit

That his peynes were **importable**;   unbearable

And certeynly the wreche was **resonable**,   sane/thinking

50 'of the illustrious King Antiochus'
51 Second-century king of Syria.
52 The apocryphal Book of Maccabees.
53 Nicanor and Timotheus, opponents of Maccabeus.

720 For on many a man dede he peyne;[54]
But fro his purpos, cursed and dampnable,
For al his smert, he nolde him noght restreyne.[55]

But bad anoon **apparailen** his host;   draw up
And sodeynly, er he was of it **ware**,   aware
God dampned al his pride and al his bost,
For he so sore fel out of his **chare**   chariot
That his lymes and his skyn **to-tare**,   were torn/rent
So that he nomore might go ne ryde,
But in a chare men aboute him bare
730 **Al forbrosed**, bothe bak and syde.   bruised all over

The **wreche** of God him smot so cruely   vengeance
That in his body wicked wormes crept ,
And therwithal he stank so horribly
That noon of al his **meyne** that him kepte.   household
Whether that he wook or elles slepte,
Ne mighte nought the stynk of him endure.
In this meschief he weyled and eek wepte,
And knew God lord of every creature.

To al his **host**, and to himself also,   army
740 Ful **wlatsom** was the stynk and the **carayne**;   loathsome; body
No man mighte him bere to ne fro,
And in his stynk and orrible payne
He **starf** ful wrecchedly, and in a mountayne.   died
Thus hath this robbour and this homicide,
That many a man made wepe and **playne**,   moan
Such **guerdoun** as that **longeth** unto pryde.   reward; belongs

54 'he did harm to many a man'
55 'he wouldn't hold himself back'

De Alexandro Magno Philippi regis Macedonie filio

of Alexander the Great son of Philip of Macedon

❦ The story of Alisaunder is so **comune** [56]   well-known
That every wight that hath discrecioun
Hath herd somwhat, or al, of his fortune.   750
Thys wyde world, as in conclusioun,
He wan by strengthe, or for his heigh renoun
Thay were glad for pees unto him sende.
The pride of man and best he **layd adoun**   put down
Wherso he cam, unto the worlde's ende.

Comparisoun yit mighte never be maked
Bitwen him and noon other conquerour,
For al this world for drede of him hath quaked.
He was of knyghthod and of **fredam** flour;   generosity
Fortune him made the heir of hir honour –   760
Save wyn and wymmen nothing might **aswage**   lessen
His heigh entent in armes and labour,
So was he ful of **lumyne** corage.   luminous/glowing

What pite were it to him, though I yow tolde,
Of Darius, and an hundred thousand mo [57]
Of kynges, princes, dukes, and **corles** holde   churls
Which he conquered, and brought unto wo?
I say, as fer as men may ryde or go
The world was his – what schold I more devyse,
For though I write or tolde yow evermo   770
Of his knighthood? It mighte nought suffise.

Twelf yer he regned, as saith Machabe,
Philip's son of Macedon he was,
That first was king in Grece, that contre.
O worthy gentil Alisaundre, alas
That ever schulde falle such a **caas**!   situation
Empoysoned of thin oughne folk thou were;
Thyn fortune is torned into an aas,
And right for the ne wepte sche never a teere.

56 There were many romance epics concerning Alexander in the Middle Ages.
57 Darius, king of Persia, was defeated by Alexander.

780 Who schal me give teeres to compleigne
       The deth of **gentiles**, and of fraunchise,   gentlefolk
       That al the worlde had in his **demeigne**;   ownership
       And yit him thought it mighte nought suffice,
       So ful was his corage of high **emprise**.   enterprise/ambition
       Allas! Who schal helpe me to endite,
       Fals infortune and poysoun to devyse,
       The whiche two of al this wo I wyte?

       By wisedom, manhod, and by gret labour
       Fro humble bed to royal mageste
790 Up roos he Julius, the conquerour
       That wan al **th'occident** by land and see,   the west
       By strengthe of hond, or elles by **trete**,   agreement
       And unto Rome made hem **contributarie**;   tributary
       And **siththe** of Rome th'emperour was he,   since
       Til that Fortune **wax** his adversarie.   became

       O mighty Cesar, that in Thessalie
       Agains Pompeus **fader thin in lawe**,   your father-in-law
       That of the orient had al the **chivalrie**   knights
       Als fer as that the day bigynnes to **dawe**,   dawn
800 Thorough thi knighthod thou hast him take and **slawe**,   slain/killed
       Save fewe folk that with Pompeus fledde,
       Thurgh which thou puttist al th'orient in awe,
       Thanke Fortune, that so wel the **spedde**.   helped

       But now, a litel while I wil **bywaile**   mourn for
       This Pompeus, the noble governour
       Of Rome, which that **flowe** fro this bataile.   fled
       Alas, I say! Oon of his men, a fals traitour,
       His heed of smoot to wynne his favour
       Of Julius, and him the heed he brought.
810 Alas, Pompey, of the orient conquerour
       That Fortune to such a **fyn** the brought.   end

       To Rome agayn **reparieth** Julius   went
       With his triumphe **laurial** ful hye,[58]   laurel

58 The laurel wreath worn by victorious generals.

But on a tyme Brutus Cassius,
That ever had to his estat envye,
Ful prively hath made conspiracie
Agains this Julius, in **subtil** wise   cunning
Cast the place in which he schulde dye
With **boydekyns**, as I schal yow **devyse**.   daggers; explain   **820**

This Julius to the capitoile went[59]
Upon a day, as he was wont to goon;
And in the capitoil anoon him **hent**   seized
This false Brutus, and his other **foon**,   enemies
And **stiked** him with **boydekyns** anoon   stuck; daggers
With many a wounde, and thus thay let him lye;
But never **gront** he at no strook but oon –   groaned
Or elles at tuo – **but if** the storie lye.   unless

So manly was this Julius of hert   **830**
And so wel loved, **estatly**, honeste;   dignified
That though his deedly woundes **sore smert**,   hurt badly
His **mantil** over his **hipes** caste he,   cloak; hips
For no man schulde seen his privete;
And as he lay **deyinge** in a **traunce**,   dying; swoon
And wiste wel that verrayly deed was he,
Of **honeste** yet had he remembraunce.   decency

Lucan, to the this story I recomende,
And to Swetoun and to Valiren also,[60]
That of the story writen, word and ende,   **840**
How that to these grete conqueroures tuo
Fortune was first frend, and **siththen** fo.   then
Ne man trust upon hir favour longe,
But **have hir in awayt** for evermo –   keep his eye on her
Witnesse on all thise conqueroures stronge.

59 The Capitol – the administrative centre of classical Rome.
60 Three Roman historians.

Cresus

❧ Off riche Cresus, **whilom** king of Lyde[61]   formerly
Of which Cresus Cirus him sore dradde,[62]
Yet was he caught amyddes al his pride,
And to the fuyr to brenne him men him ladde.
But such a rayn doun fro the heven **schadde**,   showered
850   That **slough** the fuyr, and made him to eschape;   killed
But to bewar yet grace noon he hadde,
Til Fortune on the **galwes** made him gape.   gallows

Whan he was eschaped, he couth nou*g*ht **stent**   keep from
For to bygynne a newe werre agayn.
He wende wel for that Fortune him sent
Such **hap** that he eschaped thurgh the rayn,   fortune
That of his foos he mighte not be slayn;
And eek a **sweven** upon a night he **mette**,   dream; dreamed
Of which he was so proud and eek so **fayn**,   glad
860   That in vengeaunce he al his herte sette.

Upon a tree he was set, as him thought,
Wher Jubiter him **wissch** bothe bak and side,   washed
And Phebus eek a fair **towail** him brou*g*ht,   towel
To dryen him with and therfor **wax** his pryde   grew
And to his dou*g*hter, that stood him biside,
Which that he knew in **heigh science** abounde,   academic learning
And bad hire telle what it signifyde;
And sche his dreem right thus **gan expounde**.   began to explain

'The tree,' quod sche, 'the **galwes is to mene**   gallows; signifies
870   And Jubiter **likenith** snow and rayn;   signifies
And Phebus, with his towail so clene,
Tho ben the sonne **stremes**, soth to sayn   those are; beams
Thow schalt **enhangid** ben, Fader, certayn –   hanged
Rayn shal the wasch, and sonne schal the drye.'
Thus warned sche him ful **plat** and **ek** ful playn,   clearly; also
His dou*g*hter, which that called was Phanie.

61 Croesus, king of Lydia.
62 Cyrus, king of Persia.

And hanged was Cresus, this proude king;
His **real tour** might him not **availe**;   royal tower; help
Tegredis, ne noon other maner thing,   tragedies
Ne can I synge, crie, ny **biwayle**,   mourn   880
But for that Fortune wil alway **assayle**   assault/attack
With **unwar** strook the **regnes** that ben proude;   unexpected; kingdoms
For whan men trusteth hir, than wil sche faile,
And cover hir brighte face with a **clowde**.   cloud

here endeth the monk his tale

(The Monk's Tale is ended by the interruption of the knight:
this intervention forms part of The Nun's Priest's Prologue)

THE NUN'S PRIEST'S PROLOGUE AND TALE

The knight stops the monk, saying that his tale is too gloomy, and too hard on men of wealth and position (of which he is one) for comfort. The host says that he is so bored he is almost asleep, and asks the nun's priest to tell a more cheerful tale. He attempts to cheer the nun's priest on account of the man's poor horse and poverty-stricken appearance. The nun's priest is happy to oblige with a tale.

A poor widow and her daughters live in a cottage within a small farm enclosure, with four sheep and three cows. The widow also has a beautiful, but vain, cock called Chauntecleer and seven hens, his wives, of whom his favourite is Pertelote. One night Chauntecleer dreams of a red beast with black-tipped ears which grabs and eats him. Pertelote tells him to have no fear of dreams, and they both cite authorities for and against the effectiveness of dreams. Pertelote tells her husband to go and eat some herbs to ease his digestion. The fox hides and waits in the cabbage-patch until Chauntecleer appears. He tells the cock that Chauntecleer's father (whom he once ate) sang beautifully, and wants to know if Chauntecleer can match his sire's talents. Chauntecleer starts to sing, stretching his neck and closing his eyes, and the fox grabs him. He runs off, chased by the widow and her neighbours amid general commotion. Chauntecleer tempts the fox, saying that he ought to turn round and shout defiance to the humans, which the fox does. Chauntecleer immediately breaks loose and flies up into a tree, from which he will not come down, no matter what the fox says. The priest invites his audience to take what meaning they can from the tale.

The nun's priest is a humble man, in a job – priest to a group of nuns – which carries little social status, and offers little financial reward. He challenges the educational superiority and authority of the monk using a beast fable, one of the simplest and most popular forms of story available. Although few survive in English, their popularity is attested by the large number of carvings representing foxes and other fable characters in English churches and cathedrals. In beast fable, the characters are all animals, with animal characteristics, but they also fulfil the roles of human actors. The simple narrative offers an easily understood moral lesson. Typically, however, the nun's priest's simple fable is one of the most complex tales in the collection, just as his storytelling abilities belie his humble appearance and lack of status.

There are many layers in this story; as each is peeled back (like an onion), there are other layers beneath. His narrative links the nun's priest with every other pilgrim in the company, and all their tales are touched upon in some way. The priest is particularly keen to oppose the monk, especially in his observations on gluttony (the widow didn't get problems from overeating, for example), which would also be noted by the other well-fed pilgrims. The dung cart exemplum is in the vein of the pardoner, and appears to mock the prioress's boy in a cess-pit; and the mock-heroism of Chauntecleer is opposed to the chivalric tales, such as those of knight and squire; moreover, there is a suggestion of the wife of Bath in Pertelote's manner and in her snippets from the authorities – the priest takes on the subject of marriage in his depiction of the chicken-couple. The widow and her daughters are like the nuns of his flock. There is a hint of fabliau in the double-trickery, and of the saint's life in Chauntecleer's 'miraculous' salvation. The farmyard resembles Theseus's amphitheatre, where Chauntecleer is Theseus and the widow and her daughters are the gods.

The story follows the tradition of the 'Reynard the Fox' tales, in which there is a cock called Chauntecleer and a fox, Reynard's son, called Russel. However, in this story the fox is the villain, rather than a cheeky alternative hero, as he is in the Reynard stories. If taken allegorically, the fox can be seen as the devil, skulking around the borders between earth and hell, waiting to seize Christian souls. The story does also work allegorically on the level of the Genesis/gospel story, where Adam falls from grace by means of the devil, aided by his wife (at one point Pertelote is called 'Eve'). Adam/mankind is then saved by Christ; but in this case, of course, Chauntecleer is the author of his own salvation.

It has been argued that Chauntecleer, the proud ruler and tyrant, may represent Richard II. There were those who believed that Richard had erred in following untraditional economic policies, which had led to the Peasants' Revolt of 1381, but that if he gave these up everything would be peaceful again. Chauntecleer's salvation, therefore, could be interpreted in this way. The tale can also be seen as a satire on John Gower's *Vox Clamantis* (The Voice of One Crying), an apocalyptic chronicle of the Peasants' Revolt: which represents the peasants as animals and birds. This is the only tale of Chaucer's which contains a direct reference to the Revolt; the narrator mentions the entry into London of the peasants, and the pseudonym of one of their leaders, Jack Straw. In many ways, then, this is a border tale, operating between the safe farmyard and the dangerous wood, which, however, is also the place (in the Robin Hood stories, for example) where the nature of 'Englishness' is worked out.

Chauntecleer gets his authorities mixed up, misuses and mistranslates them, and then casts them aside in favour of food and sex. Authority is rendered useless, inviting the suggestion that all learned authorities are ultimately vain, as men and women will go their own way, and that life is driven by needs other than knowledge for its own sake. This is another challenge to the scholars in the company, and particularly, again, to the monk.

Another possible identification for Chauntecleer is that he represents the poet himself. The tale is a vehicle for Chaucer's own knowledge and interests, and he may be suggesting that the poet is a crowing cock, or simply that nobody listens to a poet. The fox silences the speaker/composer (just as Phebus silences his wife and his crow), so perhaps the poet had better keep his mouth shut. The crowing cock is, however, both useful and in touch with the divine workings of the heavens, and so is the poet.

The host has revealed that the monk's name is Peter, and that the nun's priest is called John. Peter represents St Peter, the founder of the Church and therefore the voice of ultimate ecclesiastical authority. John represents St John the Evangelist, the 'disciple whom Jesus loved', who was believed to have been the author of the gospel of St John, and of the Book of Revelation. Their names, therefore, represent the nature and position of these two 'paired' pilgrims. What does this 'evangelist' preach? Like Chaucer the poet, he will not say . . . he tells the audience to sift the wheat from the chaff (another engaging farmyard metaphor) for themselves.

Key Questions

This story has many possible meanings . . . which is the most appropriate?

How does the nun's priest employ 'authorities' in the tale? Why does he do it in this way? What is important about them, or are they just being ridiculed?

Can anything be learned from a comparison between the nun's priest and the monk?

How does this story compare with other beast fables?

Topic Keywords

Beast fable as genre/ popular religion/ historical events and personalities/ philosophy and dreams/ medieval women/ medieval medicine/ medieval animals and bestiaries

Further Reading

Ann Astell, 'The Peasants' Revolt: Cock-Crow in Gower and Chaucer', *Essays in Medieval Studies*, 10, 1993, pp. 53–64

Saul Nathaniel Brody, 'Truth and Fiction in The Nun's Priest's Tale', *Chaucer Review*, 14, 1988, pp. 33–47

Martin Camargo, 'Rhetorical Ethos and The Nun's Priest's Tale', *Comparative Literature Studies*, 33, 1996, pp. 173–86

Arthur Chapin, 'Morality Ovidized: Sententiousness and the Aphoristic Moment in The Nun's Priest's Tale', *Yale Journal of Criticism*, 8, 1995, pp. 7–33

Sheila Delany, ' "Mulier est hominis confusio": Chaucer's anti-popular Nun's Priest's Tale', *Mosaic*, 17, 1984, pp. 1–8

Juliette Dor, 'Reversals in The Nun's Priest's Tale', in *Multiple Worlds, Multiple Words: Essays in Honour of Irène Simon*, edited by Hena Maes-Jelinek, Pierre Michel and Paulette Michel-Michot, Liège, English Department, University of Liège, 1988, pp. 69–77

Richard W. Fehrenbacher, ' "A yeerd enclosed al aboute": Literature and History in The Nun's Priest's Tale', *Chaucer Review*, 29, 1994, pp. 134–48

John Finlayson, 'The "povre widwe" in The Nun's Priest's Tale and Boccaccio's *Decameron*', *Neuphilologische Mitteilungen*, 99, 1998, pp. 269–73

—— 'Reading Chaucer's Nun's Priest's Tale: Mixed Genres and Multi-layered Worlds of Illusion', *English Studies (The Netherlands)*, 86, 2005, pp. 493–510

J. F. Galván-Reula, 'The Modernity of The Nun's Priest's Tale: Narrator, Theme and Ending', *Lore and Language*, 3, 1984, pp. 63–9

L. A. J. R. Houwen, 'Fear and Instinct in Chaucer's Nun's Priest's Tale', in *Fear and its Representations in the Middle Ages and Renaissance*, edited by Anne Scott and Cynthia Kosso, Turnhout, Brepols, 2002, pp. 17–30

Eric Jager, 'Croesus and Chauntecleer: The Royal Road of Dreams', *Modern Language Quarterly*, 49, 1988, pp. 3–18

Noel Harold Kaylor Jr, 'The Nun's Priest's Tale as Chaucer's Anti-Tragedy', in *The Living Middle Ages: Studies in Medieval Literature and its Tradition: A Festschrift for Karl Heinz Göller*, edited by Uwe Böker, Manfred Markus and Rainer Schöwerling, Stuttgart, Belser, 1989, pp. 87–102

Doron Narkiss, 'The Fox, the Cock and the Priest: Chaucer's Escape from Fable', *Chaucer Review*, 32, 1997, pp. 46–63

Onno Oerlemans, 'The Seriousness of The Nun's Priest's Tale', *Chaucer Review*, 26, 1992, pp. 317–28

Patrizia Grimaldi Pizzorno, 'Metaphor and Exemplum in The Nun's Priest's Tale', *Assays*, 9, 1996, pp. 79–99

Larry Scanlon, 'The Authority of Fable: Allegory and Irony in The Nun's Priest's Tale', *Exemplaria*, 1, 1989, pp. 43–68

Paul Thomas, 'Cato on Chauntecleer: Chaucer's Sophisticated Audience', *Neophilologus*, 72, 1988, pp. 278–83

Peter W. Travis, *Disseminal Chaucer: Rereading The Nun's Priest's Tale*, Notre Dame, IN, Notre Dame University Press, 2010

Edward Wheatley, 'Commentary Displacing Text: The Nun's Priest's Tale and the Scholastic Fable Tradition', *Studies in the Age of Chaucer*, 18, 1996, pp. 119–41

& here bygynneth the prologe of the nonne's prest's tale
of the kok and the hen

❦ 'Ho, Sire!' quod the knight, 'no more of this!
That ye han said is right ynough, y-wys!¹
And **mochil** more, for **litel** hevynesse   *more; a little*
Is right ynough for moche folk, I gesse.
I say for me it is a **gret disease**,   *very uncomfortable*
Wheras men han ben in gret welthe and ease
To hieren of her sodeyn fal, allas!
And the **contraire** is ioye and gret **solas**,   *opposite; wellbeing*
As when a man hath ben in pore estate,   **10**
And clymbith up and **wexeth** fortunate,   *becomes*
And ther **abydeth** in prosperite;   *remains*
Such thing is **gladsom**, as thinkith me,   *happy*
And of such thing were goodly for to telle.'
'Ye,' quod oure host, 'by Seint Paule's belle!²
Ye say right soth; this monk hath **clappid lowde**.   *made a loud noise*
He spak how fortune was **clipped** with a **clowde**   *covered; cloud*
I not never what – and als of **tregedie**   *tragedy*
Right now ye herd; and **pardy**, no remedye   *by God*
It is for to **bywayle** or compleyne   *bemoan*   **20**
That that is doon; and also it is a peyne,
As ye han said, to **hiere** of hevynesse.   *hear*
Sire monk, no more of this, so God your soule blesse!
Your tale anoyeth al this compaignie –
Such a tale is nou*g*ht worth a **boterflye**,   *butterfly*
For therinne is noon disport ne game;
Wherfore Sir monk, **Damp Pieres** by your name,   *Sir Peter*
I pray yow hertly, tel us somwhat ellis;
For sicurly, ner **gingling** of the bellis   *jingling*
that on your bridil hong on every syde –   **30**
By Heven King that for us alle dyde –

1 'you've said quite enough, thank you!'
2 The bell of St Paul's cathedral, in London.

I schold er this han falle doun for sleep,[3]

Although the **slough** had never ben so deep.   mud

Than had your tale have be told in vayn,

For certeynly, as these clerkes sayn,

Wheras a man may have noon audience,

Nought helpith it to tellen his **sentence**.[4]   speech/story

And wel I wot **the substance is in me**,   I have taken it in

If eny thing schal wel reported be.

40   Sir, say somwhat of huntyng, I yow pray.'

'Nay,' quod the monk, 'I have no **lust** for to play.   wish

Now let another telle, as I have told.'

Than spak our ost, with rude speche and bold,

And said unto the nonne's prest anoon;

'Com ner, thou prest; com ner, thou Sir John –

Tel us such thing as may our hertes glade;

Be **blithe**, although thou ryde upon a **jade**!   happy; nag

What though thin hors be bothe **foul** and **lene**?   ugly; thin

If he wil serve the, **rek not a bene**!   don't give a bean

50   Lok that thin hert be mery evermo!'

'Yis, sire; yis, hoste,' quod he, 'al so mot I go,

But I be mery, y-wis, **I wol be blamed**.'   blame me if...

And right anoon he hath his tale **tamyd**;   begun

And thus he sayd unto us everichoon,

This sweete prest, this goodly man, Sir John.

Explicit prologus

the prologue ends

her bygynneth the nonne's prest his tale

❦ A pore wydow, **somdel stope** in age,   somewhat stooping

Was **whilom** duellyng in a pore cotage   once upon a time

60   Bisyde a **grove**, stondyng in a **dale**.   wood; valley

This wydowe, of which I telle yow my tale,

Syn thilke day that sche was last a wif,   since the same

In paciens ladde a ful symple lyf,

For litel was hir catel and hir **rent**;   income

---

3 'If it weren't for the noise of the bells on your bridle I would have fallen asleep'

4 'there's no point in telling a story if you've got no audience'

For **housbondry** of such as God hir sent   *by managing*
Sche **fond** hirself, and eek hir doughtres tuo.   *kept*
Thre large sowes had sche, and no mo,
Thre **kyn**, and eek a scheep that **highte** Malle.   *cattle; was called*
Ful sooty was hir bour, and eek hir halle,   70
In which sche eet ful many a **sclender** meel –   *meagre*
Of **pynaunt saws** hir needid never a deel.   *poignant sauce*
Noon deynteth morsel passid thorugh hir throte;
Hir dyete was **accordant** to hir **cote**   *similar to; farm*
Repleccioun ne made hir never sik;   *overeating*
Attempre dyete was al hir phisik,   *moderate*
And exercise and herte's **suffisaunce** –   *sufficiency*
The goute lette hir nothing for to daunce,[5]
Ne **poplexie schent** not hir hir heed;   *apoplexy; harmed*
No wyn ne drank sche, nother whit ne reed.   80
Hir **bord** servyd bothe with whit and blak;   *table*
Milk and broun bred, in which sche fond no lak;[6]
Saynd bacoun, and som tyme an **ey** or **tweye**   *smoked; egg; two*
For sche was, as sit were, a maner deye.[7]
A yerd sche had, enclosed al aboute
With stikkes, and a drye dich withoute,
In which sche had a cok, that hight Chaunteclere;
In al the lond of crowyng was noon his **peere**;   *equal*
His vois was merier than the mery **orgon**   *organ*
On masse dayes, that in the chirche **goon**.   *plays*   90
Wel **sikerer** was his crowyng in his **logge**,   *surer; dwelling*
Than is a clok or an abbay **orologge**;   *great clock*
By nature knew he ech ascencioun
Of equinoxial in thilke toun;[8]
For wan degrees fyftene were ascendid
Thanne **crewe** he; it might not ben **amendid**.   *crowed; stopped*
His comb was redder than the fyn coral,
And **batayld** as it were a castel wal;   *battlemented*
His **bile** was blak and as the **geet** it schon,   *bill; jet*
Lik **asur** were his legges and his **ton**,   *azure (blue); toes*   100

5 'gout didn't stop her from dancing'
6 'which she was perfectly satisfied with'
7 'a sort of dairy-person'
8 That is, he knew when the sun came up and the day had irreversibly broken.

His nayles whitter than the lily flour,
And lik the burniscst gold was his colour.
This gentil cok hadde in his governance
Seven hennes, for to do al his plesaunce,
Which were his **sustres** and his **paramoures**,　　sisters; lovers
And **wonder** lik to him as of coloures,　　remarkably
Of whiche the **fairest hiewed** on hir throte　　prettiest coloured
Was **cleped** fayre damysel Pertelote.　　called
Curteys sche was, **discret** and **debonaire**　　wise; gracious

110 And **companable**, and bar hirself ful faire;[9]　　sociable
Syn thilke day that sche was seven yer old
That sche hath trewely the hert in hold
Of Chaunteclere, **loken in every lith**;　　locked in every limb
He loved hir so that wel him was therwith.
But such a joye was it to here him synge,
Whan that the brighte sonne gan to springe,
In swete accord, 'My lief is faren on londe'[10]
For **thilke tyme**, as I have understonde,　　at that time
Bestis and briddes cowde speke and synge.

120 And so byfel that in a dawenyng,
As Chaunteclere, among his wyves alle,
Sat on his perche that was in his halle –
And next him sat this faire Pertelote –
This Chauntecler **gan gronen** in his throte,　　began to; groan
As man that in his dreem is **drecched** sore;　　troubled
And whan that Pertelot thus herd him **rore**　　roar
Sche was **agast**, and sayde, '**Herte deere**,　　afraid; dear heart
What eylith yow to grone in this manere?
Ye ben a verray sleper; fy, for schame!'

130 And he anwerd and sayde thus, '**Madame**,　　my lady
I pray yow that ye take it nou*ght* agreef[11]
By God! Me **mette** I was in such **meschief**　　dreamed; trouble
Right now, that yit myn hert is **sore afright**!'　　very frightened
'Now God,' quod he, 'my **sweven** rede aright,　　dream
And keep my body out of foul prisoun!
Me mette how that I romed up and doun

9 'carried herself beautifully'
10 'My love has gone forth upon the world'
11 'don't be upset'

Withinne oure yerd, wheras I saugh a beest

Was lik an hound, and wold have **maad arrest**   grabbed me

Upon my body, and wold han had me deed.

His colour was bitwixe yolow and reed,   140

And tipped was his tail and bothe his eeres

With blak, unlik the **remenaunt** of his **heres**.   remainder; hair

His snowt was smal, with glowyng **yen tweye**,   eyes two

Yet of his look for **fer** almost I deye –   fear

This caused me my gronyng, douteles.'

'Away!' quod sche, 'Fy on yow, **herteles**!   gutless/cowardly

Allas,' quod sche, 'for by that God above,

Now have ye lost myn hert and al my love!

I can nought love a coward, by my feith,

For certis, **what so** eny womman seith,   whatever 150

We alle desiren, if it mighte be,

To have housbondes **hardy**, riche and **fre**,   bold/strong; generous

And **secre**, and no **nygard**, ne no fool,   discreet; miser

Ne him that is **agast** of every **tool**,   weapon

❦ Ne noon **avaunter**, by that God above!   braggart

How dorst ye sayn, for scham, unto your love,

That anything might make yow **afferd**?   afraid

Have ye no man's hert, and **han a berd**?   have; beard

Allas, and can ye ben agast of swevenys?

Nought, God wot, but vanite in sweven is –   160

Swevens **engendrid** ben of replecciouns,   are caused by

And often of **fume**, and of **complexiouns**   vapour; body fluids

Whan humours ben to abundaunt in a wight.[12]

Certes, this dreem which ye han met tonight

Cometh of the grete **superfluite**   excess

Of youre reede coler, parde,

Which causeth folk to dremen in here dremes

Of **arwes**, and of fuyr with reede **beemes**;   arrows; flames

Of **rede** bestis that thai wil him byte,   red

Of **contek**, and of **whelpis greet** and **lite**,   strife; dogs big and small 170

Right as the humour of **malencolie**   melancholy

Causeth in sleep ful many a man to crye

---

12 Chauntecleer must be suffering from a superfluity of humours.

For fere of **beres**, or of **boles** blake,   bears; bulls
Or elles blake develes wol hem take.
Of other humours couthe I telle also,
That wirken many a man in slep ful woo,
But I wol passe as lightly as I can.
Lo, Catoun, which that was so wis a man,[13]
Sayde he nought thus: 'Ne do no force of dremes,'[14]
180 Now Sire,' quod sche, 'whan we **fle** fro thise beemes fly
For God's love, as tak som **laxatyf** –   laxative
Up peril of my soule and of my lyf
I counsel yow the best, I wol not lye –
That bothe of **coloure** and of malencolye   choler
Ye purge yow, and for ye schol nought tarye,
Though in this toun is noon **apotecarie**, apothecary (chemist)
I schal myself tuo herbes **techyn** yow   teach
That schal be for your **hele** and for youre **prow**, health; profit
And in oure **yerd** tho herbes schal I fynde,   (farm)yard
190 The whiche han of her **proprete** by **kynde** property; nature
To purgen yow **bynethe and eek above**.   'at both ends'
Forget not this, for God's oughne love:
Ye ben ful colerik of complexioun;[15]
Ware the sonne in his ascencioun,
Ne fynd yow not **replet** in humours hote,   full
And if it do, I dar wel lay a grote,[16]
That ye schul have a **fever terciane**,   tertian fever
Or an **agu**, that may be youre **bane**.   ague; killer
A day or tuo ye schul have digestives[17]
200 Of wormes, or ye take your laxatives;
Of **lauriol**, **century** and **fumytere**, laurel; centaury; fumitory
Or elles of **elder bery** that growith there;   elderberry
Of **catapus** or of **gaytre beriis**,   euphorbia;
Of **erbe yve** that groweth in our yerd, ther **mery** is. ground ivy; pleasing
Pike hem upright as thay growe, and **et** hem in – eat

13 The *Distichs*, or sayings, of the Roman writer Cato, were used to teach grammar
  to medieval schoolboys.
14 'don't worry about dreams'
15 The cock is naturally ruled by choler, making it hot and dry.
16 'I'll bet you a groat (4d)'
17 Digestives – medicinal remedies to ease the stomach.

Be mery, housbond, for your fader **kyn**   family
Dredith non dremes – I can say no more.'
'Madame,' quod he, '**graunt mercy** of your **lore**;[18]
But natheles, as touching Daun Catoun,[19]
That hath of wisdom such a gret **renoun**,   reputation   210
Though that he bad no dremes for to drede,
By God, men may in olde bookes rede
Of many a man more of auctorite
Than ever Catoun was – so mot I the –
That al the **revers** sayn of his **sentence**,   opposite; teaching
And han wel founden by experience
That dremes ben **significaciouns**,   signs/signifiers
As wel of joye as of tribulaciouns
That folk enduren in this lif present.
Ther nedeth make of this noon argument;   220
The verray **preve** schewith it in dede.   proof
Oon of the grettest auctorite that men rede
Saith thus, that **whilom** tway felawes wente   once upon a time
On pylgrimage, in a ful good entente,
And happed so thay com to a toun
Wheras ther was such congregacioun
Of poeple, and eek **so streyt of herbergage**,   so little food
That thay fond nou*ght* as moche as oon cotage
In which that thay might bothe **y-logged** be;   lodged
Wherfor thay mosten, of necessite,   230
As for that night **depart her compaignye**,   split up
And ech of hem goth to his hostelrye,
And took his loggyng as it wolde falle.[20]
That oon of hem was loggid in a stalle,
Fer in a yerd with oxen of the plough;
That other man was logged wel ynough,
As was his **adventure**, or fortune,   chance
That us governith alle in comune.
And so bifel that long er it were day,
This oon **met** in his bed, ther as he lay,   dreamt   240

18 thank you very much; learning
19 More wisdom from Cato's *Distichs*, or sayings.
20 'as they could find it'

How that his felaw gan upon him calle
And sayd, 'Allas, for in an oxe stalle
This night I schal be murdrid ther I lye!
Now help me, deere brother, or I dye!
In alle cum to me!' he sayde.   quickly
'This man out of his slep for **fer abrayde**,   fear; awoke
But whan that he was waked out of his sleep
He **torned him**, and took of this no **keep**;   turned over; notice
Him thought his dreem nas but a vanite.

250 Thus **twies** in his sleepe dremed he,   twice
And at the thridde tyme yet his felawe
Com, as him thought, and sayd, 'I am now **slawe** –   slain
Biholde my bloody woundes, deep and wyde.
Arise up erly in the morwe tyde,
And at the west gate of the toun,' quod he,
'A **cart of donge** there schalt thou see,   dungcart
In which my body is hyd prively.
Do thilke cart **arresten** boldely –   stop
My gold caused my mourdre, **soth to sayn**.'   truth to tell

260 And told him every **poynt** how he was slayn,   detail
With a ful pitous face, pale of **hewe**.   colour
And truste wel, his dreem he fond ful trewe;
For on the morwe, as sone as it was day,
To his felawe's **in** he took the way,   lodging
And whan that he cam to this oxe stalle,
After his felaw he bigan to calle.
The **hostiller** answered him anoon   innkeeper
And sayde, 'Sire, your felaw is agoon;
Als soone as day he went out of the toun.'

270 This man **gan falle in a suspeccioun**,   became suspicious
Remembring on his dremes that he mette,
And forth he goth – no lenger wold he **lette** –   tarry
Unto the west gate of the toun, and fond
A dong cart went as it were to **donge lond**,   dung-dumping place
That was arrayed in the same wise
As ye han herd the deede man **devise**;   describe
And with an **hardy** hert he gan to crie   emboldened
Vengeaunce and justice of this felonye:[21]

21 A felony was a capital crime.

'My felaw mordrid is this same night,
And in this carte he lith heer **upright**!   stretched out   280
I crye out on the **ministres**,' quod he   governors
'That schulde kepe and reule this cite!
Harrow, allas! Her lith my felaw slayn!'
What schold I more unto this tale sayn?
The peple **upstert** and caste the cart to grounde,   rose up
And in the middes of the dong thay founde
The dede man, that mordred was **al newe**.   freshly
O blisful God! Thou art ful just and trewe!
Lo, how thow **bywreyest** mordre al day!   betrayest
Mordre wil out – certes, **it is no nay**.   it can't be gainsaid   290
Morder is so **wlatsom** and abhominable   horrible
To God, that is so just and resonable,
That he ne wold nought suffre it **hiled** be,   hidden
Though it abyde a yeer, or tuo, or thre.
Morder wil out – this is my conclusioun;
And right anoon the ministres of that toun
Han **hent** the carter and so sore him **pyned**,   arrested; tortured
And eek the hostiller so sore **engyned**,   tortured
That thay **biknew** her wikkednes anoon,   admitted
And were **anhonged** by the nekke boon.   hanged   300
Here may men se that dremys ben to **drede**.   be taken seriously
And certes, in the same book I rede,
Right in the nexte chapitre after this –
I **gabbe** nought, so have I joye or blis–   talk idly
Tuo men that wolde have passed oversee
For certeyn causes, into fer contre,
If that the wynd ne hadde ben contrarie,
That made hem in a cite for to tarie,
That stod ful mery upon an **haven** syde;   harbour
But on a day, agayn the eventyde,[22]   310
The wynd gen chaunge, and blew right as **hem list**.   they wanted
Jolyf and glad they wenten unto rest,   happy
And **casten** hem ful erly for to sayle –   planned
But herkneth! To that oon man fell a gret mervayle,
That oon of hem in his slepyng, as he lay,
Him met a wonder drem **agayn** the day.   about

22 'as evening was coming on'

Him thought a man stood by his bed's syde,
And him comaunded that he schuld abyde;
And sayd him thus, 'If thou tomorwe wende
320 Thow schalt be **dreynt**; my tale is at an ende.'   drowned
He **wook**, and told his felaw what he mette,   woke
And prayde him his **viage** to **lette**;   journey; put off
As for that day, he prayd him to abyde.
His felaw, that lay by his bed's syde,
Gan to **lawgh** and scorned him ful fast.   laugh
'No dreem,' quod he, 'may so myn herte **gaste**   make afraid
That I wil lette for to do my **thinges**.   business
I sett not a straw by thy dremynges,
For swevens been but vanitees and **iapes**.   tricks
330 Men dreme al day of owles and of apes,
And of many a **mase** therwithal –   wonder
Men dreme of thinges that never be schal;
But sith I see that thou wilt her abyde,
And thus **forslouthe** wilfully thy tyde,   lazily miss
God wot, it **reweth** me, and have good day.'   pities
And thus he took his leve and went his way;
Noot I not why, ne what **myschuance** it eyled   I don't know why; bad luck
But er he hadde half his course y-sayled,
But **casuelly** the schip's bothom **rent**   by chance; tore
340 And schip and man under the watir went,
In sight of other schippes ther byside
That with him sailed at the same tyde.
And therfore, faire Pertelot so deere,
By such ensamples olde maistow **leere**   learn
That no man scholde be to **recheles**   reckless
Of dremes; for I say the douteles
That many a dreem ful sore is for to drede.
Lo, in the lif of Seint Kenelm I rede
That was Kenulphus' sone, that noble king
350 Of Mertinrike, how Kenilm mette a thing – [23]
A litil **er** he was mordred **upon a day**,   before; one day
His mordre in his **avysioun** he say.   vision
His **norice** him **expouned** every del   nurse; interpreted

23 St Kenelm was a ninth-century boy king, who traditionally foresaw his own death
   in a dream.

His sweven, and bad him for to **kepe him wel**   look out
For traisoun – but he nas but seven yer old,
And therfore litel tale hath he told
Of eny drem, so holy was his hert.[24]
By God! I hadde **lever** than my **schert**   rather; shirt
That ye had rad his legend, as have I!
Dame Pertelot, I say yow trewely,   360
Macrobius – that writ the avisioun
In Auffrik of the worthy Cipioun –[25]
Affermeth dremes, and saith that thay been
Warnyng of thinges that men after seen.
And forthermore, I pray yow loketh wel
In the olde Testament of Daniel,
If he huld dremes eny vanyte.
Rede eek of Joseph, and ther schal ye see
Whethir dremes ben somtyme – I say nought alle –
Warnyng of thinges that schul after falle.[26]   370
Lok of Egipt the king, Daun Pharao,
His baker and his **botiler** also,   butler
Whethir thay felte noon effect in dremis.
Whoso wol seke actes of sondry **remes**   realms
May rede of dremes many a **sondry** thing.   different
Lo, **Cresus** which that was of Lydes king,   Croesus
Mette that he sat upon a tre,
Which signified he schuld hanged be.
Lo hir Andromachia, Ector's wif,
That day that Ector schulde lese his lif.   380
Sche dremed on the same night byforn
How that the lif of Ector schuld be **lorn**.   lost
If **thilke** day he went into bataille –   that same
Sche warned him; but it might nou*gh*t **availe** –   help
He wente forth to fighte, **natheles**,   nonetheless

24 'he didn't take much notice of any dream'
25 The dream of Scipio – it was first described by Cicero, who gained a reputation
   as a prophetic writer in the Middle Ages because of this. Macrobius wrote a
   commentary, and was therefore sometimes mistaken for the author.
26 Joseph and Daniel – two Old Testament dreamers and interpreters of prophetic
   dreams.

And he was slayn anoon of Achilles – [27]
But thilke tale is al to long to telle,
And eek it is neigh day; I may not duelle.
Schortly I say, as for conclusioun,
390 That I schal have of this avisioun
Adversite, and I say forthermore
That I ne telle of laxatifs no store;[28]
For thay ben **venemous**, I wot it wel –   poisonous
I hem **defye** – I love hem never a del!   defy
Now let us speke of mirthe, and **lete** al this.   leave
Madame Pertilot, so have I blis,
Of o thing God hath me sent **large grace**;   great gift
For whan I se the beaute of your face –
Ye ben so scarlet hiew about your eyyen –
400 Hit makith al my drede for to **deyyen**,   die/go away
For als **siker** as *In principio*,   sure
Mulier est hominis confusio.
Madame, the **sentence** of this Latyn is: meaning
'Womman is man's joye and man's blis;
For whan I **fiele** a-night your softe syde,   feel
Al be it that I may not on you ryde –
For that your perche is mad so narow, allas! –
I am so ful of joye and **solas**   ease
That I defye bothe sweven and drem.'
410 And with that word he **fleigh** doun fro the beem,   flew
For it was day; and eek his hennes alle,
With a chuk he gan hem for to calle,
For he had found a corn lay in the yerd.
Real he was, he was nomore aferd.   regal
He fetherid Pertelote twenty tyme,
And **trad** as ofte, er that it was **prime**.   copulated; 6am.
He lokith as it were a grim lioun,
And on his **toon** he rometh up and doun;   toes
Him deyneth not to set his foot to grounde.
420 He chukkith whan he hath a corn y-founde,

27 An episode from Dares Phrygius's *De Excidio Troiae*, the most popular medieval
   version of the fall of Troy. Hector was the champion and prince of Troy,
   Andromache his wife.
28 'I don't think laxatives do any good'

And to him rennen than his wifes alle.
Thus real as a prince is in his halle
Leve I this Chaunteclere in his pasture,
And after wol I telle **his aventure**.   what happened to him
Whan that the moneth in which the world bigan
That highte March, whan God maked first man,
Was complet, and passed were also
Syn March bygan, tway monthes and dayes tuo,
Byfell that Chaunteclere, in al his pride,
His seven wyves walkyng by his syde,   430
Cast up his **eyyen** to the brighte sonne,   eyes
That in the signe of Taurus had y-ronne
Twenty degrees and oon, and somwhat more,
And knew by **kynde**, and by noon other **lore**   nature; teaching
That it was **prime**, and crew with blisful **steven**.   six o'clock; voice
'The sonne,' he sayde, 'is clomben up on heven
Twenty degrees and oon, and somwhat more, y-wis.
Madame Pertelot, my worlde's blis,
Herknith these blisful briddes how thay synge,
And seth these freissche floures how thay springe;   440
Ful is myn hert of **revel** and **solaas**.'   joy; ease
But sodeinly him fel a sorwful **caas**,   event
For ever the latter end of joye is wo.
God wot that worldly joye is soone **ago**,   gone
And if a **rethor** couthe faire **endite**   writer; write
Hem a chronique, saufly might he write
As for a **soverayn notabilite**.   notable fact
Now every wys man let him **herkne** me,   listen to
This story is **also** trewe, I undertake,   as
As the book is of Launcelot the Lake,[29]   450
That **womman** huld in ful gret reverence.   women
No wol I torne agayn to my sentence.
A **colefox**, ful sliegh of iniquite,[30]
That in the grove had **woned** yeres thre,   lived
By heigh ymaginacioun **forncast**,   forecast
The same nighte thurgh the **hegge** brast   hedge

29 Part of the Arthurian cycle of romances; Lancelot was Arthur's 'first knight', who
   had an affair with Arthur's wife, Guinevere.
30 'fox with black-tipped tail, feet and ears'

Into the yerd ther Chaunteclere the faire
Was went, and eek his wyves, to repaire;   used to
And in a bed of **wortes** stille he lay   cabbages
460   Til it was passed **undern** of the day,   nine o'clock
Waytyng his tyme on Chaunteclere to falle,
As gladly doon these homicides all
That in **awayte lyn** to morther men.   ambush lie
O false mordrer, lurckyng in thy den!
O newe Scariot, newe Genilon!
Fals dissimulour! Greke Sinon,
That broughtest Troye **al utrely** to sorwe![31]   utterly
O Chauntecler! Accursed be the morwe
That thou into the yerd **flough** fro the **bemys**!   flew; beams
470   Thow were ful wel y-warned by thy dremys
That thilke day was perilous to the!
But what that God **forwot** most needes be,   foreordained
After the opynyoun of certeyn clerks.[32]
Witnesse on him that eny clerk is,
That in **scole** is gret **disputesoun**   university; disputation
And hath ben of an hundred thousend men;
But yit I cannot **bult it to the bren**[33]
As can the holy doctor Augustyn,
Or Boece, or the Bisschop Bradwardyn,[34]
480   Whether that God's worthy **forwetyng**   foreknowledge
Streigneth me **needely** for to do a thing.   forces..of necessity
Needely clepe I simple necessitee;   what is needful
Or elles, if fre **choys** be graunted me   choice
To do that same thing or to do it nou*gh*t,
Though God **forwot** it **er** that it was wrought,   knew in advance; before
Or if his **wityng streyneth** never a deel   knowing; forces
But by **necessite condicionel**.   conditional necessity
I wol not have to do of such **matiere**;   subject

---

31 Judas Iscariot (betrayer of Christ), Ganelon (betrayer of Charlemagne), and Sinon
    (betrayer of Troy).
32 The nun's priest is here referring to the doctrine of predestination, espoused
    particularly by John Wyclif and his (Lollard) followers.
33 'separate the wheat from the chaff'
34 St Augustine of Hippo, Boethius (writer of *De Consolatione Philosophiae*), and
    Thomas Bradwardine, a great scholar of Chaucer's own day.

My tale is of a cok, as ye schal hiere,
That took his counseil of his wyf, with sorwe,   490
To walken in the yerd upon the morwe
That he had met the dreme that I tolde.
Wymmen's counseiles ben **fulofte colde**;   very often deadly
Womman's counseil brou*gh*t us first to woo
And made Adam fro paradys to go,
Theras he was ful mery and wel at ease
But **for I noot** to whom it might displease   because I don't know
If I counseil of womman wolde blame –
Pas over; for I sayde it in my **game**.   jest
Red auctors who that trete of such **matiere**,   read; subject   500
And what thay sayn of wommen ye may heere.
These been the cokke's wordes, and not myne;
I can noon harme of womman **divine**.   make out
Faire in the **sond** to bathe hir merily   sand
Lith Pertelot, and alle hir sustres by
Agayn the sonne, and Chaunteclere so free   in
Sang merier than the **meremayd** in the see;   mermaid
For Phisiologus seith sicurly
How that thay syngen wel and merily.[35]
And so byfel that, as he cast his **ye**   eye   510
Among the wortes on a boterflye,
He was war of this fox that lay ful lowe –
Nothing ne list him thanne for to crowe,
But cryde anon, 'Cok, cok!' and up he stert
As man that was affrayed in his hert,
For naturelly a beest desireth flee
Fro his **contrarie**, if he may it see.   opposite
Though he never **er** had sayn it with his ye   before
This Chaunteclere, whan he gan it aspye
He wold han fled, but the fox anon   520
Said, 'Gentil Sire, allas! Why wol ye goon?
Be ye affrayd of me, that am youre frend?
Certes, I were worse than eny feend
If I to yow wold harm or vilonye.

---

35 A reference to the bestiary, in which animals and birds are described in terms of
   their physical and moral qualities.

I am nought come **your counsail to espye**,   to spy on you
For trewely ye have als mery a **steven**   voice
As eny aungel hath that is in heven.
Therwith ye han in musik more felynge
Than had Boece, or eny that can synge.[36]
530   My lord your fader, God his soule blesse,
And youre moder yn her gentilesse,
Han in myn hous been, to my gret ease;
And certes, Sire, ful **fayn** wold I yow please;   gladly
But for men speke of syngyng, I wol say –
So mot I **brouke** wel myn **yen tway** –   use; two eyes
Save ye, I herde never man so synge
As dede your fadir in the **morwenynge**!   morning
Certes, it was **of hert** al that he song,   from the heart
And for to make his vois the more strong
540   He wold so **peynen** him that with bothe his yen   strain
He moste wynke, so lowde he wolde crien,
And stonden on his **typtoon** therwithal,   tiptoes
And strecche forth his necke, long and smal;
And eek he was of such **discressioun**   wisdom/prudence
That ther nas no man, in no regioun,
That him in song or wisdom mighte passe.
I have wel rad in Daun Burnel th'asse
Among his verses, how ther was a cok,
For a preste's sone gaf him a knok   because
550   Upon his leg whil he was yong and nyce,
He made him for to lese his benfice.[37]
But certeyn, ther is no comparisoun
Betwix the wisdom and discressioun
Of youre fader, and of his **subtilte**.   cleverness
Now syngeth, Sire for **Seinte Charite** –   holy charity
Let se: can ye your fader contrefete?'[38]
This Chaunteciere his wynges gan to bete,
As man that couthe his **tresoun** nought espye,   betrayal
So was he ravyssht with his flaterie.

36 Boethius also wrote on the subject of music.
37 A popular fable – the cock failed to crow, and thus the young man failed to get
   up in time.
38 'let's see if you're as good as your father'

Allas, Lordynges! Many a fals **flatour**   flatterer   560
Is in your hous, and many a **losengour**   liar
That pleasen yow wel more, by my faith,
Than he that sothfastnesse unto yow saith.
Redith Ecclesiast of flaterie;
Beth war, ye lordes of her treccherie.[39]
This Chaunteclere stood heihe upon his toos,
Strecching his necke, and his **yhen cloos**,   eyes closed
And gan to crowe lowde, for the noones,
And Daun Russel the fox stert up at oones,[40]
And by the **garget hente** Chaunteclere,   throat; siezed/grabbed   570
And on his bak toward the woode him bere,
For yit was there no man that him **sewed**.   pursued
O desteny, that maist not ben **eschiewed**!   avoided
Allas, that Chaunteclere fleigh fro the bemis!
Allas, his wif **ne roughte nought** of dremis!   set no value on
And on a Friday fel al this meschaunce – [41]
O Venus, that art god of **pleasaunce**,   pleasure
Syn that thy servant was this Chaunteclere,
And in thy service did al his powere,
More for delit, than the world to multiplie –   580
Why woldest thou suffre him on thy day to dye?
O Gaufred, dere mayster soverayn,
That whan the worthy king Richard was slayn[42]
With schot, **compleynedist** his deth so sore;   by an arrow; lamented
Why ne had I nought thy **sentence** and thy **lore**   knowledge and learning
The Friday for to **chiden**, as dede ye,   chide
For on a Fryday sothly slayn was he?
Than wold I schewe how that I couthe pleyne
For Chaunteclere's drede and for his peyne.
Certis, such cry ne lamentacioun   590
Was never of ladies maad whan Ilioun

39 Possibly the biblical Book of Proverbs, or the apocryphal book of Ecclesiasticus.
40 Russel, the name of Reynard's son in the Chanson de Renart. Although little
   remains of an English version of the tradition, church carvings reveal that it must
   have been very popular.
41 Friday was Venus's day.
42 Geoffrey of Vinsauf wrote an emotional poem about the death of Richard I of
   England, the 'Lionheart'.

Was wonne, and Pirrus with his strit swerd,

Whan he hente kyng Priam by the berd[43]

And slough him – as saith us Eneydos –

As maden alle the hennes in the **clos**   pen

Whan thay had **sayn** of Chauntecler the sight.   seen

But **soveraignly** Dam Pertelote **schright**   very loudly; shrieked

Ful lowder than did Hasdrubald's wyf

Whan that hir housebond had lost his lyf,

600   And that the Romayns had **y-brent** Cartage.   burned

Sche was so ful of torment and of **rage**,   madness

That **wilfully** unto the fuyr sche **stert**,   by her own will; leapt

And brend hirselven with a stedfast hert.

O woful hennes! Right so cride ye,

As whan that Nero brente the cite

Of Rome criden the senatours' wyves,

For that her housbondes losten all here lyves

Withouten gult – this Nero hath hem slayn –

Now wol I torne to my matier agayn.

610   The sely wydow and hir doughtres tuo

Herden these **hennys** crie and maken wo,   heard; hens

And out at **dores starte** thay anoon,   doors; ran

And sayden, 'The foxe toward the woode is goon

And **bar** upon his bak the cok away!'   carried

And criden, 'Out, harrow, and wayleway!

Ha! Ha! The fox!' and after him thay ran,

And eek with staves many another man.

Ran Colle, our dogge and Talbot, and Garlond,[44]

And Malkyn, with a distaf in hir hond.

620   Ran cow, and calf, and the verray **hogges**,   pigs

So were they fered **for** berkyng of dogges,   because of

And schowtyng of the men and wymmen eke.

Thay ronne that thay thought her herte breke;

Thay yelleden as **feendes** doòn in helle.   devils

The **dokes** criden **as** men wold hem **quelle**;   ducks; as if; kill

---

43 The death of Priam is recorded in Vergil's *Aeneid*.

44 Names for dogs: Talbot is also called a Gower, a fact which has given rise to the claim that this story is an attack on John Gower, a friend with whom Chaucer later quarrelled.

The **gees** for fere **flowen** over the trees;   geese; flew
Out of the hyves came the swarm of bees.
So hidous was the noyse, a benedicite!
Certes, though Jakke Straw and his meyne[45]
Ne maden schoutes never half so **schrille**   loud/piercing   630
Whan that thay wolden eny Flemyng kille,
As thilke day was maad upon the fox.
Of bras thay brought hornes, and of **box**,   boxwood
Of horn of boon, in which thay **schryked** and thay **powped** – [46]
And ther withal they shrieked and they howped -
It semed as that heven schulde falle –
Now goode men, I pray, herkneth alle.
Lo, how Fortune torneth sodeinly
The hope and pride eek of her enemy.
This cok, that lay upon this fox's bak,   640
In al his **drede** unto the fox he spak   fear
And saide, 'Sire, if that I were as ye,
Yet schuld I sayn, as wis God helpe me,
'Turneth agein, ye proude cherles alle!
A verray **pestilens** upon yow falle!   plague
Now I am come unto this wood's syde,
Maugre youre **hede**, the cok schal heer abyde!   despite; efforts
I wol him ete, in faith, and that anoon!"
The fox answerd, 'In faith, it schal be doon!'
And whil he spak that word, all sodeinly   650
This cok brak from his mouth **delyverly**,   nimbly
And heigh upon a tree he fleigh anoon.
And whan the fox seigh that he was y-goon,
'Allas!' quod he, 'O Chaunteclere, allas!
I have to yow,' quod he, 'y-don **trespas**!   wrong
Inasmoche as I makid yow aferd
Whan I yow hent, and brought out of the yerd!
But Sire, I ded it in no wicked entent!
Com doun, and I schal telle yow what I ment.

---

45 One of the pseudonyms for a leader of the Peasants' Revolt. One of the targets of
  the peasants when they reached London was the foreign community there, and
  the Flemings fared the worst – any Fleming who could not say 'bread and cheese'
  properly was killed.
46 shrieked; whooped

660 I schal say soth to yow, God help me so!'
'Nay than,' quod he, 'I **schrew** us bothe tuo –   *curse*
And first I schrew myself, bothe blood and boones,
If thou **bigile** me any ofter than oones!   *trick*
Thou schalt no more, thurgh thy flaterye,
Do me to synge and wynke with myn ye;   *make me*
For he that wynkith whan he scholde se
Al wilfully, God let him never the!'[47]
'Nay,' quod the fox, 'but God give him meschaunce
That is so **undiscret** of governaunce,   *unwise*
670 That **iangleth** whan he scholde holde his pees!'   *chatters*
Lo such it is for to be **recheles**   *careless*
And necgligent, and trust on flaterie.
But ye that holde this tale a folye
As of a fox, or of a cok, or of an hen –
Takith the **moralite**, goode men.   *moral meaning*
For Seint Poul saith that all that writen is,
To oure **doctrine** it is y-write, I wis.[48]   *teaching*
Takith the **fruyt** and let the **chaf be stille**.   *wheat; chaff; alone*
Now, goode God, if that it be thy wille –
As saith my lord – so make us all good men,
And bring us all to his blisse. Amen.

here endeth the tale of Chaunteclere and Pertelote

47 'may God let him never thrive'
48 'everything that is written, is written for our instruction'

THE PHYSICIAN'S TALE

The physician tells a story derived from Roman historian, Titus Livius. A knight called Virginius has a beautiful daughter called Virginia, a girl remarkable for her purity and her loving obedience to her father. One day she goes to the temple, where she is watched by the corrupt and lecherous governor, Apius. Apius decides to arrange matters so that he can fulfil his lust for her. He arranges for a servant of his, named Claudius, to present a petition claiming that Virginia is in fact his servant, who was stolen from his house when a child. Apius finds in favour of Claudius, and orders Virginia to be taken into his own 'safe' custody. Virginius goes home and tells Virginia that the only way to save her purity is to kill her. She bemoans her fate, then allows her father to cut off her head. Virginius takes the head to Apius, who orders Virginius to be hanged. However, the people intervene, Apius is sent to prison, where he kills himself, and Claudius, along with everyone else involved in the trial, is hanged. Virginius is exiled.

It is difficult to determine the precise purpose of this tale. The theme is clear: it is the story of Virginia, a beautiful, chaste girl, lusted after by a man in authority, who bends the law in order to possess her unlawfully. The girl's life is the price (demanded by her father) for the preservation of her virginity. The girl's name suggests that the main purpose of the tale is to stress the importance of virginity, and that she is a theme, rather than a real person. However, she is introduced as a factual figure by the narrator, who stresses that this tale is taken from the work of a historian, Titus Livius, hereby providing an authorisation for the narrator's apparent claim that it is better to die (or to be killed) than to be unchaste.

Because there is no attempt to make the characters appear real, there is less 'reality' in this historical tale than there is in the stories which do not claim to be anything other than fictive. Apius is the archetypal unjust judge, the tyrant who bends the law to his own will for his own pleasure, Viginius is the loving but firm father, Virginia the beautiful, loving and innocent daughter, and Claudius the eternal sycophant.

Virginia's character is the result of her upbringing, that is, she is the product of her father's own virtue, his ability to bring up a girl who requires no 'maistresse'. This may be why the story begins with an admonition to those with children in their care, to bring them up properly.

Virginia's virtue is a reflection of her father's, and if this is compromised she must be destroyed. As with the reeve's miller, the daughter is the father's 'tayl', and he is raped if she is. The tale is presented by the teller as an exemplum to instruct those who are charged with the bringing up of children. It may be that Chaucer is presenting the story as a warning against putting your own shame before the life of your child.

The ending of the story seems unsatisfactory. Who are 'the people' and why do they suddenly intervene? This seems like a *deus ex machina*, a plot device to round off the story and make sure that the villains are paid in kind. Ideas of pubic outrage and the *populus* enforcing natural justice had greater meaning in the classical, Roman, world than in the medieval. In medieval English literature, it is outlaw characters who enforce natural justice on abusers of office. The power of the 'punchline' seems to have been lost in translation. Interestingly, Virginius is also punished, and thus in the end all come to grief. It makes a depressing tale, as the host points out, and is perhaps better understood in terms of Boethius's *Consolation of Philosophy*, according to which the innocent suffer through no fault of their own, and humans are the victims of chance and circumstance. This makes it difficult to give the story a Christian meaning. There is no martyr's reward for Virginia; instead, stress is laid on Virginius's pain, and his stoic ability to sacrifice his own feelings in order to preserve his public virtue.

Key Questions

They have the same name: what is the nature of the relationship between Virginia and Virginius?

What is the meaning of this story, in the context of *The Canterbury Tales*?

Whose victim is Virginia? Does Virginius deserve his punishment, or not, or is he not punished enough?

What does this story 'say' about being a ruler? Being a father? Being a daughter?

As the pilgrims argue on hearing the story, was the sacrifice worth it?

Topic Keywords

Medieval law/ Boethius and philosophy/ medieval children and families/ medieval women/ saints' lives

Further Reading

Kenneth Bleeth, 'The Physician's Tale and Remembered Texts', *Studies in the Age of Chaucer*, 28, 2006, pp. 221–4

R. Howard Bloch, 'Chaucer's Maiden's Head: The Physician's Tale and the Poetics of Virginity', in *Chaucer: Contemporary Critical Essays*, edited by Valerie Allen and Aries Axiotis, New York, St Martin's Press, 1996, pp. 145–56

John Michael Crafton, ' "The cause of everiche maladye": A New Source of The Physician's Tale', *Philological Quarterly*, 84, 2005, pp. 259–85

Lianna Farber, 'The Creation of Consent in The Physician's Tale', *Chaucer Review*, 39, 2004, pp. 151–64

Angus Fletcher, 'The Sentencing of Virginia in The Physician's Tale', *Chaucer Review*, 34, 2000, pp. 300–8

Marta Harley, 'Last Things First in Chaucer's Physician's Tale: Final Judgement and the Worm of Conscience', *Journal of English and Germanic Philology*, 91, 1992, pp. 1–16

John Hirsh, 'Modern Times: The Discourse of The Physician's Tale', *Chaucer Review*, 27, 1993, pp. 387–95

Daniel Kempton, 'The Physician's Tale: The Doctor of Physic's diplomatic "cure" ', *Chaucer Review*, 19, 1984, pp. 24–38

Daniel T. Kline, 'Jephthah's Daughter and Chaucer's Virginia: The Critique of Sacrifice in The Physician's Tale', *Journal of English and Germanic Philology*, 107, 2008, pp. 77–103

Brian S. Lee, 'The Position and Purpose of The Physician's Tale', *Chaucer Review*, 22, 1987, pp. 141–60

Linda Lomperis, 'Unruly Bodies and Ruling Practices: Chaucer's Physician's Tale as Socially Symbolic Act', in *Feminist Approaches to the Body in Medieval Literature*, edited by Linda Lomperis and Sarah Stanbury, Philadelphia, University of Philadelphia Press, 1993, pp. 21–37

Jerome H. Mandel, 'Governance in The Physician's Tale', *Chaucer Review*, 10, 1976, pp. 316–25

Sandra Prior, 'Virginity and Sacrifice in Chaucer's Physician's Tale', in *Constructions of Widowhood and Virginity in the Middle Ages*, edited by Cindy Carlson and Angela Weisl, New York, St Martin's Press, 1999, pp. 165–80

Jay Rudd, 'Natural Law and Chaucer's Physician's Tale', *Journal of the Rocky Mountain Medieval and Renaissance Association*, 9, 1988, pp. 29–45

And here bygynneth the tale of the Doctor of Phisik

❦ Ther was, as telleth Thitus Lyvius,[1]
A knight that **cleped** was Virginius,   _called_
Fulfild of honours and of worthines,
And strong of frendes and of gret riches.
A doughter he hadde by his wyf,
And never ne hadde he **mo** in al his lyf.   _more_
Fair was this mayde, in excellent beaute
Above every **wight**, that men may se,   _person_
For nature hath with sovereyn **diligence**   _care_ 10
Y-formed hir in so gret excellence,
As though sche wolde say, 'Lo! I, Nature,
Thus can I forme and **peynte** a creature   _colour_
Whan that me lust – who can me **counterfete**? _like; copy_
Pigmalion nou_gh_t, though he alwey forge and bete
To **grave** or peynte, for I dar wel sayn   _sculpt_
Appollus Zepherus schulde wirche in vayn[2]
To grave, or paynte, or forge & bete,
If thay presumed me to counterfete.
For he that is the former principal[3]   20
Hath maad me his viker general,[4]
To forme and peynte erthely creature
Right as me lust; al thing is in my **cure**   _keeping_
Under the moone that may wane and waxe,
And for my worke nothing wol I **axe**;   _ask_
My Lord and I ben fully **at accord**.   _in agreement_
I made hir to the worschip of my Lord,
So do I all myn other creatures,
What colour that thay been, or what **figures**.' _form_
Thus semeth me that Nature wolde say.   30
This mayde was of age twelf **yer** and **tway**, _years; two_

1 Titus Livius, Roman historian.
2 Appelles and Zeuxis, Greek sculptor and painter.
3 The 'first mover' – God as the intial creator of everything.
4 Vicar general, or deputy.

In which that Nature hath suche delite;
For right as sche can peynte a lili white
And **rody** as rose, right with such peynture   red
Sche peynted hath this noble creature.
Er sche was born, upon hir **limes** fre   limbs
Were **als** bright as such colour schulde be,   as
And Phebus deyed hadde hire tresses grete[5]
Y-lyk to the **stremes** of his **borned** hete;   beams; burning
40   And if that excellent was hir beaute,
A thousand fold more vertuous was sche;
And hire ne lakketh no **condicioun**   quality
That is to preyse, as by **discrecioun**.   morals
As wel in body as **goost** chaste was sche,   spirit
For which sche floured in virginite
With all humilite and abstinence,
With all **attemperaunce** and pacience   moderation
With **mesure** eek of beryng, of **array**;   moderation; clothing
Discret sche was in answeryng alway.
50   Though sche wer wis as Pallas, dar I sayn,[6]
Hir **facound** eek ful wommanly and playn,   fashioned
Noon **countrefeted termes** hadde sche   pretended phrases
To seme wys, but after hir **degre**   station
Sche spak, and alle hire wordes, more and lesse,
Sounyng in vertu and in gentilesse.   tending towards
Schamefast sche was in mayden's schamfastnesse,   modest
Constant in hert and ever **in besynesse**   doing her best
To dryve hire out of hir **slogardy**.   inertia
Bachus had of hir mouth no **maistrye**,   control
For wille and thought doon Venus encrece,[7]
60   As men in fuyr wil caste **oyle** or **grece**;   oil; fat
And of hir **oughne** vertu unconstreigned   own
Sche hath ful ofte tyme hire **seek y-feyned**   sick; pretended
For that sche wolde fleen the companye,
Wher likly was to treten of folye,
As is at festes, reveles and at daunces,

---

5 Her hair was dyed by Phoebus (the sun); that is, it was the colour of the sun.
6 Pallas Athene, Greek goddess of wisdom.
7 Bacchus, god of wine and revelry, the consumption of which increases the
   tendency to Venus, or sexual desire.

That ben occasiouns of **daliaunces**. flirting
Such thinges maken children for to be
To soone **rype** and bold, as men may se; mature/nubile
Which is ful perilous, and hath ben **yore**, for a long while 70
For al to soone may sche lerne **lore** knowledge
Of boldenesse whan sche is a wyf;
And ye maistresses, in youre olde lyf[8]
That lord's doughtres han in governaunce,
Ne taketh of my word no **displesaunce**; offence
Thinges that ben set in governynges
Of lord's doughtres oonly for tuo **thinges** – reasons
Outher for ye han kept your honeste either
Other elles ye han falle in **frelete**, weakness/frailty
And knowe wel ynough the olde daunce, 80
And **conne** forsake fully meschaunce know how to
For evermo – therfore, for Crist's sake,
Kepeth wel **tho** that ye **undertake**. those; take on
A **theof** of **venesoun** that hath forlaft thief; venison
His **licorousnesse**, and al his theves craft, criminal tendencies
Can kepe a forest best of every man –
Now kepe hir wel, for **and ye wil ye can**. you can if you want to
Loke wel to no vice ye assent,
Lest ye be dampned for your wikked entent;
For who so doth, a traytour is certayn, 90
And taketh keep of that that I schal sayn;
Of al tresoun sovereyn pestilence
Is whan a wight bytrayeth innocence.
Ye fadres and ye modres eek also,
Though ye han children, be it oon or mo,
Youre is the charge of al her **sufferaunce** patience
Whiles thay be under your governaunce.
Beth war that by ensample of youre lyvynge,
Outher by necgligence in chastisynge or
That thay ne perische, for I dar wel seye 100
If that thay doon, ye schul fulsore abeye.[9]
Under a schepherd softe and necligent

8 Women with charge of children/minors.
9 'you'll sorely regret it'

The wolf hath many a schep and lamb **torent**.   torn apart
Sufficeth oon ensample, now as here,
For I **moot** turne agein to my matiere.   must
This mayde, of which I telle my tale expresse,
So kept hirself, hir neded no maystresse,
For in hir lyvyng maydens mighte rede
As in a book, every good word and dede
110   That **longeth** unto a mayden vertuous.   belongs
Sche was so prudent and so **bounteous**,   full of goodness
Forthe which **outsprong** on every syde,   shone out
Bothe of hir beaute and **bounte wyde**,   boundless goodness
That thurgh the lond thay praysed hir **ilkoone**   every one
That loveded vertu, save envye alloone
That sory is of other men's **wele**,   good fortune
And glad is of his sorwe and **unhele**.   misfortune
The doctor made this descripcioun:
This mayde wente upon a day into the toun
120   Toward the temple with hir moder deere,
As is of yonge maydenes the manere.
Now was ther a justice in the toun,
That governour was of that regioun,
And **so bifel** this juge his **eyyen** cast   it so happened; eyes
Upon this mayde, **avysing** hir ful fast   taking notice
As sche cam forby **ther** the juge stood.   where
Anoon his **herte** chaunged, and his mood,   feelings
So was he caught with beaute of this mayde,
And to himself ful prively he sayde,
130   'This mayde schal be myn, **for** any man.'   in spite of
Anoon the **feend** into his herte ran,   immediately; devil
And taughte him sodeinly by what **slighte**   sly trick
This mayde to his purpos wynne he mighte;
For certes, by no fors, ne by no **meede**   bribery
Him thought he was not able for to **speede**,   succeed
For sche was strong of frendes, and eek sche
Conformed was in such soverayn beaute
That wel he **wist** he might hir never wynne,   knew
As for to make hir with hir body synne;
140   For which with gret **deliberacioun**,   thought/consideration
He sent after a clerk that was in the toun,
The which he knew for subtil and for bold.

This juge unto the clerk his tale hath tolde
In secre wyse, and made him to assure
He schulde telle it to no creature;
And if he dede, he schulde **lese** his **heed**.   lose; head
Whan that assented was this cursed **reed**,   advice/counsel
Glad was the juge, and made glad cheere
And gaf him giftes, precious and deere
Whan **schapen** was al this conspiracye   formed   150
Fro poynt to poynt, how that his leccherie
Parformed scholde be, ful subtilly –
As ye schul **here** afterward openly –   hear
Hom goth this clerk, that **highte** Claudius.   was called
This false juge, that highte Apius –
So was his name, for it is no fable,
But knowen for a **storial** thing notable;   historical/factual
The sentence of hit **soth** is out of doute –   truly
This false jugge goth now fast aboute
To hasten his **delit** al that he may,   pleasure   160
And so fel soone after, on a day,
This false juge, as telleth us the story,
As he was wont, sat in his **consistory**,   as he usually did; court
And gaf his **domes** upon **sondry** caas.   judgements; various
This false clerk com forth **a ful good paas**   walking very quickly
And saide, 'Lord, if that it be your wille,
As doth me right upon this pitous bille,[10]
In which I pleyne upon Virgilius,
And if he wile seyn it is nought thus
I wil prove hit, and fynde good witnesse   170
That soth is, that my bille wol **expresse**.'   explain
The juge answerd, 'Of this in his absence
I may not give **diffinityf** sentence.   final/binding
Let do him calle and I wol gladly hiere;   have him called
Thou schalt have all right and no wrong heere.'
Virginius com to **wite** the jugge's wille,   know
And right anoon was red this cursed bille.
The sentence of hit was as ye schul heere:
'To yow, my Lord, Sire Apius so deere,

10 In this case, a complaint against Virginius, pleading for redress.

180 Scheweth youre pore servaunt Claudius
    How that a knight called Virginius,
    Ageins the lawe, agens all **equyte**,   fairness
    Holdeth **expresse** ageinst the wille of me   absolutely
    My servaunt which that my **thral** is by right,   servant/slave
    Which fro myn hous was stolen on a night
    Whiles sche was ful yong; that wol I **preve**   prove
    By witnesse, Lord, so that ye yow not greve.
    Sche is nought his dou*gh*ter, what so he say –
    Wherfore to yow, my Lord the jugge, I pray,
190 **Yelde** me my thrall, if that it be your wille.'   give
    Lo, this was al the sentence of the bille.
    Virginius gan upon the clerk byholde
    But hastily, **er** he his tale tolde,   before
    And wolde have proved it as schold a knight,
    And eek by witnessyng of many a wight,
    That al was fals that sayde his adversarie.
    This cursed juge wold no lenger **tarye**,   wait
    Ne heere a word more of Virginius,
    But *g*af his jugement, and saide thus:
200 'I **deme** anoon this clerk his servaunt have;   judge
    Thou schalt no lenger in thin hous hir have.
    Go, bringe hir forth and put hir in oure **ward** –   custody
    This clerk schal have his **thral**; thus I awarde.'   servant
    And whan this worthy knight Virgineus,
    Thurgh th'assent of this juge Apius,
    Moste by force his deere dou*gh*ter given
    Unto the juge, in lecchery to lyven,
    He goth him hom and sette him in his halle,
    And **leet** anoon his deere dou*gh*ter calle,   ordered
210 And with a face deed as **aisshen** colde,   ashes
    Upon hir humble face he gan byholde,
    With fadres pite **stiking** thorough his herte,   piercing
    Al wolde he from his purpos not **converte**.   turn away
    'Doughter,' quod he, 'Virginea by thy name,
    Ther ben tuo weyes – eyther deth or schame –
    That thou most suffre; allas, that I was bore!
    For never thou deservedest wherfore
    To deyen with a swerd or with a knyf!
    O deere doughter, ender of my lif,

Which I have **fostred** up with such **plesaunce** brought; delight 220
That thou **nere** oute of my remembraunce! were not (ne were)
O doughter, which that art my laste wo,
And in this lif my laste joye also!
O gemme of chastite, in pacience
Tak thou thy deth, for this is my sentence –
For love, and not for hate, thou must be **deed**; dead
My **pitous** hond **mot** smyten **of** thin heed. full of pity; must; off
Allas, that ever Apius the **say**! saw
Thus hath he falsly jugged the today!'
And told hir al the **caas**, as ye bifore situation 230
Han herd – it nedeth nought to telle it more.
'Mercy, deere fader!' quod this mayde,
And with that word sche bothe hir armes layde
Aboute his nekke, as sche **was want to** doo. used to
The teeres **brast** out of hir **eyyen** tuo, burst; eyes
And sayde, 'Goode fader, schal I dye?
Is ther no grace? Is ther no remedye?'
'No, certeyn, deere doughter myn,' quod he.
'Than geve me leve, fader myn,' quod sche,
'My deth for to compleyne a litel space; 240
For pardy, Jeffa gaf his doughter grace
For to compleyne er he hir **slough**, allas![11] slew/killed
And, God it woot, nothing was her trespas,
But that sche ran hir fader first to se,
To welcome him with gret solempnite.'
And with that word **aswoun** sche fel anoon, unconscious
And after, whan hir **swownyng** was agoon, fainting
Sche riseth up, and to hir fader sayde,
'Blessed be God that I schal deye a **mayde**! virgin
Geve me my deth er that I have a schame; 250
Do with your child your wille, **a God's name**!' in God's name
And with that word sche prayed him ful ofte
That with his swerd he schulde smyte hir softe;
And with that word **on swoune** doun sche fel. in a swoon
Hir fader, with ful sorwful hert and **fel**, dread

11 Jephtha offered to sacrifice whatever first came out of his house on his return, in
exchange for victory; it turned out to be his young daughter.

Hir heed of **smoot**, and by the top it **hente**,   struck; seized
And to the juge bigan it to presente
As he sat **in his doom** in concistory;   in judgement
And whan the juge it say, as saith the story,
260 He bad take him and **honge him faste**;   hung him right away
But right anoon all the poeple in **thraste**   pushed
To save the knight, for **routhe** and for pite,   pity
For knowen was the fals iniquite.
The poeple anoon **had suspect** in this thing   had their suspicions
By moner of this clerke's chalengyng,
That it was by th'assent of Apius,
That wiste wel that he was leccherous;
For which unto this Apius thay goon,
And casten him in prisoun right anoon,
270 Wheras he slough himself; and Claudius,
That servaunt was unto this Apius,
Was **demed** for to honge upon a tree –   judged
But Virgineus, of his grete pite,
Prayede for him that he was exiled,
And elles certes he had ben **bigiled**.   given up to die
The **remenaunt** were anhanged, more and lesse,   remainder
That were **consented to** this cursednesse.   agreed with
Her may men se how synne hath his **merite** –   deserts
Bewar, for no man woot how God wol **smyte**   strike
280 In no degre, ne in which maner wise
The worm of conscience wol **agryse**   cause fear to
Of wicked lyf, though it so **pryve** be,   secret
That no man **woot** of it but God and he;   knows
Wher that he be **lewed** man or **lered**,   whether; learned; unlearned
He not how soone that he may be **afered**.   afraid
Therfore I **rede** yow this counseil take: advise
Forsakith synne er synne yow forsake.

here endeth the Doctore of Phisic his tale

THE PARDONER'S PROLOGUE AND TALE

The host is overcome with pity for the fate of Virginia, so he asks the pardoner to tell a happier tale to prevent him from having a heart attack. The pardoner says that he will gladly: he must have a drink while he thinks, but the host refuses; he has had enough of drunken storytellers. The pardoner tells the pilgrims about his techniques in preaching, and how he manipulates his audiences into giving him money for faked and useless pardons and relics. He has absolutely no care for the fate of their souls, his objective being only to make money to spend on his own pleasures. His theme in preaching is 'radix omnium malorum est cupiditas', but he himself is preaching only for financial gain. He gives the other pilgrims an example of his preaching.

In Flanders, there is a group of young 'rioters', who love to whore, drink and gamble. While carousing and gambling one day, they hear a funeral bell. They tell the young boy at the tavern to go and find out what the trouble is. He says that it is the funeral of someone they knew, who has been killed by a sneak thief called Death. The three rioters swear to find and kill this person, Death. They go in search of Death, and on the way they meet an old man dressed in rags. He says that he has seen Death; in fact he would really love to die, but Death will not take him. When they abuse, threaten, and press him for an answer, he tells them that they will find Death nearby, under an oak tree. They find the tree, underneath which is a large pile of gold florins. They plan to remove the florins under the cover of darkness, or people will think they have stolen the money. They draw lots to see who will go into town to fetch food and drink to sustain them while they wait. The lot falls to the youngest of the three.

While he is gone, the other two plot to kill him when he returns, so that the gold need only be divided into two parts, instead of three. The youngest, however, wants all the gold for himself, so he buys poison from an apothecary (he says he wants to kill rats) and puts it into the drink of the other two. When he returns, they kill him and inadvertently drink the poison, and so they all find death.

The pardoner then launches into his 'sales pitch', offering pardons to the pilgrims in return for money. He suggests that the host might like to pay first, but the host becomes angry and suggests that he would rather cut off the pardoner's testicles, and enshrine them in a pig's turd. It seems that they may come to blows, but the knight steps in to resolve the quarrel. The host and the pardoner exchange a kiss of peace.

In response to the host's request for something to take his (and others') thoughts away from the miserable fate of Virginia, the 'gentils' in the group fear that the pardoner (after his request for ale first) is about to tell another bawdy tale based on fabliau. Although angered by the host's refusal, the pardoner complies with the wish of the majority, and selects a morally uplifting tale instead. The pardoner's tale is an exemplum, a small story illustrating a moral theme, inviting a moral response from its audience. They were frequently used in sermons, and so this one is particularly suitable for the pardoner, who makes his living by preaching.

The theme of the story, and of the entire performance of the pardoner, is *radix omnium malorum est cupiditas*, the desire for money is the root of all evil. Although the pardoner attacks avarice, drunkenness and gluttony, he loves food, drink and money. His prologue makes clear to the audience precisely how little he cares about the content of the sermons he preaches. Their purpose is marketing, rather than instruction.

Much scholarly criticism has centred upon the question of the pardoner's gender. He is described by 'Geoffrey' as 'a geldyng or a mare', leaving open the question that he may be a eunuch, or a homosexual (although this may simply refer to the high pitch of his voice). Harry Bailly's threat to cut off his testicles may be an ironic reference to his lack of them, or to the fact that they are useless for their natural function of begetting children. Once again, Chaucer surrounds this question with ambiguity. The term 'homosexual' did not exist in Medieval English; there was no understanding that this could be a state of being, rather than a single event, an act to be committed. Apart from veiled references, there was only the crime of sodomy, the penetration of one male by another. As distinct from the other tellers of tales, it is difficult to see who the pardoner actually is at all, because the character of the pilgrimage, and of the prologue, is a man created by his own narrative. The pardoner constructs himself in words, so that the inner man is not visible, if he exists at all. The pardoner may have assumed his role so completely that he *is* the part he plays, which would accord with his physical incompleteness.

Whether or not the pardoner actually believes in God at all is another debatable point. If the pardoner is his own construct, and therefore does not exist, and he is the representative of the Church, is the Church's doctrine simply a fabrication also? Is, therefore, God himself a fabrication? In a sense he is, of course, as he is created in biblical and liturgical narrative. Just as Death did not exist for the rioters until he was named, the pardoner can only exist as a product of his own words, or as a product of Chaucer's words. In the character of the pardoner, Chaucer may be alerting the audience to the nature of their relationship with him, the writer. The pardoner's revelations about himself, and his relationship with his audiences, are very uncomfortable for the pilgrims, as for the audience of *The Canterbury Tales* in general. The pardoner holds up before them their own superstitions, greed and credulity. He even believes that they will be so affected by his tale that they will buy his pardons. The tale is extremely seductive, and makes the audience forget what they have just been told about how false the pardoner actually is. It is a measure of his self-confidence, and the sheer 'brio' of his performance, that he anticipates this. The pardoner is offering instruments of transformation as false as the Philosopher's Stone of the alchemists. He is offering an alternative way for the pilgrims to turn their dross into gold. If they were actually to buy the pardoner's wares, then they would not need to go on pilgrimage at all, and in this way the pardoner threatens the very fabric of *The Canterbury Tales*.

Key Questions

Why is the pardoner described as 'angry'? Angry about/against what or whom – the host and the pilgrims, himself, society, God?

What motivates the pardoner, and how is this reflected in his prologue and tale?

Does the pardoner represent the later medieval Church, and if so, how? Is it the pardoner, or the Church he represents, which is abusive?

Topic Keywords

Saints and relics/ medieval Church/ popular religion/ medieval sexuality

Further Reading

Joanna Beall, 'Spiritual Gold: Verbal and Spiritual Alchemy in The Pardoner's Tale and The Canon's Yeoman's Tale', *Medieval Perspectives*, 15, 2000, pp. 35–41

Robert Boenig, 'Musical Irony in The Pardoner's Tale', *Chaucer Review*, 24, 1990, pp. 253–8

John M. Bowers, ' "Dronkenesse is ful of stryvyng": Alcoholism and Ritual Violence in Chaucer's Pardoner's Tale', *Journal of English Literary History*, 57, 1990, pp. 757–84

Glen Burger, 'Kissing the Pardoner', *The Modern Language Association of America*, 107, 1992, pp. 1143–56

Janette Dillon, 'Chaucer's Game in The Pardoner's Tale', *Essays in Criticism*, 41, 1991, pp. 208–21

Carolyn Dinshaw, 'Eunuch Hermeneutics', *English Literary History*, 55, 1988, pp. 27–51

Dewey R. Faulkner, *Twentieth-Century Interpretations of The Pardoner's Tale: A Collection of Critical Essays*, Englewood Cliffs, NJ, Prentice-Hall, 1973

Alan Fletcher, 'The Topical Hypocrisy of Chaucer's Pardoner', *Chaucer Review*, 25, 1990, pp. 110–26

Allen J. Frantzen, 'The Pardoner's Tale, the Pervert, and the Price of Order in Chaucer's World', in *Class and Gender in Early English Literature: Intersections*, edited by Britton J. Harwood and Gillian R. Overing, Bloomington, Indiana University Press, 1994, pp. 131–47

Richard Firth Green, 'The Pardoner's Pants (and Why They Matter)', *Studies in the Age of Chaucer*, 15, 1993, pp. 131–45

Thomas Hahn (preface) and Marilyn Sutton (ed.), *Chaucer's Pardoner's Prologue and Tale: An Annotated Bibliography 1900–1995*, Toronto, University of Toronto Press, 2000

Mary Hamel and Charles Merrill, 'The Analogues of The Pardoner's Tale and a New African Version', *Chaucer Review*, 26, 1991, pp. 175–83

Elizabeth R. Hatcher, 'Life without Death: The Old Man in Chaucer's Pardoner's Tale', *Chaucer Review*, 9, 1975, pp. 246–52

Fred Hoerner, 'Church Office, Routine and Self-Exile in Chaucer's Pardoner', *Studies in the Age of Chaucer*, 16, 1994, pp. 69–98

Bruce Johnson, 'The Moral Landscape of the Pardoner's Tale', in *Subjects on the World's Stage: Essays on British Literature of the Middle Ages and the Renaissance*, edited by David Allen and Robert White, Newark, NJ, University of Delaware Press, 1995, pp. 54–61

Masahiko Kanno, 'Word and Deed in The Pardoner's Tale', *Studies in Medieval English Language and Literature*, 5, 1990, pp. 45–55

Steven Kruger, 'Claiming the Pardoner: Toward a Gay Reading of Chaucer's Pardoner's Tale', *Exemplaria*, 6, 1994, pp. 115–39

Heather Masri, 'Carnival Laughter in The Pardoner's Tale', *Medieval Perspectives*, 10, 1995, pp. 148–56

Robert P. Merrix, 'Sermon Structure in The Pardoner's Tale', *Chaucer Review*, 17, 1983, pp. 235–49

Joseph R. Millichap, 'Transubstantiation in The Pardoner's Tale', *Bulletin of the Rocky Mountain Modern Language Association*, 28, 1974, pp. 102–8

Roy J. Pearcy, 'Chaucer's Amphibologies and the "Old Man" in The Pardoner's Tale', *English Language Notes*, 41, 2004, pp. 1–10

James F. Rhodes, 'Motivation in Chaucer's Pardoner's Tale: Winner Take Nothing', *Chaucer Review*, 17, 1982, pp. 40–61

Gudrun Richardson, 'The Old Man in Chaucer's Pardoner's Tale: An Interpretative Study of His Identity and Meaning', *Neophilologus*, 87, 2003, pp. 323–37

Robert Sturges, *Chaucer's Pardoner and Gender Theory: Bodies of Discourse*, New York, St Martin's Press, 1999

Robert G. Twombly, 'The Pardoner's Tale and Dominican Meditation', *Chaucer Review*, 36, 2002, pp. 250–69

Warren S. Walker, 'Chaucer's Pardoner's Tale: More African Analogues', *Notes and Queries,* (new series), 10, 1972, pp. 444–5

Muriel Whitaker, 'The Chaucer Chest and The Pardoner's Tale: Didacticism in Narrative Art', *Chaucer Review*, 34, 1999, pp. 175–89

And here bygynneth the prologe of the Pardoner

❦ Owre ost gan swere **as** he were **wood**:   as if; mad
'Harrow!' quod he, "By nayles and by blood!"[1]
This was a cursed thef, a fals justice!
As **schendful** deth as herte can devise   disgraceful/terrible
So falle upon his body and his bones!
The devel I **bykenne him**, al at oones!   recognise him as
Allas, to deere boughte sche hir beaute!
Wherfore I say, that alle men may se
That giftes of fortune, or of nature,   10
Ben cause of deth of many a creature.
Hir beaute was hir deth, I dar wel sayn.
Allas, so pitously as sche was slayn!
But trewely, myn owne maister deere,
This was a **pitous** tale for to heere.   pitiful
But **natheles**, pas over – this is no fors[2]   nevertheless
I pray to God so save thi gentil **corps**,   body
And every **boist** ful of thi **letuarie**!   container; medicine
God blesse hem, and Oure Lady, Seinte Marie!
So mot I then thou art a **propre** man,   real/manly   20
And **y-lik** a prelat, by Seint Runyan!'[3]   like
Sayde I wel, can I not **speke in terme**,   use jargon
But wel I **woot** thou dost myn herte **erme**.   know; harm
I have almost y-caught a **cardiacle**!   heart attack
By **corpus boones**, but I have **triacle**,   God's bones; medicine
Other elles a draught of moyst and corny ale,
Other but I hiere anoon a mery tale,   unless I hear
Myn hert is **brost** for pite of that mayde.   burst
Thow pardoner, thou **belamy**,' he sayde,   good friend
'Tel us a tale, for thou **canst** many oon.'   Know   30
'It schal be doon,' quod he, 'and that anoon.

---

1 Blood and nails; a reference to Christ's passion.
2 'let it pass, it doesn't matter'
3 Saint unknown: these may be malapropisms, mistakes on the host's part, or the
  host may simply be making them up.

But first,' quod he, 'her at this ale stake[4]
I wil first drynke, and byt on a cake.'
But right anoon the gentils gan to crie –
'Nay, let him tellen us no **ribaudye**!   lewdness
Tel us som moral thing, that we may **leere**.'   learn
'Gladly,' quod he, and sayde as ye schal heere.
'But in the cuppe wil I me bethinke
Upon som honest tale, whil I drinke.'[5]

40   *Narrat*

                                        he tells (his story)

❦ 'Lordyngs,' quod he, 'in chirche whan I preche,
I **peyne me** to have an **hauteyn** speche,   take pains; haughty/loud
And ryng it out as lowd as doth a belle;
For I **can al by rote** that I telle.   know by heart
My **teeme** is alway oon and ever was,   theme
Radix omnium malorum est cupiditas.[6]
First I pronounce whennes that I come,
And thanne my bulles schewe I, alle and some,[7]
Oure liege lord's seal upon my patent,[8]
50 That schewe I first, my body to **warent**;   authorise
That no man be so **hardy**, prest ne clerk,   bold
Me to **destourbe** of Crist's holy werk;   hinder
And after that than tel I forth my tales.
Bulles of popes and of cardynales,
Of patriarkes and of bisshops I schewe,
And in Latyn speke I wordes fewe,
To savore with my predicacioun;[9]
And for to **stere** hem to devocioun,   stir
Thanne schewe I forth my longe cristal stoones,
60 Y-crammed ful of **cloutes** and of boones;   rags

---

4 A pole with a green garland at the top; the sign of an inn.
5 'I'll think of an honest story in the cup, whilst I'm drinking'
6 'the love of money is the root of all evil'
7 Bulls are papal documents, so called from the lead bulla or seal, with which they
   were authorised.
8 Letters patent; a form of authorisation.
9 'to spice up my sermon'

Relikes thay ben, as wene thei echoon.[10]
Than have I in **latoun** a **schulder** boon,[11]
Which that was of an holy Jew's scheep:
'Good men,' say I, 'tak of my wordes keep –[12]
If that this boon be **waische** in eny welle,   washed
If cow, or calf, or scheep, or oxe swelle
That eny worm hath ete, or worm y-stonge,
Tak water of that welle and waisch his tonge,
And it is hool anoon – and forthermore   70
Of pokkes, and of scabbe, and every sore[13]
Schal every scheep be **hool** of this welle   healed
That drynketh a draught – tak heed **eek** what I telle.   also
If that the goode man that the beest **oweth**   owns
Wol every **wike**, er that the cok him croweth,   local area
Fastynge, drynke of this welle a draught –   fasting (without eating)
As **thilke** holy Jew oure eldres taught –   the same
His beestes and his **stoor** schal multiplie;   possessions
And, Sires, also it **kelith** jalousie –   kills
For though a man be ful in jalous rage,
Let make with this water his **potage**,   soup   80
And never schal he more his wyf **mystrist**,   distrust
Though he the **soth** of hir **defaute** wist;   truth; fault; know
Al hadde sche take prestes tuo or thre.   even if
Her is a **meteyn** eek, that ye may see –   mitten
He that his honde put in this metayn,
He schal have multiplying of grayn
Whan he hath sowen, be it whete or **otes**.   oats
So that ye offre pans, or elles grootes –[14]
And men and wommen, oon thing warn I yow –
If eny wight be in this chirche now   90
That hath doon synne orrible, that he
Dar nought for schame of it **schryven** be,[15]
Or ony womman, be sche yong or old,

10 'as each of them understands'
11 shoulder; latten (form of brass)
12 'pay attention to what I say'
13 Pox, or a disease characterised by pustules, and scabies. Both are diseases typical
   of sheep.
14 The groat was a coin, worth 4*d*. (about 2p) – a lot of money in the 1390s.
15 forgiven (after confession to a priest)

That hath y-maad hir housbond cokewold,[16]
Which folk schal have no power ne grace
To offre to my relikes in this place;
And who so **fint him** out of suche blame,   finds himself
Thay wol come up and offre, in God's name,
And I **assoile** hem, by the auctorite   grant forgiveness
100 Which that by bulle was y-graunted me
By this **gaude** have I wonne every yeer   trick
An hundred mark syn I was pardoner.
I stonde lik a clerk in my pulpit,
And whan the **lewed** poeple is doun **y-set**,   unlearned; sat
I preche so as ye have herd bifore,
And telle hem an hondred **japes** more –   jokes
Than peyne I me to strecche forth my necke,
And est and west upon the poeple I **bekke**   nod
As doth a **dowfe** syttyng on a **berne**.   dove; barn
110 Myn hondes and my tonge goon so **yerne**   quickly
That is it joye to se my busynesse.
Of avarice, and of such cursednesse
Is al my preching; for to make hem **fre**   generous
To geve here **pens**, and namely unto me;   pennies/money
For myn entent is nought but for to **wynne**,   gain
And nothing for correccioun of synne.
I **rekke** never when thay ben **y-beryed**   care; buried
Though that here soules gon **a-blakeberyed**!   blackberrying
For certes, many a **predicacioun**   sermon
120 Cometh ofte tyme of evel entencioun;
Som **for plesauns of folk** and flaterie,   to amuse people
To ben **avaunced** by ypocrisie,   furthered/promoted
And som for **veinegloir**, and som for hate;   vainglory
For whan I dar not other weys debate,
Than wil I stynge him with my tonge smerte
In preching, so that he schal not **asterte**   escape
To be diffamed falsly, if that he
Hath trespast to my bretheren or to me –
For though I telle not his **propre** name,   actual
130 Men schal wel knowe that it is the same

16 'made her husband a cuckold', i.e. committed adultery.

By signes, and by other circumstaunces –
Thus quyt I folk that doon us displesaunces.
Thus put I out my venym under **hiewe**   colour
Of holynes, to seme holy and trewe.
But schortly myn entent I wol **devyse**;   reveal
I preche nothing but of coveityse.
Therfor my teem is yit, and ever was:
Radix omnium malorum est cupiditas.
Thus can I preche agayn the same vice
Which that I use, and that is avarice;   140
But though myself be gulty in the synne,
Yit can I make other folk to **twynne**   turn away
From avarice, and soone to repent –
But that is not my principal entent.
I preche nothing but for coveitise;
Of this matier it ought ynough suffise.
Than telle I hem ensamples many oon
Of olde thinges, longe tyme agoon –
For lewed poeple loven tales olde,
Which thinges can thay wel report and holde.   150
What **trowe** ye, whiles I may preche   believe
And wynne gold and silver for I teche,
That I wil lyve in povert **wilfully**?   deliberately
Nay, nay – I thought it never trewely;
For I wol preche and begge in **sondry** londes;   various
I wil do no labour with myn hondes,
Ne make basketis, and lyve therby.
Bycause I wil nought begge **ydelly**,   in vain
I wol noon of th'apostles **counterfete**.   copy
I wol have money, wolle, chese and whete,   160
Al wer it geven of the prest's page,
Or of the porest wydow in a village
And schold hir children sterve for **famyn**.   hunger
Nay, I wol drinke licour of the wyn,
And have a joly wenche in every toun.
But herkneth, lordynges, in conclusioun:
Youre likyng is that I schal telle a tale,
Now have I dronk a draught of corny ale.
By God, I hope I schal telle yow a thing

170 That schal by resoun be at your liking.[17]
For though myself be a ful **vicious** man,　　　　　full of vices
A moral tale yit I yow telle can,
Which I am wont to preche for to **wynne**.　　　　make money
Now hold your pees – my tale I wol byginne.'

Narrat

　　　　　　　　　　　　　　　　　　　he tells (his story)

🍃 In Flaundres **whilom** was a companye　　　some time ago
Of yonge folkes, that haunted folye,
As ryot, hasard, stywes, and tavernes,[18]
Wheras with lutes, harpes, and gyternes[19]
180 Thay daunce and play at **dees**, bothe day & night,　　dice
And ete also, and drynk **over her might**;　　over their limit
Thurgh which thay doon the devyl sacrifise
Whithinne the devel's temple, in cursed wise,
By superfluite abhominable.
Her othes been so greet and so dampnable,
That it is grisly for to **hiere** hem swere;　　　hear
Our blisful Lord's body thay **to-tere** –　　　rend
Hem thoughte Jewes rent hem nought ynough –
And ech of hem at other's synne **lough**.　　　laughed
190 And right anoon ther come **tombesteris**,　　dancing girls
Which that ben verray the devel's officeres,
To kyndle and blowe the fuyr of leccherie,
That is **anexid** unto glotonye.　　　　　　joined
The holy wryt take I to my witnesse,
That luxury is in wyn and dronkenesse.
Lo, how that dronken Loth, unkyndely[20]
Lay by his doughtres tuo, unwityngly –
So dronk he was he niste what he wrought.[21]
Herodes, who so wel the story sought,
200 Whan he of wyn was **repleet** at his fest,　　　full

---

17 'you will enjoy it'
18 'disorderly behaviour, gambling, bathhouses and taverns'. The bathhouse was frequented by prostitutes, and is therefore also means 'brothel'.
19 Stringed instruments.
20 Lot had sexual intercourse with his own daughters when drunk.
21 'he didn't know what he was doing'

Right at his **oughne** table gaf his **hest**   own; order
To sle the baptist John, ful gilteles.[22]
Seneca seith a good word, douteles:[23]
He saith he can no difference fynde
Betwyx a man that is out of his mynde
And a man the which is **dronkelewe**,   dead drunk
But that **woodnes** fallen in a **schrewe**   madness; evil person
Persevereth lenger than doth dronkenesse.   lasts
O glutonye, ful of corsidnesse!
O cause first of oure confusioun!   210
O **original** of oure dampnacioun,   originator
Til Crist had bought us with his blood agayn!
Lo, how dere, schortly for to sayn,
Abought was first this cursed felonye!   paid for
Corupt was al this world for glotonye!
Adam, our fader, and his wyf also,
Fro Paradys to labour and to wo[24]
Were dryven for that vice, it is no drede;
For whils that Adam fasted, as I rede,
He was in Paradis; and whan that he   220
Eet of the fruyt **defendit** of a tre,   forbidden
He was out cast to wo and into peyne.
O glotony! Wel ought us on the pleyne![25]
O, **wist a man** how many **maladyes**   if a man knew; ills
Folwith of excess and of glotonyes,
He wolde be the more **mesurable**   moderate
Of his diete, sittyng at his table!
Allas, the schorte throte, the tendre mouth,
Maketh that Est, West, North and South,
In erthe, in watir, in ayer, man to swynke,   230
To gete a sely glotoun mete and drynke!
Of this matier, O **Poul**, wel canstow **trete**;   Saint Paul; talk about
Mete unto wombe, and wombe unto mete,

22 Herod offered the dancer Salome anything she wanted, and she asked for the
   head of John the Baptist on a plate. Having given his word, Herod had to give the
   head.
23 From Seneca's Epistolae (letters).
24 The Pardoner interprets the fall of Adam as being driven by gluttony, a desire to
   eat for its own sake which made him eat the forbidden fruit.
25 'we have good reason to moan about you'

Schal God destroyen bothe, as Powel saith.
Allas, a foul thing it is, by my faith,
To say this word; and fouler is the dede,
Whan men so drynke of the whyt and rede
That of his throte he makith his **prive**,   toilet
Thurgh thilke cursed **superfluite**.   excess

240 Th'apostil, wepyng, saith ful pitously,
Ther walkith many of which you told have I –
I say it now wepyng, with pitous vois –
Thay are enemys of Crist's **croys**,   cross
Of which the ende is deth; **wombe** is her god.   belly
O wombe! O bely! O, stynkyng is thi **cod**!   bag
Fulfild of dong and of corrupcioun –
At eyther ende of the, foul is the **soun**!   sound
How gret cost and labour is the to **fynde**!   provide for
These **cokes**, how they stamp, and streyn, and grynde,[26]   cooks

250 And torne substaunce into accident[27]
To fulfille thy **licorous talent**.   lecherous gift
Out of the harde boones gete thay
The **mary**, for thay caste nought away   marrow
That may go thurgh the **golet**, softe and **soote**,   gullet; sweet
Of spicery and **levys**, barke and roote,   leaves
Schal ben his sauce maad to his delyt,
To make him have a **newe** appetit;   fresh
But certes, he that haunteth suche **delices**   delights
Is deed, ther whiles that he liveth in vices.

260 A licorous thing is wyn and dronkenesse,
Is ful of **stryvyng** and of wrecchednesse.   strife
O dronke man, disfigured is thi face!
Sour is thi breth, foul **artow** to embrace!   you are
And thurgh thi dronkenesse **sowneth** the soun,   sounds
As though thou seydest ay, 'Sampsoun, Sampsoun!'
And yit, **God wot**, Sampson drank never wyn.[28]   God knows

---

26 Much medieval cuisine consisted of highly-spiced, pulverised meat.
27 The substance of a thing is its essence, what it is in reality. The accident is the
   earthly form that it takes. This argument was the basis of the theology of the
   Mass: what appeared to be bread and wine (accident) was in fact the body and
   blood of Christ (substance). This line is, therefore, ambiguous.
28 As a Nazarite, Sampson was forbidden strong drink.

Thow fallist as it were a **stiked swyn**.	slaughtered pig
Thy tonge is lost, and al thin **honest cure**,	self respect
For dronkenes is verray **sepulture**	tomb
Of mannes witt, and his discrecioun,	270
In whom that drynk hath dominacioun –	
He can no **counseil** kepe, it is no drede.	secret

Now keep yow from the white and from the rede,
Namely fro the white wyn of Leepe
That is to selle in Fleetstreet or in Chepe;[29]

| This wyn of Spayne **crepith subtily** | is an adulterate |

In other wynes growyng faste by,

| Of which ther riseth such **fumosite** | fumes |

That whan a man hath dronke draughtes thre,

| And weneth that he be at hom in Chepe, | 280 |

He is in Spayne, right at the toun of Lepe,
Nought at the Rochel, ne at Burdeaux toun –
And thanne wol thai say, 'Sampsoun, Sampsoun!'

| But **herken** lordyngs, o word I you pray, | listen |
| That alle the soverayn actes, **dar I say**, | I dare say |

Of victories in the Olde Testament,
That thorugh the verray God omnipotent
Were doon in abstinence, and in prayere –

| Lokith the Bible and ther ye may it **hiere**. | hear |
| Loke Atthila, the grete conquerour[30] | 290 |

Deyd in his sleep with schame and dishonour,
Bleedyng ay at his nose in dronkenesse;
A captyn schuld ay lyve in sobrenesse.

| And over al this **avyse yow right wel** | take careful note |

What was comaunded unto Lamuel –[31]
Nought Samuel, but Lamuel say I;
Redith the bible and fyndeth expresly –

| Of wyn gevyng to hem that **han justice**; | sit in judgement |

No more of this, for it may wel suffice;

---

29 Mercantile areas of London, where wine was sold. Wine of Lepe is Spanish wine, used to adulterate more expensive varieties before sale. As the son of a vintner and a customs officer, Chaucer would be well aware of these sharp practices. Fine wine was exported from La Rochelle (Brittany) and Bordeaux (Gascony).

30 Atilla the Hun.

31 He had two wives at the same time.

300	And now I have spoke of glotonye,	
	Now wil I yow **defende hasardrye**.	forbid games of chance
	Hasard is verray moder of **lesynges**,	lies
	And of deceipt, of cursed **forsweringes**;	swearing oaths
	Blaspheme of Crist manslaught, and wast also	
	Of catel and of tyme; and forthermo	
	It is reproef and **contrair** of honour	opposite
	For to be halde a comun hasardour,	
	And ever the heyer he is of **astaat**,	rank
	The more is he holden **desolaat**.	of less worth
310	If that a prince use hasardrie	
	In alle governance and policie,	
	He is, as by comun opinioun,	
	Holde the lasse in reputacioun.	
	Stilbon, that was **y-holde** wis **embasitour**,[32]	
	Was sent into Corinthe with gret honour[33]	
	Fro Lacidome, to make hir alliaunce;	
	And whan he cam, him happede, **par** chaunce,	by
	That alle the grettest that were of that lond	
	Playing atte hasard he hem fond,	
320	For which, as soone as it mighte be,	
	He stal him hoom agein to his contre;	
	And saide, 'Ther I nyl nought lese my name;[34]	
	I nyl not take on me so gret **diffame**	dishonour
	Yow for to allie unto noon hasardoures.	
	Sendeth **otherwise** embasitoures,	other
	For by my trouthe **me wer lever dye**,	I would rather die
	Than I yow scholde to hasardours allye;	
	For ye that ben so glorious in honoures	
	Schal not allie yow with hasardoures	
330	As by my wil, ne as by my **trete**,'	agreement
	This wise philosophre, thus said he.	
	Lo, eek that the King Demetrius,	
	The king of Parthes, as the saith us,	
	Sent him a paire **dees** of gold in scorn,	dice

---

32 believed to be; ambassador

33 These two examples derive from the *Policraticus*, a treatise on good government written by John of Salisbury (a supporter of Thomas Becket) in the late twelfth century.

34 'I don't want to lose my reputation'

For he had used tavern ther toforn,[35]
For which he heild his **gloir** and his renoun   glory
At no valieu or reputacioun.
Lordes may fynde other maner play
Honest ynough to dryve away the day.
Now wol I speke of othes, fals and grete,   340
A word or tuo – as other bookes entrete.
Gret swering is a thing abhominable,
And fals swering is more **reprovable**.   blameworthy
The hyhe God forbad sweryng at al –
Witnes on Mathew, but in special
Of sweryng saith the holy **Jeremye**:   Jeremiah
'Thou schalt say **soth** thin othes, and not lye;   truth
And swere in **doom**, and eek in **rightwisnes**.' judgement; righteousness
But ydel sweryng is a cursednes;
Bihold, and se ther in the firste table   350
Of hihe God's **heste** honurable,   commandment
How that the secounde heste is this;
'Tak not in ydel, ne his name amys.'
Lo, he rather forbedith such sweryng
Than homicide, or many a corsed thing.
I say as by order thus it stondith;
This knoweth he that the hestes understondeth,
How that the second hest of God is that –
And forthermore I wol the telle **a plat**,   plainly
The vengance schal not parte fro his hous   360
That of his othes is outrageous.
By God's precious hert, and by his nayles,
And by the blood of Crist that is in Hayles,[36]
'Seven is my **chaunce**, and also **cink** and **tray** – call; five; three
By God's armes, and thou falsly play
This daggere schal thurgh thin herte goo!'
This fruyt cometh of **the blicchid boones tuo**:   pair of dice
Forswering, **ire**, falsnes, homicide.   anger
Now, for the love of Crist that for us dyde,
Leveth youre othis, bothe gret and smale –   370

---

35 'because he had indulged in tavern behaviour'
36 The Holy Blood of Hailes was possessed by the abbey of Hailes in Gloucestershire,
   and was one of England's most famous sites of pilgrimage.

But Sires, now wol I telle forth my tale.
These riottoures thre, of which I you telle,
Longe **erst than prime rong** of eny belle,   before 6 am.
Were set hem in a tavern for to drynke;
And as thay sat, thay herd a belle **clinke**   ring
Biforn a **corps** was caried to the grave,   corpse/body
That oon of hem gan calle unto his **knave**:   servant (male)
'Go bet,' quoth he, 'and **axe** redily   ask
What corps is, that passeth her forth by –
380   And loke thou report his name wel.'
'Sire,'quod he, 'but that nedeth **never a del**;   not at all
It was me told er ye com heer tuo houres.[37]
He was, pardy, an old **felaw** of youres;   companion
And sodeinly he was y-slayn tonight.
Fordronk as he sat on his bench upright,   'plastered'
Ther com a **prive thef** men **clepen** deth,   sneak thief; call
That in this **contre** al the peple **sleth**,   region; kills
And with his spere he smot his hert a-tuo,
And went his way withoute wordes mo.
390   He hath a thousand slayn this pestilence –
And maister, er ye come in his presence,
Me thinketh that is is ful necessarie
For to bewar of such an adversarie.
Beth redy for to meete him evermore;
Thus taughte me my **dame**, I say nomore.'   mother
'By Seinte Mary,' sayde the taverner,
'The child saith soth, for he hath slayn this yeer
Hens over a myle, withinne a gret village,   a mile away from here
Bothe man and womman, child and page.
400   I **trowe** his habitacioun be there;   believe
To **ben avysed** gret wisdom it were,   take care
Er that he dede a man that dishonour.'
'Ye, God's armes!' quod this ryottour,
'Is it such peril with him for to meete?
I schal him seeke, by way and eek by strete!
I make avow to God's **digne** boones –   worthy
Herkneth felaws, we thre ben al oones![38]

37 'two hours before you got here'
38 'we three are all one'

Let ech of us hold up his hond to other,
And ech of us bycome other's brother'
And we wil slee this false traitour deth.   410
He schal be slayne, that so many sleeth –
By God's dignete – er it be night!'
Togideres han these thre **here trouthes plight**   given their word
To lyve and deye ech of hem with other,
As though he were his oughne sworne brother;
And up thai **startyn**, al dronke in this rage,   leapt
And forth thai goon towardes that village
Of which the taverner hath spoke biforn,
And many a **grisly** oth than han thay sworn,   dreadful
And Crist's blessed body thay torent –   420
Deth schal be deed, if that thay **may him hent**.   may grab him
Right as thay wolde have torned over a style,
Whan thai han goon nought fully a myle,
An old man and a pore with hem mette.
This olde man ful mekely hem **grette**,   greeted
And saide thus: 'Lordynges, **God yow se!**'   God keep you
The proudest of the ryotoures thre
Answerd agein, 'What, **carle**! With **meschaunce**!   churl; ill luck
Why artow al **forwrapped** save thi face?   bandaged up
Whi lyvest thou in so gret an age?'   430
This olde man gan loke on his **visage**,   face
And saide thus: '**Or** that I cannot fynde   because
A man, though that I walke into Inde,
Neither in cite noon, ne in village
That wol chaunge his youthe for myn age;
And therfore **moot** I have myn age stille,   must
As long tyme as it is God's wille
And deth, allas, ne wil not have my lif.
Thus walk I lik a resteles **caytif**,   wretch
And on the ground, which is my modre's gate,   440
I knokke with my staf, erly and late,
And saye, '**Leeve** moder, let me in!   dear
Lo, how I **wane** – fleisch and blood and skyn!   fade away
Allas, whan schuln my boones ben at rest!
Moder, with yow wil I chaunge my chest –³⁹

39 'I'll give you all my possessions'

That in my chamber longe tyme hath be –
Ye, for an haire **clout** to wrap in me!   shirt
But yet to me sche wil not do that grace;
For which ful pale and **welkid** is my face.   withered
450 But Sires, to yow it is no curtesye
To speke unto an old man vilonye,
But he trespas in word or elles dede;
In holy writ ye may yourself wel rede,
'Agens an old man, **hoor** upon his hede,   white
Ye schold **arise**;' wherfor I yow **rede** –   get up; advise
Ne doth unto an old man more harm now,
Namore than ye wolde men dede to yow
In age, if that ye may so long abyde –
And God be with you, wherso ye go or ryde;
460 I moot go thider as I have to goo.'[40]
'Nay, olde cherl, by God, thou schalt not so!'
Sayde that other hasardour anoon,
'Thou **partist** nought so lightly, by Seint John!   depart
Thou spak right now of that traitour deth,
That in this contre all oure frendes sleth.
Have her my **trouth**, as thou art his **aspye** –   word; spy
Tel wher he is, or elles thou schalt dye
By God, and by that holy sacrament;
For **sothy** thou art oon of his **assent**,   truly; party
470 To schewe us yonge folk the false theef.'
'Now Sires, than if that yow be so **leef**   desirous
To fynde deth, torn up this croked way;
For in that grove I **laft** him, by my **fay**,   left; faith
Under a tree; and ther he wil **abyde**,   remain
Ne for your **bost** he nyl him nothing hyde.   boast
Se ye that **ook**; right ther ye schuln him fynde.   oak
God save yow, that bought agein mankynde –
And yow amend.' Thus sayde this olde man,
And everich of these riotoures ran
480 Til thay come to the tre, and ther thay founde
Of florins fyn of gold y-coyned rounde[41]

40 'I must go where I have to go'
41 Flemish gold coins worth three English shillings. A busshel is a large measure;
    there were lots of gold coins.

Wel neygh a seven busshels, as me thought.
No lenger thanne after deth thay sought,
But ech of hem so glad was of that sight –
For that the florens so faire were and bright –
That doun thai sette hem by that precious hord.
The yongest of hem spak the firste word:
'Bretheren, **taketh keep** what I schal say;   listen carefully
My **witte** is gret, though that I **bourde** and play.   cunning; revel
This tresour hath Fortune to us given,
In mirth and jolyte our lif to lyven;   490
And **lightly** as it comth, so wil we spende.   easily
Ey, God's precious dignite! Who **wende**   would think
Today that we schuld have so fair a grace?
But might this gold be caried fro this place
Hom to myn hous, or ellis unto youres –
For wel I **wot** that this gold is nou*gh*t oures –   know
Than were we in **heyh felicite**.   great happiness
But trewely, by day it may not be;
Men wolde say that we were theves strong,
And for oure tresour **doon** us for to honge.   order   500
This tresour moste caried be by night,
As **wysly** and as slely as it might.   carefully
Wherfore I **rede** that **cut among us alle**   advise; we draw lots
We drawe, and let se wher the cut wil falle.
He that hath the cut, with herte blithe,
Schal renne to the toun and that ful **swithe**,   immediately
And bring us bred and wyn ful prively,
And tuo of us schal kepe subtilly
This tresour wel, and if he wil not tarie,
Whan it is night we wol this tresour carie   510
By **oon assent**, ther as us liketh best.'   agreement
That oon of hem the cut brought in his **fest**,   happiness
And bad hem drawe, and loke wher it wil falle –
And it fel on the yongest of hem alle;
And forth toward the toun he went anoon,
And also, soone as he was agoon,
That oon of hem spak thus unto that other:

'Thow **wost** wel that thou art my sworne brother –   know
Thy profyt wol I telle the anoon.
520   Thow wost wel that our felaw is agoon,
And her is gold, and that ful gret plente,
That schal **departed** be among us thre;   divided
But natheles, if I can **schape** it so   arrange
That it departed were bitwix us tuo,
Had I not doon a frende's torn to the?'
That other answerd, 'I **not** how that may be.   do not know (ne wot)
He wot wel that the gold is with us **tway**.   two
What schulde we than do? What schuld we say?'
'Schal it be **counsail**,' sayde the ferste **schrewe**,   secret; evil person
530   'And I schal telle the in wordes fewe
What we schul doon, and bringe it wel aboute.'
'I graunte,' quod that other, 'withoute doute
That, by my trouthe, I wil the nought **bywray**.'   betray
'Now,' quod the first, 'thou wost wel we ben tway,
And two of us schuln strenger be than oon.
Lok, whanne he is sett, and that anoon,
Arys as thou woldest with him pleye,
And I schal **ryf** him thurgh the sydes tweye   stab
Whils thou strogelest with him, as in **game**;   play
540   And with thi dagger loke thou do the same,
And than schal al the gold departed be
My dere frend, bitwixe the and me.
Than may we oure lustes fulfille,
And play at dees right at our owne wille.'
And thus accorded ben these schrewes twayn
To sle the thridde, as ye herd me sayn.
This yongest, which that wente to the toun,
Ful fast in hert he rollith up and doun[42]
The beaute of the florins, newe and bright.
550   'O Lord,' quod he, 'if so were that I might
Have al this gold unto my self alloone,
Ther is no man that lyveth under the **troone**   throne (God's)
Of gold that schulde lyve so mery as I.'
And atte last the **feend**, our enemy,   devil
Put in his thought that he schuld poysoun **beye**   buy

42 'he turned over and over in his mind'

With which he mighte sle his felaws tweye.
For why? The feend fond him in such lyvynge
That he had leve to sorwe him to brynge,[43]
For this **witterly** was his entent.   entirely
To **sleen** hem both and never to repent,   kill   560
And forth he goth, no lenger wold he **tary**,   wait
Into the toun, unto a **potecary**;   apothecary (chemist)
And prayde him that he him wolde selle
Som poysoun, that he might his rattis **quelle**;   kill
And **eek** ther was a **polkat** in his **hawe**   also; polecat; yard
As he sayde, his **capouns** had **y-slawe**;   capons; killed
And said he wold him **wreke**, if that he might,   avenge
On vermyn that destroyed him by night.
Th'apotecary answerd, 'And thou schalt have
A thing that also – God my soule save –   570
In al this world ther nys no creature
That ete or dronk had of this **confecture**   mixture
Nought but the **mountaunce** of a **corn** of whete,   amount; grain
That he ne schuld his lif anoon **forlete**.   give up/lose
Ye, **sterve** he schal, and that in lesse while   die
Than thou wilt goon a paas not but a myle,[44]
The poysoun is so strong and violent.'
This cursed man hath in his hond **y-hent**   grabbed
This poysoun in a box, & **sith** he ran   then
Into the nexte stret, unto a man,   580
And borwed of him large botels thre;
And in the two his poysoun poured he –
The **thrid** he keped clene for his drynke;   third
For al the night he **schop him for to swynke**   intended to work
In carying the gold out of that place.
And whan this riotour, with sory grace,
Hath fillid with wyn his botels thre,
To his felaws agein **repaireth** he.   went back
What nedith it to sermoun it more?
For, right as thay had **cast** his deth bifore,   planned   590
Right so thay han him slayn, and that **anoon**.   immediately

43 'the devil found such a manner of living in him, that he was permitted to bring
   him down'
44 'quicker than you can walk a mile'

And whan this was y-doon, than spak that oon:
'Now let us drynk, and sitte an make us mery;
And **siththen** we wil his body bery.'   afterwards
And afterward it happed hem, **par cas**,   by chance
To take the botel ther the poysoun was;
And drank, and gaf his felaw drink also,
For which thay **sterved** bothe tuo.   died
But certes, I suppose that Aumycen[45]
600   Wrot never in canoun, ne in non **fen**,   chapter
Mo **wonder sorwes** of empoisonyng –   marvellous pains
Thus hadde these wrecches tuo here endyng.
Thus endid been these homicides tuo,
And eek the fals empoysoner also.
O cursed synne, ful of cursednesse!
O traytorous homicidy! O wikkednesse!
O glotony, luxurie, and hasardrye!
Thou blasphemour of Crist, with vilanye
And othes grete of usage and of pride!
610   Allas, mankynde, how may it bytyde
That to thy creatour which that the **wrought**   made
And with his precious herte blood thee bought,
Thou art so fals and so unkynde, allas?
Now good men, God forgeve yow your **trespas**;   sin
And **ware yow** fro the synne of avarice.   beware of
Myn holy pardoun may you alle **warice**,   save
So that ye offren noblis or starlinges,[46]
Or elles silver spones, broches, or rynges.
Bowith your **hedes** under this holy bulle –   bend; heads
620   Cometh forth, ye wyves, and offreth your **wolle**!   wool
Your names I entre her in my rolle anoon;
Into the blis of heven schul ye goon!
I yow **assoile** by myn heyh power,   forgive
If ye woln **offre** – as **clene** and eek als cler   make an offering
As ye were born; and Sir, lo, thus I preche;[47]
And Jhesu Crist that is our soule's **leche**   doctor

---

45 Avicenna, an authority on medicine.
46 A noble was an English gold coin, worth six shillings and eight pence: 'starling'
refers to something common and small, so 'give me a lot or a little'.
47 'I'll make you as pure and sinless as the day you were born'

So graunte yow his pardoun to receyve –
For that is best; I wol yow not deceyve.
But Sirs, o word forgat I in my tale –
I have relikes and pardon in my **male**   bag   630
As fair as eny man in Engelond,
Which were me y geve by the pope's hond.
If eny of yow wol, of devocioun,
Offren and have myn absolucioun,   absolution
Cometh forth anon, and knelith her adoun,
And ye schul have her my pardoun;
Or elles takith pardoun as ye **wende**,   go
Al newe and freissch at every town's ende;
So that ye offren, alway new and newe,
Nobles and pens, which that ben good and trewe.[48]   640
It is an honour to **every** that is heer,   everyone
That ye may have a **suffisaunt** pardoner   sufficient
T'assoile yow **in contre**, as ye ryde,   on the way
For **aventures** which that may bytyde;   happenings
For **paraunter** ther may falle oon or tuo   perhaps
Doun of his hors, and breke his nekke **a-tuo**.   in two
Loke such a **seurete** is to you alle,   security
That I am in your felaschip y-falle,
That may assoyle you, bothe more and lasse,
Whan that the soule schal fro the body passe.   650
I **rede** that oure hoste schal bygynne,   suggest
For he is most **envolupid** in synne –   enveloped/wrapped
Com forth, Sir Ost, and offer first, anoon;
And thou schalt kisse the reliquis **everichoon**!   each one
Ye, for a grote **unbocle thi purs**!'   undo your purse
'Nay, nay,' quod he, 'than have I Crist's curs!
Let be,' quod he, 'it schal not be, **so theech** –   so may I prosper
Thou woldest make me kisse thin olde breech,[49]
And swere it were a relik of a seynt,
Though it were with thi foundement depeynt![50]   660

48 A noble was a (rare) gold coin.
49 A possible reference to Becket's breeches, which were an object of veneration at
   Canterbury.
50 'though it were smeared with your own faeces'

But by the cros which that Seynt Heleyn fond,[51]
I wold I had thy **coylons** in myn hond   testicles
In stede of reliks, or of **seintuary** –   saints' relics
Let cut hem of! I wol help hem to cary –
Thay schul be schryned in an hogges tord!'[52]
This pardoner answerde nat o word,
So **wroth** he was, he wolde no word say.   angry
Now quod oure host, 'I wol no lenger play
With the, ne with noon other angry man.'

670 But right anoon, this worthy knight bygan,
Whan that he saugh that al the peple lough:
'No more of this, for it is right ynough!
Sir Pardoner, be glad and mery of cheere!
And ye, Sir Host, that ben to me so deere –
I pray yow that ye kisse the pardoner!
And pardoner, I pray yow, draweth yow ner;
And as we dede, let us laugh and play.'
Anon thay kisse, and riden forth her way.

Here endeth the pardonere's tale

---

51 St Helena, mother of the emperor Constantine, was said to have discovered the
cross of Christ in Rome.
52 'enshrined in a pig's turd'

THE SECOND NUN'S TALE

The second nun gives a short sermon on the avoidance of idleness. She will give an example of this in the life of Cecilia. She calls upon the Virgin Mary to help her, and defines the meanings of the word 'Cecilia'.

Cecilia is a noble Roman girl, a faithful Christian who wishes to remain a virgin, although she must marry, in accordance with custom. She tells her new husband, Valerian, that she has an angel who loves her, and that he will be able to see the angel, too, if he visits Pope Urban in the catacombs. Valerian does this, and an old man appears, who gives Valerian a book about the Christian faith to read. As a result of this encounter, Valerian is converted. Returning home, he meets Cecilia with an angel, who gives them each a crown of sweet-smelling roses and lilies to wear. Valerian tells his brother Tiburce about Christ. Tiburce also goes to see Urban, and is converted to Christianity. Then he, too, can see the angel. Together they make many converts, but eventually Valerian and Tiburce are executed for refusing to sacrifice to Jupiter. The officer sent to torment them is also converted and killed. Cecila buries them. Called before Almachius the prefect, and given the choice of sacrifice or death, she defends her faith stoutly. Almachius orders her to be executed by being boiled to death in a hot bath. However, she remains cold in the bath, so he sends an executioner to cut off her head. The executioner gives the three strokes allowed, but Cecilia's head is still attached to her body. She begs God to give her three days' more life, during which she preaches and makes many converts. Cecilia asks Urban to make sure that her house is converted into a church after her death. He agrees, and the church remains there 'to this day'.

This story of St Cecilia was probably written separately from *The Canterbury Tales*, and included later. Chaucer mentions in the *Legend of Good Women* that he has written a 'lyf of Seynt Cecile'. If this tale is that life, then it must have been written some time before 1386, the date of the *Legend*. Between December 1381 and December 1384 Adam Easton was installed as priest of the Church of St Cecilia in Trastevere, Rome, and it has been suggested that this was written to celebrate that occasion. As with *The Clerk's Tale*, this is written in 'rhyme royal', and attempts to elicit a strong emotional response from the reader/hearer.

The story is about the avoidance of idleness. Cecilia is a very busy person, converting people and 'translating' them from hell to heaven, from mortality to eternal life. Idleness was a positive quality in courtly love poetry (Idleness is keeper of the garden gate in *The Romance of the Rose*), perhaps in the poetry favoured by the prioress. This story is opposed to the courtly love tradition of pretty women who do little except relate to men. It is told by a 'professional' virgin, who has rejected the role of a courtly lady. It may, though, be a concealed criticism of the second nun's prioress, who fancies herself as a courtly love heroine. Life is seen as purgatory, and salvation comes through hard work. The role played by virginity both in the life of Cecilia and of the nun is obvious, but this saint is also someone who takes control of her life, and of the society around her. Unlike Griselda or Constance, she tells her husband outright that she does not want him physically, and persuades him to adopt her own point of view. Although the world around them does not change, Cecilia has shaped her own world privately, within the society of the wider world.

The nun sees herself, also, as a translator. She explains the name Cecilia using the interpretation of James of Voragine, and places herself within the tradition of male translators and commentators. Hence, she provides a bridge between one language and another, between heaven and earth, just as Cecilia does in her story. She calls herself a 'son' of Eve; this may be traditional, universal, or a political point being made by the nun. Like a son, the nun has to work; there are no men to keep her. At her trial, Cecilia argues defiantly against Almachius. Chaucer removed the trials of Valerian and Tiburce from his source (an unknown Latin life of St Cecilia and the *Legenda Aurea* – 'Golden Legend' – of the early-fourteenth-century writer Jacobus de Voragine) in order to highlight the trial, and therefore the speech, of Cecilia. The saint is not able, however, to occupy any other public space. She must make what use she can of the opportunities allowed to her by her trial and execution to make her voice heard in the public arena.

The senses, which are identified with female sexuality in romances, are used by the second nun in a different way. The ability to 'see' and to smell the flowers which represent the light, the smell and the savour of God is limited to Cecilia and those who join her, in faith, in her domestic 'privitee'. They are sign of salvation and purity, the opposite of what they represent in romance. In a similar overturning, the nun denies that virginity is unfruitful. She provides the image of the virgin's womb being a cloister, filled with nuns like herself, bringing forth faith, converts and authoritative literature. The nuns are procreative, as is Cecilia, and what they produce is children of God. Cecilia does not have children naturally, but she produces innumerable children of the faith, who are born again to a new, eternal, life, to which death is simply the bridge, the translation. Thus also the reader/hearer is translated by her story.

Key Questions

How far is the story of Cecilia a saint's life, and how far is it 'romance'?

Does the story relate to the nun's theme of idleness, and to the meanings she gives for Cecilia's name?

What is the relationship between Cecilia's story and the life of nuns, 'brides' of Christ?

How is female authority/power constructed and depicted in the story? How does this operate in relation to men? What is the relationship between public and private? How 'affective' is the story?

Topic Keywords

Female saints' lives/ women in romance/ women in society/ women in religion (nuns)/ popular religion/ the senses/ flowers and plants/ the Church in medieval Rome

Further Reading

Karen Arthur, 'Equivocal Subjectivity in Chaucer's Second Nun's Prologue and Tale', *Chaucer Review*, 32, 1998, pp. 217–31

Anne Eggebroten, 'Laughter in The Second Nun's Tale: A Redefinition of the Genre', *Chaucer Review*, 19, 1984, pp. 55–61

Marc D. Glasser, 'Marriage and The Second Nun's Tale', *Tennessee Studies in Literature*, 23, 1978, pp. 1–14

Eileen S. Jankowski, 'Chaucer's Second Nun's Tale and the Apocalyptic Imagination', *Chaucer Review*, 36, 2001, pp. 128–48

Lynn Staley Johnson, 'Chaucer's Tale of The Second Nun and the Strategies of Dissent', *Studies in Philology*, 89, 1992, pp. 314–33

V. Kolve, 'Chaucer's Second Nun's Tale and the Iconography of St Cecilia', in *New Perspectives in Chaucer Criticism*, edited by Donald Rose, Norman, OK, Pilgrim, 1981, pp. 137–74

Katherine C. Little, 'Images, Texts, and Exegetics in Chaucer's Second Nun's Tale', *Journal of Medieval and Early Modern Studies*, 36, 2006, pp. 103–33

Robert Longsworth, 'Privileged Knowledge: St Cecilia and the Alchemist in *The Canterbury Tales*', *Chaucer Review*, 27, 1992, pp. 87–96

Russell Peck, 'The Ideas of Entente and Translation in Chaucer's Second Nun's Tale', *Annuale mediaevale*, 8, 1967, pp. 17–37

Sherry L. Reames, 'The Sources of Chaucer's Second Nun's Tale', *Modern Philology*, 76, 1978, pp. 111–35

—— 'A Recent Discovery Concerning the Sources of Chaucer's Second Nun's Tale', *Modern Philology*, 87, 1990, pp. 337–61

Catherine Sanok, 'Performing Feminine Sanctity in Late Medieval England: Parish Guilds, Saints' Plays, and The Second Nun's Tale', *Journal of Medieval and Early Modern Studies*, 32, 2002, pp. 269–303

And here bygynneth the Secounde Nonne's Tale

❦ The minister and the **norice** unto vices,   nurse
Which that men **clepe** in Englisch **ydelnesse**,   call; idleness
The porter at the gates is of **delicis**,[1]   pleasures
To **eschiewe**, and by her **contrary** hire oppresse –   avoid; opposite
That is to say by **leful** besynesse –   lawful
Wel oughte we to do al oure entente,
Lest that the **fend** thurgh ydelnesse us **hente**.   fiend/the devil; seize

For he, that with his thousand cordes slye
Continuelly us wayteth to **byclappe**   tie up   10
Whan he may man in ydelnes espye,
He can so lightly cacche him in his trappe,
Til that a man be **hent** right by the **lappe**   seized; hem (of garment)
He is nou*gh*t **ware** the fend hath him in honde –   aware
Wel oughte we wirche, and ydelnes withstonde.

And though men dredde never for to deye,
Yet seen men wel by resoun, douteles,
That ydelnes is **roten sloggardye**,   rotten laziness
Of which ther cometh never good **encres**,   profit
And sin, that **slouth** her holdeth in a **lees**,   sloth; leash   20
Oonly to sleep and for to ete and drynke,
And to devour al that other **swynke**.   work for

And for to put us from such ydelnes,
That cause is of so gret confusioun,
I have her doon my faithful busynes,
After the legende in translacioun
Right of this glorious lif and passioun
Thou with thi garlond wrought, with rose and lylye;
The mene I, **mayde** and martir Cecilie.   Virgin

1 Idleness is keeper of the gate to the rose's garden in the Romance of the Rose.

30   And thou, that flour of virgines art alle,
Of whom that Bernard **lust so wel** to write,[2]   wanted so much
To the at my bygynnyng first I calle;
Thou comfort of us wrecches, do me endite
Thy mayden's deth, that wan thurgh hir merite
Th'eternal lif and **of** the feend victorie,   over
As man may after reden in hir storie.

Thou mayde and moder, doughter of thi sone,
Thow welle of mercy, synful soules' cure,
In whom that God for bountee chees to **wone**;   live
40   Thou humble and heyh over every creature,
Thow nobelest so ferforth oure nature[3]
That no disdeyn the Maker had of **kynde**,   (human)kind
His sone in blood and fleissh to clothe and wynde.

Withinne the cloyster of thi blisful sydes
Took man's schap the eternal love and pees
That of the trine compas Lord and guyde is,[4]
Whom erthe, and see, and heven **out of relees**   without end
Ay **herien**; and thou virgine **wemmeles**   worship; unsullied
Bar of thy body and dwellest mayden pure,   bore
50   The creatour of every creature.

Assembled is in thy magnificence
With mercy, goodnes, and with such pitee
That thou that art the **soune** of excellence   sun
Not oonly helpist hem that prayen the,
But often tyme, of thy benignite,
Ful frely, er that men thin helpe **biseche**,   ask
Thou **gost biforn** and art her lyfe's **leche**.   anticipates; physician

Now help, thou meke and blisful faire Mayde,
Me, **flemed** wrecche in this desert of **galle**;   miserable; bitterness
60   Thenk on the womman Canace, that sayde
That whelpes ete some of the **crommes** all,   crumbs

2 Twelfth-century writer and saint, Bernard of Clairvaux.
3 'make our nature so much more noble'
4 'threefold compass' – the three parts of the universe (heaven, earth, sea).

That from her lordes table ben y-falle;
And though that I, unworthy sone of Eve
Be synful, yet accepte my **bileve**.   faith

And **for** that faith is deth withouten **werkis**,   because; works
So for to werken give me witt and space,
That I be **quit** from **thennes** that most derk is.   saved; that place
O thou, that art so fair and ful of grace,
Be myn **advocat** in that hihe place   advocate
Ther as withouten ende is songe, 'Osanne,'   where; Hosanna   70
Thou Criste's Moder, Dou*ght*er deere of Anne.[5]

And of thi light, my soule in prisoun **light**,   illuminate
That troubled is by the contagioun   decay/sinfulness
Of my body, and also by the **wight**   power
Of everich lust and fals affeccioun.
O, heven of **refuyt**, O salvacioun!   refuge
O, hem that ben in sorwe and in destresse,
Now help – for to my werk **I wil me dresse**.   I will set myself

Yet pray I you that reden that I write,
Forgeve me that I doo no diligence   80
This ilke story subtilly to endite,[6]
For bothe have I the wordes and sentence
Of him that at the seinte's reverence
The story wroot, and folwen hir legende,[7]
And pray yow that ye wol my werk amende.

First, wol I yow the name of Seint Cecilie
Expoune, as men may in hir story se;   explain
It is to say on Englisch, 'hevene's lilie,'
For pure chastenesse of virginite,
Or for sche witnesse hadde of honeste,   90
And **grene** of conscience and of good fame;   clean
The '**soote savour** lilie,' was hir name.   sweet-smelling

---

5 St Anne, mother of the Virgin Mary.
6 'forgive me that I don't take the trouble to tell this story skilfully myself'
7 The second nun explains that she has a lif of Cecilia to use, and she is going to
    translate it.

Or Cecile is to say, 'the way of **blynde**,'   blinding
For sche ensample was, by way of techyng,
Or elles Cecily, as I writen fynde,
Is joyned by a maner **conjoynyng**   joining together
Of 'heven' and 'lya', and here in **figurynge**   a figure/word-picture
The 'heven' is sette, for thought of holynesse,
And 'lya' for hir lastyng **besynesse**.   endeavour

100   Cecili may eek be seyd in this manere,
    '**Wantyng** of blyndnes', for hir grete light   lacking
Of **sapience**, and of thilke **thewes** cleere;   wisdom; morals
Or elles, lo, this maydene's name bright
Of 'heven' and 'loos' comes, of which by right
Men might hir wel 'the heven of peple' calle –
Ensample of good and wise werkes all.

For 'leos', 'peple' in Englissh is to say,
And right as men may in the heven see
The sonne and moone and sterres every way,
110   Right so men **gostly** in this mayden free   spiritually
Seen of faith the magnanimite,
And eek the **clernes hool** of sapience,   full clarity
And **sondry** werkes, bright of excellence.   various

And, right so as these **philosofres** wryte,   learned men
That heven is swyft and round, and eek **brennynge**;   burning
Right so was faire Cecily the whyte
Ful swyft and besy ever in good werkynge,
And round and hool in good perseverynge,
And brennyng ever in charite ful bright –
120   Now have I yow declared what sche **hight**.   was called

This mayden bright Cecilie, as hir lyf saith,
Was comen of **Romayns**, and of noble **kynde**,   Romans; family
And from hir cradel up-fostred in the faith
Of Crist, and **bar** his gospel in hir mynde.   carried
Sche never **cessed**, as I writen fynde,   ceased
Of hire prayer, and God to love and drede,
Byseching him to kepe hir **maydenhede**.   viginity

And whan this mayde schuld unto a man
Y-wedded be, that was ful yong of age,
Which that **y-cleped** was Walerian,   called   130
And day was comen of hir mariage,
Sche, ful devout and humble in hir **currage**,   character
Under hir robe of gold, that sat ful faire,[8]
Hadde next hir fleissh y-clad hir an **heire**.   hair shirt

And whil the organs made melodie,
To God alloon in herte thus sang sche,
'O Lord, my soule and eek my body **gye**   preserve
Unwemmed, lest that I confounded be;
And for his love that deyde **upon a tre**.'   on the Cross
Every secound or thridde day sche faste,   140
Ay **biddyng** in hire **orisouns** ful **faste**[9]

The nyght cam, and to bedde most sche goon
With hire housbond, as oft is the manere,
And prively to him sche sayde anoon,
'O swete and wel biloved spouse deere,
Ther is a **counseil**, and ye wold it heere,[10]   secret
Which that **right fayn I wold** unto you saye,   I really want to
So that ye swere ye schul it not **bywraye**.'   give away

Valirian gan fast unto hir swere
That for no **caas**, ne thing that mighte be,   reason   150
He scholde never **mo bywreye** hire;   in future; betray
And thanne at erst thus sayde sche,
'I have an aungel which that loveth me,
That with gret love, wherso I wake or slepe,
Is redy ay my body for to kepe.

And if he may feelen out of drede
That ye me touche, or love in **vilonye**,
He right anoon wil sle you with the dede,
And in youre youthe thus schulde ye dye;

8 'which looked really beautiful on her'
9 entreating; prayers; strongly
10 'if you are prepared to listen to it'

160 And if that ye in clene love me gye,   treat
He wol yow love as me, for your **clennesse**.   Chastity
And schewe you his joye and his brightnesse.'

Valirian, corrected as God **wolde**,   wished it
Answerde agayn, 'If I schal truste the,
Let me that aungel se and him biholde,
And if that it a **verray** aungel be,   true
Than wol I doon as thou hast prayed me;
And if thou love another man, forsothe,
Right with this swerd than wol I slee you bothe.'

Cecilie answerd anoon right in this wise:
170 'If that yow **list**, the aungel schul ye see,   want
So that ye **trowe** on Crist and you **baptise**.   believe; get baptised
Goth forth to Via Apia,' quod sche,[11]
'That from this toun ne stant but myles thre,
And to the pore folkes that ther duelle
Saith hem right thus, as that I schal you telle.

Tell hem I, Cecilie, yow unto hem sent
To schewen yow the good Urban the olde,
For secre needes and for good entente;
And whan that ye Seint Urban han byholde,
180 Tel him the wordes which that I to yow tolde,
And when that he hath purged you fro synne,
Than schul ye se that aungel, er ye **twynne**.'   separate/depart

Valirian is to the place y-goon,
And right as him was taught by his **lernynge**,   what he had learned
He fond this holy old Urban anoon
Among the seynte's buriels **lotynge**;   hiding
And he anoon, withoute taryinge,
Did his message, and whan that he it tolde   repeated his message
Urban for joye his handes gan upholde.

11 The Appian Way; one of the principal routes into Rome.

The teres from his eyyen let he falle: 190
'Almyghty Lord, O Jhesu Crist,'quod he,
'Sower of chaste counseil, **herde** of us alle,   shepherd
The fruyt of thilke seed of chastite
That thou hast sowe to Cecilie, tak to the!
Loo, like a busy bee withouten gyle,
The serveth ay thin owne **thral** Cecile![12]   servant

For thilke spouse that sche took right now,
Ful lyk a fers lyoun, sche sendeth here
As meek as ever was eny lamb, to yow.'
And with that word anoon ther gan appere   200
An old man, clad in white clothes clere,
That had a book with lettres of gold in honde,
And gan **to forn** Valirian to stonde.   before/in front of

Valirian **as deed** fyl doun for drede   as if he were dead
Whan he him **say**, and he him up **hente tho**,   saw; took then
And on his book right thus he gan to rede:
'O Lord, o feith, oon God, withouten mo,   one
On cristendom and oon fader of all also,
Aboven all and over all, everywhere.'
This wordes al with golde writen were,   210
And pope Urban him cristened right there.

Valirian goth home and **fint** Cecilie   finds
Withinne his chambre with an aungel **stonde**.   standing
This aungel had of roses and of lilie
Corounes tuo, the which he **bar** in honde,   crowns; carried
And first to Cecilie, as I understonde,
He gaf that oon; and after gan he take
That other to Valirian, hir **make**.   mate/husband

'With body clene, and with unwemmed thought
Kepeth **ay** wel these corouns thre –   ever   220
Fro paradys to you I have hem brought,
Ne never moo ne schul they **roten** be,   rotten

12 'the fruit of the seed of chastity sown in Cecilia' is her potential convert, Valerian.

Ne leese her **swoote savour**, trusteth me;   sweet smell
Ne never **wight** schal seen hem with his **ye**,   man; eye
But he be chast and hate **vilonye**.   unless; evil

And thou Valirian, for thou so soone
Assentedist to good counseil also,   agreed
Say what the list, and thou schalt have thi **boone**.'   request
'I have a brother,' quod Valirian **tho**,   then
230   'That in this world I love no man so;
I pray yow that my brother may have grace
To knowe the trouthe, as I doo in this place.'

The aungel sayde, 'God liketh thy request,
And bothe with the palme of martirdom
Ye schullen come unto his blisful feste.'
And with that word, Tiburce his brother com,
And whan that he the savour **undernom**   perceived
Which that the roses and the lilies cast,
Withinne his hert he gan to wondre fast.

240   And sayde, 'I wondre this tyme of the yer
Whennes that soote savour cometh so
Of Rose and lilies, that I smelle her?
For though I had hem in myn hondes tuo,
The savour might in me no **depper** go.   deeper
The swete smel that in myn hert I fynde,
Hath chaunged me al in another kynde.'[13]

Valirian sayd, 'Tuo corouns have we,
Snow whyt and rose reed, that schinen **cleere**,   brightly
Whiche that thine eyyen han no might to see;
250   And thou smellest hem thurgh my prayere.
So schalt thou seen hem, my **lieve** brothere deere,   beloved
If it so be thou wilt, withouten slouthe,
Bilieven **aright**, and knowen verray trouthe.'   the right things

Tyburce answerde, 'Sayst thou thus to me,
In **sothenes** or in drem **herkne** I this?'   reality; hear

13 'has changed me into a different kind of person'

'In dremes,' quod Valirian, 'han we be
Unto this tyme, brother myn, y-wys,
But now at erst in trouthe oure duellyng is.'[14]
'**How wolst thou** this?' quod Tyburce, 'and in what wise?'[15]
Quod Valirian, 'That schal I the **devyse**.'   Tell   260

The aungel of god hath me trouthe y-taught
Which thou schalt seen, if that thou wilt **reneye**   renounce
The ydols and be clene, and elles nou*gh*t;
An of the miracles of these corones tweye
Saynt Ambrose in his **prefas** list to seye;[16]   preface
Solempnely this noble doctour deere
Comendeth it, and saith in this manere: recommends

'The palme of martirdom for to receyve,
Seynt Cecilie, fulfilled of God's gifte,
The world, and eek hir chamber gan sche **wyve**;   give up   270
Witnes Tyburce's and Cecilie's **shrifte**,   confession
To whiche God of his bounte wolde **schifte**   provide
Corounes tuo, of floures **wel** smellynge,   goodly
And made his aungel home the croune brynge.

The mayde hath brought this men to blisse above –
The world hath wist what it is worth, certeyn –
Devocioun of chastite to love'.
Tho schewed him Cecilie, al open and pleyn,
That all **ydoles** nys but thing in **veyn**,   idols/false gods; useless
For thay ben doumbe, and therto they ben **deve**,   deaf   280
And chargeth him his ydoles for to leve.

'Who so **troweth** not this, a **best** he is,'   believes; beast
Quod Tyburce, 'if that I schal not lye.'
And sche gan kisse his brest, that herde this,
And was ful glad he couthe trouthe espye.
'This day I take the for myn allye,'
Sayde this blisful, faire, mayde deere;
And after that sche sayde as ye may heere:

14 'we lived in dreams up to this time, but now we live in truth'
15 'how do you know this'
16 A fourth-century bishop of Milan.

'Lo right so as the love of Crist,' quod sche,
290   'made me thy brothere's wyf; right in that wyse
Anoon for myn allye heer take I the,
Sin that thou wilt thyne ydoles despise.
Go with thi brother now, and the baptise,
And make the **clene**, so that thou **mowe** biholde   pure; may
The aungel's face, of which thy brother tolde.'

Tyburce answerde and sayde, 'Brother dere,
First tel me whider I schal, and to what man?'
'To whom?' quod he, 'Com forth, with good cheere.
I wol the lede unto the pope Urban.'
300   'Til Urban? Brother myn, Valirian,'
Quod Tiburce, 'wilt thou me **thider** lede?   there
Me thenketh that it were a **wonder** dede.   wonderful

Ne **menist** thou nat Urban,' quod he tho,   mean
'That is so ofte **dampned** to be **deed**,   condemned; dead
And **woneth** in **halkes** alway, to and fro,   lives; hiding places
And dar nou*gh*t oones putte forth his heed?
Men schold him brenne in a fuyr so reed
If he were founde, or if men might him spye,
And we also, to bere him companye.

310   And whil we seken thilke divinite
That is y-hyd in heven **prively**,   secretly
Algate **y-brent** in this world schal we be.'   burnt
To whom Cecilie answerde, 'Bodyly
Men mighten wel and skilfully
This lyf to lese, myn oughne dere brother,
If this were lyvyng oonly, and noon other.

But ther is better lif in other place,
That never schal be lost – drede the nou*gh*t –
Which God's sone us tolde, thurgh his grace,
320   That **Fadre**'s sone that all thing hath **wrought**,   God the Father; made
And al that wrought is, with a skilful thought;
The **Gost**, that fro the Fader gan procede,   Holy Spirit
Hath **sowled** hem, withouten eny drede.   given them souls

By word and miracle hihe God's sone,
Whan he was in this world declared heere
That ther was other lyf ther men may **wone**.'   live
To whom answerde Tyburce, 'O suster deere,
Ne seydest thou right now in this manere:
Ther nys but oo God, o Lord, in **sothfastness**,   truthfulness
And now of thre how maystow bere witnesse?'   330

'That schal I telle,' quod sche, '**er** that I go.   before
Right as a man hath **sapiences** thre –   just; knowledges
Memorie, eyen, and intellect also –
So in oo being in divinite
Thre Persones may ther right wel be.
Tho gan sche him ful **besily** to preche   then; intently
Of Criste's **come**, and of his **peynes** teche,   coming; sufferings

And many pointes of his passioun;
How God's sone in this world was **withholde**,   made to stay
To doon mankynde pleyn **remissioun**,   forgiveness   340
That was y-bounde in synne and cares colde.
Al this thing sche unto Tyburce tolde;
And after this Tiburce, in good entente,
With Valirian to Pope Urban he wente,

That thanked God, and with glad hert and light
He cristened him, and made him in that place
Parfyt in his lernyng, God's knyght;
And after this Tiburce gat such grace
That every day he **say**, in tyme and space   saw
The aungel of God, and every maner **boone**   gift   350
That he God asked, it was **sped** ful soone.   done

It were ful hard **by ordre for to sayne**   to give a list of
How many wondres Jesus for hem wroughte;
But atte last, to tellen schort and playne,
The sergeants of the toun of Rome hem soughte,
And hem byforn Almache the prefect broughte,
Which hem **apposed**, and knew all here entente,   opposed
And to the ymage of Jubiter hem sente.[17]

17 Jupiter, chief of the Roman gods, often also associated with emperor-worship.

And saide, 'Whoso wil not sacrifise,
360 **Swope** of his **heved**: this my sentence heere.'   cut; head
Anoon these martires, that I yow devyse,
Oon Maximus, that was an officere
Of the prefecte's, and his **counceilere**,   counsellor/adviser
Hem hent, and whan he forth the seyntes ladde,
Himself he wept, for pite that he hadde.

Whan Maximus had herd the seintes' **lore**,   teaching
He gat him of his **tormentoures leve**   torturers; permission
And bad hem to his hous, withouten more,
And with her preching, er that it were **eve**,   evening
370 Thay gonne fro the tormentoures to **reve**,   seize
And fro Maxime, and fro his **fold echoone**   each one of his household
The false faith, and **trowe** in God alloone.   believe

Cecilie cam, whan it was **waxen** night,   become
With prestis that hem cristenid all **in feere**;   together/as one
And afterward, when day was waxen light,
Cecilie hem sayde, with a ful stedefast chere,
'Now, Criste's owne knyghtes, **leef** and deere,   beloved
Cast al away the werkes of derknes,
And armith you in armur of brightnes.

380 Ye han, forsothe, y-doon a greet batayle;
Youre **cours** is doon, youre faith han ye **conserved**;   race; preserved
Goth to the coroun of lyf that may not fayle.
The **rightful** jugge which that ye han served   righteous
Schal geve it yow, as ye han it deserved!'
And whan this thing was sayd, as I devyse,
Men ladde hem forth to doon the sacrifise.

But whan they were to the place y-brought –
To telle schortly the conclusioun –
They nolde **encense** ne sacrifice right nought,   burn incense
390 But on her knees they setten hem adoun,
With humble hert and sad devocioun,
And **leften** bothe here **heedes** in the place;   left; heads
Here soules wenten to the King of grace.

This Maximus, that say this thing betyde, — saw; happen
With pitous teeres tolde it anoon right — full of pity
That he here soules saugh to heven glyde, — saw
With aungels, ful of clernes and of light, — brightness
And with his word converted many a wight; — person
For which Almachius ded him so bete
With whippes of leed, til his lif gan lete. — lead; went from him 400

Cecilie him took, and buried him anoon
By Thiburce and Valirian, softely,
Withinne hire berieng place, under the stoon. — burial
And after this Almachius hastily — quickly
Bad his ministres fecche openly — servants
Cecilie, so that sche might in his presence
Doon sacrifice, and Jubiter encense. — burn incense before

But they, converted, at hir wise love
Wepten ful sore, and gaven ful credence — belief
Unto hir word, and cryden more and more, 410
'Crist, God's Sone, withouten difference,
Is verray God – this is al oure sentence – — true; witness
That hath so good a servaunt him to serve;
Thus with oon vois we trowen, though we sterve.' — die; believe

Almachius, that herd of this doynge,
Bad fecchen Cecilie that he might hir se;
And alther first so this was his axinge — first of all; question
'What maner womman art thou?' quod he.
'I am a gentilwomman born,' quod sche.
'I axe the,' quod he, 'though the it greve, — ask 420
Of thi religioun and of thi byleve.'

'Ye han bygonne your questioun folily,' — foolishly
Quod sche, 'that wolden tuo answers conclude
In oo demaunde; ye axen lewedly.' — ignorantly
Almache answerde to that similitude, — comparison
'Of whens cometh thin answering so rude?'
'Of whens?' quod sche, whan sche was y-freyned, — questioned
'Of conscience and good faith unfeyned.'

Almachius sayde, 'Takest thou noon heede
430 Of my power?' And sche answerde him this:
'Youre might,'quod sche, 'ful litel is to drede;
For every mortal man's power nys
But lyk a bladder ful of wynd, y-wis,
For with a nedele's poynt what it is blowe
May al the bost of it be layd ful lowe.'[18]

'Ful wrongfully bygan thou.'quod he,
'And yet in wrong is thy perseveraunce.[19]
Wostow nought how oure mightly princes fre
Han thus comaunded, and **maad ordinaunce**,   given an order
440 That every Cristen wight schal have **penaunce**,   punishment
But if that he his cristendom withseye,   unless
And goon al **quyt** if he wil it **reneye**?'   acquitted; renounce

'Your princes erre, as your nobleye doth,'
Quoth tho Cecilie, 'and with a **wood** sentence   insane
Ye make us gulty, and it is nought **soth**,   true
For ye that knowen wel oure Innocence.
For as moche as we doon reverence
To Crist, and for we bere a cristen name,
Ye putten on us a **crym**, and eek a **blame**.   accusation; wrongdoing

450 But we that knowen thilke name so
For vertuous, we may it not **withseye**.'   renounce
Almache sayde, '**Cheese** oon of these tuo: choose
Do sacrifice, and **cristendom reneye**   Christianity; renounce
That thou **mow** now **eschapen** by that weye.'   may; escape
At which the holy, blisful, faire mayde
Gan for to laughe, and to the jugge sayde;

'O jugge, confus in this **nycete**,   folly
Wilt thou that I refuse innocence
To make me a wikked wight?' quod sche,
460 'Lo, he **dissimuleth** heer in audience;   pretends

18 'with a needle's point all the pride of that which has been blown into it can be
laid low'
19 'you persevere in your mistake'

He starith and **woodith** in his **advertence**!'   goes crazy; confusion
To whom Almachius, '**Unsely wrecche**!   miserable wretch
Ne wostow nought how fer my might may strecche?   you know nothing of

Han nought our mightly princes to me y-given
Ye, bothe power and eek auctorite
To maken folk to deyen or to lyven?
Why spekestow so proudly than to me?'
'I speke not but stedefastly,' quod sche,
'Nought proudly; for I say, as for **my syde**   ie Christians
We haten **deedly** thilke vice of pryde.   like death   470

And if thou drede nought a soth to heere,
Than wol I schewe al openly, by right ,
That thou hast maad a ful greet **lesyng** heere.   lying
Thou saist thy princes han y-give the might
Both for to **sleen** and for to **quyken** a wight,   slay; grant life to
Thou that ne maist, but oonly lif **byreve**,[20]   take away
Thou hast noon other power, ne no **leve**.   permission

But thou maist sayn thi princes han the maked
Minister of deth, for if thou speke of moo
Thow liest; for thy power is ful **naked**.'   exposed   480
'Do way thy lewednes!' sayd Almachius tho,
'And do sacrifice to oure goddes er thou go!
I recche nought what wrong that thou me profre[21]
For I can suffre it as a philosophre'[22]

'But thilke wronges may I not endure
That thou spekis of oure goddis her,' quod he.
Cecilie answered, '**Nice** creature!   stupid
Thou saydest no word, sins thou spak to me,
That I ne knew therwith thy **nicete**,   stupidity
And that thou were in every maner wise   490
A **lewd** officer, a **vein** justise.   corrupt; false

20 'you can only take away bodily life'
21 'I don't care what wrong you accuse me of'
22 'I can be philosophical about it'

Ther lakketh nothing to thin outer eyen,
That thou art blynde for thing that we seen all,[23]
That it is stoon, that men may wel aspien –
That ilke stoon, a god thou wilt it calle.
I **rede** the, let thin hond upon it falle   advise
And **tast** it wel, and stoon thou schalt it fynde   assess
Sith that thou seest not, with thin eyyen blynde.

It is a schame that the poeple schal
500 So scorne the, and laughe at thi folye;
For comunly men woot it wel over al[24]
That mighty God is in his heven hye,
And these ymages wel thou maist **espie**   see
To the, ne to hemself, may nought profyte,
For in effect they ben **nought worth a myte**.'   worth very little

Thise wordes, and such other, sayde sche;
And he wax **wroth**, and bad men schold hir lede   angry
Hom to hir hous, 'And in hir hous,' quod he,
Brenne hir right in a bath of **flammes rede**.'[25]   red flames
510 And as he bad, right so was doon the dede;
For in a bath thay gonne hir faste **schetten**,   lock up
And nyght and day greet fuyr they under **betten**.   beat

The longe night, and eek a day also,
For al the fuyr and eek the bath's hete   despite
Sche sat al cold, and felte of no **woo**,   discomfort
Hit made hir not oon drope for to **swete**;   sweat
But in that bath hir lif sche moste **lete**,   lose
For he Almachius, with ful **wikke** entente,   wicked
To sleen hir in the bath his **sondes** sente.   orders

520 Thre strokes in the nek he smot hir **tho**,   then
The **tormentour**, but for no maner chaunce   executioner
He might nought smyte hir faire necke a-tuo;

23 'although you can see outwardly, inwardly you are blind (without perception)'
24 'it is common knowledge to all people everywhere'
25 This refers to a Roman bath, that is to a series of rooms, with a hypocaust
(central heating) system underneath – not a 'bathtub' in the modern sense.

And for ther was that tyme an ordinaunce
That no man scholde do man such **penaunce**   punishment
The **ferthe** strok to smyten, softe or **sore**,   fourth; hard
This tormentour ne dorste do no more.

But half deed, with nekke **corven** there,   cut
He laft hir lye; and on his way he went.
The cristen folk which that about hir were
With **scheetes** han the blood ful faire **y-hent**.   sheets; taken (mopped up)   530
Thre dayes lyved sche in this torment,
And never **cessed** hem the faith to teche   ceased
That sche had suffred; hem sche gan to preche.

And hem sche gaf hir **moebles** and hir thing,   possessions
And to the Pope Urban bytook hem tho,
And sayde, 'I axe this of heven Kyng;
To have **respit** thre dayes, and no mo,   rest/break
To recomende to yow, er that I go,
These soules; lo, and that I mighte **do wirche**   make
Heer of myn hous perpetuelly, a chirche.'   540

Seynt Urban with his **dekenes**, prively [26]   deacons
The body **fette**, and buried it by nighte   fetched
Among his other seyntes, honestely.
Hir hous the chirch of Seynt Cecily **yit highte**.   is still called
Seynt Urban **halwed** it, as he wel mighte,   blessed
In which unto this day, in noble wyse,
Men doon to crist and to his seint servise.

Her endeth the Secounde Nonne hir tale of the lif of Seint
Cecilie

---

26 A deacon is an assistant whose orders are below that of a priest: a deacon cannot
   consecrate the bread and wine at Mass.

THE CANON'S YEOMAN'S PROLOGUE AND TALE

As the pilgrims near Canterbury, two riders come galloping up, asking to join the company. One is an Augustinian canon and the other his servant, or yeoman. The yeoman, sweating like his horse, announces his master in courteous terms, but he then says that his master is not what he appears. He will tell the pilgrims of his master's sharp practices, and how he practises alchemy. The host notes that this must be why the canon is shabbily dressed for his position in life. Concerned for the yeoman's condition, the host asks where they live, and is told that they live in the back streets and alleys of a town. The canon comes up in order to find out what the yeoman has been saying about him. After making a futile threat to prevent the yeoman's disclosures, the canon beats a hasty retreat before the extent of his abuses can be known. The host calms the yeoman, and encourages him to speak on.

A chantry priest has a comfortable life with his mistress, a London widow. He meets a canon, who asks if he may borrow some money. The priest agrees, and loans money to the canon, who promptly pays it back. The priest is impressed, and in return the canon says he will show the priest something very useful. He sets up an experiment to make base metal into silver, and by trickery and sleight of hand makes the priest believe that he has produced a bar of silver. The priest begs for the recipe, which the canon sells to him for forty pounds. The priest will try and try, but he will never make the recipe work, and the canon leaves in a hurry with his forty pounds. The yeoman says that this is the miserable fate of those who are taken in by swindling alchemists.

There is no evidence that this tale was written and inserted later than the other tales, although the late arrival of the canon and his yeoman create the impression that this might be the case. The tale is obviously meant to 'fit' alongside the second nun's story of Cecilia, as it, too, is concerned with 'translation', only in this case it is the physical translation of base metals into gold.

The arrival of the canon and his yeoman enables 'Geoffrey' to tell his audience that the pilgrims are approaching Canterbury. They are obviously in a hurry; the canon has ridden so hard that his hat has fallen from his head, and is held at the back of his neck by its ties. We are not told which town they have come from, and the 'reason' that they are desperate to join the storytelling pilgrims seems a bit thin. Are they 'on the run'? If so, who from, and why? The arrival of the canon's yeoman reveals that a 'transformation' has taken place in the pilgrim group itself. It would seem, from the yeoman's words, that they have become local 'celebrities'. In advance of their meeting with the miracle-working saint, the host is able to perform a small miracle of his own, on behalf of the group. By taking him in, he/they are able to 'save' the yeoman from his sins, from the life of dependence and degradation to which he has been condemned. Like Sir Lancelot when he heals Sir Urry on the grail quest, the host is a very human being, but he is a 'parfit' human being, a wise ruler, who has been able to forge a community from diverse and unpromising materials. This community is a small section of humanity on its journey towards the 'holy grail' of the saint's blessing, one which is now capable (like Cecilia's household) of receiving and nurturing the 'saved'.

Here, about two miles from Canterbury, the pilgrims will have to abandon their game and remember the 'ernest' purpose of their journey. The theme of this and the second nun's tale reminds them of the 'translation' they are hoping for at the shrine of Becket, as the saint cures their physical and/or spiritual sicknesses. The alchemical processes described by the yeoman are intended to turn base metal into gold. The point is that they do not work; the pot blows up, and the actual transformation seen in the tale is a trick. The priest in the tale believes that this can happen, but he is deceived. The pilgrims must not put their trust in anyone other than God to turn their dross to gold, as the legend of Cecilia points out. As the parson will tell them, only penance, confession and absolution can provide the mechanism whereby they can be changed. Anything else merely produces a heap of rubbish. The medieval language of alchemy was framed as an alternative religious discourse, making the alchemist an apposite image for a religious charlatan. The yeoman provides an interesting and detailed introduction to the symptoms of addiction – the expectation, the thrill, and the desolation and disappointment afterwards, leading to the need for another 'fix'. There can be no true, lasting, satisfaction in anything other than God.

The transformation of base metals into gold also echoes the doctrine of transubstantiation, whereby bread and wine become the 'real' body and blood of Christ, after the celebrant says the words of consecration. In the story, this transformation, at the heart of the Church's power, is seen to be useless if carried out for financial profit. Again, this raises the question of whether a venal priest can effectively carry out this transformation, a question which strikes at the heart of the medieval Church. The priest in the tale, like many of the other clergymen in the tales and on the pigrimage, is overly interested in money. He is an abuser of his office, living with his concubine in London, making his living singing masses, rather than taking up a cure of souls. The parson represents a 'good' example of a lesser clergyman, a good man taking care of a flock . . . this priest is using his training to live a selfish life. He resembles Will in *Piers Plowman*, where such priests are introduced as abusers in Langland's General Prologue. This being so, he may be said to deserve his fate, like the victims in fabliaux. The canon is a confidence trickster, like many other ecclesiastics in the *Tales* and on the pilgrimage, but at least they are successful swindlers. The canon is not a successful spiritual entrepreneur. In terms of the pilgrimage economy, he does not make a profit. Although he is dedicated to making money, his efforts always fail. In this he also highlights the spiritual unprofitability of the other swindling ecclesiastics. None of them will reach heaven without the parson's spiritual alchemy, they will not make a profit in the spiritual economy. God cannot be bought or sold.

Key Questions

What does this story tell its audience about alchemy and 'transformation'?

Why does Chaucer introduce this character and his tale at this point in the pilgrim journey?

Is this story anti-clerical? How does it relate to the Church, its practices and beliefs?

Topic Keyword

Alchemy/ medieval theology, liturgy, heresy/ the medieval Church/ saints and miracles/ pilgrimage/ crime

Further Reading

Peter Brown, 'Is The Canon's Yeoman's Tale Apocryphal?', *English Studies*, 64, 1983, pp. 481–90

Mark Bruhn, 'Art, Anxiety and Alchemy and The Canon's Yeoman's Tale', *Chaucer Review*, 33, 1999, pp. 288–315

Michael Calabrese, 'Meretricius Mixtures: Gold, Dung, and The Canon's Yeoman's Prologue and Tale', *Chaucer Review*, 27, 1993, pp. 277–92

Jackson Campbell, 'The Canon's Yeoman as Imperfect Paradigm', *Chaucer Review*, 17, 1982, pp. 171–81

Robert Cook, 'The Canon's Yeoman and his Tale', *Chaucer Review*, 22, 1987, pp. 28–40

Donald R. Dickson, 'The "slidynge" Yeoman: The Real Drama in The Canon's Yeoman's Tale', *South Central Review*, 2, 1985, pp. 10–22

Edgar H. Duncan, 'The Literature of Alchemy and Chaucer's Canon's Yeoman's Tale: Framework, Theme and Characters', *Speculum*, 18, 1968, pp. 633–56

Bruce L. Grenberg, 'The Canon's Yeoman's Tale: Boethian Wisdom and the Alchemists', *Chaucer Review*, 1, 1966, pp. 37–54

Albert E. Hartung, ' "Pars secunda" and the Development of The Canon's Yeoman's Tale', *Chaucer Review*, 12, 1977, pp. 111–28

Britton J. Harwood, 'Chaucer and the Silence of History: Situating The Canon's Yeoman's Tale', *Modern Language Association of America*, 102, 1987, pp. 338–50

Jane Hilberry, ' "And in oure madnesse everemoore we rave": Technical Language in The Canon's Yeoman's Tale', *Chaucer Review*, 21, 1987, pp. 435–43

George R. Keiser, 'The Conclusion of The Canon's Yeoman's Tale: Readings and, Mis-Readings', *Chaucer Review*, 35, 2000, pp. 1–21

Peggy Knapp, 'The Work of Alchemy', *Journal of Medieval and Early Modern Studies*, 30, 2000, pp. 575–99

Robert Longsworth, 'Privileged Knowledge: St Cecilia and the Alchemist in *The Canterbury Tales*', *Chaucer Review*, 27, 1992, pp. 87–96

Lee Patterson, 'Perpetual Motion: Alchemy and the Technology of the Self', *Studies in the Age of Chaucer*, 15, 1993, pp. 25–57

David Raybin, ' "And Pave It Al of Silver and of Gold": The Humane Artistry of The Canon's Yeoman's Tale', in *Rebels and Rivals: The Contestive Spirit in The Canterbury Tales*, edited by Susanna Fein, David Raybin, Peter Braeger and Derek Pearsall, Kalamazoo, MI, Kalamazoo Medieval Institute Publications, 1991, pp. 189–212

And here bygynneth the tale of the
Chanoun's yeman prologus

prologue

❦ Whan ended was the lif of Seynt Cecile,
Er we fully had riden fyve myle
At Bouthtoun under Blee us gan **atake**[1]   overtake
A man that clothed was in clothes blake,
And under that he had a whit **surplice**;   surplice
His **hakeney**, that was a **pomely grice**,[2]
So swete that it wonder was to se;
It semed he hadde **priked** myles thre.   ridden (spurred)   10
The hors eek that his yeman rood upon,
So **swette** that **unnethes** might he goon,   sweated; hardly
Aboute the **peytrel** stood the **foom** ful hye –   breast-band; foam
He was of foom as **flekked** as a **pye**.   dappled; magpie
A **male tweyfold** on his **croper** lay;   double bag; crupper
It semed that he caried litel **array**,   adornment
And **light** for somer rood this worthy man;   lightly-clothed
And in myn herte, wondren I bigan
What that he was, til that I understood
How that his cloke was **sowed** unto his hood;   sewn   20
For which, whan I long had **avysed** me,   considered
I **demed** him som chanoun for to be.[3]   judged
His hat heng at his bak doun by a **laas**,   lace
For he had riden more than **trot** or **paas**;   trot; walk
He had y-pryked lik as he were **wood**.   mad
A **cloote** leef he had under his hood,   burdock
For swoot, and for to kepe his heed from hete,
But it was joye for to se him swete;
His forhed dropped as a **stillatorie**,   still
Were ful of **plantayn** and of **peritorie**,   plantain; pellitory   30

---

1 Boughton, two or three miles from Canterbury, where St Thomas's shoe was kept.
2 hackney (horse); dappled grey
3 A canon; a priest in order, living in a community – but not living in an *enclosed*
community, often working in the neighbourhood.

And whanne that he com, he gan to crie:
'God save,' quod he, 'this joly compaignye!
Fast have I priked,' quod he, 'for your sake,
Bycause that I wolde you **atake**,   overtake
To ryden in this mery companye.'
His yeman eek was ful of curtesye;
He seid, 'Sires, now in the **morwe tyde**   morning-time
Out of your ostelry I saugh you ryde,
And warned heer my lord and my soverayn,
40   Which that to ryden with yow is ful fayn
For his desport; he loveth **daliaunce**.'   banter
'Frend, for thy warnyng God geve the good **chaunce**,'   fortune
Sayde oure host, 'for certes, it wolde seme
Thy lord were wys, and so I may wel deme
He is ful **jocound** also, dar I **leye**.   merry; wager
Can he ought telle a mery tale or tweye,   he ought to be able to
With which he glade may this companye?'
'Who, sire? My lord? Ye, ye, withoute lye!
He can of merthe, and eek of jolite
50   Not but ynough; also, Sir, trusteth me,
And ye him knewe as wel as do I,
Ye wolde wonder how wel and thriftily
He couthe werke, and that in sondry wise
He hath take on him many sondry **emprise**   enterprise
Which were ful hard for eny that is heere
To bringe aboute, but thay of him it **leere**.   learn
As homely as he **ryt** amonges yow,   rides
If ye him knewe, it wolde be your **prow**.   profit
Ye nolde nought **forgon** his acqueyntaunce,   go without
60   For moche good I dar **lay in balaunce**,   put on the scales
Al that I have in possessioun,
He is a man of heigh discressioun;
I warne yow wel, he is a **passyng** man.'   marvellous
'Wel,' quod our oost, 'I pray the tel me than,
Is he a clerk or noon? Tel what he is –
Nay, he is gretter than a clerk, y-wis.'
Sayde the yeman and in wordes fewe,
Ost, of his craft somwhat I wil you schewe:
I say, my lord **can** such **subtilite** –   knows; skill
70   But al his craft ye may nought wite of me –

And somwhat helpe I yit to his **worchynge**,   works
That al this ground on which we ben ridynge,
Til that we comen to Caunterbury toun,
He couthe al clene turnen **up-so-doun**   upside down
And pave it al of silver and of gold.'
And whan this yeman hadde thus y-tolde
Unto oure oost, he seyde, 'Benedicite!
This is wonder merveylous to me,
Syn that this lord is of so heigh **prudence** –   wisdom
Bycause of which men schuld him reverence –   80
That of his worship **rekketh** he so **lite**   values; little
His over-**slop** it is not worth a myte   garment
As in effect to him – so mot I go –
It is al **bawdy**, and **to-tore** also!   dirty; torn
Why is thi lord so **slottisch**, I the preye,   slovenly
And is of **power** better clothis to **beye**?   status; buy
If that his dede accorde with thy speche
Telle me that, and that I the biseche.'
'Why? quod this yiman, 'Wherto **axe** ye me?   ask
God help me so – for he schal never the –   90
But I wol nought **avowe** that I say,   swear to
And therfor kep it secre, I yow pray.
He is to wys, in faith, as I bileve,
That that is over-don it wil nou**ght** **preve**   succeed
Aright as clerkes **sein**, it is a vice,   say
Wherfore in that I holde him **lewed** and **nyce**;   unlearned; foolish
For whan a man hath over-greet a **witte**,   intelligence
Ful ofte him happeth to mysusen itte;
So doth my lord, and that me greveth sore.
God it amende – I can say now nomore.'   100
'**Therof no fors**, good yeman,' quod oure ost,   don't worry about it
'Syn of the connyng of thi lord thou wost
Tel how he doth, I pray the hertily,
Sin that he is so crafty and so sly –
Wher duellen ye, if it to telle be?'[4]
'In the **subarbes** of a toun,' quod he,   suburbs
'Lurking in **hirnes** and in lanes blynde,[5]   hiding places

4 'where do you live, if you are able to tell me that'
5 'and in blind alleys'

Wheras these robbours and theves by **kynde**   nature
Holden here prive, ferful residence,
110 As thay that dar nou*g*ht schewen her presence;
So **faren** we, if I schal say the **sothe**.'   live; truth
'Now,' quod oure ost, 'yit let me talke to the;
Why artow discoloured on thy face?'
'**Peter!**' quod he, 'God give it **harde grace**!   by St Peter; ill luck
I am so used in the fuyr to blowe,
That it hath chaunged my colour, I trowe.
I am not **wont** in no mirour to **prie**,   used; peer
But **swynke** sore, and lerne to **multiplie**.[6]
We **blondren** ever, and **pouren** in the fuyr,   blunder; look
120 And **for** al that we faile of oure desir,   because
For ever we **lacken** oure conclusioun;   do not reach
To **moche** folk we **ben illusioun**   many; pretend
And borwe gold, be it a pound or tuo,
Or ten, or twelve, or many sommes mo;
And make hem **wenen**, atte leste weye,   believe
That of a pound we conne make tweye.
Yit is it fals, and ay we han good hope
It for to doon, and after it we grope;
But that science is so fer **us biforn**   beyond our grasp
130 We mowen nou*g*ht, although **we had it sworn**   we'd sworn to do it
It overtake, it **slyt** away so fast,   slid
It wol us make beggers atte last.'
Whil this yeman was thus in his talkyng,
This Chanoun **drough** him **ner** and herd al thing,   drew; near
Which that this yeman spak, for **suspeccioun**   suspicion
Of men's speche ever hadde this Chanoun –
For Catoun saith, that he that gulty is
Demeth al thing to be spoke of him, y-wis.   thinks
Bycause of that he gan so neigh to drawe
140 His yeman, that he herde **al his sawe**,   all he'd said
And thus he sayd unto his yeman tho:
"Hold now thi pees, and spek no wordes mo!
For if thou do, **thou schalt it deere abye** –   you'll pay dearly for it
Thow **sclaundrest** me her in this companye,   slander

---

6 work; turn base metals into gold

And eek **discoverest** that thou schuldest hide.'   reveal
'Ye,' quod oure ost, 'tel on, **what so bytyde**;   whatever happens
Of alle this **thretyng recche** the nought a myte.'   threatening; value
'In faith,' quod he, 'no more do I but lite.'
And whan this Chanoun **seih** it wold not be,   saw
But his yeman wold telle his **privete**,   private business   150
He fledde away for verray sorwe and schame.
'A!' quod this yeman, 'Her schal arise **game**!   fun
Al that I can anoon, now wol I telle,
Sin he is goon, the foule **feend** him **quelle**,   devil; kill
For never herafter wol I with him meete!
For peny, ne for pound, I wol **byheete**   praise
He that me broughte first unto that game!
Er that he deye, sorwe have he, and schame!
For it is ernest to me, by my fayth,
That fele I wel, what so eny man saith;   160
And yet for al my smert and al my greef,
For al my sorwe, and labour, and mescheef,
I couthe never leve it in no wise.
Now, wolde God my **wyt** mighte suffise   knowledge
To tellen al that longeth to that art!
But natheles, yet wil I telle you part –
Sin that my lord is goon, I wol nought spare –
Such thing as that I knowe, I wol declare.'

Narrat

he tells (his story)

❦ 'With this Chanoun I duelled have seven yer,   170
And of his science am I never the ner;[7]
Al that I hadde I have lost therby,
And God wot, so hath many mo than I.
Ther I was wont to be right freische and gay
Of clothing, and of other good array,
Now may I were an **hose** upon myn heed;   stocking
And where my colour was bothe freissche and reed,
Now it is **wan**, and of a **leden hewe**;   pale; leaden colour
Whoso it useth, sore schal he **rewe**.   repent

7 'I am none the wiser'

180 And of my swynk yet **blended is myn ye** –	I've been hoodwinked
Lo, such avauntage it is to multiplie!	
That **lyynge** science had me made so **bare**	lying; threadbare
That I have no good, wher that ever I fare.	
And yit I am **endetted** so therby,	put into debt
Of gold I have **borwed**, trewely,	borrowed
That whil I lyve schal I **quite** never.	pay back
Lat every man bewar by me for ever!	
What maner man that **casteth** him therto,	puts himself
If he continue I holde his thrifte **y-do**,	gone
190 For, so help me God, therby schal he not **wynne**,	gain
But empte his purs, and make his wittes thynne;	
And whan he, thurgh his madnes and folye,	
Hath lost his owne good in **jeupardie**,	speculation
Than he exciteth other men therto,	
To leese her good, as he himself hath do;	
For unto **schrewes** joy it is and ese	wicked people
To have here felawes in peyne, and **desese** –	discomfort
Thus was I oones **lerned of** a clerk –	taught by
Of that no charge; I wol speke of oure werk.	
200 Whan we ben ther as we schul exercise	
Oure **elvyssh** craft, we seme **wonder** wyse;	mysterious; wonderfully
Oure termes ben so **clergeal** and **queynte**.	jargon-filled
I blowe the fuyr til that myn herte feynte;[8]	
What schulde I telle ech proporcioun	
Of thinges which that we werke up and doun,	
As a fyve or six ounces may wel be	
Of silver, or som other quantite,	
And besy me to telle yow the names	
Of orpiment, brent bons, yren squames,[9]	
210 That into poudre grounden ben ful smal,	
And in an erthen pot, how that put is al;	
And salt y-put in, and also **paupere**,	pepper
Biforn these poudres that I speke of heere,	
And wel y-covered with a lamp of glas,	
And of moche other thing, what that ther was;	

8 'stoke the fire (with bellows)'

9 The yeoman lists some of the tools of the alchemist's trade: *orpyment*, burnt bones, iron, all of which are ground down and put into an earthenware pot.

And of the pot and glas **enlutyng**,	sealing
That of the aier mighte passe nothing,	air
And of the esy fuyr, and **smert** also,	strong
Which that was maad; and of the care and wo	
That we hadde in oure matiers sublymynge	220
And **amalgamynge** and **calcenynge**	bleaching; calcination
Of quyksilver, y-clept mercury crude;	
For all oure sleightes we can nought conclude:	
Oure orpiment and sublyment mercurie,	
Oure grounde **litarge**, eek on the **porfurye**,	lead monoxide; porphyry
Of ech of these of ounces **a certayn**	a number of
Nat helpeth us – oure labour is in vayn –	
No eek oure spirites **ascencioun**,	evaporation
Ne eek oure matiers that **lyn al fix adoun**,	sedimentary
Mowe in oure werkyng us no thing **avayle**,	help 230
For lost is al oure labour and **travayle**	work
And al the cost – **on twenty develway** – [10]	
Is lost also; which we upon it **lay**.	laid out
Ther is also ful many another thing	
That is to oure craft appertenyng;	
Though I by ordre hem here reherse ne can,	
Bycause that I am a lewed man,	
Yet will I telle hem **as they come to mynde**,	as I remember them
Though I ne conne nought sette hem in her **kynde**,	group/species
As bol armoniak, verdegres, boras; [11]	240
And **sondry** vessels maad of erthe and glas;	various
Oure urinals and oure descensories,	
Viols, croslets, and sublimatories,	
Concurbites, and alembikes eeke,	
And othere suche, **deere ynought a leeke**.	dear as a leek
Nat needith it to rehersen hem alle –	
Watres rubifying and boles galle,	
Arsnek, sal armoniak, and brimstoon, [12]	

---

10 'in the name of twenty devils'

11 Another list: includes verdigris, borax; then a list of vessels used by alchemists: flasks (urinals), vessels for distillation (descensories and concurbites), vials (viols), crucibles (croslets) and vessels for sublimation (sublimatories) and alembics.

12 Yet another list: waters for making other materials red (rubifying), bull's gall, arsenic, sal ammoniac, sulphur (brimstoon).

And herbes couthe I telle eek many oon,
250   As egrimoigne, valirian, and lunarie;[13]
And other suche, if that me list to **tarie**.   take the time
Oure lampes brennyng bothe night and day
To bring aboute oure craft, if that we may,
Oure fourneys eek of calcinacioun,
And of watres **albificacioun**,   whitening
Unslekked lym, salt, and **glayre of an ey**;   unslaked lime; eggwhite
Poudres **dyvers**, **aissches**, **dong**, pisse and clay;   various; ashes; dung
Cered poketts, sal petre, vitriole[14]   waxed pockets
And **dyvers** fuyres maad of woode and cole;   various
260   Salt **tartre**, alcaly and salt **preparat**,   carbonate; alkali; purified
And **combust** matieres and **coagulat**;   burnt; mixed
Cley maad with hors or man's **her** and oyle,   hair
Of tartre, alym, glas, berm, wort and argoyle,[15]
Resalgar, and oure matires **enbibing**,   ratsbane; soaking up
And eek of oure matiers **encorporing**,   compounding
And silver **citrinacioun**,   going acid yellow
Oure **cementynge** and fermentacioun,   joining together
Oure **yngottes**, **testes**, and many mo.   ingots; crucibles
I wol you telle, as was me taught also,
270   The foure spirits and the bodies seven[16]
By ordre, as ofte herd I my lord **neven**.   name
The first spirit quyksilver called is,
The secound orpiment, the thridde y-wis
Sal armoniac, and the ferthe bremstoon.[17]
The bodies seven eek, lo, hem heer anoon –
Sol gold is, and Luna silver, we **threpe**.   designate
Mars **yren**, Mercurie quyksilver, we **clepe**;   iron; call
Saturnus **leed**, and Jubitur is tyn,   lead
And Venus coper, by my fader kyn.
280   This cursed craft who so wol exercise,
He schal no good han, that may him suffise,

13 Agrimony, valerian, 'moon-wort'
14 Saltpetre, vitriol
15 Cream of tartar (the same used as a raising agent in cooking), alum crystals
   (glas), brewer's yeast, items from fermenting beer (wort and argoyle), and a form
   of arsenic.
16 Alchemists divided minerals into four 'spirits' and seven 'bodies'.
17 Orpiment, sal ammoniac and brimstone (sulphur).

For al the good he spendeth theraboute
He lese schal – therof have I no doute.
Whoso that list **outen** his folye,   reveal
Let him come forth and lerne mutiplie;
And every man that hath ought in his cofre
Let him **appiere**, and wexe a **philosofre**.   appear; a learned man
Ascauns that craft is so light to lere –   do you think
Nay, nay! God wot, al be he monk or frere,
Prest, chanoun, or eny other wight,   290
Though he sit at his book bothe day and night
In lernyng of this elvysch nice lore,
Al is in vayn, and **parde** moche more   by God
Is to lerne a lewed man this subtilte.
Fy! Spek not therof, for it wil not be –
Al **couthe** he **letterure**, or couthe he noon,   knows; booklearning
As in effect, he schal fynd it al oon –
For bothe tuo, by my salvacioun,
Concluden in multiplicacion
Y-liche wel, whan thay han al y-do;   alike   300
This is to sayn, thay fayle bothe tuo.
Yet forgat I to make rehersayle
Of watres **corosif** and of **lymayle**,   corrosive; filings
And of bodyes **mollificacioun**,   softening
And also of here **enduracioun**,   hardening
Oyles **ablucioun** and metal **fusible**,   cleansing; which fuses
To tellen al wold passen eny bible
That **owher** is; wherfore as for the best,   anywhere
Of alle these names now wil I me rest,
For as I trowe, I have yow told ynowe   310
To reyse a feend, al loke he never so **rowe**.   rough
A! Nay! Let be; thy philosophre stoon – [18]
Elixir **clept** – we sechen fast echoon;   called
For had we him, than were we **syker** ynough.   sure
But unto God of heven I make avow,
For al oure **craft**, whan we han al y-do,   knowledge
And al oure **sleight**, he wol not come us to.   craft
He hath y-made us spende moche good,

---

18 The philosophers' stone: the mysterious quest of alchemists to find the stone
   that turns base metal into gold.

For sorwe of which almost we **wexen wood**;   become; mad
320 But that good hope crepeth in oure herte,
Supposing ever,though we sore smerte,
To ben **relived** by him afterward.   relieved
Supposing and hope is scharp and hard –
I warne you wel, it is to seken ever
That future **temps**, hath made men **dissevere**   time; sever
In trust therof from al that ever they hadde,
Yet of that art thay conne nou*g*ht wexe **sadde**;   knowledgeable
For unto hem it is a bitter swete
To **demeth** it; for had thay but a **scheete**   believe; sheet
330 Which thay mighte wrappe hem in a-night,
And a **bak** to walke inne by daylight,   cloak
They wolde hem selle, and spenden on this craft;
Thay can nought **stinte** til nothing be laft,   stop
And evermore wher that ever they goon
Men may hem knowe by smel of **bremstoon**,   brimstone
For al the world thay stynken as a **goot**   goot
Her savour is so **rammyssche** and so hoot   ramlike/overpowering
That though a man fro hem a myle be,
The savour wol **infecte** him, trusteth me.   affect
340 Lo, thus by smellyng and by thredbare array,
If that men list, this folk they knowe may;
And if a man wol aske hem prively
Why thay ben clothed so **unthriftily**,   unsuitably
Right anoon thay **rounen** in his eere,   whisper
And say, if that thay espied wer,
Men wold hem slee bycause of here science.
Lo, thus this folk **bytryen** innocence!   betray
Passe over this – I go my tale unto.
Er than the pot be on the fuyr **y-do**   before; put
350 Of metals with a certeyn quantite
My lord hem **tempreth**, and no man but he.   mixes
Now he is goon, I dar say boldely;
For as men sayn, he can doon craftily –
Algate, I wot wel he hath such a name
And yet ful ofte he renneth in blame;
And wite ye how? Ful ofte **it happeth so**   it so happens
The pot to-breketh, and farwel, al is goo!
These metals been of so gret violence

Oure walles may not make hem resistence,   *container walls*
But if thay were wrought of lym and stoon;   360
They percen so, and thurgh the wal thay goon,
And some of hem synken into the grounde –
Thus have we lost bytymes many a pounde –
And some are skatered al the floor aboute;
Some lepe into the roof, withouten doute,
Though that the feend nought in oure sight him schewe,
I trow that he with us be, that schrewe!
In helle, wher that he is lord and sire,
Nis ther no more woo, ne anger, ne ire.
Whan that oure pot is broke, as I have sayd,   370
Every man **chyt** and halt him evel apayde.[19]   *chided*
Som sayd it was long on the fuyr makyng;
Some sayde, ay, it was on the blowyng –
Than was I **ferd**, for that was myn office.   *afraid*
'**Straw**!' quod the thridde, 'Ye been lewed and **nyce**!   *a straw for that; foolish*
It was nou*ght* **tempred** as it oughte be!'   *mixed*
'Nay,' quod the ferthe, 'stynt and herkne me.[20]
Bycause oure fuyr was nought y-maad of beech,
That is the cause and other noon, so theech!'[21]
I cannot telle **wher on it was long**,   *why it happened* 380
But wel I woot gret stryf is us among.
'What!' quod my lord, 'Ther is no more to doone –
Of these perils I wold be war eftsoone –[22]
I am right **siker** that the pot was **crased**.   *sure; cracked*
Be as be may, be ye nothing amased;
As usage is, let **swoope** the floor **as swithe**;[23]   *as before*
Pluk up your hertes, and beth glad and blithe!'
The mullok on an heep y-swoped was,[24]
And on the floor y-cast a **canevas**,   *canvas*
And al this mulloc in a **syve** y-throwe,   *sieve* 390
And sifted and **y-plukked** many a **throwe**.   *picked over; time*

19 'thinks he's hard done by'
20 'Shut up and listen to me'
21 'so may I thrive!'
22 'I'll watch out for these dangers another time'
23 'as we always do'
24 'What was left over was swept up into a heap'

'**Parde**!' quod oon, 'Somwhat of oure metal   by God
Yet is ther heer, though that we have nought al.
And though this thing myshapped hath a-now,
Another tyme it may be wel **ynow**;   enough
Us moste putte oure good in **adventure**   pledge/'hock'
A marchaunt, parde, may not ay endure,
Trusteth me wel, in his prosperite; [25]
Somtyme his good is drowned in the see,
400   And somtyme cometh it **sauf** unto the londe.'   safe
'**Pees**!' quod my lord, 'The nexte tyme I wol **fonde**   strive
To bring oure craft al **in another plyte**;   to a different conclusion
And but I do, Sire, let me have the **wyte**.   blame
Ther was defaute in somwhat, wel I woot.'
Another sayde the fuyr was over-hoot;
But be it hoot or cold, I dar say this,
That we concluden evermor amys;
We faile of that which that we wolden have,
An in oure madnesse evermore we rave;
410   And whan we ben togideres, everichon,
Everiche man semeth a Salamon –
But al thing which that schineth as the gold
Is nought gold, as that I have herd told;
Ne every **appel** that is fair **at ye**   apple; to the eye
Ne is not good, what so men clappe or crye.
Right so, lo, fareth it amonges us;
He that semeth wisest, by Jesus,
Is most fool whan it cometh to the **preef**;   test
And he that seemeth trewest is a theef.
420   That schul ye knowe, er that I fro yow wende,
By that I of my tale have maad an ende.[26]
Ther is a chanoun of religioun
Amonges us, wold **infecte** al a toun,   pollute
Though it as gret were as was Ninive,
Rome, Alisaundre, Troye, and other thre.[27]
His sleight and his infinite falsnesse
Ther couthe no man writen, as I gesse;

25 'a merchant can't always be successful'
26 'by the time I've finished telling my story'
27 Four great cities of the classical world: Nineveh, Rome, Alexandria, Troy.

Though that he might lyven a thousand yeer,
Of al this world of falsheed nys his peer;
For in his **termes** he wol him so wynde,   jargon   430
And speke his wordes in so sleygh a kynde
Whan he comune schal with eny **wight**,   person
That he wil make him **dote** anoon right   be under his spell
But it a feend be, as himselven is;   unless
Ful many a man hath he bygiled er this
And wol, if that he lyve may a while;
And yet men ryde and goon ful many a myle
Him for to seeke, and have his aqueintaunce,
Nought knowyng of his false **governaunce** –   behaviour
And if yow list to geve me audience,   440
I wol it telle here in youre presence.
But, worschipful chanouns religious,
Ne demeth nought that I **sclaundre** youre hous[28]   slander
Although my tale of a chanoun is;
And God forbede that al a companye
Schulde **rewe** a singuler man's folye.   suffer for
To sclaunder yow is nothing myn **entent**,   intention
But to correcten that is **mys** I ment.   amiss
This tale was not oonly told for yow,
But eek for other **moo**. Ye **woot** wel how   more; know   450
That among Crist apostles twelve
Ther was no traytour but Judas himselve;
Than why schulde **the remenaunt** have a blame   the rest/remnant
That gulteles were; by yow I say the same.
Save oonly this – if ye wol herkene me –
If any Judas in youre covent be,
Remewe him bytyme, I yow **rede**,[29]
If schame or los may causen eny drede;[30]
And beth no thing displesed, I you pray,
But in this caas herkeneth what I say.   460

28 House of religion.
29 'remove him immediately, I advise you'
30 'if you fear loss or shame'

Narrat

he tells (his story)

❦ In Londoun was a prest, an **annueler**,[31]   chantry priest
That therin dwelled hadde many a yer,
Which was so plesaunt and so **servisable**   eager to serve
Unto the wyf wheras he was at table,
That sche wolde suffre him nothing for to pay
For bord ne clothing, went he never so **gay**;   well-dressed
And spending silver had he right ynough –
Therof no force – I wol procede as now,
470   And telle forth my tale of the chanoun
That brought this prest to confusioun.
This false chanoun cam upon a day
Unto the prestes chambre, wher he lay,
Biseching him to **lene** him a certeyn   begging; lend
Of gold, and he wold **quyt** hit ageyn.   pay him back
'Lene me a mark,' quod he, 'but dayes thre,[32]
And at my day I wil it **quyte** the;   repay
And if so be that thou fynde me fals,
Another day hong me up by the **hals**.'   neck
480   This prest him took a mark, and that as **swithe**,   immediately
And this chanoun him thankid ofte **sithe**,   times
And took his leve, and wente forth his wey,
And atte thridde day brought his money;
And to the prest he took this gold agayn,
Wherof this prest was wonder glad and **fayn**.   glad
'Certes,'quod he, 'nothing annoyeth me[33]
To lene a man a noble, or tuo, or thre,
Or what thing were in my possessioun,
Whan he so trewe is of condicioun
490   That in no wise he breke wol his day;[34]
To such a man I can never say nay.'
'What!' quod this chanoun, 'Schold I be untrewe?

---

31 Paid for singing masses, usually for the souls of the departed.
32 A mark was worth thirteen shillings and four pence.
33 'it's no hardship'
34 'he doesn' fail to pay up on time'

Nay, that were **thing y-fallen of the newe!**[35]
Trouthe is a thing that I wol ever kepe   my word
Unto that day in which that I schal crepe
Into my grave, and elles God forbede –
Bilieveth this as **siker** as your Crede![36]   surely
God thank I, and in good tyme be it sayd,
That ther was never man yet evel apayd
For gold ne silver that he me lent,
Ne never **falshed** in myn hert I ment.   falsehood 500
And Sire,' quod he, 'now of my privete,
Syn ye so goodlich have be unto me,
And **kythed** to me so gret gentilesce,   shown
Somwhat to quyte with youre kyndenesse,
I wil yow schewe, and if yow lust to **lere**,   learn
I wil yow teche pleynly the manere
How I kan werken in **philosophie**;   experimental science
Takith good heed, ye schul seen wel **at ye**   with your eyes
That I wol doon a **maystry** er I go.'   mystery/wonder 510
'Ye,' quod the prest, 'ye, sire, and wol ye so?
Mary! Therof I pray yow hertily!'   by St Mary
'At youre comaundement, Sire, trewely,'
Quod the chanoun, 'and elles God forbede!'
Lo, how this theef couthe **his servise beede**!   proffer his service
Ful soth it is, that such profred servise
Stynketh, as witnessen these olde **wise**;   wise people
And that ful soone I wol it verefye
In this chanoun, roote of al treccherie,
That evermor delit hath, and gladnesse –   520
Such feendly thoughtes in his hert **empresse** –   be embedded
How Crist's poeple he may to meschief bringe.
God kepe us from his fals **dissimilynge**!   deceit
What wiste this prest, with whom that he delte,
Ne of his harm **comyng** he nothing felte.   approach
O seely prest! O sely innocent!
With coveytise anoon thou schalt be **blent**!   fooled
O graceles! Ful blynd is thy conceyt!

35 'something I've never done before'
36 The Creed – statement of Christian belief, made regularly by the believer in
    church.

Nothing art thou war of the deceyt
Which that this fox y-shapen hath to the; [37]

530
His wily wrenches. wis, thou maist not fle!   suberfuges/tricks
Wherfor, to go to the conclusioun
That referreth thy confusioun –
Unhappy n! Anoon I wil me **hie**   hasten
To tell hin unwitte and thy folye,
An ek the falsnesse of that other wrecche,
s ferforth as my **connyng** wol strecche.   ability
This chanoun was my lord, ye wolde **weene** –   assume
Sire Ost, in faith and by the Heven Queene

540
It was another chanoun, and not he,
That can an hundred-fold more subtilte;
He hath bitrayed folkes many tyme –
O, his falsnes it **dullith** me to ryme!   depresses
Ever whan I speke of his falshede,
For schame of him my cheekes **wexen** reede;   grow
Algates thay bygynne for to glowe,   at any rate
For reednes have I noon, right wel I knowe
In my visage; for fumes diverse
Of metals, which ye han me herd **reherse**,   tell you about
Consumed and wasted han my reednesse.

550
Now tak heed of this chanoun's cursednesse:
'Sire,' quod he to the prest, 'let your man goon
For quyksilver, that we it hadde anoon,
And let him bringe ounces tuo or thre;
And whan he cometh, as faste schul ye see
A wonder thing which ye saugh never er this.'
'Sire,' quod the prest, 'it schal be doon, y-wis.
He bad his servaunt fecche him his thinges,
And he al redy was at his biddynges,

560
And went him forth, and com anoon agayn
With this quyksilver – schortly for to sayn –
And took these ounces thre to the chanoun,
And he it layde faire and wel adoun,
And bad the servaunt **coles** for to bringe,   coal (charcoal)
That he anoon might go to his werkynge.
The coles right anoon weren **y-fett**,   fetched

37 'has got planned for you'

And this chanoun took out a **croselett**
Of his bosom, and schewed it the prest.   crucible
'This intrument,' quod he, 'which that thou **sest**   from
Tak in thin hond, and put thiself therinne   see
Of this quyksilver an **unce**, and her bygynne,   570
In the name of Crist, to **wax** a **philosophre**.   becom.   ounce
Ther ben ful fewe, whiche that I wol **profre**   ned man
To schewe hem thus moche of my **science**;   knoffer
For ye schul seen heer, by experience,
That this quiksilver I wol **mortifye**   stabilise
Right in youre sight anoon, withouten lye,
And make it as good silver, and as fyn,
As ther is any in youre purs or myn,
Or elles wher; and make it **malleable**,   tactile   580
And elles holdeth me fals, and unable
Amonges folk for ever to appeere.
I have a **pouder** heer, that cost me deere,   powder
Schal make al gold – for it is cause of al
My connyng, which that I you shewe schal.
Voydith youre man, and let him be **theroute**,   send away; outside
And **schet** the dore whils we ben aboute   shut
Oure privetee, that no man us aspie
Whiles wer werken in this philosophie.'
Al as he bad fulfilled was in dede;   590
This **ilke** servaunt anoon right out **yede**,   same; went
And his maister **schitte** the dore anoon,   shut
And to here labour speedily thai goon.
This prest, at this cursed chanoun's biddyng,
Uppon the fuyr anoon sette this thing,
And blew the fuyr, and busied him ful fast,
And this chanoun into the croslet cast
A pouder – **noot I** wherof that it was –   I don't know
Y-maad outher of chalk, outher of glas,
Or somwhat elles was nought worth a flye,[38]   600
To blynde with this prest; and bad him **hye**   hurry
These coles for to **couchen** al above   set down/arrange
The croislet, 'For **in tokenyng** I the love,'   to show that

38 'or something else that wasn't worth a fly'

Quod this chanoun, 'thin o... ..ne handes tuo
Schal wirche al thing wh'... ..ie prest, and was ful glad,   many thanks
'**Graunt mercy**,' qu... the chanoun bad;
And couchede c... ..as, this feendly wrecche,
And whil he ...un – the foule feend him fecche! –
This false..som took a **bechen cole**,   beechwood charcoal

610 Out of ful subtilly was maad an hole,
In ...erin put was of silver **lymayle**   filings
...unce, and stopped was withoute fayle
This hole with **wex**, to kepe the lymail in;   wax
And understondith that this false **gyn**   engine
Was not maad ther, but it was maad bifore –
And other thinges I schal telle more
Her after-ward which that he with him brought.
Er he com there, to bigyle him he thought;[39]

620 And so he dede, er thay wente atwynne –
Til he had **torned** him, couthe he nought **blynne**.   fooled; cease
It dulleth me whan that I of him speke;
On his falshede **fayn** wold I me **wreke**   gladly; avenge
If I wist how, but he is heer and there –
He is so **variant**, he **byt** no where.   variable; lives
But taketh heed now, Sires, for God's love –
He took his cole, of which I spak above,
And in his hond he bar it prively,
And whiles the preste couched bysily

630 The coles, as I tolde yow er this,
This chanoun sayde, 'Freend, ye doon amys;[40]
This is not couched as it oughte be –
But soone I schal amenden it,' quod he.
'Now let me **melle** therwith but a while –   deal
For of yow have I pitee, by **Seint Gile** –   St Giles
Ye been right hoot, I se wel how ye **swete**;   sweat
Have heer a cloth, and wype away the **wete**.'   wet
And whiles that this prest him wyped haas,

640 This chanoun took his cole – I **schrewe** his **faas**! –   curse; face
And layd it aboven, **on the mydward**   in the middle

39 'he had planned to trick him (ie the priest) before he came there'
40 'you're doing it wrong'

Of the croslet, and blew wel afterward,
Til that the coles gonne faste **brenne**.   burn
'Now geve us drinke!' quod the chanoun thenne,
'Als swithe al schal be wel, I undertake!
Sitte we doun, and let us mery make!'
And whan the chanoun's bechene cole
Was brent, al the lymail out of the hole
Into the crosselet anoon fel adoun;
And so it moste needes, by resoun,
Sins it so even above couched was –
But therof wist the prest nothing, allas!
He demed alle the colis **y-liche** goode,   alike
For of the **sleight** he nothing understood;   trick
And whan this **alcamister** saugh his tyme,   alchemist
'Rys up, Sire Prest,' quod he, 'and stonde by me;
And for I wot wel **ingot** have ye noon,   metal bar
Goth, walkith forth, and brynge a **chalkstoon**,   piece of chalk
For I wold make it of the same schap
That is an ingold, if I may have hap,
And bringe with you a **bolle** or a panne   bowl   660
Ful of water, and ye schul wel se thanne
How that oure besynes schal happe and **preve** –   succeed/profit
And yit, for ye schul have no mysbileeve
Ne wrong **conceyt** of me, in youre absence   conception
I ne wol noght be out of youre presence,
But go with you, and come with you agayn.'
The chambur dore – schortly for to sayn –
Thay opened and schette, and wente forth here weye,
And forth with hem they caryed the **keye**,   key
And comen agayn, withouten eny delay.   670
What! Schuld I tary al the long day?
He took the chalk, and schop it in the wise
Of an ingot, as I schal yow devyse –
I say, he took out of his **oughne** sleeve   own
A **teyne** of silver – evel mot he **cheeve**! –   piece; thrive
Which that was but an unce of **wight**   weight
And – taketh heed now of his cursed **slight** –   cunning
He schop his ingot in lengthe and in **brede**   breadth
Of this teyne, withouten eny drede,
So **sleighly** that the prest it nought aspyde,   slyly   680

And in his sleeve agayn he g� hyde.

And in his sleeve agayn he g⸱ ʰⁱˢ **mateere**,   material

And fro the fuyr he took⸱ith mery cheere,

And into the ingot pu⸱ he it cast

And into the wat⸱and bad this prest as fast:

Whan that hi⸱, put in thin hond and grope –

'Loke wha⸱er silver schalt, as I hope.'

Thou ⸱ of helle, schold it elles be?

W⸱ g of silver silver is, parde!

⸱tte in his hond, and tok up a teyne

⸱ silver fyn – and glad in every **veyne**   vein

⁶⁶Was this prest, whan he saugh it was so.

'God's blessyng and his Modre's also,

And **Alle Halwes** have ye, Sire Chanoun,'   All Saints

Seyde the prest, 'and I her **malisoun**,   curse

But, and ye **vouchesauf** to teche me   grant

This nobil craft and this subtilte,

I wil be youre in al that ever I may!'

Quod this chanoun, 'Yet wol I make assay

700   The secound tyme, that ye mow taken heede,

And ben expert of this; and in your neede[41]

Another day assay yourself, in myn absence,

This dicipline and this crafty science.

Let take another unce,' quod he tho,

'Of quyksilver, withouten wordes mo,

And do therwith as ye have doon er this

With that other, which now silver is.'

This prest him busyeth in al that he can

To doon as this chanoun – this cursed man –

710   Comaunded him, and faste blew the fuyr

For to come to **th'effect** of his desyr;   the objective

And this chanoun, right in the mene while,

Al redy was this prest **eft** to **bygile**;   again; trick

And for a countenaunce in his hond bar

An holow stikke – tak kep, and be war! –

In th'ende of which an unce and no more

Of silver lymail put was, as bifore

Was in his cole, and stopped with wex wel

---

41 'when you need it'

For to kepe in his limail **every del**;   every bit
And whil the prest was in his besynesse,   720
This chanoun with his stikke gan him **dresse**   attend
To him anoon, and his pouder cast in
As he ded er – the devel out of his skyn
Him torne, I pray to God, for his falshede!
For he was ever fals in **oth** and deede –   word
And with this stikke above the croslet
That was **ordeyned** with that false **jet**   prepared; 'set-up'
He styred the coles, til **relente** gan   melt
The wex agayn the fuyr; as every man
But it a fool, he woot wel it moot neede – [42]   730
And al that in the hole was out **yede**,   gone
And in to the croslet hastily it fel.
Now, good Sires, what wol ye bet then wel?
Whan that this prest thus was begiled agayn,
Supposyng **not** but **trouthe**, soth to sayn,   nothing; honesty
He was so glad, that I can nought expresse
In no maner his myrthe and his gladnesse;
And to the chanoun he profred eftsoone
Body and good – 'Ye,' quod the chanoun soone,
'Though pore I be, crafty thou schalt me fynde;   740
I warne the, yet is ther more **byhynde**.   to come
Is ther any **coper herinne**?' quod he.   copper; here
'Ye, sir,' quod this prest, 'I trowe ther be;
Elles go **bye** som, and that as **swithe**.   buy; quickly
Now, goode Sire, go forth thy way – and **hy** the!'   hurry
He went his way, and with this coper cam,
And this chanoun it in his hondes **nam**,   took
And of that copper weyed out but an ounce –
Al to simple is my tonge to pronounce
As **minister** of my witt, the **doublenesse**   servant; trickery   750
Of this chanoun, roote of cursednesse!
He semed frendly to hem that knew him nought,
But he was **fendly**, bothe in werk and thought.   devilish
It **werieth** me to telle of his falsnesse;   wearies
And natheles, yit wol I it expresse
To that entent men may bewar therby,

42 'as every man who isn't a fool knows it has to'

And for noon other cause trewely –
He put this unce of coper in the croslet,
And on the fuyr als swith he hath it set,
760 And cast in pouder, and made the prest to blowe,
And in his worching for to stoupe lowe
As he dede er; and al **nas** but a **iape** –   was not (ne was); trick
Right as him list, the prest he made his ape –
And afterward in the ingot he it cast,
And in the panne putte it atte last
Of water, and in he put his owne hond;
And in his sleeve – as ye byforenhond
Herde me telle – he had a silver **teyne**.   bar
He sleyghly took it out, this cursed **heyne**! –   thing
770 **Unwitynge** this prest of his false craft –   unaware
And in the pan's **botme** he hath it laft,   base
And in the water rumbleth to and fro;
And wonder prively took up also
The coper teyne – nought knowyng this prest –
And hidde it, and **hent** him by the brest   seized
And to him spak, and thus sayde in his game;
'Stoupeth adoun – by God, ye ben to blame!
Helpeth me now, as I dede yow **whil er**;   a while ago
Put in your hond, and loke what is ther.'
780 This prest took up this silver teyne anoon,
And thanne sayde the chanoun, 'Let us goon
With these thre teynes, whiche that we han **wrought**,   made
To som goldsmyth, and wite if it be ought;[43]
For, by my faith, I nolde, for myn hood
But if they were silver fyn and good.'[44]
And that as swithe proved schal it be,
Then to the goldsmyth with thise teynes three
Thay went and putte these teynes **in assay**   had them valued
To fuyr and hammer, might no man say nay;
790 But thay were as hem oughte be.
This **sotted** prest, who was gladder than he?   besotted
Was never brid gladder agayn the day,
Ne nightyngale in the sesoun of May;

43 'see if they're worth anything'
44 'By my hood, I wouldn't want them to be anything but fine, good silver'

Was never noon that liste better to synge,
Ne lady **lustier** in **carolynge** –   heartier; singing carols
And, for to speke of love and wommanhede –
Ne knyght in armes doon an **hardy** deede   bold
To stonde in grace of his lady deere,
Than hadde this prest this craft for to **lere**;   learn
And to the chanoun thus he spak and seyde,   800
'For the love of God, that for us deyde,
And as I may **deserve** it unto yow –   repay
What schal this **receyt** coste? Telleth now.'   recipe
'By Oure Lady,' quod the chanoun, 'it is **deere**!   dear/expensive
I warne yow wel for, Sire, I and a **freere**   friar
In Engelond ther can man it make.'
'**No fors**,' quoth he, 'Now Sire, for God's sake   no matter
What schal I paye? Telleth me, I pray.'
'Y-wis,' quod he, 'it is ful dere, I say.
Sire, at a word, if that the lust it have   810
Ye schul pay fourty pound, so God me save;
And nere the frenschipe that ye dede er this[45]
To me ye schulde paye more, y-wys!'
This prest the somme of fourty pound anoon
Of **nobles fette**, and took hem everychoon   gold coins; brought
To this chanoun for this ilk receyt –
Al his werkyng nas but fraude and deceyt –
'Sire Prest,' he seyde, '**I kepe have no loos**[46]
Of my craft, for I wold it kept were **cloos**;   close/secret
And as ye loveth me, kepeth it secre,   820
For and men knewe al my sotilte,
By God! Men wolden have so gret envye
To me bycause of my **philosophie**   learning
I schulde be deed; ther were noon other weye!'
'God it forbede,' quoth the prest, 'what seye ye?
Yet had I **lever** spenden al the good   rather
Which that I have, and elles **wax I wood**,   go mad
Than that ye schulde falle in such meschief!'
'For your good wil, Sir, have ye right good **preef**,'   outcome
Quoth the chanoun, 'and farwel! Graunt mercy!'   830

45 'if it weren't for the good turn you did me earlier'
46 'I don't want it to be known'

He went his way, and never the prest him sey
After this day; and whan that this prest scholde
Maken assay, at such time as he wolde
Of this receyt – far wel! It wold not be!
Lo thus **byjaped** and bygilt was he.   *tricked*
Thus maketh he his introduccioun,
To bringe folk to her destruccioun.
Considereth, Sires, how that in ech **astaat**   *layer of society*
Bitwixe men and gold ther is **debaat**,   *argument*
840 So ferforth that **unnethe** ther is noon.[47]   *hardly*
This mutiplying **blent** so many oon,   *fooled*
That in good faith, I trowe that it be
The cause grettest of swich **scarsete**.[48]   *scarcity*
Philosophres speken so **mistyly**   *opaquely*
In this craft, that men conne not **come therby** *understand it*
For any witt that men han **now on-dayes**;   *nowadays*
They may wel **chiteren** as doon these jayes, *chatter*
And in here termes sette lust and peyne,
But to her purpos schul thay never atteyne.
850 A man may **lightly** lerne, if he have **ought**, *easily; anything*
To multiplie, and bringe his good to **nought**. *nothing*
Lo, such a **lucre** is in this lusty game,   *financial reward*
A mannes mirthe it wol torne into **grame**,   *sorrow*
And empte also grete and hevy purses,
And make folk to purchace curses
Of hem than han her good therto y-lent!
O fy, for schame! Thay that have be brent,
Allas, can thay not fle the fuyr's hete!
Ye that it usen, I rede ye it **lete**,   *leave*
860 Lest ye **lesen** al; for bet than never is late – *lose*
Never to thrive, were too long a date –
Though ye **prolle ay**, ye schul it never fynde! *seek for ever*
Ye ben as bolde as is **Bayard** the blynde, *(name for a) horse*
That blundreth forth, and peril **casteth** noon; *foresees*
He is as bold to renne agayn a stoon
As for to go bysides in the wey –
So fare ye that multiplie, I sey.

47 'so much so that there is hardly any'
48 The yeoman is blaming alchemists for the lack of gold in the current economy.

If that youre **yyen** can nought seen aright,   eyes
Loke that youre mynde lakke nou*g*ht his sight;
For, though ye loke never so brode, and stare,   870
Ye schul nou*g*ht **wynne** upon that **chaffare**,   profit; merchandise
But wasten al that thay may **rape**, and **renne**.   grab; run
Withdrawe the fuyr, lest it so faste brenne –
Medleth no more with that art, I **mene**,   tell you
For if ye doon, youre thrift is goon ful clene;
And right as swithe, I wol yow telle heere `
What that the philosophres sein in this mateere.
Lo! Thus saith Arnold of the Newe toun,[49]
As his Rosarie maketh mencioun:
He sith right thus, withouten eny lye,   880
'Ther may no man Mercury mortifye,
But hit be with his brother knowleching'.
How that he which that first sayd this thing
Of philosophres fader was, Hermes.[50]
He saith how the dragoun, douteles,
He dyeth nought but if that he be slayn
With his brother; and that is for to sayn:
By the dragoun, Mercury, and noon other
He understood, and brimstoon be his brother,
That out of Sol and Luna were y-drawe;[51]   890
And therfore, sayde he, take heed to my **sawe**;   saying
Let no man besy him this art to seche
But if that he th'entencioun and speche
Of philosophres understonde can –
And if he do, he is a **lewed** man;   foolish
'For this sciens, and this connyng,' quod he,
'Is of the Secre of Secrets, parde.'
Also, ther was a disciple of Plato
That on a tyme sayde his maister to –

49 Arnold of Villa Nova (d. 1311) mentions the philosopher's stone in *On the Secrets of Nature*, a book used in experimental science. Another authority was the 'Thrice-Great Hermes', to whom were attributed the books of the *Corpus Hermiticum*, a compendium of writings on the scientific, astrological and mystical.
50 Hermes Tresmegistus, a legendary writer on experimental science; see note 49 above.
51 Sol, the sun; Luna, the moon.

900 As his book Somer wil bere witnesse –[52]
And this was his demaunde, in sothfastnesse:
'Tel me the name of the prive stoon.'[53]
And Plato answered unto him anoon,
'Take the stoon that Titanos men name.'
'Which is that?' quod he. 'Magnasia is the same,'
Sayde Plato. 'Ye, Sire, and is it thus?
This is *ignotus per ignotius*.[54]
What is Magnasia, good Sir, I you pray?'
'It is a water that is maad, I say,
910 Of elementes foure,' quod Plato.
'Telle me the roote, good Sire,' quod he tho,
'Of that water, if it be your wille.'
'Nay, nay,' quod Plato, 'certeyn that I **nylle**.   will not (ne wille)
The philosophres sworn were everychoon
That thay scholde **discovere** it unto man noon,   reveal
Ne in no book it write, in no manere,
For unto Crist it is so **leef** and deere   beloved
That he wil not that it discovered be,
But wher it liketh to his deite
920 Man to enspire, and eek for to defende
Whom that him liketh – lo, this is the ende!'
Than conclude I thus – **syn** God of hevene   since
Ne wol not that the philosophres **nevene**   name
How that a man schal come unto this stoon,
I **rede**, as for the beste, let it goon;   advise
For whoso maketh God his adversarie,
As for to werke eny thing in **contrarie**   against
Unto his wil, certes never schal he thrive,
Though that he multiplie **terme of al his lyve**.   all his life long
930 And ther a poynt, for ended is my tale –
God send every trewe man **boote** of his **bale**!   remedy; suffering

here endeth the chanoun's yeman his tale

52 Other manuscripts say 'senior', an Arabic writer of the tenth century; 'Somer' was
    the fourteenth-century English compiler of an astronomical/astrological calendar.
53 Philosopher's stone.
54 'the unknown *via* the more unkown'

THE MANCIPLE'S PROLOGUE AND TALE

The pilgrims are drawing very near to their goal, having reached the outskirts of Canterbury. The host, taking care of his 'flock', calls everyone's attention to the drunkenness of the cook, who is in danger of falling off his horse into the mud. The manciple offers to tell a tale instead of the cook, and makes fun of his drunken state. The cook falls off his horse, so the pilgrims have to push him back on, with great difficulty. The host permits the manciple to speak instead, although he warns the manciple against making fun of the cook, as another day the cook may get his revenge by telling others about how the manciple fixes his accounts (the manciple is purveyor for a college or institution – as in the reeve's tale). The manciple offers the cook more drink, which he takes. The host marvels at how drink can soothe arguments, and then the manciple begins his tale.

Phebus (Apollo), the greatest of knights, once lived on earth. After killing the serpent Python he always carried his bow and arrows in celebration of his victory. Phebus had a white crow, which sang like a nightingale. He kept it in a cage, and taught it to mimic the speech of anyone it heard. He also had a wife, whom he loved, and did everything he could to please her, but was careful too, in case she should commit adultery. The manciple explains that, no matter how easy its existence, no animal likes to be kept captive, and desires its freedom more than any comfort. Phebus's wife has a lover, who visits her when her husband is away. She and her lover commit adultery in the room where the crow is hanging in its cage. When Phebus returns, the crow calls him a cuckold, and relays him the details of how he has been cuckolded. In a rage, Phebus takes his bow and arrow and kills his wife, after which he is full of remorse. He breaks his instruments, along with his bow and arrows. He turns on the crow, because it incited him to kill his wife. He pulls out the crow's white feathers and takes away its beautiful voice; from henceforth all crows will be black. The crow is then kicked out of the door. The manciple recounts how his mother taught him to be careful with his speech. It is better to keep quiet than to tell a friend bad tidings. The truth should not always be told, or you will lose your friends and come to no good – 'think on the crow'.

At first sight the manciple's tale appears to be a simple 'just so' story, about how the crow got its croaky voice and black feathers. However, by setting up a relationship between the wife and the crow, the manciple highlights Phebus's treatment of both.

> Now had this Phebus in his hous a crowe . . .
> Now had this Phebus in his hous a wyf (ManT 131–140)

The statements which the manciple then advances about the unwillingness of animals to be caged and held captive, how they would rather suffer in freedom than be imprisoned in luxury, and how the she-wolf will take the 'lewedest' of wolves when she is in season, can be seen to apply to both the crow, as an animal, and to the woman, who has a close relationship with nature. No matter how well he treats them, crow and woman are Phebus's possessions, and they yearn most of all for freedom. Marriage, for the wife, is actually a cage. Her bid for freedom is the taking of a lover, although, like the wolf, he is far beneath her husband in worth and status. In the end, all she actually obtains is death, but it is a worthy cause, in that she expresses her own nature. The crow also desires to be free at all costs. This means that the ending, although it appears miserable, is actually a happy one for the captive crow; he loses his sweet voice and his pretty feathers, but he gains his freedom.

The manciple has already warned his audience about the power of words. When the cook is drunk, he says

> Of me, certeyn, thou schalt nought ben y-glosed (ManT 35)

and yet when reminded of the possibility of the cook's revenge, his words and actions become sweet again, in order to appease both his victim and the host. The manciple speaks of Plato's assertion that the essence of a thing must be contained in the word which describes it. Words are assigned to things arbitrarily, and can be altered in order to suit the needs of individuals and society, so a mistress is a 'lady' if she is noble and a 'wench' if she is not, but (says the manciple) they both lie down underneath a man. However, all is not what it may seem in the tale, because the crow's words, for example, may be carefully calculated in order to get what he wants, just as the manciple himself can use words in order to manipulate the scholars in his college, just as he can manipulate his accounts, to get what he wants out of them. He claims that he is not 'tixted wel', but this belies his ability to use words. Literacy is not simply book-learning.

Phebus, too, may not be what he seems. He is presented as the epitome of chivalry, but to kill an enemy while he is asleep cannot be described as very brave or chivalric. He then kills his defenceless wife in a fit of rage. It may be that Phebus's chivalry, like the happiness of his wife and his crow, are actually a fiction of Phebus's own imagination; he *wants* the world to be this way, and therefore it is, and the world, therefore, is Phebus-centred. After he has killed his wife, he once again restores the world to be the way he wishes it. His wife was innocent, and so was he; he was duped by the guilty crow. He punishes the crow rather than killing himself, although to the crow this is actually the reward it has sought. In this way he avoids the realisation of his own failings, and of his own guilt.

The manciple's mother's exhortation to 'think on the crow and keep your mouth shut', may be seen as sound advice, but it can also be seen as advocating the careful manipulation of words. The fact that the advice is put into the mouth of a woman, the archetypal liar, renders the advice open to suspicion, offering the likelihood that this may in fact be a form of deception. As a 'churl' the manciple represents the articulate members of the lower classes who took a prominent part in the Peasants' Revolt of 1381, and who were therefore hated and feared by people of Chaucer's social status. He, and his mother, are rendered socially and politically dangerous by their ability to use words. Chaucer, who had witnessed the events of 1381, represents the manciple as both clever and scheming, as slippery and unstable, and therefore as a threat to his society.

Key Questions

How far is the manciple revealing about himself in this story?

Who is the loser, and who the winner, in the tale? The crow appears to lose, but does it win what it really wants?

What does this story reveal about masculinity and the female? How heroic is Phebus? Is he to blame for everything? Who *is* to blame?

Does the story reflect the manciple's mother's advice? How does she compare with the other female 'advisers' in *The Canterbury Tales*? What is the importance of words? Does this impact on the function of the poet?

Topic Keywords

Medieval animals/ medieval representations of classical legend/ medieval women/ poetry as art/ masculinity/ medieval universities and colleges

Further Reading

Mark Allen, 'Penitential Sermons, the Manciple, and the End of *The Canterbury Tales*', *Studies in the Age of Chaucer*, 9, 1987, pp. 77–96

William Askins, 'The Historical Setting of The Manciple's Tale', *Studies in the Age of Chaucer*, 7, 1985, pp. 87–105

Arnold E. Davidson, 'The Logic of Confusion in Chaucer's Manciple's Tale', *Annuale mediaevale*, 19, 1979, pp. 5–11

Sheila Delany, 'Doer of the Word: The Epistle of St James as a Source for Chaucer's Manciple's Tale', *Chaucer Review*, 17, 1983, pp. 250–4

F. N. M. Diekstra, 'Chaucer's Digressive Mode and the Moral of the Manciple's Tale', *Neophilologus*, 67, 1983, pp. 131–48

Jamie C. Fumo, 'Thinking upon the Crow: The Manciple's Tale and Ovidian Mythography', *Chaucer Review*, 38, 2004, pp. 355–75

Warren Ginsberg, 'Chaucer's Canterbury Poetics: Irony, Allegory, and The Prologue to The Manciple's Tale', *Studies in the Age of Chaucer*, 18, 1996, pp. 55–89

Michaela Grudin, 'Chaucer's Manciple's Tale and the Poetics of Guile', *Chaucer Review*, 25, 1991, pp. 329–42

Peter C. Herman, 'Treason in The Manciple's Tale', *Chaucer Review*, 25, 1991, pp. 318–28

John McGavin, 'How Nasty is Phebus's Crow?', *Chaucer Review*, 21, 1987, pp. 444–58

Celeste Patton, ' "False Rekenynges": Sharp Practices and the Politics of Language in Chaucer's Manciple's Tale', *Philological Quarterly*, 71, 1992, pp. 399–417

David Raybin, 'The Death of a Silent Woman: Voice and Power in Chaucer's Manciple's Tale', *Journal of English and Germanic Philology*, 95, 1996, pp. 19–37

Brian Striar, 'The Manciple's Tale and Chaucer's Apolline Poetics', *Criticism*, 33, 1991, pp. 173–204

Eric Weil, 'An Alchemical Freedom Flight: Linking The Manciple's Tale to The Second Nun's and Canon's Yeoman's Tales', *Medieval Perspectives*, 6, 1991, pp. 162–70

Andrew Welsh, 'Story and Wisdom in Chaucer's The Physician's Tale and The Manciple's Tale', in *Manuscript, Narrative, Lexicon: Essays in Literary and Cultural Transmission in Honor of Whitney F. Bolton*, edited by Robert Boenig and Kathleen Davis, Lewisburg, PA, Bucknell University Press; London and Toronto, Associated University Presses, 2000, pp. 76–95

here bygynneth the prologe of the maunciple's tale

❦ Wot ye not wher ther **stont** a litel toun,   know; stands
Which that **cleped** is Bob up and doun   called
Under the Ble, in Caunterbury way?[1]
Ther gan our hoste for to **jape** and play,   jest
And sayde, "Sires, **what dun is in the myre!**[2]
Is ther no man, for **prayer** ne for **hyre**,   begging; paying
That wol awake our felawe al byhynde?
A theef mighte ful lightly robbe and bynde!
Se how he **nappith**! Se, for God's boones,   falls asleep   10
That he wol falle fro his hors at ones!
Is that a cook of Londoune, with meschaunce?
Do him come forth, he knoweth his **penaunce**;   punishment/forfeit
For he schal telle a tale, by my **fay**,   faith
Although it be nou*gh*t worth a **botel** hay.   bundle
Awake, thou cook! Sit up, God gif the **sorwe**!   misery
What **eyleth** the to slepe by the **morwe**?   ails; morning
Hast thou had **fleen** al night, or artow dronke?   fleas/bed bugs
Or hastow with som **quen** al night y-**swonke**,   whore; laboured
So that thou maist not holden up thyn heed?"   20
This cook, that was ful pale, and nothing **reed**,   red/flushed
Sayd to our host, 'So God my soule blesse,
As ther is falle on me such hevynesse;[3]
Not I nought why that me were lever slepe,[4]
Than the best **galoun** wyn in Chepe.'   gallon
'Wel,' quod the Maunciple, 'if that I may **doon ease**   relieve
To the, Sir Cook, and to no wi*gh*t displease
Which that her rydeth in this compaignye,
And our host **wolde** of his curteisie,   agrees
I wol as now excuse the of thy tale;   30
For, in good faith, thi **visage** is ful pale,   face

---

1 Harbledown, by the Blean forest. Blean is a village very close to Canterbury; the
   city and cathedral can be seen from the top of the hills nearby.
2 'Things are stuck (in the mud)'
3 'such heaviness fell on me'
4 'I don't know why I'd rather sleep'

Thyn eyen **daswen** eek, also me thinkith, are dazed
And wel I woot thy breth ful foule stynkith –
That scheweth eek thou art nought wel disposid –
Of me, certeyn, thou schalt nou*g*ht ben y-glosed!⁵
Se how he **ganith**, lo, this dronken wight, yawns
As though he wolde **swolwe** us anoon right! swallow
Hold **clos** thy mouth, by thy fader kynne! shut
The devel of helle sette his foot therinne!
40 Thy cursed breth effecte wil us all,
Fy stynkyng swyne foule mot the falle.
A, takith heed, Sires, of this lusty man!
Now, swete Sir, wol ye iust atte fan?⁶
Therto, me thinkith, ye beth right wel **y-schape**; suited
I trowe that ye dronken **han wyn ape**, become very drunk
And that is whan men playen with a straw.'
And with his speche the Cook wax angry & **wraw**, angry
And on the Maunciple bygan he nodde faste
For lak of speche, and doun the hors him cast;
50 Wheras he lay til that men him up took –
This was a fair chivache⁷ of a cook –
Allas, that he nad hold him by his **ladil**! ladle
And er that he agayn were in his sadil,
Ther was gret **schowvyng** bothe to and fro shoving
To lift him up, and moche care and wo,
So **unwelde** was this sory, **pallid**, **gost**. unwieldy; pale; ghost
And to the Maunciple thanne spak oure host,
'Bycause drink hath dominacioun
Upon this man, by my savacioun
60 I trow he **lewedly** tel wol his tale; badly/incoherently
For were it wyn or old moysty ale
That he hath dronk, he spekith in his nose,
And snesith fast, and eek he hath the **pose**. cold in the head
He hath also to do more than ynough

---

5 I won't gloss over your condition . . .

6 Joust at the quintain: a method of practice for mounted combat, in which the horseman aims to hit a target attached to a sack or other heavy object, which pivots round when the target is hit – the horseman must ride quickly to avoid being unhorsed by the swinging sack.

7 An armed raid of the type carried out frequently by soldiers in France during the Hundred Years' War (still in progress when Chaucer was writing).

To kepe him and his **capil** out of the **slough**,   horse; mud
And if he falle fro his capil eftsone,
Than schal we alle have ynough to doone
In liftyng up his hevy, dronken **cors**;   body
Tel on thy tale – of him **make I no fors** –   take no account
But yit, Maunciple, in faith thou art to **nyce**   fastidious   70
Thus openly to reproeve him of his vice;
Another day he wil, **paraventure**,   perhaps
Reclayme the and bringe the to lure –[8]   call you back
I mene, he speke wol of smale thinges
As for to **pynchyn** at thy **rekenynges**   quibble with; accounts
That were not honest, if it cam to **pref**.'   proof
Quod the maunciple, 'That were a gret meschief;
So might he **lightly** bringe me in the snare.   easily
Yit had I **lever** payen for the mare   rather
Which he ryt on, than he schuld with me stryve.   80
I wil not **wrath** him, also mot I thrive –   anger
That I spak, I sayd it in my **bourde**;   in jest
And wite ye what I have heer, in a gourde,[9]
A draught of wyn is of a ripe grape,
And right anoon ye schal se a good **jape**.   trick/joke
This cook schal drinke therof, if I may,
Up peyn of deth he wol nought say me nay.'
And certeinly, to tellen as it was,
Of this vessel the cook dronk fast – allas,
What needid it? He drank ynough biforn –   90
And whan he hadde **pouped** in his **horn**,   blown; drinking horn
To the maunciple he took the gourd agayn,
And of that drynke the cook was wonder fayn,   really happy
And thanked him in such wise as he couthe.
Than gan our host to **laughe wonder louthe**,   laugh extremely loudly
And sayd, 'I se wel it is necessarie
Wher that we go good drynk with us to carie;
For that wol torne rancour and **desese**   discomfort
To accord and love, and many **rancour** apese!   bitterness/quarrel
O thou Bacus y-blessid be thin name,[10]

---

8 The lure was a padded bag or piece of leather on a rope, used to 'reclaim' or
recall the hawk to its handler.
9 A drinking-vessel either made out of, or shaped like, a gourd.   10 God of wine.

100   That so canst torne **ernest** into **game**!   seriousness; play
       Worship and thanks be to thy deitee!
       Of that matier ye get no more of me –
       Tel on thi tale, Mauncipel, I the pray!'
       'Wel Sir,' quod he, 'now **herkyn** what I say.'   listen to

                         Narrat   he tells (his story)

       ❦ Whan Phebus duelt her in this eorthe adoun,
       As olde bookes maken mencioun,
       He was the moste lusty bachiler[11]
       Of al this world, and eek the best archer.
110   He slough Phiton the serpent, as he lay
       Slepyng agayn the sonne upon a day;[12]
       And many another noble, worthy dede
       He with his bowe wrought, as men may rede.
       Pleyen he couthe on every **mynstralcye**,   musical instrument
       And syngen, that it was a melodye
       To heren of his cleere vois the **soun**.   sound
       Certes, the kyng of Thebes Amphioun,
       That with his singyng wallid that citee,
       Couthe he never synge half so wel as he.
120   Therto he was the **semlieste** man   most attractive
       That it or was **siththen** the world bigan.   since
       What nedith it his fortune to **descrive**?   describe
       For in this worlde is noon such on lyve.
       He was therwith fulfild of **gentilesce**,   'gentility'
       Of honour, and of parfyte worthinesse,
       This Phebus that was flour of **bachilerie**,   young knighthood
       As wel in **fredom** as in chivalrie,   generosity
       For to **disport** in signe of victorie   enjoy (his victory)
       Of Phiton, so as telleth us the storie,
130   **Was wont to** bere in his hond a bowe.   used to
       Now had this Phebus in his hous a crowe,
       Which in a cage he fostred many a day,
       And taught it speken, as men doon a jay.
       Whit was this crowe, as is a snow-whyt swan,

       11 A knight, usually without land.
       12 Phoebus Apollo, god of music and poetry, of hunting and of the sun. The 'olde
          bookes' are probably the works of Ovid, and Python was the primeval serpent
          killed by Apollo.

And **countrefete** the speche of every man.   copy
He couthe whan he schulde telle a tale;
Ther is withinne this world no nightingale
Ne couthe by an hundred thousend del
Singe so wonder merily and wel.
Now had this Phebus in his hous a wyf,   140
Which that he loved more than his lif,
And night and day **did evermor diligence**   always tried his hardest
Hir for to please, and doon hir reverence;
Sauf oonly – if the **soth** that I schal sayn –   except; truth
Jalous he was, and wold have **kept** hir **fayn**;   imprisoned; gladly
For him were loth **bijaped** for to be –   cuckolded/fooled
And so is every wight in such degre –
But al for nought, for it availeth nou*gh*t.
A good wyf, that is clene of werk and thought,
Schuld not be kept in noon **awayt**, certayn;   strictly watched over   150
And trewely, the labour is in vayn
To kepe a **schrewe**, for it wil nought be.   wicked woman
This hold I for a verray **nycete**,   folly
To spille labour for to kepe wyves –
Thus olde clerkes writen in her lyves.
But now to purpos – as I first bigan;
This worthi Phebus doth al that he can
To pleasen hir, **wenyng** by such plesaunce,   believing
And for his **manhod**, and his **governaunce**,   manliness; bearing
That no man schuld han put him fro hir **grace**;   favour   160
But, God it woot, ther may no man **embrace**   believe
As to destroy a thing, the which nature
Hath naturelly set in a creature.
Tak any **brid**, and put him in a cage,   bird
And do al thin entent and thy **corrage**   best efforts
To foster it tenderly, with mete and drynk,
And with all the **deyntees** thou canst think;   nice things
And keep it al so kyndly as thou may,
Although his cage of gold be never so gay,
Yit hath this brid by twenty thousand fold   170
Lever to be in forest wyld and cold,   rather
Gon ete wormes, and such wrecchidness;   to go
For ever this brid wil doon his **busynes**   very best
To **scape** out of his cage, whan he may;   escape

His liberte the brid desireth **aye**.   always
Let take a cat, and foster him wel with mylk
And tender **fleisch**, and mak his bed of silk;   meat
And let him see a mous go by the wal –
Anoon he **wayveth** mylk, and fleisch, and al,   leaves
180 And every **deynte** which is in that hous,   delicacy
Such appetit hath sche to ete the mous.
Lo, heer hath **lust** his dominacioun,   desire
And appetit **flemeth** discretioun.   drives away
Also, a sche wolf hath a **vilayns kynde** –   evil nature
The **lewedist** wolf that sche may fynde,   lowest
Or lest of reputacioun, him wol sche take
In tyme whan hir lust to have a **make**.   mate
All this ensamples tel I by this men
That ben untrewe, and nothing by wommen;
190 For men han ever a **licorous** appetit   lecherous
On **lower** thing to parforme her **delit**   lesser; sexual appetite
Than on her wyves, ben thay never so faire,
Ne never so trewe, ne so **debonaire**.   sociable
Fleissch is so **newfangil**, with meschaunce,   loving of novelty
That we can in nothinge have **plesaunce**   pleasure
That souneth into vertue eny while.
This Phebus, which that thought upon no **gile**   cunning/betrayal
Deceyved was for al his jolite,
For under him another hadde sche,
200 A man of litil reputacioun,
Nought worth to Phebus in comparisoun.   nothing
Mor harm it is – it happeth ofte so –
Of which ther cometh bothe harm and woo
And so bifel, whan Phebus was absent,
His wif anoon hath for her **lemman** sent.   lover
Hir lemman! Certes, this is a **knavisch** speche! –   base
Forgiveth it me, and that I yow biseche –
The wise Plato saith, as ye may rede,[13]
The word mot neede accorde with the dede.
210 If men schal telle propurly a thing,
The word mot **corde** with **the thing werking**.   accord; what the thing is

13 Plato (the Greek philosopher) said that a word must have the same essence as
    that which it describes.

I am a **boystous wight**, thus say I;   plain man
Ther is no difference, trewely,
Bytwix a wif that is of heigh **degre**,   social status
If of hir body dishonest sche be,
And a pore wenche, other then this,
If so be thay **werke** both **amys**;   do wrong
But the gentil, in estat above,[14]
Sche schal be cleped his lady, **as in love**;   like in the love romances
And for that other is a pore womman,   220
Sche schal be cleped his **wenche** and his **lemman** –   whore; mistress
And God it wot, my goode, lieve brother –
Men layn that oon as lowe as that other![15]
Right so, bitwixe a titeles tirant
And an outlawe, or a thef **erraunt**,   criminal
The same I say – there is no difference.
To Alisaunder told was this sentence;[16]
That **for** the **tiraunt** is of gretter might   because; tyrant
By force of **meyne**, for to sle dounright,   his army
And brenne hous and home, and **make al playn** –   flatten everything   230
Lo, therfor is he cleped a capitayn!
And, for an outlawe hath so smal meyne,
And may not doon so gret an harm as he,
Ne bringe a contre to so gret meschief,
Men **clepen** him an outlawe, or a theef.   call
But for I am a man **not texted wel**,   not well read
I wil not telle of textes never a del.
I wol go to my tale, as I bigan –
Whan Phebus wyf had sent for hir lemman,
Anon thay wrou*gh*ten al her wil volage.[17]   240
This white crow, that heng always in cage,
Bihild her werk and sayde never a word.   watched their activities
And whan that **hem** was come Phebus the lord,   home
This crowe song, '**Cuckow!** Cuckow! Cuckow!'   cuckold!
'What, brid?' quod Phebus, 'What song **syngistow**?   are you singing
Ne were thou wont so merily to synge   you've never been used to
That to myn hert it was a rejoysyng

14 'but the gentlewoman, of higher social status'
15 'they both lie down under a man'
16 By his tutor Aristotle, in the Secreta Secretorum .
17 'they did everything they wanted to do'

To here thi vois – allas! What song is this?'
'By God,' quod he, 'I synge not **amys**!   inaccurately/wrongly
250 Phebus,' quod he, 'for al thy worthynes,
For al thy beaute and thy gentiles,
For all thy songes and thy menstralcie,
For al thy **waytyng**, **blered is thin ye**[18]
With oon of litel reputacioun,
Nought worth to the as in comparisoun
The **mountauns** of a gnat, so mot I thrive –   value
For on thy bed thy wif I saugh him **swyve**!'   fuck
What wol ye more? The crowe anoon him tolde
By **sadde toknes**, and by wordes bolde   detailed proofs
260 How that his wyf had doon hir leccherie,
Him to gret schame and to gret vilonye,
And told him ofte he saugh it with his **yen**.   eyes
This Phebus gan awayward for to **wryen**;   turn
Him thought his sorwful herte **brast** on tuo.   burst
His bowe he bent, and sett therin a **flo**;   arrow
And in his **ire** he hath his wif y-slayn –   anger/rage
This is **th'effect**, ther is no more to sayn.   what happened
For sorw of which he brak his menstralcye,
Bothe harp, gitern and **sauterie**,   psaltery
270 And eek he brak his arwes and his bowe;
And after that thus spak he to the crowe.
'Traytour!' quod he, 'With tunge of scorpioun
Thow hast me brought to my confusioun!
Allas, that I was born! **Why nere I deed**?
O dere wyf, O gemme of **lustyhed**!   pleasure
That were to me so sad, and eek so **trewe**   faithful
Now **listow** deed, with face so pale of hewe: lie you
Ful gulteles, that dorste I swere, y-wis!
O **racle** hond, to do so foule amys!   rash
280 O trouble wit! O ire **recheles**!,   reckless
That **unavysed** smytest gulteles!   unwary
O **wantrust**, ful of fals **suspeccioun**!   distrust; suspicion
Wher was thy wit and thy discrecioun?
Allas! A thousand folk hath racle ire
Fordoon, or dun hath brought hem in the myre![19]

18 watchfulness; 'you've been hoodwinked'
19 Been ruined or brought low by . . .

Allas, for sorw **I wil myselven sle**!' I'll kill myself
And to the crowe, 'O false theef1' sayd he,
'I wil the **quyt** anoon thy false tale! reward
Thow songe whilom as any nightyngale; you used to sing
Now schaltow, false thef, thy song **forgoon**, do without 290
And eek thy white fetheres, everichoon;
Ne never in al thy lyf **ne schaltow** speke – you will not
Thus schal men on a fals theef ben **awreke**. avenged
Thou and thin offspring ever shuln be blake,
Ne never sweete noyse schul ye make,
But ever crye agayn tempest and rayn,
In tokenyng that thurgh the my wyf was slayn!'
And to the crowe he **stert**, and that **anoon**, sprang; immediately
And puld his white fetheres, everychoon,
And make him blak; and **raft** him al his song took away from 300
And eek his speche, and **out at dore him slong** threw him out the door
Unto the devel, which I him bytake;
And for this cause ben alle crowes blake.
Lordyngs, by this ensample I yow pray,
Beth war, and **taketh kepe** what ye say. watch
Ne tellith never man, in al youre lif,
How that another man hath **dight** his wyf. had sex with
He wol yow haten mortally certeyn
Daun Salamon, as wise clerkes seyn,[20]
Techeth a man to kepe his tonge wel; 310
But as I sayd, I am **nought tixted wel**. not well read
But natheles, thus taughte me my **dame**: mother
'My sone, thenk on the crowe, in God's name!
My son, keep wel thy tonge, and kep thy frend;
A wicked tonge is worse than a **feend**. devil
My sone, fro a feend men may hem blesse.[21]
My sone, God, of his endeles goddnesse
Wallid a tonge with teeth, and lippes eek,
For man schal him **avyse** what he speek. think carefully about
My sone, ful ofte for to **mochil** speche much 320
Hath many a man be **spilt**, as clerkes teche; undone
But for a litil speche **avisily** thoughtful
Is no man **schent**, to speke generally. ruined

20 Proverbs 21:23
21 Protect by crossing themselves.

My sone, thy tonge scholdest thou restreigne
At alle tyme, **but** whan thou dost thy **peyne**   except; best
To speke of God, in honur and prayere.
The firste vertu, sone, if thou wilt **lere**,   learn
Is to restreigne and kepe wel thy tonge;
Thus lerne clerkes whan that thay ben yonge.
330 My sone, of **mochil** speking evel avised   much
Ther lasse speking had ynough suffised[22]
Cometh mochil harm; thus was me told and taught –
In mochel speche synne **wantith nought**.   lacks for nothing
Wost where wherof a **racle** tonge serveth?   do you know; reckless
Right a swerd; for kutteth and kerveth
An arm a-tuo, my dere sone – right so
A tonge cutteth frendschip al a-tuo.
A jangler is to God abhominable;   chatterer
Red Salamon, so wys and honurable.
340 Red David in his psalmes, red Senek –[23]
My sone, spek not, but with thy heed thu **bek**.   nod
Dissimul as thou were deed, if that thou heere   pretend as if dead
A jangler speke of **perilous mateere**.   dangerous subjects
The Flemyng saith, and **lere** it if the **lest**,[24]   learn; want to
That litil jangling causeth mochil **rest**.   outcome
My sone, if thou no wikked word hast sayd,
The thar not drede for to be **bywrayed**;   betrayed
But he that hath mys-sayd, I dar wel sayn,
He may by no way **clepe** his word agayn.   take back
350 Thing that is sayd, is sayd; and forth it goth,
Though him repent, or be him never so **loth**.   sorry
He is his **thral**, to whom that he hath sayd   servant
A tale of which **he is now yvel apayd**.[25]
My sone, be war, and be noon auctour newe
Of tydyngs, whether thay ben fals or trewe.
Wherso thou comest, amonges heih or lowe,
Kep wel thy tonge, and thenk upon the crowe.'

here endith the tale of the crowe

22' Of talking too much when few words will do . . .'
23 Seneca, in De Ira (on anger)
24 From a Flemish proverb.
25 'which he has lived to regret'

THE PARSON'S PROLOGUE AND TALE

The host notes that it must be ten o'clock. The light is fading, and every 'degre' of pilgrim has told a tale – except one. The host turns to the parson, asking for the final tale. The parson says that he will not tell a story; he is a southern man, and cannot alliterate. Nor is he 'textuel' like a learned clerk, but he will give them 'moralite and virtuous matiere'. The host exhorts the parson to say what he wants, but be 'fruitful' because it is getting dark. The parson then delivers a treatise on penitence . . . on the need to repent truly for one's sins, and offers details of the remedies for the seven deadly sins, one sin at a time. After this, he details how to offer penitence in order to be forgiven.

The Parson's Pale ends *The Canterbury Tales*. It would appear that it was Chaucer's intention that it should do so. This is supplied by the parson in what appears to be a sermon but is in fact a treatise on penitence. Like the rest of the tales, the parson's tale is a literary construction (intended for reading) masquerading as a speech act (intended for hearing). The pilgrims are approaching Canterbury, and need to be reminded why they joined (at least, why they should have joined) the pilgrimage in the first place. They travelled from Blean (where the manciple's tale was delivered), where the road rises from the woods, over the hill (where the University of Kent at Canterbury now stands, and where there is a panoramic view of the city and cathedral, which they would have seen), and down towards the city, possibly arriving at an inn on the main road just outside the city. Tomorrow, they will cross the river and enter the city through the gate (there is still a medieval gateway there, with the foundations of the Roman original still visible), then go through the city to the cathedral. Here they will visit the shrine of St Thomas, the knight, the parson, the ploughman and others will be blessed, the wife of Bath will obtain the final pilgrim badge for her 'set', and maybe the pardoner will find a business opportunity. To gain the maximum benefit from their visit, they will need first to confess their sins and be shriven (officially forgiven). The parson reminds them of the importance of this process, and tells them how.

The source of the tale is unknown, and there are no clues as to its date, which means that it could have been produced earlier in Chaucer's life, as were the tales of the knight and the second nun, and added when he needed an ending. It may, however (and this seems somewhat more likely), have been composed after the other tales had been completed, in order to provide a suitable ending for an already existing, although incomplete, body of work. Not enough is known about Chaucer's life (was he aware that he was dying and needed to complete the work quickly?) or about his source material, to make such a judgement possible. Within The Parson's Tale it is possible to detect two main source works, both of the thirteenth century and both by Dominican friars: the *Summa vitiorum* (Summary of Vices) of William Peyraut, and the *Summa de penitentia* (Summary of Penitence) of Raymund of Pennaforte. However, both of these works were well known in Chaucer's day, and it is highly unlikely, given his previous practice of using fourteenth-century sources, largely in French and Italian, that Chaucer would have compiled a treatise using these alone as his base. It does remain possible that he could have done this; he certainly had the linguistic ability to do it, and therefore he may have done so. What seems more likely is that Chaucer used a later source which was itself adapted from these works. This is made more likely by the awkwardness of the parson's prose, which does not demonstrate the literary poise of, for example, The Tale of Melibee, the other prose work of the *Tales*, which *was* composed by Chaucer. The parson uses a hotchpotch of authorities, biblical and patristic, laced with proverbial sayings and personal observations, in a manner typical of the contemporary sermon. His quotes are often mis-quoted and his Latin quotes are frequently mistranslated or elaborated (for example, his extension of Revelation 3:20, where Christ's invitation to the sinner to open the door of his heart and allow Him in for dinner is carried well beyond the biblical original), as if the parson is incapable of making a biblical reference without unbiblical elaboration. This, of course, is part of Chaucer's ambiguous characterisation of the speaker, and demonstrates that, whatever the source, the final result is uniquely the writer's own. The parson, as a character, is the most fulsomely praised by 'Geoffrey' the pilgrim (and, by implication, by the writer himself), and yet even he is offered up for judgement, and implied – if gentle – criticism, by the tale which he tells and the manner of its telling.

The use of prose indicates that this is a serious, didactic message, as the parson has indicated in his prologue. He will not tell a 'tale' for entertainment, or 'game'. Instead, he delivers a treatise, or 'sermon' on sins, vices and the 'remedies' by which they can be cured. The steps offered by the parson as means to a true 'translation' are contrition (being sorry), confession (oral, to a priest) and absolution (again, by a priest).

During the course of his tale, he manages to indict most of the other pilgrims, with the possible exception of his brother, the ploughman, and the knight. Some of the vices he mentions include: desiring public precendence (wife of Bath, tradesmen); gluttony and drunkenness (cook, miller, franklin, pardoner); pride in knowledge (clerk, monk); excess of dress (squire, pardoner); marital infidelity and courtly love (franklin, wife of Bath); vanity (prioress); avarice (pardoner, reeve); sexual immorality (miller, friar, summoner); homicide (shipman); theft (man of law, physician, reeve, manciple, summoner); abuse of clergy (friar, pardoner); hypocrisy (doctor, merchant, and just about everyone else with the exception of the ploughman and the knight); and the telling of fables ('Geoffrey' and the nun's priest). There are many others; how many of the pilgrims can you detect in the parson's 'sin list'? These people all need to take the three steps to obtain the blessing of God and St Thomas, and achieve the goal of their pilgrimage, personal transformation from base metal into pure gold. Having read the tales and digested their meaning, so also do we, the readers.

Key Questions

How many of the pilgrims and their tales can been seen reflected in The Parson's Tale?

What can The Parson's Tale reveal about popular religion in later medieval England, and about the teaching of the Church on penitence and the seven deadly sins?

How appropriate is The Parson's Tale at this point in *The Canterbury Tales*?

Topic Keywords

Medieval theology/ popular religion/ the medieval Church

Further Reading

Judson Allen, 'The Old Way and the Parson's Way: An Ironic Reading of The Parson's Tale', *Journal of Medieval and Renaissance Studies*, 3, 1973, pp. 255–71

Thomas Bestul, 'Chaucer's Parson's Tale and the Late-Medieval Tradition of Religious Meditation', *Speculum*, 64, 1989, pp. 600–19

Laurie Finke, 'To Knytte up al this Feste: The Parson's Rhetoric and the Ending of *The Canterbury Tales*', *Leeds Studies in English*, 15, 1984, pp. 95–107

John Finlayson, 'The Satiric Mode and The Parson's Tale', *Chaucer Review*, 6, 1971, pp. 94–116

Wendy Harding, 'The Function of Pity in Three Canterbury Tales', *Chaucer Review*, 32, 1997, pp. 162–74

Albert E. Hartung, 'The Parson's Tale and Chaucer's Penance', in *Literature and Religion in the Later Middle Ages: Philological Studies in Honor of Siegfried Wenzel*, edited by Richard G. Newhauser and John A. Alford, Binghamton, NY, Medieval and Renaissance Texts and Studies, 1995, pp. 61–80

Linda Tarte Holley and David Raybin, *Closure in the Canterbury Tales: The Role of The Parson's Tale*, Medieval Institute Publications, Kalamazoo, Western Michigan University, 2000

Carol Kaske, 'Getting around The Parson's Tale: An Alternative to Allegory and Irony', in *Chaucer at Albany*, edited by Rossell Robbins, New York, Franklin, 1975, pp. 147–78

Frances McCormack, *Chaucer and the Culture of Dissent: The Lollard Context and Subtext of The Parson's Tale*, Dublin and Portland, OR, Four Courts Press, 2007

Michael Olmert, 'The Parson's Ludic Formula for Winning on the Road (to Canterbury)', *Chaucer Review*, 20, 1985, pp. 158–68

Charles A. Owen Jr, 'What the Manuscripts Tell Us about The Parson's Tale', *Medium Ævum*, 63, 1994, pp. 239–49

Lee W. Patterson, 'The Parson's Tale and the Quitting of *The Canterbury Tales*', *Traditio*, 34, 1978, pp. 331–80

Paul G. Ruggiers, 'Serious Chaucer: The Tale of Melibeus and The Parson's Tale', in *Chaucerian Problems and Perspectives: Essays Presented to Paul E. Beichner*, edited by Edward Vasta and Zacharias P. Thundy, Notre Dame, IN, and London, Notre Dame University Press, 1979, pp. 83–94

Judi Shaw, 'Corporeal and Spiritual Homicide, the Sin of Wrath and The Parson's Tale', *Traditio*, 38, 1982, pp. 281–300

Krista Sue-Lo Twu, 'Chaucer's Vision of the Tree of Life: Crossing the Road with the Rood in The Parson's Tale', *Chaucer Review*, 39, 2005, pp. 341–78

Chauncey Wood, 'Speech, the Principle of Contraries, and Chaucer's Tales of The Manciple and The Parson', *Mediaevalia*, 6, 1980, pp. 209–22

And here bygynneth the prologe of the parsoun's tale

❦ By that the Maunciple had his tale endid,
The sonne fro the south line is descendid[1]
So lowe, that it has nou*gh*t **to my sight**   as far as I can see
Degrees nyne and twenty as in hight.[2]
Ten **on the clokke** it was, as I gesse,   o'clock
For eleven foote, or litil more or lesse
My schadow was, at thilke tyme of the yere,
Of which feet, as my lengthe parted were,
In sixe feet equal of proporcioun.[3]   10
Therwith the moone's exaltacioun –
I mene Libra – alway gan ascende,
As we were entryng at a town's ende;
For which our host, as he was wont to **gye**   direct
As in this **caas**, our joly compaignye,   situation
Sayd in this wise, 'Lordings **everichoon**,   each one
Now lakketh us no more tales than oon.
Fulfilled is my **sentens**, and my decre –   judgement
I trowe that we han herd of ech **degre** –   social status
Almost fulfilled is myn **ordynaunce**.   decree   20
I pray to God, so geve him right good **chaunce**   fortune
That telleth to us his tale lustily.
Sir Prest,' quod he, 'artow a **vicory**?   vicar
Or artow a **persoun**? Say soth, by my fay;   parson
Be what thou be – ne breke nought oure play,
For every man save thou hath told his tale;
Unbocle, and schew us what is in thy **male**,   unbuckle; bag
For trewely me thinketh by thy chier
Thou scholdist wel knyt up a gret matier.[4]
Tel us a tale anoon, for cokke's boones!'[5]   30
This persoun him answerde al at oones,

1 The sun has gone down
2 The sun was less than twenty-nine degrees above the horizon.
3 At this time of the year, his shadow was eleven feet long at this time of night.
4 'You should be able to provide a conclusion for an important subject'
5 'for cock's (ie. God's) bones'

'Thow getist fable noon y-told for me;
For Poul, that writes unto Thimothe,
Repreveth hem that **weyveth** sothfastnesse,   reproves; desert
And tellen fables, and such wrecchednesse.
Why schuld I sowen draf out of my fest,
Whan I may sowe whete, if that me lest?[6]
For which I say, if that yow lust to hiere
Moralite and vertuous matiere,
40   And thanne that ye wil **give me audience**;   listen to me
I wol ful fayn, at Crist's reverence,
Do yow **plesaunce leful** as I can.   lawful pleasure
But trusteth wel, I am a **suthern** man;   southern
I can not geste; rum, raf, ruf, by letter;[7]
Ne, God wot, rym hold I but litel better.
And therfor, if yow lust, I wol not **glose** –   use obscure speech
I wol yow telle a mery tale in prose,
To **knyt up** al this fest, and make an ende;   bring an end to
And Jhesu, for his grace, wit me sende
50   To schewe yow the way in this **viage**   journey
Of thilke perfyt glorious pilgrimage,
That **hatte** Jerusalem celestial;[8]   is called
And if ye **vouchesauf**, anoon I schal   grant
Bygynne my tale, for which I yow pray
Telle your **avis** – I can no better say.   opinion
But **natheles**, this meditacioun,   nevertheless
I put it **ay** under correccioun   always
Of clerkes, for I am not **textuel**[9]
I take but the **sentens**, trustith wel –   meaning
60   Therfor I make protestacioun
That I wol stonde to correccioun –
Upon this word we han assented soone,
For as it semed, it was for to done[10]
To enden in som vertuous sentence,

6 'why should I sow chaff from my feast, when I may sow wheat, if I want to?'
7 A reference to alliterative poetry, identifying it with the North of England. 'I
  don't know how to write a 'geste' in 'ram, rum, ruf, by letter'
8 The New Jerusalem, site of God's throne in the Book of Revelation
9 Educated in many learned texts
10 'it was the best thing to do'

And for to geve him space and audience.
And **bad** ourre host he schulde to him say   ask
That alle we to telle his tale him pray.
Our host hadde the wordes for us alle;
'Sir Prest,' quod he, 'now faire yow bifalle![11]
Say what yow **lust**, and we wil gladly hiere.'   like   70
And with that word, he said in this manere;
'Telleth,' quod he, 'your meditacioun,
But haste yow – the sonne wol adoun.
Beth **fructuous**, and that in litel space,   fruitful
And to do wel, God send yow his grace.'

*State super vias & videte et interrogate de semitis antiquis
que sit via bona et ambulate in ea et inuenietis
refrigerium animabus vestris & cetera*[12]

❦ Owre swete Lord God of heven, that no man wil perische, but wol
that we comen alle to the knowleche of him, and to the blisful lif that is
perdurable, amonestith[13] us by the prophet Jeremye, that saith in this
wise: 'Stonde upon the weyes and seeth & axeth of olde pathes, that is
to sayn of old sentence, which is the good way, and ye schul fynde
refresshyng for youre soules & cetera.'

Many ben the wayes espirituels that leden folk to oure Lord Jhesu
Christ and to the regne of glorie, of whiche weyes ther is a ful noble way
and ful covenable[14] which may not faile to man ne to womman, that
thorough synne hath mysgon fro the right way of Jerusalem celestial, and
this wey is cleped[15] penitence. Of which men schulden gladly herken
and enquere with al here herte, to wyte what is penitence, and whens it
is cleped penitence, and in what maner, and in how many maners been
the acciones or workynges of penaunce, and how many spieces ben of
penitences, & which thinges apperteynen and byhoven to penitence,
and which thinges destourben penitence.

Seint Ambrose saith that penitence is the pleynyng of man for the gult

11 'may good things happen to you'
12 See below for the parson's translation of this text from Jeremiah 6:16
13 eternal, admonishes
14 suitable, proper
15 called

that he hath doon, and no more to do onything for which him oughte to pleigne. And som doctour saith, 'Penitence is waymentynge of man that sorweth for his synne, and peyneth himself for he hath mysdoon'. Penitence, with certeyn circumstaunces, is verray repentaunce of man that holt himself in sorwe and in woo for his giltes; and for he schal be verray penitent, he schal first bywaile the synnes that he hath do, and stedfastly purposen in his hert to haven schrifte of mouth,[16] and to doon satisfaccioun, and never to do thing for which him oughte more to bywayle or to complayne, and to continue in goode werkes – or elles his repentaunce may nought avayle. For, as saith Seint Isidore, 'He is a japere and a gabber, and no verray repentaunt, that eftsoone doth thing for which him oughte to repente'. Wepynge, and nought for to stynte to doon synne, may nought availe;[17] but natheles, men schal hope that at every tyme that men fallith, be it never so ofte, that he may arise thorugh penitence, if he have grace. But certeyn, it is gret doute; for, as saith Seint Gregory, 'Unnethe arist he out of his synne that is charged with the charge of yvel usage'.[18] And therfore, repentaunt folk that stinte for to synne and forlete synne, er that synne forlete hem, Holy Chirche holt hem siker of her savacioun.[19] And he that synne, and verraily repentith him in his last ende, Holy Chirche yit hopeth his savacioun, by the grete mercy of Oure Lord Jhesu Crist, for his repentaunce – but take the siker way.

And now, sith that I have declared yow what thing is penitence, now schul ye understonde that ther ben thre acciouns[20] of penitence:

The first is, that if a man be baptised after that he hath synned. Seint Augustyn saith but if he be penitent for his olde synful lif, he may not bygynne the newe, clene lif; for certes, if he be baptised withoute penitence of his olde gilt, he receyveth the mark of baptisme but nought the grace, ne the remissioun of his synnes, til he have repentaunce verray. Another defaut is this; that men doon deedly synne after that thay haue receyved baptisme. The thridde defaute is that men fallen into venial synne after here baptisme, fro day to day. Therof saith Seint Austyn, that penitence of goode men and of humble folk is the penitens of every day.

The spices[21] of penitence ben thre; at oon of hem is solempne, another

16 oral confession (confessing to a priest)
17 'Weeping, and not ceasing to do sin, isn't any good'
18 'He who is guilty of continual sinning may hardly rise out of his sin'
19 'Holy Church considers them sure of their salvation'
20 actions, ie ways in which penitence can happen
21 species, types

is comune, and the thridde is pryve. Thilke penaunce that is solempne is
in tuo maners; as is to be put out of Holy Chirche in Lente for slaughtre
of childre, and such maner thing; another is whan a man hath synned
openly, of which synne the fame is openly spoken in the contre, and
thanne Holy Chirche by juggement streyne[22] him to doon open penaunce.
Comun penaunce is that prestes enjoynen men comunly in certeyn caas
as for to goon peraduenture naked in pilgrimage, or barfot. Prive
penaunce is thilk that men doon alday for prive synnes, of whiche we
schryve us prively, and receyven prive penaunce.

Now schalt thou understonde what bihove and is necessarie to verray
perfyt penitence, and this stondith in thre thinges: contricioun of herte,
confessioun of mouth, and satisfaccioun. For whiche saith Seint John
Crisostom, 'Penitence distryne man to accepte benignely every peyne
that him is enjoyned; with contricioun of herte and schrift of mouth,
with satisfaccioun and werking of all maner humblete'. And this is
fruytful penitence agayn thre thinges in which we wrathe Oure Lord
Jhesu Crist; this is to sayn, by delit in thinking, by rechelesnes in speking,
by wicked, synful werkyng. Again these thre wickid gultes is penitence,
that may be likned unto a tre. The roote of this tre is contricioun, that
hydith hiim in the hert of him that is verray repentaunt. Right as the
roote of a tree hidith him in the eorthe, of the roote of contricioun
springe a stalk that bereth braunches and leeves of confessioun, and
fruyt of satisfaccioun. For whiche Crist saith in his gospel, 'Do digne[23]
fruyt of penitence. For by this fruyt may men knowe this tree, and nought
by the roote that is hyd in the hert of a man, ne by the braunches, ne the
levys, of confessioun'. And therfore Oure Lord Jhesu Crist saith thus, 'By
the fruyt of hem schul ye knowe hem'.[24]

Of this roote eek springeth a seed of grace, the which seed is mooder
of sikurnes,[25] and this seed is egre[26] and hoot. The grace of this seed
springe of God, thorough remembraunce of the Day of Doom and of the
paynes of helle. Of this matier saith Salomon, that in the drede of God
man forlete[27] his synne.[28] The hete of this seed is the love of God, & the
desiring of the joye perdurable; this hete drawe the hert of man to god,
and doth him hate his synne. Forsothe, ther is nothing that serveth so
wel to a child as the milk of his norice,[29] ne nothing is to him more

---

22 constrain/force   25 'mother of security'   28 Proverbs 16:6
23 worthy   26 bitter   29 wet-nurse
24 Matthew 7:20   27 abandons

abhominable than the milk whan it is melled with other[30] mete. Right so, the synful man that loveth his synne, him semeth it is to him most swete of enything, but fro that tyme he love sadly Oure Lord Jhesu Crist, and desireth the lif perdurable, ther nys to him nothing more abhominable; for sothly, the lawe of God is the love of God. For which Davyd saith, 'I have loved thy lawe, and hated wikkednesse and hate'. He that loveth God, keepe his lawe and his word. This tree saugh the prophete Daniel in spirit upon the avysioun[31] of Nabugodonosor, whan he counseiled him to do penaunce.[32] Penaunce is tre of lif to hem that it receyven, and he that holdeth him in verry penitence is blessed, after the sentence[33] of Salomon.

In this penitence or contricioun, men schal understonde foure thinges; that is to sayn, what is contricioun, and how he schulde be contrit, and what contricioun availeth to the soule. Thanne it is thus; that contricioun is the verray sorwe that a man receyveth in his herte for his synnes, with sad purpos to schryve him and to doo penaunce, and never more to don synne. And this sorwe schal be in this maner, as saith Seint Bernard, 'It schal be hevy and grevous, and ful scharp and poynaunt, for he hath wrathed and agilt him that brought him with his precious blood, and hath delyvered us fro the bondes of synne, and fro the cruelte of the devel, and fro the peynes of helle'.

The causes that oughten to moeve a man to contricioun ben vj:[34] first, a man schal remembre him of his synnes, but loke that thilke remembrance be to no delyt of him by no way, but gret schame and sorwe for his gilt. For Job saith that synful men doon werkes worthy of confessioun,[35] and therfor saith Ezechie,[36] 'I wol remembre all the yeres of my lif in bitternesse of myn herte'. And God saith in Apocalips,[37] 'Remembre yow from whens that ye ben falle'; for biforn that tyme that ye synned ye were the children of God[and lymme of the regne of God,[38] but for youre synne ye be woxe thral and foul, and membres of the feend, hate of aungels, sclaunder of Holy Chirche, & foode of the fals serpent, perpetuel matier of the fuyr of helle, and yet more foule and abhominable; for ye trespassen so ofte tyme as doth the hound that tourneth to ete his spewyng, & yet ye ben fouler, for youre longe continuyng in synne and youre synful usage, for whiche ye ben roten in youre synne as a beest in

---

30 mixed wth other food   33 judgement   36 King Hezekiah. Isaiah 38:15
31 prophetic dream   34 six   37 Revelation 2:5
32 Daniel 4:7ff.   35 Proverbs 12:4   38 the kingdom of God

his donge. Suche maner of thoughtes make a man have schame of his synne, and no delit. And God saith by the prophete Ezechiel, 'Ye schul remembre yow of youre weyes, & thay schal displese yow sothly'.[39] Synnes ben the way that leden folk to helle.

The secounde cause that oughte make a man to have disdeyn of his synne is this; that, as seith Seint Petre, 'Whoso do synne is thral of synne, and synne put a man in gret thraldom'[40] And therfore saith the prophete Ezechiel, 'I went sorwful, in disdeyn of myself'. Certes, wel oughte a man have disdeyn of synne, and withdrawe him fro that thraldom and vilonye. And lo, what saith Seneca in this matiere.[41] He saith thus: 'Though I wiste that God nere man schulde never knowe it, yit wold I have disdeyn for to do synne'. And the same Seneca also saith, 'I am born to gretter thinges than to be thral to my body, or than for to make of my body a thral'. Ne a fouler thral may no man ne womman make of his body, than give his body to synne, and were it the foulest cherl or the foulest womman that lyve, and lest of value; yet is thanne synne more foul and more in servitute. Ever fro the heigher degre that man fallith, the more he is thral, and more to God and to the world vile and abhominable. O, goode God! Wel oughte a man have gret disdayn of such a thing that thorough synne, ther he was free, now is he maked bonde! And therfore saith Seint Austyn, 'If thou hast disdayn of thy servaunt if he agilte or synne, have thou an disdeigne that thou thiself schuldist do synne. Tak reward of thy value, that thou be nought to foul in thiself'. Allas! Wel oughte men have disdeyn to be servauntes & thralles to synne, & sore ben aschamed of hemself that God of his endeles goodnes hath set hem in heigh estate, or geven hem witte, strength of body, hele, beaute, prosperite, and bought hem fro the deth with his herte blood, that thay so unkindely ageinst his gentilesce quyten so vileynsly, to slaughter of her oughne soules. O, goode God! Ye wommen that ben of so gret beaute, remembreth yow of the proverbe of Salomon, that saith he likene a fair womman that is a fool of hir body to a ryng of gold that were in the groyn of a sowe; for right as a sowe wroteth[42] in everich ordure, so wrootith sche hir beaute, in stynkyng ordure of synne.[43]

The thridde cause that oughte moeve a man to contricioun is drede of the Day of Doome,[44] & of the orrible peynes of helle; for as Seint Jerom

39 Ezechiel 20:43
40 servitude: 2 Peter 2:19
41 on this subject

42 grubs about
43 Proverbs 11:22
44 Doomsday, or the Last Judgement

saith, 'At every tyme that I remembre of the Day of Doom I quake; for whan I ete or drinke, or what so that I doo, ever seme me that the trompe[45] sowneth in myn eere: Rise ye up, that ben deede, and cometh to the Juggement''. O, goode God! Mochil[46] ought a man to drede such a juggement, ther as we schul be all; as seith Seint Poul, 'Biforn the sete of our Lord Jhesu Crist, wher as he schal make a general congregacioun, wher as no man may be absent; for certes, ther avayleth non essoyne, ne excusacioun'.[47] And nought oonly that, oure defaute schal be openly knowen; and as Seint Bernard saith, 'Ther schal no pleynyng avayle ne no sleight; we schuln give rekenyng of every ydel word'.[48] Ther schulle we have a juge that may nought be disceyved ne corrupt, and why? For certes, alle oure thoughtes ben descovered as to him; ne for prayer ne for meede[49] he nyl not be corupt. And therfor saith Salomon, 'The wrath of God ne wol nought be corupt'. And therfor saith Salomon, 'The wrath of God ne wol nought spare no wight, for praier ne for gift'.[50] And therfore at the Day of Doome ther is noon hope to eschape. Wherfor, as Seint Anselm seith, 'Ful greet anguisch schuln the synful folk have at that tyme; there schal the stern and the wroth Juge sitte above, and under him the horrible pit of hell open to destroye him that not byknowe[51] his synnes, which synnes openly ben schewed byforn God and biforn every creature; and on the lift syde mo develis than herte may thynke, for to hary and to drawe the synful to pyne of helle; and withinne the hertes of folk schal be the bytyng conscience, and withouteforth schal be the world al brennyng. Whider schal thanne the wrecched synful man flee to hyden him? Certes, he may not hyde him – he moot come forth and schewe him'. For certes, as seith Seynt Jerom, 'The erthe schal caste him out of him, and the see also, and the aer also, that schal be ful of thunder-clappes and lightnynges'.

Now sothly, whoso wel remembrith him of these tydynges, I gesse his synne schal not torne him to delit, but to gret sorw, for drede of the peyne of helle. And therfore saith Job to God, 'Suffre Lord, that I may a while biwayle and wepe or I go, withoute retournynge to the derk lond covered with derknes of deth to the lond of mysese and of derknesse, wheras is the schadow of deth, wheras is noon order ne ordinaunce, but

45 the trumpet, announcing the Day of Judgement
46 greatly/much
47 'no leave of absence, nor excuse': Romans 14:10
48 'there no pleading will be of help, nor any cunning; we shall account for every idle word'
49 bribe   50 Proverbs 6:34   51 acknowledge

grislich drede that ever schal last'. Loo, her may ye see that Job prayed respit a while, to wepe and biwayle his trespas; for forsothe, oon day of respit is bettre than al the tresor in this world. And forasmoche as a man may aquyte himself byforn God by penaunce in this world, and not by tresor, therfore schuld he praye to God giue him respit a while to wepe and to waile his trespas; for certes, al the world nys but a litel thing at regard of the sorw of helle.

The cause why that Job calleth helle the lond of derknes; understondith that he clepith it lond or eorthe for it is stable, and never schal fayle: derk; for he that is in helle hath defaut of light material, for certes the derke light that schal come out of the fuyr that ever schal brenne schal torne him to peyne that is in helle, for it schewith him to thorrible develes that him tormenten: covered with the derknes of deth; that is to sayn, that he that is in helle schal have defaute of the sight of God. For certes, the sight of God is the lif perdurable; the derknes of deth ben the synnes that the wrecchid man hath doon, whiche that stourben him to see the face of God, right as a derk cloude doth bitwixe us and the sonne: lond of mysese; bycause that there ben thre maner of defautes agains thre thinges that folk of this world han in this present lif; that is to sayn honures, delices, and richesses. Agayns honours; han they in helle schame and confusioun, for wel ye witen that men clepyn honure the reverence that men doon to the man; but in helle is noon honour ne reverence; for certes, no more reverence schal be doon to a kyng than to a knave. For which God saith by the prophete Jeremie, 'Thilke folk that me displesen schul be despit'.[52] Honour is eke cleped gret lordschipe. There schal no wight serven othir, but of harm and torment. Honour eek is cleped gret dignite and heighnes; but in helle schulle that be al fortrode of develes, and God saith orrible develes schuln goon and comen upon the heedes of dampned folk, and this is for als moche as the heyher that thay were in this present lif, the more schuln thay ben abasid and defouled in helle.

Agayns riches of this world schuln thay han mysese of povert. This povert schal be in iiij[53] thinges: in defaut of tresor; of which, as David saith, 'The riche folk that embraseden and onedin in al here herte the tresor of this world, scholn slepen in the slepyng of deth, and nothing schuln thay fynde in her hondes of al her tresor'.[54] And moreover, the mysease of helle schal be in the defaut of mete and drink; for God saith

52 1 Samuel 2:30   53 four   54 Psalm 75:6

thus by Moyses, 'Thay schul be wasted by hunger, and the briddes of helle schuln devoure hem with bitter deeth, and the galle of the dragoun schal be her drink, & the venym of the dragoun here morsels'.[55] And forthermoreover her misease schal be in defaut of clothing, for thay schul be naked in body as of clothing, save of fuyr in which thay brenne, and other filthis, and naked schuln thay be of soule. Wher ben thanne the gaye robes, and the softe scheetis, and the smale schirtes? Lo, what saith of hem the prophete Isaye: 'Under hem schuln be strewed mothis, and here couertours[56] schuln ben of wormes of helle'.[57] And forthermorover, here disease schal be in defaute of frendes, for he is not pouere that hath goode frendes; but here is no frend, for neither God ne no creature schal be frend unto hem, and everich of hem schal hate other with dedly hate. 'The sones and the doughtres schuln rebellen agayns the fader and the mooder, and kynrede agayns kynrede, and chiden and despisen everich of hem other, bothe day and night', as God saith by the prophete Michias.[58] And the lovyng children, that whilom loveden so fleisschlich everych other, wolden everych of hem eten other, if thay mighten. For how schulden thay loven hem togider in the peyne of helle, whan thay hated everich of hem other in the prosperite of this lif? For trustith wel, her fleisshly love was dedly hate; as saith the prophete David: 'Whoso that love wickidnes, hateth his soule; and whoso hatith his oughne soule, certis he may not love noon other wight in no manere'.[59, 60] And therfore in helle is no solace, ne frendschipe, but ever the more flesshly kynredes that ben in helle, the more cursynge, the more chydynges, and the more deedly hate ther is among hem.

And fortherover, thay schul have defaute of all manere delices; for certis, delices ben the appetites of thy fyve wittes: as sight, hieryng, smellyng, savoring, and touching. But in helle here sight schal be ful of derknesse and of smoke, and therfore ful of teeris; and her hieryng ful of waymentyngge and of grintynge of teeth, as saith Jhesu Crist, 'Her nosethurles[61] schuln ben ful of stynkyng stynk', and as saith Ysaye the prophete, 'Here savoringe schal be ful of bitter galle, and touchyng of al here body y-covered with, fuyr that never schal quenche, and with wormes that never schuln deyen, as God saith by the mouth of Ysaie.[62] And for also moche as thay schuln nought wene that thay may deyen for peyne,

55 Deuteronomy 32:24
56 bedcoverings
57 Isaiah 14:11
58 Micah 7:6
59 Psalm 10:6
60 Isaiah 24:9; 66;24
61 nostrils
62 Isaiah

and by here deth fle fro peyne, that may thay understonde in the word of
Job, that saith, 'Ther as is the schadow of deth'. Certes, a schadow hath
the liknesse of the thing of which it is a schadow, but the schadoew is
nought the same thing of whiche it is schadowe; right so fare the peyne
of helle. It is like deth for the horrible anguisshe; and why? For it peyneth
hem ever as though men scholden deye anon, but certes thay schul not
deye. For as saith Seint Gregory, 'To wrecchid caytifs schal be give deth
withoute deth, and ende withouten ende, and defaute withouten faylinge;
for here deth schal alway lyven, and here ende schal evermore bygynne,
and here defaute schal not fayle. And therfore saith Seint John the
Evaungelist,[63] 'Thay schul folwe deth and thay schuln nought fynde him,
and thay schul desire to deyen and deth schal flee fro hem.

    And eek Job saith that in helle is noon ordre of rule; and albeit that
God hath creat al thing in right ordre, but alle thinges ben ordeyned and
noumbred, yit natheles thay that ben dempned been nought in ordre, ne
holden non ordre; for the eorthe schal bere hem no fruyt. For as the
prophete David saith, 'God schal destroye the fruyt of the eorthe as for
hem, ne watir schal give hem no moysture, ne the aier non refreishing, ne
fuyr no light'.[64] For, as seith Seint Basile, 'The brennyng of the fuyr of
this world schal God give in helle to to hem that ben dampnyd, but the
light and the clernesse schal be geve in hevene to his children; right as
the goode man geve fleisch to his children, and bones to his houndes'.
And for thay schul have noon hope to eschape, saith Seint Job, atte laste,
that, 'ther schal horrour and grisly drede duelle wiouten ende'.

    Horrour is alway drede of harm that is to come, and this drede schal
ever duelle in the hertes of hem that ben dampnyd, and therfore han that
lorn al here hope for vij[65] causes: first; for God that is here Jugge schal be
withoute mercy to hem, ne thay may not please him, ne noon of his
halwes,[66] ne thay may give nothing for here raunsoun, ne thay have no
voice to speke to him, ne thay may not fle fro payne, ne thay have no
goodnes in hem that thay may schewe, to delivere hem fro peyne. And
therfore saith Salomon, 'The wikked man deye, and whan he is deed he
schal have noon hope to eschape fro peyne'.[67] Whoso wolde, thanne wel
understonde these peynes, and bythynk him wel that he hath deserved
thilke paynes for his synnes; certes, he schulde have more talent to

---

63 Note the similarity with the Pardoner's Old Man. Revelation 9:6
64 Psalm 106:34   65 seven   66 saints   67 Proverbs 11:7

sikyn[68] and to wepe, than for to synge or pleye. For as that Salamon saith, 'Whoso that hath the science to knowe the peynes that ben establid and ordeynt for synne, he wolde make sorwe'. Thilke science, as saith Seint Austyn, maketh a man to wayment in his herte.

The fourthe poynt that oughte make a man have contricioun is the sorwful remembraunce of the good that he ha left to doon heer in eorthe, and eek the good that he hath lorn. Sothly, the goode werkes that he ha left, eyther thay been the goode werkes that he wrou*g*ht er he fel into deedly synne, or elles thai ben the goode werkes that he dede er he fel into synne, ben amortised and astoneyed and dullid by ofte synnynge, that othere goode werkes that he wrou*g*hte whul he lay in dedly synne been outrely deed as to the lif perdurable in heven. Thanne thilke goode werkes that ben mortified by ofte synnyng, which goode werkes he dede whiles he was in charite, ne mow never quyken agayn withouten verray penitence. And therof saith God by the mouth of Ezechiel, that, 'if the rightful man retourne agayn fro his rightwisnesse and werke wikkednesse, schal he live? Nay, for all the good werkes that he hath wrought ne schuln never be in remembraunce, for he schal dye in his synne'.[69] And upon thilke chapitre saith Seint Gregory thus, that, 'we schuln understonde this principally that whan we doon dedly synne, it is for nought thanne to reherse or to drawe into memorie the goode werkes that we han don biforne this tyme'; that is to say, as for to have therby the lif perdurable in heven. But natheles, the goode werkes quiken agayn and comen again and helpen, and availen to have the lif perdurable in heven whan we han contricioun. But sothly, the good werkes that men doon whil that thai ben in deedly synne, thay may never quyken; and albeit that thay availen not to have the lif perdurable, yit avaylen thay to abrigging[70] of the peyne of helle, or elles to gete temporal riches, or elles that God wol the rather enlymyne[71] and lightene the hert of the synful man to have repentaunce, and eek they availen for to usen a man to do goode werkes, that the feend have the lasse power of his soule.

And thus the curteys Lord Jhesu Crist ne wolde nought no good werk be lost, for in somwhat it schal availe. But for als moche as the goode werkes that men don whil thay ben in good lif ben amortised by synne folwyng, and eek sith that all the goode werkes that men doon whil thay ben in dedly synne been outrely deede as for to have the lif perdurable,

68 sigh
69 Ezechiel 18:24

70 lessening
71 illumine

wel may that man that no goode werkes werkith synge thilke newe freisch song, '*J'ay tout perdu moun temps & moun labour*'[72] For certis, synne byreveth a man bothe goodnes of nature, and eek the goodnes of grace. For sothly, the grace of the Holy Gost fareth lik fyre that may not ben ydel; for fuyr, as it forletith his werkyng and faile anoon, and right so, whan the grace faile, than lesith the synful man the goodnes of glorie, that oonly is byhight[73] to goode men, that labouren and werken. Wel may he be sory thanne, that owe al his lif to God as longe as he hath lyved, and eek as longe as he schal lyve, that no goodnes ne hath to paye with his dette to God, to whom he owe al his lyf. For trusteth wel, he schal give accompt, as saith Seint Bernard, of alle the goodes that han be geven him in this present lif, & how he hath hem dispendid; nat so moche that ther ne schal not perische an heer of his heed, ne a moment of an hour ne schal not perische of his tyme, that he ne schal give of it a rekenyng.

The vte[74] maner of contricioun that moeveth a man therto is the remembraunce of the passioun that Oure Lord Jhesu Crist suffred for us, and for oure synnes. For, as seith Seint Bernard, 'Whil that I lyve I schal have remembraunce of the passioun that Oure Lord Jhesu Crist suffred for us in preching, his werynesse in travayling, his temptacioun, whan he fastid, his longe wakinges whan he prayde, his teeres whan he wepte for pite of good peple, the wo and the schame and the filth that men saide to him, of the foul spittyng that men spitten on his face, of the buffetis that men gaf him, of the foule mowes and of the reproues that men to him saiden, of the nayles with whiche he was nayled to the cros, and of al the remenaunt of his passioun that he suffred for my synnes, and nothing for his gilt. And ye schal understonde that in man's synne is every maner ordre of ordinaunce turned upso doun; for it is soth that God & resoun, and sensualite, and the body of man, be so ordeyned that everich of these iiij schulde have lordschipe over resoun, and resoun over sensualite, and eek over the body of man. And why? For sensualite rebellith thanne agayns resoun, and by that way lesith resoun the lordschipe over sensualite and over the body. For right as resoun is rebel to God, right so is bothe sensualite rebel to resoun and the body also. And certis, this disordynaunce and this rebellioun Oure Lord Jhesu Crist bought upon his precious body ful deere. And herkeneth in which wise.

72 'I have wasted my time and my labour'
73 granted   74 fifth

For as moche as resoun is rebel to God: therfore is man worthy to have
sorwe and to be deed. This suffred Oure Lord Jhesu Crist for man, and
after that, he was bytryed of his disciple, and destreyned and bounde, so
that the blood brast out at every nayl of his hondes, as saith Seint Austyn.
And fortherover, for as mochil as resoun of man wol nought daunte
sensualite whan it may, therfore is man worthy to have schame. And this
suffred Oure Lord Jhesu Crist for man whan thay spitten in his face. And
fortherover; thanne forasmoche as the caytif body of man is rebelle bothe
to resoun and sensualite, therfore it is worthy the deth. And this suffred
Oure Lord Jhesu Crist for us upon the croys, wheras ther was no part of
his body fre withoute great peyne and bitter passioun. And al this suffred
Jhesu Crist that never forleted. So mochil am I streyned for the thinges
that I never deservyd, and to moche defouled for schendschip[75] that man
is worthy to have. And therfore may the synful man wel seye, as saith
Seint Bernard, 'Acursed be the bitternesse of my synne, for which ther
moste be suffred so muchel bitternesse'; for certis, after the dyvers
discordaunces of oure wickednes was the passioun of Oure Lord Jhesu
Crist ordeyned in divers thinges, as thus.

Certis, sinful man's soule is bytraysid of the devel by coveitise of
temporal prosperite, and scorned by disceyt whan he cheseth fleischly
delytes, and yit is it tormentid by impacience of adversite and byspit by
servage and subjeccioun of synne, and atte last it is slayn finally. For this
discordaunce of synful man was Jhesu Crist first bytraised, and after was
he bounde, that com for to unbynden us fro synne and of peyne. Than
was he scorned, that oonly schulde be honoured in alle thing, of alle
thinges. Than was his visage, that oughte be desired to be say of al
mankynde, in which visage aungels desiren to loke, vileynsly byspit.
Thanne was he scorned, that nothing had agilt. And fynally, thanne was
he crucified and slayn. Thanne was accomplised the word of Ysaye, 'He
was woundid for oure mysdede, and defouled by oure felonyes'.[76] Now,
sith Jhesu Crist tok upon him thilke peyne of all oure wikkednes, mochil
oughte synful men wepe and bywayle, that for his synnes schulde God's
sone of hevene al this endure.

The vj[te] thing that oughte to moeve a man to contricioun is the hope
of thre thinges; that is to sayn, forgevenes of synne and the gifte of grace
wel for to do, and the glorie of heven with which God schal guerdoun[77]
man for his goode deedis. And for als moche as Jhesu Crist geveth us
these giftes of his largesse, and of his soverayn bounte, therfore is he

75 ruin   76 Isaiah 53:5   77 reward

cleped '*Jhesus nazarenus rex iudaeorum*'[78] Jhesus is for to say saveour or savacioun, of whom men schal hope to have forgevenes of synnes, which that is proprely savacioun of synnes. And therfore seyde the aungel to Joseph, 'Thou clepe his name Jhesus, that schal save his poeple of here synnes'.[79] And herof saith Seint Petir, 'Ther is noon other name under heven that is geve to any man by which a man may be savyd, but oonly Jhesus'.[80] *Nazarenus* is as moche to say as, florisching, in which a man schal hope that he that geve him remissioun of synnes schal give him grace wel to doo, for in the flour is hope of fruyt in tyme comynge, and in forgivenes hope of grace wel to do. 'I was at the dore of thin herte,' saith Jhesus, 'and cleped for to entreth; he that openith to me schal have forgeuenes of synne. I wol entre in to him by my grace, and soupe with him by the goode workes that he schal doon, whiche werkes be the foode of God, and he schal soupe with me by the grete joye that I schal give him.'[81] Thus schal man hope that for his werkis of penaunce God schal give him his regne,[82] as he behetith him in the gospel.

Now schal man understonde in what maner schal be his contricioun. I say, it schal be universal and total; this is to say, a man schal be verray repentaunt for alle his synnes that he hath doon in delyt of his thought, for delit is ful perilous. For ther ben tuo meners of consentyng of affeccioun; whan a man is moeved to synne & delitith him longe for to thinke on that synne, and his resoun aparceyve wel that it is synne agayns the lawe of God, & yit his resoun refreyne not his foule delit or talent, though he se wel apertly[83] that it is agenst the reverence of God; although his resoun consente not to do the synne in dede, yit, sayn some doctours, delyt that duellith longe, it is ful perilous, albeit never so lite. And also a man schulde sorwe namely for al that he hath desired ageyn the lawe of God with parfyt consentynge of his hert and of his resoun, for therof is no doute that it is dedly synne, that it nas first in man's thought & after that in his delit, and so forth into consentyng and into dede. Wherfore say I, that many men repente hem never for suche thoughtes and delites, ne never schrive hem of hit, but oonly of the dede of grete synnes outward. Wherfore I say that suche wickid delitis and wickid thoughtes ben subtile bigiours of hem that schuln be dampned. More-over, man oughte to sorwe for his wicked wordes, as wel as his wikked

---

78 Jesus of Nazare king of the Jews (one of the titles placed above Jesus on the
   cross by order of Pilate)
79 Matthew 1:21   80 Acts 4:12   81 Revelation 3:20
82 'kingdom . . . as he promises him'   83 openly

dedes; for certis, the repentaunce of a singuler synne, & nought repente of alle his other synnes, may nought availe. For certis, God Almighty is al good, and therfore he forgeveth al, or elles right nought; and herof seith Seint Augustin, 'I wot certeynly that God is enemy to every synnere'. And how, thanne? He that observe oon synne, schal he have remissioun of the remenant of his other synnes? Nay; and fortherover, contricioun schulde be wounder sorwful an anguisschous, and therfore give him God pleinly his mercy. And therfore, whan my soule was anguissheous withinne me, I hadde remembraunce of God, that my prayer mighte come to him. And fortherover, contricioun most be continuelly, and that a man have stedefast purpos to schryve him and for to amende him of his lyf. For sothly, whil contricioun lastith, man may ever hope of forgevenes, and of this come hate of synne, that destroyeth synne bothe in himself and eek in other folk, at his power. And therfore saith David, 'He that loven God hatith wikkidnesse'[84] for trustith wel, for to love God is for to love that he loveth and to hate that he hatith.

The laste thing that a man schuld understonde in contricioun is this: wherof availith contricioun. I say, that somtyme contricioun delivereth man fro synne, of which David saith, 'I say,' quod David, 'that is to say, I purposid fermely, to schryve me, and thou, Lord, relesidist my synne'.[85] And right so as contricioun destruyeth the prisoun of helle and makth wayk and feble the strengthes of the develes, and restorith the gift of the Holy host and of all vertues, and it clensith the soule of synes, and delivereth the soule fro the peynes of helle, and fro the companye of the devel, and from the servage of synne, and restorith it to alle goodes espiritueles, into the companye & communioun of Holy Chirche. And fortherover, it makith him that somtyme was sone of ire, sone of grace. And alle these thinges he provith by Holy Write, and therfore he that wil sette his herte to these thinges, he were ful wys. Forsothe, he scholde not thanne in al his lyf have corrage to synne, but given his body and al his herte to the service of Jhesu Crist, and therof do him homage; for certis, oure swete Lord, Jhesu Crist, hath sparid us so debonerly in oure folyes, that if he ne hadde pite of man's soule, sory songe mighte we alle synge.

---

84 Psalm 96:10
85 Psalm 31:5

Explicit prima pars. Incipit secunda pars eiusdem[86]

❦ The secounde partye of penitence is confessioun; that is, signe of contricioun. Now schul ye understonde what is confessioun, and whethir it oughte needes be doon or noon, and which ben convenable to verray confessioun. First schalt thou understonde that confessioun is verey schewing of synnes to the prest; this is to sayn, verray.[87] For he moot schewe him of all the condiciouns that ben longynge to his synne as ferforth as he can; al mot be sayd, and nought excused ne hyd, ne forwrappid; and nought avaunte him[88] of his goode werkis. And forthermore, it is necessary to understonde whens that synnes springe, and how thay exersen, and which they ben. Of the springing of synnes, Seint Poul saith in this wise, that 'Right as by a man synne entred first into this world, and thorough that synne deth, right so thilke deth entred into alle men that synneden';[89] and this man was Adam, by whom that synne entred into this world whan he brak the commaundement of God.[90] And therfore he that first was so mighty that he schulde not have deyed, bicam sithe on that he most needis deye, whethir he wolde or noon, and al his progenie that is in this world, that in thilke manner synneden. Loke that in the estate of innocence, whan Adam and Eve makid were in paradys, and nothing schame ne hadden of hir nakidnesse; how that the serpent, that was most wily of all other bestis that God hadde makid, sayde to the womman, 'Why comaundid God to yow ye schulde nought ete of every tree in paradys?' The womman answerde, 'Of the fruyt,' quod sche, 'of the trees in paradys we feede us; but sothly, of the fruyt of the tre that is in the myddil of paradis, God forbad us for to eten, ne not touche it, lest peraventure we schulde deye.' The serpent sayde to the womman, 'Nay, nay, ye schal not drede of deth; forsothe, God wot that what day ye ete therof youre eyen schal open, and ye schul ben as Goddis, knowing good and harm.' The womman saugh the tree was good to feedyng and fair to eyen, and delitable to sight. She tok of the fruyt of the tree and eet it, and gaf to hir housbond, and he eet it; and anoon the eyyen of hem bothe openeden; and whan that thay knewe that thay were naked, thay sowede of fige leves in maner of breches to hiden here membris.

Here may ye see that dedly synne hath first suggestioun of the feend, as scheweth here by the neddir,[91] and aftirward the delit of the fleisch,

---

86 'the first part ends: the second part of this begins'
87 true   88 boast   89 Romans 5:12   90 Genesis 3   91 adder

as scheweth here by Eva and after that the consentyng of resoun, as schewith by Adam. For trustith wel, though so were that the feende temptid oon; that is to sayn, the fleissch hadde delit in the beaute of the fruyt defendid, yit certes til that resoun, that is to say Adam, consentid to the etyng of the fruyt, yit stood he in th'astaat of innocence. Of thilk Adam took we thilke synne original, for of him flesschly descendit be we alle, and engendrit of vile and corrupt intiere. And whan the soule is put in oure body, right anoon is contract original synne; and therfore be we all y-born sones of wrathe and of dampnacioun perdurable, if it nere baptism that we receyven which bynymeth us the culpe.[92] But forsothe, the peyne duellith with us as to temptacioun, which peyne highte concupiscence. And this concupiscence, whan it is wrongfully disposed or ordeyned in man, hit makith him to coveyte; covetise of fleisschly synne by sight of his eyyen as to erthely thinges, and eek coveityse of heighnesse as by pride of herte.

Now as to speke of the first coveitise; that is concupiscence after the lawe of oure membris, that is nought obeissant to God that is his Lord, therfore is fleissch to him disobeisant thurgh concupiscence, which that yit is cleped norisshing of synne. Therefore al the while that a man hath in him the peyne of concupiscence, it is impossible but he be tempted somtyme, and moeved in his fleisch to synne, and this may not faile as longe as he liveth. It may wel wexe feble and faille by vertu of baptisme, and by the grace of God thorough penitence, but fully schal it never quenche, that he schal somtyme be moeved in himself, but if he were al refreydit by siknes, or by malice of sorserye or colde drinkes. For what saith Seint Poul: 'The fleissch coveitith agayn the spirit, and the spirit agayn the fleisch; thay ben so contrarie and so stryven that a man may nought alwey do as he wolde'.[93] The same Seint Poul after his penaunce in watir and in lond; in watir by night and by day in gret peril, and in gret peyne in lond and in famyne, and in thurste and colde, and clothles; oones almost stoned al to the deth, yit saide he, 'Allas, I caytif[94] man! Who schal delyvere me fro the prisoun of my caytif body?' And Seint Jerom, whan he long tyme had woned in desert, wheras he hade no compaignye but of wilde bestes, wheras he hadde no mete but herbes, & water to his drink, ne non bed but the nakid erthe. For which his fleisch was as blak as an Ethiopen for hete, and neigh destroyed for cold, yit sayde he that the brennyng of lecchery

92 'takes away our guilt'		93 Galatians 5:17		94 wretched: Romans 7:24

boylid in al his body. And therfore Seint John the Evaungelist saith, 'If that we sayn we be withoute synne, we deceyue oursilf, and trouthe is nought in us'.[95]

Now schal ye understonde in what maner that synne waxith and encresceth in a man. The firste thing is thilke norisching of synne of which I spak byforn; thilke concupiscence. And after that come the suggestioun of the devel; this is to sayn the devel's bely, with which he bloweth in man the fuyr of fleisschly concupiscence. And after that a man bythink him whethir he wol don it or non, thilke thing to which he is tempted; and thanne if that a man withstonde the feend it is no synne, and if so be he do not so, thanne feeleth he anoon a flame of delit; and thane it is good to be war and kepe him wel, or ellis he wil falle anoon into consentyng of synne, and thanne wol he do it, if he may have tyme, and space, and place. And of this mater saith Moyses by the devel in this maner, 'The feend saith, 'I wol chace and pursewe the man by wickid suggestiouns and I wil hent him by moevyng or steryng of synne',[96] and I wil parte my prise or my pray by deliberacioun, and my lust schal be accomplisit in delit; I wil drawe my sword in consentynge. For certes, right as a swerd departith a thing in tuo parties, right so consentyng departeth God fro man, and thanne wol I sle him wi my hond in dede of synne.' Thus saith the feend'. For certis, thanne is a man al deed in soule, and thus is synne accomplisid by temptacioun, by delit, and by consentyng; and thanne is the synne cleped, actuel.

Forsothe, synne is in two maneres; over it is venial, or dedly synne. Sothly, whan man lovith any creature more than Jhesu Crist our creatour, thanne it is dedly synne. And venial synne is if a man love Jhesu Crist lesse than him oughte. Forsothe, the dede of this venial synne is ful perilous, for it amenisith[97] the love that men schulde have to God more and more. And therfore, if a man charge more himself with many suche venial synnes; certes but if so be that he somtyme discharge him of hem by schrifte, thay may ful lightly amenise in him al the love that he hath to Jhesu Crist; than in this wise skippith venial into dedly synne. For certes, the more that a man chargith his soule with venial synnes, the more is he enclyned to falle in deedly synne. And therfore, let us nought be negligent to descharge us of venial synnes, for the proverbe saith that, 'Many smale makith a gret'; and herken this ensample: a grett wawe of the see cometh somtyme with so gret a violence that it drenchith[98] the

---

95 I John 1:8   96 Exodus 15:9   97 diminishes   98 drowns

schip, and the same harm doon somtyme smale droppis of watir that entri thurgh a litil creves into the thurrock,[99] and into the botme of a schip, if men be so negligent that thay descharge hit nought by-tyme; and therfore, although ther be difference betuene these tuo causes of drenching, algates the schip is dreynt. Right so farith it somtyme of deedly synne and of anoyous venial synnes, whan thay multiplien in a man so gretly that thilke wordly thynges that he love, thurgh which he sinne venially, is as gret in his herte as the love of God; yit is it venial syne. And deedly synne is whan the love of eny hing weyeth in the hert of a man as moche as the love of God or more. Dedly synne is as saith Seint Austyn, 'Whan man torne his hert from God, which that is verray soverayn bounte that may not chaunge, and flitte and give his herte to a thing that may chaunge and flitte; and certes, that is everything save God of heven. Forsothe, if that a man give his love the which that he owith to God with al his herte, unto a creature, so moche he reveth from God, and therfore doth he synne. For he that is dettour to God yelde not his dette; that is to sayn, al the love of his hert.

Now sithe man understondith generally which is venial synne; thanne is it covenable to telle specially of synnes whiche that many man perauenture ne demith hem no synnes, and schryue him not of the same thinges, and yit natheles thay ben synnes. And sothly, as clerkes writen, this is to say at every time that man etith or drinkith more than suffiseth to the sustienaunce of his body, in certeyn he do synne; and eek whan he spekith more than it needith he doth synne. And eek whan he herkeneth nought benignely the pleynt of the pore, eek whan he is in hele of body and wil not faste whan other folk fasten withouten cause resonable, eek whan he slepith more than needith, or whan he cometh by thilk enchesoun to late to Holy Chirche or to other werkes of charite, eke whan he useth his wyf withoute soverayn desir of engendrure, to th'honour of God and for th'entent to yelde his wyf the dette of his body, eek whan he wil not visite the sike and the prisoner if he may, eek if he love wyf or child or other worldly thing more than resoun require, eek if he flatere or blaundisshe more than him oughte for eny necessite, eek if a man menuse or withdrawe the almesse of the pouere, eek if he apparaylith his mete more deliciously than it nedith, or ete it to hastily by licouresnes, eek if he talke of vanitees at chirche or at God's service, or that he be a talkere of ydil wordes of vanite or of vilonye; for he schal yelde of hem acount at the Day of Doome, eek whan he heetith or assure to do thinges that he may

99 bilge

nought performe, eek whan that by lightnes or foly he myssaith or scorneth his neighebor, eek whan he hath eny wicked suspeccioun of thing that he wot of it no sothfastnesse; these thinges, and mo withoute nombre, ben synnes, as saith Seint Austyn. Now schal men understonde that albeit so that noon erthely man may eschiewe alle venial synnes, yit may he refreyne hem by the brennyng love he hath to Oure Lord Jhesu Crist, and by prayeres and by confessioun and other goode werkes, so that it schal but litil greve. For as saith Seint Austyn: 'Yif a man love God in such a maner that al that ever he do is in the love of God or for the love of God verraily, for he brenneth in the love of God; loke how moche that a drope of watir that fallith in a furneys ful of fuyr annoyeth or greveth, so moche annoyeth a venial synne unto a man that is perfyt in the love of Jhesu Crist'. Men may also refreyne venial synne by receyvyng of the precious body of Jhesu Crist, by receyvyng eek of holy water, by almes dede, by general confessioun of *Confiteor*[100] at masse and at complyn, and blessing of bisschops and of prestes, and by other goode werkis.

Now it is bihovely thing to telle whiche ben dedly synnes; that is to sayn, chiveteyns of synnes, as alle thay renne in oon loos, but in divers maners now ben thay cleped chiveteyns, forasmoche as thay ben chief and springers of all othere synnes. Of the roote of these seven synnes, thanne is pride the general synne and roote of all harmes. For of this roote springen general braunches, as ire, envye, accidie or sleuthe, avarice or coveitise to commune understondynge, glotonye and leccherie. And everich of these synnes hath his braunches and his twigges, as schal be declarid in here chapitres folwinge; and though so be that no man can telle utterly the nombre of the twigges and of the harm that cometh of pride, yit wol I schewe a party of hem, as ye schul understonde. Ther is inobedience, auauntyng, ypocrisie, despit, arragaunc, impudence, swellyng of hert, insolence, pertinacie, veinglorie, and many another twigge that I cannot telle ne declare. Inobedient is he that disobeieth for despyt to the commaundements of God, and to his sovereigns, and to his gostly Fader. Avauntour is he that boste of the harm or of the bounte that he hath don. Ypocrisy is he that hyde to schewe him such as he is, and scheweth him such as he not is. Despitous is he that hath desdayn of his neighebour; that is to say, of his even- Cristen,[101] or hath despit to doon that him ought to doon. Arragaunt is he that thinketh that he hath thilke bountees in him that he hath not, or wene that he schulde have hem by desert, or elles he deme that he is that he is not. Impudent is he that for

---

100 'I confess'   101 fellow-Christian

his pride hath no schame of his synne. Swellyng of hert is whan a man rejoysith him of harm that he hath don. Insolent is he that dispisith in his juggement alle other folk as to regard of his valieu, and of his connyng, & of his spekyng, and of his beryng. Elacioun is whan he may never suffre to have maister, ne felawe. Impacient is he that wil not ben y-taught ne undernam of his vices, and by struyf werreth trouth witynge, and defendeth his folie. Contimax[102] is he that thorough his indignacioun, and agains everych auctorite or power of hem that been his soverayns. Presumpcioun is whan a man undertakith and emprisith that him oughte not to do, or elles that he may not doo; and that is cleped surquidrye. Irreverence is whan men doon not honour ther as hem ought to doon, and wayte to be reverenced. Pertinacie is whan man defendith his folye and trusteth to moche to his owne witte. Vainglorie is for to have pomp and delit in temporal heighnes, and glorifie him in worldly estaat. Jangelyng is whan a man spekith to moche biforn folk, & clappith as a mille, and taketh no keep what he saith. And yit is ther a prive spice of pride that wayte first to be saluet ther he saliewe, al be he lasse worth than that other is, paradventure, and eek wayteth or desireth to sitte above him or to go above him in the way, or kisse pax, or be encensed, or gon to the offringe biforn his neighebore, and hath such a proud desir to be magnified and honoured toforn the poeple.

Now ben tuo meners of pride; that oon is heighnes withinne the hert of a man, and that other is withoute. Of which sothly these forsayde thinges and mo than I have said aperteynen to pride that is in the hert of a man; and that other spices of pride ben withoute; but netheles that oon of thise spices of pride is signe of that other, right as gay leueselle[103] at the taverne is signe of wyn that is in the celer. And this is in many thinges, as in speche, and conteinaunce, and in outrageous array of clothing. For certis, if ther hadde be no synne in clothing, Crist wolde not so soone have notid and spoke of the clothing of thilke riche man in the gospel. And saith Seint Gregorie that precious clothing is coupable for dere of it, and for his schortnes, and for his straungenes, and disgisines, and for the superfluite, or for the inordinat skantnes of it. Allas! Many man may sen as in oure dayes the synful costlewe array of clothing which that makid is so dere, to harm of the poeple, not oonly the cost of embrowdyng the gyse endentyng of barryng, swandyng, palyng or bendyng,[104] and sembable wast of cloth

102 contumacious
103 Bush or garland, sign of a tavern
104 Different heraldic devices; all forms of 'stripe'

in vanite. But ther is also costlewe furring in here gownes, so mochil pounsyng of chiseles to make holes, so moche daggyng of scheris,[105] for with the superfluite in lengthe of the forsaide gownes trayling in the donge and in the myre, on hors and eek on foote, as wel of man as of womman, that al thilke traylyng is verray, as in effect, wasted, consumed, thredbare and rotyn with donge, rather than it is geven to the pore to gret damage of the forsaide pore folk, and that in sondry wise; this is to sain, that the more that cloth is wastid, the more most it coste to the poeple for the scaresenes; and forthermore, if it so be that thay wolde give such poinsed and daggid clothing to the pore folk, it is not convenient to were to the pore folk, ne suffisaunt to meete here necessite to kepe hem fro the desperaunce of the firmament.[106]

Upon that other syde, to speke of the horrible disordinat scantnes of clothing as ben these cuttid sloppis, or anslets,[107] that thurgh her schortnes ne covere not the schamful membre of man, to wickid entent. Alas! Som men of hem schewen the schap and the boce[108] of the horrible swollen membres, that seme like to the maledies of hirnia in the wrapping of here hose, and eek the buttockes of hem, that faren as it were the hinder part of a sche-ape in the fulle of the moone. And moreover the wrecchid swolen membres that thay departe here hosen in other colours; as is whit and bliew, or whit and blak, and blak and reed, and so forth; and semith it as by variaunce of colour that half the party of his privy membris ben corrupt by the fuyr of St Antony, or by cancre,[109] or by other such meschaunce. And yit of the hynder partye of here buttokes, it is ful horrible for to see. For certis, in that partie of here body ther as thay purgen her stynkyng ordure, that foule party schewe thay to the poeple proudly, in despyt of honeste; which honeste that Jhesu Crist and his frendes observeden to schewen in his lif.

Now as of the outrageous array of wommen; God wot that though the visage of some of hem seme ful chaste and debonaire, yit notifye thay in here array of attyre licorousnesse and pride. I say not that honeste in clothing of man or womman is uncovenable, but certis, the superfluite or disordinat skantnes of clothing is reprevable. Also the synne of here ornament or of apparaille as in thinges that aperteynen to rydyng, as in to many delicat horses that ben holden for delyt, that thay ben so faire, fat,

105 The fashionable cutting of slashes in clothing
106 'to keep out the weather'
107 short coats, or jerkins
108 outline   109 'St Anthony's Fire, or cancer'

and costlewe, and also many a vicious knave mayntened bycause of hem, and in to curious harnoys, as in sadelis and bridlis, cropours and peytrell, couered with precious clothing and riche barres, and plates of gold and of siluer. For which God saith by Zacharie the prophete, 'I wol confounde the ryders of such horsis'.[110] These folk take litil reward of the ryding of God's sone of heven and of his harneys whan he rode upon an asse, and hadde noon othere harneys but the clothing of his disciples newe, ne rede I not that ever he rode on other beest. I speke this for the synne of superfluite, and nought for resonable honeste whan resoun it requirith.

And fortherover, certes thay ben of litil profyt or of right no profyt, and namely whan that meyne is felenous and daungerous to the poeple by hardynesse of lordschipe, or by way of offices. For certes, such lordes selle thanne here lordschipe to the devel of helle whan thay susteyne the wickidnes of here meyne; or elles whan these folk of lowe degre as is thilke that holden hostilries, and susteyne the thefte of here hostilers; and that is in many maneres of disceytes. Thilke maner of folk ben the flyes that folwen the hony, or elles the houndes that folwen the carayn.[111] Suche forsayde folk strangelen spririteuelly here lordschipes, for which thus saith David the prophete, 'Wikked deth moot come upon suche lordschipes, & God geve that thay moot descende into helle adoun, for in here houses ben iniquites and schrewednesses and not God of heven';[112] and certes, but thay do amendement, right so as Jacob gaf his benisoun to Laban by the service of God and to Pharao by the service of Joseph,[113] Right so God wil geve his malisoun to suche lordschipes as susteynen the wikkednes of her servauntes, but thay come to amendement.

Pride of the table apperith ful ofte; for certes, riche men ben cleped to feste and pore folk ben put away and rebuked. Also in excesse of divers metis and drinkis, and namely of suche maner of bake metis, brennyng of wilde fuyr and peynted and castelid with papire and semblable wast, so that it is abusioun for to thinke; and eek in greet preciousnes of vessel & in curiousnesse of vessel, and of mynstralcye by the which a man is stired the more to delitis of luxurie, if so be that thay sette her herte the lasse upon Oure Lord Jhesu Crist. Certeyn, it is a synne, and certeinly the delites mighte be so grete in the caas that men mighte lightly falle by hem into dedly synne. The espices that sourdren of pride, sothely whan thay sourdren of malice ymagined and avised aforn cast, or elles of usage,

110 Zechariah 10:5   111 carrion   112 Psalm 54:16
113 altered: Harley 7334 says 'god . . . pharao . . . jacob . . . balan', which does
    not make sense in the biblical context.

ben dedly synnes it is no doute. And whan they sourden by frelte unavysed sodeinly, and sodeinly withdrawe agayn; als be thay grevous synnes, I gesse thay ben not dedly.

Now mighte men axe, wherof pride sourde[114] and springe. I say, somtyme it springith of the goodes of nature, and som tyme of the goodes of grace. Certes, goodes of nature stonden outher in goodes of body or goodes of soule. Certis, the goodes of body ben hele[115] of body, strenge, deliverance, beaute, gentrie, fraunchises. Goodes of nature of the soule ben goodes wit scharp, understondyng, subtil engyn,[116] vertu naturel, good memorie. Goodes of fortune been richesses, highe degrees of lordchipes, preisyng of the poeple. Goodes of grace been science, power to suffre, spirituel trauaile, benignite, vertuous contemplacioun, wistondyng of temptacioun, and semblable thinges, of whiche forsayde goodes, certes, it is a ful gret foly a man to pryden him in any of hem all.

Now as for to speke of goodes of nature; God wot that somtyme we have hem in nature as moche to oure damage as to oure profit. As for to speke of hele of body; certes, it passith ful lightly, and eek it is ful ofte enchesoun of the siknesse of the soule; for God wot the fleissch is a gret enemy to the soule, and therfore the more that oure body is hool, the more be we in peril to falle. Eke for to pride him in his strengthe of body it is a foly; for certes, the fleisch coveytith again the spirit, and ay the more strong that the fleisch is the sorier may the soule be, and over al this strengthe of body and worldly hardynes causeth ful ofte many a man to peril and meschaunce. Eek for to pride him of his gentrie is ful gret folye, for often tyme the gentrie of the body bynymeth the gentry of the soule; and we be all of oon fader and of oon moder, & all we ben of oon nature; roten and corrupt, riche and pore. Forsothe oon maner gentry is for to prayse, that apparailleth man's corrage with vertues and moralitees, and mak him Crist's child; for trustith wel over what man that synne hath maistry, he is a verray cherl to synne.

Now ben ther general signes of gentilesse; as schewyng[117] of vice & rybaudrie and servage of synne, in word, in werk and countenaunce, and usinge vertu, curtesie and clennes, and to be liberal; that is to sayn, large by mesure,[118] for thilke that passith mesure is foly and synne. And another is to remembre him of bounte that he of other folk hath resceyved; another is to be benigne to his goode subjectis, wherfore as saith Senek,

---

114 arises   115 health   116 intelligence
117 avoiding   118 in moderation

'Ther is nothing more covenable to a man of heigh estate than debonairte and pite'. And therfore, thise flies that men clepen bees, whan thay make here king, thay chesen oon than hath no pricke wherwith he may stynge. Another is a man to have a noble herte & a diligent, to atteigne to hihe vertuous thinges. Certis also, who that pridith him in the deedes of grace is eek an outrageous fool, for thilke giftes of grace that schulde have y-torned him to goodnes and medicyene torne him to venym and to confusioun, as saith Seint Gregory. Certis also, whoso pridith h[m in the goodes of Fortune, he is a ful gret fool; for somtyme is a man a gret lord by the morwe that is a caytif and a wrecche er it be night, and somtyme the riches of a man is cause of his deth. Somtyme the delice[119] is cause of his grevous maledye, thurgh which he deie. Certis, the commendacioun of the poeple is somtyme ful fals and ful brutil for to trust; this day thay prayse, tomorwe thay blame. God woot, desir to have commendacioun of the poeple hath causid deth of many a busy man.

Now, sith so is that ye han herd and understonde what is pride and whiche ben the spices of it, and whens pride sourde and springe; now schul ye understonde which is the remedy agayns pride, and that is humilite or meekenes, that is a vertue thurgh which a man hath verray knowleche of himself, and holdith of himself no pride, ne pris, ne deynte as in regard of his desertes, considering evermore his frelte.[120] Now ben ther thre maners of humilite; as humilite in hert, another is humilite in his mouth, the thridde is in his workes. The humilite in his herte is in foure maners; that oon is whan a man holdith himself not worth biforn God of heven, another is whan he despiseth no man, the thrid is whan he ne rekkith nought though a man holde him nought worth, the ferth is whan he holdeth him nought sory of his humiliacioun. Also the humilite of mouth is in foure thinges; in attempre speche and in humbles of speche, and he byknowith with his own mouth that he is such as him thenkith that he is in herte; another is whan he praisith the bounte of another man and nothing therof amenusith.[121] Humilite eek in werk is in foure maneres; the first is whan he puttith other men toforn him, the secounde is to chese lewedest[122] place over al, the thrid is gladly to assente to good counseil, the ferthe is gladly to stonde to award[123] of his sovereyns, or of him that is in heigher degre – certeyn, this is a gret werk of humilite.

119 living for pleasure
120 'no pride, value or worth in respect of what he deserves, considering evermore his (human) frailty'
121 holds back/lessens   122 least/lowest   123 decision/decree

De inuidia [124]

❦ After pride, now wol I speke of the foule synne of envye, which that is, as by the word of the philosophre, 'Sorwe of other men's prosperite. And after the word of Seint Austyn, is it sorwe of other men's wele, & ioye of other mennes harm. This foule synne is platly agayns the Holy Gost, albeit so that every synne is agayn the Holy Gost; yit natheles, for as moche as bounte apeerteyne proprely to the Holy Gost and envye proprely is malice, therfore is it proprely agayns the bounte of the Holy Gost.

Now hath malice tuo spices; that is to sayn, hardnes of hert in wickednes, or ellis the fleisch of man is so blynd that he considereth not that he is in synne, which is the hardnes of the devyl. That other spice of envye is whan a man warie [125] trouthe, and wot that it is trouthe; and eek whan he warieth the grace that God hath geve to his neighebor, and al this is by envye. Certes than is envye the worste synne that is, for sothely all other synnes ben somtyme oonly agayns oon special vertu, but certes envye is agayns all vertues and agayns al goodnes, for it is sory of all the bountees of his neighebor. And in this maner it is divers from all the synnes, for wel unnethe is ther any synne that he ne hath som delit in himself, sauf oonly envye, that ever hath in itself anguisch and sorwe. The spices of envye ben these; ther is first sorwe of other men's goodnes and of her prosperite, and prosperite is kyndely matier of joye; thanne is envye a synne agayns kynde. [126] The secounde spice of envye is joye of other men's harm, and that is proprely lik to the devyl, that ever rejoye him of men's harm. Of these tuo spices cometh bacbityng, and this synne of bakbytyng or detreccioun hath certein spices, as thus: Som man praiseth his neighebor by a wickid entent, for he makith alway a wickid knowtte [127] atte last ende; alway he makith a, 'but,' at the last ende, that is thing of more blame than worth is al the praysing. The secounde spice is that, if a man be good and do or saith a thing to good entent, the bacbiter wol torne al thilke goodnes up-so-doun to his schrewed entent. The thridde is to amenuse the bounte of his neighebor. The ferthe spiece of bakbytyng is this: that if men speke goodnes of a man, than wil the bakbiter seyn, 'Parfay, yit such a man is bet than he,', in dispraysing of him that men praise. The fifte spice is this; for to consente gladly and herken gladly to the harm that men speke of other folk. This synne is ful gret, and ay encresith after th'entent of the bakbiter.

---

124 'of envy'   125 opposes   126 nature   127 point

After bakbytyng cometh grucching or m[ur]muracioun. And somtyme it springith of impacience agayns God, and somtyme agains man. Agayns God is it, whan a man grucchith agayn the pyne of helle, or agayns poverte, or of losse of catel,[128] or agayns reyn or tempest, or elles grucchith that schrewes han prosperite or ellis that goode men han aduersite; and all these thinges schulde men suffre paciently, for thay come by rightful juggement and ordinaunce of God. Somtyme come grucching of avarice, as Judas grucched agens the Maudeleyn whan sche anoynted the hed of Oure Lord Jhesu Crist with hire precious oynement. This maner murmur is swich as man grucchith of goodnes that himself doth, or that other folk doon of here owne catel. Somtyme cometh murmur of pride, as whan Symon the Pharise grucchid agayn the Maudeleyn whan sche approchid to Jhesu Crist and wepte at his feet for hir synnes. And somtyme it sourdith of envye, whan men discovereth a man's harm that was prive, or bere him on hond that that is fals. Murmuryng eek is ofte among seruaunts, that grucchen whan here soverayns bidden hem to doon leeful thinges, and forasmoche as thay dar nought openly withstonde the comaundements of here soverayns, yit wol thay sayn harm, and grucche and murmure prively for verray despit; whiche wordes men clepe 'the Devel's Paternoster' but that lewed men calle it so. Somtyme it cometh of ire, of prive hate that norische rancour in herte, as I schal declare. Thanne cometh eek bitternes of herte, thorough which bitternesse every good deede of his neighebore semeth to him bitter and unsavery. But thanne cometh discord, that unbyndeth alle maner of frendschipe. Thanne cometh scornynge of his neighebor, al do he never so wel, thanne come accusyng, as whan man seketh occasioun to annoyen his neighebore, which that is lik the craft of the devel, that waytith bothe night and day to accuse us alle. Thanne cometh malignite, thurgh which a man annoyeth his neighebor prively if he may; and if he not may, algate his wikked wille schal nought wante as for to brenne his hous prively, or empoysone him, or sleen his bestis prively, and sembable thinges.

Remedium contra invidiam [129]

❦ Now wol I speke of the remedies agayns thise foule things and this foule synne of envye. First is the love of God prindipal, and lovynge of his neighebor as himself. Sothely, that oon ne may nought be withoute that other. And truste wel that in the name of thy neighebour thou schalt

128 goods   129 'remedy against envy'

understonde the name of thy brother, for all we haue oon fader fleisschly and oon mooder, that is to sayn Adam and Eva, and eek oon Fader spirituel, & that is God of heven. Thy neghebor artow holden for to love; that is to sayn, bothe to savacioun of lif and of soule, and moreover thou schalt love hym in word, and in benigne amonestyng and chastising, & comforte him in his annoyes, and praye for him with al thin herte; & indede thou schalt love him in such wise that thou schalt do to him charite, as thou woldist it were doon to thin oughne persone; and therfore thou schalt doon him noon harme in wikked word, ne damage him in his body, ne in his catel, ne in his soule, by wicked entising of ensample. Thou schalt nought desiren his wif, ne noone of his thinges.

Understonde eek that in the name of thy neighebor is comprehendid his enemy. Certes, man schal love his enemy by the commaundement of God, and sothly thy frend schalt thou love in God. I sayde thin enemy; forsothe God nolde nought receyve us to his love that ben his enemyes. Agains thre maner of wronges that his enemy doth to him he schal do thre things as thus; agayns hate and rancour of herte he schal love him in herte; agayns chydyng and wicked wordes he schal pray for his enemye; agains wikked dede of his enemy he schal doon him bounte. For Crist saith, 'Loveth youre enemyes, and prayeth for hem that yow chacen and pursewen, and doth bounte to hem that yow haten'.[130] For sothely, nature driveth us to love oure frendes and parfay, oure enemyes han more neede to love than oure frendes. For sothely, to hem that more neede have; certis, to hem schul men do goodnes. And certis, in thilke dede have we remembraunce of the love of Jhesu Crist that dyed for his enemys. And inalsmoche as thilke love is more grevous to parforme, so moche is the more gret remedye & meryt; and therfore the lovyng of oure enemy hath confoundid the venym of the devel. For right as the devel is confoundid by humilite, right so is he woundid to the deth by love of oure enemy. Certis, thanne is love the medicine that castith out the venym of envye fro man's hert. The spices of this part schuln be more largely declared in here chapitres folwynge.

De ira [131]

❧ After envye wol I descryven the synne of ire; for sothely whoso hath envye upon his neighebor, anoon he wol comunly fynde him a matiere of wrathe in word or in dede agayns him to whom he hath envie. And as wel

130 Matthew 5:44   131 'of anger'

cometh ire of pride as of envye, for sothly he that is proud or envyous is lightly wroth. This synne of ire, after the descryvyng of Seint Austyn, is, 'Wikked wille to ben avengid by word, or by dede'. Ire, after the philosofer, is, 'The fervent blood of man y-quiked in his hert, thurgh which he wolde harm to him that him hatith'; for certes, the hert of man by schawfyng[132] and moevyng of his blood waxith so trouble that he is out of alle juggementes of resoun. But ye schal understonde that ire is in tuo manere; that oon of hem is good, that other is wikke. The goode ire is by jalousy of goodnesse, thurgh which a man is wroth with wikkidnes; and therfore saith a wise man that ire is bet than play. This ire is with deboneirete, and it is wroth without bitternes; not wroth with the man, but wroth with the mysdedes of the man, as saith the prophet Devid, 'Irascimini, & nolite peccare, & cetera'.[133]

Now understonde that wikked ire is in tuo maners; that is to sayn, sodeyn ire or hastif ire, withoute avysement and consenting of resoun; the menynge and the sentence of this is that the resoun of a man ne consentith not to thilke sodein ire, and thanne is it venial. Another ire is ful wicked, that cometh of felony of herte, avysed & cast biforn with wickid wille to do vengeaunce, and therto his resoun consentith, and sothely this is deedly synne. This ire is so displesaunt to God that it troublith his hous and chace the Holy Gost out of man's soule, and wastith and desroyeth the liknes of God; that is to say, the vertu that is in man's soule, and put in him the liknes of the devel, and bynymeth the man fro God, that is his rightful Lord. This ire is a ful greet plesaunce to the devel, for it is the devel's fornays, that is eschaufid with the fuyr of helle. For certes, right so as fuyr is more mighty to destroye erthely thinges than eny other element, right so ire is mighty to destroye all sprituel thinges. Loke how that fuyr of smale gledis,[134] that ben almost ded under asshen, wolden quicken agayn whan thay be touched with brimstone; right so ire wol evermore quyken agayn whan it is touched by pride, that is covered in man's herte. For certes, fuyr may nought come out of nothing, but if it were first in the same thinge naturelly, as fuyr is drawe out of flintes with steel. Right so as pride is often tyme mater of ire; right so is rancour norice and keper of ire. Ther is a maner tree, as saith Seint Isydore, that whan men maken fuyr of thilke tree and cover the colis with asshen, sothly the fuyr of it wol lasten al a yer or more. And right so fareth it of rancour whan it oones is conceyved in the hertis of som men;

132 heating
133 'be ye angry, and do not sin, etc...': Psalm 4:5   134 coals

certein, it wol lasten fro oon Estren day until another Ester day and more. But certis, thilke man is ful fer fro the mercy of God al thilke while.

In this forsaide devel's fornays ther forgen thre schrewes; pride, that ay blowith and encresth the fuyr by chidyng and wickid wordis; thanne stont envye, and blowith the hoot iren upon the hert of man with a paire of longe tonges of rancour; and thanne the sinne of contumelie or strif, and cheste[135] and baterith and forgeth by vileyns reprevynges. Certes, this cursed synne annoye bothe to the man himsilf and eek to his neighebor; for sothely, almost al the harm that eny man do to his neighebour cometh thurgh wrathe. For certis, outrageous wrathe doth al that ever the devyl him comaunde, for he ne spareth neyther for Crist ne his Moodir, and in his outrage, anger, and ire, allas! Ful many oon at that tyme felith in his herte ful wikkedly bothe of Crist and eek of all his halwes. Is nat this a cursed vice? Yis, certis. It bynymeth fro man his witte and his resoun, and al his deboneire lyf spirituel that scholde kepen his soule. Certes, it bynymeth eek God's dewe lordschipe and the love of his neighebor; hit stryveth eek alday agayns trouthe. It reveth him eek the quiete of his hert, and subvertith his herte and eek his soule.

Of ire cometh these stynkynge engendrures; first hate, that is olde wrathe; discord, thurgh which a man forsakith his olde frend that he hath loved ful longe; and thanne cometh werre, and every maner of wronge that man do to his neighebor in body or catel. Of this cursed synne of ire cometh eek manslaughter, and understonde wel that homicidie, that is manslaughter, is in divers wise: som maner of homicidie is sprirituel and som is bodily. Spirituel manslaughter is in sixe thinges: first, by hate, as saith Seint John, 'He that hateth his brother is an homicide'.[136] Homicide is eek by bakbytyng, of whiche bakbiters saith Salomon that thay have twaye swerdes with whiche thay slen here neighebors. For sothely, as wikke is to bynyme his good name as his lif. Homicidy is eek in gevyng of wikkid co[nseil by fraude, as for to geve counseil to areyse wicked and wrongful custumes and taliages,[137] of whiche saith Salomon, 'Leoun roryng and bere hungry ben like to the cruel lordschipes in withholdyng or abrigging of the schipe, or the hyre or the wages of servauntes, or ellis in usure or in widrawyng of almes of pore folk'. For whiche the pore man saith 'Feedith him that almost dye for hunger; for sothely, but if thou feede him, thou sleest him';[138] and eek these ben dedly synnes.

135 argument   136 1 John 3:15   137 forms of taxation or imposition
138 Proverbs 28:15

Bodily manslaughter is whan thou sleest him with thy tonge, in other manere, as whan thou comaundist to slen a man or elles givest counseil to slee a man. Manslaughter in dede is in foure maneres: That oon is by lawe, right as a justice dampnith him that is coupable to the deth. But let the justice bewar that he do it rightfully, and that he do it nought for delit to spille blood, but for keping of rightwisnes. Another homicidy is doon for necessite, as whan a man sleth another him defendaunt,[139] and that he may noon other wise eschape fro his deth. But certeynly, if he may escape withoute slaughter of his adversarie and sle him, he doth synne, and he schal bere penaunce as for dedly synne. Ek if a man by caas or aduenture schete an arwe or cast a stoon with which he sleth a man, he is an homicide. Eke if a womman by negligence overlye[140] hir child in hir sleping, it is homicide and deedly synne. Eke whan a man distourbith concepcioun of a child, and makith a womman outher bareyn by drinke of venenous herbis, thugh whiche sche may nought conceyve, or sle a child by drynkes, or elles putteth certeyn material thinges in secre place to slee the child, or elles doth unkyndely synne by which man or womman schedith here nature in manner or in place, theras the child may nought be conceyved, or ellis is a womman have conceyved and hurt hirself, and sle the child, yit is it homycidie. What say we eek of wommen that mordren here children for drede of worldly schame? Certes, it is an horrible homicidy. Homicidy is eek if a man approche to a womman by desir of lecchery, thurgh the which the child is perischt, or elles smitith a womman wytyngly, thurgh which sche slee hir child. Alle these ben homicides.

Yit cometh ther of ire many mo synnes, as wel in word as in werk & thought; as he that arettith[141] upon God, and blamith God of thing of which he is himself gulty, or despisith God and all his halwes, as doon these cursed hasardours in divers cuntrees. This cursed synne don thay whan thay felen in here herte ful wickidly of God and his halwes. Also, whan thay treten unreverently the sacrament of the auter,[142] thilke synne is so gret that unnethe may it be relessed, but that the mercy of God passith alle his werkes, and is so gret and so benigne. Thanne cometh of ire that anger whan a man is scharply amonested in his schrifte to forlete synne; thanne wol he be angry and answere hokerly[143] and angrily, and defenden or excusen his synne by unstedefastnesse of his fleisch; or elles

---

139 'whilst defending himself' (ie in self-defence)

140 lie upon (ie crush)

141 lays blame upon

142 'sacrament of e altar' at is, e Mass

143 impatiently

he dede it to holde companye with his felawes, or ellis he saith the fend
entised him, or elles he dide it for his youthe, or ellis his complexioun is
so corrageous[144] that he may not forbere, or ellis it is desteny, as he saith
it cometh him of gentilesce, of his auncetrie, and semblable thinges. All
these maner of folk so wrappen hem in here synnes at thay wol nought
deliver hemself, for sothely no wight that excuse him wilfully of his
synne may nought be delivered of his synne, til that he mekely biknoweth
his synne.

After this thann come sweryng, that is expres agayns the comaunde-
ment of God, & this bifall often of angir and of ire. God saith, 'Thou
schalt not take the name of thy Lord God in vayn or in ydil';[145] also, Oure
Lord Jhesu Crist saith by the word of Seint Mathew, 'Ne wol ye not swere
in alle manere; neither by heven, for it is God's trone; ne by the eorthe,
for it is the benche of his feet; ne by Jerusalem, for it is the cite of a gret
king; ne by thin heed, for thou may nought make an her whit ne blak; but
saye by youre word, 'Ye, ye', and, 'Nay, nay', and what it is more, it is of
evel'.[146] Thus saith Jhesu Crist. For Crist's sake, swereth not so synfully in
dismembring of Crist for Crist's sake, by soule, herte, boones and body;
for certes, it seme that ye thenke that cursed Jewes ne dismembrit nought
y-nough the precious persone of Crist, but ye dismembre him more. And
if so be that the lawe compelle yow to swere, thanne reule yow after the
lawe of God in youre swering, as saith Jeremie, chapter iiij: 'Thou schalt
kepe thre condiciouns; thou schalt swere in trouthe, in doom, and in
rightwisnes';[147] this is to sayn, thou schalt swere so. For every lesyng[148] is
agayns Crist, for Crist is verray trouthe, and think wel this; that euery gret
swerer not compellid lawfully to swere, the wounde schal not departe fro
his hous whil he use such unleful sweringe. Thou schalt eek swere in
doom whan thou art constreigned by thy domesman to witnesse the
trouthe. Eek, thou schalt not swere for envye, ne for favour, ne for mede,
but for rightwisnesse, for declaring of it to worship of God and helping
of thin even-Cristen. And therfore euery man that takith God's name in
ydil or falsly swerith with his mouth, or elles takith on him the name of
Crist and callith himself a cristen man, and lyve agayns Crist's lyvyng and
his teching, alle thay take Crist's name in ydel. Loke eek what saith Seint
Peter; Actes, chapter iiij, '*Non est aliud nomen sub coelo, & cetera*' There is
noon other name, saith Seint Peter, under heven, ne geven to noon men,

144 'he is so temperamental at he couldn't help himself'
145 Exodus 20: the Ten Commandments.
146 Matthew 5:34   147 Jeremiah 4:2   148 lie

in which thay mowe be saved; that is to sayn, but in the name of Jhesu Crist.[149] Tak heede, eek, how the precious name of Crist, as saith Seint Poule *ad Philippenses* ij: *In nomine Jhesu & cetera*,[150] that in the name of Jhesu every of hevenly creatures, or erthely, or of helle, schulde bowe and tremble to heeren it nempned.

Thanne semeth it that men that sweren so horribly by his blessed name that thay despise it more bodyly than dede the cursed Jewes, or elles the devel, that tremblith whan he heerith his name. Now certis is, that swering, but it be lawfully doon, is so heihly defendid. Moche wors is forswering falsely, and yit needeles. What say we eek of hem that deliten hem in swering, and holden it a gentery or manly dede to swere gret othis, and what of hem that of verray usage ne cessen nought to swere grete othis, al be not the cause worth a strawe? Certes, this is horrible synne. Sweryng sodeynly without avysement is eek a gret synne. But let us now go to thilke horrible sweryng of adjuracioun and conjuraciouns, as doon these false enchauntours or nigromanciens, in bacines ful of water, or in a bright swerd in a cercle, or in the schulder bon of a scheep. I cannot sayn, but that thay doon cursedly and dampnably agains the faith of Holy Chirche. What say we of hem that bilieven on divinailes, as by flight or by nois of briddes, or of bestes, or by sort, by geomancie, by dremes' by chirkyng of dores, or crakking of howses, by gnawyng of rattis and such maner wrecchidnes? Certes, al this thing is defended[151] by God and Holy Chirche, for whiche thay ben accursed til thay come to amendement that on such filthe bisetten here bileeve. Charmes for woundes or malady of men or of bestes, if thay take any effect, it may be peraduenture that God suffreth hit for folk schulde geve the more faith and reverence to his name.

Now wol I speke of lesynge, whiche generally is fals signifiaunce of word in entent to desceyven his even-Cristen. Som lesyng is of whiche ther come noon avauntage to noon wight, and som lesyng torneth to the ease or profit of som man and to damage of another man. Another lesyng is for to save his lif or his catel; of delit for to lye, in which delit thay wol forge a long tale and paynte it with alle circumstaunces, wheras the ground of the tale is fals. Som lesyng cometh for he wolde susteyn his word; som lesyng come of rechelesnes withoute avisement, and semblable thinges.

149 This is a translation of the latin verse just given: Acts 4:12
150 'in the name of Jesus etc . . . ': Philippians 2:10
151 forbidden

Lat us now touche the vice of flaterie, which come not gladly, but for drede or for coveitise. Flaterie is generally wrongful preysing. Flaterers ben the devel's norices, that norisschen his children with mylk of the losingerie. Forsothe, Salomon saith that flaterie is worse than detraccioun, for somtyme detraccioun makith an hawteyn[152] man be the more humble, for he dredith detraccioun. But certes, flaterie makith a man to enhaunsen his hert and his countenaunce. Flaterers ben the devel's enchauntours, for thay maken man to wene of himself that he is like to that he is nought like. Thay ben like Judas, that bitraied God to selle him to his enemye, that is the devel. Flaterers ben the develes chapeleyns, that singen ay, '*Placebo*'.[153] I rekene flaterers in the vice of ire, for ofte tyme if oon man be wroth with another, thanne wol he flatere som man to mayntene him in his querel.

Speke we now of such cursyng as cometh of irous herte; her malisoun generally may be said every maner power of harm. Such cursyng bireveth man fro the regne[154] of God, as saith Seint Poule; and ofte tyme such cursyng wrongfully retourneth agayn to his owne nest. And over all thinges men oughten eschewe to cursen here oughne children, and give to the devel here engendrure, as ferforth as in hem is; certis, it is gret peril and gret synne.

Let us thanne speke of chydynge and reproche, which that ben ful grete woundes in man's hert, for they unsewe the semes of frendchipe in man's herte. For certis, unnethe may a man plainly ben accordid with him that him openly revyled, reproed and disclaundrid. This is a ful grisly synne, as Crist saith in the gospel, 'And takith keep now that he that reproveth his neighebor'; outher he reprovith him by som harm of peyne; thanne tornith the reproef to Jhesu Crist, for peyne is sent by the rightwis sonde of God and by his suffraunce, be it meselrie[155] or many other maladies; and if he repreve him uncharitably of synne as, 'Thou holour! Thou dronkelewe harlot!' and so forth, thanne aperteyne that to the rejoysing of the devel, that ever hath joye that men doon synne. And certis, chidyng may nought come but out of a vilein's herte, for after the abundaunce of the herte speketh the mouth ful ofte. And ye schal understonde that loke, by any way, whan any man schal chastise another, that he bewar; he may ful lightly quiken the fuyr of anger and of wrathe which that he schulde quenchen, and peraduenture sleth that he mighte chastise with benignite. For, as saith Salamon, 'The amiable tonge is the tree of lif';[156] that is to

---

152 proud/vain   153 'I will please'   154 kingdom: 1 Corinthians 6:10
155 leprosy   156 Proverbs 15:4

sayn, of life espirituel; and sothely, dislave tonge sleth the spirit of him
that repreve and also of him which is repreved. Lo, what saith Seint
Augustyn, 'Ther is nothing so lik the fende's child as he that ofte chideth'.
Seint Poule seith eek, 'I, servaunt of God, bihove nought to chide'; and
though that chidyng be a vilein's thing bitwixe all maner folk, yit is it
certes more uncovenable bitwix a man and his wif, for ther is never rest.
And therfore saith Salomon, 'An hous that is uncovered & droppyng and
a chidyng wif ben like; a man that is in dropping hous, in many partes
though he eschiewe the dropping in oon place, it droppeth on him in
another place. So farith it by a chyding wyf; but sche chide him in oon
place, sche wol chide him in another'.[157] 'And therfore better is a morsel
of bred with joye than an hous ful of delices, with chyding',[158] seith
Salomon. Seint Poul saith, 'O ye wommen, be ye sugettis to youre hous-
bondes, as bihoveth in God, and ye men, love youre wyves'.[159]

Afterward speke we of scornyng, which is a wikked thing and sinful,
and namely whan he scornith a man for his goode workes For certes,
suche scorners faren lik the foule toode,[160] that may nought endure the
soote smel of the vine roote whan it florischith. These scorners ben
partyng-felawes[161] with the devel, for thay han joye whan the devel wynne,
and sorwe whan he lese. Thay ben adversaries of Jhesu Crist, for thay
haten that he love; that is to say, savacioun of soule.

Speke we now of wikked counseil, for he that wickid counseil give, he
is a traytour; for he deceyve him that trusteth in him, ut Achitofel ad
Absolonem.[162] But natheles, yet is his wikkid counseil first agens himself;
for, as saith the wise man, 'Every fals lyvyng hath this proprete in himself;
that he that wil annoye another man, he annoye first himself. And men
schul understonde that man schulde noughte take his counseil of fals
folk, ne of angry folk, ne of folk that loven specially to moche her oughne
profyt, ne in to moche worldly folk, namely in counselyng of soules.

Now cometh the synne of hem that sowen and maken discord amonges
folk, which is a synne that Crist hateth outrely, and no wondir is, for God
died for to make concord; and more schame do thay to Crist than dede
thay that him crucifiede. For God love bettre that frendchipe be amonges
folk, thanne he dide his owne body, which that he gaf for unite. Therfore
ben thay likned to the devel, that ever ben aboute to make discord.

Now comith the sinne of double tonge, suche as speken faire biforn

---

157 Proverbs 27:15   158 Proverbs 17:1
159 Colossians 3:18   160 toad   161 partners
162 'thus Achitofel and Absolom'

folk and wikkely bihynde, or elles thay make semblaunt as though thay speke of good entencioun or ellis in game & play, and yit thay speke in wikked entent.

Now cometh the wreying of counseil, thurgh which a man is defamed; certes unnethe may he restore that damage.

Now cometh manace, that is an open foly; for he that ofte manace, he threttith more than he may parfourme, ful ofte tyme.

Now cometh idel wordes, that is withoute profyt of him that spekith the wordes, and eek of him that herkeneth tho wordes. Or elles ydel wordes ben tho that ben needeles or withouten entent of naturel profyt, and albeit that ydel wordes ben somtyme venial synne, yit schulde men doute hem. For we schuln give rekeninge of hem bifore God.

Now comith jangeling, that may nought be withoute synne, as saith Salomon, 'It is a signe of apert folie';[163] and therfore a philosophre, whan men askid him how men schulde plese the poeple, and he answerde, 'Do many goode werkes and spek fewe jangeles'. After this cometh the synne of japes, or japerie, as folk doon at the gaudes[164] of an ape. Suche japes defendith Seint Poule. Loke how that vertuous and holy wordes conforten hem that travailen in the service of Crist; right so conforten the violent wordes and knakkis and japeries of hem that travayle in the seruice of the devyl.

These ben the synnes that cometh of ire, and of other synnes.

Remedium contra iram[165]

❧ Remedye agayns ire is a vertu that men clepen mansuetude;[166] that is, debonairetee, and eek another vertu that men clepe pacience or suffraunce. Debonairetee withdrawith and restreigneth the stiringes and the moevynges of man's corrage in his herte in swich manere that they ne skippe nat out by angre, ne by ire. Suffraunce suffrith swetely alle the anoyaunce and the wronges that men doon to man outward. Seint Jerom seith thus of debonairtee, that, 'It doth noon harm to no wight, ne seith; ne for noon harm that men doon ne sayn, he ne eschaufith[167] nought agayns resoun. This vertu comith somtyme of nature, for as seith the philosopher, 'A man is a quik thing by nature, debonaire and tretable to good-nesse; but whan debonairetee is enformed of grace, thanne is it the more worth'.

163 Ecclesiastes 5:2   164 tricks   165 'remedy against ire (anger)'
166 meekness   167 gets hot ('under the collar')

Pacience, that is another remedye agayns ire, is a vertu that suffreth swetely every man's good-nes, and is nat wroth for noon harm that is doon to him. The philosopher seith that pacience is thilke vertu that suffreth deboneirely alle the outrages of adversitee and every wikked word. This vertu makith a man lyk to God, and makith him God's oughne dere child, as seith Crist. This vertu destroyeth thyn enemy, and therfore saith the wise man, 'If thou wolt venquishe thyn enemy, lerne to suffre'. And thou shalt understonde that man suffreth foure manere of grevances in outward thinges, agains whiche he moot have foure manere of pacience. The firste grevaunce is of wikkede wordes. Thilke suffrede Jhesu Crist withoute grucching, ful paciently, whan the Jewes despised and reproved him ful ofte. Suffre thou therfore paciently, for the wyse man saith, 'If thou strive with a fool, though the fool be wroth or though he laughe, algate thou shalt have no reste'.[168] That other grevaunce outward is to have damage of thi catel; theragayn suffred Crist ful paciently, whan he was despoyled of al at he hadde in his lyf, and that nas but his clothis. The thridde grevaunce is a man to have harm in his body; that suffred Crist ful paciently in al his passioun. The ferthe grevaunce is in outrageous labour in werkis. Wherfore I say that folk that rnaken hir servaunts to travaile to grevously or out of tyme as on halydayes, sothely they doon gret synne. Hereagainst suffred Crist ful paciently, and taughte us pacience, whan he bar upon his blisful schulder the croys upon which he shulde suffre despitous deth. Here may men lerne to be pacient, for certes, nought oonly Cristen ben pacient for the love of Jhesu Crist and for guerdoun of the blisful life that is pardurable, but the olde paynymes that never were cirsiten comaundedin and useden the vertu of pacience.

A philosopher upon a tyme, that wolde have bete his disciple for his grete trespas for which he was gretly amoeved, and brought a yerde to scoure the child;[169] & whan the child saugh the yerde, he sayde to his maister, 'What thenke ye to do?' 'I wolde bete the,' quod the maister, 'for thi correcioun.' 'For sithe,' saide the child, 'ye oughte first correcte youresilf, that han lest al youre pacience for the gilt of a child!' 'Forsothe,' quod the maister, al wepyng, 'thou saist soth; have thou the yerde, my deere sone, and correcte me for myn impacience.' Of pacience cometh obedience, thurgh which a man is obedient to Crist and to alle hem to which him oughte to be obedient in Crist. And understonde wel that

168 Proverbs 29:9   169 'brought a stick to beat the child'

obedience is parfyt, whan a man doth gladly & hastily, with good herte outrely, al that he scholde do. Obedience is generally to parforme the doctrine of God and of his soveraignes to whiche him oughte to ben obeissant in alle rightwisnes.

❦ After the synne of envye and ire, now wol I speke of accidie,[170] for envye blendith[171] the hert of a man, and accidie makith him hevy, thoughtful and wrawe. Envye and ire maken bitternes in herte; which bitternesse is mooder of accidie, the anguische of a trouble hert. And Seint Augustine saith, 'It is annoye of goodnesse and annoye of harme'. Certes, this is a dampnable synne, for it doth wrong to Jhesu Crist inasmoche as it bynymeth the service that we ought to do to Crist with alle diligence, as saith Salomon. But accidie doth noon such diligence; he doth alle thing with anoy and with wraweness, slaknes, and excusacioun, and with ydelnes & unlust, for which the book saith, 'Acursed be he that doth the service of God necligently'.[172] Thanne is accidie enemy to every astaat of man, for certes th'estat of innocence as was th'astate of Adam biforn that he fel into synne, in which estat he is holden to worche, as in herying[173] and honouryng of God. Another astat is th'estate of sinful man, in which estate men ben holden to labore in praying to God for amendment of her synnes, and that he wolde graunt hem to rise out of here synnes. Another estaat is th'estate of which he is holde to werkis of penitence; and certes, to alle these thinges is accidie enemye, contrarie, for it loveth no bysynes at al. Now certis, this foule synne accidie is eek a ful gret enemy to the liflode of the body, for it hath no purveaunce agens temporel neccessite, for it forslowthith and forsluggith, and destroyeth all goodes temporels by rechelessnes. The ferthe thing is that accidie is like hem that ben in the peyne of helle, bycause of her slouthe and of her hevynes, for thay that ben dampned ben so bounde that thay may nought wel do, ne wel thenke. Of accidie cometh first that a man is annoyed and encombrid for to do eny goodnes, and makith that God hath abhominacioun of such accidie, as saith Seint John, 'Now cometh slouthe, that wol suffre noon harnes ne no penaunce'. For sothely, slouthe is so tendre and so delicat, as saith Salomon, that he woll suffre noon hardnes ne penaunce; and therfore he schendeth[174] al that he doth.

Agayns this roten-hertid synne of accidie and of slouthe, schulden

170 sloth   171 deceives   172 Jeremiah 48:10   173 worshipping
174 ruins/destroys

men exercise hemself to do goode werkes, and manly and vertuously cacchen corrage wel to do, thinking that Oure Lord Jhesu Crist quiteth every good dede, be it never so lyte. Usage of labour is a ful greet thing, for it makith, as saith Seint Bernard, the laborer to have stronge armes and harde synewes; and slouthe maketh hem feble and tendre.

Thanne cometh drede to bygynne to werke eny goode deedes; for certes, who that is enclined to don synne, him thinkith it is so gret emprise for to undertake to doon werkes of goodnes, as saith Seynt Gregory.

Now cometh wanhope; that is, despair of the mercy of God, that cometh somtyme of to moche outrageous sorwe, and somtyme of to moche drede, ymagynynge that he hath do so moche synne that it will not availe him, though he wolde repent him and forsake synne. Thurgh which despeir or drede he abandoneth al his herte to alle maner synne, as seith Seint Augustin; which dampnable synne, if that it continue unto his lyve's ende, it is cleped, 'synnyng of the Holy Gost'. This horrible synne is so perilous that he that is despaired, ther is no felonye ne no synne that he doutith for to do, as scheewed wel by Judas. Certes, the mercy of God is ever redy to the penitent, and is above alle his werkes. Allas! Cannot a man bythenk him on the gospel of Seint Luk, wheras Crist saith that as wel schal ther be joye in heven upon a synful man that doth penitence, as upon nynety and nyne that ben rightful men that needen no penitence? Loke forther in the same gospel; the joye and the fest of the goode man that had lost his sone whan the sone with repentaunce was torned to his fader. Cannot thay remembre eek that, as saith Seint Luk xxiij; how that the thef that was hangid biside Jhesu Crist sayde, 'Lorde, remembre of me whan thou comest into thy regne'? For sothe saith Crist, 'Today thou schalt be with me in paradis'. Certis, ther is noon so horrible synne of man that it may in his lif be destroyed with penitence, thorugh the vertue of passioun of the deth of Crist. Allas, what needith it man thanne to be despaired, sith that his mercy is so redy and large? Aske, and have.

Thanne cometh sompnolent; that is, sluggy slumbring, which makith a man ben hevy and dul in body and in soule, and this synne cometh of slouthe; and certes, the tyme that by way of resoun man schulde nought slepe, that is, by the morwe, but if ther were cause resonable. For sothely, the morwe-tyde is most covenable to a man to say his prayers and for to thenk upon his God, and to honoure God and to geve almes to the pore that first cometh, in the name of Crist. Lo, what saith Salomon, 'Whoso wol by the morwe arise and seeke me, schal fynde'.[175] Than cometh

175 Proverbs 8:17

negligence, that rekkith of nothing. And how that ignoraunce be moder of all harm, certes, necgligence is the norice. Necligence doth no force whan he schal doon a thing, whethir he do it wel or baddely.

Of the remedy of these tuo synnes, as saith the wise man, that, 'He that dredith God, he sparith nought to do that him ought to don; and he that lovith God wol do diligence to plese God by hs werkis, and abounde himself with alle his mightes wel for to doon'.[176] Thanne comith ydelness, that is the gate of all harmes, and ydil man is like an hous that hath noone walles; the develes may entre on every syde, or schete at him at discovert[177] by temptaciouns on every side. This ydelnes is the thurrock[178] of alle wickid vileyns' thoughtes and of alle jangles, tryfules and of alle ordure[179] Certes, the heven is geven to hem that wol laboure, and nought to ydil folk. Eke David saith that, 'Thay ne ben not in the labour of men, ne thay schul not be whipped with men',[180] that is to sain, in purgatorie. Certis, thanne semeth it that thay schal be tormentid with the devel in helle, but if thay don penitence.

Thanne comith the synne that men clepe *tarditas*,[181] as whan a man is so latrede or tarying er he wil torne to God; and certis, that is a gret foly. He is like him that fallith into the diche and wol not arise. And this vice cometh of a fals hope that he thinkith he schal lyve long, but that hope fayleth full ofte. Thanne comith laches;[182] that is he when he bigynneth any good werk, anoon he wol forlete it and synte, as doon thay that han eny wight to governe, and ne take of hem no more keep anoon as thay dyde eny contrarie or eny anoy. These ben the newe schepherdes, that leten her schep wityngely go renne to the wolf that is in the breres, or don no force of her oughne gouernaunce. Of this cometh povert and destruccioun, bothe of spirituel and of temporel thinges. Thanne cometh a maner of coldenesse, that freseth al the hert of man. Thanne cometh undevocioun, thurgh which a man is so blunt &, as saith Seint Bernard, he hath such a langour in soule that he may neyther rede ne synge in Holy Chirche, ne heere, ne thinke on deuocioun in Holy Chirche, ne travayle with his hondes in no good werk that nys to him unsavory and al. Thanne waxith he slowe and slombry, and soone wol be wroth, and soone is enclined to hate and to envye. Thanne cometh the synne of

---

176 Ecclesiastes 7:19
177 'shoot at him through the opening (undefended)' – the Parson is imagining the devils as archers, as at a medieval seige.
178 bilge (of a ship). The hidden place below where rubbish is placed.
179 filth/shit   180 Psalm 72:5   181 lateness   182 laziness

worldly sorwe such as is clepid *trisitita*,[183] that sleth man, as saith Seint Poule.[184] For certis, such sorwe werkith to the deth of the soule & of the body also, for therof cometh that a man is anoyed of his oughne lif; which sorwe schorteth ful ofte the lif of a man, or that his tyme is come by way of kynde.

Agains this horrible synne of accidie, and the braunches of the same, there is a vertu that is cleped fortitudo, or strengthe; that is affeccioun thurgh which a man despiseth all noyous thinges. This vertu is so mighty & so vigurous that it dar withstonde mightly, and wisely kepe himself from perils that be wicked, and wrastil agains the assautes of the devel; for it enhaunsith and endorceth the soule, right as accidie abateth it and makith it feble. For this fortitudo may endure by long sufferaunce the travailes that ben covenables. This vertu hath many spices; the first is cleped magnanimite, that is to sayn, gret corrage. For certis, ther bihoveth gret corrage agains accidie, lest that it ne swolwe not thi soule by the synne of sorwe, or destroye it by wanhope. This vertue makith folk undertake harde and grevous thinges by his owne wille, wilfully and resonably; and foralsmoche as the devel fighteth agaynst a man more by queyntise and by sleight than by strengthe. Therfore many a man schal ageinstonde him by witte, and by resoun, and by discrecioun. Thanne is ther the vertu of faith and hope in God and in his seintes to acheuen and to accomplice the goode werkes in the which he purposith fermely to continue. Thanne cometh seurte or sikernes, and that is whan a man doutith no travaile in tyme comyng of good werk that a man hath bygonne. Thanne cometh magnificence; that is to say, whan a man doth and performith grete wekes of goodnesse that he hath bygonne, and that is th'end why that men scholden do goode werkes. For in the accomplising of grete goode werkes lith the grete guerdoun. Thanne is ther constaunce; that is, stablenes of corrage, and this schulde ben in herte by stedefast faith, and in mouthe, and in berying, and in cheer and in deede. Eek, ther ben mo special remedies agayns accidie in dyvers werkis and in consideracioun of the peyne of helle, and of the joye of heven, and in the trust of the hyhe grace of the Holy Gost that wil geve him might to parforme his good entent.

183 sadness
184 2Corinthians 7:10

De avaritia[185]

❧ After acccidie, I wil speke of avarice and of coveytise; of which synne for sothely saith Seint Poule that, 'The roote of alle eveles & harmes is coveytise',[186] and that, 'The hert of man is confoundid in itself and troublid, and that the soule hath lost the comfort of God,. thanne seekith he an ydel solas of worldly thinges'. Avarice, after the descripcioun of Seint Austyn, is, 'A likerousnes in hert to have erthely thinges'. Some other folk sayn that avarice is for to purchase many erthely thinges, and nothing geve to hem that han neede. And understonde that avarice ne stont not oonly in lond ne in catel, but somtyme in science and in glorie, and eny maner outrageous thinges, is avarice. And the difference bytwixe avarice and coveytise is this; covetise is for to coveyte suche thinges as thou hast not, and avarice is a synne that is ful dampnable, for al holy writ curseth it and spekith agayn that vice. For it doth wrong to Jhesu Crist, for it bireveth him the love that men to him owen, and turnith it bakward agayns al resoun, and makith that the avarous man hath morre hope in his catel than in Jhesu Crist; and therfore saith Seint Poule *ad Ephes*[187] that an averous man is in the thraldom of ydolatrie. What difference is ther bitwen an ydolaster and an avarous man, but that an ydolaster peradventure hadde but a mawment; and certes, the synne of mawmetrie is the firste thing that God defendith in the ten comaundements, as berith witnes in *Exodus cap. xx*,[188] 'Thou schalt have noone false goddes biforn me, ne thou schalt make to the no grave thing. Thus is he an averous man that loveth his tresor toforn God. And an idolaster, thurgh his cursed synne of avarice and coveytise, comen these harde lorschipes thurgh whiche thay ben destreyned by talliages, custumes, and cariages, more than here duete of resoun is, and elles take thay of here bondemen amercimentes which mighte more resonably ben callid extorciouns than mercymentis; of whiche mersyments and raunsonyng of bondemen some lordes' stywards sayn that it it rightful, 'forasmoche as a cherl hath no temporal thing that it nys his lorde's', as thay sayn.[189] But

---

185 Of avarice   186 Timothy 6:10   187 Ephesians 5:5   188 Exodus 20:3
189 The parson is referring to forms of imposition, mostly financial but sometimes in the form of goods or labour, enforced by lords upon their tenants. These are taxation, payments for transportation and tolls on the transportation of goods, and amercements, impositions laid down by (in this case local, feudal, courts presided over by the lord or his representatives. Bondmen are villeins, or unfree tenants. In the years following the Black Death of 1348/9 and again in 1362,

certes, thise lordeschipes doon wrong that bireven here bondemen thinges that thay never gave hem. Augustinus;[190] 'Sloth is the condicioun of thraldom, and the first cause of thraldom is sinne'. Genesis v;[191] 'Thus may ye seen that the gilt deserved thraldom, but not nature.' Wherfore these lordes schulden nought to moche glorifie in here lordschipes, sith that by naturel condicoun thay ben nought lordes over thralles, but for thraldom com first, by the desert of synne. And fortherover, ther as the lawe sayth that temporel goodes of bonde folk been the goodes of her lordschipes; ye, that is to understonde, the goodes of the emperour, to defende hem in here right; but not to robbe hem ne to reve[192] hem. And therfore seith Seneca, 'Thi prudence schulde live benignely with thi thralles. Thilke that thay clepe thralles ben God's poeple, for humble folk ben Crist's frendes; thay ben contubernially[193] with the Lord. Thenk, eek as of such seed as cherles springen, of such seed springe lordes. As wel may the cherl be saved as the lord. The same deth that takith the cherl, such deth taketh the lord. Wherfor I rede, do right so with thy cherl, as thou woldist thi lord dide with the if thou were in his plyt. Every sinful man is a cherl, as to synne.

I rede the certes, thou lord, werke in such a wise with thy cherles that thay rather love the than drede the. I wot wel ther is degre above degre, as resoun is, and skil it is, that men don her devoir theras it is dewe; but certes, extorciouns and despit of oure undirlinges is dampnable. And forthermore, understonde wel that conquerours and tyrauntes maken ful ofte thralles of hem that born ben of als royal blood as byn thay that hem conqueren. This name of thraldom was never erst couth[194] til Noe sayde that his sone Chanaan schulde be thral of his bretheren for his synne.[195] What say we thanne of hem that pylen[196] and doon extorciouns to Holy Chirche? Certis, the swerdes that men geven first to a knight whan he is newe dubbyd signifieth faith, and that he schulde defende Holy Chirche; and as seith Seint Austin, 'Thay ben the devel's wolves that stranglen the scheep of Jhesu Crist'. And doon wors than wolves, for sothely, whan the wulf hath ful his wombe, he stintith to strangle scheep; but sothly the

---

these impositions became harsher, and the attempts to control unfree tenants much stricter, due to the high demand for labour and the shortage of supply. These strict controls and exactions were among the grievances of the peasants during the 1381 Peasants' Revolt.

190 *De Civitate*, Book Nine (added in other manuscripts, but not in this one)

191 Book of Genesis, Chapter Five   192 take from

193 close to   194 known

195 Genesis 9:25   196 steal from

pilours and the destroyers of the goodes of Holy Chirche ne doon nought
so, for thai stinte never to pile.

Now, as I have sayd; sith so is that synne was first cause of thraldom,
thanne is it thus that ilke tyme that al this world was in synne. Thanne
was al this world in thraldom and in subjecciounb But certis, sith the
tyme of grace com, God ordeyned that somme folk schulde be more
heigh in estaate and in degre, and somme folkes more lowe, and that
everich schulde be served in here estate and in degree. And therfore in
somme contrees there thay ben thralles, whan thay han turned hem to
the faith, thay make here thralles free out of thraldom. And therfor,
certis, the lord oweth to his man that the man owith to the lord. The
pope callith himself servaunt of servauntes of God. But forasmoche as
the staat of Holy Chirche ne might not han be; nor the commune profit
might nought have ben kepte, ne pees, ne reste in erthe, but if God had
ordeynde som man of heiher degre and some men of lower; therfore
was soveraignte ordeyned to kepe, and to mayntene and defende, her
underlynges or her sujectis in resoun, as ferforth as it lith in her power,
and not to destroye ne confounde hem. Wherfore I say that thilke lordes
that be like wolves that devouren the possessioun or the catel of pore
folk wrongfully withoute mercy or mesure; thay schul receyve, by the
same mesure that thay han mesured to pouer folk, the mercy of Jhesu
Crist, but if it be amendid.

Now cometh deceipt bitwixe marchaunt and merchaunt; and thou
schalt understonde that marchaundise is in many maneres. That oon is
bodily, and that other is gostly, that oon is honest and leful, and that
other is dishonest & unleful. Of thilke bodily marchaundise that is
honest and leful is this; that theras God hath ordeyned that a regne or a
cuntre is suffisaunt to himself, thanne is it honest an leful that of the
abundaunce of this contrre be men helpe another cuntre that is more
needy. And therfore ther moote be marchaunts to bringe fro that oon
cuntre to that other her merchaundise. That other marchaundise, that
men hauntyn with fraude and treccherie and decipt, with lesynges and
fals othis, is cursed and dampnable. Espirituel marchaundise is proprely
symonie, that is ententyf desire to beye thin espirituel, that is, thing that
apperteyneth to the seintuarie of God and to the cure of the soule. This
desir, if so be that a man do his diligence to parforme it, albeit that his
desire take noon effect, yit is it to him a dedly synne; and if he be ordrid,
he is irreguler.[197] Certis, symonye is cleped of Symon Magus, that wolde

197 'if he receives holy orders, this is irregular/illegal'

han bought for temporal catel the gifte that God had given by the Holy Gost to Seint Petir and to th'apostlis; and therfore understonde that bothe he that sellith and he that bieth things espiritueles ben cleped Symonials, be it by cate, be it by procurement, or by fleisshly prayere of his frendes, either fleisshly frendes or spirituel frendes; fleisshly in tuo maneres; as by kynrede or other frendes.[198] Sothely, if thay pray for him, it is not worthy & able. If he take the benefice, it is symonie, and if he be worthy & able it is non.

That other is whan man or womman prayen for folk to avaunce hem oonly for wikkid fleisshly affeccioun, that thay have unto the persone, and that is ful symonye. But certis, in service, for which men geven thinges espirituels unto hir servaunts, moote he be honest and ellis not; and eek that it be withoute bargaynynge, and that the persone be able. For as saith Seint Damase, 'Alle the synnes of this world, at the regard of this synne, is a thing of nought'. For it is the gretteste synne that may be, after the synne of Lucifer and Antecrist. For by this synne God forlesith the chirche, and the soule that he bought with his precious blood, by hem that geven chirches to hem that ben not digne.[199] For thay putten in theves that stelen the soules of Jhesu Crist, and destroyen his patrimoygne. By suche undigne prestis and curates han lewed men han lasse reverence of the sacrament of Holy Chirche, and such geveres of chirches putten out the children of Crist and putten into the chirche the devel's oughne sone. Thay sellen soules that lambes schule kepe, to the world that stranglith hem, and therfore schul thay neuer have part of the pasture of lambes, that is the blisse of heven.

Now cometh hasardrie with his appertenaunce, as tables and rafles,[200] of whiche cometh deceipt, fals othis, chidynges and alle reveynes,[201] blasphemyng and reneying of God and hate of his neighebors, wast of goodes, mispendyng of tyme, and somtyme manslaughter. Certes, hasardours ne mowe not be withoute gret synne whil thay haunte that craft. Of avarice cometh eek lesynges, thefte and fals witnesse and fals othis, and ye schul undirstonde that these be grete synnes, and expresce agains the comaundements of God, as I have sayd. Fals witnesse is in word and eek in dede. In word; as for to bireve thin neighebor his good name by thy witnessinge, or bireve him his catel or his heritage[202] by thy fals witnesse, whan thou for ire or for meede, or for envie berest witnes, or accusist him or excusist him by thy fals witnes, or ellis excusist thiself falsly. Ware

198 Acts 5:18   199 worthy
200 'table- and dice-games'   201 theft   202 inheritance

yow, questemongers[203] and notaries! Certis, for fals witnessynge was Susanna in ful gret sorwe and peyne, and many another mo.

The synne of thefte is eek expresse agayns God's hestis, & that in tuo maners; coporel and sprituel. Corporel; as for to take thy neighebour's catel agayns his wille, be it by force or by sleight, be it by mette or by mesure, by stelyng eek of fals enditements upon him and in borwyng of thin neghebore's catelle in entent never to paye, and in semblable thinges. Espirituel thefte is sacrilege; that is to sain, hurtynge of holy thinges, or of things sacred of Crist. Sacrilege is in tuo maneres; that oon is by reasoun of holy place, as chirches or chirchehawes.[204] For whiche every vilein's synne that men doon in suche places may be clepid sacrilege, or every violence in semblable place. Also, they that withdrawen falsly the rightes that longen to Holy Chirche. And generally sacrilege is to reue holy thing fro holy place and unholy thing out of holy place, or holy thing out of holy place.

Remedium contra Avariciam[205]

❧ Now schul ye understonde that the relevyng of auarice is misericorde, and pite largely taken. And men might axen why that misericord and pite is relievyng of avarice. Certes, the avaricious man schewith no pite ne misericorde to the needeful man, for he delitith him in kepyng of his tresor and nought in the rescowing ne relievyng of his even-Cristen, & therfore speke I first of misericord. Thanne is misericord, as saith the philosopher, 'A vertu. by which the corrage of a man is stired by the myseise of him that is mysesed', upon which misericorde folwith misericord in parforming of chariteable werkis of misericord. And certes, these moeven men to the misericord of Jhesu Crist, that gaf himself for oure gult, and suffred deth for misericord, and forgaf us our original synne, and therby relessid us fro peyne of helle and amenusid the paynes of purgatorie by penitence, and geveth grace wel to do, and at the laste the joye of heven. The spices of misericorde ben for to love and for to give, and eek for to forgive and for to relesse, and for to have pite in herte and compassioun of the meschief of his even-Cristen, and eek chastise theras neede is.

Another maner of remedye agains avarice is resonable largesse, but sothely here bihovith the consideracioun of the grace of Jhesu Crist, and

203 those who conduct inquests/questioners
204 churchyards   205 remedy against avarice

of his temporel goodes, and eek of his goodes perdurable that Crist gaf us, and eek to have remembraunce of the deth that he schal resceyve, he noot not whanne; and eke he schal forgon al that he hath, save oonly that he hath dispendid in goode werkes. But foralsmoche as some folk ben unresonable, men oughte to eschiewe foly largesse, than clepen wast. Certes, he that is fool large ne giveth nought his catel. Sothely what thing that he giveth for vaynglorie, as to mynstrals and to folk for to bere his renoun in the world; he hath synne, and noon almes. Certes, he lesith foule his goodes that sekith with the gift of his good nothing but synne. He is like to an hors that sekith rather to drynke drovy[206] watir and trouble than for to drinke watir of the welle that is cleer. And forasmoche as thay give theras thay schuld not giue, to hem appendith thilke malisoun that Crist schal give at the Day of Doom to hem that schal be dampned.

De gula[207]

❦ After avarice cometh glotenye, which is expresse eke agayns the comaundement of God. Glotenye is unresonable and desordeyned coveytise to to ete and to drynke. This synne corruptid al this world, as is wel schewed in the synne of Adam and of Eva. Loke, eek, what saith Seint Poul of glotouns: 'Many,' saith Seint Poul, 'gon, of whiche I have ofte said to yow, and now I say it wepyng, that th'enemyes of the cros of Crist, of whiche th'ende is deth, and of whiche her wombe is here God, and here glorie in confusioun that so saveren erthely thinges'.[208]

He that is usaunt to this synne hath many spices. The first is dronkenes, that is th'orrible sepulture[209] of man's resoun. And whan man is dronken he hath lost his resoun, and this is dedly synne. But schortly, whan that a man is not wont to strong drinke and peraduenture ne knowith not the strengthe of the drynk, or hath feblesse in his heed, or hath travayled, thurgh whiche he drynkith the more, and be sodeynly caught with drynke; it is no dedly synne, but venial. The secounde spice of glotenie is whan the spirit of a man wexith al trouble for drunkenesse, and bireveth him his witte and his discressioun. The thridde spice of glotouns is when a man devoureth his mete and hath no rightful maner of etyng. The ferthe is whan, thurgh the grete abundaunce of his mete, the homours of his body been distemprid. The fifth is the idilnes by to moche drinking, for which a man somtyme forgetith by the morwe what he dide at eve or on the night bifore. In other maner ben distinct the

206 dirty   207 of gluttony   208 Philippians 3:18   209 sepulchre/tomb

spices of glotonye after Seint Gregory: The firste is for to ete or drynke byfore tyme to ete; the secound is whan man giveth him to delicate mete or drinke; the thridde is whanne man takith to moche therof, over mesure; the ferthe is curiosite, with gret entent to make and apparayle[210] his mete; the fifte is for to ete to gredely. These ben the fyve fyngres of the devel's hand, by whiche he drawith folk to synne.

❦ Agayns glotonye is the remedie abstinence, as saith Galien. But that hold I nought meritorie, if he do it oonly for the hele of his body. Seint Austyn wol that abstinence be don for vertu and with pacience. 'Abstinence,' he saith, 'is litil worth but if a man have good wille therto, and but it be enforced by pacience and by charite, and that men doon it for God's sake and in hope to have the blisse of heven'. The felawes of abstinence ben attemperaunce, that holdith the mene in alle thinges; eek schame, that eschiewith al dishoneste; suffisaunce,[211] that seeketh noone riche metes ne drynkes, ne doth no force of to outrageous apparaillyng of mete; mesure also, that restreyneth by reson the dislave appetit of etyng; sobernes also restryneth the outrage of drinke; sparing[212] also, that restreyneth the delicat wille to ete at the lasse leysir

De luxuria[213]

❦ After glotonye thanne cometh leccherie, for these two synnes ben so neih cosyns that ofte tyme thay wol not departe, *unde Paulus ad Ephes,*[214] *'Nolite inebriari vino & c'*. God wot, this wynne is full displesaunt thing to God, for he sayde himself, 'Do no leccherie';[215] and therfore he putte gret peyne agayn this synne. In the olde lawe, if a womman thral were take in this synne sche scholde be beten with staves to the deth, and if sche were a gentilwomman sche schulde be slayne with stoons, and if sche were a bisschop's doughter sche schulde be brent, by God's comaundement. Fortherover, for synne of leccherie God dreinte al the world at the diluvie,[216] and after that he brent fyve citees with thonder-layt,[217] and sonk hem into helle.

Now let us thanne speke of thilke stynkyng synne of leccherie that men clepen advoutry of weddid folk, that is to sayn if that oon of hem be

210 decorate   211 sufficiency   212 frugality   213 of lechery
214 'hence Paul, in his epistle to the Ephesians; 'Do not become drunk
     with wine etc.'
215 Exodus 20:14   216 the Flood   217 lightning

weddid, or elles bothe. Seint John saith that advouterers schuln be in helle, in watire brennyng of fuyr and of brimston; in fuyr for the leccherie; in brimston, for the stynk of her ordure. Certis, the brekyng of this sacrament is an horrible thing; it was makid of God himself in paradis, confermed of Jhesu Crist, as witnesseth seint Mathew, 'A man schall lete fader and mooder and take him to his wif, and thay schul ben two in oon fleisch'.[218] This sacrament bitokeneth the knyttyng togider of Crist and of Holy Chirche. Nat oonly that God forbad advoutrie in dede, but eek he comaunded that thou scholdest nat coveyte thy neyhebor's wif. 'In this heste,' seith Seint Austyn, 'is forboden al maner coveytise to do leccherie'. Lo, what seith Seint Mathew in the gospel; that, 'Who so seth a womman to coveytise of his lust, he hath doon lecchery with hir in his herte'.[219] Here may ye se that nought oonly the dede of this synne is forboden, but eek the desir to do that synne. This cursed synne annoyeth grevously hem that it haunten; and first to here soule, for he obligith it to synne and to pyne of the deth that is perdurable; unto the body annoyeth it grevously also, for it dreyeth him and wastith him & schent him, and of his blood he makith sacrifice to the devel of helle. It wastith eek his catel and his substaunce, and certes if that it be a foul thing a man to waste his catel on wommen, yit is it a fouler thing whan that for such ordure wommen dispende upon men here catel and here substaunce. This synne, as saith the prophete, byreveth man and womman her good fame and al here honour, and it is ful pleasaunt to the devel, for therby wynneth he the moste pray of this world. And right as a marchaunt deliteth him most in chaffare that he hath most auauntage of, right so delitith the feend in this ordure.

This is the other hond of the devel with fyve fyngres to cacche the poeple in his vilonye. The first fynger is the foule lokyng of the foule womman and of the foule man, that sleth right as a basiliskoc[220] sleth folk by the venym of his sight; for the coveytise of eyen folwith the coveytise of the herte. The secounde fynger is the vileyn's touchinge in wikkid manere; and therfore saith Salomon that who so touchith and handelith a womman, he farith like him that handelith the scorpioun, that syngith and sodeinly sleth thurgh his envenmynge, as whoso touchith warm picche[221] it schent his fyngres. The thridde is foule wordes, that farith lik fuyr that right anoon brenneth the herte. The ferthe is the kissyng; and

---

218 Matthew 19:5   219 Matthew 5:28
220 Basilisk: was supposed to kill with his stare   221 pitch

trewely he were a greet fool that wolde kisse the mouth of a brennyng oven or of a forneys, and more fooles ben thay that kyssen in vilonye. For that mouth is the mouth of helle, and namely thise olde dotard fooles holours;[222] yit wol thay kisse, though thay may nought do. Certis, thay ben like to houndes; for an hound, whan he cometh to a roser[223] or by other bussches, though he may nought pisse, yet wil he heve up his leg and make a countenaunce to pisse. And for that many man weneth he may not synne for no licorousnes that he doth with his wif; certis, that oppinioun is fals. God wot, a man may sle himself with his owne knyf and make himself dronke of his oughne tonne. Certis, be it wif or child or eny worldly thing that he lovyth biforn God, it is his maumet[224] and he is an ydolastre. Man schulde love his wyf by discrescioun, paciently and attemperely, and thanne is sche as it were, his suster.

The fyfte fynger of the devel's hond is the stynkyng dede of leccherie. Certes, the fyue fyngres of glotony the devel put in the wombe of a man, & his fyve fyngres of lecchery, bygripeth him by the reynes[225] for to throwe him into the fourneys of helle, thereas they schuln have the fuyr and the wormes that ever schal lasten, and wepyng and wayling, scharp humger and thurst, grislines of develes that schul al to-tere hem withoute respit and withouten ende. Of leccherie, as I sayde, sourdren[226] divers spices of fornicacioun that is bitwen man and womman that ben nought maried, and this is dedly synne and against nature, al that is enemy and destruccioun to nature. Parfay, the resoun of a man tellith him wel that it is dedly synne, foralsmoche as God forbad leccherie, and Seint Poule gevith hem that regne that is due to no wight but hem that doon synne dedely.[227] Another synne of lecchery is for to bireve a mayden of hir maydenhede, for he that so doth, certes he casteth the mayden out of the heighest degre that is in the present lif, and birevith hir thilke precious fruyt that the book clepith the hundrid fruyt.[228] I can geve it noon other name in Englisch, but in Latyn it is y-clepid *centesimus fructus secundum Hieronymum contra Jovinianum.*[229] Certes, he that so doth is cause of many harmes and vilenyes, mo than eny man can rekene. Right as he somtyme is cause of alle the damages that bestis doon in the feeld, that brekith the hegge of the closure, thurgh which he destroyeth that may not be restored; for certes, no more may maydenhode be restored than an arm that is smyten fro the body retourne agayn to waxe.[230] Sche may

---

222 lechers   223 rosebush   224 idol   225 loins, guts
226 spring   227 Galatians 5:19   228 'the fruit that is a hundred-fold'
229 ' . . . according to Jerome Against Jovinian'   230 grow

have mercy, this wot I wel, if sche do penitence, but never schal it be that sche nas corrupt. And al be so that I have spoke somwhat of advoutre, yit is it good to speke of mo perils that longen to advoutre, for to eschiewe that foule synne.

Advoutrie in Latyn is for to sayn, approaching of other man's bed thorugh the which that whilom[231] were oon fleisch abandone here bodyes to other persones. Of this synne, as saith the wise man, many harmes cometh therof. First, brekyng of faith; and certes, faith is the keye of cristendom, and whan that faith is broke and lorn sothely cristendom stont veyn, and withouten fruyt. This synne is eek a theef, for theft is – generally to speke – to reve a wight his thing agayns his wille. Certis, this is the foulest thefte that may be, whan a womman stelith hir body from hire housbonde and geveth it to hire holour, to defoule hire & stelith hir soule fro Crist and gevith it to the devel. This is a fouler thefte than for to breke a chirche and stele chalises,[232] for these advouterers breke the temple of God spirituelly, and stelen the vessel of grace that is the body and the soule. For whiche Jhesu Crist schal destroyen hem, as saith Seint Poule.[233] Sothely, this thefte doubtyd gretly Joseph whan that his lord's wyf prayde him of vilonye when he saide, 'Lo, my lady, how my lord hath take to me under my warde al that he hath in this world; ne no thing of his power is oute of my power, but oonly ye that ben his wyf; and how schuld I do thanne this wikkidnes and synne so horribly agayns God and my lord. God it forbede'. Alas, al to litel is such trouthe now y-founde!

The thridde harm is the filthe thurgh which thay breken the comaundement of God and defoule the auctor of here matrimonye, that is Crist; for certis, insomoche as the sacrament of mariage is so noble and so digne, so moche is it the grette synne for to breke it; for God makid mariage in pardys in th'estat of innocence, to multiplie mankynde to the service of God, and therfore is the brekyng the more grevous. Of which breking cometh fals heires oftetymes, that wrongfully occupien men's heritage, and therfore wolde Crist putte hem out of the regne[234] of heven, that is heritage to goode folk. Of this breking cometh eek oftetyme that folk unwar wedden or synnen with her kynrede, and namely these harlottis that haunten a comune gonge[235] whereas men purgen her entrayles of her ordure. What say we ek of putours,[236] that lyven by the orrible synne of putrie, & constreyne wymmen – ye, som with his oughne

---

231 formerly
232 chalices – the cups (usually silver), in which the wine is administered at Mass.
233 1Corinthians 3:17   234 kingdom   235 lavatory   236 pimps

wyf or his child – as don these baudes, to yelde hem a certeyn rente of
here bodily putrie. Certes, these ben cursede synnes! Understonde eek
that avoutrie is set gladly in the Ten Comaundements bitwixe man-
slaughter and thefte, for it is grettest thefte that may be; for it is thefte of
body and soule, and it is lik to homicidie, for it kerveth a-tuo hem that
first were makid oone fleisch. And therfore by the olde lawe [237] of God
thay scholde be slayn. But natheles, by the lawe of Jhesu Crist, that is the
lawe of pite, whan he sayde to the womman that was founde in advoutri
and schulde have ben slayn with stoones aftir the wille of the Jewes as
was her law, 'Go,' quod Jhesu Crist, 'and have no more wille to synne'.[238]
Sothely, the vengeaunce of avouterye is awardid to the peyne of helle,
but if be destourbed by penitence.

Yit ben ther mo spices of this cursed synne, as whan that oon of hem
is religious or ellis bothe, or for folk that ben entred into ordre as sub-
dekin, or prest, or hospitalers; and ever the higher that he be the gretter
is the synne. The thinges that gretly aggreggith her synne is the brekyng
of here avow of chastite whan thay resceyued ordre, and fortherover is
soth that holy ordre is chefe of all the tresor of God and is a special signe
and mark of chastite, to schewe that thay ben joyned to chastite, which
that is the moste precious lif that is. And eek these ordred folk ben special
traytours of God and of his poeple, and whil thay ben suche traytours
here prayer avayleth not to the poeple. Prestis ben aungels, as by the
dignite of here misteris, but forsothe Seint Poul saith that Sathanas
transformeth him in an aungel of light.[239] Sothely, the prest that hauntith
dedly synne, he may be likened to the aungel of derknes, and he semeth
aungel of light; but forsothe he is aungil of derknes, which ben the sones
of Beliel, that is the devel. Belial is to say, withoute juge, and so faren thay
thay thynke hem fre and han no juge, no more than hath a fre bole that
takith which cow that him liketh in the toun. So faren thay by wommen,
for right as a fre bole is ynough for al a toun, right so is a wikked prest
corrupcioun ynough for al a parisch, or for al a contray. These prestes, as
saith the book, 'Ne conne not the mistery of presthode; the poeple ne
God ne knowe thay not'.[240] Thay holde hem nought apayed, as saith the
book, of soden fleissch that was to hem offred; but thay tooke by force
the fleissch that is raw. Certes, so these schrewes holde hem not appayed
with rosted fleissch and sode fleissh[241] with whiche the poeple feeden
hem in gret reverence, but thay wil have raw fleisch of folk's wyves and

---

237 The Old Testament law (of Leviticus and Deuteronomy)   238 John 8:11
239 2 Corinthians 11:14   240 1 Samuel 2:13   241 roasted . . . boiled

here doughtres. And certes, these wommen that consenten to here harlotrie don gret wrong to Crist and to Holy Chirche and Alle Halwes and to Alle Soules, for thay bireven alle these hem that schulde worschipe Crist and Holy Chirche and praye for Cristen soules. And therfor han suche prestis & here lemmans eeke that consenten to here leccherie the malisoun of al the Court Cristian,[242] til thay come to amendement.

The thridde spice of advoutry is somtyme bitwix a man and his wif, and that is whan thay take noon reward in her assembling[243] but only to the fleischly delit, as seith Seint Jerom, and ne rekke of nothing but that thay be assemblid bycause that thay ben maried. Al is good ynough, as thinkith hem. But in suche folk hath the devel power, as saith the aungel Raphael to Thoby; for in here assemblyng thay putten Jhesu Crist out of her herte and given hemself to alle ordure. The ferthe spice is the assemble of hem that ben of here kynrede, or of hem that ben of oon affinite, or elles with hem with whiche here fadres or here kynrede han delited in the synne of leccherie. This synne makith hem like houndes, that taken noon heede of kynrede. And certes parenteal[244] is in tuo maneres; eyther gostly, as for to dele with her godssib,[245] for right so as he that engendrith a child is his fleisshly fader, right so is his godfader his fader espirituel. For which a womman may in no lasse synne assemble with hir gossib than with hire oughne fleischly fader or brother. The fifte spice is thilke abhominable synne of which that no man is openly rehersed in holy wryt; but though that holy writ speke of horrible synne, certes holy writ may not be defouled no more than the sonne that schyneth on a dongehul.[246] Another synne apperteneth to lecchery that cometh in slepyng, & this synne cometh ofte to hem that ben maydenes, and eek to hem that ben corrupte; and this synne men clepen pollucioun, that cometh in iiij maners.[247] Somtyme of languisschynge of the body, for the humours ben to ranke and to abundaunt in the body of man; somtyme of infirmite, for the feblenesse of the vertu retentyf,[248] as phisik maketh mencioun; and somtyme for surfete of mete and drynke; somtyme of vilein's thoughtes that ben enclosed in man's mynde. Man moste kepe him wisely, or elles may men synne grevously.

Now cometh the remedye agens lecchery, and that is generally chastite

---

242 ecclesiastical court (for the enforcement of moral law)
243 sexual intercourse   244 incest
245 godparents, or those closely related to them; or the godparents of one's children.
246 homosexual activity   247 'wet' dreams
248 The 'vertu retentif', or powers of fluid retention, fail – allowing seminal fluid
    to escape.

of wikkedhede, and continence, that restreyneth all the disordeigne[249] moevynges that comen of fleischly talentes. And ever the gretter meryt schal he han that most restryneth eschaufynges of ordure of this synne; and this is tuo maneres, that is to sayn chastite of mariage, chastite of widewhede. Now schalt thou understonde that matrimoigne is leful assemblynge of man and womman, that resceyuen by vertu of the secrement the bond thurgh which thay may not be departid in al here lif; that is to say, whil thay lyven bothe. This, as saith the boke, is a ful gret sacrement; God makid it, as I have said, in paradis, and wolde himself be born in mariage; and for to halwen mariage he was at the weddyng wheras he turnede watir into wyn, which was the first miracle that he wrought in erthe biforn his disciples. The trewe effect of mariage clensith fornicacioun and replenischeth Holy Chirche of good lynage; for that is the ende of mariage, and it changith dedly synne into venyal bituixe hem that ben weddid, and it makith the hertes al one as wel as the bodyes. This is verray mariage that was furste blessed by God er that the synne bigan, whan naturel lawe was in his poynt in paradis; and it was ordeyned that oon man schulde have but oon womman, and oon womman but oon man, as saith Seint Augustyn by many resouns. First, for mariage is figured bitwixe Crist and Holy chirche. Another is for a man is heed[250] of a womman; for if a womman had mo men than oon, thanne schulde sche have mo hedes than oon, & that were an horrible thing biforn God. And eek a womman myghte nought please many folk al at oones; and also ther ne schulde never be pees & rest among hem, for everich wolde aske his oughne thing. And fortherover, no man schulde knowe his oughne engendrure,[251] ne who schulde have his heritage, and the womman scholde be the lasse loved fro the tyme that sche were joyned to many men.

Now cometh how that a man schulde bere him with his wif, and namely in tuo thinges; that is to sayn, in sufferaunce and in reverence; and that schewed Crist whan he made first womman. For he ne made hire not of the heed of Adam, for sche schulde not to gret lordschipe have – theras the womman hath the maistry, sche makith to moche disaray. Ther nedith non ensample of this; the experience of this day by day oughte suffice. Also, certes God ne made nought womman of the foot of Adam, for sche ne scholde nought be holden to lowe, for sche cannot paciently suffre. But God made womman of the ribbe of Adam, for womman schulde be felawe unto man. Man schulde bere him to his wif in faith, in trouthe and in loue; as saith Seint Poule, 'A man schulde

249 involuntary/uncontrolled   250 head   251 natural children

love his wif as Crist loved Holy Chirche, that deyed for it' – so schulde a man for his wyf, if it were neede.

Now, how that a womman schulde be subject to hire housbonde; that tellith Seint Peter iij c;[252] first in obedience. And eek, as saith the decre, 'A womman that is a wif, as long as sche is a wif, sche hath noon auctorite to swere ne to bere witnesse without leve of hir housbonde, that is hir lord. Algate he schulde be so by resoun. Sche schulde eek serve him in al honeste, and ben attempre[253] of hir array. I wot wel that thay schulde sette here entent to please her housbondes, but nought by here queyntise of array. Seint Jerom saith that, 'Wyves that ben arrayed in silk and in purpre ne mowe nought clothe hem in Jhesu Crist.'[254] Loke what saith Saint John eek in the same matier. Seint Gregori saith eek that no wight sekith precious clothing ne array, but oonly for veynglorie, to ben honoured the more biforn the poeple. It is a gret folly a womman to have fair array outward and hirsilf to ben foul inward. A wyf schulde eek be mesurable in lokyng, and in beryng, and in laugheing; and discrete in all hir wordes and hir dedes, and above alle worldly thinges sche schulde love hir housebonde with al hire herte, and to him to be trewe of hir body; so scholde an housebonde eeke ben trewe to his wif. For sith that al the body is the housebond's, so schulde here herte ben, or elles ther is bitwixe hem tuo as in that no parfyt mariage.

Thanne schal men understonde that for thre things a man and his wyf mowe fleischly assemble. The first is in entent of engendrure of children to the service of God; for certis, that is the cause fynal of matrimoyne. The secounde cause is to yelden everych[255] of hem his dette unto other of his body, for everych of hem hath power of his oughne body. The thridde is for to eschiewe leccherie and vileynie. The ferthe forsothe, is dedly synne; as to the firste, it is meritory. The secounde also; for as saith the decre, that, 'Sche hath merit of chastite that yeldith to hir housebonde the dette of hir body; ye, thogh it be agayn hir likyng and the lust of hir hert'. The thridde maner is venial synne, and trewly, scarsly may eny of these be withoute venial synne, for the corrupcioun and for the delit. The forthe maner is for to understonde as, if thay assemble oonly for amorous love and for noon the forsayde causes, but for to accomplise thilke brennynge deliyt, thay rekke never how ofte. Sothely, it is dedly synne, and yit with sorwe some folk wole more peyne hem for to doon than to her appetit suffiseth. The secounde maner of chastite is to ben a clene widewe, and to eschiewe the embrasynges of men and disiren the embrasynges of Jhesu Crist. These ben tho that han ben wyves and han forgon here housebondes, and eek wommen that han doon leccherie and be relieved by penitence. And certis, if that a wyf couthe kepe hir al chast by licence of hir housebonde, so that sche geve non occasioun that he agilt, it were to hire a gret merit. Thise maner wymmen that observen chastite moste be clene in herte, as wel as in body and in thought, and mesurable in clothing & in countenaunce, abstinent in etyng and drynkyng, in speche and in dede; and thanne is sche the vessel or the boyst[256] of the Blessed Magdaleyne, that fulfillith Holy Chirche ful of good odour. The thridde maner of chastite is virginite, and it bihoveth that sche be holy in herte and clene of body; and thanne is sche spouse of Jhesu Crist, and sche is the lif of aungels. Sche is the preysyng of this world, and sche is as these martires in egalite[257]; sche hath in hir that tongue may nought telle. Virginite bar Oure Lord Jhesu Crist, and virgine was himselve.

Another remedy agayns leccherie is specially to withdrawe suche thinges as given occasioun to thilke vilonye, as is ease, and etyng and drynkyng. For certes, whan the pot boylith strongely, the beste remedye is to withdrawe the fuyr. Sleping eek longe in greet quiete is eek a greet norice unto leccherie. Another remedye agayns leccherie is that a man or a womman eschiewe the companye of hem by whiche he doutith to be tempted; for albeit so that the dede be withstonde, yit is ther gret temptacioun. Sothely, a whit wal, although it brenne not fully by stikyng of a candel,[258] yet is the wal blak of stiking of a candel. Ful oftetyme I rede that no man truste in his oughne perfeccioun, but he be strenger than Sampson or holiere than Davyd, and wiser than Salomon. Now after that I have declare yow the seven dedly synnes as I can, & some of here braunches and here remedyes; sothely, if I couthe I wolde telle yow the Ten Comaundements, but so heigh a doctrine I leve to divines. But natheles, I hope to God thay ben touchid in this litil tretys, everich of hem alle.

❦ Now, forasmoche as the secounde part of penitence stant in confessioun of mouth, as I bigan in the first chapitre, I say Seint Austyn saith, 'Synne is every word and every dede, and al that men coveyten agayn the lawe of Jhesu Crist, and this is for to synne in herte, in mouthe, and in dede by thy fyve wittis, that ben sight, heeryng, smellyng, tastyng,

258 'putting a candle against the wall'

or sauoryng, or felyng. Now it is good to understonden the circum-
staunces that aggreggen[259] moche to every synne. Thou schalt considre
what thou art that dost the synne; whethir that thou be male or female,
old other yong, gentil or thral, fre or servaunt, hool or seek, weddid or
sengle, ordrid or unordred, wys or fool, clerk or seculer; is sche of thy
kyn bodily, or gostly, or noon, if eny of thy kynrede have synned with
hire or noon, and many mo thinges. That other circumstaunce is whether
it be don in fornicacioun or in advoutry or incest, or noon, or mayden or
noon, in maner of homicide or non, horrible grete synne or smale, and
how long thou hast continued in synne. The thridde circumstaunce is
the place wher thou hast don synne; whether in other men's houses or
in thin owne, in feld or in chirche or in chirchhawe, in chirche dedicate
or noon. For if the chirche were halowed, and man or womman spill his
kynde[260] within, it is enterdited[261] til it be reconsiled by the bischop, and
the prest scholde be enterdyted that dede such a vilonye to terme of al
his lyf, & scholde no more syng no masse; and if he dede he schulde do
dedly syne at every tyme that he song masse. The ferthe circumstunce is
by which mediatours, as by whiche messagers, or for entysement or for
consentement to bere companye with felaws. For many a wrecche, for to
bere companye, wol go to the devel of helle, for thay that eggyn or
consentyn to the synne ben parteneres of the synne, and of the damp-
nacioun of the synnere. The fyfte is how many tymes that he hath synned;
if it be in his mynde, and how ofte that he hath falle, for he that ofte
fallith in synne despiseth the mercy of God and encresceth his synne,
and is unkynde to Crist, and he waxith the more feble to withstonde
synne, and synneth the more lightly and the latter arisith, and is the
more eschiewe to schrive him. And namely to him that hath falle agayn
in here olde folies, eyther thay forleten her confessours al utterly, or ellis
thay departen here schrifte in divers places;[262] but sothely, such departed
schrifte hath no mercy of God of his synnes. The sixte circumstauce is
why that a man synneth, as by which temptacioun or by excityng of other
folk, or if he synne with a womman by force or by hir owne assent, or if
the womman maugre hir heed[263] hath ben enforced[264] or noon. This
schal sche telle for coveytise or poverte, & if it was hire procuryng or
noon, and all such maner harneys. The vij circumstaunce is in what

259 increase   260 'spill' their body fluids
261 interdicted; that is, it is polluted by sacrilege, and may not be used as a church
     again until it is purified.
262 'they confess parts of their sin in different places'
263 'despite her own resistance'   264 raped

maner he hath don his synne, or how that sche hath suffred that folk han doon to hire. The same schal the man telle pleynly all the circumstaunces, and whether he have synned with commune bordeal womman[265] or noon, or doon his synne in holy tyme or noon, in fastyng tyme or noon, or biforn his schrifte or after his latter schrifte, and hath peradventure broken therby his penaunce enjoyned therfore, by whos help or by whos counseil, by sorcery or by other crafte – al moste be told.

Alle these thinges, after thay be grete or smale, engreggen the consciens of a man; and eek the prest that is the jugge may the better ben avysed of his jugement in givyng of thy penaunce, and that is after thy contricioun. For understonde wel, that after the tyme that a man hath defouled his baptisme by synne, if he wol come to savacioun ther is noon other wey but penitence and schrifte of mouthe, and by satifaccioun, and namely by tho tuo. If ther be a confessour to which he may schryve him, and the thridde if he have lif to parforme it; thane schal men lokeit and considre that if he wol make a trewe and a profitable confessioun, ther moste be foure condiciouns.

First, it moste ben in sorweful bitternesse of herte, as sayde the King Ezechie[266] to God, 'I wol remembre me alle the yeres of my lif in bitternes of myn hert'. This condicioun of bitternes hath fyve signes. The first is that confessioun moste be schamefast, not for to covere ne hyde his synne, but for he hath agultid his God and defouled his soule. And herof saith Seint Augustyn, 'The herte tremblith for schame of his synne', and for he hath gret schamefastnes, he is digne to have gret mercy of God. Such was the confessioun of the publican that wolde nought heve up his eyyen to heven, for he had offendid God of heven; for which schamefastnes he had anon the mercy of God. And there saith Seint Augustyn that, 'Such schamefast folk ben next forgevenes of remissioun'.

The secounde signe is humilite of confessioun, for therby God forgiveth the synnes; he alone hath the power. And this humilite schal ben in herte and in signe outward; for right as he hath humilite to God in his herte, right so schulde he humble his body outward to the prest that sittith in God's place. For which in no manere, sith that Crist is soverayn and the prest is his mene and mediatour betwix Crist and the synnere, and the synner is the lasse as by way of resoun; thanne schulde nought the confessour sitte as lowe as the synnere, but the synnere schulde knele biforn him or at his feet but if maladye distourbid it, for he schal take no keep who sittith there, but in whos place that he sitteth. A man that hath

265 'brothel woman' ie prostitute   266 Hezekiah: Isaiah 38:15

trespassed to a lord, and cometh for to axe him of mercy and to maken his accord, and settith him doun anoon by the lord; men wolde holde him outrageous, and not worthy so soone for to have mercy ne remissioun.

The thridde signe is that thy schrifte schulde be ful of teeris; if men may wepe with his herte. Such was the confessioun of Seint Peter; for after he hadde forsake Jhesu Crist he wente out and wepte ful bitterly.[267] The ferthe signe is that he lette nought for schame to schewen his confessioun. Such was the confessioun of the Magdaleyn, that spared for no schame of hem that were at the feste to go to Oure Lord and byknowe[268] to him hire synne. The fifte signe is that a man or a womman be obeisaunt to resceyve the penaunce that him is enjoyned, for certis Jhesu Crist for the gultes of oon man was obedient to his deth. The other codicioun of verray confessioun is that it hastily be doon; for certes, if a man had a dedly wounde, ever the lenger that he taried to warisch himself, the more wolde it corrupte and haste him to his deth, and eek the wounde wolde be the worse to hele. And right so fareth synne that long tyme is in a man unschewed. Certes, a man oughte soone schewe his synne for many causes, as for drede of deth that cometh sodeinly and not certeyn what tyme it schal come, or ben in what place. And eek the drecchyng of oon synne drawth another; and eek the lenger he tarieth, the ferther is he from Crist; and if he abyde unto his laste day, skarsly may he schrive him or remembre him of his synnes or repente, for the grevous malady of his deth. And forasmoche as he hath not in his lif herkened Jhesu Crist whan he hath spoken, he schal crien to Jhesu Crist at his laste day and scarsly wol he herken him.

And understonde that this condicioun moste have foure thinges. Thy schrifte moste ben purveyed byforn and avysed; for wikked haste doth no profyt, and that a man can schryve him of his synnes – be it of pride or of envye, and so forth – alle the spices and the circumstaunces, and that he have comprehendid in his mynde the nombre and the gretnes of his synne, and how longe he hath lyen in synne, and eek that he be contrit of his sinnes and in stedefast purpos, by the grace of God, never eft to falle in synne; and eek that he drede and countrewayte[269] himself, and that he flee the occasiouns of synne to whiche he is enclyned. Also, that thou schalt schrive the of all thin synnes to oon man, and nat a parcel to oon man and a parcel to another man. That is understonde in entent to parte thy confessioun of thy soule, for certes, Jhesu Crist is enterely al good; in him is noon imperfeccioun, and theerfore outher he

267 Matthew 26:75   268 reveal/tell   269 keep watch over

forgiveth al parfitly, or elles never a del[270]. I say nought if ther be assigned
to thy penitencere[271] for certein synne that thou art bounde to schewe
him al the remenaunt of thy synnes of whiche thou hast ben schryven of
thy curate, but if it like the of thin humilite; this is no departyng of
schrifte. Ne I say not thereas I speke of divisioun of confessioun, that if
thou have licence to schryve the to a discret and to an honest prest wher
the likith, and eek by the licence of thy curate, that thou ne maist wel
schrive the to him of all thyn synnes. But let no synne be byhnde untold,
as fer as thou hast remembraunce. And whan thou schalt be schrive to
thi curate, telle him eeke al thy synne that thou hast doo syns thou were
last y-schryvne. This is no wikkid entent of divisioun of schrifte.

Also, thy verrey schrifte askith certeyn condiciouns. First that thou
schrive the by thy fre wille, nought constreyned ne for schame of folk, ne
for maladye or such thing. For it is resoun that he that trespassith with
his fre wille, that by his fre wille confesse his trespas; noon other man
schal telle his synne, ne wrathe him with the prest for his amonestynge to
lete synne[272] The secounde condicioun is that thy schrifte be laweful; that
is to sayn, that thou that schrivest the, and eek the prest that herith thy
confessioun, ben verrayly in the feith of Holy Chirche, and that a man be
nought despaired of the mercy of Jhesu Crist as Caym or Judas. And eek
a man moot accuse himself of his owne trespas, and not another; but he
schal blame and wite himself of his oughne malice of his synne, and noon
other. But natheless, if that another man be occasioun or ellis enticer of
his synne, or that the estate of a persone be such thurgh which his synne
aggreggith, or elles that he may not playnly schryve hym but[273] he telle the
person with which he hath synned; thanne may he telle it so that his
entent be nought to bakbyte the persone, but oonly to declare his con-
fessioun. Thow schalt nought eke make no lesyng[274] in thy confessioun
for humilite, to sayn that thou hast don synnes of whiche thou were never
gulty, as Seint Augustyn saith, 'If thou bycause of humilite makest
lesynges on thiself, though thou were not in synne biforn, yit art thou
thanne in synne thurgh thy lesynges'. Thou most schewe thy synne by
thyn oughne propre mouth but thou woxe dombe, and not by no lettres,
for thou that hast don the synne, thou schalt have the schame. Thou
schalt not eek peynte thy confessioun by faire subtil wordes to cover the
more thy synne, for thanne bigilist thou thisself and not the prest. Thou
most eelle it platly, be it never so foul ne so horrible. Thou schalt eek

270 not at all   271 confessor   272 'admonishing to forsake sin'
273 unless   274 lie

schrive the to a prest that is discrete to counsaile the. And thou schalt
nought schryve the for veineglorie ne for yprocrisie. Thou schalt not eek
renne to the prest sodeinly to telle him lightly thy synne, as who tellith a
tale or a jape,[275] but buysily and with gret devocioun, and generally
schrive the ofte. If thou ofte falle, ofte thou arise by confessioun. And
though thou schryve the ofter than oones of synne of which thou hast
ben schriven, it is the more merite; and as saith Seint Augustyn, 'Thou
schalt have the more lightly relessyng and grace of God bothe of synne
and of payne. And certes, oones a yer atte lest way, it is laweful to be
houselyd, for sothely oones a yer alle thinges renovelen.[276]

De tertia parte penitentiae[277]

❦ Now have I tol of verray confessioun, that is the secounde partye of
penitence. The thridde partye of penitence is satisfaccioun, and that
stondith generally in almesdede and bodily peyne. Now ben ther thre
maner of almesdede; contricioun of herte, where a man offereth himself
to God; the secounde is to have pite of the defaute of his neighebor; the
thridde is in geving of good counseil and comfort gostly and bodily,
where men han neede, and namely in sustenaunce of men's foode. And
take keep that a man hath neede of clothing and of herberwe.[278] He hath
neede of charitable counseil and visityng in prisoun and malady, and
sepulture of his dede body. And if thou may not visite the needeful with
thy persone, visite by thy message and by thy giftes. These ben general
almesses[279] or werkes of charite of hem that han temporal riches or
discrecioun in counselynge. Of these werkes schalt thou hieren at the
Day of Doom. This almes schalt thou doon of thin oughne propur
thinges, and hastily and prively[280] if thou maist. But natheles, if thou
maist not do it prively, thou schalt nought forbere to do almes though
men se it, so that it be nought don for thank of the world but oonly for
thenk of Jhesu Crist. For as witnessith Seint Mathew c. v, 'A cite may not
ben hid that is set on a mountayn; ne men light not a lanterne and put
it under a buisschel, but men sette it on a candel-stikke to lighte the men
in the house. Right so schal youre light lighten biforn men, that men may
se oure goode werkes and glorifien oure Fader that is in heven'.[281]

---

275 joke
276 'it is the law's demand that you take communion at least once a year, for truly
    once a year are all things renewed'   277 of the third part of penance
278 lodging   279 almsdeeds   280 secretly   281 Matthew 5:14

Now as to speke of bodily peyne. It is in prayere, in wakinges, in fastynges, in veruous techinges. Of orisouns[282] ye schul understonde that orisouns or prayeres is for to seyn a pitous wil of herte, that redresseth in God and expressith it by word outward; to remoeven harmes, and to have thinges espirituel & durable, and somtyme temporel thinges, of whiche orisouns in the orisoun of the Paternoster[283] hath Oure Lord Jhesu Crist enclosed most thinges. Certis, it is privileged of thre thinges in his dignite than any other prayer, for Jhesu Crist himself maked it; and it is schort, for it schude be couth the more lightly, and forto withholde it the more esily in herte and helpe himselfe the oftere with this orisoun, and for a man schulde be the lasse wery to say it, and for a man may not excuse to lerne it; it is so schort and so easy; and for it comprehendith in itself all goode prayeres. This exposicioun of this holy praier, that is so excellent and so digne, I bitake to these maystres of theology. Save thus moche wol I sayn; whan thou prayest that God schulde forgive the thy gultes as thou forgivest hem that they gulten to the, be ful wel ware that thou be not out of charite. This holy orisoun amenisith eek venial synne, and therfore it appendith specially to penitence. This praier moste be trewely sayd and in verray faith, and that men pray to God ordinatly,[284] discretly & devoutly, and alway a man schulde putte his wille to be subject to the wille of God. This orisoun moste eek be sayd with greet humblesse and ful pure and honestly, and nought to the annoyaunce of eny man or womman. It moste eek be continued with the werkis of charite. It avayllith agayns the vices of the soule, for as seith Seint Jerom, 'By fastyng ben saved the vices of the soule'.

After this thou schalt understonde that bodily peyne stant in wakyng. For Jhesu Crist saith, 'Wakith and prayeth, that ye ne entre not into temptacioun'.[285] Ye schul understonde that fastynge stont in thre thinges: in forbering of bodily mete and drink and in forberyng of worldly jolite, and in forbering of worldly synne; this is to sayn, that a man schal kepe him fro dedly synne in al that he may. And thou schalt understonde eek that God ordeyned fastyng, and to fastyng appurteynen foure thinges: Largesce to pouer folk, gladnes of hert espirituel, not to ben angry, ne annoyed, ne grucche for he fastith, and also resonable hour for to ete by mesure; that is to sayn, a man schulde not ete in untyme,[286] ne sitte the lenger at his mele for he fastith.

Thanne schal thou understonde that bodily peyne stant in discipline or

---

282 prayers   283 'Our Father', ie the Lord's Prayer   284 in a proper fashion
285 Matthew 26:41   286 'at the wrong time'

teching; by word, or by writyng, or by ensample. Also in heires weryng or of stamyn or habejeons[287] on her naked fleisch for Crist's sake, and suche maner penaunce. But ware the wel, that such maner penaunce of thyn fleissch make nought thin herte bitter or angry, or anoyed of thiself.; for better is to cast away thin hayre than for to caste away the swetnes of Jhesu Crist. And theerfore seith Seint Poule, 'Clothe yow as thay that ben chosen of God, in herte of misericorde, debonairete, sufferaunce, and such maner of clothing',[288] of the which Jhesu Crist is more appayed than of haires or of hauberkis. Than is discipline eek in knokking on the brest, in scourgyng with yerdes,[289] in knelynges, in tribulacioun, in suffring paciently wronges that ben doon to him, and eek in pacient sufferaunce of maledies or lesyng of worldly catel or of wif or of child, or of othir frendes.

Thanne schalt thou understonde which thinges destourben penaunce, and this is in foure thinges; that is drede, schame, hope and wanhope, that is desperacioun. And for to speke first of drede, for which he weneth that he may suffre no penaunce. Ther agayns is remedye for to thinke that bodily penaunce is but schort and litel, at the regard of the peyne of helle that is cruel and so long that it lastith withouten ende. Now agains the schame that a man hath to schryve him, and namely these ypocrites that wolde be holde so parfyt that thay have no neede to schryve hem agayns that schame, schulde a man thinke that by way of resoun that he hath not ben aschamed to do foule thinges, and that is confessioun. And man scholde eek think that God seeth alle thy thoughtes and thy werkes; to him may nothing be hyd ne covered. Men schulde eek remembre hem of the schame that is to come at the Day of Doom to hem that ben nought penitent and schriven in this present lif. For alle the creatures in heven, in erthe and in helle, schuln seen apertly al that he hydith in this world.

Now for to speke of hem that ben so negligent and slowe to schryve hem, stant in tuo manerres. That oon is that he hopith for to lyve longe and for to purchace moche riches for his delyt, and thanne he wol schrive him and, as he saith, he may as him semith tymely ynough come to schrifte. Another is the surquidrie[290] that he hath in Crist's mercy. Agains the firste vice, he schal thinke that ourre lif is in no sikernesse,[291] and eek that al the riches in this world ben in adventure[292] and passen as a schadowe on the wal; and as saith Seint Gregory, that it apperteyneth to the grete rightwisnes of God that never schal the peyne stynte of hem

---

287 hair shirts, coarse woollen shirts or shirts of mail
288 Colossians 3:12   289 sticks   290 arrogance
291 security   292 'on loan'

that never wolde withdrawe hem fro synne, her thankes, but ay continue in synne; for thilke perpetuel wille to doon synne, schul thay have perpetuel peyne. Wanhope is in tuo maneres. The firste wanhope is in the mercy of Crist; that other is that thay thinke thay mighte nought longe persever in goodnesse. The firste wanhope cometh of that he demyth that he synned so highly and so ofte, and so longe layn in synne that he schal not be saved. Certis, agens that cursed wanhope schulde he thenke that the passioun of Jhesu Crist is more strong for to unbynde than synne is strong for to bynde. Agains the secounde wanhope he schal thinke that als ofte as he fallith, he may arise agayn by penitence. And though he never so longe have leyn in synne, the mercy of Crist is alway redy to resceyve him to mercy. Agains the wanhope that he thinkith he schulde not longe persevere in goodnesse, he schal thinke that the febles of the devel may nothing doon, but men wol suffre him. And eek he schal have strengthe of the help of God and of al Holy Chirche, and of the proteccioun of aungels, if him list.

Thanne schal men understonde what is the fruyt of penaunce. And after the word of Jhesu Crist, it is the endeles blisse of heven, ther joye hath no contrariete of wo, ne of penaunce ne grevance. Ther alle harmes ben passed of this present lif. Ther as is the sikernesse fro the peyne of helle. Ther as is the body of man, that whilom was so foul and derk, more cleer than the sonne; ther as the body, that whilom was seek, freel, and feble, immortal – and so strong and so hool that ther may nothing empeire it. Ther nys neyther honger, thurst, ne colde; but every soule replenisched with the sight and the parfyt knowyng of God. This blisful regne may men purchace by poverte espirituel, and the glorie by lowenes, the plente of joye by hunger and thurst, and reste by travaile, and the lif by deth and mortificacioun of synne – to which life he us bringe that bought us with his precious blood. Amen.

THE 'RETRACTION'

This small text appears at the end of *The Canterbury Tales* in all of the manuscripts which contain the ending of The Parson's Tale. It is obviously a form of closure, but it is unclear whether the 'litel tretise' mentioned is *The Canterbury Tales* as a whole or just The Parson's Tale. There is also the problem that other works are mentioned, which gives rise to the suggestion that this may be two 'epilogues', one for The Parson's Tale/ *Canterbury Tales*, and another for some other work, or works. It seems highly unlikely that Chaucer would refer to an enterprise such as *The Canterbury Tales* as a 'litel tretise', as it is neither little, nor a treatise. If *The Canterbury Tales* were in some 'approved' complete form on Chaucer's death, he might have written a conclusion for it. If, however, it was not, and was put together after his death, then a conclusion may not have been written. The content is problematic for modern readers, as Chaucer appears to be renouncing the works that have become most popular. The fact is that modern readers judge according to different sets of values, both moral and literary, from those applied to literature by fourteenth- and fifteenth-century readers/hearers. In other words, we like the more 'humanist' of Chaucer's productions, and we do not wish to imagine him as a conventional fourteenth-century Christian. He may or may not have been, but the chances are, unfortunately for us, that he was, and that, whatever his feelings may have been during his life, faced with death and the unknown, he accepted the 'insurance' offered by the Church for the faithful and the penitent. Whatever was originally intended, The 'Retraction' makes a fitting codicil to The Parson's Tale. It is the end of a pilgrimage.

Further Reading

Tita Baumlin, 'Theology and Discourse in The Pardoner's Tale, The Parson's Tale and The Retraction', *Renascence*, 41, 1989, pp. 127–42

James Dean, 'Chaucer's Repentance: A Likely Story', *Chaucer Review*, 24, 1989, pp. 64–76

Matthew Wolfe, 'Placing Chaucer's Retraction for a Reception of Closure', *Chaucer Review*, 33, 1999, pp. 427–31

❦ Now pray I to yow alle that heren this litel tretis or reden, that if ther be anything that likes hem, that therof thay thanke Oure Lord Jhesu Crist, of whom procedith alle witte and al goodnes. And if ther be enything that displesith hem, I pray hem that thay arette it to the defaute of myn unconnyng, and not to my wille, that wolde fayn have sayd better if I hadde connyng. For the book saith, 'Al that is writen, for oure doctrine is writen'.[1] For I biseke yow mekely, for the mercy of God, that ye pray for me, that God haue mercy on me, and forgeve me my giltes; and nameliche my translaciouns, and of endityng in worldly vanitees, which I revoke in my retracciouns as is the Book of Troyles, the Book also of Fame, the Book of 25 Ladies,[2] the Book of the Duchesses, the Book of Seint Valentine's Day and of the Parliment of Briddes, the Tales of Caunturbury, all thilke that sounen into synne; the Book of the Leo,[3] and other bokes if thay were in my mynde or remembraunce, and many a song and many a leccherous lay. Of the whiche Crist, for his grete mercy, forgive me the synnes.

But of the translacioun of Boce, De consolacioun, and other bokes of consolacioun, and of legend of lyues of seints, and Omelies, and moralitees, and devocion; that thanke I Oure Lord Jhesu Crist and his Moder, and alle the seintes in heven, bisekyng hem that thay fro hennysforth unto my lyve's end send me grace to biwayle my gultes, and to studien to the savacioun of my soule; and graunte me grace and space of verray repentaunce, penitence, confessioun, and satisfaccioun, to don in this present lif, thurgh the benigne grace of Him that is King of Kynges and Prest of alle Prestis, that bought us with his precious blood of his hert, so that I moote be oon of hem at the Day of Doom that schal be saved *qui cum Patre*.[4] Amen.

1 Romans 15:4
2 The Legend of Good Women
3 Unknown: a 'lost' work of Chaucer, although well enough known in his own time to be worth mentioning in his retraction
4 'Who with the Father and the Son and the Holy Spirit lives and reigns now and forever'